Composers in the Movies

JOHN C. TIBBETTS
Foreword by Simon Callow

Composers in the Movies

STUDIES IN MUSICAL BIOGRAPHY

Yale University Press
New Haven &
London

Published with assistance from the Mary Cady Tew Memorial Fund.

Set in Sabon type by Keystone Typesetting, Inc.
Printed in the United States of America by Sheridan Books.

Library of Congress Cataloging-in-Publication Data
Tibbetts, John C.
Composers in the movies : studies in musical biography / John C. Tibbetts ; foreword by Simon Callow.
p. cm.
Includes bibliographical references and index.
ISBN 0-300-10674-2 (alk. paper)
1. Composers in motion pictures. I. Title.
PN1995.9.C553T53 2005
791.43′68780922—dc22
2005004689
A catalogue record for this book is available from the British Library.

The paper in this book meets the guidelines for permanence and durability of the Committee on Production Guidelines for Book Longevity of the Council on Library Resources.

10 9 8 7 6 5 4 3 2 1

This book is dedicated to Dr. Nancy B. Reich, biographer of Clara Wieck-Schumann, who has unselfishly and unstintingly opened to me many doors to the world of music and musicians, and to Kevin Brownlow, whose endeavors in the service of film history have shown us all the way

For new songs a new lyre is needed. . . .
Will the cinema be that new lyre with strings of light?
— *Abel Gance,* Prism, *1930*

Contents

Foreword

SIMON CALLOW

Biographical dramatization is a tricky business. I've been involved in it for most of my career, playing the Great Dead in a surprising number of plays, documentaries, and films; I've even written two spectacularly bad biographical plays myself. Quite often the Great Dead in question have been artists of one sort or another; twice I have played composers (three times, if you count Emanuel Schikaneder in the film version of *Amadeus,* who — as well as being the first Viennese Hamlet, an original clown, and an impresario of genius — was a prolific songwriter). For me this has been a perfectly logical development: From childhood, biography has been my favorite form of literature, and the key works of my youth were the Lives of the Great Composers, suitably romanticized (and duly sanitized) accounts of the canonic masters from Bach to Tchaikovsky, which showed their heroic struggle to make great art in the face of an indifferent or hostile world. Their lives and their works were inextricably intertwined: when they were sad, their music was sad; when they were happy, their music overflowed with joy.

As soon as I was offered the part of Mozart in the original London stage production of Peter Shaffer's play *Amadeus,* I immediately recognized my favorite boyhood genre: the story was not sanitized (in fact, it was rather conspicuously the opposite), but it was still romanticized. It was the drama of the artist's struggle against the forces of philistinism, in this case attached to a parable about the injustice of the unequal distribution of genius. Shaffer framed his story within a theatrical framework of dazzling flamboyance, cunningly using the music with unerring instinct to heighten the drama. All of this was somewhat at the expense of musicology but greatly to the advantage of drama; the effect of Shaffer's outrageous theatrical audacity was, paradoxically, profound, even for those who came to sneer. The play created a new myth of the artist failed by his own character (or lack of it), the artist who wouldn't (or couldn't) play the game; but the audible evidence of his sublime genius made the story unbearably poignant. Shaffer's masterstroke, from a theatrical point of view, was to have the story narrated by the villain: everything we saw of Mozart was told to us by Antonio Salieri, who has fair claims to being considered the unreliable narrator to end all unreliable narrators. Indeed, according to Shaffer's original scheme, this element would have been demonstrated even more forcefully than it was by having not a note of Mozart's music played as he actually wrote it; it too would have been filtered through Salieri's poisoned memory. In practice, this idea proved to be too difficult to realize effectively, and instead the passages, alternately sublime and exuberant, that Shaffer had so skillfully chosen, unaltered, turned a whole generation of theatergoers to whom Mozart's music had hitherto been merely pretty into convinced Amadeaphiles, even Amadeamanes.

Interestingly, when Milos Forman came to make his film from the play, he used a great deal more music than had ever appeared in the stage version and turned the film into more of a joint biography of the two composers than had been the case on stage, where Mozart is very much the shorter of the two roles. Shorter but perhaps more vivid, as Mozart is viewed by lightning, sudden shafts of hectic, hysterical brilliance alternating with equally sudden ascents into the sublime or descents into despair. There was no linear progression to the role: he was simply the sum of Salieri's fevered and embittered recall. Film being — despite the recent and rapid rise of the fantasy epic — essentially a realistic medium, considerable attention in both the screenplay (by Shaffer and Forman) and the acting was given to realizing the psychological truth of the character; an attempt was made to render Mozart credible on his own terms. Theater — or certainly the theater of Shaffer and that of most dramatists before the arrival of Ibsen — exists so much in the realm of gesture that this would have been an impossible undertaking on stage.

The injunction to me by the play's director, Peter Hall, when we started rehearsals — "I have to believe at all times that he was capable of writing the overture to *The Marriage of Figaro*" — became the central task of my performance, while pushing the parameters of Shaffer's outlandish creation as far as possible. The idea was to make the audience feel to the fullest Salieri's exasperation at having to endure Mozart's behavior, while being frustrated by Salieri's inability to see beyond it to the supreme artist within.

I suspect that this is an essentially theatrical ploy, one that would probably not work on film. It was certainly one that the film version eschewed. Rather, Forman's film returned to the realm of myth-making, of telling a great and at the same time very human story in terms of vivid simplification. Significantly, Shaffer and Forman actually invented an incident that we know *not* to have happened — the dictation by Mozart to Salieri of the *Requiem*. Everything in the play *could have* happened: Shaffer had merely filled in the gaps in our knowledge of Mozart's life. But this invention discarded — as Shakespeare had discarded them in his history plays — the known facts in favor of dramatic manipulation, and deeply satisfying it was. *Non era vero ma era ben trovato.* The addition of a gloriously achieved recreation of late eighteenth-century Vienna and an almost continuous and headily beautiful musical soundtrack completed the conquest of the audience. The film became the Mozart Experience and put the two-hundred-year-old composer onto the best-selling lists for the first time, effortlessly pushing former chart-toppers Beethoven, Mahler, and Tchaikovsky to one side.

To one degree or another, almost every film described in this book's vivacious and thorough survey of the field takes flight into the realm of myth-making. Somehow inevitably, the moment a reconstruction of events is attempted, the dramatist's hand starts to play fast and loose with reality. The reason for this is pretty simple: composing as such, like most artistic activities, is drudgery, and — unlike painting — one that it is hard to represent on the screen or stage. To watch even a genius compose is like watching paint dry — with the difference that once the paint has dried, one has something to look at. Even while the paint is wet, one has something to look at; in the case of Henri-Georges Clouzot's great film about Picasso, it is the process that is so fascinating. To some extent that is reproducible on film in a musical context — again, perhaps the supreme example is in *Amadeus*, when Mozart takes a trite little march of Salieri's and turns it into "Non piu andrai" from *Figaro* — but the drama, the elevation, the intensity of the music is rarely present in its creation.

And this is the difficulty. It is a reasonable expectation that the events depicted in the life of Beethoven should be Beethovenian, that Chopin's should be Chopinesque, Tchaikovsky's Tchaikovskian. In reality, their lives rarely reflected their music. So the lives are bent, adjusted, manipulated to achieve the desired effect. It is easy for the purist to despise the results, but in my view a film that uses the composer's story, or a version of it, to evoke his or her spirit, is perfectly legitimate; all that matters is how it is done. Thus Tony Palmer's monumental *Wagner* (1983) reproduces the experience of watching one of the composer's operas, even to the extent of including a number of *mauvais quart d'heures* among the delirious inspirations. Ken Russell's *The Music Lovers* (1970) seems to me to be perfectly Tchaikovskian, in both its occasional vulgarities and its visual inventiveness, while the same director's *Mahler* (1974), alternately crude and self-consciously literary, misses his subject by a mile. That of course is merely my taste.

It is worth observing, however, that dialogue is the undoing of most musical biopics, from *Song without End*'s "George Sand — gee, a girl in pants!" to *Mahler*'s "but Alma, don't you see? The andante of the Sixth Symphony — it's you!" On the other hand, the few passages of dialogue in Anna Ambrose's witty, tender *Handel: Honour, Profit and Pleasure* (1983), in which I myself played the composer, limit themselves to swiftly conveyed narrative detail. Even better is Russell's *Elgar* (1962), still the greatest of all composer films, in which there is no dialogue whatsoever; and both the Handel and Elgar films set out to embody rather than to explain the spirit of the composer, his age, his world, and his emotional frame of reference. It is also true that playing composers offers remarkable opportunities to actors, who in themselves can sometimes suggest the essence, the vision of the music. Jean-Louis Barrault in *La Symphonie Fantastique* (1942), Max Adrian as Delius in Russell's *Song of Summer* (1967), and, perhaps most startlingly, Innokenti Smoktunovsky in Dimitri Tiomkin's lumbering and witless *Tchaikovsky* (1971) in their performances suggest deep insight into the work.

The musical biopic, it seems to me, is an art form of rich potential that in an age of increasing cinematic flexibility, both of form and of image, has only begun to be explored. This book by John C. Tibbetts is a wonderful guide to the follies and the splendors of what should be regarded as the infant years of musical biography on film.

Acknowledgments

Sometimes a writer seeks out a subject and runs with it. This book, however, sought *me* out, shook me by the scruff of the neck, kicked at my heels, and so bedeviled me that I finally cried for mercy. Doubtless, the many colleagues and friends involved will be relieved to know it's finished at last. (Do I dare confess to them that this investigation is just a beginning?) At any rate, to them and so many others go my profoundest thanks for patiently putting up with my longstanding inquiries about that most curious breed of biographical films — the composer biopic.

First of all, I owe the very existence of this book to Harry Haskell, former editor of Yale University Press, who took seriously what must at first have seemed a preposterous subject for a "serious" study. His successor, Lauren Shapiro, along with copyeditor Amy Smith Bell, received the baton without flinching and have patiently seen the project through.

Among the many historians and educators, from the disciplines of music and cinema alike, who heard me out with some bemusement and even an occasional degree of seriousness about a subject that has been largely marginalized over the years, I particularly want to thank Dr. Nancy B. Reich and the late Dr. Peter Ostwald, esteemed biographers of Clara Wieck-Schumann and Robert Schumann, respectively, for their unstinting advice and assistance in contacting many of the musicians and scholars interviewed in this book. My thanks also go to film historians Kevin Brownlow and the late William K. Everson, who shared late-night conversations and films from their private collections; editors David Culbert of *The Historical Journal of Film, Radio, and Television*, Richard T. Jameson, formerly of *Film Comment*, James M. Welsh of *Literature/Film Quarterly*, Michael Saffle, editor of many anthologies about music and media, and Shirley Fleming of *The American Record Guide* — all of whom first encouraged and published some of my early findings. I must also thank the dean of humanities scholars, Professor Jacques Barzun, whose generous advice in the initial years of my research has guided me through some torturous conceptual issues.

I have also found unexpected — but welcome — encouragement from many other scholars and specialists who, to one degree or another, have also pursued this topic: Robert Winter of UCLA, who has included in his classes some of the films discussed in this book; Leon Botstein of Bard College, whose annual Bard Music Festivals have added so much to the synergistic study of music and media; Christopher Gibbs, also of Bard College, whose Schubert research has added so much to our understanding of the processes of the public constructions of composers' lives; Adrienne Block of the City University of New York, who invited me to speak on these topics before a seminar in 2002; Deane Root of the Stephen Foster Archive and Performing Arts Center in Pittsburgh, who took so much time to talk about Foster lore and movies; Alan Walker of McMaster University, who invited me to a Stockholm Liszt Conference to talk about Liszt movies; song historians Eric Sams and Rufus Hallmark, who opened my eyes (and ears) to the programmatic implications of the art song tradition; Albert Boime, art historian at UCLA, whose inexhaustible knowledge of Romanticism ultimately fed into many of this book's topics; Berlioz biographers Hugh Macdonald, Kern Holoman, and Katherine Reeve, who taught me how much Hollywood owes to the dramatic innovations of the French master; popular culture historians Charles Hamm, David Beveridge, Michael Beckerman, and novelist Josef Skvorecký, whose contributions to my *Dvořák in America* revealed the far-reaching consequences of the multicultural revolution in late-nineteenth-century America; Miles Kreuger of the Institute of the American Musical in Los Angeles, who first told me about *Blossom Time;* Tony Williams of Southern Illinois University at Carbondale, who brought *The Story of Gilbert and Sullivan* to my attention; William A. Everett of University of the Missouri–Kansas City, who shared the manuscript of his forthcoming biography of Sigmund Romberg; Mike Nevins of St. Louis University, who shoehorned the films of Tex Ritter (!) into this discussion; Joe Gomez, whose pioneering work on Ken Russell guided so much of my own research; and Schubert enthusiasts Janet Wasserman and Richard Morris, who generously shared their research and their Schubert newsletters.

Many happy hours have been spent talking shop with musicians and film-makers about movies and music. My thanks to composers Philip Glass and the late Virgil Thomson; pianists Charles Rosen, Joerg Demus, the late Eugene Istomin, Leslie Howard, Andras Schiff, Vladimir Ashkenazy, Ruth Laredo, Cyprian Katsaris, and Claude Frank (whose one-man interpretation of MGM's *Song of Love* has enlivened many private parties for years!); and conductors Wolfgang Sawallisch, Christoph Eschenbach, David Zinman, Leonard Slatkin, and John Nelson. Filmmakers Ken Russell and Tony Palmer not only granted me many hours of their time and permitted access to many of their films, but they helped me contact important personages pertinent to their careers, such as former BBC and London Weekend Television (LWT) producer Humphrey Burton, LWT producer Melvyn Bragg, actor and entrepreneur Simon Callow (who wrote the foreword to this book), and actor Ronald Pickup, who (second only to Mr. Callow) has impersonated more artists and historical figures than anyone else. Other filmmakers who agreed to interviews include Austrian director Fritz Lehner, whose *Mit meinen heissen Tränen* (*With My Hot Tears*) was one of the great "discoveries" I encountered while researching this book; and David Devine, whose estimable Canadian-based "Great Composers" series has brought classical music to younger viewers.

Film research centers and archives on both sides of the Atlantic have been extremely helpful. In England, I was assisted at the National Film and Television Archive of the British Film Institute (BFI) in London by Olwen Terris and Kathleen Dickson in Research Viewings, Janet Moat in Paper Holdings, and Gavin Beattie, senior cataloguer of the BFI Collections. Guy Strickland and Jeff Walden were very helpful at the BBC Written Archives Centre, at Caversham Park, near Reading. And Susan Dunford provided research copies of LWT films through Granada Media. In California I also wish to thank the staff at the Margaret Herrick Library, the Academy of Motion Picture Arts and Sciences in Beverly Hills for their help, including Fay Thompson and Barbara Hall of Special Collections and Michelle McKenzie of the Photographic Special Collections. My thanks also goes to Noelle Carter of the Warner Bros. Archive at USC's Hoffman Research Annex in Los Angeles and to Ned Comstock of the USC Cinema-Television Library, also in Los Angeles. At the University of Kansas Music and Dance Library, chief librarian and old friend Jim Smith was always on hand to locate that elusive article or book. And thanks to Dick May, of Warner Bros. in Burbank, for showing me that curious MGM short, *Heavenly Music:* I was told it would change my life and, indeed, it did.

To the many colleagues who took the time to read early drafts of this book, I express my appreciation for their many corrections and suggestions — Professors Greg Black of the University of Missouri–Kansas City; Tom Leitch of the University of Delaware; Stan Singer of Scottsdale Community College; Peter Rollins of Oklahoma State University; and Chuck Berg, John Sweets, John Gronbeck-Tedesco, Catherine Preston, and Rodney Hill of the University of Kansas. Any errors and miscalculations that remain must be laid at my doorstep, not theirs.

Finally, I owe much to those boon companions and lifelong friends, Christine Whittaker, archivist emeritus of the BBC, the aforementioned James M. Welsh of *Literature/Film Quarterly,* and Los Angeles–based scholar Frank T. Thompson, whose unfailing encouragement and good-humored assistance have helped me past those occasional times when energies flagged, the image dimmed, and the music failed. And to Mary Blomquist and Marilyn Heath: I hope I have justified your confidence in me. To you and to all the others, I can only say — "Now read this book, *see* the movie, and *hear* the music!"

Introduction
The Lyre of Light

O! The one life within us and abroad, which meets all motion and becomes its soul—a light in sound, a sound-like power in light, rhythm in all thought.
— *Samuel Taylor Coleridge, "The Eolian Harp"*

History as "Image"

Dramatizations in the movies of historical events and famous people possess a power, a vitality, and an enduring image quite distinct from the history books. Who can forget Laurence Olivier as Richard III, Henry Fonda as Abraham Lincoln, George C. Scott as General Patton, and — especially relevant to this book — Tom Hulce as the naive and foolishly giggling composer Wolfgang Amadeus Mozart in the popular *Amadeus* (1984)? Professional historians may chronicle their subjects with greater detail, precision, and accuracy, but they can scarcely hope to convey their portraits with a comparable degree of graphic, personal, and emotional vividness. Mark C. Carnes, professor of history at Barnard College and Columbia University, and secretary of the Society of American Historians, acknowledges that historical films speak "both eloquently and foolishly," that their "fabrications" may go unnoticed and their "truths" unappreciated, "but they have spoken, nearly always, in ways we find fascinating. . . . Their final product gleams, and it sears the imagination."[1] Carnes does not speak for all professional historians, to be sure; but he perhaps speaks to most of the people who enjoy movies.

That historical films and biopics construct peculiarly persuasive images has been demonstrated over and over again. Oliver Stone's *JFK* (1991) is a particularly compelling example. Its depiction of conspiratorial plots behind the Kennedy assassination was so visually persuasive that to this day it arouses controversy and threatens to overshadow the findings of the Warren Commission. Thus, even in light of recent findings that continue to prevail against the "conspiracy theory," the majority of viewers continue to privilege the film's glamour over the more mundane, factual alternatives. Arguably, had the *JFK* screenplay only been published, rather than realized on film, it might be forgotten today. The pictures have spoken louder than historians' words. The urgent question arising from this, as it will over and over again throughout the pages of this book, is whether the "truth" of a pictorial speculation should be allowed some degree of legitimacy alongside the historical record. Can the two coexist?

"The time will come in less than ten years," predicted American filmmaker D. W. Griffith shortly after the release of his *Birth of a Nation* (1915), "when the children in public schools will be taught practically everything via moving pictures. Certainly they will never be obliged to read history again."[2] If not yet completely fulfilled, that prophecy has been echoed more recently by historical novelists and media theorists as diverse as Gore Vidal and Marshall McLuhan. Indeed, for better or worse, many history teachers frequently complement their classroom instruction with movie screenings, and video distributors increasingly are targeting their products to educational institutions. Robert A. Rosenstone, professor of history at the California Institute of Technology, admits that today "the chief source of historical knowledge for the majority of the population — outside of the much-despised textbook — must surely be the visual media, a set of institutions that lie almost wholly outside the control of those of us who devote our lives to history."[3] And Carnes concludes ruefully, "For many, Hollywood History is the only history."[4]

That "history," then, for the viewers of the films discussed in this book, includes half-truths and stereotypes about composers that have achieved a measure of popular currency. They include, for example, allegations that Mozart was murdered by Antonio Salieri; that Franz Schubert left his Eighth Symphony unfinished; that Frédéric Chopin died saving Poland from tsarist tyranny; that young Johannes Brahms played piano in brothels; that Richard Wagner was a kind of artistic vampire; that Richard Strauss was a Nazi; that Stephen Foster based his songs on the chants of African-American dock workers; that John Philip Sousa wrote "Stars and Stripes Forever" for the Spanish-American War effort; and that ragtime music — the most indigenous of American art forms — was the creation of white, classically trained musicians.

Certainly, these composer biopics — respectively, Miloš Forman's *Amadeus* (1984), Paul Stein's *Melody Master* (1942), Charles Vidor's *A Song to Remember* (1944), Tony Palmer's *Brahms and the Little Singing Girls* (1996), Ken Russell's *Lisztomania* (1975), *Dance of the Seven Veils* (1970), Sidney Lanfield's *Swanee River* (1939), Henry Koster's *Stars and Stripes Forever* (1952), and Henry King's *Alexander's Ragtime Band* (1938) — are among the many that have been consigned by many critics and historians to the margins of cinematic discourse.[5] "There is a hideous vulgarity, indeed, about all these pictures based on composers' lives," wrote Graham Greene in 1939, after viewing a French dramatization of the life of Ludwig van Beethoven. "The human melodrama belittles the music all the time like programme notes so that . . . [the] music becomes only a sentimental illustration to sentimental dialogue."[6] Composer Richard Strauss lived long enough to fear the worst, when he commented on the biographical and musical transgressions of an operetta about Schubert: "As long as something like *Lilac Time* is possible, no one can say that composers have any real protection."[7] Strauss didn't know the half of it — years later he, too, would fall "victim," to director Ken Russell's *Dance of the Seven Veils.*

Undaunted, I make no apology for my own personal affection and regard for these films. In the first place they contain wonderful music, music that plays its own part in enhancing the image and enlivening the biography. To that end I can only echo "Corsino's Toast" in that curious collection of stories and sketches by Hector Berlioz, *Evenings with the Orchestra:* "Here's to Music, gentlemen, her reign has come! She protects the drama, dresses up comedy, glorifies tragedy, gives a home to painting, intoxicates the dance, shows the door to that little vagabond, the ballad opera, mows down those who oppose her progress, flings out the window the representatives of routine."[8] Moreover, in the main, these films *are* well made, benefiting from the full resources of the Hollywood studio system and the idiosyncratic brilliance of impassioned European individualists like the aforementioned Russell, Tony Palmer, Miloš Forman, Mike Leigh, Renato Castellani, Gérard Corbiau, and others discussed in this book. Furthermore, an examination of the production records of many of these films confirms that exhaustive time and money were expended on researching and compiling thick volumes of factual, biographical data (even if the results often seem to contradict that). Thus, any alterations in the historical record were made deliberately, according to the working contexts of industry and consumer exigencies and demands. And we should never discount the allure of the ready-made prestige of a celebrated artist's name as a validation of studio respectability. "I want to bring culture and taste, in the form of enlightenment, to the masses," proclaimed MGM studio chief Louis B. Mayer.[9] This is no idle boast. Try as I might to smile cynically at that old pirate, I am forced to admit he achieved his ambition, perhaps in spite of himself. Millions of viewers have been introduced in dramatic fashion to lives and musics they otherwise might never have encountered. This writer is one of those millions.

A personal note is in order. As a boy growing up in a small Kansas town, I was greatly impressed by a late-night television broadcast of Charles Vidor's *A Song to Remember* (1944), a "life" of the Polish pianist/composer Chopin, starring Cornel Wilde. Its vivid hues, heightened drama, and exciting musical presentation were unforgettable. That moment when Chopin's Technicolor blood splashed on the piano keys during his fateful concert tour (surely the best remembered albeit most notorious moment in the entire oeuvre) was particularly startling. As a result, for years thereafter I embarked on a search for more information about Chopin. I attended concerts and haunted record stores trying to identify the music I had heard. I even fell upon James Huneker's biography of Chopin and eagerly devoured its overheated effusions (which rivaled those of the film!).[10] As the years passed, I encountered more composer biopics and was similarly stunned by the delirious waltz sequences of Julien Duvivier's *The Great Waltz* (1938); James Cagney's recreation of George M. Cohan's "Give My Regards to Broadway" routine in Michael Curtiz's *Yankee Doodle Dandy* (1942); the musical dictation of the paralyzed Frederick Delius (Max Adrian) to his amanuensis Eric Fenby (Christopher Gable) in Russell's *Song of Summer;* the last gasps of Mozart (Tom Hulce) as he dictated the "confutatus maledictus" to Antonio Salieri (F. Murray Abraham) near the end of *Amadeus;* and the shadow of Joseph Stalin's gigantic statue looming over the pathetic, shuffling figure of Dmitry Shostakovich (Ben Kingsley) in Palmer's *Testimony* (1987).

As I began to distinguish between the historical record and the filmic dramatizations, it was clear, of course, that great liberties had been taken. It was a challenge to juggle fact and fiction, much as one might process a piece of contrapuntal music, attending to first one then the other of the melodic strands, decentering and privileging each in turn. It was no use trying to reconcile story with history. It was a lot more rewarding to enjoy their doubled pleasures as a synergy, a cooperation, a polyphony of separate but related elements. At the very least, one might come to regard these films as if they were wayward children who, with the best of intentions, sometimes stumble and break things. They may be a nuisance at times, but they bring fresh per-spectives to our lives. Like parents, we viewers must practice tolerance while warily remaining on the watch. Support them, yes, but don't let them stray too far.

History as "Story"

Since Herodotus and Thucydides, historians and storytellers alike have pondered the intersections of fact, fiction, and speculation. Historian Simon Schama quotes a remark by the eminent mid-nineteenth-century English man of letters, Thomas Babington Macaulay, in 1828 to the effect that historiogra-phy is a negotiation between the "map" of factual data and the "painted landscape" of public and private speculation. "Macaulay viewed history as a relentlessly contested battleground between regiments of analysts and story-tellers," writes Schama, "with him stuck in a no-man's land as the polemical bullets whistled over his head."[11] Three of the twentieth century's foremost fabulists — Jorge Luis Borges, Italo Calvino, and Luigi Pirandello — have imag-ined the search for the truth of history and biography as a kind of fantastic quest. In Borges's short story "The Garden of Forking Paths," the trip takes us into a maze-like garden, where we lose our way amid a tangled continuum consisting of "an infinite series of times, in a growing, dizzying net of diver-gent, convergent and parallel times."[12] In Calvino's "Cities and Desire — 3" we visit the city of Zobeide, the site of a quest for an elusive, beautiful woman. In their dreams several men, separately and individually, pursue this woman until she disappears into the winding streets of a mysterious white city. Upon awak-ening, the dreamers determine that by building a simulacrum of this dream city, they can capture her. They lay out the streets and, at the very spot where the woman had eluded them, "arrange spaces and walls different from the dream, so she would be unable to escape again." Yet, for all their efforts to contain her, they never see her again. Ultimately, they only encounter — and recognize — each other.[13] And Pirandello's play *Right You Are (If You Think So)* explores the baffling mystery of a woman whose identity shifts and changes, according to the testimonies of those who presume to know her.[14] She herself appears at the end of the last act but refuses to resolve the dilemma: "For myself, I am nobody," she announces. "Make of me what you will." The response — indeed, the only possible response — comes from the character of Mr. Laudisi, who all along has stood apart from the proceedings and watched in bemusement at the growing confusion. He does the only thing a reasonable person can do in the face of paradox: he laughs.

Historians and cultural theorists sympathetic to the kinds of films outlined in this book — variously categorized as "docudramas," "meta-histories," "virtual histories," "counterfactuals,"and so on — formulate admittedly tortuous but compelling arguments of their own concerning their interstices of history and fantasy. This book chooses neither to contest nor to contribute to such learned disquisitions. But it is necessary briefly to acknowledge them. Rosenstone in *Revisioning History,* for example, has argued that it is a mistake to condemn historical films and biopics out of hand for their historical transgressions; rather, they should be taken "on their own terms as a portrait of the past that has less to do with fact than with intensity and insight, perception and feeling, with showing how events affect individual lives, past and present." He adds: "To express the meaning of the past, film creates proximate, appropriate characters, situations, images, and metaphors."[15] History may thus be comprehended as a *story,* an *interpretation,* asserts Hayden White, Presidential Professor of Historical Studies at the University of California at Santa Cruz, "because it is here that our desire for the imaginary, the possible, must contest with the imperatives of the real, the actual."[16] The historical record may be either so fulsome as to demand exclusion of certain facts as "irrelevant to the narrative purpose" or so sparse as to demand reconstruction of an event "by filling in the gaps in this information on inferential or speculative grounds." Either way, historical narrative is thus "necessarily a mixture of adequately and inadequately explained events, a congeries of established and inferred facts."[17]

These interpretations may take account of or allude to the *public constructions* of history that, while not necessarily claiming factual basis, possess their own kind of legitimacy, borne out of their widespread repetition, variability, and appeal. Biographical subjects are polysemic texts, open to ongoing processes of signification and resignification, nexes of cultural processes and interpretations. They are open, as cultural historian Leo Braudy has noted in his classic study of fame, *The Frenzy of Renown,* to the constantly renewed interpretations and meanings of successive generations, "even though that meaning might be very different from what they meant a hundred or a thousand years before." Braudy concludes: "Such people are vehicles of cultural memory and cohesion. They allow us to identify what's present with what's past."[18] Meanwhile, informed speculation interrogates the all too porous historical record, fills in the holes, plugs the gaps, and squints hard at accepted truths. They insist, explains historian Niall Ferguson, on reconstructing the determining conditions of events. They reenact, dramatize, embellish, even rewrite the past — not only according to informed and dramatized speculations, but also according to their own makers' empathetic contacts with the subject.

Thus, in the absence of confirming proof, as well as contradictory evidence — and taking as examples a few of the biopics already cited — it may not be probable but it is at least *possible* that Salieri poisoned Mozart, that Schubert never finished his Eighth Symphony, that Chopin's burning Polish patriotism drove him to an early death, that a young Brahms played piano in brothels, that Wagner stole many of his musical ideas from Liszt and Berlioz, that Strauss collaborated actively with the Nazi Party, that Shostakovich was a closet dissident in Soviet Russia, and that Foster gained inspiration for his songs from the chants of black dockworkers. "In short," Ferguson explains, "by narrowing down the historical alternatives we consider to those which are *plausible* — and hence by replacing the enigma of 'chance' with the calculation of *probabilities* — we solve the dilemma of choosing between a single deterministic past and an unmanageably infinite number of possible pasts. The counterfactuals we need to construct are not mere fantasy: they are simulations based on calculations about the relative probability of plausible outcomes in a chaotic world."[19] Maybe, as many writers have radically suggested, the South really did win the Civil War, or, as proposed in Russell's *Dance of the Seven Veils,* Strauss really was a Nazi (in political accommodation if not in practice).

Writer Melvyn Bragg confirmed this method based on probability and intuition while writing the script of Russell's *The Music Lovers* (1970), a film about Pyotr Tchaikovsky: "You're *betting* on things, really, trying to imagine how the characters behave and what they say. It wasn't a difficult bet. Ken and I would talk about these things all the time, and then I would go away and write; and as I wrote, I would firm up my convictions and write it that way. You might call it deep intuition, if you were polite."[20] Russell himself, as will be seen in later chapters, frequently relies on this imaginatively intuitive process.

Mythic and Public Constructions of Genius

Since the Renaissance, and culminating in later nineteenth-century Romanticism, artists of every stripe had come to be regarded as heroic figures of protean, even supernatural energies, whose supreme accomplishments were held to be *inventions* rather than imitations. They themselves were subjected to considerable invention on the part of their biographers, acolytes, and friends. "What is important to us," writes Rutgers University professor of philosophy Peter Kivy in *The Possessor and the Possessed,* "is not what may be true about the nature of Handel's genius, or Mozart's or Beethoven's, but what was taken for truth by those who were in the process of constructing the concept of musical genius."[21] Anecdotal accuracy was irrelevant, declare Viennese historians Ernst Kris and Otto Kurz in their classic 1934 investigation of the intersections of art history and psychoanalytical theory, *Legend, Myth, and Magic in the Image of the Artist:* "The only significant factor is that an anecdote recurs, that it is recounted so frequently as to warrant the conclusion that it represents a typical image of the artist."[22] In other words, public history claims its own reality. It functions as a kind of counterpoint to the historical life.

The two primary models for these mythic constructions, against which other composers would be measured to greater and lesser degrees, were George Frideric Handel and Wolfgang Amadeus Mozart. Handel was the first composer to be admitted to the pantheon of artistic genius (hitherto reserved for literary icons Homer, Milton, and Shakespeare) and the first to benefit from artist biographies.[23] As Kivy explains, Handel was mythologized as the self-possessed genius who sets his own rules. Rooted in the writings of the Roman philosopher Longinus, this myth held that a true genius was an active creator, a "possessor" endowed with an unusually powerful mind and apt to violate artistic rules in pursuit of his goals. The artist was revered, Kivy continues, more for his originality than for his imitative talent, more for "deviating from the rules of art than in adhering to them."[24] The artistic products of this type of genius are sublime rather than beautiful: "These are the acts of men, not the deliverances of gods."[25] Thus, egotism, indomitable will, eccentricity, even madness frequently attend the "possessor."

The "possessor" myth was inherited early in the nineteenth century by Ludwig van Beethoven—the Romantic personification of the democratic revolt against the restrictions of class divisions and musical conventions. Kivy explains that Beethoven's status as genius, conferred upon him by the Romantics and by his first biographers,[26] gave him the right to break conventions and formulate new models that other, nongeniuses may subsequently follow. "No artist that I know of more perfectly exemplifies this than Beethoven," writes Kivy, "for no artist that I know of was more vilified in his lifetime, or more admired afterward, for breaking the artistic commandments, of which music, perhaps, has more than its fair share."[27] And it might be argued that Berlioz, Pierre Boulez, Claude Debussy, Charles Ives, Liszt, Gustav Mahler, Arnold Schoenberg, Roger Sessions, Shostakovich, Igor Stravinsky, Tchaikovsky, and Wagner and extended the myth into the later nineteenth and twentieth centuries.

By contrast, Mozart represents the musical genius as a "possessed," hence passive, genius. Rooted in Plato and later espoused in Schopenhauer, this "possession" theory holds that the muse, or God, speaks through the poet. This has led to the "Amadeus myth" of the genius who is naïve and rather childlike, but who is gifted with prodigious "natural" talents and who creates with seemingly no effort at all. It was Mozart's associates and early biographers who first presented him in this light (and it is the image that dominates Peter Shaffer's play and film *Amadeus,* as will be discussed elsewhere in this book).[28] "What a sad and great destiny it is to be an artist!" wrote Liszt appositely in 1837 at the height of his public celebrity. "He certainly does not choose his vocation; it takes possession of him and drives him on. . . . He creates an impenetrable solitude within his soul [where he] contemplates and worships the ideal that his entire being will seek to reproduce."[29] Parenthetically, there is a measure of disingenuousness in this remark, considering Liszt was the most self-propelled of musicians and composers, who established single-handedly not only the celebrity status of the performer but also a proto-modernist direction in music. Anton Bruckner, John Cage, Antonín Dvořák, Schubert, Robert Schumann, and later popular composers Foster, W. C. Handy, Irving Berlin, Jerome Kern, George Gershwin, Bob Dylan, and the songwriting team of John Lennon and Paul McCartney are among the seemingly naive, "possessed" geniuses who fit conveniently into this category.

Neither of these antimonies in itself would prove to be suitable for the movies' construction of musical genius, particularly for the agendas of the Hollywood studios. Neither category was responsive to populist responsibilities. The "possessed" genius was too detached from worldly affairs, and the "possessor" genius was too arrogant and overriding to respect societal and artistic conventions. It was only in Kivy's third category — the hard-working craftspersons (such as Johann Sebastian Bach, Franz Joseph Haydn, Felix Mendelssohn, Nikolai Rimsky-Korsakov, Virgil Thomson, and the Tin Pan Alley and Broadway tunesmiths) — that both manifestations of genius might achieve the equipoise, the balance between the two extremes, that could be best impressed into the service of popular entertainment. Thus, the movies construct a paradigm of the composer — as well as of the creative artist in general — who struggles to express and contain within himself or herself the antinomies of the "possessed" and the "possessor" types of genius. Parenthetically, this paradigm, with many variations, can also be found in the many celebrity biopics of athletes, entertainers, scientists, politicians, soldiers, and so on. Ultimately, they are all brothers under the skin.

Musical Canons

Meanwhile, the growth and proliferation in the nineteenth and early twentieth centuries of music publishing, instrument manufacture, and concert management increased the public consumption and familiarity with another canon — that of particular classical and popular works. Cultural historian William Weber, in "Mass Culture and the Reshaping of European Musical Taste, 1770–1870," examines the process by which a pantheon, or "canon," of great lives and works was first established. Whereas as late as 1840 most Viennese and Parisian concertgoers had scoffed at the idea that the greatest music might lie already in the past, by 1860 things had radically changed. Orchestra conductors/entrepreneurs like Mendelssohn in Leipzig, Otto Nicolai in Vienna, Francois Habeneck in Paris, and John Ella in London consolidated programs of "classics" by dead composers that possessed for publishers the stabilizing virtues of lower costs and audience familiarity. "The worship of the masters spread like a lofty canopy over all of European musical life, over concerts large and small, high and low."[30] Today, that canon goes under the rubric of the classical "Top 40" marketed in numerous advertisements, record sales, and broadcast programs.

Late in the nineteenth century, Chicago conductor Theodore Thomas, Boston publisher John Sullivan Dwight, and such New York–based entrepreneurs, musicians, and critics as Anton Seidl, Henry Krehbiel, and Jeannette Thurber played key roles in transplanting the "classical" canon to American shores. Dwight, an influential critic and journalist, had fought for decades to promote in his *Dwight's Journal of Music* the establishment of an American opera company and a great symphony orchestra that "would epitomize and disseminate the highest musical standards," to perform a "sacralized art" that would "create in time the taste which would patronize and reward it." Public concerts and recitals would serve a conservator function, "to keep the standard master works from falling into disregard, to make Bach and Handel, Haydn and Mozart and Beethoven, Schubert, Mendelssohn, and Schumann, and others worthy of such high companionship continually felt as living presences and blessed influences among us." In his efforts to form a Chicago Orchestra, Thomas proclaimed his determination to perform "the great works of the great composers"; he dubbed Bach, Handel, Mozart, and Beethoven "sons of God!" Thus, "the great works of the great composers greatly performed, the best and profoundest art, these and these alone," he insisted, would form the core of his repertory.[31] In New York, meanwhile, conductor Seidl led the way in establishing the Wagnerian operatic repertoire, Thurber imported Dvořák to head the newly established National Conservatory of American Music, and Krehbiel kept his journalist's pen at the ready to promote all these activities.[32]

High and Low

Such attitudes and endeavors, writes American music historian Charles Hamm, were part and parcel of the emergence of tightly stratified class structures in the United States in the second half of the nineteenth century: "Classical music became more and more associated with the cultural and economic elite; the very notion that one body of music is superior to all others and can be understood and 'appreciated' only by a small, privileged segment of the population is in itself elitist. The American people were perceived as being split into 'us' and 'them,' and in a way that was judgmental." Moreover, continues Hamm, "this cultural divide corresponded to ethnic and national divisions as well: most of the elite were of Anglo-Saxon descent, most 'others' were Irish, Italian, black, German, Scandinavian, and soon Central European and southern Mediterranean."[33] However, as will be seen throughout this book, the boundaries of these cultural antimonies would subsequently alter and blur, in no small measure due to the numerous biopics of classical and popular composers.

Inevitably, when the new century introduced the disseminating technologies of phonographs, radio broadcasting, and motion pictures, the hard and fast divisions in American attitudes toward "high" and "low" culture began to break down. As music critic and commentator Joseph Horowitz has pointed out in his book *The Post-Classical Predicament,* a new breed of cultural spokespersons "tutored a broader, more passive audience" than that reached and instructed by Krehbiel and Dwight. "The listener does not have to be a tutored man or person technically versed in the intricacies of the art of composition," opined *New York Times* critic Olin Downes, "to understand perfectly well what the orchestra [is] saying to him."[34]

The nationwide promotion of a canon of classical "great works" flourished in such books as George Marek's *How to Listen to Music over the Radio* (1937) and *A Good Housekeeping Guide to Musical Enjoyment* (1949) as well as in the writings of Downes; in network radio broadcasts of opera performances, concerts by Toscanini's NBC Orchestra, and music programs like Walter Damrosch's *Music Appreciation Hour;* and in the "swing" adaptations of the classics by bandleaders such as Freddy Martin, Claude Thornhill, Benny Goodman, and Artie Shaw. Damrosch's NBC broadcasts alone, begun in 1928, were said to reach seven million students in seventy thousand schools within the next decade. Horowitz quotes NBC chief David Sarnoff as dubbing Damrosch "America's leading ambassador of music understanding and music appreciation." (Hollywood certainly took notice of Damrosch's grandfatherly, popular image, casting him "as himself" in several films, including the George Gershwin 1946 biopic *Rhapsody in Blue* and the Ernest R. Ball 1944 biopic *Irish Eyes Are Smiling.*) These popularizers, furthers Horowitz, "fostered a new elitism: to participate in the exclusive aura of Great Music became a democratic privilege."[35]

The introduction of sound technology in the film industry likewise facilitated and accelerated this process. "People's appreciation of music [has been] raised quite a bit in the last four years," noted American operetta composer Sigmund Romberg, who worked in Hollywood in the 1930s. "They have learned to like the better class of music. . . . [I]t is to the movies that we owe this sense of appreciation. [They have presented] real music and the movie-going public learned to like it."[36] Indeed, the earliest experiments in synchronized sound, Edison's Kinetophone process in 1913 and 1914, Lee DeForest's Phonofilms of the mid-1920s, the Fox Movietones of the late 1920s, and Warner Bros. Vitaphone short subjects from 1926 to 1929 brought to moviegoers programs modeled after the kinds of mixtures of classical and popular music long since established on vaudeville bills — the juxtaposition of opera singers and classical instrumentalists, including Giovanni Martinelli and Mischa Elman, with music hall and Broadway stars such as Al Jolson and Fanny Brice.

The time was right for Hollywood to appropriate the classical canon of "great lives" and "great works," strip away some of its elitist posturings, and commodify and market it to a mass audience. Beethoven, for example, could no longer be "sold" as a colossal genius whose "sublimity was so overwhelming that it compels one's awe and reverence as well as one's admiration."[37] Rather, he and the other canonical composers had to be modified and reconfigured into recognizable and accessible individuals who redirected and consolidated the antimonies of their genius — "possessed" and "possessor" — into the service of the social welfare and cultural aspirations of the community at large. As music teacher Joseph Elsner tells Chopin in *A Song to Remember*, "A man worthy of his gifts should grow closer to those people as he grows more great."

Their music must be likewise commodified into a tuneful kind of "classical greatest hits," such as Beethoven's "Ode to Joy," Schubert's "Unfinished Symphony" and "Ave Maria," Liszt's "Liebestraum" ("Song of Love") Johann Strauss Jr.'s "Blue Danube" and "Tales of the Vienna Woods" waltzes, Rimsky-Korsakov's *Scheherazade*, and Brahms's "Lullaby" — to cite just a few among thousands of examples — and condensed, adapted in a variety of instrumentations, and deployed as "shorthand" emotional and thematic cues to accompany and enhance the dramatic contexts for silent and sound films.[38] Thus, they function in several capacities: They serve as extradiegetic "background" music in cartoons (especially the Carl Stalling–composed scores for Warner Bros. cartoons[39]) and genre films (horror films and romantic fantasies like the pastiches of Liszt, Schumann, and Berlioz tunes in the horror film *The Black Cat* [1934] and Dmitri Tiomkin's compilation of Debussy tunes in the romantic fantasy *Portrait of Jennie* [1948]). They are heard as "themselves" in musical films about real and fictional classical instrumentalists and singers

The composer Erich Wolfgang Korngold (right) demonstrates conducting techniques to Alan Badel, who portrays Richard Wagner, on the set of *Magic Fire* (1954). (Courtesy Photo-fest/Republic Pictures)

(such as the many opera films and musicals starring Lawrence Tibbett, Grace Moore, Lily Pons, José Iturbi, Leopold Stokowski, Jascha Heifitz).[40] And they provide the "soundtracks" to the lives of composers (such as the many biopics examined in this book). In sum, Hollywood exploits and confirms the enduring familiarity and popularity of the musical canon.

At the same time Hollywood applied the classical composer paradigm to the tunesmiths of Tin Pan Alley, establishing a popular "canon," if you will, responsive to the late-nineteenth-century preachments of composer Dvořák, the pioneering work of ethnomusicologist Arthur Farwell, the increased dissemination of music by the rapidly growing sheet music industry, and the proliferation of player piano rolls, nickelodeons, and phonographs. American music at this time was quickly finding its own indigenous voice, or constellation of voices. "The new American school of music must strike its roots deeply into its own soil," wrote Dvořák in a letter to the *New York Herald* on 28 May 1893. The "Negro melodies," the "red man's chant," the "plaintive ditties" of immigrants will commingle into "the natural voice of a free and vigorous

Director George Cukor (right) confers on the set with Dirk Bogarde, who portrays Franz Liszt in *Song without End* (1960). (Courtesy Photofest/Columbia Pictures)

race."[41] In *St. Louis Blues* (1958) the African-American composer Handy (Nat King Cole) declares, appositely: "The music I play is the music of our people. It's not mine, it's theirs. I was born with this music in me." Fueled by a New World's instincts and mentored by Old World traditions, the screen incarnations of Foster, George Gershwin, Handy, Kern, and others rose above the mere status of tunesmiths to the level of spokespersons for the rapidly evolving American Dream.

The Peoples' Music

In sum, Hollywood was determined to bring the classical composer and the popular songwriter — the Old World and the New — together in a *juste-milieu* synergy or equilibrium. There were ethical and moral lessons here: The classical composer must bow to the dictates of "the people," and the popular composer must strive for the legitimacy of the "classics." The extraordinary individual must not overreach himself, because success has a price, and the humble artist must strive for social and cultural improvement, lest he sink into frustration and mediocrity. In other words, those "possessed" geniuses must climb out of their ivory tower and industriously pursue the American work ethic; and those "possessor" figures must relinquish their autonomy and blend their voices with those voices around them. These antimonies must meet, as it were, somewhere in between. "America is a mixture of things that are very old with more that is new," a classically trained teacher tells George Gershwin (Robert Alda) in *Rhapsody in Blue* (1946). "Your nature has the same contradictions, ideals and material ambition. If you can make them both serve, you will give America a voice."

Thus, the similarities in these films between Hollywood's constructions of Schubert and Foster, between Liszt and Gershwin are not accidental. They border on identity. Their collective portraits are like the composite drawings found in police files, whose faces are collations of "types" of eyes, ears, noses, chins, and hairlines gathered together from sundry disparate sources. Composers, statesmen, inventors, athletes, artists, soldiers, and the like are not specific individuals existing at specific times, but collective entities for all times that function as catalysts of social, political, and cultural change. They refract contemporary issues and concerns through the filters of the past; they provide escape routes into nostalgia; and, in sum, they subsume the complexities and contradictions of biography into texts that are entertaining, informative, and accessible. Moreover, they reflect another, more immediate kind of history — that is, the corporate contexts of the movie studios, the personal agendas of the filmmakers, the pressures of the star system, the exigencies of budgets, the interventions of censorship, the expectations of targeted audiences, and so on.

Program Notes

This book is intended to appeal not only to specialists in music history and film history but also to the many general viewers and readers who enjoy in biopics the special confluences of both music and film. Chapters One and Two examine in detail a substantial representation of Hollywood and foreign biopics of classical and popular composers made during the studio era (1930–1960). Chapters Three and Four examine at length the composer biopics of two prolific and highly idiosyncratic British filmmakers: the irrepressible Ken Russell, a controversial figure whose more recent composer biopics have unjustly been overlooked in scholarly and popular studies, and the extraordinary Tony Palmer, an extremely important but unaccountably neglected figure in contemporary cinema studies. Both Russell and Palmer usher the composer biopic into the postmodern attitude and sensibility. Their films *struggle against history*, to paraphrase Rosenstone. They employ subjective intervention, invent micro-narratives as alternatives to history, and raise questions about the validity of their own texts.[42] Chapter Five investigates many more independent and experimental films and video productions that are less easily categorized and located. For every popular work like *Amadeus,* for example, there are relatively unknown biopics such as *The Debussy Film* (1965), *Testimony* (1987), and *Mit meinen heissen Tränen* (1987). They, too, deserve our attention.

However, this book is only a beginning. The subject of the composer biopic is far broader than at first might be supposed. For example, there were many such films made during the era of the silent film. The absence of a synchronized soundtrack did not preclude films such as Henry Roussell's Chopin film, *Waltz de l'adieu* (1928)—a film explored later in this book—from supplementing their stories with musical cue sheets for the theater-house musicians. Sorely needed, moreover, is an examination of French, Italian, Russian, Scandinavian, and Spanish composer biopics. And particularly lamentable is the conspicuous absence in current scholarship of the role composer biopics have played in the political and propaganda agendas of Nazi Germany in the 1930s and in the Russian and Eastern European communist regimes during the Cold War.[43]

What this book is *not* is a history of *performer* biopics, of which Hollywood has produced many. Conspicuously absent here, for reasons of economy of space as much as the need to maintain the parameters of the composer model, are jazz biopics such as *Young Man with a Horn* (1950), *The Glenn Miller Story* (1954), *The Benny Goodman Story* (1955), and *Bird* (1988), as well as pop and rock and classical performer pictures such as *The Jolson Story* (1946), *The Great Caruso* (1951), *The Helen Morgan Story* (1957), *Lady Sings the Blues* (1972), *The Doors* (1991), and so on. To be sure, most of these films display elements of the composer paradigm discussed in this book, and the interested reader is advised to turn to Krin Gabbard's estimable book, *Jamming at the Margins,* which devotes a chapter to the examination of many of these titles.[44]

The Chase Is On

Finally, as we examine in these pages dramatizations of composers' lives and works, we find ourselves examining Macaulay's maps and paintings, chasing down Borges's garden of forking paths, running through the streets of Calvino's white city, and harking to Laudisi's laughter. We may well wonder in the end if this search for the "truths" of fact and fiction alike is a doomed quest; that it might leave us, as Schama has lamented, "forever chasing shadows, painfully aware of their inability ever to reconstruct a dead world in its completeness, however thorough or revealing their documentation." We fear we may even find ourselves "forever hailing someone who has just gone around the corner and [is] out of earshot."[45] Maybe Laudisi's laughter is on *us* (it's an ancient mirth, after all). Ultimately, we might find ourselves sharing the fascination biographer James Boswell had for his great subject, Dr. Johnson — we may be really seeking a likeness of *ourselves*.

The Classical Style
Composers in the Studio Era

In our time the public takes the initiative and asks for all the family secrets, all the details of one's private life. Do you have the semblance of a reputation? Then people want to know the color of your bedroom slippers, the cut of your dressing gown, the kind of tobacco you prefer, and what you call your favorite greyhound. The newspapers, eager to profit from this pitiable curiosity, heap anecdote upon anecdote, falsehood upon falsehood, and cater to the idle amusement of the salons [which welcome] the vilest gossip, the silliest slander, with unprecedented alacrity.

— Franz Liszt, 1837

Studio Systems

The canon of classical composers already discussed in the Introduction — Ludwig van Beethoven, Frédéric Chopin, Franz Liszt, Franz Schubert, Robert Schumann, Pyotr Tchaikovsky, Richard Wagner, and others — first reached American and British screens at the precise time that the studio system in Hollywood and England was at its peak, and when the popularity of movies was at its height. Many film historians refer to this time, roughly 1930–1960, as the "classical period" of the studio system. By no means coincidentally, it also was the "golden age" of the composer biopic, both classical and popular (the popular songwriter biopics are discussed in Chapter Two).

The American film industry was dominated by the vertically integrated "Big Five" studios (MGM, Paramount, Warner Bros., RKO, and Twentieth Century-Fox), by the "Little Three" studios (United Artists, Universal, and Columbia), and by smaller, independent studios (such as Republic and Disney). Under the supervision of the moguls — Louis B. Mayer, Harry Cohn, Darryl F. Zanuck, Jack Warner, Walt Disney, and others — and through their respective distribution networks and theater chains, a "consistent system of production and consumption, a set of formalized creative practices and constraints, and thus a body of work with a uniform style, a standard way of telling stories, from camera work and cutting to plot structure and thematics" was established. This oligopoly would not break down until the mid-1960s, when the Supreme Court–mandated divestiture of studio-owned theaters effectively ended it.[1]

At the same time British producers and supervisors like Michael Balcon and J. Arthur Rank began in the mid-1930s to bring Hollywood-style centralized control and factory production principles to their own industry of hitherto scattered production entities. The Rank Organization came to embrace the Ealing, Gainsborough, Gaumont-British, and London-Denham studios; several exhibition chains, such as the Odeon theaters; and the distribution outlets of General Film Distributors. Despite repeated protestations from Balcon that they were making intrinsically "British" pictures — promoting a national cinema, as it were — Balcon, Rank, and others were in reality shaping their pictures to be as commercially attractive as possible to the American market.[2]

Thus, the American and British biopics in general — although a minor genre numbering substantially fewer titles than melodramas, westerns, and horror films — were shaped by and subjected to similar pressures and standards. Because most of them were joint productions, cofinanced and released through the distribution outlets of both countries, these biopics revealed a kinship in theme and structure that answered to the same personal and political agendas of producers and writers, the exigencies of the star system, the restrictions of the censorship codes, and the economic necessity of appealing to the widest possible audience base.[3] In sum, asserts film historian George F. Custen in his pioneering study of biopics, they "reduce their lives to a mass-tailored contour for fame in which greatness is generic and difference has controllable boundaries."[4]

From 1930 to 1960 Hollywood led the way in sheer numbers of biopics with, according to Custen, an estimated 300 features, 227 of which came from the 8 major film studios and 14 from independent production entities, like

Republic and Monogram. One-quarter of these pictures focused on artists and entertainers (many of the composer biopics discussed in this book were created during the last two decades of this period). Twentieth Century-Fox produced the most with 14, followed by MGM with 13.

The British film industry, by contrast, whose markets were one-quarter the size of the American markets and whose theaters were dominated by American films, produced far fewer biopics. Current research has yet to tabulate their precise number, but they included a variety of prestigious patriotic and artistic efforts, such as Alfred Hitchcock's *Waltzes from Vienna* (Johann Strauss, Jr., 1933); Alexander Korda's *The Private Life of Henry VIII* (1933), *Rembrandt* (1936), and *That Hamilton Woman* (Admiral Nelson and Lady Hamilton, 1943); Rank's *The Great Mr. Handel* (1942) and *Bad Lord Byron* (1951); the team of Frank Launder and Sidney Gilliatt's *Young Mr. Pitt* (1942) and *The Story of Gilbert and Sullivan* (1953); and Ronald Neame's *The Magic Box* (William Friese-Greene, 1951).

Representative American and British composer biopics released during the classical period are arranged for discussion in this chapter in roughly chronological order: *Waltzes from Vienna* (1933, Gaumont-British), *Blossom Time* (1936, British-International), *The Great Waltz* (1938, MGM), *The Melody Master* (1941, United Artists), *The Great Mr. Handel* (1942, Rank-GWH), *A Song to Remember* (1945, Columbia), *The Magic Bow* (1946, Rank/Universal-International), *Song of Love* (1947, MGM), *Song of Scheherazade* (1947, Universal-International), *The Story of Gilbert and Sullivan* (1953, British Lion–London Films), *Magic Fire* (1954, Republic), *Song without End* (1960, Columbia), and two Disney biopics, *The Peter Tchaikovsky Story* (1959) and *The Magnificent Rebel* (1962). Each film is briefly synopsized, its dramatic discourse compared with the factual biographical record, and its contemporary contexts and critical reaction measured. The end of this chapter is reserved for an investigation of the censorial restraints imposed on each film.

Based on the paradigm of the composer subject established in the Introduction, these works reveal the following commonly held agendas: (1) They conform the "life" so as to make it congruent with the narrative structures and formulas common to romantic melodramas, musicals, westerns, horror films, and so on. (2) They "normalize" and contain the artist's life, depicting him or her, on the one hand, as a somewhat marginalized individual struggling against stifling societal conformism and, on the other, as a citizen striving to compose a "song of the people" that reflects, confirms, and celebrates the community's own commonly held experiences. (3) They tailor the artist's life to the prevailing screen images of the actors that appear in the cast. (4) They cater to the "prestige" ambitions of the studio producers. (5) They "adjust" the life against possible litigiousness from relatives of the subject (an especially important consideration in the Tin Pan Alley biopics discussed in Chapter Two). And (6) they pluck the musical texts out of their historical contexts and, in addition to exploiting their familiarity and performance values, transmute them into collages and pastiches deployed via the programmatic and leitmotif techniques of late-nineteenth-century "Romantic" composers.

This last agenda needs some elaboration. Reconfiguring classical music into a motion picture soundtrack strips away its autonomy, wrenches it from its original historical frame, and subordinates it to an extradiegetic role in the narrative discourse. Assigning specific meanings to the music—a musico-dramatic strategy derived from the leitmotif system of opera composer Richard Wagner[5]—imposes programmatic connotations upon the viewer and promotes what cultural historian Theodor Adorno rather grandly terms "conditioned reflexes"—"a system of response-mechanisms wholly antagonistic to the ideal of individuality in a free, liberal society."[6] It is the great irony of the classical composer biopics, writes historian Carol Flinn, that the greatest music ever written should merely be used to repeat or reinforce the action in the image—"it should not 'go beyond' it or draw attention to itself *qua* music. After all, it was only 'background' music.'" Thus, no matter how distinguished the score, "it is not successful unless it is secondary to the story being told on the screen."[7] This judgment needs some qualification, however; inasmuch as the *performative* aspects of the music do on occasion become an important part of the biopics.

Deploying these practices in composer biopics and other film projects were a number of European- and Eastern European–trained composers who emigrated to Hollywood and brought with them what historian Tony Thomas has dubbed the traditions of the "Mittel-Europa Strain" of late-nineteenth-century classical music.[8] For example, Dimitri Tiomkin, famous for his western scores (*High Noon,* 1951, and *Red River,* 1948), studied at the St. Petersburg Conservatory of Music under Alexander Glazunov and Felix Blumenthal; Miklos Rozsa, noted for his many Korda and MGM historical films (*The Jungle Book,* 1938, and *Ben Hur,* 1959), studied at the Franz Liszt Academy in Budapest and under Hermann Grabner at the Leipzig Conservatory of Music; Erich Wolfgang Korngold, a Viennese wunderkind who made his Hollywood reputation scoring Errol Flynn vehicles (*Robin Hood,* 1939, and *The Sea Hawk,* 1940), was encouraged in his studies by no less than Richard Strauss, Gustav Mahler, and Giacomo Puccini; Constantin Bakaleinikoff studied at the Moscow Conservatory before coming to America to work as a music director for MGM, RKO, and Paramount; and Max Steiner, another Viennese prodigy who grew up under the influence of his famous grandfather, Maximilian Steiner (the impresario of the Theatre an der Wien), and who studied with Mahler, became the most prolific composer in Hollywood, creating for RKO, David O. Selznick, and Warner Bros. the scores for such classics as *King Kong* (1933), *Yankee Doodle Dandy* (1942), and *Gone with the Wind* (1939).[9] Less well known but also deserving attention is Heinz Roemheld, head of Universal studio's music department, who had studied music in Berlin.

Finally, the composer biopic confronts the unique challenge of visualizing the actual creative process. "Plays about musicians or writers have one insurmountable problem in common," observes commentator Patrick O'Connor. "It is the least dramatic situation imaginable to show the artist at work, sitting at his desk, or at the keyboard. He must pace the floor, throw tantrums, be tormented by doubts, tear his hair. That is how the creative life seems to audiences, or so [authors and filmmakers] suppose."[10] Actor Simon Callow, who portrayed Mozart in the original stage production of *Amadeus,* agrees: "It's nonsensical, when you think about it. Maybe you can show something that *stimulates* creativity, but what about the interior process itself? Where does *that* come from? Very few filmmakers or playwrights seem to be interested in the actual question of creativity. And maybe that's true of 80 percent of the people. That sort of thing is probably done best in a novel. Oddly, it might be easier to visualize creative bankruptcy. We all can share in *that* feeling!"[11] Like the biographical aspects of the subject, the mystery of musical creativity itself has to be contained within the parameters of a mass audience's experience and understanding. Without such containment, declares UCLA art historian Albert Boime, "We risk the stereotype of the mad artist — creativity as some kind of disease or psychological aberration. This indicates our underlying fear and anxiety about creativity. Hollywood has to use stereotypes as a way of negotiating that fear."[12] For example, as the following discussion illustrates, composer biopics deploy visual strategies that reveal musical inspiration deriving from nature, folk traditions (the "voice of the people"), the emotions (love, hate, sorrow, frustration, triumph, and so on), and the divine (spiritual inspiration).

A Selection of Films

Blossom Time (1936), a British biopic about Franz Schubert (1797–1828), adapts to the screen the paradigm of the publicly constructed artist's life, which has its roots in Schubert's own day. It is the model of the dramatized "life" that has continued to manifest itself, with variations not only in the many theatrical and film biographies about Schubert that have appeared in the past century—more plays, operettas, and films have been produced about Schubert than any other composer, excepting only Franz Liszt and Johann Strauss, Jr.—but also in the biopics of the other classical and popular composers discussed throughout this book.

At first glance Schubert's life scarcely seems suggestive of such far-reaching dramatic implications. Born in Vienna in 1797, he grew up in the humble household of a schoolmaster, sang as a boy in the Imperial Chapel's choristers, and, after a desultory attempt at teaching in his father's school, decided to pursue a composing career. Although he was encouraged by a small circle of artists and writers, many of his major works—including operas, symphonies, religious music, and chamber works—failed to find a wide public and remained unpublished. Indeed, he held only one public concert of his works, on March 26, 1828. Only his prodigious output of songs and dance music was well known in his lifetime. Schubert traveled seldom, never held an official appointment, never married, earned only enough to survive, and died in 1828 at age thirty-one of typhoid and complications of tertiary syphilis.

Ironically, the gaps in our knowledge of Schubert's life and the seemingly modest surface of his activities—not to mention the commercial viability of his glorious melodies—were among the very factors that attracted dramatists. Even before his death, his life and music were already being wrenched from his private space and thrust into the more public arena of collective myth. "The externals of Schubert's life," writes historian Robert Winter, "its brief span, the prodigious output, the lack of public turning points—invited writers to create a make-believe world bathed in nostalgia, a world where genius overcomes poverty and people have no sweat glands. For a century that was constantly reminded of its loss of innocence, Schubert offered a source of refuge and comfort."[13] Contemporary accounts, memoirs, and anecdotes from friends and colleagues labeled him as a kind of cherubic idiot savant—"a guileless child romping among giants," as Schumann famously observed, a modest, relatively untutored *schwammerl* ("little mushroom") who sat in coffeehouses and effortlessly improvised dance tunes for his amiable circle but who was unlucky in life and love and who died young, impoverished and neglected. "Unfortunately," writes biographer Brian Newbould, "fiction often being hardier than fact, this concoction had an enduring influence on the popular conception of Schubert as a man and composer which has still not been eradicated."[14] This lament will be heard countless times throughout these pages, as will the counterargument—that the various literary, theatrical, and cinematic incarnations of *Blossom Time* have brought Schubert and his music to the very public he so avidly, but unsuccessfully, courted during his own tragically brief lifetime.

No matter that revisionist historians (Maynard Solomon is one recent out-standing example) point to a very different reality. They reference the gay subculture in which Schubert may have moved, his apparent lack of interest in women,, the moods of alienation and suicide expressed in his letters, the egomaniacal outbursts among his friends, the relative degree of success in publishing much of his music, the innovative/problematic nature of his last experimental compositions, and the controversies over the precise cause of his death.[15] Yet, it is the highly sentimentalized fiction that first attracted popular favor, was consolidated by Schubert's first biographer, Heinrich Kreissle von Hellborn, and given its fullest elaboration by George Grove in 1882.

After the turn of the twentieth century this public construction of Schubert's life was incarnated in a novel by Rudolf Bartsch called *Schwammerl* (1912), which was adapted into a *singspiel* in 1916, *Das Dreimäderlhaus* (*The House of Three Girls*). In this variation on *Cyrano de Bergerac,* Schubert is a penni-less young composer who courts Hannerl, the youngest of three sisters. But she is in love with Herr Schober, an aristocrat who has impressed her with his singing of, ironically, a Schubert song. Heartbroken, Schubert can find solace only in his music. In some versions of the story, after losing the girl, Schubert composes "Ave Maria" on his deathbed; in other versions, he leaves behind him an "unfinished" work, the Eighth Symphony — that musical emblem of thwarted hopes and unfulfilled love.

Das Dreimäderlhaus enjoyed an eighteen-month run in Vienna and toured in revivals for several decades thereafter. In London the show's book and music were slightly altered and retitled *Lilac Time*; in Paris it was known as *Chanson d'Amour;* and in America in a 1921 Sigmund Romberg–Dorothy Donnelly adaptation, it was retitled *Blossom Time* (the generic title I use throughout this discussion). This American version, for which Romberg se-lected and adapted several new Schubert songs, brought Romberg his first great stage success (see Chapter Two for a discussion of Romberg and the film that purported to tell *his* life story, *Deep in My Heart*). Schubert is a poor, unrecognized composer who loves Mitzi, the daughter of a gentleman living in the apartment below him. Because she loves his music, he writes her a love song and asks his best friend, Schober, to sing it to her. Schubert plays the piano and Schober sings the song. But Mitzi only has eyes for Schober and rushes into his arms and confesses her love. In an act of self-sacrifice, Schubert plays cupid to the young lovers. At the end, a sick and heartbroken Schubert realizes he can never win the girl. He decides, as a result, not to finish the symphony he has been writing for Mitzi. Left alone, he finds consolation only in his music. On his death bed, he hears a chorus of angels singing his last song, "Ave Maria." Among the adapted Schubert songs, in addition to "Ave Maria," was "Song of Love," derived from the second theme of the first movement of the Eighth Symphony, and the celebrated "Ständchen," or "Serenade," from the song cycle *Schwanengesang*. *Blossom Time* was a spectacular success and ran for 592 performances in its first Broadway run. For years thereafter it crisscrossed the country in numerous touring productions.

Here is a Schubert representative of the "possessed" aspect of the aforementioned paradigm of genius—the individual who, as film historian Thomas Elsaesser explains in his study of classical biopic formulas, "is both within and outside given ideological discourses, who belongs to his age and in some sense transcends it."[16] In his classic study of the history of fame, *The Frenzy of Renown,* cultural historian Leo Braudy observes that this person's celebrity status "allows the aspirant to stand out of the crowd, *but with the crowd's approval*; in its turn, the audience picks out its own dear individuality in the qualities of its heroes."[17] And as Rutgers University professor of philosophy Peter Kivy notes in *The Possessor and the Possessed,* he is someone who is divinely possessed, a "Liederfuerst": "It is not the poet who speaks but the Muse or the God *through* the poet"; and, to a lesser extent, he is the individual who by his very nature breaks rules and remains alienated from society ("The greatest natures are the least immaculate").[18] The seeming paradox is put most succinctly by the character of Joseph Elsner to Frédéric Chopin in another biopic discussed later in this chapter, *A Song to Remember:* "A man worthy of his gifts should grow closer to the people as he grows more great." By no means coincidentally, this may also be construed as reflecting the situation of the individual filmmaker who works within the collaborative studio system but who strives to exercise a degree of personal creativity.

The British film version of *Blossom Time* (American title: *April Romance*) was directed by Paul Stein and brought popular Austrian opera star Richard Tauber to the screen in his most famous stage role. Tauber's Schubert is a poor, plainspoken, and modest little man, a teacher and composer, who falls in love with Vickie (Jane Baxter), the beautiful daughter of the local dancing master. Determined to marry her, Schubert plans to finance the wedding with a concert program of his songs. The affair is a great success, but Vickie, who has been unaware of his feelings, now rejects his proposal. She is in love with a dashing soldier, Count von Hohlenberg (Carl Esmond), whom she cannot marry because of a rule prohibiting professional soldiers to marry beneath their class. Realizing that Vickie's happiness is more important than his own, Schubert hides his tears and intervenes with the Archduchess to overturn the law and allow the lovers to marry. Schubert sings his own "Ave Maria" at the church wedding. At the end he retires alone to his garret, his song still echoing in his ears.

The "possessed" side of the paradigm is intact: Schubert is a genius but his gifts are more instinctive than learned (indeed, as the passive vehicle of the Muse, he hardly seems to compose at all). He lives alone in a garret, but his populist identity is confirmed by his contacts with a convivial circle of friends in the taverns. His music, moreover, particularly "Ave Maria," can be sung in the church or in the streets, appealing to both the spirit and the heart. (It should be noted that the song popularly known as "Ave Maria" was composed three years *before* Schubert's death and has no overt churchly connections.)[19] There is a Great Love but it must ultimately be sacrificed to his work. He dies of a broken heart, neglected and impoverished, but he leaves behind the consolation of a wealth of melody that will delight and enrich the world.

The music itself — consisting primarily of selected songs (the major symphonic, chamber, and piano works are ignored) — is cleverly adapted by the musical arranger, G. H. Clutsam, to function as both source music and soundtrack accompaniment to the diegesis. The tunes are given new lyrics, arranged for modern instrumental ensembles, and assigned specific biographical meanings as they appear and reappear in a variety of shifting contexts. Several of them, including "Dein ist mein Herz," "Ungeduld," and the "Ständchen" are either sung in their entirety by Tauber (whose ear-splitting "Dein ist mein Herz" sounds more threatening than endearing) or heard in orchestral guise. "Das Wandern," for example, is used as a marching tune for Schubert's students on a country outing. The last of his piano impromptus is transformed into a gypsy dance in a tavern. A song from *Die Schöne Müllerin* is quickened into a brisk promenade in a ball scene. And the perennially popular "Ave Maria" connotes Schubert's religious convictions. The point is clear, as Schubert biographer Christopher Gibbs declares sardonically, "Schubert's music becomes the soundtrack for mythological narratives of his life. . . . [It is] fragmented and fetishized." It is a presumption that has persisted to this day, Gibbs continues: "Even with so many miserable circumstances, Schubert's music laughs through its tears and the maudlin conflation of his life and works in myriad biographies and fictional treatments makes readers past and present weep."[20]

Another Schubert film, the joint British-American *Melody Master* (alternatively titled *New Wine*), released by United Artists in 1941, is a more ambitious film, but it utilizes the *Blossom Time* paradigm in several of its plot points and in its use of music. This Schubert (Alan Curtis) is a handsome, ambitious, but penniless composer who learns that he can redeem his failures in life and love only through the spiritual power of music. The story begins in Vienna. In this version Schubert quits his job as a teacher and flees to Hungary to avoid conscription in the army of the King of Naples. He finds work on a sheep ranch, where he falls in love with the beautiful estate owner, Anna (Ilona Massey), who, like a modern-day Delilah, educates him in the proper techniques of wool-shearing. Together they return to Vienna, where he intends to pursue a career as a composer. Impoverished but happy, Schubert furiously scribbles out page after page of music. But the publisher Tobias Haslinger rejects his compositions. "It's not the kind of music I'm interested in," Haslinger says. "People will remember, not buy, the music. I tell you, in my opinion, it may go in one ear and out the other. It may become popular very fast, but it will be forgotten even faster. My clients are the great orchestras, the salons of the nobility. Do you think they would play such music? It's too thin. It's not in the classical form." Ever impractical, in words that will be echoed by numerous other composers in biopics to come, Schubert retorts, "I don't care if people buy my music, as long as they sing it."

But Anna is determined to keep up the fight. "Franz is struggling against an indifferent world," she tells some friends. "I won't let him give up. The world must acclaim him. That is my future." Accordingly, she clandestinely visits Beethoven (Albert Basserman[21]), the reigning king of music in Vienna. The aging but flirtatious composer is delighted to entertain this beautiful young lady but initially unwilling to hear her pleas. When she angrily protests, Beethoven relents and takes a Schubert manuscript to his piano, murmuring to himself, "Wait—good thing I'm deaf." As he turns the pages, a series of brief excerpts from the Eighth Symphony ("Unfinished") are cleverly and seamlessly joined together on the soundtrack. At length, now agitated with excitement, he turns to Anna. "This is not the end. Where are the other pages? This Symphony is *unfinished*. Why? Is Schubert sick? For years amateurs have annoyed me with bad music; but here is someone with divine fire. This man is a genius!" Anna is overwhelmed. She agrees to return to Schubert and tell him that when the symphony is finished, the great Beethoven will meet with him.

But a few weeks later, when he hears the news of Beethoven's death, Schubert resolves to return to teaching. "I've wasted too much time chasing rainbows," he declares to Anna. "Now I've come to my senses. I don't think you'll find my being a professor ridiculous. I can't go on drifting, borrowing, leading a shiftless, aimless life. I'll go to the registrar this instant and take out our marriage license. And we'll be together, always." Anna is dismayed. Resigned to the fact that marriage will stifle Schubert's composing, she leaves. "If I stay, he would soon hate me," she explains in a letter to Schubert's friend, the coachman. "I love him far too deeply to accept such sacrifice. He must return to his music. I shall always pray for his success."

Schubert, now alone, retires to his garret. "A man must turn his face to God," he murmurs, gazing at a wall painting of the Madonna and Child.

The strains of "Ave Maria" well up on the soundtrack as he bends to his music paper.

Confirming the redemptive power of Schubert's music for generations to come is the addition of a modern framing story, wherein an unnamed young man and woman (Kenneth Ferrill and Ann Stewart), each disappointed in their respective love lives, accidentally meet and fall in love at a Schubert Memorial Concert at Carnegie Hall. As they listen to the music (excerpts from the *Rosamunde* incidental music, the Eighth Symphony, orchestrations of the song "Dein ist mein Herz," and a waltz from Opus 33), the scene crosscuts to incidents in the historical narrative. When the lovelorn Schubert finds consolation in writing his "Ave Maria," the film returns to Carnegie Hall as the orchestral rendition of that song resounds through the cathedral-like auditorium. Overcome with emotion, the young couple exchange rapt glances, and she gives him her phone number. Schubert's music has fulfilled its destiny and inspired their love. "Think what he would have written had he not died so young," the man says, rather irrelevantly.

The film embellishes the *Blossom Time* paradigm with allegations that Schubert was a discontented and inept teacher; that he avoided conscription by fleeing to a Hungarian sheep farm; that his beloved broke off their affair *only* because she didn't wish to interfere with his composing career; that the publisher Haslinger refused to publish his works; that Beethoven saw the manuscript of the Eighth Symphony; and that the symphony remained unfinished because of Schubert's disappointment in marriage. It is instructive to note that these plot points considerably heighten the drama of what is otherwise a more modest historical record: Schubert did indeed teach primary school, but it was in his father's school where, by all accounts, he was strict and reliable. He was not eligible for conscription, because his short stature was under the minimum for military service. Moreover, there was no military operation at that time going on in Naples, where Joachim Murat had been recently delegated king by Napoleon. (Schubert had been harassed by the authorities only because he was a friend of Johann Senn, a political liberal, who was arrested and detained in 1820. Schubert was also arrested but not detained). Schubert did go to Hungary as a young man, but not to avoid military conscription; rather, he spent a summer tutoring the daughters of Count Johann Karl Esterházy of Galanta. He never returned to teaching because by 1818 he was making a living, albeit scantily, by composing music for meager commissions. The only "Anna" in Schubert's life was Anna Froehlich, whom he met in 1822 and for whom he composed his popular "Serenade." (Biographer Charles Osborne speculates that she and her sisters may have been the inspiration for the *Blossom Time* paradigm.)[22] Schubert's relations with Haslinger were relatively good; and late in life he also published through another firm, the Mainz company of B. Schott. The Eighth Symphony remained unfinished for a variety of reasons, none of which had anything to do with career frustrations. Indeed, it may have been "finished" after all.[23] Whether he ever met Beethoven has occasioned much conjecture.[24]

Biographical facts notwithstanding, as late as the 1950s the *Blossom Time* paradigm was still in evidence in two German biopics, *Ein Leben in Zwei Setzen* (1953) and Das *Dreimäderlhaus* (1958).[25] In spite of the sternly revisionist depiction of Schubert in Fritz Lehner's *Mit meinen heissen Tränen* (1987) — examined in the last chapter of this book — the straightforward *gemütlich* image of the "little mushroom" will likely continue on well into the twenty-first century. "As long as something like *[Blossom Time]* is possible," said Richard Strauss, "no one can say that composers have any real protection."[26]

When the mantle of Vienna's dance master passed from Schubert to Johann Strauss, Jr. (1825–1899), the *Blossom Time* paradigm found a new candidate, although the story would find a happier ending this time. At first glance Strauss scarcely seems the tragic, lovelorn figure embodied by Schubert; yet the glitter of his Viennese milieu, the captivating waltzes, and an ill-starred love life suggest their distant artistic and emotional kinship. Strauss's early successes as a composer and orchestra leader had been hard won against the bitter objections of his composer father, the reigning "Waltz King" of Vienna. Moreover, beyond the glare of his public celebrity and globe-trotting concertizing was a man divided in his political loyalties toward the Hapsburg Empire, unhappy in his affairs, unfulfilled in his marriages, and afflicted by chronic depression and numerous phobias. Paradoxically, for a man whose career transpired in the full glare of public celebrity, relatively little is known of Strauss's private life, inviting biographers and dramatists to flesh out their own details.[27] In the final analysis here was an artist who could echo Schubert's populist credo in *The Melody Master* ("I don't care if people buy my music, as long as they sing it") with his own declaration, "There must be something in [music] for everybody's taste . . . the people in the gallery must get something they can easily remember and take home."[28]

The movies naturally took notice. Among the many dramatizations of Strauss's life are two biopics that appeared in the 1930s, one made in England by Alfred Hitchcock, the other in America by the French émigré director Julian Duvivier. Like *Blossom Time*, Hitchcock's *Waltzes from Vienna* (released in America as *Strauss' Great Waltz*) began as a German stage musical by Heinz Reichert and Ernst Marischka, moved to London and America (where it played at the Radio City Center Theatre), and finally fell into the hands of the

Gaumont-British studios, where it was adapted to the screen by Guy Bolton and Alma Reveille with musical supervision by Erich Wolfgang Korngold. Esmond Knight duplicated his stage role as Strauss, and Jessie Matthews, just then on the verge of superstardom (her "breakout" film, *Evergreen,* was soon to be released), portrayed the love interest, Rasi.

One of the least known of Hitchcock's films, *Waltzes from Vienna* is quite different in plot and tone from the more characteristic series of thrillers that dominated his career after 1934, beginning with *The Man Who Knew Too Much.* "The enterprise was a desperate one from the start," declares biographer Donald Spoto, "and it justified Hitchcock's later statement that this was the lowest ebb of his career."[29] Moreover, Matthews has since dismissed it in her autobiography.[30] As a result, it has been regarded as an aberration in both their careers. At this writing it is unavailable (only a 35-millimeter print is available to scholars at the archives of the British Film Institute). A calmer appraisal of the film, however, reveals a work worthy of revival, which possesses considerable wit and charm.[31] Of particular interest to this study is its subversion of the *Blossom Time* paradigm with typically Hitchcockian satiric asides, sly erotic twists, a secondary plot about the bitter rivalry between Strauss the elder and Strauss the younger, and the deployment of Straussian tunes.

Strauss, Jr., is a struggling young composer who has been relegated literally to second fiddle in the orchestra of his celebrity father. "You don't share the general enthusiasm for my compositions," accuses Sr. (Edmund Gwenn). "You're wrong," replies Jr. "Nobody loves your music more than I do. But every artist must march forward. He can't afford to stand still and admire." Sr. is miffed. "You think I'm already at a standstill, a back number? But I understand *you* were thrown out of your lodgings last month, because your neighbors couldn't stand to listen to your improvisations."

Impoverished and desperate for a break, young Strauss is reduced to working in the bakery owned by the father of his girlfriend, Rasi. She chides him for chasing his dreams of music when he should be more practical about earning a living. One day Strauss meets the Countess Helga von Stahl, who promises to promote his music if he will agree to write a tune to a poem she's writing about the Danube River. He complies and dedicates it to her. In turn, she contrives a scheme to have his new "Blue Danube" waltz played at Dommayer's Beer Garden, where the prominent music publisher Drexler will hear it. The Countess lures the unsuspecting Sr. away from the podium so Jr. can conduct the work. It is a triumphant moment for the young man — until his outraged father reappears. "This is still *my* orchestra," he says. "Listen to the people calling for me." Drexler intervenes. "I beg your pardon, Herr Strauss," he says. "They're not calling for you; they're calling for your son." Amid the crowd's exhortations for Strauss the younger to return to the podium, the father snarls sarcastically, "The late Strauss and his illustrious son."

All this is not lost on the jealous Rasi, who resents Strauss's obvious affections for the Countess and his ambitions to leave the bakery. He protests, "I've given up everything for you. All my dreams. And now I've started on a career as artist with gingerbread and chocolate cakes!" In desperation, Rasi turns to the Countess for support. But the Countess is supportive of Strauss's musical career. "If he listens to you now," she warns Rasi, "he'll never amount to anything." Rasi resigns herself to the fact that Strauss will choose his career over her.

Back in his apartment, Strauss finds the Countess, who has come to congratulate him on his success at the beer garden. They kiss. Alerted to the budding romance, the Countess's husband bursts into the room. But Rasi, repentant over her selfishness toward Strauss, arrives just in time to escort the Countess away by a back stair and take her place. When the Count sees Rasi instead of his wife, his suspicions are allayed. The ruse has worked, and Strauss can return to Rasi.

In the last scene Strauss, Sr., sits alone in the beer garden. He has been literally toppled from the podium, deposed from the seat of power, as it were. A woman comes up to him and requests an autograph. He regards her for a moment, then signs his name. After another pause he adds "Senior" beside it — a tacit confirmation that he has accepted his son as his equal.

There are hints of the essential Hitchcock here. He teases proscriptions by the British Board of Film Censors against adultery (see the conclusion of this chapter for a fuller examination of the censorship code) by suggesting the affair between Strauss and the Countess in a farcical, rather than graphic, manner. There is the use of doubled characters — that is, father and son, significantly reflecting in this instance the paradigm of composer's struggle against social conformity for artistic independence; and Rasi and the Countess, reflecting the duality of the working girl and the wealthy dilettante. Class divisions are debunked, both in the witty counterpointing of aristocratic life with the bemused asides of the servants; and in the contrasting of the artificial divisions between Strauss the elder's stuffy, conventional concert music with his son's more lively and "populist" dance music. As if to confirm Strauss the younger as a people's artist rather than an elitist composer, he is shown composing the "Blue Danube" waltz — the principal diegetic and extradiegetic leitmotif of the film — while working in the bakery. In a montage blend of image and sound, Strauss watches as a baker tosses fresh-baked rolls into the apron of a fellow worker. He listens to the whirling crank of the dough-beater. He picks up the rhythm and begins humming the tune. The crank turns faster, the batter spatters his face, and the melody quickens. Strauss excitedly turns to Rasi and sings her the completed tune.[32] Thus, artistic inspiration is fused with working practicalities. Strauss is both musical genius and regular guy — a sure-fire "recipe" for musical bakers!

The film betrays its theatrical origins at times. Its tableau-like character groupings, artificially stylized sets, frontally presented action are quite charming. Preserving the musical sense of the original operetta, Korngold's adaptations of Strauss's waltzes have a primarily diegetic function as source music that is either sung by Matthews or performed by the Strauss orchestra (strategies praised by historian Charles Barr as prophetic indications of Hitchcock's later use of music in *Rear Window* and *The Man Who Knew Too Much*).[33] And the light and airy filigree of the sets resembles the scenic décor found in later period films by Max Ophuls. Only in the set piece of the film, Strauss's conducting of his "Blue Danube" waltz, is the otherwise static camera unleashed. The orchestra performance is, properly enough, foregrounded and visually amplified through the elaborately choreographed camera moves of cinematographer Glenn MacWilliams — the whole thing counterpointed by cutaways to shots of the pleased Countess and the sobbing Rasi.

Although we may see it in hindsight as more than just a footnote in Hitchcock's career, *Waltzes from Vienna* elicited only tepid responses from American critics at the time. "Despite a capable cast," reported the *New York Herald,* "the production somehow misses fire, giving evidence of rather ineffectual production."[34] And *Motion Picture Daily* noted: "Here is a film that will charm music lovers because of the immortal compositions of the two Strausses, father and son; but except for this there is little else in the way of entertainment. American audiences will probably fail to appreciate what little humor is presented."[35]

But the public's appetite for Johann Strauss biopics was undiminished. *The Great Waltz,* the first American cousin to *Waltzes from Vienna,* was released by MGM in November 1938 to great acclaim. The *Motion Picture Herald* noted, "It is not a highbrow screen offering to which only the intelligentsia may be bidden. . . . It is essentially a mass attraction."[36] And *Film Daily* agreed that "classical music" was given "a tremendous wide appeal to the pop elements as well as the lovers of classical music."[37] The *Variety* critic applauded Dmitri Tiomkin's musical arrangements "as one of the memorable achievements of this kind presented on the screen," which "has been selected for its haunting quality and is treated with fine dignity and respect."[38] And the critic for the

MGM's *The Great Waltz* (1938), a life of Johann Strauss, Jr., displayed Hollywood's typically sumptuous production values. (Courtesy Photofest/MGM)

Motion Picture Herald wrote that the film was "magnificently staged, picturesque and artistically wrought," with a set design that "minutely reflect[s] the splendor and glory of Vienna during the time of Strauss' mature life."[39]

The Great Waltz was based on an operetta of the same name with book by Moss Hart, which had premiered at Radio City on 22 September 1934. (It is unclear at this writing if this particular operetta is related in any way to the source material for the Hitchcock film.) Its European credentials were impeccable — it was adapted and written by Austrian émigré Walter Reisch, who had had experience with composer biopics and classical music-related films in his native country (he wrote a silent film, *Ein Walzer von Strauss*, in 1925); musically supervised by Tiomkin; performed by Austrian songstress Milija Korjus; and directed by the acclaimed, recently imported French director Duvivier.[40] Studio chief Mayer himself greenlighted the picture as an opportunity to pursue his avowed duty, as he saw it, "to bring culture and taste, in the form of enlightenment, to the masses."[41]

In this Hollywood version Strauss (Fernand Gravet) works in a bank instead of a bakery, his potential infidelity involves an opera singer instead of a countess, and his "breakthrough" tune is not "Blue Danube" but "Tales of the Vienna

Woods." Of the rivalry with his father, there is nary a trace. The story is allowed to carry forward to Strauss's involvement with the Viennese Revolution of 1848 and beyond, to his last years as the Waltz King idol of Vienna at the end of the century. By contrast to the quaint theatrical artifice of the Hitchcock film, this version is served up in an extravagantly cinematic concoction of dazzling camera work and spectacular image-and sound montage sequences.

The action begins in Vienna in the mid-1840s. After quitting his job at a bank, twenty-year-old Strauss assembles an orchestra of unemployed musicians to perform his waltz music to the Viennese masses. It is evident that his music is not merely the product of academic study and aristocratic patronage; rather, it comes directly from the people and the world around him. For example, the celebrated "Tales of the Vienna Woods" sequence depicts the composer inspired by a morning coach ride through the MGM back lot (doubling for the Vienna Woods). Accompanied by the celebrated opera diva, Carla Donner (Korjus), he listens to the triple-time clopping of Rosie the horse, the tweeting of the birds, the piping counterpoint of two peasant's flutes, the blaring horn of a passing coachman, and the trilling of the coach driver's harmonica. A tune begins to take shape. The harmonica launches into a riff, the triple-time meter accelerates, the birds twitter on the downbeat, and Strauss begins to hum a fragment of the melody. Donner completes the phrase. Both voices blend, and soon Strauss and Donner are standing up in the coach, gesticulating wildly as they belt out the "Vienna Woods" theme.

Likewise, the famous "Blue Danube" waltz is composed under the most mundane of circumstances: As Strauss sits on the dock and watches the dawn come up over the river, he listens intently to the tooting of the harbor boats, punctuated by the slapping sounds of the washerwomen scrubbing laundry against the stones. Gradually, as strains of the music well up on the soundtrack, an elaborate visual montage ensues, consisting of shots of printing presses cranking out the sheet music in many languages, string players performing in the concert hall, and dancers in many ethnic costumes whirling across dance floors.

Music like this levels all classes into a delirious democracy of dancers, entranced in common by Strauss's "Verzückungswalzer" ("Bewitching Waltzes"). This is reinforced by another of the film's set pieces, Strauss's debut at the Dommayer Beer Garden. The place is empty when he and his band first take up their instruments. It is only when Donner drops in and joins in the music that the citizens outside in the surrounding public square begin to take notice. Gradually, one by one, curious shopkeepers, aristocrats, and servants alike cluster about the doors. As the music mounts in intensity, the trickle of visitors becomes a stream. Soon the place is packed with whirling dancers. A rousing rendition of a Strauss polka (with lyrics provided by Oscar Hammerstein II) drives performers and dancers into a frenzy. Photographed by Oscar-winning cinematographer Joseph Ruttenberg, the sequence is one of Hollywood's most delirious displays of virtuoso camera work and editing.

Meanwhile, Strauss the democrat turns revolutionary as he and the "people" march to the barricades in the 1848 insurrection against Austrian tyranny. The new young emperor, Franz Joseph, quietly appears and asks Strauss what they are rebelling against. "Why?" answers Strauss, not recognizing his interrogator, "because tyranny and oppression—it's written on those banners out there—can't you read?" The emperor replies softly, "And how are *you* oppressed, Mr. Strauss?" To which the composer sniffs, "Oh, never mind that. If you know what's good for you, you'll sneak out the back way." He tweaks the emperor's nose and is promptly arrested.

But woe unto Strauss when he forgets his humble origins. His affair with Donner bespeaks his seduction by professional and class opportunism. In the end, after Donner abandons Strauss, the composer returns apologetically to wife, Poldi, the baker's daughter (Luise Rainer), and home. "You can't find happiness in rich palaces," confesses a repentant Strauss, "or in hearts covered with gold braid, or behind false, painted laughter."

In the final scene, late in the 1890s, the aging Strauss, now at the end of his career, has a reunion in the Imperial Palace with Franz Joseph. The emperor escorts him to a window, through which is seen a huge crowd of people paying their respects. "Vienna is giving you the love you gave Vienna," he says. He confers upon Strauss the honorary title "King of Vienna." It's a neat consolidation of the antimonies of the classical composer paradigm—the man of the people is also the aristocrat of art; and the private dreamer is privileged to speak in the voice of the people.

According to the opening title, *The Great Waltz* "dramatizes the spirit rather than the facts of [Strauss's] life." That "spirit" was obviously tailored for contemporary 1930s audiences. For example, the film's references to the citizens' rebellion against Austrian tyranny,[42] perfunctory as they are, do point up the fact that the film was made at the time of the Nazi Anschluss, when the Johann Strauss Society in Vienna was banned.[43] This was not lost on the critic for the *Fox West Coast Bulletin,* who acknowledged that "the picture has a modernity unusual in costume drama"[44] Moreover, it is clear that that "spirit" is also in keeping with Depression America's unemployment crises. Strauss's pickup orchestra of shopkeepers and unemployed citizens resembles those other musicians' ensembles organized at MGM by Mickey Rooney and Judy Garland in their Busby Berkeley vehicles ("Hey, kids, let's put on a *show!*") and at Universal Studios in the Deanna Durbin vehicle, *One Hundred Men*

The Great Waltz dramatized a tense romantic relationship between Johann Strauss, Jr. (Fernand Gravet) and a fictitious character named Poldi (Luise Rainer). (Courtesy Photofest/ MGM)

and a Girl. And the swing stylings of the music they perform function in the same way as the waltzes and polkas in Strauss's time — they unify disparate audiences of young and old, from all economic and social classes, in a democratic expression.

Many elements of the historical Strauss are deemed extraneous to the film and have been omitted — chiefly, as already noted, the bitter musical rivalry between Strauss and his father and the political squabbles that further divided their relationship.[45] Strauss's affairs and his three marriages — to Henrietta Treffitz ("Jetty") in 1862; to Angelika ("Lili"), a singing student much younger than he in 1878; and to Adele in 1887 — are simplified into the figures of his wife, Poldi, and mistress Carla Donner. (A Strauss biopic that would more frankly deal with his many affairs and marriages would appear much later, in 1954, with the Austrian film *Ewiger Waltz* (*Eternal Waltz*).[46] As for the music, although the debut at Dommayer's Beer Garden has historical verification,[47] important dates of the key compositions have been rearranged: "The Vienna Woods" and "Blue Danube" were actually composed much later than the 1840s, in 1867.[48]

A few critics rejected the whole business. Franz Hoellering, writing in *The Nation,* dismissed the film as "phony, awkwardly written, and, with the exception of the woods sequence, as unoriginal as it is crudely directed."[49] Others, like the critic writing in *Stage,* attacked the actors: "A sleek Fernand Gravet, an over-frivolous and too-too-zealous Miliza Korjus, and a harassed and unhappy Luise Rainer play an obvious and sometimes embarrassingly ineffectual drama of wife versus opera star."[50]

If the populist sentiments and Jewish heritage of Strauss were deemed by American filmmakers as an appropriate protest against the turmoil of the Nazi Anschluss in 1938, the figure of George Frideric Handel (1685–1759), a transplanted German, was appropriated by British filmmakers to speak on behalf of besieged Britain in 1942. Norman Walker's *The Great Mr. Handel,* scripted by L. Dugarde Peach and Gerald Elliott and produced by Rank's GWH Productions, was essentially a wartime film intended to bolster patriotic sentiments among its viewers. Released to embattled Londoners at the height of the Blitz, it wears its British nationalism on its sleeve and makes of the composer a proper British patriot. At the same time, as I discuss below, here is a Handel who embodies and balances the antimonies of the "possessor" of will and industry (the populist figure) and the "possessed" of divinely inspired genius (the transcendent genius).

The Great Mr. Handel depicts the composer's London years, spanning his assumption of British citizenship in 1727; his association with the theatrical producer, John Jacob Heidegger; the wrangles over the patronage of King George II and Frederick, Prince of Wales; the contests between rival opera companies; the relationship with singer Susanah Cibber; and the composing of *Messiah* in 1742 (with the attendant controversy about allowing actors to sing from New Testament texts).

In a parley with a church bishop the German-born Handel (Wilfrid Lawson) consolidates his Englishness, his artistic agenda, and his spiritual values in one neat package: "Pardon, but I am even more certainly an Englishman than yourself, my Lord Bishop. I am English by Act of Parliament. You are English by no act of your own. I am English by choice. I think it better suitable that I compose anthems for England's King. I know my Bible well. I choose texts myself." At the same time the film must confirm Handel's status as a man of the people. The monumental image of the solemn and heavy-jowled genius is set aside, for the most part, in favor of a very human, social figure, the associate and friend of aristocrats, singers, servants, and street vendors alike. To a degree this is consonant with commentator A. Craig Bell's assessment of the historical Handel, who displays "the temper of temperamental prima donnas

. . . [who was] the first composer to scorn patronage, to stand alone and independent and, by sheer integrity, persistence and genius, to compel society, from king to commoner, to accept him, together with his art, on his own terms and as their equal."[51] In the film his servant, the Scotsman Phineas (Hay Petrie), is his Sancho Panza. Handel walks the streets, inspired by the ditties of the flower vendors and the fishmongers. Despite his own financial straits, he opens his house and his pantry to orphaned children and persuades his creditors to assist him in establishing a hospital for foundlings. Invited to come to London to premiere his new *Messiah,* he insists on employing the services of a "common" actress, Mrs. Cibber (Elizabeth Allan), as a soloist. "An actress singing a sacred work?" asks the astonished Mrs. Cibber. "An actress believes in God," Handel replies. "Is that strange?" As she auditions her role, the lamplighters and shopkeepers outside gather outside the window in hushed reverence.

The set piece of the film is Handel's composing of *Messiah.* Occupying fully one-third of the running time, it is an ambitious attempt to capture in a complex montage of image, words, and music the processes of creation—not Handel as the "possessor" figure who consciously transforms the voice of the people into an art form, but as the "possessed" and passive servant of God. Slumped at his desk, transfixed in the grip of inspiration, Handel views through his window a succession of tableaux vivant, each derived from a biblical passage and accompanied on the soundtrack by appropriate excerpts from the *Messiah* music. When faithful Phineas arrives with food, Handel ignores him and mutters, "I saw the firmament open, the glory of all heaven before me, the great God himself. . . . Never have I known such happiness. He who gave me this work to do will give me strength to do it." Handel bends back to his work, muttering, "Now leave me." As he continues to watch through the window his visions of the Christ story—the manger scene, the gathering of the apostles, the crucifixion, the Resurrection and ascension into Heaven—we get the distinct impression that he, like us, is *watching a movie,* an elaborate costumed panoply of characters and events that, tastefully done as it is, is nonetheless just this side of a Cecil B. DeMille biblical epic. Three days pass. Finally, the exhausted Handel puts aside his pen and tells Mrs. Cibber, "I heard the voice, the voice imperative; and it said, 'Write.' And I asked, 'What shall I write?' And straightaway the answer was put into my hands. And here is the fruit of my laboring." Capping the entire sequence is the performance at the Royal Opera House, Covent Garden, 1742, when nobility and common folk alike—yes, including two of Handel's orphaned charges— stand up during the "Hallelujah Chorus." A concluding title says it all: "Seest thou a man diligent in his business? He shall stand before kings."

To be sure, in circumstances like this, Handel's genius must ultimately be

The Great Mr. Handel (1942) was a British patriotic wartime film, with Wilfrid Lawson as Handel and Elizabeth Allan as Mrs. Cibber. (Courtesy Photofest)

presented as more than just the copying of the street songs of the vendors. For studio chief Rank, here was a perfect opportunity to indulge not only in patriotic sentiments, but in a religious agenda he had been pursuing with the GHW production company, which had been formed as part of what has been called the British "Religious Film Movement."[52] Writing something like *Messiah* must be depicted as more divine inspiration than mere diligence and hard work. Biographer Newman Flowers, in his *George Frideric Handel: His Personality and His Times*, would reaffirm this in 1948 in a prose passage that rivals — and indeed seems to have been drawn from — *The Great Mr. Handel:* "It was the achievement of a giant inspired, the work of one who, by some extraordinary mental feat, had drawn himself completely out of the world, so that he dwelt — or believed he dwelt — in the pastures of God. What happened was that Handel passed through a superb dream. He was unconscious of the world during that time, unconscious of its press and call; his whole mind was in a trance. . . . 'I did think I did see all Heaven before me, and the great God himself!' he exclaimed. . . . For twenty-four days he knew those uplands reached only by the higher qualities of the soul."[53]

Ironically, as Bell observes, Handel traditionally fits into no convenient nationalist category: "The great cosmopolitan, he is claimed by no nationality as its own. German-born, Italian-adopted, English-bred, he stands apart, solitary and unique. His position, while being a measure of his all-embracing universality, puts him out of court for the more chauvinistic musicologist, being too German for the Italians and too Italian for the Germans and English." Even in his adoptive country, England, where his best-known music is set to English texts, his true greatness is realized "in a limited and unsatisfactory way."[54]

In addition to its wartime credentials, *The Great Mr. Handel* was, like its Hollywood counterparts, consciously crafted as a "prestige" picture that would appeal to a mass audience. "The decision to make the film was an effort on my part to study J. Arthur Rank's desire to make better films for the public," recalled director Norman Walker, "which was not too well served at the time. I convinced [Rank] there was a ready-made public in the choir and musical societies who every year drew vast audiences. So we got together with our script writers and musical director and succeeded in writing a script that pleased Mr. Rank; and he whole-heartedly agreed with me that it should be made in color."[55] American critics were generally enthusiastic. "It is an eye-and-ear filling gem which will delight the audiences for which it was attended," wrote the *Hollywood Reporter*. "Wilfrid Lawson gives a brilliant performance as Handel, making the composer a living human being."[56]

Less reverential portraits of Handel would have to wait decades before the release of three more biopics—Tony Palmer's *God Rot Tunbridge Wells!* (1985), Anna Ambrose's *Honour, Profit, and Pleasure* (1985), and Gerard Corbiau's *Farinelli* (1985) (see Chapter Five for more discussion on these films).

Another composer conscripted by biopics into service as a wartime patriot was Frédéric Chopin (1810–1849). Columbia Pictures's *A Song to Remember*, filmed in 1944 and released in early 1945, was directed by Charles Vidor and featured the young and virile Cornel Wilde as the frail and consumptive composer. Written and produced by Sidney Buchman, with music adaptation by Miklos Rozsa and piano performances by José Iturbi, the Polish composer is depicted not as the morbidly sensitive aesthetic of the Parisian salons, but as a fiery Polish patriot who abjures a life of artistic self-indulgence and political neutrality for the sake of the Polish struggle against tsarist tyranny. *A Song to Remember* is not only the best remembered of all Hollywood composer biopics, but its savvy blend of fact and fiction, its lush Technicolor palette, sumptuous production values, and bewitching exploitation of Chopin's music—as both soundtrack score and diegetic performance—qualifies it as the touchstone of the classical studio biopic. The film is examined in detail in the next chapter.

If the American star system demanded that a swashbuckling Cornel Wilde should bring machismo in his impersonation Chopin, then the British star system upped the ante a year later in casting the dashing Stewart Granger as Chopin's contemporary, the notorious virtuoso violinist Niccolò Paganini (1782–1840), in *The Magic Bow*. This Rank production, released in America through Universal-International, was directed by Bernard Knowles, with musical assistance on the soundtrack by violinist Yehudi Menuhin. Granger's Paganini is quite the rascal, a cynical joke always on his lips, his sword at the ready, and beautiful women by his side—a cross between Scaramouche and Beau Brummell (indeed, Granger would soon be on his way to Hollywood, where he would play both roles in subsequent MGM movies).

Few composers have led lives so shrouded in myth and gossip, a lot of it self-generated. Paganini, like other icons of the Romantic age, such as Napoleon, Byron, and Brummell, says Leo Braudy, exercised "a sincere willingness to stage themselves theatrically and premeditatively."[57] According to biographer Jeffrey Pulver, "He bent all his efforts to wind himself in a chrysalis of romance and at the end only succeeded in achieving sensational calumny." Indeed, continues Pulver, "his audiences outside of the court circle, typical of their romantic era, expected a certain amount of theatrical sensationalism on the platform. . . . For this reason he began to cultivate an inscrutable expression of sphinx-like mystery, to allow his hair to grow long and curl unrestrainedly about his shoulders, to thrust his right foot well forward and rest the weight of his body on his left hip in a most unnatural—even grotesque—manner."[58] Included among the many legends associated with Paganini are an angel's visitation at birth, tales that he had spent several years in prison, allegations of spectacularly amorous exploits, and the rumors that his super virtuosity with the violin was the result of a pact with the Devil.[59]

The reality is hardly less sensational. Born in Genoa in 1782, Paganini spent much of his boyhood subjected by his father to a merciless, occasionally abusive regimen of violin study. An ambitious young virtuoso, he separated from his father and went to Lucca, where he fell into gambling habits that cost him his priceless Stradivarius violin (which he had previously won in a sight-reading competition sponsored by the painter Antonio Pasini). Assisted by a friend and business manager named Luigi-Guglielmo Germi, he embarked on extensive concert tours, eventually receiving the title of Chevalier of the Order of the Golden Spur by Pope Leo XII. Subject to some dispute among his biographers are the identities of some of the women with whom he allegedly

Dashing Stewart Granger mimed Niccolò Paganini's violin virtuosity to the off-screen performances of Yehudi Menuhin in *The Magic Bow* (1946) (Courtesy Photofest)

had affairs — among them are Marie Elisa Bonaparte, Napoleon's eldest sister; the Princess of Lucca and Piombo; Angelina Cavanna, a Genoese woman who became pregnant and took him to court for damages (he served a short period of jail time); the Baroness Helena von Feurbach, a married woman who offered to leave her husband, until Paganini grew tired of the affair; and Antonia Biachi, a singer with whom he had a child and who subjected him to a series of violently jealous episodes. As a composer, Paganini's output was limited. After the celebrated *Twenty-Four Caprices*, completed around 1809, and his First Violin Concerto (1811–1817), his work, suggests biographer G. I. C. De Courcy, showed little development and was generally sacrificed to his career as a virtuoso: "While the possession of such amazing gifts, together with his meteor-like course through Europe at the meridian of his life as a 'virtuosis in excelsis,' undeniably contained the stuff of romance, he dissipated so many of his best years by frittering away his talents that his career, viewed as a whole, was by no means so romantic as that of Liszt, who shares virtuoso honors with him."[60]

Obviously, Paganini's notoriety presents a striking contrast to the other composer subjects so far discussed — particularly the frail, retiring, socially correct Chopin. However, the *Blossom Time* paradigm is at work, even here. By the time *The Magic Bow* reaches its conclusion below, Paganini will prove to be a brother under the skin with Chopin, Schubert, Strauss, and Handel.

The Magic Bow begins in Genoa, Italy, in 1800, against the backdrop of Napoleonic invasion. The young virtuoso Paganini leaves his drunken father to seek his fortune in Parma, where he wins a Stradivarius violin in a competition sponsored by the painter Pasini. "With this violin I can talk to the world," he smiles. Assisted by Germi (Cecil Parker), an unemployed lawyer he has met on the road, he embarks on a concert career. "Each note of your music has cash value," insists the canny Germy. "Properly presented you might become famous. You need a manager." But Paganini's attempts to win over Parma society in a concert held in the salon of the French nobleman Count de Vermond, consisting of the "Carnival of Venice" variations and a melody from his First Violin Concerto (which henceforth will function as the picture's "love theme"), are rebuffed by a rudely inattentive audience. "Where I come from, people know how to behave," he angrily tells the Count's daughter, Jeanne (Phyllis Calvert). In a huff Paganini heads for the gaming tables, where he loses his Stradivarius.

A concert performance of the First Violin Concerto is interrupted by the arrival of Napoleon's troops. Paganini quips, "They're late for my concert; they should have come sooner." He ignores the intrusion and continues playing. Impressed, Jeanne realizes she is falling in love with him. However, Jeanne's mother will not approve her marrying beneath her station and arranges a marriage instead with one of Napoleon's officers, the Vicomte de la Rochelle (Dennis Price). Jeanne is in a difficult position: A refusal to marry according to Napoleon's mandate could damage Paganini's career. The violinist greets the news sarcastically: "There's no room for people like me in your world," he says. "Go on, marry him and fill the nursery full of pale-faced, aristocratic parasites." Sorrowfully, she leaves as Paganini picks up his violin and plays the Big Theme one last time for her.

Back on the road, Paganini takes up with a comely wench named Bianchi (Jean Kent). Together, with Germi, they embark on a succession of concerts, depicted in a montage of shots of posters, coach wheels, musical performances (where he performs excerpts from Tartini's "Devil's Trill" Sonata and a concerted version of the last of the "24 Caprices," and adoring crowds (where he overhears the remark "They say he's in league with the Devil!"). Inevitably, he glimpses Jeanne in the crowd. Her jealous fiancé calls him out. The two men fight a duel, in which Paganini's hand is wounded.

Back home in Genoa, Paganini nurses his wounds and his broken heart. "I can't keep [Jeanne] out of my music," he confesses to Germi. Bianchi puts aside her jealousy and visits her rival, telling her of Paganini's love and that only she, Jeanne, can restore his spirits. At this moment, Paganini is summoned before the Pope for a command Vatican concert. Paganini is doubtful at first, but he yields to advice from his mother: "You'll not fail, my son. We'll all be there, willing the magic back into your bow." After kneeling before the Pope and accepting a Knighthood, Paganini takes up baton and bow and launches into the last movement of Beethoven's Violin Concerto. Overwhelmed by emotion, Jeanne, who just happens to be in attendance, announces to her fiancé that she must return to Paganini. The violinist, meanwhile, begs permission from the Pope to play one last composition. "It's a melody that came to me when I kneeled in prayer," he says. The Pope replies, "Your prayer may yet be answered." Forthwith, he begins to play a melody, *the* melody. Jeanne smiles. The orchestra obligingly joins in.

The obligatory Big Theme of the First Violin Concerto has done its work. All will be well in love and art.

Like the other composers discussed in these biopics, this version of Paganini is a combination of quixotic artist and democratic citizen, a lovelorn fellow who finds consolation only in his music. His dashing manner and aristocratic flair (courtesy of Granger) find their complements in his "other half," Germi's Sancho Panza–like sidekick. As a man of the people, he's a working stiff—his special gifts as a *composer* take second place to his profession as a *performer*. "With this violin I can talk to the world," he declares. Except for an early scene when he improvises on "La Campanella," he hardly seems to compose at all. At first, his skill and irrepressible bravado defy all obstructions, including Napoleon himself (an event, of course, that never could have happened, inasmuch as the emperor occupied Italy in 1797, much earlier than the time period depicted in the film). But Cardinal Michelotto stands by with the kind of warning issued to so many composers in these classical and popular biopics: "Remember, success is a heavy burden to carry. Poverty is a burden that is carried by man; success must be borne alone." Thus, when fame and fortune separate him from the common folk, Paganini lapses into a crippling depression, symbolized by his lamed hand. Only through a spiritual rejuvenation blessed by the Pope himself can he regain his art, his common touch, and his Great Love. She, of course, is Jeanne, who as an aristocrat has been forbidden to marry Paganini but who in her determination to leave the Vicomte for Paganini—with the complicit approval of rival Bianchi—has declared her own freedom from the class constraints that had kept them apart. Paralleling and counterpointing all this, of course, is the Big Theme, which wells up periodically on the soundtrack or leaps to Paganini's violin, courtesy of sound-track arranger Ernest Irving.

A barrage of studio publicity boasted of the film's vaunted authenticity — including an exact reproduction of the interior of the Vatican and Granger's expert synchronizing of his bowing technique with Menuhin's playing ("Every spare minute of his time in the studio he spent locked in his dressing room with his violin and records by Menuhin"). Viewers were also assured that not only was Granger a man's man in real life — he served in the Black Watch during the war — but that "both highbrow music lovers and admirers of popular ballads will have the unique opportunity of hearing Yehudi Menuhin play the entire violin score for the picture."[61] And his pairing with costar Calvert, moreover, was designed to appeal to British audiences already familiar with their work together in two previous films, *Madonna of the Seven Moons* (1944) and *The Man in Grey* (1943).

American critics rightly greeted *The Magic Bow* as the first cousin of the Hollywood biopics. "The violin playing doesn't compensate for the parade of dramatic clichés," opined reviewer Jack D. Grant in the *Hollywood Reporter*.[62] And the critic in the *Daily Variety* handily sniffed out the story formula, noting: "The story resolves itself into the too familiar one of a man loved by two women, one a socialite, the other a gutter graduate with a heart of gold."[63]

Inevitably, perhaps, the pain, anxiety, and disillusionment of the immediate postwar years would catch up with composer biopics. MGM's *Song of Love* (1947), the next Hollywood entry in the series, a dramatization of the storied romance between Robert Schumann (1810–1856) and the pianist Clara Wieck (1819–1896), invests the *Blossom Time* paradigm with the lurid style of the film noir of the late 1940s. "On his fingertips, the Love of Music," proclaimed one advertisement, "and on her lingering lips, the Music of Love!" Other headlines blared: "She FELL IN LOVE . . . and trouble. . . with a MAD GENIUS!"[64]

Song of Love is an A-list release starring Katharine Hepburn (fresh from her pairing with Spencer Tracy in *Sea of Grass*), Paul Henreid (who had just portrayed a classical cellist in *Deception,* 1946), and, as Johannes Brahms, Robert Walker (who had appeared as Jerome Kern in *Till the Clouds Roll By,* 1946). The screenplay by Irmgard von Cube and Allan Vincent was based on an unproduced play by Bernard Schubert and Mario Silvia. Artur Rubinstein provided the piano performances. It was directed by studio mogul Mayer's favorite contract director, Clarence Brown, who had already made several biopics, including *Conquest* (1937), about Napoleon and Marie Walewska, featuring Greta Garbo and Charles Boyer; and *Edison the Man* (1940), starring Spencer Tracy. The classically trained Bronislau Kaper supervised the music, William Steinberg and Alfred Scendre conducted the concert sequences, and Rubinstein provided the piano performances.

"In this story of Clara and Robert Schumann, of Johannes Brahms and Franz Liszt," cautions an opening title card, "certain necessary liberties have been taken with incident and chronology. The basic story of their lives remains a true and shining chapter in the history of music." This bright promise notwithstanding, consider the challenges the *real* Schumann story presented to the proprieties of classical Hollywood romance: Since his youth, Schumann was chronically subject to extreme pathological states and repeatedly considered — and finally attempted — suicide; he died in an asylum, hopelessly insane, his demise possibly abetted by tertiary syphilis. The great love of his life, the piano prodigy Clara Wieck, whom he married after a stormy courtship against the bitter resistance of her father, broke with convention by continuing her concert career despite the demands of husband and family. And during Schumann's institutionalization she may have had an affair with her husband's protégé, Brahms.

How to suggest but at the same time ultimately "contain" these "troublesome" events?

After an opening credit sequence with young Clara performing Liszt's First Piano Concerto, she announces to the crowded hall (among them, the King of Saxony and his son) she will play an encore, "Traumerei," by an unknown composer named Robert Schumann. Backstage moments later, Clara's father, Friedrich (Leo G. Carroll), who is acting as her concert manager and promoter, angrily rebukes her and repeats his objections to her relationship with Robert. The composer intervenes with a speech that conveniently establishes the backstory of his studying with Friedrich and his attentions toward Friedrich's daughter, who is eleven years younger than Robert. "We intend to marry," he declares to Friedrich. "Your objections are good enough, I suppose. Heaven knows, I'm older than she is. I'm unknown; she's famous and all that. You might mention, though, the possibility of making her happy. When did you ever try that? I've seen you dominate her, break her spirit as if you enjoyed it. Why? Because it meant better business at her concerts." Friedrich retorts that he will block the romance in court, if necessary. But at the judicial proceedings, the judge is swayed by Franz Liszt's testimony about Schumann's noble character and by Clara's own heartfelt pleas: "Give us our freedom, Your Worship. The freedom to live together under the same sky, and did if we must, together, where our hands can touch. I love him, proudly, immodestly, everlastingly."

After the wedding, Clara and Robert ascend three flights of stairs to their flat, where Robert presents her with his newly composed love song, "Widmung" ("Dedication"). "It's all I can give you," he says, as together they sit at the piano, their hands interlocked on the keys. "It's the days of my life—the happy days, the other days. How the sun rose where you were standing; how it sets when you say goodnight. It's me; it's yours."

Time passes. Nine years later, in 1849, the Schumann house bustles with children and music. A young man named Johannes Brahms has just arrived and, after witnessing in bewilderment the chaos of housekeeping and children underfoot, seats himself at the piano and auditions his music for Robert. "There is no one, Professor Schumann," says Brahms, "with whom I'd rather study." He launches into the G-minor Rhapsody; but his attention is soon distracted by Clara's entrance. Later, while Brahms settles in to the household, functioning as part-time nursemaid and willing Schumann protégé, Clara argues that she must be allowed to resume her concert career—interrupted since their marriage—not for her sake but for the welfare of the family. "I couldn't stand it any longer," she says, "watching you, day after day, year after year, struggling to make ends meet—working, grinding, killing yourself. For what? For me, for the children, for the landlord. I can make the money so easily, because I'm a performer, nothing else. What I do is here today and forgotten tomorrow. But you create, Robert, the things you do will last forever. You must be free to write your music." He replies resignedly, "Music to which no man will listen." But her rejoinder is quick: "Music which the angels will be proud to sing."

Another supporter is Liszt (Henry Daniell). He invites the publisher, Tobias Haslinger, to a soiree at which he will perform (and to which he also has invited the Schumanns). After banging out a Hungarian Rhapsody, he launches into a paraphrase of Robert's "Dedication." But Clara is upset with Liszt's flashy pyrotechnics. She seats herself at the keyboard and plays a more modest version of the song. "You're a brilliant artist, Franz," she says as she plays. "I envy you. I wish I had the power to translate the commonplace into such stupendous experience. But [this is] love, Franz, as it is—no gilt, no glitter, just love, unadorned. Do you know what I mean?" The room is silent. The guests are astonished at Clara's rebuke. "Well, Franz, she insulted you," murmurs Liszt's companion. He pauses a moment, then replies, "She did much worse than insult me, my dear; she *described* me!" Only Daniell could deliver such a line with the requisite dry hauteur!)

Meanwhile, Brahms, who has been nursing in secret his infatuation with Clara, resolves to quit the Schumann home. When Clara presses him for an explanation, he confesses that he loves her, but because of his loyalty to Robert, he must leave. When apprised of the situation, Robert is not surprised. "I was afraid that was coming," he tells her quietly. "Why, Clara dear, what did you expect? You go around like an angel — innocent, busy, shining, you make yourself so necessary to people that it shocks you when you find out they can't get along without you. Perhaps he'll get over it. He's young." Brahms leaves.

All this time, Schumann has been wrestling with inner turmoil of a different kind. Alone in his darkened room, he has been playing on the piano dissonant chords and tortured fragments of a melody. The doctor looks in. "What was that music I heard you playing?" he asks — "a strange sort of melody. Perhaps it's the dissonances, but it's not at all like your usual thing." Distracted, Schumann answers that it is based on a poem called "The Cursed Forest," about a flower that blooms scarlet because it has been drenched in human blood. "It's horrid in a way; but it happens to people, too, sometimes, you know." In subsequent scenes Schumann suffers aural hallucinations, painful, protracted, ringing sounds that drive him to distraction. They grow in frequency and intensity until, during a concert in which he conducts his *Faust* music, he breaks down completely, flailing about on the platform like a marionette whose strings have been cut. He drops the baton and collapses.

The next time we see Robert he is an asylum. He tells the visiting Clara that he's been working. "I'd like to play for you something I've just written," he declares. I wrote it for you." Whereupon he plays the "Traumerei," the self-same piece Clara had played as an encore years before. "It's beautiful, Robert," she says tearfully. Robert abruptly bangs out a dissonant chord.

Five years after Schumann's death Clara meets Brahms in an outdoor café. He renews his protestations of love and proposes marriage. She gazes lovingly at him. But when a strolling violinist begins to play Schumann's "Dedication" theme, she recovers herself and retreats from Brahms's gaze. They both now realize that her love for Schumann will forever come between them.

The picture ends with Clara, now a white-haired lady, performing once again Schumann's "Traumerei." Above in the box sits the new king of Saxony. He is the same person who as a little boy had listened so appreciatively in the film's opening scene. Once again, he rests his chin on his hand, an eloquent reminder not just of a similar gesture so many years before but of the musing tilt of the head and hand that is so characteristic of Schumann himself.

Song of Love reflects Hollywood's preoccupation at the time with aberrant behavior and disturbed psychological states, which was just then being realized in that genre and style that French critics have dubbed "film noir." Fed by

Song of Love (1947) was MGM's tribute to the great romance between Robert Schumann (Paul Henreid) and Clara Wieck (Katharine Hepburn). (Courtesy Photofest/MGM)

wartime disillusionment and subsequent Cold War paranoia, practiced by European émigré filmmakers who were master practitioners of expressionistic themes and techniques, and encouraged by the then fashionable trend of psychoanalysis, movies were preoccupied with psychopathic killers (Hitchcock's *Shadow of a Doubt,* 1943; Raoul Walsh's *White Heat,* 1949), phony patriots (Preston Sturges's *Hail the Conquering Hero,* 1944), shell-shocked soldiers (John Huston's documentary *Let There Be Light,* 1946), corrupt politicians (Robert Rosson's *All the King's Men,* 1949), and psychiatric case histories (Hitchcock's *Spellbound,* 1945; Anatole Litvak's *The Snake Pit,* 1949; and Mitchell Leisen's *Lady in the Dark,* 1944). Why not a "mad" musician? Up to now mad musicians had been stock villains, from the various incarnations of *The Phantom of the Opera* (including the newest version with Claude Rains in 1943) to the John Brahm thriller, *Hangover Square* (1945), about a deranged homicidal pianist. But what about a new species of mad artist — not the stereotypical villain but a more sympathetic, psychologically complicated character?

The psychiatric thriller was coming into its own, report film historians Stephen Farber and Marc Green in their study *Hollywood on the Couch.* *Spellbound* and *Lady in the Dark,* particularly, brought psychoanalytic theory (no matter how simplified and hoked up) to the masses: "Many of these works were devised by artists who were not just long-term habitués of the couch but evangelical crusaders for the Freudian cause."[65] The celebrated Karl

Menninger, of the Menninger Clinic in Topeka, Kansas, along with an influx of German Freudians, led the way in introducing psychoanalysis to the denizens of the film colony. Indeed, as humorist S. J. Perelman sardonically noted at the time, "The vogue of psychological films started by *Lady in the Dark* has resulted in flush times for the profession, and anyone who can tell a frazzled id from a father fixation had better be booted and spurred for an impending summons to the Coast."[66]

If ever there were a composer tailor-made for such a noirish, psychologically inflected film, it was Schumann. To this day he remains a fascinating yet elusive character, a troubled genius whose music embodied all the dreams, fancies, and ambiguities of German Romanticism. Ever since his death in the Bonn-Endenich Asylum in 1856, gallons of ink have been spilled and numerous theories and countertheories have flown about regarding the exact nature of his mental illness, the affliction of his right hand, the problems beneath the surface of his "ideal" marriage to Clara, the alleged coded meanings buried in his music, the possible affair between Brahms and Clara, and his treatment during his twenty-eight months in the asylum.[67]

The theme of genius as a form of madness — an extreme example of the "possession" myth — had always lurked beneath the *Blossom Time* paradigm. In *The Possessor and the Possessed*, author Kivy points out that the Romantic age, influenced by the writings of Schopenhauer, regarded poetic inspiration as a kind of madness. "In the throes of poetic creation the poet is literally no longer himself," Kivy writes, "the result of the poet being used by the god as the god's conduit." This freedom from the dominance of the will may bring the poet to a childlike state: "One way of characterizing a genius, then, is to describe him as someone who manages to retain the child's dominance of intellect over will into maturity. The genius, in other words, is simply an old child."[68]

So far, we have seen this "possession" paradigm in the Schubert operettas and films, and to a lesser degree in the portrayals of Strauss and in the Handel of *The Great Mr. Handel*. It will resurface when we consider biopics about Mozart, Stephen Foster, W. C. Handy, and Anton Bruckner later in this book. Certainly, Schumann himself — particularly in his youthful infatuation with the works of German writers Jean Paul Richter and E. T. A. Hoffmann — regarded his mental instability not so much as a mental and physical pathology but a Romantic condition he called "melancholia," both an affliction and a blessing, to be borne and to exploit. This contributed, by no means coincidentally, to his lifelong preoccupation — even obsession — with childhood and childlike states of mind. Indeed, he became the supreme example of the artist who not only located and identified the "childlike" aspects within himself but also expressed them in the service of music for and about children.[69]

However, it was understood that a major prestige release from MGM, starring headliners Hepburn, Henreid, and Walker, would have to "contain" the darker implications of the Schumann "problem," as it is generally known. The availability of the production files in the MGM archives provides useful information about the considerations that went into this containment process.[70] The studio research on Schumann's life and work and his relationships with Clara and Brahms is exhaustive and fills several thick bound volumes. Whatever changes were wrought in the screenplay were intended and not based on ignorance.

Memos, treatments, and scripts spanning 26 July 1945 to 24 August 1946 reveal much indecision about how to handle the film's story, tone, and music. "Loyalty of Clara to Robert and his ideals is the most important feature of the film," advised script supervisor Ivan Tors, "as well as the strength she gains through love and suffering." However, from the outset, Tors was worried about what he called "a potential weakness" of the downbeat tone of the Schumann story. "Sometimes it's too gloomy," he wrote. "The ending is unsatisfactory. The picture starts with a hope for happiness and ends with loneliness." Tors suggested employing a flashback technique to keep the two moods in balance. "The story could open at a Schumann festival when Clara, a gracious old lady, plays 'Traumerei.' She's moved by the enthusiastic reaction of the audience and by memories of the past. She can see herself as a young girl in Leipzig when she listened secretly at Schumann's door when he was engaged in composing the melody." After a succession of memories, the story would return to Clara at the piano. "This proves to the audience that in spite of her loneliness at the ending, this gray-haired lady had an exciting and sometimes very happy and full life." Later memos reveal second thoughts, however: Maybe the flashback technique should be abandoned for a linear chronology. Maybe Clara should be a little girl, or a young woman, at the opening concert. Should she play Beethoven's "Moonlight Sonata" or a concerto by Chopin, Beethoven, or Liszt? What to do about Clara's career obsessions? How can Brahms's and Clara's love for each other be suggested but not made explicit? Should Brahms be present with Clara when Schumann dies? Should Clara reunite with Brahms in their old age? And how should Schumann's mental problems be suggested?

The first story treatments indicate that the picture would include an elaborate staging of Schumann's suicide attempt during the Düsseldorf Carnival of 1854—an event in real life that surely demanded the Hollywood treatment:

Deranged and disheveled, Schumann would rush through clouds of confetti and a crowd of costumed figures. Auditory and visual hallucinations-distorted musical sound and the tolling of a bell-would assail him. He would follow a mysterious, caping figure in harlequin costume toward the river and his doom. As late as 24 August 1946, that sequence was still intact in the script. However, there is no record of such a scene actually being filmed. Certainly it does not appear in the released version. Perhaps it was axed due to budgetary restrictions or, more likely, because the depiction of a suicide attempt would be too problematic for the censors.

Ultimately, Schumann's psychological problems, the tensions in the marriage, his suicide attempt, the controversial relationship between Clara and Brahms would be negotiated in accordance with the Production Code's restrictions on the depiction of deviant behavior, adultery, and suicide. Deeper, more candid on-screen examinations of the Schumann story would have to wait until two later biopics, Peter Schamoni's *Spring Symphony* (1985) and Peter Ruggi's *Schumann's Lost Romance* (1996), and two biographical novels, J. D. Landis's *Longing* (2000) and Janice Galloway's *Clara* (2002).[71]

It is thus illustrative of Hollywood's storytelling agendas to see how the finished film contains the problematic historical record. As per Tors's instructions, *Song of Love* is determined to portray the Schumann relationship as one of unwavering love and devotion. This is suggested at the outset, not just by Clara's passionate declaration at the court proceeding, but by their duet performance on their wedding day of the "Dedication" theme, when in close-up Clara places her hands over his. The screen depiction of Clara's untrammeled love for her suitor flies in the face of the facts of her vacillating loyalties, toward both him and her father and her avowed doubts and chronic ambivalence regarding a future with Robert. References to issues that disrupted the relationship and outraged her father — Robert's incipient alcoholism, his womanizing, the possibilities of a syphilitic infection — are omitted entirely (as is the crisis engendered by his damaged hand, which curtailed a promising concert career). The potential scandal of a mature man falling in love with a mere child (she was only eleven years old when they first met) is sidestepped by the casting of an obviously mature Katharine Hepburn in the role. Moreover, the film would have us believe that after the marriage, Clara's desire to return to the concert stage was an unselfish gesture to allow Robert time to compose. The truth is that she was determined to pursue her career on her own terms, regardless of the demands of homemaking and childbearing and regardless of the protestations of Robert, who alternately found himself either confined to the duties of house-husband back home during her tours or unwilling companion on the road, frustrated by the lack of opportunity to compose. In sum,

Clara Schumann (Katharine Hepburn) considers an affair with Johannes Brahms (Robert Walker) in *Song of Love* (1947). (Courtesy Photofest/MGM)

the conflicts between his and her professional aims frequently disturbed the harmonious union that legend (and Hollywood) would have us believe.

The business with Brahms is likewise sanitized out of all recognition. The most passionate moment between them transpires at the moment when Brahms, torn by his love for Clara and duty to Robert, decides to leave the Schumann home. As he packs his shirts into his suitcase, Clara remonstrates with him to stay and puts the shirts back in the drawer. But at the moment when he overtly confesses his love, she slowly takes the shirts back out of the drawer and replaces them into his suitcase. It is a telling moment. Although the historical record suggests that throughout their lives Brahms and Clara cherished a platonic and mutually nurturing relationship, it is also probable that early in their acquaintance there was genuine passion on both sides, which may have flared up precisely during the time of Schumann's incarceration[72]—not coincidentally at the very time when the film discreetly removes Brahms from the scene.

Likewise simplified, suggested, or expunged outright is the full extent of Schumann's mental instability.[73] His psychological abnormalities lent the film a generally "noirish" tone, but beyond that their specific pathology was side-stepped, lest they make him seem another "mad" artist, like the murderous

Mr. Bone in *Hangover Square* or Eric the Phantom in the various versions of
The Phantom of the Opera. Thus, the film elides any discussion of the history
of insanity that ran in Schumann's family, the disabling severity of his chronic
bipolar affective disorders, the syphilitic infection that compounded his mental and physical deterioration, his homicidal threats against Clara at the time
of his breakdown, and the gruesome details of his incarceration and debili-
tated condition during the last twenty-eight months of his life.[74] Instead, the
film implies his attacks came on only late in his career and were probably the
result of overwork and mental strain. And excepting Clara's last visit, no
scenes are set in the asylum.

Aside from a particularly egregious musical anomaly—namely, the selection of Clara's performance of the Liszt's First Piano Concerto under the
opening credits (curious, considering that Clara was never on good terms with
Liszt and that this particular concerto was not premiered until 1855, many
years after the film's opening concert)—many of the minor departures from
the musically correct record can claim at least a modicum of historical and
dramatic justification. The "Traumerei" (from the *Kinderscenen*, Opus 15),
which Clara plays as an encore in her opening scene, was indeed composed in
1838, during the latter stages of their courtship. Composer-arranger Kaper's
selection of a "love theme," so endemic to the Hollywood classical style, has
justification here—"Widmung" ("Dedication") was composed as part of a
cycle of songs called *Myrthen*, Opus 25, which he presented to Clara as a
wedding present. The scene where Liszt plays his own flashy version of it (he
did indeed write a piano transcription of the song) establishes an effective
contrast between his virtuosity and Clara and Robert's own aversion to flamboyant embellishment.

Assigning incipient madness to Schumann's piano piece "Cursed Forest"
(better known as "Verrufene Stelle," or "Haunted Spot," from the piano cycle
Waldscenen, Opus 82) is no more or less defensible than any other "problematic" music written late in his life, say, the last movement of the Cello Concerto, the whole of the Violin Concerto, or choral works such as the *Scenes
from Faust*. These and other works have been relentlessly probed for signs of
mental instability, with no definitive conclusions forthcoming as yet.[75] And
while "Verrufene Stelle" was composed in 1848 at a time of relative serenity in
Schumann's interior world, it *is* indeed an unsettling little thing and proves to
be eerily effective in the context of the scene in the film. "It is used to divulge
the first signs of Schumann's mental collapse," explains music director Kaper.
"Through its oddness, Schumann's mental disintegration is brought into dramatic significance."[76] (Amusingly, the film demands that Schumann bang it
out in discordant fragments, as if the piece in itself weren't sufficiently sinister.)

What music Brahms auditioned for the Schumanns in his first visit to their Düsseldorf home in September 1853 is not known with certainty—perhaps the Second Piano Sonata, the Scherzo, Opus 4, some early songs. The selection of the G-minor Rhapsody, Opus 79, No. 2, though, is wrong, since it was composed much later in 1877; however, its passionate intensity, which prefigures Brahms's love for Clara, warrants its inclusion here.

The breakdown scene, which transpires during a performance of *Faust,* contains at least a kernel of truth. While in actuality, Schumann's breakdown transpired under far different circumstances, as we know, there is some justification here in that there are several documented instances of Schumann's miserable failures as a conductor in Düsseldorf. Moreover, the aforementioned *Faust* does testify to Schumann's longstanding preoccupation and identification with Johann Wolfgang von Goethe's drama of the collapse of poetic and personal ideals and the promise of final spiritual redemption. Schumann's playing of what he claims is a "new" piece during Clara's visit to the asylum (but which is only the same "Traumerei" he had written years before) speaks to several truths—that is, that Schumann did not compose any new music during his incarceration and that he had regressed to occasional childlike states.

Critical reception was mixed. *New York Times* critic Bosley Crowther attacked the film's "cloying clichés" and found it too obviously imitative of its immediate MGM successor, *A Song to Remember:* "It takes the lives of famed musicians—Robert and Clara WieckSchumann and Johannes Brahms—laces them into the clichés of false and sentimental romance" and "saccharine-sweet little glimpses of episodes in their domestic life—familiar troubles with the servant, laughing anxieties over the kids and touching necessities of rebuffing the romantic advances of 'Uncle Brahms.'"[77] On the other hand, the usual "liberties with regard to incident and chronology" were forgiven by the *Hollywood Reporter,* "since the purpose was entertainment above documentation, no fault can be found with the free adaptation." Hepburn's performance was "easily the best she has done in recent years," and Henreid's Schumann was "appealing though dolorous, with his best scenes the ones where he realizes he cannot escape the cloak of madness that is descending upon him."[78]

In retrospect, *Song of Love,* despite its shortcomings, is a prime demonstration of classical Hollywood's cultivation of classical music's built-in prestige factor. "MGM really felt it was presenting something intellectual and of a high cultural order," says historian William K. Everson. "If a studio like that felt it was making money on "Dr. Kildare" films and Red Skelton vehicles, it then felt it had to do something classy once in a while. I honestly feel that in films like these, in spite of the fact that history is distorted and diverted to a very contrived plot, they really felt they were adding to the cultural status of

Hollywood."[79] At the same time the film's desperate attempts to reconcile the extremes of Schumann's disordered world to the narrow confines of "respectable" Hollywood corresponds rather neatly to the Schumann's own lifelong struggles to construct "normalcy" out of the chaotic conditions of his life and personality.

Nothing could present a greater contrast to *Song of Love* than *Song of Scheherazade,* also released in 1947, an episode in the life of Nikolai Rimsky-Korsakov (1844–1908). This colorfully whimsical, light-hearted concoction presumes to add one more tale to the *1001 Arabian Nights*—"Did you hear the one about the young Russian sailor on shore leave who falls in love with a beautiful Arabian dancer?" Released by Universal-International, the film is written and directed by Walter Reisch and stars Jean-Pierre Aumont as Nikolai Rimsky-Korsakov and Yvonne de Carlo as the fictitious Cara de Talivara, his lover. This Technicolor extravaganza extends the biopic formula into the realm of a standard Hollywood-style musical fantasy. Indeed, it is best described this way by one of the characters in the story: "An opera by Nicholas Rimsky-Korsakov. A Comic Opera: The curtain rises. A woman in man's clothes, a Big Love, a Young Hero, a Beautiful Heroine. I wonder, though, who is the Clown?"

Indeed, the film's plot might have been lifted from one of Rimsky-Korsakov's many fanciful operas: The year is 1865. Young Rimsky-Korsakov is a cadet in the Russian Naval Academy, homeward bound from a world cruise aboard the clipper *Almaz*. When the ship is becalmed in a Moroccan port, the despotic Captain Vladimir Gregorievitch (Brian Donlevy) turns the cadets loose for shore leave. He has special orders for Rimsky-Korsakov, who has professed more interest in music than in sailing: "Put away the pen and music paper, go ashore, be a man, and have adventures." But all Rimsky-Korsakov can think about is finding a piano to perform music he has recently written during the cruise. Stumbling upon an instrument in the villa of Madame de Talivara (Eve Arden), he and his companion, Dr. Klin (Charles Kullman), launch into a rendition of the newly composed "Song of India." Later, in the Café Oriental, he is attracted to an exotic dancer (Yvonne de Carlo), who tells him the legend of the Sultana Scheherazade, the storyteller. He learns the dancer is in reality Cara, the respectable daughter of Madame de Talivara, who is performing in secret in the cafe. A rival for Cara's attentions is RimskyKorsakov's whip-wielding shipmate, Prince Meschetsky. Their enmity results in a vicious duel with bullwhips. RimskyKorsakov is victorious. But it still takes some time before the naïve young sailor realizes that Cara has fallen in love with him. Moreover, she confesses her ambition to dance some day in the St. Petersburg

Ballet. Reluctant to leave her behind when his ship is ordered to set sail, and anxious to further her career, he contrives to bring her aboard in sailor's disguise. The ruse is discovered when the men are ordered to strip for a swimming drill. Cara is put ashore and RimskyKorsakov takes tearful leave of her. In an epilogue, set in St. Petersburg, RimskyKorsakov, having ended his naval service, conducts a *"Scheherazade"* ballet. In the meantime, his beloved Cara returns to dance the lead role.

It takes only a moment to trace the bare modicum of historical fact behind all this. The early chapters of Rimsky-Korsakov's memoir, *Chronicle of a Musical Life,* written over several decades and first published in 1908, relate in some detail his preparations to follow family tradition and become an officer in the Russian Navy. In 1856 at age twelve he was sent to the Naval College at St. Petersburg. Six years later he began a three-year world cruise as midshipman on the clipper ship *Almaz,* under the "timid" rule of one Captain Zelyony (a man "rather too free with his hands," hints RimskyKorsakov darkly). Ports of call include New York City, Rio de Janeiro, Cadiz, Marseilles, and Genoa. Far from constituting his formative musical inspiration, as the film suggests, the cruise aroused RimskyKorsakov's interest in foreign lands but dampened his artistic ambitions. "Thoughts of becoming a musician and composer gradually left me altogether," he wrote. "Distant lands began to allure me, somehow, although, properly speaking, naval service never pleased me much, and hardly suited my character at all." By the time the cruise had ended, "music had been wholly forgotten, and my inclination toward artistic activity had been stifled." His musical studies, desultory at best so far, would not begin in earnest until the years following the cruise.[80]

Of course, Hollywood will have none of *that*. Rimsky-Korsakov will embody the dual nature of the composer paradigm — he will fall in love, dispatch his rival with the bullwhip, and generally behave as "one of the guys," while at the same time succumb to the inspiration of the dances and songs of the common folks he meets in the Moroccan port city.

Advertised as "A Pleasure Treasure in Torrid Technicolor," *Song of Scheherazade* is overlong and rather chaotic in its jumble of incidents, characters, and a variety of musics. Young de Carlo dances an Arabian slave dance and a Russian ballet number. Arden delivers her patented arsenal of quips and wisecracks. Donlevy's chain-smoking ship's captain takes particular pleasure appearing bare-chested on deck among his deck hands (reprising for the alert moviegoer his earlier role as the villainous "Sergeant Markoff" in *Beau Geste,* 1939). Metropolitan Opera tenor Charles Kullman periodically belts out a vocal arrangement of "Song of India" (courtesy of music director Miklos Rozsa and lyricist Jack Brooks). And, when he's not snapping his bull whip,

Aumont displays skills with piano, violin, and harmonica in performances of "Flight of the Bumblebee" and the "Prince and Princess" love theme from *Scheherazade* (which appears repeatedly throughout as the film's primary thematic material).[81]

None of it makes the slightest sense, of course. But the film is not without its charms. In particular, the opening scenes aboard ship, announced by a bugler's playing of the fanfare from *Le Coq d'Or*, have a snap and verve that is winning. The whip fight is startlingly vicious, and the *Scheherazade* ballet (staged by Arthur Murray) prefigures the elaborate balletic numbers in many Hollywood musical films to come, such as Vincente Minnelli's *The Pirate* (1948) and *An American in Paris* (1952). Aumont, whose credentials were properly macho (the pressbook boasts that he won the Croix de Guerre with a tank unit fighting in the Sudan in 1940) delivers a likeable performance that in look and manner resembles that of a young Danny Kaye. And the muted, pastel color palette and beautifully stylized set design are always a pleasure to watch.

Rozsa's elaborate arrangements of Rimsky-Korsakov's music deserve special mention and a place of honor alongside the pastiches of Chopin themes he employed in *A Song to Remember,* Tiomkin's adaptations of Strauss's waltzes in *The Great Waltz,* and Kaper's work in *Song of Love.* Freely reconfigured and reorchestrated themes come and go in a seamless flow, serving as simultaneously background and source music in several of the singing and dancing numbers. For example, the *Capriccio Espagnole* and *Scheherazade* have been converted into quasi-ballet scores, the first in Madame de Talivara's soiree and the second in the climactic St. Petersburg concert.[82] Most strikingly (as it were), themes from *The Russian Easter Overture* underscore the dramatic whip fight between Rimsky-Korsakov and Prince Mischetsky. If nothing else, Rozsa's work supports the notion that RimskyKorsakov's musical style — foregrounding melodies against a relatively simple and unobtrusive ground of blocks and strata of sound while avoiding competing melodic lines — can be fairly considered as a proto-film music.[83]

"Never is it said that *Song of Scheherazade* is a fact," astutely observed Jack D. Grant in the *Hollywood Reporter,* "but something of the sort could have been. . . . The story is a bubble that should never have been taken seriously. It is the music that counts." Gene Arneels in *Motion Picture Daily* applauded its commercial quality: " 'Scheherazade' is decidedly designed to hurdle the commercial limitations of classical music, with its whimsical and wholly flavorsome approach. No monumental tribute to a great composer, the film is bantam-weight, but yet is mirthful and carefully made."[84]

Finally, the question asked by Captain Gregorievitch at the beginning of this discussion must be answered: "Who is the Clown?" A likely candidate is not a character in the story, but director-scenarist Walter Reisch, who has already been mentioned in this chapter. He was an Austrian émigré whose work before his arrival in Hollywood in the late 1930s consisted primarily of biopics about composers, including a silent film, *A Waltz by Strauss* (1925), and the script for a Schubert film, *Leise flehen eine Lieder* (1933, Austria; American title: *Unfinished Symphony*). And it will be recalled that as a contract writer in Hollywood, Reisch scripted *The Great Waltz. Song of Scheherazade* was his directorial debut. However, according to Reisch, although it got good reviews, he himself was treated terribly by the critics. "I suffered very much under the effects of it for years and years," he recalled. "If you make a picture with 'Flight of the Bumble Bee' in it . . . you are leaving yourself wide open for criticism. Today, I accept it with a certain sense of humor. But the studio people just didn't believe in my direction [as a consequence], and I never got a picture to direct in Hollywood again."[85] This dismal ending to a directorial career would never have been allowed in Rimsky-Korsakov's operas!

W. S. Gilbert (1836–1911) and Arthur Sullivan (1842–1900), two contemporaries of Rimsky-Korsakov, brought their own brand of fairy-tale whimsy and "topsy-turvydom" to the British and American operetta stage. Directed by Sidney Gilliat and starring Robert Morley and Maurice Evans as Gilbert and Sullivan, respectively, *The Story of Gilbert and Sullivan* was produced in 1953 by British Lion and distributed in America by London Films. More of a "backstage" musical than *Song of Scheherazade*, it is an ambitious, expensively mounted portrait of the popular light opera team, who have collectively assumed their place alongside Handel and Sir Edward Elgar as institutions in English music history. The storyline spans the years 1875–1900, from *Trial by Jury* to the death of Sullivan in 1900. It begins with the decision of Gilbert and Sullivan to devote their careers to collaborating on light operas; continues through their glory years with *The Sorcerer, H.M.S. Pinafore, Iolanthe, Ruddigore, The Mikado, The Yeoman of the Guard*, and *The Gondoliers*; and concludes with the death of Sullivan just before the opening night of the revival of *The Yeoman of the Guard*.[86]

The legendary contentious relationship between the amiable Sullivan and the irascible Gilbert is nicely outlined in two key scenes: First, during a boating party they argue over whose work has taken second fiddle to the other; and second, after the success of *The Gondoliers*, disputes break out over D'Oyly Carte's (Peter Finch) diverting of profits for the purpose of restoring of the Savoy Opera House. In the first scene Sullivan announces he wishes to write a grand opera and asks Gilbert if he would write the libretto. Gilbert objects, declaring that opera is "a triumph of sound over sense." Sullivan counters that

Robert Morley and Maurice Evans portray W. S. Gilbert (left) and Arthur Sullivan in *The Story of Gilbert and Sullivan* (1953). (Courtesy Photofest)

it is *his* music that has taken second place to Gilbert's words. "I can assure you that time after time I've had to reduce my music to a mere 'rum-te-tum,'" he says, "so that every syllable of yours can be heard at the back of the gallery." Gilbert retorts, "While my words have been consistently drowned by your first fiddle and all the other confounded fiddles!" And so on. The argument continues as the two men sit down, with their backs to each other, Gilbert finally declaring, "If we work together, we must work as master and master, not as master and servant" (while an offstage chorus all the while declaims: "They are both Englishmen").

The second exchange transpires after Gilbert has returned from vacation only to learn that large sums of money are being diverted from his earnings to restore the Savoy Opera House. His outrage is countered by Sullivan. "For more than fifteen years our three names have been linked in harmony wherever our operas are played," he says. "You've often said that 'Gilbert and Sullivan' are as much a national institution as Westminster Abbey. And here we are, quibbling over the price of a carpet." The always politically tactful

Helen D'Oyly Carte breaks in: "Gentlemen, please remember that you are quarreling in the very theatre built out of your success. Why don't you take a leaf out of your own book, *The Gondoliers,* Act Two — 'Free from every kind of passion / Some solution we must find.'" (Whereupon the film cuts to the onstage chorus declaiming those very words.) But the argument continues, with Gilbert declaring, "We all know the carpet is only a symptom of the disease which has been rotting the fabric of this partnership since 1883." He fires a parting shot at D'Oyly Carte as he leaves: "I think it is a mistake to kick down the ladder by which you have risen."

Sullivan's besetting ambition to compose "serious music" and Gilbert's insistence on remaining loyal to comic opera nicely constitute both halves of the classical biopic paradigm — the artist whose genius is a compound of artistic and populist qualities (I stop just short of hauling out the Quixote–Sancho Panza dichotomy). Sullivan's lofty ambitions are tempered by Gilbert's more practical considerations; Gilbert's absurdities are modified by Sullivan's lofty example.[87] On one hand, Sullivan's dream of being a "serious" composer is abetted by his snooty fiancée, Grace (an episode based on fact)[88]. "You were taught by a pupil of the great Beethoven himself," she reminds him. "You must learn to dedicate yourself to your art, religiously, like the great master. The theater is not your world." But when Sullivan sheepishly leaves grand opera to return to stage music, she turns on him angrily. "You are squandering your gifts on triviality. It is wrong and wicked. I saw you there, bobbing and bowing; and although I could scarcely believe my eyes, I saw that you were *proud* of it. You actually *liked* it." She departs, leaving Sullivan to console himself with a bottle of wine.[89] (This kind of antipopulist sentiment has been heard before, particularly in the Schubert and Chopin biopics already discussed, and will be heard again in the biopics about many of the Tin Pan Alley composers, such as Foster, Handy, and George Gershwin.) And when Sullivan is summoned before Queen Victoria to be knighted, the queen admits that his opera *Ivanhoe* has earned her admiration, but it is a command performance of *The Gondoliers* that she *really* has on her mind.

For his part Gilbert is afflicted with a penchant for theatrical absurdities, which is branded by Sullivan as "topsy-turvydom."[90] It is only at Sullivan's urging — and because as a practical man Gilbert needs to keep the partnership together — that he strives for a more sophisticated artistry, producing the libretto of *The Mikado.* In the end he, too, is presented to the queen, and he, too, is knighted. The aspirations and works of the two men meet somewhere in between these antimonies, resulting in a kind of composite "creator" of the operettas.

The music is generously represented and imaginatively staged by members of the D'Oyly Carte Opera Company (including the estimable Martyn Green) with the London Symphony Orchestra conducted by Sir Malcolm Sargent. The technical adviser is Miss Bridget D'Oyley Carte. Included are lengthy chunks of *Trial by Jury* (virtually the entire "Now, Jurymen, Hear My Advice"), *Pinafore* ("I Am Little Buttercup" from Act I and "I Am an Englishman" from Act II), *The Pirates of Penzance* (Gilbert and Sullivan themselves perform an impromptu song), *Ruddigore* (the "Ghost Scene" from Act II), and *Iolanthe* ("The Lord Chancellor's Song" in Act I).

Frequent use of parallel editing wittily counterpoints onstage and offstage action: A scene from the opening night of *Iolanthe* is crosscut with a nervous Gilbert walking about the streets and peering into the pubs, periodically consulting his watch. And the comic antics of *The Mikado* are contrasted with the ponderous solemnity of a scene from Sullivan's oratorio, *The Golden Legend*. A particular highlight has Gilbert demonstrating the action of *The Gondoliers* on his tabletop toy theater: as the camera moves in tight on the cardboard cutout characters, the scene dissolves to the stage action as Marco and Giuseppe sing "We're Called Gondolieri."

Few composer biopics can rival the entertainment savvy and biographical respectfulness of *The Story of Gilbert and Sullivan*. And few such films surpass its genuinely moving penultimate scene: During the revival of *Yeoman of the Guard*, Gilbert arrives backstage determined to reconcile with the ailing Sullivan, who by now is terminally ill and confined to a wheelchair. They agree to appear together for a curtain call on opening night. Later, however, Sullivan's manservant appears with the news that his master is near death and unable to appear. As the music of Jack Point's song "Merryman and His Maid" is heard onstage, the sorrowing Gilbert silently retreats backstage and slowly takes his leave out the stage door.

"[*The Story of Gilbert and Sullivan*] embodies a tradition of historical pageantry in British filmmaking that film historians have tended to dismiss as static, wooden and word-bound," writes commentator Geoffrey O'Brien. "However, it looks better now than anyone might have expected. The very traits once characterized as Stiff Upper Lip Cinema—the absence of high emotion or flamboyant gesture, the dry and carefully researched presentation of historical background, the tone balanced between blithe good humor and unflinching decorum in the face of life crises—have receded sufficiently into the past to seem rather bracing."[91] In sum, it can hold its head high alongside the 1999 masterpiece by Mike Leigh, *Topsy-Turvy*.

Perhaps no composer represented in this chapter, save Beethoven, held out to the movies a purer example of the "possessor" myth of genius than Richard Wagner (1813–1883). The almost universal image of Wagner remains still today that of an egomaniacal, ruthlessly opportunistic, manipulative, anti-Semitic sybarite who forged new forms of music drama and a harmonic vocabulary that placed him in the forefront of what came to be called the revolutionary "New Music" of the second half of the nineteenth century. It is difficult to find a positive view of Wagner the man. Critic Jonathan Lieberson's general assessment is typical: "He was a consummate borrower, a self-important braggart with an opinion on every subject, something of a crank (though probably not a bore), and treacherous in love. He was not merely a charming rascal, a lesser *Hochstapler,* but unquestionably a genuine swindler, indifferent to the feelings of others, calculating, ruthless, and coarse."[92] To be sure, suggests biographer Barry Millington, these extreme views are unjust to a degree and need to be tempered.[93]

Born illegitimately into a lower-middle-class home, Wagner received only sporadic music education as he stubbornly pursued a musical career in the face of poverty and public indifference. A self-starter and an indefatigable worker, he surmounted daunting circumstances to establish himself as the foremost and most influential opera composer of his day. His revolutionary politics, moreover, kept him a perpetual exile, fleeing from place to place, ruthlessly and opportunistically currying favor as he went with any prospective patrons and artistic supporters who presented themselves. His dream of a new form of Music Drama was fulfilled when, with the financial support of his young patron, King Ludwig II of Bavaria, he built a Festspielhaus designed to produce his colossal four-part opera cycle, *The Ring of the Nibelungs,* in 1876. Meanwhile, his private life was a shambles, as his scandalous affairs ruined one marriage and led to another, to his second wife, Cosima Liszt. His publicly vented anti-Semitism did little to endear him to the musical establishment, and it aroused controversy that divides his partisans and enemies to this day. To the end, he remained a canny promoter and mythologizer of his own life and work. No filmmaker has approached, much less surpassed him in that respect.

Many have tried, however. A string of aborted, failed, or incomplete biopics have straggled along in Wagner's wake (see the discussion in Chapter Five of Tony Palmer's *Wagner,* 1983, for an overview). Every genre or category of films has its "might-have-beens," its "what-if?" projects. *Magic Fire* (1954), an ambitious "life" of Wagner, is such a biopic. If ever a composer film deserved to be compared with Erich von Stroheim's mutilated *Greed* (1924), it is *Magic Fire.* Which is to say, we may never know what the original version of this epic production was like, inasmuch, like Stroheim's film, it has been cut, recut, and savaged beyond recognition. By the time the picture reached American theaters, its two-and-a-half-hour length had been reduced by more than an hour

Magic Fire (1954) brought Alan Badel and an international cast to the story of Richard Wagner. (Courtesy Photofest/Republic Pictures)

and its depiction of the *Ring* cycle to a few minutes of screen time. "When I had to compress sixteen hours of the *Ring* into five minutes," recalled émigré composer and Hollywood veteran Erich Wolfgang Korngold, who supervised the music, "that was already drastic, but now that they have cut it down to four minutes—that's too much."[94] Shot in many authentic European locations, it was directed by the German émigré filmmaker and Hollywood veteran William Dieterle, adapted from a story by Bertita Harding, supervised by music director Korngold, and featured Alan Badel as Wagner, Yvonne de Carlo as Minna Wagner, Rita Gam as Cosima Liszt, Carlos Thompson as Franz Liszt, and Gerhard Riegmann as King Ludwig II.

What survives is a story continuity as choppy as the truncated musical selections. The story begins in Magdeburg in 1834, when Wagner successfully auditions for the conductorship of the Magdeburg Stage and Opera Company. Later, restless and dissatisfied, he moves to Paris with his new wife, Minna. "A new age needs new music!" he tells her. "One day I shall conduct my own opera and conquer the world!" In a meeting with the two leading lights of the city, composer Giacomo Meyerbeer and virtuoso pianist Franz Liszt, he reiterates his ambitions: "I don't want arias, duets, ballets—they interfere with the actions. I intend my operas to be dramatic symphonies—music-dramas, I call them." As Liszt obligingly plays excerpts from the score of *The Flying Dutchman*, Wagner continues his music lecture: "No doubt you noticed there were several themes that were played again and again. I call them 'leitmotifs.' Each character is expressed by a particular theme."

But creditors catch up with Wagner and he soon finds himself in a debtors' prison. After his release he conducts his *Dutchman* in Dresden. Applause is generous, although the Dresden king advises the composer, "Don't make it so long next time." Relations with the king cool quickly when Wagner is implicated in the 1848 Dresden Uprisings. He flees to Weimar, where Liszt provides him safe harbor and conducts a program of numbers from the new *Lohengrin*. His status as political refugee with a price on his head impels him to find asylum in Zurich with some wealthy friends, Otto and Mathilde Wesendonk. As he settles in to a comfortable cottage on the Wesendonk estate, Wagner begins a clandestine affair with Mathilde. He asks her to come away to Paris with him. "I'm nothing without you," he declares. "I see my soul in your eyes, my angel." But Minna discovers the affair and bitterly denounces Wagner. Otto quietly asks Wagner to leave his house. Once again, he finds himself on the road, alone.

Back in Paris, he disregards Liszt's sage advice to insert a ballet into the second act of *Tannhäuser*. As a result, the production is disrupted by a claque of anti-Wagner partisans. Meanwhile, his hopes for a reunion with Mathilde are dashed when Liszt's daughter, Cosima (Rita Gam) — the wife of his conductor, Hans von Bülow — informs him Mathilde has decided to remain with her husband. She then counsels him to put Mathilde out of his mind: "You have no right to destroy yourself for a woman."

Thirteen years later, Wagner's fortunes take a turn for the better. He is granted amnesty and his sagging career is bolstered by the unexpected appearance of young King Ludwig II of Bavaria, who invites Wagner to take charge of his opera house in Munich. "I shall do everything in my power to make you happy," Ludwig enthuses. "I shall surround you with such splendor the gods will envy you." With the change in fortunes and sumptuous creature comforts, Wagner grows increasingly arrogant. Cosima alone understands him, declaring: "Everyone who comes too close to you is consumed by the magic of your fire." Ludwig, in the mean time, is delighted with the command performance of Wagner's new opera, *Die Meistersinger*. But his ministers are alarmed at the enormous sums the king is flinging at Wagner. "It's madness to spend the country's wealth for theatrical purposes," they tell Wagner. "No sacrifice is too great for the cause of art," he retorts. They angrily denounce him as "a corrupting influence on our young monarch. Either you leave or the King must abdicate."

In Wagner's time of trial, Cosima confesses her love for him and offers to leave her husband, von Bülow. Wagner, startled, objects at first: "Hans is my friend. You know my feelings for you, but you cannot go with me." But after a moment's reflection, he changes his mind and embraces her in a passionate kiss. "I shall lead you on to higher and higher achievements," promises

Cosima. "I shall make you forget everything you gave up." Despite Liszt's vehement objections, Wagner and Cosima are married and take up residence in Triebschen. The outbreak of the Franco-Prussian War disrupts domestic harmony, however, and Wagner resolves to return to Germany. His long-held dream of a colossal cycle of four operas based on the Ring of the Nibelungs is finally realized when King Ludwig is persuaded to help subsidize his Festspiel-haus in Bayreuth.

February 1883. Aging and sick, Wagner determines to finish one more op-era, *Parsifal*. But its controversial religious nature elicits attacks from the church, and Liszt, now an abbé, arrives to voice his objections. But when he hears Wagner describe the plot and play a few musical excerpts, he is over-whelmed; he seats himself at the piano and engages in a musical duet with his old friend. Indeed, so powerful is the music that when Cosima enters the room, Liszt impulsively embraces her in a new spirit of reconciliation. Mo-ments later, Wagner dies of a heart attack.

In a final act of devotion, Cosima closes the cover of her husband's piano for the last time.

It is curious that in 1954, at a time when the world was fully aware of Hitler's dubious appropriation of Wagner's music, the collapse of the Aryan dream, and the revelations of the Holocaust — it is very strange that *Magic Fire* fails to mention Wagner's notorious anti-Semitism and avoids any hint of his Aryan ideologies. Blame the ever-present Production Code's strictures, as will be discussed later in this chapter.

Nonetheless, there is evidence that *Magic Fire* on occasion does address the more problematic aspects of the "possessor" myth. The protagonist, por-trayed by Alan Badel, emerges as an outright cad and manipulator who elicits not an ounce of sympathy from the viewer. Credit the script with a brave attempt to peel at least some of the varnish off the typically valorized com-poser paradigm. For example, when he is confronted by Liszt regarding the affair with his daughter, Cosima, the dialogue strikes to the heart of Wagner's ruthless opportunism and rampant egomania.[95]

> LISZT: There are things in life not even a genius should do.
> WAGNER: Franz, what has happened nobody could have prevented.
> LISZT: Nonsense! Save your feeble excuses which only point out your pam-pered ego.
> WAGNER: My pampered ego? I seem to remember that the pious and respect-able Abbé Liszt was once as successful in the boudoir as on the concert stage. Naturally, in later years one's youthful indiscretions can be minimized by taking the cloth.

LISZT: I don't deny deserving that. But I have paid for that. I'm still paying. If you could only see yourself in that fancy dress of yours. The velvet jacket and the Rembrandt cap. What an absurd masquerade! I would have never thought you capable of such humbug. But I don't blame you for hankering after riches when you had nothing but want. However, stealing the wife of the man who worshiped you as a god is abominable."

Not even Cosima's attempt to justify Wagner's behavior — "artists are but tools in the hands of their demons; ask yourself what matters in the face of his work, his music" — can soften *that* diatribe! Moreover, the script's attempts to soft-pedal Wagner's womanizing by portraying Minna as a spiteful harridan and Mathilde and Cosima as the aggressors in the case fail to convince. And Wagner's own description of *Parsifal* — "I'm trying to take what's best in all religions to show their common path to salvation — through suffering, compassion, sacrifice, and renunciation" — rings pretty hollow by the time the final curtain falls.

It is difficult to determine just what Republic producer Herbert J. Yates was thinking when he green-lighted this film. In the absence of studio production records, we can only speculate that perhaps here was one more example of the time-honored tradition of a Hollywood producer grasping at the built-in prestige value of classical music. Certainly by the early 1950s Yates's studio, a charter member of what has come to be known as "Poverty Row," was more famous for its John Wayne and Gene Autry cowboy movies, stunt serials, and Vera Hruba Ralston vehicles than for its A-list features. A mogul of the old school, Yates had managed to produce only a handful of prestige pictures, including the modestly budged Stephen Foster biopic, *Harmony Lane* (1934), Orson Welles's *Macbeth* (1948), and John Ford's *The Quiet Man* (1951).[96] Already in financial straits at the time *Magic Fire* went into production, the studio hoped to take advantage of money that had been frozen in German banks after World War II. Yates visited Germany at this time and announced in an interview that Republic would make a "film of George [*sic*] Wagner, a love story with some music."[97]

Korngold came on to the project avowedly to prevent Republic from perpetrating what he called the "hatchet job" he felt had been wrought on other Hollywood biographies. "When I accepted William Dieterle's invitation to supervise the musical shaping of his Richard Wagner film *Magic Fire*," he recalls, "I did it with the understanding that it would be my artistic intention to use Wagner's music in its original form, without adding a single bar to satisfy the demands of the 'background music' or changing the orchestration of the opera excerpts actually performed."[98] Certainly there is evidence of careful and loving attempts to shoot lengthy operatic scenes in authentic European locations with a wonderful cast of singers, including Leonie Rysanek, Hans Hopf, Otto Edelmann, and Annelies Kupper, under the direction of Professor Rudolph Hartmann, director of the Munich Bavarian State Opera. Indeed, it has been estimated that in the original version there were at least fifty minutes of uninterrupted music. However, only remnants of scenes remain from *The Flying Dutchman,* the "Venusberg Music" from *Tannhäuser,* and the third act of *Die Meistersinger.* Thus, pursuant to the dictates of the classical paradigm and budget the performative aspects of the music are ultimately subordinated to the storyline. The scant four minutes allowed for a succession of glimpses of the sixteen-hour *Ring of the Nibelungs* amply attest to that.

These musical restrictions notwithstanding, Republic seems to have been determined to wrench a pop tune out of the score. Korngold's son, George, explains: "Half way through shooting, a reel of magnetic film arrived from Hollywood marked 'Main Title Song.' I played it when my father was not present and found that it contained a pop arrangement of the 'Siegfried Idyll' complete with a crooned vocal and disrespectful reharmonization of Wagner's chord structures. The lyrics were something on the line of 'Magic Fire, you're my heart's desire." When director Dieterle learned of this, he threatened to quit the picture if the song were used. The song was pulled. "Later, when the film was completely finished, I played this travesty for my father who was amused but not really shocked because he knew that anything was possible in Hollywood and that at least he had protected Wagner to the best of his abilities."[99]

Today, *Magic Fire* can be seen only in its badly mutilated version. Moreover, the color process utilized in the film, a rather dubious process called "Trucolor," has faded over the years into a blotchy palette of rusty red-and-brown hues. Originally seen theatrically as a second feature at cheap movie houses, it is now relegated to late-night television reruns. In an era before "directors' cut" releases, *Magic Fire* was never a candidate for a restored, "original" version, and it is not likely to be one now. A few scraps of music and some patches of images are all that remains. Wagner would have to wait thirty more years before Tony Palmer's *Wagner* (1983) would restore him to at least a semblance of his proper shape and sound (see Chapter Five).

Classical composers first entered American homes and "played" to American families in the television era with several biopics originally produced for Walt Disney's weekly television series and expanded for theatrical release. *The Peter Tchaikovsky Story* was directed by Charles Barton, written by Otto Englander and Joe Rinaldi, and cast Grant Williams, fresh from his triumph in *The Incredible Shrinking Man* (1957), as Pyotr Tchaikovsky (1840–1893). It was telecast on 30 January 1959 as a kind of curtain raiser, or promotional hype, for Disney's forthcoming animated feature, *Sleeping Beauty*, which, it was announced, was to use Tchaikovsky's music. The broadcast marked the first time a television program was simulcast in stereo — since FM stereo did not yet exist, one channel was aired on an AM station and the other on an FM station. Although director Barton might seem a curious choice for such a project — his previous work included Buster Crabbe westerns and Abbott and Costello features — he was a veteran of television directing and had won Uncle Walt's trust with several successful Disney projects, including the *Zorro* and *Spin and Marty* series. Alas, there is no extant scholarship dealing with his involvement in the Tchaikovsky project.[100]

Toss aside the story of the historical Tchaikovsky, a man troubled from his student years by his sexual ambivalence and ill-starred romantic liaisons (including a disastrous marriage to a woman of dubious reputation); whose relationship with his mysterious patron, Nadejda von Meck, smacked of a mutual smarmy opportunism; and who died under circumstances that aroused cries of foul play. Instead, Hollywood had already sanitized and contained the Russian master in a 1948 Allied Artists picture, *Song of My Heart*, directed and written by Benjamin Glazer, starring Frank Sundstrom as the composer, with piano performances provided by José Iturbi. Needless to say, all mention of the composer's sexual ambivalence was omitted.[101] Not until Ken Russell's *The Music Lovers* (1970) would the subject be tackled with a degree of frankness (see Chapter Five).

Disney's version of Tchaikovsky is an inspired tunesmith, disappointed in love and consoled only by his music, in the best *Blossom Time* tradition. He is first seen as a precocious child so emotional about music that after hearing his nanny's rendition of the "Sleeping Beauty" story, he awakens in the middle of the night with tunes running through his head. Forbidden to play sports by his family, he sits instead by his window, conducting music to himself so vigorously that he thrusts his hand through the pane. His ambition to be a composer is temporarily sidetracked when his mother dies and the grief-stricken boy goes to work at the Ministry of Justice. After meeting pianist Anton Rubinstein, his interest in music rekindles and he resumes his music studies. Meanwhile, his hopes to marry the beautiful Desiree Artot (Narda Onyx), an Italian soprano, are dashed when she leaves him for another man.[102] Moreover, his music for *Swan Lake* receives poor reviews. After spending some time abroad nursing his wounds, Tchaikovsky returns to Russia, where he resumes work on his dream to compose music for *Sleeping Beauty*. The ballet enjoys a great success with "the people," commoners and aristocrats alike, and the composer settles down to enjoy his status as a major force in the world of music.

Disney's biopic about Beethoven (1770–1827), *The Magnificent Rebel,* was filmed on location in Vienna and telecast in two parts for Disney's first experiment in color television, *Walt Disney's Wonderful World of Color,* on 18 and 25 November 1962 (it was released theatrically overseas the year before). It was directed by Georg Tressler, written by Joanne Court, and musically supervised by Heinz Schreiter. Again, pursuant to the Schubert paradigm, this Beethoven joins Tchaikovsky as a composer whose music brings him closer to the hearts of the people while offering solace from disappointed love. The story opens in 1792, when the young composer (Carl Boehm) arrives in Vienna to study with Franz Joseph Haydn (Ernst Nadheny). Beethoven is a truculent fellow who proclaims his identification with the democratic politics of the invading Napoleon by announcing, "Napoleon will free the people and I will free music!" At a concert for Prince Lichnowsky he meets the beautiful Countess Giulietta Guicciardi (Giulia Rubini). Impressed by his music, Giulietta seeks him out for music lessons. Their friendship soon turns to love, but her father objects to her being involved with a man beneath her station ("But there is great nobility in your music," Giulietta assures him).

Beethoven, who has already composed his "Moonlight" Sonata for her, determines to forget Giulietta by devoting himself to music. While wandering in the woodland, he is newly inspired to write a symphony. Back in his rooms, the landlord's peremptory knock provides a convenient motto for the work (da-da-da-DUHHHMMM). His Fifth Symphony completed, he is heartened by its enthusiastic reception. But fate intervenes. The onset of deafness in 1812 ruins his conducting career, and the subsequent premiere of his opera, *Fidelio.* Moreover, Napoleon's appearance in Vienna forces Beethoven to leave the city. Broken and distraught, he escapes to a small town where he meets Stephen, a blind boy who pumps the church's organ. Newly inspired by the boy's determination to overcome his infirmity, Beethoven returns to composing and writes his Ninth Symphony. The public joyfully greets its premiere. "This is just the beginning," declares a stentorian narrator voice, "a sound that came from the heart and burst into music could not be silenced! His was a life that would be remembered as long as music and courage and greatness are remembered!"

Like all Beethoven movies, excepting *Beethoven Lives Upstairs* (1992) — see Chapter Six — *The Magnificent Rebel* flirts with the identity of the elusive "immortal beloved" (in this case identified as Giulietta Guicciardi).[103] It generally reflects the biographical constructions of the composer already seen in two previous foreign films, Abel Gance's *Un grand amour de Beethoven* (France, 1938) and Walter Kolm-Veltee's *Eroica* (Germany, 1949). Gance's Beethoven (Harry Baur), which recasts the composer in Gance's own image, was the epitome of the Heroic Artist whose disappointments in love with the "immortal beloved" (here identified as Guicciardi) and struggles with physical affliction result in a search for "the higher expression of the spirit," as Gance put it.[104] Likewise, *Eroica* (which also identified Guicciardi as Beethoven's elusive "immortal beloved") likewise insisted that it was only through Beethoven's disappointment in love that he was able to pursue his art. "I don't know whether it is in me to make another person happy," Beethoven (Ewald Balser) moans. "Am I not entitled to give and receive love like everyone else?" To which his friend, Therese von Brunswik replies, "God has chosen you to speak to all mankind. No one should come between you and the world. You must not give your love to just one. It is your fate to remain lonely."

From Gance to Kolm-Vetee to Disney, this image of Beethoven confirms the deification that had already been under construction since his own lifetime. For a more candid, if not altogether more historically accurate assessment of Beethoven's struggles with life and art, the world would have to wait more than two decades for Paul Morrissey's *Beethoven's Nephew* (1987) and Bernard Rose's *Immortal Beloved* (1994).[105]

Disney's Tchaikovsky and Beethoven films became convenient armatures upon which to hang some elaborate location shooting, the popularizations of a handful of compositions (generous portions of Tchaikovsky's *Sleeping Beauty* and Beethoven's "Moonlight" Sonata, *Fidelio,* and the Ninth Symphony), fodder for the weekly television series, promotion for other Disney projects, and, most significant, what has come to be known as the "Disney version" of life and art. They joined the many classical composers and cultural properties Disney had already commodified in his constructions of popular entertainments, ever since Mickey Mouse shook hands with Leopold Stokowsky in *Fantasia*.[106] These were lives — and music — that must be tidied up and sanitized, just as the "Main Street, U.S.A." attractions at the Disney theme parks cleaned up the irregularities and blemishes of his own Midwest childhood.[107] "Disney film not only 'cleans up' history and political struggles, nature and culture, gender and sex/uality," writes the editors of that estimable book, *From Mouse to Mermaid: The Politics of Film, Gender, and Culture* "but elevates sanitization to pedagogy." Thus, the Tchaikovsky and Beethoven biopics, conceived and targeted for prime-time television family audiences, emerge as "Disneyfied" versions of the complexities and more marginalized aspects of these composers' lives. Tchaikovsky and Beethoven were ready to join the stable of composers who composed the soundtrack to Disney's world.[108]

The classical period of composer biopics was on the wane by the time Columbia Pictures's *Song without End,* an American-British production about the life and music of Franz Liszt (1811–1886), was released in 1960. It featured

British actor Dirk Bogarde as Liszt, Capucine as the Princess Carolyne von Wittgenstein, Genevieve Page as Marie d'Agoult, and was directed by Charles Vidor and George Cukor. The classical studio style that had dominated American and British screens for decades—and which had significantly influenced commercial filmmaking throughout the world—was being challenged in the late 1950s by alternative approaches to production and narrative structure in the French New Wave, the collapse of the vertically integrated studio system in Hollywood, the weakening of the American and British censor codes, and the introduction of new technologies related to the television medium (such as single-system sound, portable 16-millimeter cameras, improved light-sensitive film, telephoto lenses, and so on). In other words, *Song without End,* in style and substance, was already a museum piece by the time it reached the theater houses.

It could be fairly stated that *any* attempt in the classical studio era to translate the phenomenon that was Liszt to the screen was doomed to failure. A self-promoter from the beginning, by the time Liszt was in his mid-twenties he had already established himself not only as the reigning supreme virtuoso among pianists but as a Byronic figure, cloaked—like his contemporary, violinist Paganini—in the mantle of sin, sex, and public notoriety. Yet, paradoxically, he was also drawn to the spiritual life, eventually taking Holy Orders in the Roman Catholic Church. Thus, he was both "possessor" and "possessed" —by turns. On one hand, he was the architect of his own public image of flamboyant performer and the forger, with Wagner, of the so-called "Music of the Future." On the other hand, he was subservient to the folk music of his Hungarian heritage and the ancient musical traditions of liturgical music. By the time of his death in 1886, Liszt had long since been victimized by his own celebrity, subjected to a degree of gossip and notoriety that continues to obscure the real qualities of his music.

As if prescient of what was to come at the hands of filmmakers, according to Alan Walker, author of the definitive three-volume Liszt biography, Liszt himself was wary about future commentators and biographers: "Liszt himself entertained no illusions about his biographers," writes Walker. "They often irritated him, and for good reason; some of them . . . had a genuine talent for invention. Occasionally, Liszt corrected their effusions. By the time he had reached old age, however, he was resigned to his fate: the groundwork for that generous supply of misinformation, half-truth, and legend which taints the Liszt literature to this day."[109] It has also "tainted," to borrow Walker's term, the many movies that have either featured Liszt as the principal player of his own drama, or a secondary character involved in the lives of other artist. Indeed, I would argue that more movies involving Liszt have been made than about any other composer, excepting only Schubert and Strauss.

Examples are plentiful. There is Liszt as the serene aristocrat of the piano, with a walk-on cameo role in the 1943 version of *The Phantom of the Opera*. He is the cynical roué we have seen in *Song of Love;* the sweetly romanticized traveling musician in early scenes in Max Ophus's *Lola Montez* (1955); the unselfish entrepreneur who introduces Chopin to George Sand's salon in *A Song to Remember;* the rigidly respectable abbé we have seen in *Magic Fire;* the outrageous proto–rock star in a film discussed in Chapter Four of this book, Ken Russell's *Lisztomania* (1975); the ruthless opportunist in Visconti's *Ludwig* (1972) and Tony Palmer's *Wagner* (1983), also discussed in Chapter Five; and the hen-picked husband of James Lapine's *Impromptu?* (1991), discussed in Chapter Six.[110] Ever variable and always unpredictable, he might have been the subject for Byron's lines in *The Vision of Judgment:*

> The moment that you had pronounced him *one,*
> Presto! His face changed, and he was another;
> And when that change was hardly well put on,
> It varied, till I don't think his own mother
> (If that he had a mother) would her son
> Had known, he shifted so from one to t'other. (line LXXVII)

Determined to depict all these personae, *Song without End* instead gives us a veritable mulligan stew of a character, whose outlines are blurred and whose character is indeterminate.

Despite Columbia's publicity hype — "The shocking loves, the scandalous life of a sinner torn between flesh and the devil!" — *Song without End* winds up a pretty dull affair. Hollywood is at it again, holding out the enticements of sin and sex, only to indulge at the last minute in an act of *cinematicus interruptus*. Little in this biopic does more than vaguely suggest the spectacular popularity, creative frenzies, sensual excesses, and inner torments of the composer-pianist who, contemporary Robert Schumann observed, combined "splendour and tinsel."[111] As Liszt himself cautioned, in words that might have been heeded much later by the watchdogs of the Production Code office, "Who would venture to speak explicitly about anything today? It would be in poor taste and set a bad example."[112]

The screenplay, by Oscar Millard, spans Liszt's affair with Marie d'Agoult in the late 1830s in Paris, his concert tour to raise money for Hungarian flood victims, the split with d'Agoult and the meeting with Princess Carolyne Wittgenstein, relationships with other composers (Lyndon Brook as Wagner, and Alex Davion as Chopin), the futile attempts to win papal consent in Rome to Carolyne's divorce, and the renunciation of worldly pleasures as Liszt enters a monastery in the late 1850s.

Interwoven throughout are Liszt's vacillations over a career devoted to the

In *Song without End* (1960) Dirk Bogarde's Liszt is a handsome virtuoso torn between the sacred and the profane. (Courtesy Photofest/Columbia Pictures)

pleasures of fame and flesh and the spiritual calling of the church. "It's difficult to be either good or bad," he tells his mother. "I'm part gypsy, part priest. When I'm alone, I want the world; when I have the world, I want the peace and seclusion of a monastery. I'm at war with myself. Mother, pray tonight. . . . Pray for your son." Late in the film, he tells the Grand Duchess of Weimar of his plans to abjure the concert platform: "This may surprise you, Madame, but my heart has never been on the concert stage. My tendency to vulgar exhibitionism, which you were too polite to qualify by so many words, is misleading. I despise my career as a virtuoso." His affair with d'Agoult goes stale at her repeated, nagging reminders that she sacrificed her respectability by leaving her husband to live with him. "It's a debt I'll pay in guilt," he retorts, "and boredom, and self-disgust." The only way he can get away from her is to embark on his series of concerts to benefit his fellow Hungarian flood victims. Later, Princess Carolyne takes charge. Her chilly demeanor contrasts with d'Agoult's more smarmy qualities. Carolyne regards her rival with open hostility. "Did he drive you to Paradise," she sarcastically inquires of Marie. "No, Madame," Marie riposts meaningfully, "he doesn't know the road." Liszt wisely avoids this interchange altogether by escaping to the street, where he joins a band of gypsies in an impromptu concert.

The difficulties Liszt and Carolyne have in securing her divorce from Rome take up the last third of the picture. Although Carolyne's husband agrees to a divorce, the archbishop says Rome will not allow it. He orders the lovers never to meet alone again. But Carolyne's protestations at the Vatican win a reversal, and the two make their marriage plans. However, on the eve of their wedding, the Holy Council cancels the promised annulment. Carolyne explains to the astonished Liszt that perhaps God never intended them to be together. "I was sent to you only to lead you back to Him," she concludes piously, echoing the agendas of the Hollywood Production Code. Liszt dons black robes and enters a monastery. In the film's last scene, he ascends to the organ loft and plays "Un Sospiro" while Carolyne kneels below in silent prayer.

The critics were tepid in their praise. Writing in *Variety*, Saul Ostrove noted that the picture "obviously was made to please as many people as possible and it will do that. Music lovers will be satisfied, general film fans will appreciate the picture's scope, and Capucine, who is being publicized heavily in the press, will stir interest."[113] James Powers in the *Hollywood Reporter* singled out Bogarde, who was suitably "dashing and romantic." Powers continued, "He is more British than European, however, and does not seem as authoritative as the role should be."[114]

The film's gestation goes back almost a decade, the title changing every year as Hollywood grappled with modifying Liszt's "traveling circus life," as he described it, to the more politely genteel proportions of the film frame—*Dream of Love* in 1953, *The Franz Liszt Story* in 1954, and *The Magic Flame* in 1959. By contrast to Oscar Millard's semifictitious screenplay, Hollywood as usual was concerned with depicting authentic surface details and locations. Cameras were taken on location to Rome and France, where many of the events actually transpired. The international cast seems to have been chosen to take advantage of their British and European accents. Bogarde purportedly devoted his entire time away from the set learning to simulate keyboard performance (the piano was actually played by Liszt specialist Jorge Bolet). And to be sure, Bogarde's expert miming of the scene in which he plays Chopin's B-flat Scherzo is quite amazing. But such authenticity has its limits. Bogarde's orchestra conducting consisted of a lamentable series of spasmodic arm wavings. And although he was soon to acquire a reputation for sensitive screen roles in British films—the homosexual in distress in *Victim* and the decadent valet in *The Servant* would appear in the next two years—for now, Bogarde was here merely a dashing pretty boy whose hair must never turn white (as Liszt's did) in later life.

A pop tune is in order, of course. Filling the bill is the "Un Sospiro," the third of Liszt's *Etudes de Concert.* Its assigned meanings of faith and love and its deployment throughout the soundtrack as a leitmotif resembles the appropriation of similar themes cited in biopics discussed earlier in this chapter, notably the "Ave Maria" in *The Melody Master,* the Third Etude of Opus 10 in *A Song to Remember,* the theme from Paganini's First Violin Concerto in *The Magic Bow,* the theme of the Prince and Princess in *Song of Scheherazade,* and so on. It appears with alarming frequency, both as source music and background score, arranged by Harry Sukman and Roger Wagner for piano, full orchestra, and chorus. Published by Columbia Pictures Music Corporation under the title "Song without End," it featured lyrics by Ned Washington:

> Eternal light, shine unto me!
> That it may guide me close to thee
> To gaze upon thy countenance
> Forever more.

Another melody, derived from the "Consolation," No. 3, was published, also with lyrics by Washington. According to the movies, Liszt not only wrote the soundtrack to his own life, but its "hit" tunes as well.

Censored Lives

Song without End suffered many censorial changes on its way to the theaters. No opportunity was lost in emphasizing the victory of Liszt's spirituality—read that, the victory of the censors—over his more carnal hungers. It is no accident that all the women in his life—his mother, Marie, Carolyne, the Grand Duchess—are depicted as divining and encouraging his finer instincts. In reality, although Liszt's conflicts between flesh and the spirit were real enough, they were hardly resolved as handily as they are here (indeed, they may never have been resolved at all). Despite the references in the dialogue to his hedonistic life, there is little visual evidence of it on screen. In reality, his affair with Marie—which lasted roughly from 1833 to 1839 and which saw the birth of three illegitimate children and her extensive collaboration with him in all matters musical and literary—was lived out in the full public glare of his concertizing years.[115] His relationship with Carolyne, which began at their first meeting in Kiev in 1847 and endured for the rest of their lives, was likewise obviously, if relatively discreetly, lived out in their Altenburg residence, amid

the social and artistic milieu of Weimar. Far from being an unqualified determination to marry, their plans were plagued by many doubts and hesitations on
both sides. The story of their attempts to gain an annulment from Carolyne's
marriage to Prince Nicholas is a long and convoluted one, as evidenced by the
exhaustive researches of biographer Walker.[116] Liszt's assumption in July 1865
of minor orders of the priesthood (doorkeeper, lector, exorcist, and acolyte) —
which in the film seems a final renunciation of worldly ways — was nothing of
the kind. He never took orders of celibacy, and he led an active secular as well as
churchly life for the rest of his days.[117]

The production files of *Song without End* reveal that the Hollywood censors kept tight rein over potential problems in the depiction of these worldly
and spiritual affairs. A particularly telling series of memos from Joseph Breen
of the Production Code Administration (PCA) to Columbia producer Harry
Cohn, dispatched during the preliminary story treatments of 1954–1955, reveals concern about several issues. The first is a request for clarification about
the church's role in annulments in a case like Liszt's and Carolyne's. The second concerns the Code's strictures regarding the subject of adultery: "We have
consistently required, under the Code, that stories of adultery stay away . . .
from actual scenes in bedrooms." Third, Liszt's scandalous behavior must not
be rationalized in any of the dialogue "because he is a genius, apart from
the rest of men." Moreover, those who criticize Liszt's excesses must *not*
come off as "stiff-backed and social snobs"; conversely, those who encourage
such behavior must *not* seem to be "tolerant, more humane, and, generally,
much more desirable than those who resist the adultery." Later, in 1959,
Geoffrey M. Shurlock, who had taken over the reins of the PCA from Breen
five years before, advises producer Samuel J. Briskin that Marie's line "I have
never regretted being your mistress" be deleted, and that "the sex affair" with
her suggested in the script "would be difficult to justify, even within the framework of this story. In our opinion, Liszt's rather free relationship with women
is quite thoroughly established, without need for dramatizing it almost casually, as seems to be the case here. We ask that you consider simply dropping this scene." In addition, pursued Shurlock, "Please be advised that open-
mouthed or excessively lustful kisses are unacceptable under the Code."[118]

This gambit of alluding to but not overtly depicting such "problematic" issues and scenes stands at the heart of the strategies by which the PCA and
the British Board of Film Censors (BBFC) contained the "problematic" aspects
of the aforementioned composers' lives, much as it did with all the other
studio-released films of the period. Adultery, licentiousness, homosexuality,
suicide, and political radicalism are among the plot elements in many of these

composer biopics that had to be monitored and restricted. According to British film historian Kevin Brownlow, British censorship, no less than the American agenda, "has been extremely strict" since its inception in 1913. "In the 1930s and 1940s audiences were protected to a ridiculous degree. The BBFC was not legally binding — it was set up by the film industry — but a theatre's supply of films might cease if it was ignored." In addition to the BBFC, there were also the local Watch Committees to deal with, "who could occasionally be liberal but were often fiercer than the BBFC."[119]

An enormous amount of recent scholarship has sifted through Hollywood's PCA files and other censorial agencies, like the Catholic Legion of Decency, to ascertain these patterns of containment, particularly in the social problem films of the 1930s like the gangster and "fallen women" cycles, the wartime propaganda films of the 1940s, and the proliferation of politically themed films of the postwar period.[120] Composer biopics, perhaps due to their less privileged status among today's critics and historians, are seldom mentioned, if at all. Yet, the fabrications, sidesteps, and outright distortions just noted in *Song without End* and the other biopics in this chapter are prime examples of Code and BBFC policies coming to bear on biopics. Indeed, the sometimes marginalized personality traits, sexuality, and creative energies of composers constituted exceptionally troublesome challenges to the censors.

Before the American Ratings System was instituted in 1968, Hollywood filmmakers had been forced to devise strategies to target the widest possible audience, all the while suggesting more "adult" themes appealing to a narrower, more sophisticated demographic. Regulating these activities was the Production Code, which was written in 1930 and administered rigorously in 1934 with the establishment of the Production Code Administration office under the leadership of Breen. "A basic premise of this code was that movies did not enjoy the same freedom of expression as the printed word or theatrical performances," writes Gregory D. Black in his exemplary *Hollywood Censored*. "This most democratic of art forms had to be regulated . . . because movies cut across all social, economic, political, and educational boundaries."[121] As historian Richard Maltby demonstrates in his witty dissection of Code strategies, the Code was implemented to render narratives "chameleon-like, adaptable, resilient, and accommodating" to differing components of the viewing audience. Malby writes, "A movie's inclusion of contradictions, gaps, and blanks allowed it to be consumed as at least two discrete, even opposing stories going on in the same text." Putting it another way, it could render the "objectionable" to some viewers "unobjectionable" to others. "Having chosen not to divide its audience," Maltby continues, "Hollywood was obliged to devise a system that would allow 'sophisticated' viewers to read whatever they liked into a formally 'innocent' movie, so long as the producers could use the mechanics of the Production Code to deny that the sophisticated interpretation had been put there in the first place."[122]

Thus, the Code required that any suggestion of Schubert's homosexuality in *The Melody Master* must be limited to fleeting, suggestive scenes among Schubert's male companions, like the episode in which a conscripting officer confronts them in a beer hall and describes them as "chambermaids" and accuses one of them as being a "butterfly" who "crochets like a dream"; and the scene where a barmaid offers to marry Schubert and thus save him from conscription: "I guess I'm just a coward," he replies; "I'll take the army." Likewise, the captain of Rimsky-Korsakov's ship in *Song of Scheherazade* struts about bare-chested, declaring defiantly that *no women* will ever board his ship (save the one who, ironically, turns out to be in drag). RimskyKorsakov, meanwhile, remains steadfastly and suspiciously oblivious to the aggressive advances of Cara for most of the picture.[123]

Although political references are generally to be avoided, particularly in the years immediately preceding and during World War II, we have already seen how allusions to the Nazi Anschluss and Stalinist totalitarianism were negotiated in *The Great Waltz* and *A Song to Remember*. "Here and elsewhere, the showing of scenes of revolutionists will very likely be rejected in a number of foreign countries," advised Breen in a memo dated 11 May 1938, regarding the depiction of Strauss's participation in the 1848 uprisings. In another memo, dated 17 May 1938, he also ordered the deletion of some of the students' words, such as "We want free press — down with tyranny!"[124]

But the greatest challenge, as we have seen in *Song without End*, was the sexual license alleged to be present in the lives of many composers. Regarding *The Great Waltz*, a letter from Breen to producer Mayer dated 16 February 1935 expressed concern with Strauss's affair with singer Carla Donner. "Inasmuch as Strauss is a married man, we believe it will be necessary to omit from these episodes all action of Strauss and Carla kissing each other." A later memo, dated 13 May 1938, repeated the proscription of "any suggestion that there is an adulterous relationship between Carla and Schani [Strauss]." Similarly, in *A Song to Remember,* Breen objected to any graphic depiction of the affair between Chopin and George Sand (see the case study in Chapter Two).

Tchaikovsky's homosexuality, as might be expected, could never be countenanced by the Code. Censors issued warnings to director Benjamin Glazer, while preparing *Song of My Heart* "of the necessity of handling all situations very carefully in view of the known fact that Tchaikovsky was a sex pervert. It is for this reason that we felt any emphasis on the fact that he led a 'woman-less' life would be highly objectionable." Glazer was further admonished that "sex perversion, or any inference of it, is forbidden."[125] Needless to say, any such allusions are scrupulously avoided in the Disney version.

Nothing, it seems, escaped the Code's purview. Scenes in early script drafts of *Song of Love* depict the birth and the nursing of Clara Schumann's baby. Breen's memo to MGM studio chief Mayer, dated 5 September 1946, cautions against "any undue emphasis on the pains of childbirth" and advises that "this scene of Clara nursing the baby will be shot with great care." Director Clarence Brown's solution constitutes one of the film's more fondly remembered scenes: Clara has come offstage between encores. She seats herself, her back to the camera, and cradles the baby in her lap. The only suggestion of nursing is a close-up of the baby's toes, curling up in perfect bliss.[126] In *Song of Scheherazade* even dance routines fell victim to the scowling Breen. In a letter to one of the studio heads at Universal, dated 3 January 1946, Breen complained that dancer Cara's gyrations "should avoid any objectionable or indecent movements of the body in the actual dance routines."[127]

The same thematic and narrative paradigms discerned in the classical composer biopics of the American and British studio era, 1930–1960, also shape the biopics of popular songwriters from that same period. As is discussed throughout Chapter Three, the "lives" of American songwriters Foster, Handy, Berlin, Gershwin, and others — all inhabitants of that semimythical place known as Tin Pan Alley — reveal an essential kinship with their classical brethren on the other side of the street. Putting it whimsically (but not altogether inaccurately), Schubert and Strauss, under their new identities of Foster and Handy, transform the waltzes of Biedermeier Vienna to the folk music and popular songs of post–Civil War America. Liszt's Parisian salon performances of his Hungarian Rhapsodies will find their New World counterparts in Gershwin's Carnegie Hall performance of "Rhapsody in Blue." And Gilbert and Sullivan's contentious relationship will be echoed in that of Bert Kalmar and Harry Ruby. It's a synergy that could find its apotheosis only in Hollywood.

2

A Song Remembered
Frédéric Chopin Goes to War

"A man worthy of his gifts should grow closer to those people as he grows more great. Fight harder for them with that same genius."
— *Joseph Elsner to Frédéric Chopin in* A Song to Remember *(1945)*

"*A Song to Remember* is destined to rank with the greatest attractions since motion pictures began," proclaimed the advance publicity from Columbia Pictures — "seven years in the making . . . , seven years of never-ending effort to bring you a glorious new landmark in motion picture achievement. It means not only prestige but money in the box-office till." Viewers were assured, "As long as lovers love and as long as dreamers dream, their story will be remembered."[1]

Aside from the expected Hollywood publicity hype, however, there were some grains of truth in the prophecy. *A Song to Remember,* a "life" of the celebrated Polish composer Frédéric Chopin (Cornel Wilde), released in the waning months of World War II, deserves pride of place among the dozens of biopics about classical and popular composers produced during the height of Hollywood's studio period in the 1930s and 1940s. Despite its highbrow profile, it scored at the box office through its entertaining blend of fact and fiction, its patriotic message to contemporary wartime audiences, and its bewitching exploitation of Chopin's music (doubtless heard for the first time by

A Song to Remember (1944–1945) was a Technicolor Columbia picture, casting Cornel Wilde (Frédéric Chopin) opposite Merle Oberon (George Sand). (Courtesy Photofest/Columbia Pictures)

millions of audience members). "It achieves . . . the praiseworthy aim of bringing the concert hall to the film theatre," noted Sherwin Kane in *Motion Picture Daily,* "where it is certain to be welcomed by the patrons of both."[2] And writing in 1949, four years after the film's release, Chopin's biographer Herbert Weinstock attributed directly to the film the "suddenly increased popularity" of Chopin's great A-flat Major Polonaise, Opus 53, fragments of which are heard throughout the picture: "José Iturbi's brash, insensitive performance of this flashy and vital piece," Weinstock wrote, "was at once taken to the hearts of thousands of people who had otherwise only a remote — and either awed or disdainful — interest in serious music."[3]

The *Hollywood Reporter* greeted *A Song to Remember* as a welcome addition to the recently imported European screen biographies of Beethoven, Schubert, and Handel: "It is the first venture in this field by American film makers and is a magnificent success. . . . It is one of the finest and most beautiful screen productions yet given to the world, and in the field of music films of its kind it stands alone."[4] Other critics were equally enthusiastic. *Variety* reported, "This dramatization of the life and times of Frédéric Chopin (1810–1849), the Polish musician-patriot, is the most exciting presentation of an artist yet achieved on the screen."[5] *Film Daily* contended that "no Holly-wood film has succeeded so signally in providing a medium for the projection of a music master's art."[6] However, the film's casual concern for historical and biographical accuracy, as I examined later in this chapter, outraged other commentators. Particularly notorious was a wholly fabricated penultimate sequence wherein the disease-ravaged Chopin embarks on a suicidal concert tour to aid Polish freedom fighters. He hunches over the piano. He sweats profusely. He labors on and on in an increasing frenzy. He coughs spasmodically. Suddenly, a spot of blood spatters onto the keyboard. . . .

That shot of Technicolor blood splashing across the snow-white keys has lingered long in the memories of many viewers, critics, and musicians and music historians for whom the film has acquired the status of high kitsch (admittedly, the same holds true for me, who, as a startled ten-year old, first saw it many years ago on television).[7] Several contemporary critics were impressed. "The amazing passage covering the lengthy montage of Chopin's final tour is an unforgettable achievement," wrote the *Hollywood Reporter* on 18 January 1945, "not only in film but in musical history." Other critics were not. " 'A Song to Remember' is not a motion picture to remember," objected the *New York Herald Tribune*. "Its two-hour Technicolor contemplation of Frédéric Chopin's life is a gilded screen biography whose hero conforms to all the Hollywood conventions governing historical celebrities."[8] And the *New York Times* condemned the script as "a dramatic hodge-podge, which provides absolutely no conception of the true character of the composer."[9]

Despite these critical differences, *A Song to Remember* went on to garner six Oscar nominations that year, including Actor (Cornel Wilde), Music Score (Miklos Rozsa), and Cinematography (Tony Gaudio). It continues to earn healthy rental receipts today.[10] Yet, one looks in vain in serious studies of history and biography on film for anything more than a passing reference to the film.[11] In addition to the scholarly and critical neglect of biopics in general, a substantial number of Columbia Pictures production files, which could throw much needed light on the film's inception, production, and reception, have either disappeared or are unavailable.[12] Most inexplicable is the film's absence in any discussions of World War II movies, a body of films to which *A Song to Remember* most decidedly belongs.

The Chopin Myths

The canonical status of Frédéric Chopin was secure long before Hollywood brought him to the movie screen. At the very moment of his death, on 17 October 1849, two photographers burst into his rooms and set up photographic equipment. When they attempted to move Chopin's bed nearer the window to catch the dawn light, they were escorted to the door. The few images they did capture were poorly exposed, but, according to biographer Benita Eisler, "they had already claimed the deathbed as public domain. . . . These larval paparazzi announced the end of Chopin's world of aristocratic privacy and discreet patronage."[13] Indeed, according to the late Chopin specialist Arthur Hedley: "The process of viewing him and his art through a kind of distorting lens . . . went on at ever-quickening pace during the second half of the nineteenth century."[14]

There is some confusion in this mythmaking: today, Chopin is regarded either as a frail, sickly, vaguely androgynous composer drooping languidly over his slender little nocturnes and preludes, or as a bold Polish patriot, thundering away at his polonaises, defiantly proclaiming the pain and glory of his war-wracked country. The "masculinity" of his person and his music seems always to have been in dispute. "A male composer who wrote in 'feminine' genres like the nocturne for domestic settings like the salon confuses our sense of the boundaries of gender," writes Jeffrey Kallberg in his study of gender constructions in Chopin's music.[15]

These sometimes contradictory images had been under construction long before Chopin's demise. Three years before, novelist George Sand (1804–1876), with whom Chopin had a nine-year liaison, published *Lucrezia Floriani,* which contained a thinly disguised portrait of him as one "Prince Karol," an exasperatingly selfish, morbidly sensitive, implicitly asexual, and chillingly aloof character. The novel precipitated outrage among Chopin's friends, although the composer kept his feelings to himself.[16] Three years later, Franz Liszt's affectionate biographical study, *F. Chopin,* contained flights of rhetorical fancy that embellished Chopin's spotless character, his selfless patriotism, his physical elegance, and his spiritually sanctified death throes. Typical of Liszt's effusions is this example: "His whole appearance reminds one of the unbelievable delicacy of a convolvulus blossom poised on its stem—a cup divinely coloured but so fragile that the slightest touch will tear it." As for the liaison with Sand, Liszt asserted it produced in Chopin's heart "a delight, an ecstasy, which fate grants only once to the most favored."[17] Such exaggerations and poetic effusions paled before the work of biographer James Huneker, whose *Chopin: The Man and His Music,* published in 1900, may lay claim to the purplest prose ever committed to paper. The process was complete by 1952, when, despite the appearance in the meantime of more sober biographical studies by Friedrich Niecks in 1888 and Herbert Weinstock in 1949, pianist Alfred Cortot urged that we cling to the legend, not the reality, of the man: "It is this legendary Chopin that we must cherish. By disregarding the deprecatory facts of his daily life, but going to the heart of the essential truth, we preserve the image of a Chopin who answers all our aspirations, a Chopin who existed in a world created by his imagination, who had no other existence save that of his dreams . . . who by the outpourings of his genius was able to immortalize the dreams and longings of countless human souls."[18]

Chopin Goes Hollywood

Like his life, Chopin's music reached the general public in a variety of venues, some of them rather dubious. In his lifetime, over his objections, his work was published with what he called "stupid titles," such as "The Zephyrs," "The Infernal Banquet," "Minute Waltz," "Raindrop Prelude," and "Butterfly" and "Winter Wind" études.[19] The ballet *Chopiniana* (later retitled *Les Sylphides*), one of the most enduringly popular of all ballets, was introduced by Michel Fokine in 1908, and it orchestrated the piano music to accompany a series of tableaux drawn from the composer's life. Song writers hit pay dirt by writing lyrics for some of his melodies. For example, the second theme from the *Fantasie Impromptu* for piano had been recast by songwriters Harry Carroll and Joseph McCarthy as "I'm Always Chasing Rainbows" for the 1918 Broadway show *Oh, Look!* As is discussed later in this chapter, Buddy Kaye and Ted Mossman appropriated the theme from the great A-flat Polonaise, Opus 53, for the wartime hit song "Till the End of Time."[20] And cartoon character Andy Panda performed his own version of the celebrated A-flat Polonaise in Walter Lantz's cartoon, "Musical Moments from Chopin" (1945).[21]

Feature films, in the meantime, were appropriating Chopin's music for a variety of purposes. In MGM's *Romance* (1930), for example, a Greta Garbo vehicle, the E-flat nocturne served as an elegant accompaniment to the story of a young actress's affairs. By contrast, MGM's *A Picture of Dorian Gray* (1945), based on the Oscar Wilde novel, deployed the Twenty-Fourth Prelude, Opus 28, as a sinister foreshadowing of the moral collapse of the eponymous Gray.[22] Warner Bros.'s *In Our Time*, released a few months before *A Song to Remember*, quoted on its soundtrack many Chopin melodies (including the so-called military polonaise, Opus 40) to represent Polish patriotism in the face of the Nazi invasion in September 1939.

One of the first biopics was a silent film, Henry Roussell's *Waltz de l'adieu* (France, 1928), subtitled as "A Page in the Life of Chopin," which dramatized Chopin's (Pierre Blanchar) romantically frustrated attachment to Marie Wodzinska. In more recent years, James Lapine's revisionist *Impromptu* (USA, 1991) concentrated on the early years of Chopin's (Hugh Grant) affair with George Sand (Judy Davis). And Tony Palmer's *The Strange Case of Delfina*

Potocka (1998), about which more is related in Chapter Five, examined the composer's controversial liaison with another woman in his life, the eponymous Countess Potocka.

A Song to Remember was filmed in 1944 and released in early 1945. It was a Columbia Pictures release directed by Charles Vidor, written and produced by Sidney Buchman, with music adaptation by Miklos Rozsa and (uncredited) piano performances by José Iturbi. Because of the absence of Columbia studio records, details of its production history are sketchy. As early as 1938, according to the *Hollywood Reporter,* plans were afoot for Columbia's leading director, Frank Capra, to helm the film with Spencer Tracy and Marlene Dietrich in the leading roles of Chopin and his inamorata, George Sand. Eventually, as preliminary titles like *Tonight We Dream, The Song That Lived Forever,* and *The Love of Madame Sand* were discarded, the project went to a Hungarian-born émigré Charles Vidor, who had just directed Columbia's stylish Rita Hayworth musical, *Cover Girl,* and the roles to Cornel Wilde and Merle Oberon. There are claims, neither of them definitive, that the Oscar-nominated screenplay had its origins in a novel, *Polonaise* by Doris Leslie, or in an original story by Ernst Marischka.[23]

The casting of robust, athletic Wilde was intended to allay fears any viewers might have had concerning the prevailing stereotypes of Chopin. A relative unknown at the time — he had appeared in several B pictures in light romantic roles, like the Sonja Henie vehicle *Wintertime* (1943) — Wilde was just now coming into his own as a macho leading man. Taking advantage of his background as a champion-class fencer, publicity releases described him as an actor who yearned for sword and doublet and who spent his off-screen time engaging in fencing exercises with fellow cast members. "Although Cornel never touches hand to sword hilt in the movie," proclaimed one press release, "there are sundry nobles and others who do carry swords. . . . It is that kind of picture."

At the same time, the studio promised anyone wary of elitist "classical music" that Chopin's music consisted of "all-time hit tunes" that were not at all "highbrow." Although their original titles might be unfamiliar, viewers were assured they are better known "under the titles of popular tin pan alley song hits of today and yesterday." Chopin was thus positioned as a proto-pop songwriter "who has furnished the basic melodies for more modern and popular song writers than any music-maker in history."[24] According to Morris Stoloff, the studio's chief music producer, Chopin's music, "though played for the aristocrats of his time — the early nineteenth century — was drawn from the peasant music of Poland, Chopin's birthplace, and is felt and understood by anyone with a heart."

Most significant, the film's depiction of the Polish composer as abjuring a life of artistic self-indulgence and political neutrality for the sake of the Polish struggle against tsarist tyranny held a profound significance for its wartime audiences. Before examining this point, it is necessary to examine how *A Song to Remember* negotiated the many myths that had already accrued around the life and work of Chopin.

A Song to Remember begins with the eleven-year-old Chopin studying music in his native Warsaw. From the outset he's seen as a hot-headed Polish patriot, banging angrily on the piano after witnessing Russian troops hauling Polish prisoners away to Siberia. "My dear boy," counsels his music teacher, Joseph Elsner (Paul Muni), "music and freedom are like one. They both belong to the world. A real artist wants freedom in every country." Seeing an ally in his teacher, the boy promptly enlists Elsner's complicity in the meetings of a secret band of revolutionaries. "Life, liberty, and the pursuit of happiness is every man's birthright," declares the revolutionary leader. Fifteen years pass. Chopin, now a handsome young man, is invited to perform at the salon of Count Wodzinska. But when the new Russian Governor-General of Poland arrives, Frédéric starts up from the piano and vehemently declares, "I do not play before tsarist butchers!" He abruptly leaves the room.

Fleeing the tsarist authorities, Chopin, accompanied by the loyal Elsner, flees to Paris, carrying with him a pouch of Polish soil given him by a lady friend and fellow revolutionary named Kostancia. Elsner had already suggested that a series of Parisian recitals might raise money to aid the Polish cause, and now Chopin determines to carry out the plan. But his recital debut is ruined when he learns of the incarceration, torture, and death back in Poland of his revolutionary friends, Titus and Jan. Overcome with sorrow, he breaks off his performance and quits the room. The concert is a disaster and the reviews are scathing. But he receives an invitation to visit the home of the Duchess of Orleans, George Sand (Merle Oberon), the notorious young female novelist who smokes cigars and dresses in the masculine attire of trousers, vest, and top hat. She is so impressed that she promptly takes over his career management and, with the aid of Franz Liszt, arranges for his next concert at her salon. In a clever ruse, she contrives with Liszt to begin the recital, but under cover of the dim light of the room, Chopin takes his place at the keyboard. When the lights go back up, it is he who receives the acclaim of the crowd.

Sand's first advice to her new protégé is to suppress his patriotic impulses because they will impede the true calling of his art and his career. "Shut the world out," she urges, "[find with me] a place apart, away from the petty struggles of men." Elsner intervenes. "I see trousers on a woman," he warns Chopin. "I know that woman has a will of her own. I have ears. I know about her reputation. Books that shock the world and laws of conduct designed for herself." Chopin ignores his old friend and follows Sand to the island of Majorca, where he will compose away from the "causes" and struggles of petty worldly affairs. "Your genius is for creating music for smaller men to play," says Sand. "Follow that genius, Frédéric, or you are lost, and everything with it. Be selfish with that genius. Stay here, write music." But Chopin cannot entirely get away from haunting reminders of his countrymen's struggles back home. At the piano he huddles against the chill, a shawl about his shoulders, and toys idly at the keys with the unfinished polonaise that has been pre-occupying him of late. "I'm not in the mood for waltzes and graceful studies," he says. Sand, alarmed at the possibility of his renewed patriotic duties, once again angrily denounces the tune.

Meanwhile, back in Paris, Elsner frets, forgotten and impoverished. He is still waiting for that patriotic polonaise Chopin promised him years before. Upon Sand's return, Elsner seizes an opportunity to visit her to learn how his absent friend has been doing. Elsner reminds her that Chopin has a duty to raise money to support the cause of Polish freedom. "Concerts are out of the question," she retorts. "He's too ill for that. He couldn't stand the strain of concerts now or at any time in the future. His purpose is to serve his own work." Elsner is aghast. "You're a lady of very strong will, used to having her way in all things," he responds sharply. "But I shall not see you have this way with Frédéric."

Later, after learning from the visiting Konstancia of tsarist atrocities back in Poland, Elsner confronts Chopin and flings another pouch of Polish earth on the table. "Your genius is a rare gift," he declaims. "So many ordinary people seem to be robbed to make one such man. A man worthy of his gifts should grow closer to those people as he grows more great. Fight harder for them with that same genius. But you are a waste of that gift, a man who has lost all sense of decency and honor."

But Sand isn't through yet. She denounces political causes in general and describes the sacrifices she has had to make as an artist and a woman to serve the purest aims of her art. But her words are drowned out as Chopin goes to the keyboard and thunders out the polonaise theme. At last, his mind is made up. He will go on a concert tour to raise money for the release of his im-prisoned countrymen. In the ensuing montage sequence, Chopin travels from concert hall to concert hall — Rome, Berlin, Vienna, Amsterdam, Stockholm, London — growing steadily weaker from his exhausting labors. Finally, as the final chords of his polonaise die out, he staggers away from the piano and collapses backstage. Elsner entreats Sand to come to the dying composer. "I think not," she answers haughtily. "Frédéric is mistaken to want me. I was always a mistake. I certainly do not belong there now. Good day, monsieur." (Actually, this decision comports with history: Sand did indeed refuse to attend the dying Chopin.) In the final screen version it is his compatriot, the loyal Konstancia, not Sand, who will come to his bedside.

Chopin breathes his last in a spiritually serene moment that is transfigured by an arching overhead camera movement that encloses in its gentle embrace a carefully composed tableaux grouping of mourners (a mythic construction wholly at odds with the reality of Chopin's horrible last moments). In an adjoining room in the background, Liszt softly plays the C-minor Nocturne, Opus 48, No. 1. Attentive to its elegiac strains, Chopin whispers, "It's like coming home." He expires.

Censorship and Containment

Hollywood's containment and "normalization" of Chopin's life, which led to a construction of his masculine and patriotic identity — all the while reconfiguring and deploying his music to confirm that identity — is the primary agenda at work here. It directs and shapes the film's numerous historical and musical alterations and fabrications.

A Song to Remember, no less than other Hollywood films of the day, came under the purview of the censors of the Production Code Administration (PCA) and its "Code." Especially problematic was the open affair between Chopin and the French novelist Sand. The complexities of the nine-year relationship, spanning roughly 1838–1847, have long fascinated and intrigued biographers and commentators. There is considerable dispute as to what degree Chopin and Sand found in each other mutual sexual fulfillment and creative support (as popular myth alleges) and to what extent the relationship proved to be dysfunctional, even mutually destructive (as some other historians claim). Chopin's contemporaries were in general agreement about Sand's overtly "masculine" role in the relationship. According to many reports, she treated Chopin as her "little one"; she "devoured" him. Indeed, as Sand's friend, novelist Balzac, once pronounced, "All in all, she is a man, so much the more so because she wants to be one; because she has given up the role of a woman and is no longer one."[25] Sand's biographer, Curtis Cates, speculates that a sexual component to the relationship was probably limited to just one or two years. "We can only surmise — for the documentary evidence is lacking — that [Sand] had found the physical act of lovemaking with Chopin considerably less exalting than his music."[26] Moreover, as Chopin biographer

Benita Eisler contends, their breakup in 1848 had nothing to do with squabbles over patriotic duty, as *A Song to Remember* alleges (indeed, patriotic issues seem never to have been subject of discussion between them) but with a variety of petty and extremely nasty disputes, involving, among other things, turmoil in the private lives of Sand's children, Maurice and Solange. By this time, Eisler continues, Sand had taken on another lover and was beginning to treat Chopin "like one of the aged domestics, recently dismissed after years of service."[27] William G. Atwood, in his study of the relationship, *The Lioness and the Little One,* takes rather a different view, placing much of the blame for the failed relationship on Chopin's hyper-critical temperament and his meddlings in Sand's family affairs.[28]

Of course, Hollywood would have none of this. An examination of PCA files reveals that Code overseer Joseph Breen closely monitored over several years the progress of the script's depiction of the Chopin-Sand affair. To begin with, any suggestion of the other romantic liaisons in Chopin's life — notably, with Maria Wodzinska and Delfina Potocka — would be deleted. Similarly there should be no backstory about Sand's other affairs, particularly with the young poet Alfred de Musset (although he puts in a cameo appearance early in the film), or the affair that immediately preceded her relationship with Chopin, a liaison with Felicien Mallefille, a former inamorata of Sand's so jealous of Chopin that he stalked the two lovers and threatened them with violence. As for Sand and Chopin, aside from the suggestion that they were living together, and apart from a chaste kiss and a touch of the hand, there were to be no suggestions of an actual sexual liaison.

"From the standpoint of the Production Code," Breen wrote to Columbia producer Harry Cohn in a memo dated 19 July 1943, "what is needed is a definite and affirmative voice for morality in connection with the illicit relationship between Chopin and Sand. There should be a definite and specific condemnation of this relationship, in order thus to show that the relationship is wrong; that it is not condoned, nor justified, nor made to appear right and acceptable." Accordingly, Breen recommended deletion of lines like Sand's declaration "We make our own laws — and break them if we like" and the alteration of Elsner's remark "To be a great artist one must first be a great man" to this substitution: "One must first be a great man and a *decent* man." However, subsequent drafts of the script failed to convince Breen that his admonitions were being followed. "We continue to be of the opinion that this story is entirely unacceptable under the provisions of the Production Code," he scolded in a memo dated 13 January 1944, "because it is a story of illicit sex without sufficient compensating moral values. . . . We must insist that such an element be injected into the story if the finished picture is to be approved. This

With George Sand in *A Song to Remember* is dashing Franz Liszt
(Stephen Bekassy). (Courtesy Photofest/Columbia Pictures)

condemnation of the sinful relationship between these two characters should
come from Elsner in one or two of the scenes between himself and Sand." (And
we recall instances already cited in the dialogues between Elsner and Sand.)
Moreover, Breen was anxious to delete a scene suggesting that the dying Chopin invite Sand to see him. That would suggest "a complete lack of regenera-
tion on his part." Rather, "it would be very helpful from our standpoint if the
action were to be reversed; if Sand were to apply for admission to the death
chamber only to be turned away."[29]

Meanwhile, Chopin's masculine agency must be bolstered up, even at the
expense of historical accuracy. The stereotypical image of his effeminate, perhaps androgynous nature, his chronic bad health, and his diminutive stature —
his passport declares he was a shade under five feet tall and weighed less than a
hundred pounds — demanded redress. Although there are no studio records
available to prove the point, other composer biopics of the day — notably

Fox's *Swanee River* (1939) and *Stars and Stripes Forever,* two Twentieth-Century Fox biopics about, respectively, Stephen Foster and John Philip Sousa —have left paper trails demonstrating that the studios typically took great care to lend (or outright invent) masculine characteristics to "normalize" their otherwise dull and unprepossessing artist protagonists.[30] In the case of *A Song to Remember,* Chopin's sturdy patriotism must be signified at the outset; his trip to Paris part of a plan to raise money for the Polish cause, his music, and his fatal concert tour confirm his masculine agency, and the emasculation he suffers during the liaison with Sand is no more than a temporary aberration.

Ironically, in reality it was Sand, not Chopin, who was the political animal. Born Aurore Dupin into a well-to-do family, she was notorious not only for her scandalous novels and unconventional behavior and dress—indulging tastes for cigars, men's clothes, and openly sexual adventures—but also for her vocal and active attacks on the French conservative establishment. She was the child, as well as the victim, of the Revolution of 1830, which promised freedoms for all but delivered only bourgeois conformity and denied equal rights to women. Her always outspoken republican sympathies led to a lifelong call for liberation from the tyrannies of class, gender, economic, and political injustice. She called for the collapse of Louis-Philippe's July Monarchy in 1848 and actively supported the revolutionary provisional government; she lived long enough to denounce the bloodbath of the Commune of 1871.[31]

But in the contexts of 1940s Hollywood, Sand must undergo a "feminization," and in the process she is both victimized and demonized. It would not do to depict her as she probably was, in fact, the woman who literally wore the pants in their relationship and who was a major force in French society and politics. To be sure, there was nothing new about the presence on screen of aggressive, cross-dressing females. Marlene Dietrich in *Morocco* (1930), Greta Garbo in *Queen Christina* (1933), and Katharine Hepburn in *Christopher Strong* (1933) and *Sylvia Scarlett* (1935) are among the many earlier examples. But as Mary Ann Doane writes in her study of "the woman's film" in 1940s wartime America, an ideological and gender shift of women in society and in the work force lent a new contemporary relevance—and accompanying anxiety—to images like this.[32]

Here, Sand's "masculine" identity is exposed as a sham. She is constructed as a predatory, apolitical female in male disguise. Although she wears trousers and a top hat in her first scene—when she announces to Chopin, "I want you to promise me you'll execute all my orders"—she soon spirits him away from public life in Paris to isolation in Nohant and the Valldemosa Monastery on the island of Majorca, where she abandons this masculine pose and dons a succession of spectacular gowns—ranging from a white formal dress to sev-

eral elaborately ornamented dressing gowns — as well as a desperately possessive attitude. This ambiguous variety of gendered garb and behavior identifies her as part female and part male — possessing a "mixed sexual body," as
Doane terms it.[33] Initially depicted as a dynamic, pro-active agent in Chopin's
career, Sand now stiffens into a morbidly possessive woman who blocks his
public career. Masculine action is supplanted by a clinging feminine passive
aggressiveness. A stark, grim-faced figure cloaked in black, she refuses to
allow him to perform publicly, imprisoning him instead to the domesticized
confines of her own salon.

Moreover, as already noted, she disdains Chopin's "causes." She rejects his
patriotic, large-scale, more traditionally masculine music as "that Polonaise
jumble which shuts me out completely" and insists he stick to the smaller,
innocuous, more traditionally gendered "feminine" salon pieces such as nocturnes, waltzes, and preludes.[34] In a key scene, while she attacks Elsner's
patriotic sentiments, the sounds of Chopin in the next room playing his "Ber-
ceuse" — a prettily ornamented genre piece that is the epitome of the salon
style — appropriately underscore her remarks.

In sum, Sand assumes the Hollywood stereotype of the chilly, selfishly grasping, possessive, ultimately destructive female typical of other "women's" melodramas of the day, notably Jean Negulesco's *Humoresque* and John Stahl's
Leave Her to Heaven (both 1946), starring Joan Crawford and Gene Tierney,
respectively.[35] "The genre of the female victim occurred simultaneously with
that of the Evil Woman," writes feminist critic Marjorie Rosen. "It may be no
coincidence that the plethora of these films coincided with female acquisition of
economic and social power in life. . . . Avarice and controlled loathing more
often than passion dictated the carnage wrought by Fatal Women."[36] Although
it is clear the film intends to demonize her for 1940s audiences, Sand is seen
today in a more sympathetic light, as the victim of a woman's attempts to break
out of the restrictive boundaries of her gender. "No one knows this human
jungle better than I," she angrily declares to Chopin: "No one ever fought more
bitterly to survive in it. To have some talent and ambition and to be a woman. I
buried them all, wrote behind a man's name, wore trousers to remind them I
was their equal. Yes! I was as moral as they were — no more and no less. Maybe
you think it didn't cost the woman something to do it, year after year in the face
of contempt and slander. But there was a reward to remember. I ruled my own
life. And what I set out to do, I did. A thousand weaklings came to me to draw
me into their hopeless causes, to ask me to lift their misbegotten lives at the
waste of my own. I'd see every last one rotting first!" Seen today, it's a remarkable speech, Sand's testament as well as her obituary. In hindsight, it may also be
regarded in its own way as a reflection of the status of many creative women in

Hollywood, who, like director Dorothy Arzner and screenwriter Frances Marion, fought their way, with varying degrees of success and sacrifice, to break
into the male-dominated Hollywood establishment.

Meanwhile, it is up to Chopin's fussy, bumbling, comic sidekick, Joseph
Elsner, to see through Sand's façade and divine the danger she poses to Chopin. "I see trousers on a woman," he warns Chopin (eloquent of the masculine
anxiety of the 1940s as much as the 1840s). "I know that woman has a will of
her own." It is up to him, not Chopin, to rebuke her: "You're a lady of very
strong will," he declares sternly, "used to having your way in all things. I shall
have *my* way here, Madame!" Indeed, his blandishments, combined with a
visit by Chopin's former Polish revolutionary colleague, the beauteous Konstancia (who in her own activist agendas resembles Sand[37]), and the sight of
that pouch of Polish earth are enough to restore Chopin to his senses. He
recovers his masculinity by rejecting Sand, finishing his polonaise, and taking
to the road on his suicidal concert tour. All the while, despite the best efforts of
the Hollywood makeup artists to transform the robust Wilde into a sick and
gaunt victim of an unspecified disease (Chopin died of tuberculosis), audiences
were not fooled. Even at his sickest and most hen-pecked, Wilde's nascent
virility has reassured viewers throughout the film that at any moment he might
leave his sick bed, burst out of his flowered waistcoat, and storm the tsarist
barricades.

This construction of Chopin's patriotism was just as spurious as that of
Sand's apolitical aesthetics. In reality, patriotism played little if any role in
Chopin's personal life after leaving Poland in 1829, and that his decision to
emigrate to Paris was motivated by career ambitions. No matter that he immediately gallicized his given name, Fryderyk, to Frédéric; that there was no
Elsner by his side to prod his conscience (he never saw Elsner again after
leaving Poland); and that except for a single benefit performance in London
the last year of his life, he never embarked on a concert tour to assist the Polish
cause. If anything, his patriotic fervor (or lack of it) was criticized in his own
time by his countryman, the Polish poet and patriot Adam Mickiewicz, who
accused Chopin of wasting his talent on the aristocracy instead of using it
to speak out against tyranny. And although he dutifully contributed money
to Polish causes, he continued giving lessons to Russian aristocrats passing
through Paris.[38] It was only after his death that he returned to Poland (at his
instructions, his heart was removed and sent back to Warsaw).

If Chopin must be reduced for a large chunk of the picture to a relatively
passive role in the clutches of the predatory Sand, at least his patriotic polonaises and stormy études recur periodically as ongoing reminders and reas-
surances of his patriotic commitment. By contrast to the "feminine" nocturnes,

the stormy C-minor Etude ("Revolutionary") originally earned its sobriquet when Chopin composed it after hearing of Warsaw's conquest by the tsarist armies. According to biographer Tad Szulc, "He did react with a paroxysm of fury and despair that he recorded in his diary."[39] And the polonaises, particularly the great A-flat, Opus 53, always connoted Polish national pride.[40] Accordingly, the film's music director, Miklos Rozsa, strategically deploys their melodies as a series of leitmotifs functioning both diegetically and extra-diegetically, in performance scenes and on the soundtrack.[41] For example, the aforementioned étude in C minor functions as a cry of pain for the Polish victims of tsarist repression. We first hear it in orchestral guise as Chopin bolts from the presence of the governor general at the Wodzinska salon. And it reappears in variously instrumented versions every time there is a reference to Polish sufferings. By contrast, the plaintive melody from the so-called Raindrop Prelude (Opus 25, No. 15) is associated with the pouch of Polish earth that Chopin carries away with him. The lovely theme from the third étude in E major (also from Opus 10) is first heard when Chopin meets Sand, and is heard thereafter as an emblem of his love for her. And, from the outset, the melody of the heroically declamatory A-flat Polonaise, Opus 53, is attached to the theme of patriotic duty.

Rozsa's deployment of this polonaise theme ingeniously reinforces each stage of Chopin's developing patriotic commitment. After its introduction in an arrangement for piano and orchestra under the Columbia logo, it reappears periodically in fragments and variants in major and minor modes, in an ingenious array of instrumentations—at times cleverly counterpointed by a few measures of the tumultuous eleventh étude in A minor, Opus 25, and at other times by themes from the First Piano Concerto. In a beautifully staged scene in the salon of the publisher Pleyel, Chopin performs it as a duet with Liszt. "A Polonaise!" exclaims Liszt. "The spirit of Poland! Magnificent! And you play it with the spirit of a patriot!" Later, at his first Paris concert, upon hearing of the deaths of his Polish friends, Chopin interrupts his playing of Beethoven's "Moonlight Sonata" with a few brusque measures of the polonaise. Aware of its significance to Chopin, Sand never fails—as has already been demonstrated—to dismiss it. Everywhere, fleeting references to the polonaise persist on the soundtrack (serving as Chopin's internal diegesis), always nagging at him, even while he's comfortably ensconced with Sand at Nohant and Majorca. Elsner frets all the while, wondering when Chopin will stop composing waltzes and nocturnes and finish the damned thing. At last, as Sand rants against Chopin's decision to return to the concert stage, Chopin picks out the polonaise theme again, his playing growing louder and louder as his determination is fixed, until it fairly drowns out her discouraging words.

Finally, the polonaise also plays a crucial role in the most elaborate of the performance sequences. The climactic montage depicting Chopin's desperate recital tour to raise funds for the release of Polish prisoners is a masterpiece of the seamless blending of diegetic source music and extradiegetic background music. It begins with a breath-taking straight cut from Chopin's playing of the introductory measures of the polonaise in Sand's room to a public performance in the concert hall—at which point the music shifts abruptly to the opening measures of the eleventh étude from Opus 25 (a clever and dramatically effective juxtaposition of the two pieces). The ensuing interplay of sights (a variety of playbills from Paris, Amsterdam, London; close shots of hands on the keyboard; shots of Chopin's perspiring brow) and sounds (a seamless medley of orchestrated snatches from the polonaise, a "Waltz-Brilliante" (Opus 40, No. 1), the Second Scherzo, another polonaise (the "Military," Opus 40, No. 1), the C-minor Etude, and a culminating reprise of the A-flat Polonaise (whose completed version is heard at last), reveals a steadily weakening Chopin, blanched and strained, his colorful waistcoat replaced by a severe black coat, the ebony cravat tightly knotted at his neck, the collar pulled tightly up his neck. And yes, there's the notorious moment when Chopin coughs Technicolor blood onto the piano keys.

Chopin at War

The correlations between *A Song to Remember*'s constructions of Chopin's masculinity and patriotism and the contemporary contexts of World War II were not lost on critics of the day. A number of commentators called attention to the story's relevance to current events in Poland. *Film Daily*, for example, noted its "potent appeal to the present-day conscience of the underlying theme of Poland's fight for freedom."[42] Writing in hindsight in his book-length study of biopics, George Custen confirms that "Frédéric's artistic and social conscience and his presence allows the Polish liberation theme to be showcased at a time when Poland was under Nazi oppression, and contemporary classical musicians from war-torn countries (like Italy's Arturo Toscanini and Poland's Artur Rubinstein) were mixing music and Allied propaganda in their public performances."[43]

Since the Pearl Harbor disaster, Hollywood was quickly shifting from what had been a reluctance to promote American involvement in the war to active on-screen support of that participation. The newly formed Office of War Information (OWI) mandated motion pictures to depict the war "not merely as a struggle for survival but a 'people's war' between fascism and democracy, the crusade of Vice President Henry A. Wallace's 'Century of the Common

Man.' "[44] By late 1942, notes Thomas Schatz in his study of 1940s Hollywood, "about one-third of the features in production dealt directly with the war; a much higher proportion treated the war more indirectly as a given set of social, political, and economic circumstances." A spate of "conversion" films unabashedly appealed to patriotic commitment. They were designed, assert Gregory D. Black and Clayton R. Koppes in their study of wartime Hollywood, "to focus attention upon key problems which the people must decide, the basic choices which the people must make."[45] This constituted a "conversion" in another sense in that standard narrative paradigms were undergoing transformations. Genre formulas of crime thrillers, women's melodramas, and backstage musicals were reformulated into espionage thrillers and resistance dramas. The traditional Hollywood narrative that had heretofore emphasized individual protagonists working toward the goals of a successful career and a romantic "coupling," or sexual attachment, was being retooled into a new narrative paradigm, wherein "the individual had to yield to the will and activity of the collective (the combat unit, the community, the nation, the family); and coupling was suspended 'for the duration,' subordinated to gender-specific war efforts that involved very different spheres of activity." In other words, concludes Schatz, "the war effort created radically different requirements, indefinitely postponing the climactic coupling while celebrating the lovers' dutiful separation and commitment to a larger cause."[46]

Immortal Sergeant (1944) and *Casablanca* (1942) are cases in point. At the end of the former, Henry Fonda's character, who has hitherto vacillated about his patriotic duty, talks about the cruel necessity of war: "If I want . . . anything worthwhile in life, I've got to fight for it. That's not a bad thing for a man to find out, is it? Or for a nation, either, for that matter, to fight." And against *Casablanca*'s background of the eve of the Pearl Harbor attack the transformation and redemption of the politically neutral (but former Loyalist in the Spanish Civil War) Rick Blaine (Humphrey Bogart) into a self-sacrificing freedom fighter — with the strains of "La Marsaillaise" ringing in his ears — remains the most celebrated exemplar of that agenda.[47]

Hardly less effective for its contemporary American audiences, if less noted today, was the relevance of Chopin's decision to forsake the safe aesthetic cocoon of political neutrality and embark on a suicidal concert tour, his polonaise serving as a rallying cry for the Polish cause. Like Rick, caught in the crossfire of debate between the cynical Renault and the idealistic Czech patriot, Victor Laszlo, Chopin must choose between the aesthetic self-indulgence of Sand and the nationalist conscience of Elsner. Indeed, although discussion of *A Song to Remember* as a *wartime-related* film is nowhere to be found in the standard histories of World War II cinema, it is not a stretch to regard

Chopin as Rick in period waistcoat and top hat, whose patriotic message is targeted to audiences in 1944. Both proclaim the populist message mandated by the OWI, so eloquently reflected in Elsner's words: "A man worthy of his gifts should grow closer to the people as he grows more great." In so doing, both not only recover their patriotic identity, but, in abjuring the seductions of sex, they also regain the Hollywood ideal of masculinity.

In order to track further the film's relevance to wartime audiences, it is necessary to compare events in Poland in Chopin's lifetime with the fate that befell Poland at the time of the film's production and release. During Chopin's boyhood, Poland had been fragmented by a series of partitions mandated by the Congress of Vienna in 1815. Under the benevolent despotism of Tsar Alexander I, Poland had no sovereignty but enjoyed a relatively favorable position as compared with the iron rule Russia imposed elsewhere. However, with Alexander's death in 1825 and the accession a few years later of the autocratic Nicholas I, all this changed. Poland soon became a police state. Censorship reigned, universities were closed, and the tsar's secret police spied on radical student activities. A counterrevolution transpired in 1848, as it did in other countries, notably Austria, France, Germany, and Italy, but it was crushed.

Flash forward to the twentieth century. As a result of the collapse of the Austro-Hungarian monarchy in 1918, Poland had proclaimed its independence. However, with the outbreak of hostilities in the late 1930s, Poland found itself once again torn apart. Hitler attacked Poland in September 1939, precipitating Britain's and France's entry into the growing war. In accordance with the infamous Nazi-Soviet Pact, Russian forces moved in from the east and partitioned off the nation. The Polish government went into exile for the duration of the war, while Russia recognized a puppet government, the Polish Committee of National Liberation. Later, when the Poles rose against the Nazis in Warsaw in June 1944, Russian assistance was not forthcoming and the Nazis crushed the resistance. Soon the situation would reverse and it would be Russia's turn to take over the country, dimming prospects of a postwar independent Polish regime.

This was the historical context of events during the making of *A Song to Remember*. Indeed, production was not yet completed when the Warsaw Uprising was crushed and Soviet Russia prepared to assume total dominance. Thus, it is not difficult to trace in the depiction of a Russian enemy in Chopin's time a parallel with real-life events in 1944. Audiences would have understood that immediately, but they would also have perceived the distinction the film makes between Stalin's Communist regime and the Russian *people* — a subtlety likewise explored in other Hollywood Russian-related films of the period, notably, *Song of Russia* and *The North Star,* where, as historian Robert Fyne has observed, American audiences could sympathize with the heroic struggles of the peasants of the Motherland against fascism, while, at the same time, distrust, even despise, the Communist leaders' iron rule over Poland.[48] Thus, it is particularly significant that in *A Song to Remember* a Polish patriot tells Chopin that the real enemy of Poland is *tsarist repression* — read that: Stalinist tyranny — not the Russian people themselves. "They tell us that the Polish people and the Russian people are enemies," the patriot declares. "Except for those leeches under the tsar, they aren't enemies at all. In fact, they get along quite well together. Strange, isn't it? — tyrants must have something in common, to teach our peoples to hate each other."

One gauge of the effectiveness of transforming Chopin into a World War II hero, in effect, can be seen in the continued association of the celebrated A-flat Polonaise with wartime patriotism. One year after the release of *A Song to Remember,* the polonaise was once again "inducted" into American patriotic service when it was appropriated by songwriters Buddy Kay and Ted Mossman as a pop song called "Till the End of Time," which quickly became the anthem of postwar returning servicemen. It was thus recognized when it was quoted in the credit sequence of Edward Dmytryk's postwar drama *Till the End of Time* (1946).

At first glance it seems strange that a producer like Harry Cohn, a former song plugger on Tin Pan Alley, who seemingly had no interest in classical music and politics, and who generally preferred action and comedy pictures, would have countenanced such an overt blend of classical music and political ideology. Yet, it should be remembered that Cohn, like other Hollywood moguls, recognized the prestige factor of classical music. He had already demonstrated this in a number of vehicles he tailored for opera star Grace Moore, like the hugely successful *One Night of Love (1934),* which blended well-known arias with popular ballads. The results, as described by studio historian Rochelle Larkin, "mixed lumps of Puccini and the like into a pancake batter of plot thickeners such as the nice American girl, European settings, playboys, yachts, and glamour."[49] Moreover, significantly, Cohn selected Sidney Buchman as writer-producer of *A Song to Remember.* For years Buchman had held a privileged position as Cohn's favorite writer at Columbia and had already established his "social message" credentials with the satiric but inherently patriotic *Mr. Smith Goes to Washington* (1939) for Frank Capra. According to Capra's biographer, Joseph McBride, "Buchman brought his political convictions to the *Chopin* script, responding eloquently to the composer's commitment [*sic*] to the cause of Polish independence."[50] Buchman's leftist politics — he became a Communist Party member in late 1938 — would later get him in trouble with the House UnAmerican Activities Committee (HUAC) investigations.[51] Hindsight confirms that Buchman's fingerprints are all over the political activism of *A Song to Remember*.

Coda

It should be noted, in conclusion, that the ideological battle over Chopin's body and reputation neither began nor ended with *A Song to Remember*. On 19 September 1863, in retaliation for a bomb attempt on the life of Warsaw's Russian governor, Russian troops set fire to the residence of Chopin's sister and brother-in-law. Most of Chopin's letters written to his parents were consumed in the flames. Immediately after the liberation of Poland from Nazi occupation, the Soviet authorities proclaimed that a newly politicized image of Chopin would once again prevaile in the "new" Poland, a Chopin constructed in accordance with the party's agendas. But when a woman named Paulina Czernicka, a self-taught musician and admirer of Chopin, came forward with a packet of letters allegedly by Chopin to her ancestor, the Countess Delfina Potocka, the authorities were outraged.[52] The letters revealed a Chopin whose anti-Semitic sentiments, petty bigotries, and erotic obsessions were decidedly contrary to the officially sanctioned and sanitized image. Subsequently, Czernicka's reputation and veracity were attacked in the public press. She died mysteriously in 1949, an apparent suicide. Chopin scholars Adam Zamoyski, Arthur Hedley, Adam Harosowski, and Tad Szulc have reported that the debate over the authenticity of the letters and the circumstances of Czernicka's death has raged for decades.[53] Tony Palmer's docudrama *The Strange Case of Delfina Potocka* (1999) begs the issue of the documents' authenticity but alleges that the Polish-Soviet authorities were directly responsible for Czernicka's demise.

A Song to Remember quickly established itself as something of a benchmark for composer biopics to come. References and comparisons to it appeared repeatedly, for example, in critical notices of subsequent pictures like *Song of Love* (1947) about Robert and Clara Schumann, *Song of Scheherazade* (1947) about Nikolai Rimsky-Korsakov, *Magic Fire* (1954) about Richard Wagner, and *Song without End* (1960) about Franz Liszt. For the British filmmaker Ken Russell, however — today's preeminent practitioner of the composer biopic — *A Song to Remember* marked a point of departure for his own work. "I didn't think too much of the big Hollywood movies about composers that were coming out at that time," Russell recalled in a 2003 interview. "They seemed like nothing more than nonsense to me. I didn't associate them with art or music. They had become a cliché. Too often you never got a sense of the *art*, just people in costumes doddering around. I'm more interested in the *spiritual* and *poetic* and *creative* side of such subjects."[55]

Still, the dramatization of Chopin's music in *A Song to Remember* remains a cherished memory for those who saw it when America was at war, and for those, like the present writer, who thrilled to it in their youth. For them, at the very least, as the pop song suggests, the song has ended—but the melody lingers on . . .

3

The New Tin Pan Alley
Hollywood Looks at American Popular Songwriters

"When does a man cease just to write hit songs and become part of the music and a nation? That's what's happened to you — You've graduated from Tin Pan Alley! I want to see you in Carnegie Hall. I want to hear your music at its peak. I want a symphony orchestra to play it."
— *Lillian Harris to Sigmund Romberg in* Deep in My Heart *(1954)*

When George M. Cohan got an advance peek at the Warner Bros. movie about his life, *Yankee Doodle Dandy* (1942), he exclaimed, "My God, what an act to follow!" As if daunted by the very notion, he died two months later, on 29 May 1942. His astonishment at what Hollywood had wrought was disingenuous. He had conspired with the filmmakers to unleash upon the viewing public not his life, but the life that could have been, or should have been — the kind of life, as his daughter Georgette declared, "Daddy would like to have lived!"[1]

Yankee Doodle Dandy is but one of dozens of Hollywood biopics purporting to tell the story of the great American popular songwriters, from Stephen Foster to the tunesmiths of Tin Pan Alley and the Broadway musical show. Despite their public celebrity, relatively little was known about their private lives. As far as Hollywood was concerned, this was as it should be.[2] Filmmakers, sometimes assisted by the composers themselves, could recast them into any desired shape and construct a weave of fact and fiction, sacrificing bio-graphical detail to the glory of the music itself. These pictures, like their classi-cal composer counterparts discussed in the preceding chapter, came in a flood, from roughly the 1930s to the late 1950s, from the major studios — MGM, Columbia, Paramount, Warner Bros., and Twentieth Century-Fox — produced by heavyweights like Arthur Freed, Hal Wallis, and Darryl F. Zanuck. They boasted big budgets, glossy production values, lots of music, and major stars. If the prestige of the classical pantheon had been and continued to be a factor in its marketability, the allure of the Tin Pan Alley composers — success and money — was even more potent. The year after Irving Berlin published "Alex-ander's Ragtime Band," for example, his royalties amounted to more than $100,000, and a decade later he was worth $4 million. In their peak years during the 1930s, Cole Porter, Richard Rodgers, and Lorenz Hart each earned more than $500,000 annually from their songs alone. Jerome Kern was wealthy enough to pursue his passion for rare book collecting, amassing librar-ies worth millions. And George Gershwin enjoyed a lifestyle that rivaled that of the movie stars whose company he cultivated.

Their songs were songs of love. Hollywood, always preoccupied with ro-mantic stories, took notice. According to musical theater historian Edward Pessen, in his recent study of Tin Pan Alley songs, about 85 percent of them were about love in all its bewildering, bewitching, and heart-breaking variety. There were the sentimental ballads and ragtime songs of the first generation of "Alley" composers, W. C. Handy (1873–1958), Paul Dresser (1856–1906), George M. Cohan (1878–1942), Gus Edwards (1879–1945), and Irving Ber-lin (1888–1989); the Irish-inflected ballads of Ernest R. Ball (1878–1927); the light classical songs of operetta composers Victor Herbert (1859–1924), John Philip Sousa (1854–1932), Rudolf Friml (1879–1972), and Sigmund Rom-berg (1887–1951); and the smart, sophisticated music from Jerome Kern (1885–1945), Cole Porter (1891–1964), and the songwriting teams of George Gershwin (1898–1937) and Ira Gershwin (1896–1983), Richard Rodgers (1902–1979) and Lorenz Hart (1895–1943), and Bert Kalmar (1884–1947) and Harry Ruby (1895–1974). In one way or another, they all created a uniquely American expression out of the disparate voices of Old World tradi-tions and New World vernacular. While paying lip service to the flux and change of contemporary realities, they cast occasional loving, backward glances at a simpler, rural past.[3]

If occasionally the biopics of these Tin Pan Alley tunesmiths flirted with historical truth, more often they catered to public constructions of myth and anecdote. For example, *Yankee Doodle Dandy* (1942) perpetuated the legend that Cohan (James Cagney) was born on the Fourth of July; *Swanee River*

(1939) claimed that Foster (Don Ameche) introduced and sang "My Old Kentucky Home" with E. P. Christy's minstrels; *Stars and Stripes Forever* (1952), that Sousa (Clifton Webb) wrote "Stars and Stripes Forever" for the Spanish-American War effort; *Till the Clouds Roll By* (1946), that Kern (Robert Walker) learned everything he knew from a student of Johannes Brahms; *Words and Music* (1948), that lyricist Hart (Mickey Rooney) sang duets with Judy Garland; *Night and Day* (1946), that a battle-scarred Porter (Cary Grant) wrote the title song while convalescing in a World War I hospital; *Three Little Words* (1950), that Kalmar and Ruby preferred magic tricks and baseball games, respectively, to writing songs; and *Alexander's Ragtime Band* (1938) — a thinly disguised biopic of Berlin — that ragtime was introduced and first popularized in 1915 by a white, classically trained violinist.[4] Moreover, there was no trace of Jewish ethnicity in the lives of Dresser, Romberg, George Gershwin, Kern, and Berlin; no indication of the racism that hampered the career of black composer Handy; no direct references to Porter's homosexuality; and little evidence anywhere that African Americans made any contributions to the shaping of ragtime and jazz.

Ironically, considering the plethora of films touching on the subject of songwriting, audiences learned little about the workings of Tin Pan Alley. According to the aptly titled *Tin Pan Alley* (1940), which chronicled the career of the fictitious songwriting team of "Harrigan and Calhoun" (John Payne and Jack Oakie), all the songwriters were white, Protestant, and in search of beautiful singers to "put over" their tunes.[5] The serious grind of writing, plugging, and publishing songs along the Alley is reduced to the following scrap of dialogue:

> QUESTION: What's happening on Tin Pan Alley?
> ANSWER: The same old grind — Irving Berlin is still ringing the bell with every number.
> QUESTION: Is Anna Held still packing them in at the Casino?
> ANSWER: Yes, dear; and the Statue of Liberty is still packing them in at Bedloe's Island!

Rhapsody in Blue and *Night and Day* (both 1946) depict their respective composers, George Gershwin and Porter, working as song pluggers playing new songs for prospective customers at publishing companies like Jerome H. Remick's. When they persist in playing their own music instead of that of other composers, they are fired.

With a few notable exceptions mentioned in this chapter, the process of songwriting itself apparently consisted merely of the composers sitting down to an old upright and accidentally stumbling upon a few notes, which, in a subsequent furious montage of images, are instantly transformed into a full-fledged show number, replete with sumptuous strings, blaring brass, and high-stepping chorines. The success of these men was the product not so much of genius but of good old American pluck: "When you have something and you know you have it, nothing can keep you down," explains Harrigan.

A Tale of Two Industries

Like the biopics of classical composers discussed in Chapters One and Two, these Tin Pan Alley films were also the direct results of the very structure and purpose of the Hollywood classical studio system, 1930–1960. In many respects Hollywood and Tin Pan Alley were joined at the hip. Since the beginning of the twentieth century, both had been participating in the fashioning of an indigenous, nationally homogeneous culture — "reinventing America," as today's parlance would have it. Both, in their beginnings, were centered in New York City and environs. The first movie studios such as Edison, Biograph, Vitagraph, and Warner Bros. were based in lower Manhattan, Flatbush, Queens, and New Jersey. Even after the studios relocated their production facilities on the West Coast, they retained their corporate offices in New York.

In the years just before the turn of the twentieth century, the popular music publishing business consisted of a small cluster of companies in the Union Square section of New York, on East Fourteenth Street, between Broadway and Third Avenue, in what was then the heart of the theater district. Before that time such occupations as composers, lyricists, and popular music publishers did not exist. Music publishers were either classical publishers, music store owners, or local printers who printed sheet music along with other commodities like books, posters, and magazines. But as historian David A. Jasen recounts in his invaluable *Tin Pan Alley,* the establishment in 1891 of the International Copyright Law, which protected American works published abroad, and the appearance in the 1890s of a dynamic new breed of publishers — namely, Edward B. Marks, Max Dreyfus, Leopold Feist, the Witmark brothers, and others — changed everything.[6] Using promotional strategies, like the hiring of top song pluggers and performers (rather like the star system soon to be employed by the movie studios), they hustled vaudeville performers and orchestra leaders with the sentimental ballads of Charles K. Harris ("After the Ball") and Dresser ("On the Banks of the Wabash, Far Away"); they marketed the show scores of Herbert and Cohan and the syncopated "coon" songs of the increasingly popular black composers and entertainers, such as Bert Williams; and, later, to the burgeoning record industry, which had begun to sell flat discs commercially in 1897. By 1900 many publishers had relocated uptown to Twenty-Eighth Street, near Fifth Avenue. Dubbed "Tin Pan Alley" by the composer Monroe H. Rosenfeld, the area came to represent the music publishing industry in general. Music historian Charles Hamm, in his classic *Yesterdays: Popular Song in America,* notes, "By 1900 control of the popular-song industry by these new publishers was virtually complete, and it was a rare song that achieved mass sales and nationwide popularity after being published elsewhere."[7] The term stuck, even though subsequent centralized locations kept moving uptown, toward West Forty-Second Street and, eventually, to Fifth-Sixth Street (where the Great White Way is still to be found).

Both industries were shaped and dominated by a multiethnic and predominantly first-generation immigrant community located primarily in lower Manhattan.[8] And both developed efficient systems for the mass production and distribution of their products — in the instance of Tin Pan Alley, in the powerful publishing houses; and in Hollywood, in the monolithic movie studios — vertically integrated structures controlling movies' production, distribution, and exhibition, organized by men like Adolph Zukor, Louis B. Mayer, Darryl F. Zanuck, and William Fox. Inevitably, these two industries developed a synergistic relationship, each depending upon, and exploiting, the other. Warner Bros., for example, took control of Witmarks, MGM bought into the Robbins Music Corporation, RKO obtained Leo Feist, and Paramount established its own Famous Music Corporation. By the dawn of the talking picture, it has been estimated that 90 percent of America's most popular songs were film-related. Tin Pan Alley and film entrepreneurs shared in common an understanding of public taste, an expertise in merchandising and marketing stemming from their backgrounds in sales and retail, and, as the 1920s and 1930s wore on, a willingness to promote a "mainstream" American fantasy that had only a tenuous connection to contemporary realities and controversies of labor unrest, Depression woes, women's issues, sex and violence, and racial and ethnic issues.

Even if these entrepreneurs themselves were barred from the "real corridors of gentility and status in an America still fraught with anti-Semitism," as cultural historian Neal Gabler states in his *An Empire of Their Own: How the Jews Invented Hollywood,* they could fashion in their songs and in their films "a new country — an empire of their own, so to speak. . . . They would create its values and myths, its traditions and archetypes."[9] A cultural language was evolving that became common currency all across the nation, the result of the "commingling" of disparate and ethnic influences that Antonín Dvořák had predicted in 1893 — of high and low culture, Old World classicism, and New World multiculturalism.[10] It appropriated them all but remained bound to none.[11]

The biopic genre played its own part in this process of assimilation. It brought the lives and works of popular songwriters into the lower slopes of a pantheon hitherto reserved exclusively for their classical brethren. A suitable introduction to this process can be found in two Hollywood films from the mid-1940s — the Oscar-winning MGM two-reel short subject *Heavenly Music* (1943) and Howard Hawks's Danny Kaye vehicle, *A Song Is Born* (1948).

In *Heavenly Music* swing composer Ted Barry's (Fred Brady) petition for entry into Heaven's hallowed Hall of Music is greeted with derision by the spirits of Beethoven, Wagner, Tchaikovsky, Brahms, Chopin, Paganini, and Johann Strauss, Jr. Stung by their haughty response, Ted declares, "I've written sweet stuff, boogie-woogie, Dixieland, jump music for the hepcats, but solid, eight-to-the-bar, with plenty of schmaltz." Unimpressed, they demand he audition his music for them. Ted sits at the piano and plays one of his tunes. Tchaikovsky angrily objects that it is a "steal" from his "Waltz of the Flowers," and he moans, "Everybody makes money with my music except me." Ted wryly reminds him that everybody steals from everybody. A more positive response is elicited by Ted's next tune, when, suddenly inspired, the composers step forward and perform a classical variant of the tune, each in his own distinctive style. At length, the whole ensemble joins in and breaks it out in a full-blown swing band interpretation, complete with a blast from Gabriel's horn. "Just because Ted's music is modern," conclude the composers, "and just because it sounds new to your ears, that doesn't mean it's bad music. After all, isn't it the melody that counts? You can play a good melody in any style, modern or classical!"

Ted's petition for admission into the Hall of Music is approved.

If *Heavenly Music* brought popular tunes into the Pantheon, *A Song Is Born* performs the same service for folk music and jazz. A stellar cast of performers — Benny Goodman, Lionel Hampton, Gene Krupa, Mel Powell, Charlie Barnet, Tommy Dorsey, Louis Bellson, and members of the Golden Gate Quartet — broadcast a radio program that subjects a simple, folk-like tune to a series of riffs, varying it as an African tribal dance, a Latin samba, a black spiritual, a popular song, and, finally, a piece for jazz combo. Never identified, the "folk melody," ironically, is nothing of the sort; in actuality, it is the "Largo" theme from Antonín Dvořák's Symphony in E minor ("From the New World").[12] Classical, folk, swing, jazz, and popular songs lose their distinctive and idiosyncratic qualities in the assimilation process that is the American melting pot. "Very little corresponds to current jazz history," writes State University of New York film professor Krin Gabbard about this sequence in *Jammin' at the Margins.* "The 'art' of jazz is retrospectively validated by referencing the American *folk song* that supposedly inspired the European masters."[13] Both *Heavenly Music* and *A Song Is Born* thus provide perfect metaphors for the transformations, transmutations, and fusions among popular and classical forms that abound in Hollywood films during the classical studio era (even cowboy crooner Tex Ritter challenged the classics on his own terms).[14]

The Tin Pan Alley Paradigm —
Stephen Foster and Sigmund Romberg

The biopics in this chapter are vehicles for a New World update of the aforementioned Old World "Blossom Time" paradigm. The Tin Pan Alley songwriters are depicted as the latter-day incarnations of Franz Schubert, Johann Strauss, and others. The new albeit related paradigm derives from the Warner Bros. pioneering talkie classic *The Jazz Singer* (1927). One might go so far as to suggest that in its essentials, *The Jazz Singer* is *Blossom Time* in ragtime and blackface.[15]

Stripped to its essentials, *The Jazz Singer* is a collection of interrelated antimonies — tradition and assimilation, the Old World and the New, father and son, and the sacred and the profane. A Jewish cantor's son, Jakie Rabinowitz (Al Jolson) struggles to escape his ethnic heritage and the musical traditions of the synagogue (the "Kol Nidre") in his search for fame as "Jack Robin," a popular blackface performer singing jazz on Broadway ("Toot Toot Tootsie"). In the end, after acceding to his father's dying request to sing the Kol Nidre in the synagogue, Jack returns in triumph to sing "Mammy" at the Winter Garden Theatre. "In freeing himself from the social constraints of religious orthodoxy," writes John Mundy, in *Popular Music on Screen,* "and from the literal and symbolic Law of the Father, Jack offers up an image of a new America in which energy, hard work and spontaneity are seen as the democratic antidote to the cloying hypocrisies of religious and social tradition."[16] This is a bit overstated. Jack's "victory" is not exactly that of the rebel overturning tradition, nor is his "jazz" an authentic African-American musical expression; rather, in that "commingling" of elements Dvořák had predicted thirty-four years before, Jack's Jewishness has been "whitened" and his music has become a concatenation of minstrel tune, jazz riff, Hebraic chant, and popular song — in short, the new soundtrack of contemporary America.

Most of the Tin Pan Alley biopics discussed here display variations of this "Jazz Singer" formula: The composer protagonist, of indeterminate ethnicity, is young, handsome, ambitious, and dreadfully in earnest. When forced to choose between his instinctive genius for New World vernacular music and his ambitions for the seductive prestige of the Old World classical establishment, he overreaches and falls victim to vaulting ambition, quirks of fate, a weakness to drink, and an ill-starred romance. The Old World option deflects him away from "the people." The New World option uproots him from the nourishing soil of tradition and respectability. Either way, he loses his social, cultural, and emotional balance. Looking on is the Great Love, an exceptionally sympathetic woman who anguishes at her wayward lover's struggle. And, of course, there is a Great Song that needs to be sung. It is only when the composer learns to fuse the classical and the vernacular that he reunites with his Great Love, composes at last his Great Song, reconnects to the community, and achieves the true fulfillment of his genius and his manhood.

We see the dynamics of this paradigm fully fleshed out in two seemingly disparate biopics, *Swanee River* (1939), the story of Stephen Foster, and *Deep in My Heart* (1954), the story of Sigmund Romberg. *Swanee River* constructs Foster as the prototypical American popular composer, the native-born "possessed" genius of humble rural origins — rather naive, relatively untrained, supremely sensitive to ethnic vernacular — whose misguided ambitions for "classical" legitimacy temporarily derail his true artistic calling. *Deep in My Heart* begins at the other extreme: It portrays the European émigré, Romberg, as a "possessor" figure, cosmopolitan and worldly wise, learned and adept in the traditions of the Old World classics, who, as an adopted American, struggles to reconcile his elitist sensibilities with the jazzy popular idioms of American popular song stylings.

Twentieth Century-Fox's *Swanee River,* directed by Sidney Lanfield and starring Don Ameche as Foster, was neither the first nor the last of the Foster biopics, but it is the most famous. Studio chief Zanuck had already produced a series of biographical films about celebrated historical figures during his tenure at Warner Bros. and Twentieth Century Films, including several George Arliss vehicles, including *Disraeli* (1931) and *Cardinal Richelieu* (1935). His agenda was clear. As biographer George F. Custen has observed, Zanuck was fighting "the American cultural hierarchy" that was "opposed to placing the power to interpret high art in the hands of the vulgarians who ran the movie studios."[17] As one of those "vulgarians," Zanuck was prepared to reconstitute the lives and works of celebrated public figures into images congruent with the experiences and expectations of his viewing public — and, by implication, with himself.

Now in the late 1930s, with political and social tensions at every hand, at home and abroad, Zanuck turned his attention away from biographies of foreign notables and toward the enshrinement of prototypical *American* lives from the recent past, with *Jesse James* (1939), *The Story of Alexander Graham Bell* (1939), and *Young Mr. Lincoln* (1939). At the same time, he added *Alexander's Ragtime Band* (1938) and *Swanee River* to the list, inaugurating a notable series of composer biopics (many of them in Technicolor) about Foster and his successors, Tin Pan Alley composers Dresser, Ball, Berlin, Sousa, and others. They held out splendid opportunities for biography, spectacle, music, and romance, all encapsulated in a nostalgic American past. On film, these lives were sanitized and reconstituted, according to Custen, so that references to specific ethnic origins and traditions were eliminated, "as if all Americans sprang fully socialized from a small town in the Midwest."[18] At the same time, their extraordinary talents were endorsed. "We could have it both ways," explains Custen. "The viewer could relate to the 'normal' aspects of the private life . . . while venerating their unusual achievements."[19] "Our main drama," Zanuck declared, "lies in [the subject's] fight against the world to convince them he had something great, and then to protect his ownership."[20] This could also be the credo for the true "author" of these films, not the screenwriters, not the directors John Ford, Henry King, and others — but Zanuck himself.

Foster was America's first professional popular songwriter, arguably the most famous American composer of the nineteenth century. Born on 4 July 1826, in what is now Pittsburgh, to a Scotch-Irish family, Foster pursued songwriting against the wishes of his family and despite a limited formal training. The popularity of his "breakthrough" song, "Oh! Susanna," in 1848, his first song to be associated with the Christy Minstrels, encouraged him to pursue a professional songwriting career. It became an anthem for the '49ers Gold Rush and the Temperance movement, and it was translated into languages ranging from Hindi to Chinese.

More than two hundred songs poured out in a seemingly endless stream. Many of them reveal a composer torn between the New World minstrel vernacular tradition of "Ethiopian" and "plantation" songs — the nineteenth-century popular equivalent to the ragtime rage that would sweep across America at the turn of the century — and the Old World "white man's music" of classical and sentimental parlor songs. However, Foster's difficult marriage to Jane McDowell, a weakness for drink, and poor business dealings (he gave away "Oh! Susanna" to a publisher who made more than $10,000 from it) brought about a sharp decline in his fortunes. In 1860 he moved to New York City, where a string of hack songs failed to revive his career. After being abandoned by his wife, he plunged deeper into poverty and drink. His final days were spent alone in a Bowery hotel room, where he fatally gashed his head as the result of a fall. At the time of his death at age thirty-eight, on 13 January 1864, he had only thirty-eight cents in his pocket. He left behind one last song, destined to become a posthumous classic, "Beautiful Dreamer."

Comparisons with Franz Schubert are obvious. Like Schubert, the surface details of Foster's life seem unprepossessing fare for a motion picture. "[Foster's] life was not in itself especially eventful or significant," writes historian Fletcher Hodges, Jr. "Stephen as an individual meant little, but that which he contributed has a national significance."[21] Like Schubert, there are major gaps in the biographical record. Foster left no autobiographical statement, and details of his marriage and the record of the last four years of his life, while he lived in New York City, are missing. Both were the master songwriters of their respective times and countries, conflicted by, on one hand, a "natural" bent for popular songs and, on the other, the desire for status and legitimacy with a more refined, "serious" music; both were rather passive figures victimized by unfortunate business dealings and frustrated by ill-starred romances; both died young and impoverished under tragic circumstances; and both, in general, seem to be prime examples of the "possessed" myth of genius, whose dreamy, other-worldly natures ill-equipped them to survive in the real world.

As had happened with Schubert, the mythologization of Foster's life and work began with the manipulative practices of relatives and friends. What Foster authority Deane Root, curator of the Stephen Collins Foster Memorial in Pittsburgh, Pennsylvania, has described as "a highly charged" and sentimental biography published in 1896 by his older brother and literary executor, Morrison ("the high priest" in the "cult of family loyalty"), romanticized and distorted the historical record because of the family's shame at Foster's failed marriage, his drunkenness, and his sorry end.[22] It asserts that Foster was an untutored genius, that he longed for the past and sentimentalized the Old South, that he was sympathetic to the institution of slavery, that he was hopelessly impractical and inept in his business dealings, and that his wife was principally at fault for a disastrous marriage. Morrison compounded the book's distortions by altering and destroying key family documents — material referencing Foster's ties with abolitionist groups, for example, and details about Foster's marital problems — that might have corrected or countered these allegations. Biographer Ken Emerson alleges that Morrison's daughter, Evelyn Foster Morneweck, also withheld information from Foster's chief biographer, John Tasker Howard, whose book, *Stephen Foster: America's Troubadour* (1934), is "invaluable but occasionally misleading."[23]

It is this mythic "life," rather than the strict historical record, that best suited Hollywood. Four years before Zanuck's *Swanee River,* Republic Pictures, which was generally known for its cowboy movies and stunt serials, got the ball rolling when it released *Harmony Lane,* directed by Joseph Santley and starring Douglass Montgomery as Foster, Joseph Cawthorne as Professor Henry Kleber, and William Frawley as E. P. Christy.[24] This variant of the "Blossom Time" paradigm depicts Foster as a "possessed" genius inspired by the vernacular black spirituals he hears in the country churches. But his determination to become a songwriter is discouraged by his mentor, Kleber, who persuades him to write a symphony instead. After hearing "Oh! Susannah," Kleber sniffs, "It might be popular for a day, a month, a year, but it's rhythmic emotion, pathos, that you want to cultivate. Maybe some day you'll write something that'll live forever." Meanwhile, disappointed when his true love,

Don Ameche portrayed Stephen Foster opposite Al Jolson as the minstrel E. P. Christy. (Courtesy Photofest/Twentieth Century-Fox)

Susan, marries another man, Foster drifts into an unhappy marriage with social climber Jane McDowell. She likewise disparages his songs. After years of enduring her nagging, he leaves her. Besieged by debts, plagued by alcoholism, and rejected by his publishers, he spends his last days in a New York garret room, dreaming of his lost love, Susan. At his death Foster leaves behind mourning friends and his last masterpiece, "Beautiful Dreamer." (Not content with just this one version of Foster's life, Republic would release yet another Foster picture in 1951, *I Dream of Jeanie*.)[25]

By the time *Harmony Lane* went into release, Zanuck was already planning his own *Swanee River*. The Fox research department dispatched a team of researchers to the Foster Archives in Pittsburgh, Pennsylvania, who then turned over their findings to screenwriters John Tainter Foote and Philip Dunne. "The people at Fox came here to research the picture," recounts Root, "then they threw everything out and rewrote his life!"[26]

A perusal of *Swanee River*'s production records in the Twentieth Century-Fox archives reveals the lengths Zanuck and his writers went to rework the clay of this particular genius into a shape that embodies both the "possession" myth of a passive genius and the "possessor" myth of the more masculine American populist.[27] A series of story conference memos bearing Zanuck's penciled annotations, dating from 31 May to 11 August 1939, reveals the process: On one hand, in a memo dated 31 May 1939, Zanuck argues that Foster (like Franz Schubert) should "always have a song running through his mind. When he's in the throes of creation he forgets everything and everybody — the song is the most important thing in the world." On the other hand, in a later memo dated 6 June, Zanuck urges, "We cannot depend on the songs alone. . . . We must tell our story in terms of guts and excitement and punch." According to another memo dated 11 July, he cautions against making Foster into "a conscious genius, [because] audiences will not accept him." Rather, he's "an interesting, colorful guy — full of weaknesses, irresponsible as hell, always doing the wrong things and then being sorry afterwards."

Aware of the proscriptions of the Production Code regarding the subject of alcoholism — a letter from PCA administrator Joseph Breen dated 12 August directed "that every care will be taken to keep Foster's drinking and drunkenness to the minimum necessary for characterization or plot motivation" — and concerned about the ignominy of Foster's death from an accidental fall, Zanuck declared in a memo dated 7 June: "We must fight every minute from letting this become a depressing story. Stories of that type spell box-office suicide." Instead, citing the dramatic climax of his own previous Fox biopic starring Don Ameche, *Alexander Graham Bell* (1938), Zanuck urged his writers to provide Foster some sort of dramatic victory. "We must root for Foster — create a pull for the finish."

The resulting portrait bears strong resemblances to *Harmony Lane,* although the production is much more elaborate. *Swanee River* begins with Foster (Ameche) as a struggling young composer torn between the inspiration, on one hand, of the chants of the black stevedores working on the docks of Louisville, Kentucky — "It's — it's music from the heart, from the heart of a simple people . . . by jingo!, the only real American contribution to music" — and the ambition, on the other, supported by his venerable German émigré music teacher, Professor Kleber (Felix Brassart), to compose music in the time-honored classical tradition. Against his parent's wishes, Foster leaves his desk job and pursues a career in music. But while his "Negro songs" find favor with minstrel man E. P. Christy (Al Jolson) and popular audiences, the public performance of his classical-styled *Suite* for chamber ensemble is a dismal failure. Foster and Kleber both learn a lesson. "Stephen can write American folk songs," opines Kleber, "but classical composition needs another kind of training. I don't want to see a first-class Stephen Foster turned into a tenth-rate Beethoven." Now estranged from his wife, Jeanie, Foster relocates to New

York, where more rejections and loneliness lead him to indulge his "weakness" (the film's euphemism for his alcoholism). He dies, but not before he fulfills his true genius by returning to the wellsprings of his art and writing "Old Black Joe" for a dying black servant (and not before he reunites for a few last moments with the beloved Jeanie). We are left with the assurance that his musical legacy is secure when Christy's performance of "Old Folks at Home" brings tears to the eyes of a memorial benefit concert audience.

As Fletcher Hodges, Jr., curator of the Foster Hall Collection at the time, noted, "*Swanee* River [is] a disappointment to curators, librarians, historians and research workers interested primarily in biographical accuracy."[28] Root admits, decades later, "Many people who walk into this Collection have seen *Swanee River* and have an image of Foster that is completely at odds with the image I have of him from my experience working with the Collection. Contrary to the myths perpetuated in that film, he was a very well educated composer and knew what he was about. The big mistake he made in his career was to let Christy put Christy's name on the cover of 'Old Folks at Home,' which he quickly realized was a mistake — and which he tried to correct."[29]

Root insists that the historical Foster approached his songwriting not as a vague and dreamy endeavor, but as a business, and he had to do so without benefit of performing rights organizations or fully protective copyright laws. His mentor, Kleber, was not the elitist snob as depicted but something of an impresario who specialized not just in classical music but genteel parlor ballads and polite dances and who passed along to Foster an acquaintance with a wide repertoire of scores from the European masters. Foster's own attempts to write "classical" music — in reality, paraphrases of operatic arias and European dances in works like his *The Social Orchestra* — were not rejected by public and critics but published, praised, and repeatedly reprinted. Foster never actually met Christy in person. And it was Kleber, not Christy, who presided over Foster's memorial concert.

Moreover, continues Root, Foster's first-hand knowledge of the Old South was limited. He never traveled below the Mason-Dixon line. As a child, he briefly visited Augusta, Kentucky, along the Ohio River. And he took a single boat trip to New Orleans in 1852. His primary contacts with blacks came from growing up in Pittsburgh, at that time a major stop on the Underground Railroad, where he was exposed to the sizable black community of freedmen, escaped slaves, and families of slaves. (Curiously, not once in his career did he write a song alluding to Pittsburgh.) Through connections with his wife, Jane, he was conversant with and sympathetic to abolitionist activities.[30] He sought to "elevate" the minstrel tradition and create an original, distinctively American music by combining what he knew of black music with elements from the various national or ethnic styles then circulating. He divined their common threads, observes Root: "The pain of leaving a loved one back home and coming to a new land, perhaps never to see each other again; the longing for self determination, free from political oppression, the right to live in dignity, and to die in peace; the longing to be surrounded by family amidst the oppressive loneliness of life. These became the themes of his songs."[31] The result was a music calculated to appeal to the widest possible public.

Swanee River's containment of the more complex and "problematic" aspects of Foster's personal life elicited a mixed critical and popular response. A *Variety* review noted, "There is no ugliness in the picture, no repellent realism, even in the scenes where Foster hits the bottom as a saloon pianist and lives in squalor after the unconquerable addiction to drink." However, some members of the viewing public held a different view. They objected to *any* indication of Foster's alcohol consumption. In the *Swanee River* production file are packets of angry letters from teachers, musicians, and private citizens directed to PCA administrators Joseph Breen and Jason Joy. They were apparently provoked by a column by Hedda Hopper in the *Los Angeles Times,* dated 4 September 1939 (before the film's release), in which she speculated, "I wonder if it's smart to make the Stephen Foster of American memories such a drunkard on the screen?" A typical reaction was registered by one Lela Mason, a music supervisor from the College of Education of the University of Kentucky, dated 23 October 1939: "In my schools, the picture will be ignored insofar as discussion or my advising children to attend is concerned. I hope some day you become fully aware of the possibilities for pictures of a life which should be remembered for its power to produce beauty." And a letter from the National Congress of Parents and Teachers threatens to blacklist the picture.

Clearly, as both *Harmony Lane* and *Swanee River* demonstrate, genius must be normalized and chastened if it falls into elitist tendencies, succumbs to bad habits, ignores the needs of the common folk, and rejects romance for the sake of career ambitions. And yes, the distressing, realities of the African-American slave experience that form a context for Foster's life and work must be replaced with a more cozy and comforting series of outrageously patronizing and (perhaps unintended) racist stereotypes.[32]

MGM's Romberg biopic, *Deep in My Heart,* was directed by Stanley Donen, written by Leonard Spiegelgass (after a novel by Elliott Arnold), and starred Jose Ferrer as Romberg, Merle Oberon as Dorothy Donnelly, and Doe Avedon as Lillian Harris. The lavish Technicolor production — the title is derived from a song in Romberg's operetta, *The Student Prince* (1924) — drew upon the full resources of the studio, with an all-star supporting cast, including Cyd Charisse,

Gene Kelly, Howard Keel, Jane Powell, and Metropolitan Opera star Helen Traubel, to tell the story of a Hungarian immigrant musician whose popular songs and operettas brought him fame and fortune on Tin Pan Alley and on Broadway.

The timing of *Deep in My Heart's* release is significant. Operettas and light musical comedies — definitions of the form, derived from the *Singspiel* of Germany, the *Opera Bouffe* of France, and the comic opera of England, vary, according to the source[33] — had always been prime material for Hollywood adaptations, since the first days of the talking picture in 1927 through 1930. Their blends of operatic stylings, lyric waltzes, vaguely European settings, sophisticated tone, and unabashed sentiment and nostalgia proved a potent formula at the boxoffice.[34] Now, in the early 1950s, MGM and other studios were releasing new versions of classic works. Warner Bros. remade *The Desert Song* in 1953, the third version since its 1929 and 1943 productions; and MGM released three new filmed operettas, Jerome Kern and Oscar Hammerstein II's *Show Boat* in 1951 (the third adaptation to date); Rudolf Friml's *Rose Marie* in 1954 (the second adaptation since the classic Jeanette MacDonald–Nelson Eddy version in 1936); and Romberg's *The Student Prince* in 1953. Clearly, the time was right for a biopic about Romberg, who, with Rudolf Friml and Victor Herbert, was the foremost exponent of American operetta. (Herbert had already been the subject in 1939 of a tepid biopic from Paramount entitled *The Great Victor Herbert*.)[35]

Although Hungarian-born Romberg had been a fixture in the American musical scene for forty years, relatively little was known about his early years in Vienna. In a novelized biography, *Deep in My Heart* (1949), for which he served as an "adviser," it was claimed he abandoned a career as a railroad engineer to study in Vienna with operetta master Victor Heuberger and later serve as assistant manager at the famous Theater an der Wien, home of so many famous operetta first nights. Substantiating evidence, however, is absent.[36] What is indisputable is that Romberg emigrated to New York in 1909 and found employment as a pianist in a fashionable New York restaurant, Bustanoby's, at Thirty-Ninth Street off Broadway. This led to a longtime association with the Broadway revue impresarios, the Shubert brothers. Despite his experience and talents for light opera, it was his facility for foxtrots, marches, and various dance styles that first established him on Tin Pan Alley. Increasingly dissatisfied, however, with what he came to feel was a distraction from his more "legitimate" true calling, he composed *Maytime in 1917*, an operetta-styled musical show. It transferred to American locales the Austrian settings of its original, *Wie einst im Mai,* and gave Romberg the opportunity to blend the usual rags and minstrel-related tunes with a more European-inflected musical style.

"The music was largely Viennese," writes historian Gerald Bordman, "tempered throughout with subtle American softenings [and minimizing] the use of recitatives, extended choral passages, and overflowing finales."[37] The same could be said for the succession of Broadway hits that followed during the next ten years, written in collaboration with librettists Dorothy Donnelly and Oscar Hammerstein II, including *Blossom Time* (1921), which brought Schubert melodies like "Ave Maria" and the "Serenade" (from the first movement of the Eighth Symphony) to American playgoers (see the discussion in Chapter One); *The Student Prince* (1924), the ultimate Ruritanian, bittersweet romance with standouts like "Serenade" ("Overhead the Moon Is Beaming") and the "Drinking Song"; *The Desert Song* (1926), an exotic concoction of desert settings and vaguely Eastern-inflected songs like the title song and "One Flower Grows Alone in Your Garden"; and *The New Moon* (1928), a story set in New Orleans at the time of the French Revolution, with hits "Lover Come Back to Me" and "Stouthearted Men." Hollywood beckoned, and by 1930 Romberg was writing original operettas for the movies, including the popular *Viennese Nights* (1930). He spent the wartime years conducting concerts and programs of light classical music and arrangements of his operetta melodies. By the time of his death in 1951, Romberg had written more than sixty shows for the theater and movies.

The Romberg of *Deep in My Heart* emerges as both a composer and a performer, exploiting the energy if not exactly the singing and dancing talents of the versatile Jose Ferrer. The story begins in New York in 1911 at the Café Vienna on Second Avenue. Proprietress Mrs. Anna Mueller (Helen Traubel) is proud of her new Vienna-trained star performer, "Romy," as she affectionately nicknames Romberg. "He plays here like it is Vienna," she boasts. One day, a ragtime publisher pops in long enough to admonish Romberg to ditch the Old World stuff and go for the latest pop stylings. "The customers want modern, up-to-date, uptown stuff," he says, "not that Viennese oom-pah stuff. You are 'last year' in fourteen languages!" He shows Romy a fistful of ragtime sheet music publications, including a song called "Choo-Choo to Chicago." "Baboons play songs like this," sniffs Romberg. The publisher retorts, "Baboons with rhythm. Baboons that do the Bunnyhop and The Squeeze. They don't dance ONE-two-three, ONE-two-three; it's one-TWO, one-TWO. Today a song's gotta be like a grizzly bear dancing on a tack."

Nonetheless, Romy promptly dashes off a jazzy "Leg of Mutton Dance," dutifully accompanied by a singing and dancing Mrs. Mueller. "I don't understand one word of it," he says ruefully. But the song is an instant sensation. Disgusted with the pittance he is given by his publisher, Romy approaches J. J. Shubert (Walter Pidgeon) with his new song, "Softly, as in a Morning Sunrise." To his horror, the song is given a full-scale Broadway revue treatment, uptempo, with high-stepping chorines, stair-step fashion shows, and flying pieces of floral scenery. "I don't want to write songs for galloping horses," complains Romy. He demonstrates the way it *should* be performed, with the assistance of Mrs. Mueller's full-throated voice and measured tempo. The result is a classic contrast between New World smirk and Old World schmaltz.

Meanwhile, Dorothy Donnelly (Merle Oberon), a beautiful actress and talented writer, has come in to his life. Freely offering him the fruits of her Broadway experience, she counsels him to temper his anger and advises him to stay with Shubert, produce a few hits, and gain the clout he needs to do better things. "Don't you find it strange a Viennese should write love songs for America?" he asks Donnelly. She replies, "No, love is love in Middle Europe and America. . . . With a few Shubert hits under your belt, there'll be nothing to stop you." Romy responds with an operetta, *Maytime,* and Donnelly uses her influence with J. J. Shubert to get it produced.

Maytime is a hit. The money pours in. Romy moves uptown and surrounds himself with luxuries. Success goes to his head, and he tries to produce his next show himself, a pretentious effort entitled *Magic Melody.* The neon lights on the marquee fade. The show is a disaster. Bankrupted, he returns to the Shubert fold, chastened. "I'm a smart-aleck," he announces. "I've learned my lesson. Do you by chance need some tunes for your next show?" Newly reconciled to his calling as a popular composer, he goes to the Saranac resort to work in peace on his next show, something called *Jazza-Doo.* In the process he meets a prim, snobbish woman named Lillian Harris (Doe Avedon). She rebuffs his advances: "You live in a world of vulgarity and jazz," she sniffs. He retorts, "Gilbert and Sullivan, even Puccini, compose for the people who pay to hear their music—just as I do. I'm not embarrassed by trying to please them."

But Romy has fallen for her and, as if modeling his life after the Schubert of *Blossom Time,* the lovelorn Romy is forced to find solace in his music. He and Donnelly write a new show, *The Student Prince.* Despite its success, his frustration continues over what he feels is a waste of his talent in frivolous shows. But Lillian, returning after a long absence, is so impressed with *The Student Prince* that she now declares Romy to be the love of her life. Such is the power of music. "Where could I go that I wouldn't hear your music and see your face?" she asks. "Men and women and boys and girls, in New York and

Iceland and Arabia, too, I guess, will be singing and playing what came out of the depths of you."

The happy moment is tempered by the fact that loyal Dorothy Donnelly has contracted a fatal illness. Despite her imminent demise, she and Lillian conspire in their efforts to urge Romy to follow his ambition toward light opera. "When does a man cease just to be a songwriter and become a composer?" Lillian asks. "When does a man cease just to write hit songs and become part of the music and a nation? That's what's happened to you, Romy — You've graduated from Tin Pan Alley! I want to see you in Carnegie Hall. I want to hear your music at its peak. I want a symphony orchestra to play it." Romy is aghast. "That's out of the question," he scoffs. "My stuff was not meant for Carnegie Hall. It was meant for singing and dancing and making love. It doesn't belong on the concert stage. Perhaps it doesn't belong anywhere, anymore."

But there *is* a Carnegie Hall concert, with Romy both conducting the symphony orchestra from a podium set on the right side of the stage (enabling him to keep an eye on the audience as well as the players) and playing the piano for Helen Traubel's performances of "Stouthearted Men" and "When I Grow Too Old to Dream" (from his film score for the 1934 MGM film *The Night Is Young*). Addressing the upscale audience, Romberg declares, "This music isn't highbrow music and it isn't lowbrow music. Perhaps it might be called 'middlebrow' music. It belongs in the heart."

Deep in My Heart joins *Rhapsody in Blue* and *Till the Clouds Roll By* in depicting the creation of a uniquely American kind of light opera. Indeed, as William A. Everett asserts in his study of Romberg: "The operettas which Romberg composed during the 1920s form a very important chapter in the development of the American musical theater, as they form a link between the central-European operetta tradition and the mature American musical."[38] All of them, in their own way, fulfill Dvořák's prophecy about the "commingling" of disparate voices in the formation of a uniquely American cultural expression.

Taking its cue from Elliott Arnold's fictionalized biography of Romberg, *Deep in My Heart* (1949), the MGM film constructs a mythology for Romberg much in the same way Stephen Foster's friends and first biographers mythologized his life. Arnold's book, written with the unacknowledged assistance of Romberg himself, presents a portrait of the artist that is the flipside of Foster: Romberg is an artist with Old World respectability and training striving to assimilate into his music the vernacular of a New World. Unlike Foster, he succeeds in this ambition; but like Foster, he grows frustrated in his endeavors. Humbled in the realization that he has abandoned his true calling, he resolves to create a populist expression that blends his gifts for old and new

MGM's *Deep in My Heart* (1954), starring Jose Ferrer as Sigmund Romberg, was a cavalcade of song and dance numbers. (Courtesy Photofest/MGM)

music. His wife's rebuke is but one of many similar reprimands to the "possessor" geniuses that resonate through the oeuvre of movie biopics: "Humility is necessary if your music is going to continue to have something in it to reach people's hearts."[39] His triumph comes with his Carnegie Hall concert (a scene copied almost detail for detail and word for word from the book). He achieves in his lifetime what was denied Foster — the successful assimilation of classical and popular art.

The climactic Carnegie Hall concert sequence is a standard part of the Tin Pan Alley biopic formula. As I discuss below, almost all of the Tin Pan Alley tunesmiths aspire to, and achieve, this stamp of legitimacy. Here, however, it reverses the outcome of Foster's disastrous salon concert in *Swanee River*. Romberg's triumph and Foster's failure only point to the essential features of both aspects of Hollywood's Tin Pan Alley paradigm: Romberg is the "possessor" figure who, through industry and adaptability, gains a certain legitimacy by reconfiguring Old World stylings into his popular songs. Foster, for his part, is the "possessed" figure whose tragedy resides in his inability to transcend his social circumstances and personal shortcomings. In Hollywood parlance, Romberg gets the girl and Foster doesn't; Romberg earns applause and wealth in his lifetime, and Foster only finds frustration and poverty. But both leave a legacy: Foster and the black composers of the next generation, in particular, W. C. Handy and Will Marion Cook, point the way toward the assimilation of the "Ethiopian melodies" and "plantation songs" of the black culture into the white consumer mainstream. In biographer Emerson's words, "[Foster] blazed the trail that eventually led to Tin Pan Alley."[40]

Although many of the surface details are grounded in the historical record — the Vienna Café (which stands in for Bustanoby's restaurant); the "Leg of Mutton" dance (which was an early Romberg foxtrot); his associations with the Shuberts, writer Dorothy Donnelly, and spouse Lillian Harris; the symphony orchestra concerts (which indeed included Carnegie Hall); his chronic discontents with his relatively lowly status as a pop song stylist — the film's portrait of a brash, hustling go-getter, an accomplished pianist and dancer, an ardent wooer of Lillian, and a spokesperson for the musical classical establishment are all elements carefully crafted to construct the epitome of the cosmopolitan, reassuringly masculine artist. Moreover, as in Arnold's book, all traces of Romberg's Jewishness have been erased in the film's determination to "whiten" the image of the mainstream American composer (an erasure that Romberg himself participated in).[41]

Other details are carefully designed to embroider this image. Metropolitan Opera headliner Helen Traubel's character of the fictitious Mrs. Mueller lends both a cozy "family value" to the story and the desired operatic "weight" and classical legitimacy to Romberg's songs. (Traubel admits in her autobiography, *Saint Louis Woman,* that she was amused to be greeted by the critics as "Newcomer of the Year": "This was a prime chortle to me, since I had been 'newcoming' ever since 1939, about fifteen years before.")[42] Unfortunately, there are no references to *Blossom Time,* the operetta that first brought him fame in 1921. It seems the Shubert brothers refused to grant MGM studios permission to allude to or quote from the work.

There was disagreement about the casting and the performances. On one hand, Jack Moffitt in the *Hollywood Reporter* enthused: "Not since Jimmy Cagney played George M. Cohan in 'Yankee Doodle Dandy' has a theatrical personality been presented with the zest and flair that Jose Ferrer brings to the role of Sigmund Romberg. . . . But the big news of the production is Helen Traubel. Don't let her great fame as an opera singer fool you. She sings popular music with never a classical 'tra-la-la.' . . . Miss Traubel has the common touch. She will appeal to all those who like beer, baseball games, and hot dogs."[43] A discouraging word, however, was heard from the *Newsweek* critic, who regretted that the "Serenade" from *The Student Prince* was "lunged out *fortissimo*" by William Olvis, and that "Softly as in a Morning Sunrise" and

"Auf Wiedersehen" was entrusted to "the noble Wagnerian vocal chords of Helen Traubel, formerly of the Metropolitan Opera Company, which is like firing balloons from siege guns."[44] Most critics agreed that Doe Avedon's portrayal of a snobbish, boring Lillian Harris is surely one of the least appealing heroines in the history of screen romance.

The Populist Mandate

The other Tin Pan Alley composers represented in this chapter are also portrayed as conflicted between ambitions to pursue single-mindedly either an American vernacular or an elitist tradition. In either case, their self-centered indulgences jeopardize their true populist calling. You can almost sense a Hollywood scenarist off in the wings, shaking his finger reprovingly at such temerity: What'll the folks in the audience say? They must effect a compromise or reconciliation between the two. Thus, when George M. Cohan (James Cagney) in Warner Bros.'s *Yankee Doodle Dandy* (1942) fails in his ambitious attempt to write a dramatic, nonmusical play, he becomes the laughingstock of Broadway; and only when he publicly denounces his own show does he regain his artistic balance. In Fox's *Alexander's Ragtime Band* (1939), Alexander's (Tyrone Power) High Art pretensions are rebuked by the saloon singer, Stella (Alice Faye): "Maybe I don't know the tripe they play up Snob Hill, but I know what they like down here; and that's more than you'll ever know." Subsequently, a dutifully chastened Alexander reunites with Stella after shrewdly blending the best of both worlds by dressing up ragtime in symphonic clothes for a Carnegie Hall concert. In Warner Bros.'s *Rhapsody in Blue* (1946) George Gershwin's first attempt to write a "Negro Opera," called *Blue Monday,* is soundly rejected as audience members leave in boredom and confusion. Publisher Max Dreyfus (Charles Coburn) grumbles, "Gershwin must have lost his mind." Even the more sympathetic Paul Whiteman (played by himself) advises, "George, it's great, but it doesn't belong in this kind of a show." Elsewhere in the film, none other than Maurice Ravel is on hand to remind Gershwin (Robert Alda) of the real genius of his populist, vernacular gifts. His words are an echo of Kleber's to Foster in *Swanee River:* "Gershwin, if you study with me, you'll only write second-rate Ravel instead of first-rate Gershwin. . . . Now tell me, how did you get your inspiration for your rhythm?"[45]

In MGM's *Words and Music* (1948) the usually effervescent Larry Hart (Mickey Rooney) goes into a funk whenever he falls in love and tries to write serious romantic lyrics. When asked by partner Richard Rodgers (Tom Drake) about his problem, Hart replies: "No more love songs, that's all; just those fast, bright things from here on in." Later, Hart confesses sardonically, "I'm just a guy that writes lyrics, runs away, hides, has a few laughs, comes back and writes . . . lyrics."[46] In *Three Little Words* (1950) attempts by lyricist Bert Kalmar (Fred Astaire) to write a "legitimate" play result in the disastrous breakup of his partnership with composer Harry Ruby (Red Skelton). In Fox's *Stars and Stripes Forever* (1952) John Philip Sousa (Clifton Webb) abandons writing art songs when he finds out that one particularly mournful effusion, "My Love Is a Weeping Willow," comes off better when quickened into march tempo and retitled "Semper Fidelis." Later, a newly enlightened Sousa proclaims, "Our job, our only job will be to put on a good show. Which means that if our audiences prefer 'Turkey in the Straw' to 'Parsifal,' we'll play 'Turkey in the Straw.' " In MGM's *Till the Clouds Roll By* (1946) Jerome Kern (Robert Walker) is congratulated by none other than Victor Herbert (Paul Maxey) for his populist musical achievement: "You've got a song to sing. Look down at that city, Jerry. It's made up of millions of people. And music has played a part in all their lives. Lullabies, love songs, hymns, anthems." A misty-eyed Kern replies, "It makes me feel grateful, and very humble." (Even the cab driver, to whom Kern tells his life story, pronounces his admiration for *Show Boat:* "That was a swell show!"). The worst comeuppance, of course, is reserved for the snootiest songwriter of them all, Cole Porter (Cary Grant) in Warner Bros.'s *Night and Day* (1946). When Porter disdains the "people's music" — "I'm fed up with the riverboats, honky-tonks, and music counters" — his wife deserts him, his friends disappear, and he endures a terrible riding accident. Later, suffering brings him enlightenment, and, after writing "Don't Fence Me In" for Roy Rogers, he returns to hearth, home, and songwriting.[47]

Sharing in the songwriters' comeuppance are their Old World mentors. We've already met the model of this character, Foster's teacher, Professor Kleber.[48] In *Alexander's Ragtime Band* the wholly fictitious Professor Heinrich (Jean Hersholt) monitors the performances of his classically trained violinist pupil "Alexander" with this stern advice: "You did very well, my boy, but your pizzicato, we still have to work on it." Later, however, when Alexander gives a ragtime concert in Carnegie Hall — the newspaper headline reads, "POPULAR MUSIC OUT TO WIN HIGHBROW RECOGNITIONS" — an enlightened Heinrich occupies a box seat and nods his approval. In *Rhapsody in Blue* it's Professor Otto Franck (Albert Basserman), a former pupil of Johannes Brahms, who putters about in his study among the busts and paintings of Schubert and Beethoven, while disapproving young Gershwin's attempts to "improve on the classics" with jazzy riffs. Eventually, he gives way to the grudging acceptance of his pupil's true calling: "I have such hope for you, my boy," he confesses finally. "America is a growing country, a mixture of things that are very old with more that is new. Your nature has the same contradictions, ideals and material ambition. If you can make them both serve, you will give America a voice." On his deathbed, Professor Franck listens to the radio broadcast of a concert performance of Gershwin's *Rhapsody in Blue,* after which he dutifully expires with a peaceful smile on his face.[49] In *Till the Clouds Roll By* an academically trained composer and arranger named "James Hessler" (Van Heflin) takes one look at his new pupil, Jerome Kern, and declares: "The trouble with you songwriters is that all you ever think about is making money. You never think about doing anything big or worthwhile. . . . No, all you fellows want to do is write sugary little tunes and make a lot of money." But Hessler changes his tune, so to speak, in the face of Kern's genius, and, after abandoning his own symphony, collaborates with him on his musical shows. Finally, on his death-bed, Hessler confesses to Kern: "You were writing the real music, the folk music of America. Thanks, Jerry, for letting me stick around." Gasping his last, Hessler concludes, "It looks like a time for strings," and the film's sound-track obediently wells up in a funereal burst of violins.[50]

Even if other biopics don't feature Old World mentor figures such as Hein-rich, Kleber, Franck, and Hessler, there is always the *implication* of one. For example, in *Night and Day,* Monte Woolley (who plays a Yale professor inex-plicably named "Monte Woolley") fits the professorial model; and in *Stars and Stripes Forever* a bearded, monocled Clifton Webb (who looks for all the world like he strayed in from the latest "Mr. Belvedere" picture) does double duty, alternately functioning as a March King and a High Art Counsellor.

Friendly Persuasions and Rewritten Lives

As has been noted earlier in this chapter, the Tin Pan Alley biopics were shaped by the same pressures of the classical studio system as were the classical music films — the established agendas of producers and writers, the exigencies of the star system, the restrictions of the censorship codes of the Hays and Breen Offices (reinforced in mid-1934 by proddings from the Catholic Legion of Decency), and the dictates of marketing research and audience demograph-ics. And, like their classical music brethren, they exploited the name recogni-tion and prestige of their composer subjects.

In addition, it must again be noted that living composers like Berlin, Cohan, Kern, and Porter actively participated in the fictionalizing of their lives. With-out question, Berlin was the most influential, most prolific, and most successful American songwriter of the twentieth century. Born Israel Baline in Western Siberia in 1888, the son of a cantor, he and his family emigrated to America four years later, where they settled in the Jewish quarter of New York's Lower East Side. Despite his lack of education and formal music training, he worked his way up from singing waiter and song plugger on Tin Pan Alley, to staff lyricist for the Ted Snyder Company, to a partnership in his own publishing company in 1921, to international renown for his numerous ragtime songs, sentimental ballads, and patriotic anthems. Berlin, whom Zanuck regarded as "show business incarnate, his life story the history of popular entertainment," first came to Twentieth Century-Fox in 1936 to write the music for an Alice Faye vehicle, *On the Avenue*.[51] It was not a happy experience for him, but it did lead to an invitation to write the scenario for his own life story, *Alexander's Ragtime Band*.

Convinced his life held no real dramatic value, and disinclined to refer to his Jewish background and early experiences at "Nigger Mike's" club on New York's Lower East Side, Berlin fabricated a different "life" for Hollywood. He constructed himself as "Alexander," a classically trained WASP clarinetist who scores with the ragtime-inflected "Alexander's Ragtime Band" in a New Orleans honky-tonk in 1915, makes his way to Broadway, enlists in the army at the outbreak of World War I, goes to Camp Upton (where he meets a songwriter named Irving Berlin), and ultimately winds up at Carnegie Hall, where he conducts a symphonic arrangement of "Alexander's Ragtime Band."[52]

Fox's production chief, Zanuck, rejected the script, complaining of its lack of a romantic interest (Berlin had omitted references to his two marriages). Discouraged, Berlin withdrew from the writing process, allowing scenarists Kathryn Scola and Lamar Trotti to take over and further embellish his biography. The story that emerged retained some of Berlin's plot points but transferred the story's opening to San Francisco's Barbary Coast, cast Tyrone Power as "Alexander," and brought in Alice Faye as the honky-tonk songstress who can't make up her mind between Alexander and his songwriting friend, Charlie Dwyer (Don Ameche). Ironically, Berlin's name, which appears above the title, is referred to only once in the film, when it is seen on the sheet music cover of the title song. The resulting film, directed by Henry King, cost $2 million, featured thirty Berlin songs — ranging from the early songs like the title number, patriotic World War I ditties like "It's Your Country and My Country," 1920s hits like "A Pretty Girl Is Like a Melody," and the 1938 present with new Berlin songs like "Walking Stick" and "Now It Can Be Told" (composed especially for Faye) — and received six Oscar nominations. *Alexander's Ragtime Band* was the closest Berlin ever got to a biopic of his own.[53]

Grace Kahn, the widow of songwriter Gus Kahn, served as the technical adviser on *I'll See You in my Dreams* (1951). She was in a unique position to oversee the facts of her husband's life and career, having collaborated with him on his first published song hit, "I Wish I Had a Girl." After Gus's death in 1941, Grace was approached by several producers who wished to bring her husband's story to the screen, but she rejected all of their ideas as "too fictional." When a family friend, Louis Edelman, a producer at Warner Bros., pitched her with his idea of filming the "true story" of Gus Kahn, Grace accepted his offer. The script was eventually written by Mel Shavelson and Jack Rose, and Gus Kahn was portrayed by Danny Thomas, in what was only his fourth feature film role.

Even with Grace's hard line against "fictional" scripts, in the final analysis *I'll See You in My Dreams* is no more factual than most biopics. She did ensure, however, that there were moments in the film that retained at least some degree of authenticity. For example, she made a cameo appearance in the film as an audience member applauding Doris Day's rendition of "I Wish I Had a Girl" in a scene depicting a banquet in honor of Grace and Gus Kahn (and even made sure that the scene was filmed at the Beverly Wilshire Hotel, in the same banquet room where the actual testimonial had been held in 1939). These touches don't make the film any more accurate of course, but they do invest it with a modicum of emotional veracity.

My Gal Sal (1942), the story of songwriter Paul Dresser, was originally conceived by Dresser's younger brother, the famous novelist Theodore Dreiser. He wrote a memoir, "My Brother Paul" in 1919 and sold it to Twentieth Century-Fox for $35,000, which included the rights to Dresser's songs. One would have expected a gritty, realistic portrait from Dreiser, the author of such celebrated — and controversial — novels as *Sister Carrie* (1900) and *An American Tragedy* (1925). Certainly his brother, Indiana-born Paul Dresser, composer of the phenomenally popular songs "On the Banks of the Wabash" and "My Gal Sal," had led a singularly tragic life. After rejecting his father's plans to follow him in the ministry, he had run away to a medicine show. Later, after adventures as a vaudeville and minstrel show performer, he found great success in New York as a songwriter of sentimental Gay '90s ballads. But his career went into severe decline as a result of poor management, the growing trend in popular taste away from sentimental ballads toward ragtime, the desertion by his wife, and his fatal addiction to drink. He died in 1906, alone, forgotten, and broke.

Yet, despite the fact that the title card read "Theodore Dreiser's *My Gal Sal*," Dreiser left the project after submitting some preliminary story ideas, few of which survived in the finished film. What appears on the screen bears instead the unmistakable imprint of studio chief Zanuck and screenwriters Seton I. Miller, Darrell Ware, and Karl Tunberg. Zanuck made it clear to them that the story needed more comedy and that Dresser would not die in the end, as originally written; instead, the revised story opted for a conventional happy ending. Moreover, the eponymous Sal would no longer reference Sallie Walker,

My Gal Sal (1942) bore little resemblance to Theodore Dreiser's original story treatment of the life of his brother, songwriter Paul Dresser (Victor Mature). (Courtesy Photofest/Twentieth Century-Fox)

an Evansville, Indiana, prostitute of Dresser's acquaintance, but a fictitious musical comedy actress, Sally Elliott.[54] The finished film, Zanuck wrote in a memo, "sticks to the facts of Dreiser's [*sic*] life as closely as we can be expected to stick to them."[55]

My Gal Sal begins as Dresser (Victor Mature) abandons his ministerial calling and goes to work with a traveling medicine show. His flirtation with the beautiful Mae (Carole Landis), the daughter of his boss, is interrupted when he meets the famous vaudeville entertainer, Sally Elliott (Rita Hayworth). He pursues her to New York, where he establishes himself on Tin Pan Alley with his song "On the Banks of the Wabash." After a series of bickerings and reconciliations the suddenly famous Dresser scorns his rural roots and goes "uptown" with a vengeance, purchasing expensive clothes and consorting with a bunch of high-class aristocrats, including a dalliance with a countess. He eventually comes to his senses, however, proposes marriage to Sally, and composes his most famous song for her.

None of this, innocuous as it now seems, came to the screen easily. A series of scripts were subjected to the censors at the Production Code Administration. Colonel Jason Joy of the PCA warned at one point: "We regret to advise that the present script is unacceptable under the provisions of the Production Code. The unacceptability lies in the fact that the lead, Paul, has indulged in various sex affairs without the proper compensating moral values, and, hence, a picture based on the story could not be approved. It is essential that the present characterization of Paul be changed from that of a man who frequently indulges in sex affairs," followed by a long list of proscriptions, including references to Dresser's affair with the medicine show girl, Mae ("The action of Mae kissing Paul hungrily, with the dissolve, seems to suggest a flavor of seduction, which could not be approved in the finished picture"); "Paul's line, 'You're getting to be a pretty big girl' will be unacceptable if it refers to Mae's breasts or buttocks"; and "Mae's line: 'You've got *all* you're going to get out of me!' which must be rewritten to get away from its sex suggestiveness." Other advice from Joy included: "drinking, except where absolutely necessary for plot motivation or proper characterization" must be minimized; and a scene with a tailor "must not be characterized as a 'pansy,' particularly with regard to the line: 'It's a pleasure to make clothes for someone with a figure like yours, Mr. Dresser.' And there must be no hint that Paul expects to have an affair with Sally."[56]

Ironically, since only a couple of Dresser's songs seemed to outlive him, songwriters Leo Robin and Ralph Ranger were brought in to write more tunes in "the Dresser ditty style," such as "Here You Are," "Oh, the Pity of It All," "Me and My Fella 'Neath a Big Umbrella" and "On the Gay White Way." *My Gal Sal* is that rare biopic in which not only are the facts of the composer's life mostly jettisoned, but so are the songs that, presumably, made him of interest in the first place.

Despite such evidence to the contrary, a few critics thought they saw Dreiser's hand in the finished film. They even considered *My Gal Sal* to be more honest and hard-hitting than the typical composer biopics of the day. *Variety* mistakenly wrote that Dreiser gave "a seemingly authentic picture of his brother's struggles to be a songwriter back in the high buttoned shoe era."[57] And the *Hollywood Reporter*'s critic found that "the author is not too complimentary in depicting the musical career of the older, headstrong Paul who ran away from home to join medicine shows and carnivals, eventually to end up in New York as one of the most popular songwriters of his era. Yet the character of Paul is more human for the frankness of Dreiser's account and gains stature through the unabashed brashness of Victor Mature's portrayal."[58] A few days later *Variety*'s "Walt" added, "Dresser's life is far from sugar-coated in its cinematic unreeling as narrated by novelist-brother Dreiser. . . . There's too much footage consumed in unnecessary episodes and incidents that might have been historically correct for the times, but not important to a straight line presentation of a musical drama."[59] Even Dreiser himself nodded his approval, eliciting this remark from Dreiser biographer Richard Lingeman: "How Dreiser could say that Twentieth Century-Fox had done well by his story is difficult to imagine. Perhaps, after the years of futile attempts to sell a movie, he was relieved to have his name connected with something — and a commercially successful picture at that."[60]

Particularly revealing insights into the extent to which *living* composers worked to influence the screenplays of their own lives may be gained from the examples of Ruby, Cohan, Kern, Porter, Rodgers, and Gershwin. In late 1949 Ruby, of the songwriting team of Kalmar and Ruby, assured MGM producer Jack Cummings that he would cooperate in the writing of a screenplay for what became *Three Little Words*. He approved the casting of Fred Astaire to portray his late partner, Bert Kalmar; Astaire had known the songwriting team from his Broadway days, when he and his sister, Adele, modeled their routines on Kalmar's vaudeville act). In an interview Ruby claimed that the film presented at least a semblance of the truth of his relationship with Kalmar: "I guess you know what happened — if you watch the Late Show, you can see the picture *Three Little Words* which Jack Cummings made of our life story. Fred Astaire played Bert, and Red Skelton played me. Quite an improvement — for me, that is."[61]

Cohan's biopic, *Yankee Doodle Dandy,* is of course one of the most beloved films in the American cinema. Cohan not only collaborated with Warner Bros., he enthusiastically went about helping the writers discard the facts of his life in favor of a far more upbeat fiction. He was just as pleased with the product as everyone else was — and continues to be to this day. Viewers knew or cared little about the truth of Cohan's life — and even if they did, they certainly found few traces of it in this rousing patriotic pageant. What they did find was a relentlessly cheerful "cavalcade" of the music of Cohan spread over an upbeat, often moving framework that managed to capture the mood of its own time, 1942, even more clearly than it expertly recreated the America of the early twentieth century.

And that is exactly the way Cohan wanted it. By 1941 Cohan, who had not written a musical play on Broadway since 1928 and who had been unsuccessful in his foray into early talkies, was hungry for a comeback.[62] He still had enough clout that when he signed a contract with Warner Bros. for a musical biography, he stipulated that he retain script approval and that Cagney play the leading role. Like Irving Berlin before him, Cohan wished to avoid anything too close to his private life and personal obsessions — in this case, his rabid antiunionism (such as his bitter opposition to the Actors Equity Strike of 1919), his two marriages to Ethel Levey and Agnes Nolan (there are also indications that Cohan may have been married *four* times), his bitter battles with critics, and so on.

Robert Buckner wrote the original script, based upon many hours of interviews and conversations with Cohan. From the beginning, the studio knew that trouble might lie ahead because of Cohan's participation. As producer Hal Wallis wrote to studio chief Jacob Wilke: "The actual story of Cohan's life might offer a great many difficulties in transference to the screen. . . . Cohan's life was just a succession of one play after another and offered little variety in the way of incident of possibilities for dramatization. Another is Cohan's personal life which you must realize would be difficult to incorporate in a picture. . . . [W]e do not wish to be bound by any agreement whereby we will have to reproduce the life of George M. Cohan actually, nor do we want to be forced to submit the script for final approval by Cohan. What we want to do is to make a broad adaptation of Cohan's life, fictionalizing wherever we deem necessary."[63]

Because the studio feared that Cohan would try to exert too much influence on the film, a letter was drafted to the song and dance man, dated 21 April 1941, which affords a revealing glimpse into the machinations behind the crafting of a Hollywood biopic: "We do not wish to make your domestic life the main theme of the picture, but it is such an important and essential part of a man's life that its complete exclusion is very likely to result in an unbalanced story. We are willing to follow any questions which you may have on this problem, either to ignore it completely or else to represent it as you wish. We could eliminate any reference to your first wife and depict only your present wife. If possible, we would like to include the children. . . . As I said, we are completely willing and anxious to fit our story to your own personal wishes, and if you should disapprove of any representation of your family life, we will forget it at once."[64]

Cohan read Buckner's first script with great interest—then tossed it aside and immediately countered with one of his own, numbering 170 pages. Cohan's revision removed most of the domestic details and created a fictional girl friend, "Agnes," whom he meets after his retirement from the stage. As Cohan explained to Buckner in a lengthy telegram: "The . . . romance should not start until much later in the story for reasons that you possibly can understand without my going into details. To my mind the only sweetheart your hero can have in the early stages is the theatre itself. He is too much in love with his work and ambitions to find romance elsewhere until he is well on his way to success."[65] Note that Cohan refers to himself as "your hero" and treats his romantic life as if he were writing an entirely fictional work — which, of course, he was. And to give an idea of what might have been, here is one self-referential scene from Cohan's script, dated 6 June 1941:

> (A BELLBOY with "an infectious grin" approaches COHAN in a hotel.)
> BELLBOY: I'd like to work for you someday, Mr. Cohan.
> COHAN: Would you, kid? Swell. What can you do?
> BELLBOY: I can dance a little. Want to see me?
> COHAN (smiling): Not now. But come around when you grow up.
> BELLBOY: Thanks!
> (COHAN starts to walk away, then turns). By the way son, what's your name?
> BELLBOY: Cagney — Jimmy Cagney.[66]

Although Cohan went on to say to Buckner that he "sincerely hope[d] you are in no way offended because of my blunt way of putting things," Buckner was understandably annoyed at Cohan's having essentially tossed Buckner's script away. In exasperation, Buckner wrote to Hal Wallis about his predicament: "It is not now a question simply of blending some of his script to ours, Hal. This won't work at all because our stories are written from totally different viewpoints. Ours was a screenplay, a picture. His is an autobiography, a rambling series of stereopticon slides that don't slide. I think Cohan has completely violated the promise of his contract, to give us enough leeway with facts to make an interesting motion picture."[67]

Eventually, a compromise story was hammered out (Robert Buckner and Edmund Joseph received screenplay credit on the film), in which were added a composite sweetheart-wife named "Mary" (Joan Leslie), a moving death scene for Jerry Cohan (Walter Huston), and some anecdotal details (such as a meeting with Eddie Foy, portrayed by Eddie Foy, Jr.). Counterpointing these fictions were the authentic re-creations by Cagney and vaudevillians William Collier and Johnny Boyle of the staging of the classic "Peck's Bad Boy" and routines from *Little Johnny Jones,* including "Give My Regards to Broadway." The framing device of a meeting with President Roosevelt — like the flag-waving patriotism of the "Grand Old Flag" number — was directly calculated to bolster the morale of audiences still recovering from the shock of Pearl Harbor.[68]

Another example of collusion on the part of the nominal subject of the biopic is *Till the Clouds Roll By,* a dramatization of the life of Jerome Kern. The opening title card pretty well sums up the reverential attitudes toward the composer's life, promoted by the subject's family and friends: "This story of Jerome Kern is best told in the bars and measures, the quarter and grace notes of his music — that music that sings so eloquently his love of people, love of

Robert Walker traded in the waistcoat of Johannes Brahms for the business suit of songwriter Jerome Kern in MGM's lavish *Till the Clouds Roll By* (1946). (Courtesy Photofest/MGM)

country, love of life. We who have sung it and will sing it to our children can only be grateful that he gave his life to music — and gave that music to us." The producer of *Till the Clouds Roll By*, Arthur Freed, and the writer, Guy Bolton, were both longtime admirers and associates of Kern. Bolton had been a friend and collaborator with Kern since 1915, when they began their run of the legendary Princess Theatre shows. Freed was a Tin Pan Alley graduate himself, an accomplished lyricist who had been with MGM since 1929, writing such memorable hits as "Singin' in the Rain" and "You Are My Lucky Star." Freed had known Kern since 1917, when they met during the run of *Oh, Boy!* It was Freed who first approached Kern about the possibility of bringing his life to the screen. Later, after Kern's death, Freed assured his widow, Eva, "Jerry Kern was always an ideal of perfection to me, as an artist, as a showman and as a friend."[69] Freed and Bolton also collaborated on *Words and Music*. Their contract with Richard Rodgers and the estate of the late Lorenz Hart granted them script approval.[70]

When Kern was approached by MGM, he initially balked. He had guarded his private life from the public too long to readily consent to what he regarded as a potential invasion of his private life. Besides, he quipped, his relatively dull life would not be an interesting subject. "If you tell the truth," he said, "it'll be the dullest picture in the world."[71] When the studio executives persisted, Kern finally granted permission but with the stipulation that his story be largely fictitious, confining itself to a few well-known anecdotes. Writers Bolton and George Wells took him at his word.[72]

In the first draft of the script, dated 4 October 1945, the story begins with a radio tribute to Kern, which includes Frank Sinatra singing "Old Man River" from *Show Boat*. Kern, who has been asleep in the garden of his California home, misses most of the show. He is awakened for a surprise party and hears the last part of the broadcast on the radio. The radio announcer begins to tell Kern's story. At this point the script calls for a flashback to Kern's youth, after which the remainder of his life story unfolds. By the time the final script was completed (dated 10 January 1946), the radio show idea had been dropped. Instead, this new script begins with a lengthy digest version of *Show Boat* (in which, at the command of censor Joseph Breen, the word "nigger" was changed to "colored folks").[73] After this review of Kern's greatest triumph, the story settles into a conventional — and spurious — version of Kern's biography, leaving the door open for numerous production numbers, including Sinatra performing "Old Man River." Although Kern fully supported — even encouraged — the fictionalizing of his life, we will never know what he thought of the finished film. He died in 1945, several months before *Till the Clouds Roll By* was released.

"Why quibble about the story?" asked *Variety* critic "Abel." "It's notable that the Kern saga reminds us of the current Cole Porter [*Night and Day*] release — both apparently enjoyed a monotonously successful life. No early-life struggles, no frustrations, nothing but an uninterrupted string of Broadway and West End show success."[74] "Abel" wasn't the only viewer to note the similarities between *Night and Day* and *Till the Clouds Roll By*. Porter himself seems to have been highly aware of them as well. In his negotiations for the scripting of his own biopic, *Night and Day*, Porter, like Kern, willingly signed away his rights to a factually accurate account. Encouraged by his wife and mother, Porter agreed to a contract that paid him $270,000 and stipulated that "it is understood that Producers in the development of the story . . . upon which the photoplay shall be based shall be free to dramatize, fictionalize, or

Cary Grant and Alexis Smith brought
a highly romanticized version of the
life of Cole Porter to Warner Bros.'s
Night and Day (1945). (Courtesy
Photofest/Warner Bros.)

emphasize any or all incidents in the life of the Seller, or interpolate such
incidents as Producers may deem necessary in order to obtain a treatment of
continuity of commercial value."[75]

Porter had his reasons. This not only cleared the way for a strapping Cary
Grant and a youthful, elegant Alexis Smith to play the diminutive, balding
Porter and his older wife, Linda, but it provided Porter the opportunity to
construct a movie "life" that could confirm the public image he so avidly
sought. After all, he never had been averse to fictionalizing his own life, and he
had already expended considerable energy in embellishing and embroidering
it. "Considering the numerous fibs about himself that Cole had foisted on
an unsuspecting public for decades," writes biographer Charles Schwartz,
"one could hardly expect a Hollywood film biography to come any closer to
the truth."[76]

Problematic as far as Hollywood was concerned, for example, were inconvenient realities such as the substantial inheritance that allowed Porter a life of
relative ease, his many extramarital affairs, his indulgence in the New York–
Paris–Beverly Hills cafe society, and career successes that had come to him
easily. Accordingly, producer Hal Wallis ordered that the script depict scenes
suggesting Porter's solid work ethic, sturdy individuality, and heterosexual
attachment to Linda. This "new," more populist Porter now bravely rejects his
grandfather's support, declaring, "I can't come back here and live on your
money and all the time wonder what would've happened if I'd gone out on my

own." Later, adrift in Tin Pan Alley and on Broadway, Porter lives hand to mouth while struggling to get his shows produced. Then, after the outbreak of World War I interrupts the run of his show *See America First* — "I guess it was just one of those things," the disappointed Porter muses meaningfully as he emerges from the darkened theater — he enlists in the French Army and is wounded during an enemy artillery barrage. Coming to his rescue is his wife-to-be, Linda, who just so happens to be serving as a nurse in the local hospital. She promptly assists him in writing the song "Night and Day." The subsequent rifts in the marriage with Linda are to be explained away not by Cole's lusts for other partners but by his all-consuming obsession with his musical shows. "You shouldn't have gotten married in the first place," scolds Porter's friend, Monte Woolley (played by himself). "In the second place, as long as you did, act like a husband instead of a guy who shouldn't have gotten married in the first place!" As for the riding accident in 1937 that disabled Porter for the rest of his life, even Hollywood couldn't have devised anything more appropriate to its purposes. Here was the ideal opportunity to confirm through suffering his nobility and strength of character. In all the foregoing ways, insisted Wallis, Porter and his work could be seen as "springing from the heart of a normal American homelife."[77]

The sometimes ribald — even risqué — nature of Porter's stage shows and lyrics were also something of a problem. While wildly popular on the stage, were still too much for the screen. For example, a letter from the Production Code's Joseph Breen to Jack Warner cautioned against suggesting a "strip-tease" in the "My Heart Belongs to Daddy" sequence. A later memo, from 20 August 1945, detailed the items of clothing and the order of their removal in this number. One Arthur Houghton advised, "We have informed [the dance choreographer] that it was decidedly an unacceptable strip tease, that we would report to the staff in the morning about our visit, and told him how unacceptable the showing of underwear was at all times."[78] Two weeks later, Breen wrote to Jack Warner listing problematic words in the Porter songs: "hell" in "Blow, Gabriel, Blow;" "cocaine" in "I Get a Kick out of You;" "she strayed" in "Miss Otis Regrets;" and "in the all-together" in "Let's Not Talk about Love." "It is of great importance," Breen scolded, "that you make the eliminations suggested herein in as much as this material is almost certain to be eliminated by Censor Boards everywhere."[79]

But the biggest problem still had to be addressed — Porter's sexuality. Specifically, Porter was gay in an era when coming out of the closet was tantamount to professional suicide. He had carried on the pretense of a heterosexual public life while maintaining an actively gay private life. Moreover, his marriage to

Linda was probably a marriage of mutual convenience, as she allegedly carried on affairs of her own.[80] The subject of homosexuality, as has been pointed out in Chapter One, if not exactly forbidden by the Motion Picture Production Code, was certainly discouraged.[81] Thus, it was in Porter's best interests to support Wallis's determination to "normalize" his sexuality. If Porter were forbidden by the script to look at another woman, now he was also abjured not to look at another *man*. As the script tap dances around these issues, the effect is occasionally rather comic, intended or otherwise. Witness this exchange in the finished film between Porter and a singer in a sheet music store:

> GIRL: I work with lots of piano players. They make propositions. They're always trying. You haven't made a single pass. You treat me as if I were a lady. Frankly, Mr. Porter, I resent it!
> PORTER: I never realized. Here, have a sandwich.
> GIRL: I know I've got natural attributes. I'll be frank, Mr. Porter, you've got natural attributes, too. Seems a shame we can't "attribute" with each other.
> PORTER: You're extremely attractive, Carol. But you're not eating your sandwich.

The production of *Night and Day* seems to have been an unpleasant one for everyone involved — except Porter himself. Jack Moffitt, who first brought the idea to Warner Bros. and wrote the initial script, was highly critical of ensuing drafts. There was a great deal of tension between Cary Grant and director Michael Curtiz over changes in dialogue and bits of "stage business." The production schedule record of 29 September 1945 shows that Curtiz "stormed off the set at 3:30 AM" after arguing with Grant. Curtiz also had a rough time with costar Jane Wyman, who complained that she was "little more than an extra," while Curtiz insisted that she was padding her part shamelessly.[82] Further, Grant seems to have tried to exert influence on more than simply his own dialogue. Unit Manager Eric Stacey wrote on 5 September 1945, "I don't think there is a set in this picture that has not been changed by Cary and it has cost this studio a terrific amount of money."[83] All that Sturm und Drang was not reflected in the film itself, however, and Porter was highly satisfied at the idealized version of his own life. The critics liked it, too, while admitting its distance from the facts.

"The film," wrote a critic for the *Hollywood Reporter,* "is obviously less concerned with a note-by-note Porter history than with using parts of his career as a framework for a cavalcade of his deft lyrics and tunes. . . . Now not once during the entire progress of the hit parade does any character stop to admire the miracle of the genius of the man the picture celebrates. This is a major virtue seldom encountered in film biographies. Other biographers please note."[84] *Variety* put it a little more succinctly: "Story is billed as 'based on the career of Cole Porter' — which means that a lead character is given the name of 'Cole Porter' and put through the sequences of the standard biographical film."[85]

MGM's new Porter biopic, *De-Lovely*, released in 2004 and starring Kevin Kline and Ashley Judd as Cole and Linda, brings Porter into the new century of revisionist biography. His homosexual proclivities are openly depicted, and wife Linda is portrayed as a tolerant and understanding companion who objects to his behavior only when it becomes increasingly inconvenient and/or indiscreet. Of particular interest is a scene wherein Cole and Linda attend a screening of *Night and Day*. As the the "real" Porters confront their fictionalized screen counterparts, they marvel at the film's climactic reunion between Grant, hobbling on crutches, and a tearful Smith. After the screening, Kevin Kline's Porter remarks to Ashley Judd's Linda, "If I can survive that, I can survive anything. Why did Linda come back to him?" The response: "Because he's Cary Grant." They walk on for a few more moments. "Well," says Porter, "at least they gave us a happy ending." As a piece of metacinema, scenes like this, scripted by Jay Cocks, function as a revisionist critique of not just *Night and Day* but the sanitizing formulas of the standard classical Hollywood biopic in general.

Just as Porter assisted the studio in making a "biography" that had little or no relation to the facts of his life, so too did Richard Rodgers cooperate with MGM in the production of *Words and Music* (1948). As early as 1944, only a few months after Hart's death, the studio began planning a biography or "cavalcade" on the lives and music of Rodgers and Hart. On 25 September 1946, a contract was arranged with Rodgers, who was the executor of the Hart estate. He fully intended to smooth over some of the rough spots of the career and character of his partner. Rodgers was granted approval of the script, and a studio memo stated that "reasonable consideration" would be given to Rodgers's "suggestions."[86] Perhaps as a safeguard against the practice of composing additional music (as had happened in *My Gal Sal*), it was also stipulated contractually that "Loew's may not change Rodgers and Hart's music and not interpolate numbers written by others."[87]

The script was assigned to Guy Bolton, a prolific Broadway producer and playwright. He began tailoring the screenplay to Frank Sinatra, who was to play Rodgers, and Gene Kelly, who was cast as Hart. The working title was "The Lives of Rodgers and Hart," since *Words and Music* had already been registered by the Fox Film Corp. and had already been used as the title of a 1929 movie musical starring Helen Twelvetrees and featuring a brief appearance by a young John Wayne (still billed as "Duke Morrison"). MGM had to ask Fox for a waiver on the title, which was finally granted in 1946. By that time, Sinatra and Kelly had been replaced by Tom Drake as Rodgers and Mickey Rooney as Hart.

Rodgers's intention to be as honest as possible about Hart's personal problems ran afoul of the Production Code office. A censor named "Jackson" complained to Louis B. Mayer, "There seems to be an unnecessary amount of references to liquor and drinking in this script."[88] In an earlier letter, dated 7 April 1948, Jackson urged "that you cut down any emphasis on liquor and drinking, possibly substituting hors d'oeuvres as a prop to replace liquor."[89] In addition to Hart's drinking, there was also the then inconvenient fact of his homosexuality. According to many who knew him, Hart was more open and "out of the closet" than many men of his era, but homosexuality was still a taboo subject for the movies. Thus in *Words and Music*, Hart is given a female love interest, "Peggy McNeil" (Betty Garrett). In the final analysis, despite the censorial restrictions of the studio system of the 1940s, the problematic aspects of Hart's life are treated with a surprising frankness. *Words and Music* may be no more factual than most composer biopics, but in many ways it seems the most honest of them all.

Not that the critics seemed to care, or even notice. "It's the tunes, not the lives of the individuals, that are remembered, and Metro has showcased the old heart-warmers beautifully," enthused *Variety's* critic.[90] The *Hollywood Reporter* agreed: "It is such an outstanding job in the revue department that one gladly forgives the story — which doesn't matter."[91] And *Variety* chimed in again, the next day: "The saga of Rodgers and Hart itself is neither very interesting nor exceptional. . . . While details are freely reshuffled, the yarn is strikingly sound from an overall psychological view, catching Hart's early zest for life and its gradual change to a to a tragic chase after a happiness he couldn't achieve, a chase that led to his death in 1943 at age of 47."[92] Perhaps not surprisingly, Oscar Hammerstein does not appear in this film at all, despite the fact that Rodgers broke up his partnership with Hart, two years before Hart's death, to work with Hammerstein on a remarkable string of Broadway (and later movie) hits such as *Oklahoma!, Carousel,* and *The Sound of Music.*

Rhapsody in Blue, a Warner Bros. biopic about George Gershwin, benefited at least in part from supervision by George's brother and lyricist, Ira, who turned over their rights to George's story to Warner Bros. in 1941 for $100,000. Ira explained to Gershwin biographer Elsie Goldberg that, as of 1940 the studio was interested only in the rights to the music "in a so-called cavalcade." He continued: "They were not interested in me as a screen writer because my specialty was lyrics and because even if I had had a screen playwright credit, they felt the subject was too close to me and I would be too sensitive and tentative wherever liberties had to be taken."[93] A few months later, Ira wrote to Goldberg again: "Since the summer of 1941 I have had nothing to do officially with the film nor have I received any compensation after being paid for my rights. However, I am naturally interested and whenever I am called about this or that item or asked about a certain song etc., etc., I try to be helpful. After all I want to see a good picture which although fictionalized and telescoped to a great extent is still about my brother and contains his music and a good many of my lyrics."[94] Actor Herbert Rudley was eventually cast to play Ira Gershwin. "[Ira Gershwin] said he didn't have any suggestions about how to play him," Rudley later said. "I told him I guessed the characterization would be a lot of Rudley and very little Gershwin, and he said that was all right."[95]

However, Warner Bros.'s $100,000 did buy ten weeks of Ira's time, during which he was to consult with two screen writers, Robert Rossen and Katherine Scolar. Later, playwright Clifford Odets was brought onto the project, and he interviewed Ira's mother and other friends of George's. "The time [Odets] spent with me," Ira wrote, "was devoted mostly to playing records of Gershwin music so he could acquaint himself with all the musical possibilities. Outside of our immediate family and an occasional character like Oscar Levant, the rest of the cast is entirely fictional, as is the love story, etc. There are some things in it my family and I will undoubtedly argue about and I'm sure the Warners will listen to reasonable protests but in the last analysis they have absolute final say on story, cast and choice of music. . . . Naturally it will not be an actual documentary film on George but if the director captures some of George's personality and if whatever music that is used is well done I'll settle for that."[96] For his part, Odets wrote to Jack Warner, promising, "This story should make a distinguished and entertaining picture. If it does not do so it is solely the fault of the writer (unless, of course, someone puts in Mickey Rooney to play Gershwin!)."[97]

Robert Rossen's experience with *Rhapsody in Blue* was not an entirely happy one. After working on the script for five weeks, he complained of his difficulties with the project in a memo: "If you tell the true story, it is dull. If you intend, as I attempted to do in an outline that I made for Mr. Wallis, it strays too far from the truth and makes the story anything but the life of Gershwin. Thus far, I have found it impossible to become enthusiastic over any invented material. I am bearing in mind the fact that Gershwin's death is only a recent thing, and that incidents in his life are still well known to many people who are alive and who have taken part in that life. For the past week, ever since I spoke to Mr. Wallis, I have been getting together scenes that would dramatize the story outline that I suggested. But I cannot seem to be able to make them hang together. They just don't have meaning and collapse in front of me."[98]

Odets didn't have a much easier time of it. In a letter to Jack Warner, he wrote: "Truthfully, this job is no cinch. There is a vast amount of disconnected and extremely undramatic material in the life of Gershwin. It is almost the matter of the old joke about the song writer — 'and then I wrote my next hit!' In other words, I have started from scratch."[99] Still later, writer Sonya Levien was brought in to polish the screenplay. Of all the writers actively involved in the process, it was she who had the closest personal and professional connection to George Gershwin. Levien had worked with the composer in Hollywood and had been a good friend during his last days.[100] Levien, Howard Koch, and Elliot Paul were the only writers who ultimately received screen credit on *Rhapsody in Blue*.

To the studio, the Gershwin hits were always more important than the biographical facts. In a letter to the studio's music director, Leo Forbstein, producer "R. J." had this to say regarding the use of music: "We may paraphrase, adapt, arrange, transpose, add to or subtract from any or all of same and can use the same for incidental scoring and may interpolate other music by way of incidental music whether such interpolated music has been composed by George Gershwin or not. . . . As to any interpolated music and as to changing the basic melody of any of Gershwin's compositions, we must first get Ira Gershwin's approval."[101] Although the finished product was essentially a fiction based on the life of George Gershwin, *Rhapsody in Blue* was filled with incidental touches of authenticity. Eight original members of the Paul Whiteman Orchestra were assembled for the scenes in the Aeolian Hall where "Rhapsody in Blue" was first performed. Hazel Scott, famed black pianist and singer, played herself in the Paris scene performing "My Man." Several paintings by George Gershwin were used in the film. His actual table/desk was used in the composing scenes.

These touches aside, *Rhapsody in Blue* struck virtually no one as an authentic telling of George Gershwin's life. Many critics went out of their way to point out the film's many inaccuracies. Barry Ulanov, editor of *Metronome,* pointed out a few of the howlers:

> Gershwin is represented as a man of 25 or 30 working at Remicks, although he was actually 16. He sells himself to Max Dreyfus of Harms on the basis of "Swanee," though he really didn't write the song until two years after joining Dreyfus' staff. Dreyfus sells the song to Al Jolson over the phone at this same time, two years before it was written, though Jolson actually didn't pick up "Swanee" until three years after that, a year after it was first written and

performed. Gershwin's major music teacher is called Professor Frank, though his name was actually Charles Hambitzer; his age is doubled to permit Albert Basserman to shake melodramatically through the role [Basserman, it will be recalled, had portrayed Beethoven four years before in the Schubert biopic *Melody Master*]. But Hambitzer died at 37 and wasn't likely to have sported white hair and the halting gait of an 80-year-old. Furthermore, he was known to have thoroughly disapproved of popular music rather than making a compromising acceptance of it, which the teacher does in this film. In connection with his part, there is some crude melodrama: he dies listening to a broadcast of "Rhapsody in Blue" from the Aeolian Hall concert at which it was introduced by Paul Whiteman. But this was February, 1924, radio was only three and a half years old, and concerts were not being broadcast from remote locations. Two entirely false romances are introduced in the film and into Gershwin's life, in order to serve Warners' fanciful conception of "real life" and its contractual obligations, perhaps, to its female stars. At the piano of a Paris night club, in 1925, sits Hazel Scott (called by her own name) playing "The Man I Love," "Fascinatin' Rhythm," and "I Got Rhythm." Hazel was three years old at the time; "I Got Rhythm" wasn't written until 1930.[102]

Other critics were not quite so exhaustive in their objections, but they tended to be just as adamant. The *Hollywood Reporter* called the film "pretty dull" and promised that "audiences will get a feeling of having been cheated out of a movie and dragged into listening to Gershwin numbers."[103] Bosley Crowther, writing for the *New York Times*, wrote: "The craftsmen who made the picture were apparently so utterly confused by the complex nature of the subject — or so determined to show a 'genius' type — that their profile of Mr. Gershwin is a hobbled and vague affair. . . . Robert Alda plays Mr Gershwin in an opaque, mechanical way which gives little intelligence of the character — and not much more of the way he really looked."[104]

Problematizing Ethnicity and Gender

The peak studio years in Hollywood, as we have seen, contributed to a collective fantasy on screen that not only "whitened" America but also diminished feminine agency. For example, Foster's Jeanie, Porter's Linda, "Alexander's" Stella, and Kern's Eva, to cite but a few examples, were women who were present primarily to perform the songs and/or provide their men with inspiration and support (except when they were chiding them for neglecting domestic duties for professional goals). They were never professional composers in their own right.[105]

Gender, racial, and ethnic identities were blurred, if not outright erased, as a result of the assimilation processes depicted in the Tin Pan Alley biopics, beginning with *The Jazz Singer* (as they were in the majority of Hollywood's mainstream pictures). One looks in vain for a trace of ethnicity in the portraits of Berlin, Kern, Hart, and Gershwin. Even Ernest Ball's "biography," *Irish Eyes Are Smiling* (1944), while reveling in the Irish-themed songs that Ball wrote with various lyricists and performers (notably Chauncy Olcott), ignored Ball's Irish background entirely, portraying him simply as an All-American tunesmith who just happened to turn out hits like "Mother Machree," "Ireland Is Ireland to Me," and "When Irish Eyes Are Smiling." This is all the more puzzling, given Hollywood's traditional eagerness to embrace blarney of any sort.

If Hispanics, Jews, Native Americans, African Americans, and other minorities and people of color appeared at all, they were, with few exceptions, secondary characters (like servants, maids, and other "faithful family retainers") — caricatures that served as the targets of stereotyped humor. The situation with African-American characters and black culture generally was particularly problematic and requires extended examination. Few biopics give any indication that there were any black publishers or composers on the Alley, or that white composers benefited from connections and/or affiliations with them. "Because blacks could not entirely be denied their role in the genesis of jazz and swing," writes historian Krin Gabbard, "filmmakers had to acknowledge their importance without departing from the entrenched practice of denying black subjectivity."[106]

Thus, on the rare occasions when African Americans appear, they merely serve as a kind of obbligato to the main action. In *Swanee River,* for example, they supply musical cues for Foster's writing of "Oh! Susanna" and "Old Black Joe." In *Stars and Stripes Forever* they dutifully obey Sousa's injunction to accompany him in a performance of "Battle Hymn of the Republic."[107] This sort of appropriation of black culture by a white consumer class is spelled out in no uncertain terms in *Till the Clouds Roll By.* Whereas in the prologue, a black performer, Caleb Peterson, sings "Old Man River" with a simple and moving dignity, in the finale a white-garbed Frank Sinatra takes over the song, with amusing and disturbing results. Standing atop a white pillar, surrounded by a vast pink-and-white art deco set and surrounded by a bevy of leggy chorines, young Frankie croons out the song in his smoothest manner (endowing the words "*jest* keeps rolling along" with a little too much emphasis). Critic James Agee was appalled by this White Apotheosis, objecting to its "misplaced reverence," as if it were a musical translation of the Emancipation Proclamation: "This I realize is called *feeling* for music," Agee wrote, but "for that kind of feeling I prefer W.C. Fields' cadenzas on the zither."[108]

More difficult to classify are those occasions when viewers can't precisely determine a performer's racial identity. There was nothing accidental about this feat of Hollywood sleight of hand. The staging of the "Blue Monday Blues" number in *Rhapsody in Blue* utilizes a whole complement of dancers and singers who are dressed and made-up in a manner carefully calculated to keep viewers guessing about their racial identity (historian Gabbard's claim that the performers are wearing blackface is not convincing).[109] And in *Stormy Weather,* an all-black musical revue purporting to chronicle the career of legendary black tap dancer Bill "Bojangles" Robinson, skin color seems to be relatively incidental, if not irrelevant, to the plot. At first glance this survey of twenty-five years of African-American music might seem to be the black alternative to *Alexander's Ragtime Band.* On closer inspection, however, the two films display not only a resemblance but a marked similarity. As film historian Gerald Mast has pointed out, with the exception of Fats Waller's gutsy rendition of "Ain't Misbehavin'," "black life and entertainment look no different from white life and entertainment in the Fox films that survey the same turf with the same plot."[110] Most of the music numbers "take the high white road," like those featuring Cab Calloway in his trademark white tails, the Nicholas Brothers in their impeccable tuxedos, the Katherine Dunham Dancers in their stylish ballet, and a light-skinned Lena Horne in her "I Can't Give You Anything But Love" number.[111]

During all this time, only twelve biopics about nonwhite Americans appeared, and only one was about a black composer. *St. Louis Blues,* a Paramount film directed by Allen Reisner and released in 1958 on the occasion of W. C. Handy's death, would seem at first glance to be a landmark film in the history of biopics. Alone among the period's biopics, it foregrounds an African-American composer; traces the rise of the blues as a popular American music form; boasts an all-black cast, including Nat "King" Cole as Handy, Eartha Kitt as blues singer Go Go Germaine, Pearl Bailey as Handy's Aunt Hagar, Juano Hernandez as Handy's father, and Ella Fitzgerald as herself; and depicts the rise of a musically untutored black artist from poverty and obscurity to wealth and acclaim. In the public's mind, at least, Handy was to the blues what Foster was to the vernacular ballad and Scott Joplin was to ragtime.

Handy was born in Florence, Alabama, in 1873, the son of a minister in a church-going community that frowned on secular music. "My father was a preacher," he recalls in his autobiography, *Father of the Blues* (1955), "and he was bent on shaping me for the ministry. Becoming a musician would be like selling my soul to the devil."[112] As a teenager, he joined a band but kept it a secret from his disapproving parents. In 1892 he took a temporary teaching job in Birmingham and married four years later. Thereafter, the

restless Handy lived, taught, and worked in many places, including Evansville, Indiana; Henderson, Kentucky; Clarksville, Mississippi; Chicago; and
St. Louis. It was a rough life, and the impoverished Handy learned the realities behind that sorrowful, plangent music he heard along the Mississippi
River, known as the "blues." "Southern Negros sang about everything," he recalled. "Trains, steamboats, steam whistles, sledge hammers, fast women,
mean bosses, stubborn mules—all become subjects for their songs. . . . [This
music] consisted of simple declarations expressed usually in three lines and set
to a kind of earth-born music that was familiar throughout the Southland."

He didn't relocate to Memphis until 1909 at age thirty-six, where he performed in a number of venues, including Dixie Park and the Alaskan Roof
Garden. Meanwhile, he was composing, and three years later he wrote and
published "Memphis Blues," a landmark event in the popularization of blues
music. In 1915 he became only the second black artist to establish a music
publishing company, Pace & Handy (later the Handy Brothers Music Company). After relocating the business to Tin Pan Alley in New York City, he
published his most famous song, "St. Louis Blues." Its popularity was phenomenal, and it has been subsequently praised by African-American poet
Langston Hughes as "the greatest American song written in our time [which]
would someday be the basis for great ballets and sonatas."[113] At the same
time, Handy composed and arranged dozens of spirituals and church hymns.
On 15 February 1919 he consolidated his new "respectability" when he joined
James Reece Europe and the Clef Club Orchestra in a program of blues and
jazz at a Carnegie Hall concert. "It was no longer possible," writes historian
Albert Murray, "to restrict blues music to the category of folk expression."[114]
For the rest of his life, Handy worked tirelessly to promote and disseminate
blues and ragtime music. His own music was performed not just in popular
venues, but by symphony orchestras in many concert halls across America.
"Handy looked at folk songs as source material for the creation of something
bigger and better," writes historian Hugues Panassie. "[He] adopted the white
folklorists' approach to folk songs as material to be mined and transmuted
into something more respectable and grand."[115] Chronically afflicted with a
visual disability, Handy went totally blind late in life after suffering a subway
station accident. He died in 1958.

Handy's work had first come to the screen in 1929, when independent
filmmaker Dudley Murphy produced a two-reel Photophone short subject, *St.
Louis Blues,* in which Bessie Smith recreated for the cameras her celebrated
interpretation of the eponymous song. Nine years later Paramount studios
approached Handy about a feature-film dramatization, but nothing came of
it. (A 1939 Paramount Dorothy Lamour vehicle by that name has nothing to

do with the Handy story.) By the time Paramount did succeed in bringing a Handy biopic to the screen, in 1958, his autobiography had been published. The film script by Robert Smith and Ted Sherdeman, while observant of some of the book's main features, departed from it in significant ways.

Most of the movie's action takes place in Memphis, which, contrary to Handy's account, is depicted as his lifelong home (a suggestion doubtlessly welcomed and endorsed by the Memphis Chamber of Commerce). Young William's interest in secular music is indeed violently discouraged by his reverend father, as Handy's book alleged, who angrily brands jazz and blues as "the Devil's music." So obdurate is the good Reverend, that Handy has to pursue his interests in secret, signing on to perform with a fictitious singer named Go Go Germaine (Eartha Kitt) at a notorious (and likewise fictitious) nightspot called the Big Rooster Club. Handy is smitten with Germaine, but his marriage proposal is turned down. Germaine is convinced of Handy's genius, if not his romantic attractions, and decides to take his songs to New York City. The disconsolate Handy remains behind in Memphis.

Suddenly, without warning, Handy suffers an inexplicable attack of blindness (references to his failing eyesight are absent in Handy's book). In an episode wholly fabricated by the screenwriters, he turns to composing church hymns out of penance for betraying his father's religion. One day while performing one of his new hymns at a church service, he miraculously regains his sight. Inspired by this recovery, and newly determined to pursue his blues music, he leaves Memphis and goes on the road to perform his music from town to town.

Back in Memphis, news reaches Handy's family that his "St. Louis Blues" is scheduled on a concert program in the prestigious Aeolian Hall in New York City (site of the legendary, self-proclaimed "Experiment in Modern Music" concert on 12 February 1924 that introduced George Gershwin's *Rhapsody in Blue*)[116]. It is a glittering, upscale event, featuring the all-white New York Symphony orchestra in evening dress conducted by that presumably esteemed European artist, Constantin Bakaleinikoff (an amusing detail, considering that in real life Bakaleinikoff was a studio composer for Paramount studios)[117]. "This is Aeolian Hall," whispers Go Go Germaine to the arriving Handy family. "No dancing, no drinking. People pay three dollars and thirty cents a seat and listen to great music." After the concluding Mendelssohn's Third Symphony, Bakaleinikoff steps forward to make an announcement regarding the next selection on the program. "Ladies and gentlemen," he begins, "you ask why the Symphony Orchestra would play the blues. . . the only pure art form to originate in America. Only in the art of a new folk music is America pre-eminent. One man, more than any others, is responsible for that fact, W. C. Handy."

Whereupon the orchestra launches into a full-blown symphonic arrangement of "St. Louis Blues." Handy steps forward, dapper and trim in his tuxedo, to sing the lyrics. It is a triumphant occasion, even if the only African Americans present are Handy and his family, who are relegated to a backstage peek at the proceedings. Fade out. "[The Father] is won over," dryly remarks historian Gabbard, "at least in part by the majesty of the symphony hall and the spectacle of white men in tuxedos playing violins."[118] There is at least a kernel of truth in this climactic sequence. In his autobiography Handy reports that Paul White-man played the "St. Louis Blues" in concert arrangements several times, once at Carnegie Hall, and again in 1936 at the Hippodrome. Introducing it was the well-known composer and writer Deems Taylor, whose quoted words bear a similarity to the speech given in the film by Bakaleinikoff.[119]

St. Louis Blues is obviously cut from the same cloth as the other Tin Pan Alley biopics discussed in this chapter. Most obviously, it displays significant parallels with the *Blossom Time–Jazz Singer* paradigm already cited, wherein a young artist struggles against class and ethnic prejudice in his effort to legitimize vernacular music. Handy embodies the by now familiar "possessed" paradigm, an African-American version of Franz Schubert and Stephen Foster. His music comes from an instinctive response to the immediate world around him, not from formal training and Old World imitations. (In this regard, at least, Handy's autobiography supports this contention.)[120] He is a curiously passive, lovelorn creature, marginalized by society and condemned — until the very end, at least, when he is taken up and endorsed by the New York classical establishment — to find solace and fulfillment only in his single-minded devotion to his music. (Significantly, there is no mention in the film of Handy's business endeavors, of his publishing firm, and of his indefatigable labors in behalf of the popularization of blues music. His passive genius rather than his more masculine, activist industry is privileged.)

Handy's racial identity has been mostly erased. As Gabbard points out with heavy irony, *St. Louis Blues* bears a significant affinity with another jazz-related Paramount film that year, the Elvis Presley vehicle *King Creole*. Nat "King" Cole's Handy is the inverse of Presley, writes Gabbard, "a restrained black man acting 'white' rather than a shameless white man acting 'black.' "[121] Moreover, Cole's stiffly formal and sacralized concert rendition of "St. Louis Blues" is not altogether dissimilar from Sinatra's "whitened" rendition of "Old Man River" in the climactic scene in *Till the Clouds Roll By*. That Handy is an African American living and working in a black community in the racist, segregationist South is scarcely apparent. There is nary a hint of bigotry and oppression — a striking departure from the oppressive social milieu and numerous racist incidents described in Handy's autobiography. In the film

Handy seems unaware of the painful origins of blues music. Indeed, the only moment when he acknowledges it as a distinctly black expression comes in a brief declaration he makes to his father: "The music I play is the music of our people. It's not mine, it's theirs. Are our people evil because they sing other songs besides hymns? I was born with this music in me."

What that music really *is*, however, what relation it bears to the milieu in which Handy lived, and what it contributed to American mainstream music is ignored altogether. Ultimately, as we have seen, his blues are sanitized and clothed in symphonic garb for the edification of white musicians and the white folks in the audience of the hallowed precincts of Aeolian Hall. Its rough edges and gritty textures are smoothed out and rendered acceptable to the predominantly white middle-class audiences of the American movie-going public.

The star system is a crucial factor in the conception, execution, and reception of *St. Louis Blues*. Obviously, it is tailored to Cole's image and talents. Perhaps, as Gabbard claims, only the presence of Cole enabled it to be made at all: "Cole functioned as a healthy alternative to the unsavory image of the drug-crazed, psyched-up black jazz artist that had been thoroughly inscribed on the American mind by the late 1950s."[122] A comfortable, familiar, non-confrontational presence, viewers knew him either from his television variety series that had premiered the year before (a breakthrough in network television), his career in the early 1940s as an esteemed jazz artist, his previous appearances in the films *The Blue Gardenia* (1953) and *China Gate* (1957), among others, or as a popular singer identified with such mainstream classics as "The Christmas Song."

Accordingly, Hollywood was quick to exploit the alleged similarity of Cole's and Handy's backgrounds. Cole claimed that the issue of religious music versus popular music was one that he had confronted in his own life and that made him identify with Handy. "Both of us were the sons of ministers," Cole said, "and both our fathers firmly disapproved of our playing jazz. It took a long time before my father became reconciled to my singing, as it did with Mr. Handy."[123] And, like the Handy of the film, Cole was known as the composer and singer of many of his own songs (his "Straighten up and Fly Right" was for him the "breakthrough" equivalent of Handy's "St. Louis Blues"). Thus, he, too, played a significant role in bringing jazz and the image of the black artist into the mainstream of American entertainment.

Although the earnestness and good intentions of *St. Louis Blues* are beyond dispute, the sad fact is that the end product, including Cole's performance, is a stiff, stodgy, and bloodless affair. "The life, times and music of the late W.C. Handy, from age 10 to 40, are dealt with carefully, respectfully, and more slowly than is good for the project," wrote critic William R. Weaver in *Motion*

Picture Daily. "The filming is done with a care bordering on reverence."[124] "The cast is all-Negro, except for very minor roles," wrote *Variety*'s "Powr." "A real and successful effort has been made to avoid any possible charge of 'Uncle Tom' in the characters. But for this reason or others, the result is such a genteel portrayal of life in Memphis in the early years of this century that you might wonder why the Negroes ever sang the blues. The blues certainly came in part out of the spirituals that expressed the deep and justified melancholy of the Negro. They came from laborers' folk songs, but they also came from the honky-tonks, the bordellos and the bistros, and this is barely indicated."[125]

Before leaving this subject, it is worth noting that an alternative to the "whitening" strategies of *St. Louis Blues* is depicted in a relatively unknown, independently produced film with an all-black cast called *Broken Strings* (1940), directed and written by Bernard B. Ray and distributed by International Roadshow Pictures. Not a biopic about a real-life musician, *Broken Strings* is yet another variant of *The Jazz Singer* paradigm, only the fictional protagonist here is not Jewish but black. Violinist Johnny Williams's (William Washington) passion for swing music runs him afoul of his father, Arthur (Clarence Muse), a renowned classical violinist who has lost the use of his left hand in an automobile accident. Like the Reverend Handy, Arthur is determined to block his son's ambitions. "I'll drill the skill of the Masters into you and drive out the spirit of jazz," he sternly admonishes Johnny, "if I have to make you practice twenty hours straight." But young Johnny is undaunted. "I'd like to play like a bird flies, up and down, winging and swinging through the air — no control, just music," he declares, whereupon he and his accompanist launch into a "swing" version of Antonín Dvořák's famous "Humoresque." "You're desecrating a classic," growls Arthur, "committing a crime against music." When Johnny learns he can win enough money in an amateur radio contest to pay for his father's hand operation, he enters the competition. The ensuing radio concert parallels the Carnegie Hall concert in *St. Louis Blues*. In words echoing Bakaleinikoff's declaration of the virtues of the blues, the radio producer steps to the microphone and says, "We are considered one of the most musical peoples on earth, because we have suffered. Music washes away from the soul the dust of everyday life. There's beauty in all music — classical, swing, jazz." As his father listens grudgingly in the audience, Johnny interrupts his classical performance with some "hot" jazz riffs and wins the prize money. His father reluctantly breaks into applause — only to discover that he has suddenly recovered the use of his hand. The healing of his infirmity symbolizes the reconciliation with his son and validates the vernacular expression of his people. "My heart still belongs to the Masters," the proud father declares, "but look what swing has done for me!"

Whereas the Handy of *St. Louis Blues* compromises his blues music to the European classical stylings of a symphony orchestra — at the risk of losing its black identity altogether — Johnny wins a victory in the liberation of his swing music from its classical constraints. Classical music does not function as a desired end here, as it seems to do in *St. Louis Blues;* rather, as commentator Adam Knee claims, it is a point of departure: Johnny's improvisations demonstrate that "[swing] represents a means of escape from a broader social oppression" that classical music represents. Black identity is privileged and retained in the face of assimilation.[126]

They Write the Songs

As was seen in the chapter about classical composer biopics, the visualization of the creative process is a continuing challenge for filmmakers. Consistent with the biopic paradigm, creativity has to be "normalized" and rendered understandable to the average viewer. The long hours of a composer's training in composition, harmony, and instrumentation would seem to play little part in the visualization process. Instead, a favorite Hollywood ploy was to place the composer in a setting whose sights and sounds could be counted upon to stimulate a creative response, provoking in the inspired artist a sort of musical "automatic writing" (evoking the paradigm of the "possessed" composer outlined earlier in these pages). "Every time I pick up a law book," explains Porter in *Night and Day* to his mother, "I hear a tune. Every contract I read turns into a lyric. I don't know how it happens or where it comes from. But there it is." In *Swanee River,* after listening to the chants of black slaves unloading a merchant ship, Foster rushes into a saloon to bang out "Oh! Susanna" on the piano.[127] In *Yankee Doodle Dandy,* when Cohan hears a trumpet call at a World War I rally, "Over There!" is instantly born. In a burst of imaginative reconstruction in *Till the Clouds Roll By,* Kern's scenarists depict him writing "Old Man River" while in Memphis, his interior monologue accompanying his nocturnal walk along the banks of the Mississippi River: "I walked along the river that night, with the river wind in my face and the taste of it on my lips. And I stood there, listening. The sudden excitement was thrilling to me, listening to the song of a river that makes its way right through the heart of America. and the voice of that river was the laughter, the tears, the joys, the sorrows, the hopes of all Americans."[128]

And, in a similar situation, in *Stars and Stripes Forever,* Sousa strides the deck of a ship under foggy night skies, musing to himself: "Suddenly, as I paced the deck, I began to sense the rhythmic beat of a band playing in my head, ceaselessly, echoing and re-echoing the most distinct melody. Though I did not

Clifton Webb gave a stiff upper lip to John Philip Sousa in Darryl F. Zanuck's *Stars and Stripes Forever* (1952). (Courtesy Photofest/Twentieth Century-Fox)

know it then, my brain band was composing my most popular march—not one note of which, once I had transferred it to paper, would ever be changed."

In *Tin Pan Alley,* Jack Oakie spends most of his screen time trying to fashion lyrics to a catchy tune. Determined that the words should refer to a geographical place name, he tries a variety of two- and three-syllable options, including "Dixie," "Hawaii," "Ireland," "Australia," and "Bermuda" ("Bermuda, lovely Bermuda, where the onions and the lilies scene the air"). It's not until near the end of the film, when our frustrated lyricist stumbles over the name of his pal's girl friend, "Katie," that the song achieves its final, familiar form: "K-K-K-Katie." A similar strategy is deployed in *Three Little Words,* wherein the title song appears throughout the first two-thirds of the picture only as a melodic fragment attached to a succession of (ultimately) discarded lyrics. It is only at the very end, during an argument between Kalmar and Ruby, that the "three little words" of the title are finally adopted as the rightful lyrics. Lest we dismiss this example of fortuitous bi-association as just another Hollywood hallucination, we should remember that more than one song standard has evolved under similar circumstances.[129]

By far the most elaborate and (in my opinion) beautifully crafted creative "reconstructions" in these films — at least in a cinematic sense — are two set pieces in *Night and Day* and *Rhapsody in Blue*. In the first Porter is convalescing from wartime wounds in a French hospital (as explained earlier, a wholly fictitious scene). A high-angle shot reveals him in his dressing gown sitting at the piano, his cane resting against the bench, a clock ticking audibly in the stillness. Absently, he strikes a note on the keyboard. He repeats it. When the clock interrupts and strikes the hour, he imitates the sound in the bass register. As if in a trance, he speaks: "Like the tick-tick-tock of the stately clock as it stands against the wall." A pause. Rain spatters against the window. Porter touches the keys again, intoning, "Like the drip-drip-drop of the raindrops when the summer shower is through. So a voice within me keeps repeating — you, you, you!" His hands sweep across the keyboard. At that moment his wife-to-be, Linda, enters the room and turns out the lights. Seating herself beside him, she joins in and declaims: "Night and day — " He instantly finishes the phrase: " — You are the one." Another pause. He murmurs to her, "It's giving me much trouble." They chat a few moments as he fiddles with the tune. Impulsively he kisses her. He unexpectedly modulates the phrase and exclaims, "Wait a minute! I think I've got it!" The music swells up extradiegetically on the music track, fully instrumented, as the camera retreats up and away from the scene.[130]

The sequence depicting George Gershwin's creation of his famous *American in Paris* music is an imaginative traversal of space and time, a blend of diegetic performance and nondiegetic soundtrack music that cleverly elides almost ten minutes from the original score. It is, in short, a proto-music video: On a bright morning, the composer is seated in his Paris apartment, listening through the open window to the street sounds below. A car horn blares. Gershwin goes to the piano and taps out a three-note musical correlative. Without a pause, he leans forward and inscribes the title, "An American in Paris," on the music paper. As the now fully instrumented music wells up on the soundtrack, the scene dissolves to a train station. A montage of shots, seen from Gershwin's subjective point of view, follows the arrival of a traveler, the transfer of his bags (labeled "G.G.") to a waiting taxi, and a drive through the streets and boulevards. Cut back to Gershwin's studio (the time is later in the day). The composer gestures with his hands, as if conducting the soundtrack orchestra. Dissolve to a view of Notre Dame as the music's mood and pace assumes a more stately quality. Again, from the subjective point of view, our traveler alights from the cab and enters a hotel lobby, where he signs the register "George Gershwin." Cut to a street scene as the trumpet wails its memorably bluesy melody as we amble past an outdoor cafe. Cut to a ballet performance as the trumpet theme shifts to the strings (Gershwin's shadow is thrown against the wall of his box seat). Cut back to Gershwin's studio again: It's twilight now and the composer has left the piano to stand at the window. Back to Paris again, the Folies Bergere, as the raucous brass theme accompanies a line of high-kicking dancers. Cut to streams of water flowing along a brick pavement. Cut back to Gershwin's studio, as he signs his name to the music. Finally, cut to a concert hall where Walter Damrosch concludes a performance of the music. Perhaps significantly, this sequence is visualized roughly in accord with the programmatic notes that Deems Taylor and Gershwin wrote for the work's premiere.[131]

The Show *Is the Thing*

Many critics were distressed at the narrative formulas and historical distortions in these films: *The New Yorker* complained about the "exasperating cliches" and the "foolish attempts to inject synthetic melodrama" into the life of Kern; *Time* lamented *Swanee River*'s superficial treatment of Foster's creative moments ("In pictures about composers a vacant look, head noddings and rhythmic hand flourishes denote musical inspiration"); and *New York Times*'s Bosley Crowther complained that in *Rhapsody in Blue* "there is never any true clarification of what makes [Gershwin] run, no interior grasp of his nature, no dramatic continuity to his life. The whole thing unfolds in fleeting episodes, with characters viewing the genius with anxiety or awe, and the progression is not helped by many obvious and telescoping cuts." In the opinion of other critics, however, the quality of these films' *showmanship* was their mot juste.[132] Studio chief Zanuck remarked on several occasions that unless the distortions and errors in a film were particularly outrageous, or unless the history in question was too recent to be tampered with, most viewers would care only about a given film's entertainment value. For example, in a story conference memo regarding his Sousa picture, *Stars and Stripes Forever,* Zanuck insisted not on biographical accuracy so much but on pursuing an entertainment formula that had proven itself on previous biopics: "Actually, it can be a sort of combination of *Swanee River* and *My Gal Sal,* and it should be told in those terms, using the biographical framework of *Yankee Doodle Dandy.*"[133]

Thus, it is worth noting that some critics were willing to forgive *Yankee Doodle Dandy* its free and easy manner with the historical record. *Variety* wrote: "While the narrative is not wholly biographical, it is so steeped in the life and the legend of George M. Cohan as to have substantial accuracy about the man and the Broadway figure who might appropriately be termed the music laureate of his American day."[134] The *Hollywood Reporter* agreed:

"Chronologically, the picture takes several liberties with dates, but no one should mind. It is the spirit of the piece and its times that really count, a spirit captured superbly by Cagney's Cohan."[135] And *Variety*'s "Abel" wrote "that Robert Buckner, and his co-scripter, Edmund Joseph, jazzed up a little of the latter-day chronology is beside the point—that, too, is so much additional showmanship. What matters if one or another show preceded this or that of Cohan's many successes."[136] Critic Philip T. Hartung seemed to be speaking on behalf of American audiences when he remarked about *Rhapsody in Blue:* "In spirit the film succeeds in its purpose although the facts are selected and readjusted for dramatic unity, and characters are even invented to further the story and action."[137]

Even more interesting is the fact that even the more knowledgeable members of the trade endorsed the fictionalization of the world they knew. Songwriter Harry Ruby wrote to producer Arthur Freed upon seeing the Kern film, *Till the Clouds Roll By:* "In my opinion, it is the best picture of that kind thus far made and it is the way all pictures, having for their subject a composer, should be made."[138] Because *Till the Clouds Roll By* bears virtually no resemblance to the facts of Kern's life—of which Ruby would have been aware—his comment shows an enthusiastic embrace of fantasy over reality, of invention over history.

Which Life?

In conclusion, as was noted at the outset of this chapter, these biopics partake of what today is called a postmodernist "metahistorical" interrogation of the elusive meanings of biography and historical events. They engage the knowing viewer in an amusing game of peekaboo with fact and fiction. It's a game many of us willingly subscribe to. An amusing example in *Words and Music* demonstrates the point: Larry Hart (Mickey Rooney) throws a lavish party in his Hollywood estate ("Who built this place, Metro-Goldwyn-Mayer?" he quips). Among the attendees is Judy Garland, appearing as herself. Immediately, she and Hart launch into a song and dance rendition of "I Wish I Were in Love Again." Think about it. It's not so much that Hart and Garland probably never danced together (that's a justifiable quibble but hardly an important consideration). Rather, remember that this 1948 film has situated this particular scene in the mid-1930s. Garland would have been a child of thirteen, up way past her bedtime. But we accept the scene because we know she's not dancing with Hart but with Mickey Rooney. This is a "reality" that overrides the fictive "reality," because we've seen them perform so many times together in previous films (made for MGM, of course). In hindsight the moment even acquires a special poignancy when we realize it was to be the *last* time they were to appear together on screen.

Which are we to believe — the lives that these late songwriters actually led (to paraphrase a Porter song), or, as we saw at the outset with Cohan, the lives they would *wish* to have lived? When these worlds collide, we're invited to acknowledge both rather than choose just one. Perhaps the best course is to follow the immortal Yogi Berra's advice: "When you come to a fork in the road, take it!"

4

"Just an Innocent Bystander"
The Composer Films of Ken Russell

> *A man has some reason for selecting the subject of another man; and the chances are that his reason, even if perfectly reasonable, will be highly personal; and sometimes personal to the point of being perverse. There is always a possible association of a monograph with a monomania.*
> — *G. K. Chesterton*

The Wand of Youth

The telecast on 22 November 2002 on London Weekend Television of Ken Russell's *Elgar: Fantasy of a Composer on a Bicycle* brings full circle the career of a filmmaker who has gained fame and notoriety for his many biographical dramatizations of composers.[1] His breakthrough *Elgar* of forty years before, broadcast on BBC's *Monitor* television program, had inaugurated a unique sensibility in the conception and crafting of biography, art, and ideas on film—an imaginative interplay of fact and fantasy that continues to influence filmmakers today. Throughout his long career Russell's antic imagination, canny exploitation of music, dazzling showmanship, and controversial pose have conveyed to theater and television audiences worldwide insistently idiosyncratic interpretations of the lives and music of Béla Bartók (1881–1945), Arnold Bax (1883–1953), Anton Bruckner (1824–1896), Claude Debussy

(1862–1918), Frederick Delius (1862–1934), Edward Elgar (1857–1934), Franz Liszt (1811–1886), Gustav Mahler (1860–1911), Bohuslav Martinu (1890–1959), Serge Prokofiev (1891–1953), Richard Strauss (1864–1949), Pyotr Tchaikovsky (1840–1893), and Ralph Vaughan Williams (1872–1958).[2] Needless to say, they are not the only films from Russell's oeuvre to benefit from his lifelong passion for classical music; even his nominally non-musical projects for television and film, like his portraits of poets and painters, are flooded with musical references that inform and enhance their images. "Only Stanley Kubrick, among major contemporary filmmakers," writes music critic and historian Joseph Horowitz, "treats music with something like the respect and understanding Russell accords it."[3] Music is inextricably a part of his life and his art. It has always "spoken" to him in a language that he has appropriated as uniquely his own — all the more astonishing in that to this day, Russell admits he cannot read a note of music.[4] In his own experience and sensibility he declares, like one of his composer subjects, Mahler, "From Beethoven onward no music exists that does not have an inner program."[5]

It is entirely appropriate that in the twilight of his career, Russell would return to the subject of Elgar, with whom he shares an affinity bordering on identity. Like Elgar, he has been haunted all his life by the emotional and narrative implications of music he encountered in his youth. And, like Elgar, he has returned frequently to the countryside of his boyhood, the edge of the New Forest (a region just above the Isle of Wight and east of Bournemouth and fifteen miles west of Southampton, England) — an area proximate to and not unlike Elgar's beloved Malvern Hills — for locations for his films. In this context Elgar's words might well be Russell's: "The trees are singing my music, or am I singing theirs?" Russell recalls: "I've used this location many times, beginning with my first *Elgar,* and mostly for *The Music Lovers, Valentino,* and the film I did on Bruckner. The rolling wheat fields, the birch trees, the lakes and pine trees have served me well."[6]

Since Russell's youth, Elgar's music, along with the music of many other classical composers, has been bound up with the flickering images of motion pictures. "I first realized at the age of eleven, what power there could be when the right music went with the right image," he recalls. "I absorbed all those American films with scores by [Erich Wolfgang] Korngold. I appreciated the overall effect of the music and the pictures. And I used to give film shows in my dad's garage on a little hand-cranked Pathescope Ace 9.5 millimeter projector, coupled with some of the classical music I was hearing. The films generally were 'Felix the Cat' and Charlie Chaplin shorts. Then I realized you could get extension arms for the projector and show feature films. So, the next

Filmmaker Ken Russell at his home in East Boldre, Brockenhurst. (Courtesy John C. Tibbetts)

Christmas I looked around for feature movies and found some German Expressionist films. Later, with the War on, it was rather strange that I was showing these films — titles like Fritz Lang's *Metropolis* and *Siegfried* — in my dad's garage while we were being bombed by the Hun! But art knows no frontiers, so it didn't worry me too much. But it was ironic that while Siegfried was slaying the fire-breathing dragon on the screen, the Sons of Siegfried were raining down incendiary bombs all around us!"

In addition to Elgar's *Enigma Variations,* an early favorite, other music suggested itself as accompaniment to his film screenings. "One of the gramophone records I possessed had a march by [Edvard] Grieg on one side and a march by Sir Arthur Bliss from *Things to Come* on the other. I discovered quite by accident that when the modern march by Bliss coincided with *Metropolis,* that the whole screen came alive. And similarly, when Siegfried was slaying the dragon, the trumpets in the Grieg absolutely brought the scene to life yet again.[7] That's as far as my discovery went, and it wasn't until Tchaikovsky's music hit me a few years later that I got the final message of the power of music and its ability to evoke images. Something that's particularly exciting is the opportunity I have to play about with particular pieces of music, and what I think about them in the light of what I know about their composition. In a film I did much later about Gustav Holst's *The Planets,* I didn't have to use a single word of dialogue."[8]

Years later music again played a defining role in Russell's life. He had entered the Merchant Navy as Sixth Officer on a cargo ship and later volunteered to serve in the Royal Air Force. The war concluded, he returned home sick and disillusioned with the whole experience. "My next big discovery about music came when I was recovering after the war from a nervous breakdown," he says. "Back home, I just sat like a vegetable in the armchair. My mother did the vacuuming around me, and the radio would be on, for week after week. One day, something began to impinge on my consciousness. Lo and behold, it was a piece of music. It was such music that I had never heard in my life, and it brought me to. It made me wake up. I thought, I have to find out what this is called! It turned out to be the slow movement from Tchaikovsky's B-flat Minor Piano Concerto. After pumping up the flat tires to my bicycle, which had lain dormant for several months, I pedaled like mad to the nearest record shop and bought the record. And that was the beginning of my 'vision' — hearing music and seeing pictures at the same time. And I suddenly realized that Tchaikovsky's symphonic poems could be mini-movies. For instance, when I heard *Romeo and Juliet,* the whole thing flashed before my eyes. Tchaikovsky himself once said that he put his whole life into his *Pathetique* symphony."

It was at this time that Russell also began experimenting with another kind of musical experience — dance. He was determined to pursue a ballet career, he remembers, "only because I couldn't get into the movies. I studied at the Shepherd's Bush Ballet Club and had five years' training under Michael Strosigiev at the Imperial Mariensky Ballet. He used to beat me mercilessly with a very hard stick on the buttocks, shouting, 'Shoemaker! Shoemaker!, which I gather is the worst Russian swear word you can possibly utter. Hence, my interest in sado-masochism! I played Dr. Coppelius just like Dr. Caligari. I terrified matinee audiences in every southern seaside resort in England in 1949! In *Giselle* I played the Duke and wore black tights and a feather hat and a papier-mâché hunting horn. After that I was in the British Dance Theatre, so-called because it was full of Germans. We went on the road with a ballet called *Born of Desire,* to one of Grieg's *Lyric Pieces.* I was an ugly boy in bare feet. The program notes took longer to read than to watch the ballet. My mum was in the audience one time and shouted out, 'You can tell Ken's a peasant because he can't afford shoes. Ha! Ha!' "

The British Broadcasting Corporation Films

Dance does indeed play an important part in Russell's subsequent film oeuvre. One of his earliest short films for the BBC was *The Light Fantastic* (1960), a survey of dance in England, from ballroom to Morris dance; and one of his best BBC feature-length biopics is *Isadora Duncan, the Biggest Dancer in the World* (1966), starring Vivian Pickles. Moreover, as an amateur filmmaker, Russell was experimenting with musical subjects and with creative ways of conjoining film images with music. His Chaplinesque comedy short, *Peepshow* (1956), had a pianola accompaniment; *Lourdes* (1957), a documentary about the famous Catholic Shrine, borrowed music from Benjamin Britten's *Prince of the Pagodas* ballet; *Amelia and the Angel* (1957), a short fantasy, used popular tunes played on Victorian music boxes; and the seldom seen *Gordon Jacob* (1959) was a portrait of the contemporary British composer.

When these short films came to the attention of the approving Norman Swallow, assistant head of films at the BBC, the thirty-two-year-old Russell was recommended to Humphrey Burton (who in later years would become head of the BBC's Music and Arts Programmes) and producer Huw Wheldon, who was in charge of the arts program *Monitor*. And so it was that the most important and fruitful creative relationships in Russell's life began. Between 1959 and 1961 he worked on a series of fifteen-minute documentaries for Wheldon. Their relationship, while stormy at times, would prove to be crucial to Russell's emergence as a mature filmmaker. "If Ken Russell has any one model for the externals of his mature persona," writes biographer John Baxter, "it is surely this industrial *paterfamilias* [Wheldon], with his boundless physical vitality and philosopher's faith in the certainties of art."[9] Russell now acknowledges the significant impact of Wheldon's tutelage: "Wheldon was my guru. He shaped me, knocked me into shape. Taught me to think, taught me to speak, taught me to write. And inspired me in general." Russell had already had his eye on the *Monitor* program for some time, as he recalls in his autobiography, *Altered States:* "Here was a forty-five minute programme on the arts which actually dealt with esoteric themes in an accessible and exciting way. *Monitor* was one of the most prestigious programmes on television. I thought it was the best; I wanted to be part of it."[10]

Predictably, music played an important element in Russell's biographical documentaries, including *Poet's London* and *Cranks at Work* (profiles of poet John Betjeman and choreographer John Cranko, respectively). But it was with the forty-five-minute *Prokofiev: Portrait of a Soviet Composer,* broadcast on 18 June 1961, that the thirty-two-year-old Russell first embarked on what would become his signature series of composer films. There were few, if any, precedents to guide him in this sort of endeavor. "I didn't think too much about the big Hollywood movies about composers that were coming out at the time, like *A Song to Remember,*" he recalls. "They seemed like nothing more than nonsense to me. I didn't associate them with art or music. Later, with Huw Wheldon at the BBC, I was looking to do something quite different. The first music documentary I made for the BBC was on Prokofiev."[11]

Portrait of a Soviet Composer was broadcast on *Monitor* on 18 June 1961. Russell's preliminary treatment spelled out the theme: "To tell the story of a child of the Revolution who fell out of favour with Uncle Stalin when he refused to turn out muzak glorifying the USSR. At the same time it's about the responsibility of the artist to his public."[12] In a memo to the head of films, dated 7 April 1959, Swallow supported Russell's project: "My original faith in him remains, and has indeed increased by his work for Monitor. . . . In my own opinion this money would be well spent, and I would like to encourage Russell to make a complete film for us before very long."[13] However, in a memo dated 1 June 1959, he voiced an objection that would soon echo all too often in the ambitious filmmaker's ears: "This kind of thing would be much more effective if the people concerned were *suggested* rather than literally seen."[14] It provoked an argument Russell is fond of recalling: "For my visuals, I used mostly USSR documentaries. That was all I was allowed to do. I did say to Huw that it would be wonderful to show Prokofiev walking around in exile, very lonely and very disconsolate. Huw said, 'He's dead!' I said, 'Yes, I know he's dead!' He asked me if I had any moving pictures of him; and I said no, no movies. He said, 'It's impossible! We make documentaries here, we want the truth. We can't dress somebody up and pretend he's Prokoviev [*sic*]!' I said, 'I don't see why not; but could I just show his reflection in a pond?' He said, 'Only if it's a muddy pond, and you stir it up!' So, that was that. He did also let me show the pianist's hands on the piano, because that was almost an abstract kind of image."

Ironically, in addition to the use of Wheldon's voice narrative and many photos supplied by the Moscow State Archive of Literature and Art, Russell also appropriated footage from Sergei Eisenstein's *October* (1927), a reenactment of the storming of the Winter Palace (scenes that have been subsequently deployed in countless documentaries as actual representations of the Revolution). The fictive scenes cleverly mesh with archival images and music excerpts: A mother's hands guide a boy's fingers across the keyboard while playing a four-hand version of Schumann's "Wild Hunt"; at the St. Petersburg Conservatoire in 1904 the boy Prokofiev's studies are conveyed by means of brief shots of hands writing on music paper, a ticking metronome, a blurred rain-swept window. His initial notoriety in 1914 with the First Piano Concerto is accompanied by shots of bearded officials clucking disapprovingly ass the camera tracks across the sounding board of a piano.[15] Archival stills and film are used in montages depicting his 1918 visits to America and France — shots of skyscrapers, feet pounding the pavement, jostling pedestrians, taxi cabs, bunches of congratulatory flowers, and exotically costumed dancers, backed throughout by music from *The Love for Three Oranges*. Later scenes depicting Prokofiev's return to Russia employ newsreel images of Soviet industrial development — children in the factories, a stage setting backed by an enormous hammer-and-sickle flag, the building of the Volga Canal — backed by music from the Seventh Piano Sonata and the Sixth Symphony. The sad, later years of the semiexiled composer's country life are conveyed by shots of trees, watery reflections, and hands turning the pages of a book.

Despite the documentary detachment of much of this, something of Russell's political and artistic empathy with Prokofiev is in evidence. Prokofiev is initially viewed as sympathetic to the strictures of the officially sanctioned socialist realism: "From 1941 Prokofiev may have been writing music to order," intones the narrator, "but it was music that came from the heart. Like everybody else, he wanted to win the war, to cry defiance. He did it with music." Later, however, after the banning of Prokofiev's Sixth Symphony and during the denunciations by Zhdanov of Prokofiev, Shostakovich, and others at the 1948 Conference of Musicians and Composers, Wheldon's voice-over bitterly pronounces, "Prokofiev was told that he was lacking in real understanding of Soviet realism and Soviet humanity. . . . He had behaved characteristically at the meeting and sat with his back to Zhdanov." Finally, living in disrepute and semiexile, his first wife deported by the party to a work camp, Prokofiev returns to the music he wants to write. The narrative voice quotes his words: "Composing is like shooting at a moving target. Only by aiming ahead, at tomorrow, will you avoid being left behind at the level of yesterday's music. I have striven for clarity. At the same time, I have scrupulously avoided palming off familiar harmonies and tunes. That is where the difficulty of composing clean, straightforward music lies. The clarity must be new, not old."

This is clearly Russell's testament as well, one that is echoed many times in the works and words of his later films. His lifelong attempts to balance personal expression and formal clarity with the seductive lure of new forms is played out against the constraints of political censorship and critical hostility. At the same time, the issue of creative license is already being raised here. For example, Prokofiev biographer Harlow Robinson has rejected Russell's depiction of Prokofiev's presence at the Zhdanov denunciations.[16] To this, and to so many other allegations of historical inaccuracies to come in Russell's films, it may be necessary to register objections, as commentator Joseph Gomez has stated, "but ultimately such observations have little to do with the film as Russell conceived it, and should not be part of the criteria for judging it."[17] Russell's first composer biography was indeed well received. "I believe it to be much the most important thing we have done this year," wrote Wheldon to the deputy editor of *The Observer* on 5 June 1961. "It really does do what we are trying like anything to bring off; and that is to make the apparently unsellable vivid. All our best things have this feature — that in advance they would appear to be dead ducks."[18]

This burst of enthusiasm was as nothing compared with the acclaim that greeted Russell's next composer film, *Elgar*. Again, Burton produced and Wheldon voiced the soundtrack commentary. "The odd thing is that Hollywood has neglected the Elgar story," wrote Burton in the *Radio Times* for 10–16 November 1962, "because it has all the ingredients of a rags to riches epic — tradesman's son marries Major-General's daughter and ends up Master of the King's Musick." None of this was lost on Russell. He had been considering for some time a narrative about Elgar the provincial dreamer, the son of a piano-tuner, who through talent, perseverance, and the help of his loyal wife becomes the musical voice of Edwardian England. The story turns darker with the disaster of the Great War, the death of his wife in 1920, his retreat in middle age to the countryside of his youth, and his death at seventy-six in 1934. From the very beginning, Russell found in this story an important thematic device he had noticed in the Prokofiev biography — and that he would exploit many times in his subsequent composer films — the theme of a sensitive temperament so haunted by the scenes and ideals of a romanticized youth that he strives (usually unsuccessfully) for the rest of his days to recapture and sustain them.

While acknowledging that the BBC is interested in abandoning "the straightforward documentary approach for something like a feature film," Burton reiterated objections to Russell's suggestions about using actors. Spoken dialogue should be avoided, Burton wrote in the same memo, in favor of the dramatic visualization of music: "You have the music of Elgar, music which mirrors the opulence and optimism of Edwardian England and at the same time pin-points the emotions of a single complex personality."[19] And Wheldon warned that dramatizations could result in a product that "will seem hollow, like cardboard, as most of them do."[20] As late as July 1961, Russell himself was confused about how to proceed with a project that was nominally a documentary but that cried out for dramatic enhancement. "For some considerable time now I have wanted more than I can say to make a film about Sir Edward's life and music," he wrote to Elgar's daughter, Carice Elgar Blake, "but there are so many riches here that it is not easy to decide on the ideal approach."[21] But in the end Russell won important concessions from his producers. "In the next film I did, *Elgar*," Russell recalls, "Huw finally allowed me to show people impersonating Elgar from his boyhood to old age. They could only be seen in medium to medium-long shot, and they weren't allowed to speak." Wheldon by now was expressing his enthusiasm, pronouncing the shooting script "terrific" and predicting that "this film is likely to come off in a big way."[22]

Thus, employing the same concept of blending archival images, newsreel footage, and spoken narrative with dramatic reenactments (featuring actors Peter Brett and George McGrath as, respectively, the mature and the elderly Elgar in several wordless sequences), interpolated location scenes shot in the Malvern Hills, Elgar's birth cottage at Birchwood Lodge Farm and Worcester Cathedral, *Elgar* was broadcast as the 100th Monitor Program on 11 November 1962. Highly romantic in conception and execution, it utilizes several repeating musical excerpts — most notably the *Introduction and Allegro for Strings* — as binding structural elements. Burton, writing in the BBC magazine, *Aiel,* credits Russell with this idea: "The significant episodes in his life in terms of story-telling seemed to stem naturally from this basic musical structure."[23] Thus, the celebrated opening shots of a young boy galloping on a pony across the Malvern Hills area of Worcestershire, to the background music of Elgar's *Introduction and Allegro for Strings* are repeated, with variations, throughout.[24] With each return to the Malverns he is depicted, variously, as a student on a bicycle, a newly engaged swain astride a donkey, a husband on a bicycle, a father with his daughter flying a box kite and tumbling down the Malvern slopes, and, finally, an aging widower alone in his motorcar. And music from the "Nimrod" episode of the *Enigma Variations,* already noted as a favorite of Russell's, is quoted several times in the film, notably in conjunction with Elgar's stroll through a cathedral-like stand of pines in the Malverns; the occasion of his first public celebrity (as close-ups of his walking trousers dissolve into a pair of silk hose); and finally at the very end, as the dying Elgar listens to a phonograph recording while gazing out a window and imagining scenes of his youth.

Predictably, Russell's tendency to editorialize and interpolate political elements ran him into trouble. As he did with Prokofiev, he depicts Elgar as initially supportive of putting his music to patriotic service. Against newsreel footage of street parades, the narrator informs us that his imperial march in honor of Queen Victoria's Diamond Jubilee, written in 1897, inflames the public's appetite for imperial glory: "It was frankly popular music and it matched the mood of the day." But again, as in the Prokofiev film, Elgar's artistic fervor turns to disillusionment with the carnage of war. As newsreel footage of cheering crowds and proud military processions shifts to images of slaughter and mutilation in the Great War (including a procession of blinded and wounded soldiers staggering single file, supporting hands on each other's shoulders), the familiar music and words of Elgar's "Land of Hope and Glory" underpin the sequence in a tragically ironic counterpoint. "Official music had become an abomination," says the narrator. "The words were not his and he disapproved of them. They were too jingoistic. And there was a time when he could not bear what had virtually become a second national anthem." The music reaches its peroration against shots of graveyards and ranks of crosses and monuments.

A few protesting voices were immediately raised. An unsigned article in *Time and Tide* from November 1962 rejected Russell's implication that Elgar was a pacifist and that he abhorred the aristocracy. Mrs. Elgar-Blake was quoted as claiming her father was certainly *not* a pacifist.[25] Producer Wheldon also objected, and he insisted some of the aforementioned scenes be deleted. "It is Elgar's beliefs that counted, not Ken's or mine. And on this Ken and I, as we frequently did, had what you might call an editorial row."[26] Russell fiercely defends the scene: "I did take care to put right Elgar's feelings about the Great War. . . . His 'Pomp and Circumstance March, No. 1' had been appropriated for propaganda purposes under the title 'The Land of Hope and Glory.' Jingoistic words were put to it, and he didn't approve of that. He hated that, in fact."[27]

Despite the film's success and its garnering of a Screenwriter's Guild Award, Russell was not satisfied: "The film was all too lovely, like a TV commercial for the Malvern Hills! I was perhaps too much in love with the man's music to see what really produced it."[28] Indeed, excepting for a few voice-over references to Elgar's depressive moods — "His illnesses became chronic . . . and to his wife he sometimes talked of suicide" — it was a generally sunny and respectful portrait, enlivened by the aforementioned editorial flourishes and a sporadically irrepressible humor, like images of Elgar's hillside tumbles, his kite-flying, and his explosive experiments in soap-making. Fifteen years later Russell was already talking of a remake, in which he would show "the darker side of his life as well as the lyrical, colorful side. . . . This time I would want to depict the complete man, 'warts and all,' as they say."[29] For that Russell would have to wait many years later, as is explored later in this chapter.

Russell's complaints notwithstanding, it is unjust to undervalue his first *Elgar* film because it lacks the free-form interpretive fantasies of his later composer films. Rather, operating within *Monitor*'s aesthetic and political constraints, it emerged a fully realized project on its own terms. Nothing quite like its blend of documentary fact and interpretive flair had ever been seen before. It demonstrates the first appearance, but not the last, of a thematic and structural strategy that will be developed in all his subsequent films: three aspects of Elgar are thrown into high relief — the historical figure, the myth that figure has created, and Russell's own vision of the subject.[30] Thus, the historical Elgar is sometimes in conflict with the public myth, which in turn is inflected and frequently debunked by Russell's own interpretive insights. "People liked the Elgar film because, for a start, he doesn't look like an artist," says Russell. "Here was a composer who looked like a cavalry officer, the epitome of the upright British gentleman. . . . [But] he's a bit of a failure and people are on the side of anyone likely to overcome failure."[31]

Not only did *Elgar* win a higher audience reaction index than any other *Monitor* documentary yet made,[32] but its four broadcasts in the 1960s played a large part in a reawakening of interest, popular and scholarly, in Elgar himself. "After the appearance of my film," recalls Russell, "new recordings started to be issued from the record companies, with images from my film on the jackets." This stands in stark contrast to the state of things in 1962, when only two full-scale biographies were in print and recordings of the choral works and early wind music were either few in number or nonexistent. Following Russell's film, Elgar has even been the subject of a novel, *Gerontius,* published in 1989.[33]

Russell's next composer film, *Bartók,* telecast on *Monitor* on 24 May 1964, remains one of his most unjustly neglected works. He subordinates his already apparent tendencies toward visual flamboyance to the service of his subject, crafting an unvarnished, even starkly limned portrait of Bartók's painful last years.[34] Newsreel footage, archival photographs, and visualized musical fantasies flash back to his early years as a Hungarian nationalist, his pioneering work as a collector of folk music, his flight from Nazi oppression, and, finally, his final days struggling to survive socially and artistically in the hostile, sterile environment of New York City. In my opinion Russell is never better than in some of these sequences, when he works against his own grain, as it were — that is, reigning in his flamboyant fantasies in the service of an artistic effect that is severe and almost painfully ascetic. The black-and-white photography of cameraman Charles Parnell is stunning. It's as if Federico Fellini had attempted — and succeeded — in making a film in the manner of Carl Dreyer.

By this time Russell had won an important concession from Wheldon. "I pushed the envelope further in my next film on Bartók," says Russell. "I was allowed to show a close-up of someone who purported to be Bartók, the actor Boris Ranevsky. Boris really did look like him (he was unknown at the time, which helped). But he still wasn't allowed a voice." That very silence works to the film's advantage. This Bartók is a stranger in a strange land, a stiff and lonely sixty-year-old man, utterly impoverished, entrapped in the steel and glass canyons of New York City, buried in the claustrophobic subways, bewildered by the crush of the streets. He had fled his native Hungary and his family in 1940, fully aware that he might never return. "Bartók remained permanently lonely here," his biographer and friend Agathe Fassett would write later, "since he was not the kind to transplant well, and every step was made harder — for although he did not know it, soon after he arrived the seed of his fatal illness, leukemia, was within him, and wherever he went he was followed by the doom of his tightly numbered years."[35]

Static, carefully composed shots of Bartók sitting alone in a white-walled room overlooking New York City are juxtaposed to a succession of wordless fantasies visualized to the music of the *Miraculous Mandarin* pantomime ballet, the "Night Music" sequence from the second movement of the Third Piano Concerto, the opera *Bluebeard's Castle,* excerpts from the adagio of the *Music for Strings, Percussion, and Celeste,* and the "Intermezzo Interroto" from the *Concerto for Orchestra.* By turns erotic and violent (the knife fight in the *Mandarin* sequence), fantastic (images of a rocket launch behind one of Bluebeard's doors), eerie and sinister (black-clad figures moving up and down gliding escalators to the "Celeste" music), and earthy (a montage of peasants, goat herders, whirling dancers, and rearing horses to the *Concerto*), music and image work together to support a portrait of an active, even tumultuous inner world contrasted with the composer's stolid, chilly exterior demeanor. "The visuals and the music work together in suggesting that these Bartók compositions mirror the violence and alienation of the contemporary world," writes biographer Joseph Gomez. "Russell emphasizes Bartók's view of himself as an alien in a hostile world."[36]

"I allowed myself license to recreate events in Bartók's life," comments Russell, "such as when he prowls through the woods with a flashlight looking for insects, and when he takes the underground in New York (which he hated).[37] That sequence is pretty scary — it scared *me* while I was doing it! And I had fun with the *Bluebeard's Castle* sequence, with the rocket launch and all of that. I was just adding some of my own impressions to what I knew about Bartók. A lot of people ask me where I found those wonderful images of Hungarian peasants on horseback. They were from a famous Hungarian film called *Hortobargy,* which I had seen in London when I was a young lad. It was made by the man who used to run the Academy Cinema in Oxford Street."

The recurring scenes of Bartók listening to the phonograph not only serve as a source of diegetic music, a kind of conduit into the musical sequences, they also capture the paradox that was Bartók's interest in ethnomusicology: here was a man very much aware that the phonographic technology of the urban industrial society he despised was, ironically enough, the very technology that enabled him to preserve the folk music traditions of a preindustrial culture.[38] Thus, Russell effortlessly suggests what commentator Leon Botstein has described as Bartók's search for a synthesis "between the self-consciously radical aspirations of aesthetic modernism and a sentimental preindustrial construct of the world."[39]

According to an audience research report conducted by *Monitor* on 25 June 1964, the telecast of *Bartók* "aroused plenty of active interest (to some small degree hostile, but chiefly of a very appreciative kind) among viewers in the sample audience. Bartók's music, as many made plain in comment, is of the order they would describe as controversial and far from easy to understand." Although the eroticism of the *Mandarin* scene was singled out as "very distasteful to some viewers," the report concluded that "the quality of Ken Russell's film-making was the subject of very warm praise and, indeed, the photography throughout was noted as most expressive of atmosphere and mood."[40]

"I like the Bartók film a lot," says Russell. "It had a lot of drama. And the music — well, the music from *The Miraculous Mandarin* is the most sensual, erotic music that I know.[41] That clarinet that comes in three times is pure sex. Bartók was in reality a very sexy dude. The film got really close to the man, I think."

First telecast on 18 May 1965 as part of the BBC's *Monitor* series, *The Debussy Film* was introduced by a disclaiming subtitle, "Impressions of the French Composer." It was Russell's first fully realized BBC composer biopic — "one of Russell's major contributions to the art of film biography," according to biographer Gomez.[42] One of Russell's most significant and influential films, it has long been unseen and is currently unavailable, which accounts for its neglect in recent scholarship.[43] For reasons not entirely clear, no copies are in distribution, and none are available for screening at the British Film Institute.[44] This is particularly regrettable, inasmuch as it represents several important breakthroughs in Russell's oeuvre. It was his first feature-length television biopic — more a *film* than an arts program (Russell has said that all of his biopics "were really feature films masquerading under the banner of TV documentaries")[45]. It was the first time that he used actors speaking lines in their impersonations of real-life people. It was the first time he indulged in a highly personalized experiment in metacinema. And, no less significantly, it was the first time he worked with coscenarist Melvyn Bragg, inaugurating a personal and professional association that continues to this day.[46] When questioned today about *The Debussy Film*, Russell casts a wink about its significance as a personal statement. "It reflects everything that was going on at the time, with the BBC, with Melvyn, my cast members, myself — everything and everybody![47]

The Debussy Film is a movie within a movie. "I made it clear that it wasn't to be a biography of Debussy," recalls Russell, "but that it was about a film

company making a *movie* about Debussy. It wasn't actor Oliver Reed portraying Debussy, it was Oliver Reed portraying *himself* preparing to play the part
of Debussy. This conceit allowed me to examine the very process of making a
biopic. It also helped me get around the BBC's restrictions on using actors to
portray composer." A dazzling tour de force, Russell takes us backstage to
meet his cast and crew. The director (Vladek Sheybal) and actors (Reed as
Debussy; Sheybal as his friend and mentor, Pierre Louÿs; Annette Robertson
as Debussy's mistress, Gabrielle Dupont; Penny Service as his first wife, Rosa-
lie Texier; and Isa Teller as his second wife, Madame Emma Bardac) go about
their daily business, shooting scenes and discussing and debating the details of
their roles. By implication, we are also witnessing Russell's own struggles to
make *his* Debussy film. In both the film within a film and Russell's film, historical fact, dramatic reenactment, and production history overlap and interpene-
trate to the extent that one is sometimes indistinguishable from the other. Any
confusion we encounter in separating the two, and in identifying which is
which, is entirely to the point. *The Debussy Film* is Russell's *8½.*

Visual fantasies counterpoint the music of *Le Martyre de Saint Sébastien, La
Mer,* the ballet *La Boite a joujoux, L'après-midi d'un faune,* and the *Danse
sacrée et profane.* To those who complain that he takes considerable interpretive liberties, Russell points out that Debussy himself wanted his music to be
like paintings in sound. Russell is merely extending the process: "I've always
felt justified in taking a piece of music and doing my own 'paintings in sound,'
even if it's something totally different from what the composer may have
intended."

The emerging portrait of the historical Debussy — as well as of the actor and
director making the film about Debussy — is of a brilliant but ruthlessly opportunistic artist who shamefully manipulates those around him in the pursuit of
art and commercial success. "Artists are dogmatic and pig-headed," says Russell. "It's not nice, but that's how it works. Yes, Debussy was probably one of
the few total geniuses of music. And like all the composers I've made films
about, he had these two sides of genius and selfishness. It can't be reconciled;
it's just a fact of existence. I don't think there's any reason why they should be
reconciled." Russell pauses, eyes twinkling. He assumes an ingenuous pose.
"But who am I to say so? Just think of me as the conduit, the lightning conductor of these things. Just an innocent bystander. Somebody once said Debussy
was 'just a musician.' I wouldn't mind if they said something like that about
me — 'He was just a filmmaker.' "

Song of Summer, a biopic about English composer Frederick Delius, was telecast on 15 September 1968. Its spare, exquisite conjunction of music and

London Weekend Television producer Melvyn Bragg worked with Ken Russell as scenarist and presenter on many films. (Courtesy John C. Tibbetts)

image, stunning location photography in England's Lake District, intelligent script, and superb performances justify it as, as biographer Ken Hanke has claimed, "the most completely successful and mature of Russell's BBC output."[48] It appeared on the heels of his second theatrical film, the spy thriller *Billion Dollar Brain,* and just after another of his BBC biopics, *Dante's Inferno* (a group portrait of Dante Gabriel Rossetti and his circle). It also marked Russell's great discovery of the Lake District. This area of spectacular hills, valleys, and lakes in the far northwestern corner of England would prove to be Russell's "promised land," as he put it in his autobiography, *Altered States.* Among the later composer films, *Song of Summer, Dance of the Seven Veils, Mahler, Arnold Bax, Bruckner, The Secret of Dr. Martinu,* and the new *Elgar* would all be filmed "in a magic land that at the sound of a clapper board turned into Iceland, Norway, France, or Bavaria, or even itself."[49]

The first stirrings of the Delius project appear in a letter from Estelle Palmley, secretary of the Delius Society to Kenneth Adam, director of television at Television Centre: "I am sure Delius' most eventful life before settling down at

Grez would be of great interest to a wide audience."[50] Five months later Russell is considering such a project in a letter to Geoffrey Cornell: "I have often thought of doing a film on Delius, whose music attracts me immensely. There are many pitfalls to the story, however."[51]

True enough. Compared with the romantically stalwart Elgar and the indulgently hedonistic Debussy, Delius seemed intractably remote and unsympathetic, a personality closer to the chilly Bártok than to anyone else. Too much of his music, including the *Requiem* and most of his operas, was unknown in England in his lifetime. The general opinion was that he was not "English" at all. He had left England for Germany and France while still a relatively young man, and his music reflected links with the French and Wagnerian schools rather than to any English tradition. And there was the issue of Delius's disabling illness, which left him paralyzed and blind in his last years in France at Grez-sur-Loing — an unprepossessing subject at that time for a television project. In truth, the illness was syphilis, something not as yet known to the general public.

"Well, boys, it won't be pretty," Russell said, undaunted, "but this is how a man lived and worked and was."[52] Although he was initially nervous about public reactions to the syphilis issue, Russell would eventually insist that references to the disease and his dissolute activities in Paris be included. Objections were raised by Delius's niece, Mrs. Vessey. In a letter to Russell dated 22 August 1968, producer Norman Swallow tried to assuage Russell's fear of a legal injunction. "This is certainly not enough cause for the injunction you fear," Swallow wrote. "I'm sure that the risk is non-existent. What [Mrs. Vessey] could do, however, is probably prevent the film from being shown abroad." A week later Swallow dispatched another letter with the good news that upon seeing the script, a solicitor had assured him that "there's no case whatever for the niece to prevent the film being shown."[53]

While casting the role of Delius, Russell insisted on an appropriate physical type: "Delius was always frail and there is nothing we can do about it," he told an aspiring actor who proved to be too robust, Felix Aylmer, in a letter dated 19 February 1968 (Max Adrian would get the part). "The nurse used to fling him over his shoulder and carry him about the house as if he were a bundle of feathers. Apparently, even his wife could lift him."[54] Initially, only Delius's early years were to be depicted, his boyhood in Bradford, his work at the Solano orange groves in Florida, and his taking up serious musical studies at the Leipzig Conservatory. A more ambitious idea was to have Delius's amanuensis, Eric Fenby, return to Grez after Delius's death and recall via flashbacks incidents in their relationship. Ultimately, these two approaches were combined in a detailed treatment by Anthony Wilkinson and dated 27 November

1967, in which Delius's years with Fenby at Grez triggered flashbacks of Delius's life — scenes at the boyhood home, the family's Wool and Noil Company; the years spent at the Solano Grove in Florida; the music lessons with Ward in Jacksonville; vacations hiking in Norway; a period spent in an artists' colony in Paris; and the composer's final move to Grez. These flashbacks "would contain situations of great visual beauty which allow the use of extended passages of music."[55] Most of these flashbacks would eventually be discarded, as were suggestions for incidents depicting visits to Grez by friends (the painter James Gunn and the conductor Sir Thomas Beecham) and Delius's trip to London to attend a Delius Festival.

An important source for any screen treatment was a memoir entitled *Delius As I Knew Him,* by the composer's amanuensis, Fenby, first published in 1936 and revised in 1981. Fenby had initially written an appreciative letter to the blind, partially paralyzed composer in 1928. After receiving an amicable response, Fenby offered his services to assist him in composing: "To be a genius as this man plainly was," recalled Fenby, "and have something beautiful in you and not be able to rid yourself of it because you could no longer see your score paper and no longer hold your pen — well, the thought was unbearable!"[56] What resulted, after almost five years of painful and tedious artistic collaboration, were a handful of memorable works (including the work that would serve as the title of Russell's film). Two years after Delius's death in 1934, a sadder and somewhat disillusioned Fenby published his book, a respectful but unvarnished portrait of the difficulties attendant upon living and working with Delius. "It was irksome for a young man to go on regulating his life according to the whims of a sick man," Fenby wrote candidly of his experiences. "Those five years had taught me that it is not wholesome and good for a youngster to live for long periods in an atmosphere of sickness and depression if he would keep his spirit."[57]

Although Russell was attracted to Fenby's candid and personal tone, so like Russell's own approach to his composer subjects, he was ambivalent at first about referencing it. "When I first took on the Delius film, *Song of Summer,* I tried to do it without Eric Fenby, who had been Delius['s] secretary and amanuensis in the last years of his life," remembers Russell. "But I couldn't come up with a satisfactory script. It was always too sentimental, hopeless. But when I read Fenby's wonderful book about his association with Delius, I knew it had to be a part of the project, somehow. This rather naïve fellow from Yorkshire went to France and lived in the Delius house in Grez for four or five years and managed with great difficulty to wrestle three or four masterpieces out of Delius'[s] tortured brain. I spoke to Fenby and got permission to use the book." Indeed, according to Russell, Fenby actively participated in the writing

Christopher Gable and Max Adrian as Eric Fenby (left) and Frederick Delius in Ken Russell's *Song of Summer* (1967). (Courtesy Photofest)

of the final script. "I'd ask Fenby about a particular event and he'd just tell me the dialogue for it. . . . We changed a few lines, but most of the script was taken from his recollections of their own conversations."[58]

Russell hews scrupulously to the details of Fenby's recollections, including the evenings at Grez with Delius and his wife, Jelka, listening to phonograph records (including the Revellers's rendition of "Old Man River"); frankly observed the physical details of Delius's syphilitic condition; the hilarity of Percy Grainger's visit; the flashback of Delius being carried up a mountain in Norway to view a sunset; and the bedside readings of books by Mark Twain. Some of Delius's rants seem to be verbatim transfers from the book, witness his attacks on religious music ("Given a young composer of genius, the surest way to ruin him is to make a Christian of him.") and his advice to Fenby against marrying ("No artist should ever marry. He should be as free as the winds. Amuse yourself with as many women as you like, but for the sake of your art never marry one."). Even what seems to be a "Russell touch" — Jelka's sprinkling of rose petals over Delius's corpse — derives directly from Fenby's account. Fenby confirmed this in 1974: "I have often been asked whether or not the sprinkling of rose petals over his body was a touch of Ken Russell's fantasy. No, that actually happened at daybreak that morning. Strange, perhaps, to English ways, but it was Jelka's wish, and she did it herself from the a wheelchair."[59]

To be sure, Russell makes the most of many opportunities to lend visually imaginative wings to the musical sequences. It is startling, for example, to find a film about Delius opening with a scene of the young Fenby playing organ accompaniment to a Laurel and Hardy silent film (actually, a scene from their 1936 movie *Way out West*). When Percy Grainger literally "drops in" on Delius, his race around the garden is accompanied by the sprightly "Country Gardens." Particularly electrifying is a scene when Delius laboriously crawls down a corridor toward the camera, the incandescent music from *The Walk to the Paradise Garden* blazing away on the soundtrack. It is a perfect evocation of the triumph of spirit over the frailties of flesh. And in the aforementioned scene with Jelka scattering flower petals over Delius's corpse, the soundtrack swells to the lyric splendor of "Song of Summer."

Just as Fenby had emerged in the pages of his book as both observer and participant in the Delius story, he was now likewise to serve in the same dual function with Russell. Thus, *The Song of Summer,* like his book, would be Fenby's story as much as Delius's. But it would be in many ways an unpleasant reminder of a time that was "disturbingly life like," as he put it.[60] "I told Fenby he must come along to the shoot," recalled Russell, "but he said no, he didn't want to interfere with Chris Gable, the actor playing him. But when I told him he was welcome to show up anytime without announcing himself in advance, he did come. He arrived when we were shooting the scene where the wheelchair bound Delius, played by Max Adrian, first welcomes Fenby. I remember that scene well: Delius demands to know something about Fenby's musical background. And Fenby innocently replies, 'I play for the films, Laurel and Hardy.' Delius explodes, 'LAUREL AND HARDY!?' 'Yes,' says Fenby, not realizing what he was getting into, 'and then I go down to the beach and I listen to the bands playing British music.' Of course, Delius explodes again — 'British music!? I don't know British music! There's no such thing! Trust in the Lord! That was the ruin of Elgar, poor man!' At that point in the scene, as I was saying 'Cut!' I heard sobbing. We looked around, and there was Fenby, just come, unbeknownst to anyone. He was moved to tears. He said, 'That was exactly how it was — and it was *horrible!*' " Fenby's own recollection of the moment is touching:"On my arrival I found Russell immersed in directing a 'retake' of my first meeting with Delius. . . . But this was too much for me — the voice, the inflection, the image of Delius sitting there, a rug over his knees, with a greet screen about him, slowly extending his hand in welcome. I lived that momentous moment again, I am unashamed to say, and not without tears."[61]

Russell always says that the making of each of his films is a learning experience, and he was learning quickly of the central significance of the psychic scars Fenby retained from his years with Delius. "It became obvious to me that he was very divided in his feelings about Delius," says Russell; "that he loved the music but that he felt his life had been ruined by the man; and that his own composing career had been sacrificed. Who knows how good a composer he might have been?" Indeed, here was the real story Russell was looking for, one that he could identify with—not so much a story about Delius's triumph as a composer but about Fenby's tragic failure as an artist. Fenby, a newly converted Catholic, had paid a terrible price to bring to his generation the life and music of a composer whose talent he thought greater than his own. Ironically, on the evidence of the music dictation sessions so painstakingly recorded in the book, and scrupulously documented in the film, it can be argued that the resulting music was as much Fenby's as Delius's. Commentator Philip T. Oyler has argued this point: "My opinion is that he made himself so familiar with Delius's music that he guessed the *sort* of theme that Delius would write himself and that, when he played it, Delius agreed to it. . . . Delius himself confessed to me that he did not know what he had composed and what Eric had!"[62] Nonetheless, Fenby's own creative energies have remained largely unrecognized. Ken Hanke sums up Fenby's fate: "Fenby has lived Delius ever since, . . . [but] he's never been able to shake him off his back."

It is tempting at this point to speculate about the parallels and correspondences between Fenby and Russell. To what degree is Fenby's story Russell's own? Can the sort of personal artistic sacrifice Fenby made in the service to Delius be compared with Russell's lifelong efforts to place his talents in the service of artist biographies? Can Fenby's largely unrecognized creative contributions to the Delius music be correlated to the interpretive—Russell would call it "intuitive"—and imaginative vision Russell brings to all his films? Can the identification with Delius that has dogged Fenby's subsequent professional life be compared with the associations in the public mind linking Russell to the many composer subjects of his films? And, fairly or not, in the special instance of *Song of Summer*, will Russell be remembered primarily for his Delius film as Fenby has been for his Delius associations?

Like Fenby, Russell came from a strong Catholic background. "It's the most Catholic film I've ever done," he has said. "Sacrifice is the central pivot of the Catholic faith and one of the best things about it."[63] Certainly, variations on this theme are everywhere in Russell's biopics, and it is obvious that Russell himself has devoted a considerable part of his career to the service of composer biographies. However, Russell is always idiosyncratically Russell, whatever the nature of the individual project, and there is no danger of his falling victim, or suborning himself, to the material, as Fenby had done. Thus, although Russell has been frequently criticized for the interpretive license of many of his more flamboyant visual fantasies, they nonetheless remain his most celebrated or notorious works, subject always to comment but never to indifference or neglect. As for the place of *Song of Summer* in Russell's oeuvre, it is likely that it will continue to be cited as among his supreme artistic achievements.

No examination of *Song of Summer* is complete without special mention of the superbly conceived and enacted sequences in which Delius and Fenby collaborate on music composition. We find in Russell's marvelous reenactments of these dictation sequences — arguably the film's dramatic and musical highlights — revealing glimpses of the typically strenuous, at times combative, give-and-take nature of artistic collaboration. "What was fascinating to me was their method of working," says Russell (who enjoys taking on the parts of both Delius and Fenby as he talks). "It afforded me a chance to dramatize the very processes of creation. Fenby never forgot those dictation sessions with Delius. It was a weird process. They would argue and taunt each other and all that. Delius would begin by teasing him — 'Well, come along, Fenby; what are we going to do today? Let's take up that piece that you thought we *might* do.' Fenby would reply with the taunt, 'No, Delius, I didn't think it was up to your usual standard.' 'What!?' Delius would splutter, 'you didn't think it was up to my usual standard! — What are you saying?' 'Well, I have to be honest, Delius, though there are some fine things — .' Delius would then try to sing some of the notes and Fenby would exclaim, 'Delius, you're going too fast — I can't keep up!' And so on. So I was able to write out in the script this kind of banter and the kind of collaborative process that Fenby described. The actors were able to really get into those scenes."

Song of Summer won the strongest reviews of any Russell film to date. Writing in *The Guardian* on 17 September 1968, Stanley Reynolds wrote that the relationship between Russell and the BBC "would seem to be an ideal one" and that "one wonders if ever a commercial company will be able to produce such a relationship. Moreover, Russell "is able to constantly tread the narrow margin between exaggeration and real art." Critic Henry Raynor in *The Times* applauded a degree of restraint in the film not seen recently in Russell's work: "He does not, as he has permitted himself to do in much of his recent work, self-indulgently allow images to detach themselves from the matter in hand, and live an exciting but irrelevant life of their own. This programme joins Mr. Russell's study of Elgar as a work which forces us to forgive him his occasional excesses."[64] Russell's own boss, John Culshaw, head of music programs for BBC Television, congratulated him in a letter dated 24 July 1968: "[It is] the best film I have ever seen about a composer."[65] Meanwhile, Russell need not have worried about the reception from Delius fans and colleagues. In a letter dated 23 September 1968, Estelle Palmley, who had first voiced the possibility of a Delius film, thanked the BBC for such "a happy result" and called the film "a masterpiece for television."[66] And Fenby himself voiced his enthusiasm in a letter to Russell dated 16 September 1968: "Thank you for your truly marvelous realization of my book. . . . More than ever you have proved yourself a great artist; the brilliance of your direction and profound insight into the strange story in which I found myself involved were so completing [sic] convincing that the total effect was of seering [sic] beauty. . . . Christopher [Gable] was so astonishingly true and so sensitive that I can forgive him his accent! . . . I shudder at what [the film] might have been in other hands!"[67] To which Russell replied in a letter two days later, "My worst fear was that I hadn't done justice to you, so you can imagine how relieved and gratified I was when I heard the news."[68]

The subtitle of Russell's most notorious composer biopic, and the one least frequently seen today, *Dance of the Seven Veils,* aptly sums up what was in store for unsuspecting viewers of the BBC *Omnibus* broadcast of 15 February 1970: "A Comic Strip in Seven Episodes on the Life of Richard Strauss." The disclaimer issued before the broadcast was equally revealing: "It's been described as a harsh, sometimes violent caricature of the life of the composer, Richard Strauss. This is a personal interpretation by Ken Russell of certain real and many imaginary events in the composer's life. Among them are dramatized sequences about the war and the Nazi persecution of the Jews, which include scenes of considerable violence and horror."

Russell was approaching the summit of his career, with a series of popular and innovative BBC films and the acclaimed, recently completed D. H. Lawrence adaptation, *Women in Love,* behind him. The Strauss film was to be his last, and only BBC film in color for more than a decade. From the beginning, after being approached by John Culshaw, head of the BBC Music Department, Russell had been opposed to a conventional handling of Strauss, whose life and music had been fraught with artistic and political controversy. This was a man who, after all, had witnessed a succession of important political and artistic changes in modern Germany. Born in 1864, he quickly became known as a rival to Mahler in his orchestral skills and formally innovative tone poems. He saw an emperor come and go. He survived the trials and tribulations of the Weimar Republic in the 1920s. He endured the period of National

Socialism in the 1930s. He was "de-Nazified" in the immediate postwar years. And he died in 1949, long since a musical conservative hostile to decades of modernist music. By turns described as a "genius" by his friends and as a "decadent" and "leg-puller" by his enemies, he lived long enough to see the critics who had pronounced him an artistic visionary in his ardent youth now condemn him as a commercial sellout in his stodgy old age.

When Russell received a preliminary screen treatment by Henry Reed, he felt its routine chronological treatment was ill-suited to the style he had been developing, beginning with *The Debussy Film*. "His life has proved too large and complex to do in the way we had planned," he wrote in a memo dated 20 March 1969. "The only way, in fact, we can seem to make it work is by illustrating his life in choreographic terms to an accompaniment to his music. In short, it is all dancing and no acting."[69] Accordingly, he prepared a treatment of his own, organized in seven sections, "each of which is introduced by Strauss himself (and sometimes possibly his wife) addressing the audience." Except for the scene where Strauss and his wife make love to the music of the *Domestic Symphony* (a scene not in the original proposal), this treatment was conveyed relatively intact to the screen.[70] Just three days before the broadcast, Russell was quoted in *Radio Times:* "It's a *comic* strip; it's not a profound, serious, dramatic reconstruction of Strauss' life. I felt it was time to get up off our knees and take a lighter view of someone as an artist. He seemed to lend himself to this sort of treatment. He took himself very seriously. . . . All the dialogue, except for about three lines, is his own."[71]

The viewing public and several critics, however, took it *very* seriously. The BBC received a flood of outraged mail and telephone calls. Critics took aim. James Thomas in the *Daily Express* one day after the broadcast opined, "It was as if a man was being destroyed before the eyes of millions." Writing in *The Times,* John Russell Taylor charged, "Clearly, Mr. Russell doesn't like Strauss, though whether on aesthetic or moral grounds or on both is not immediately apparent. . . . Its Strauss is entirely fictitious, an invented figure on which to hang certain fantasy pictures inspired by the music."[72] A report issued by the BBC's television director to the Board of Governors twelve days after the broadcast stated, "No one could watch the film for more than a minute or so without realizing that this was certainly not an attempt at a balanced biographical reconstruction." The report goes on to examine particularly controversial elements, such as the music's "unbridled sensuality," Strauss's "propagation of Nietzschean philosophy," his "support of the Nazis," and the film's "bestiality of unrestrained sexual licence [*sic*]." The report concluded that the violence was, if anything, "an understatement of what actually happened"; and that "the film was a major work of creation by a greatly gifted director, which dealt

seriously with profound issues."[73] It was even suggested in Parliament that the
BBC be denounced for the broadcast. Strauss's son, Dr. Franz Strauss, threatened legal action in a letter to Huw Wheldon on 19 March, demanding the
film "be withdrawn and buried in the BBC archives."[74]

Meanwhile, a BBC Audience Research Report dated 3 March 1970 notes
that while the film was praised by some viewers as "a brilliant masterpiece for
television," others denounced it as "one of the most horrible films ever seen."
This last group complained they could see no merit whatever in this "distorted" portrait of Strauss, "which not only contained a savage and vitriolic
attack on the man but 'desecrated' his music with scenes of such nightmarish
horror and brutality that they felt physically sick. One viewer acutely observed that the film 'told one less about Strauss than about Ken Russell.' " The
BBC responded with an "equal time" broadcast of a public forum in which
critics and musicians debated the merits of the composer and the film.[75] As for
Russell, he is quoted as remarking, "The members of the television audience
are all asleep in their armchairs. It's a good thing to shake them up; even if it's
only as far as the telephone."[76] Ultimately, the film was embargoed because of
actions by the Strauss family. At this writing, it is still unavailable for theatrical
screening.

"Yes, I've had my share of controversy," says Russell, looking back on the
furor. "Not since its first broadcast has my *Dance of the Seven Veils* been seen.
It was never shown again, from that day to this. The music publishers freaked
out. Maybe it was coincidental, but the next week the BBC held a program of
pundits saying that my film was rubbish; that Strauss was never a Nazi; and so
forth. There was a huge outcry. Mary Whitehouse, a well-known public activist, wanted to sue me. She found she could only sue the land cable transmitting
the program. Then Huw Wheldon made a speech in the Houses of Parliament
defending the film and my right to say what I felt. That was a great moment. I
have no bitterness about that—if it rains you get wet."

Dance of the Seven Veils is divided into seven parts, or "veils," each of which
is loaded with intertextual references to a wide variety of music and films. In
the first, "The Superman," in a parody of the figure of Leopold Stokowsky in
Disney's *Fantasia,* the young Strauss (Christopher Gable) mounts the podium
to the music of *Also Sprach Zarathustra.* "The dead end of mankind is approaching," he announces. "Into the squalid epoch, I will reveal the Superman." After leaving his cave and entering the world of men, where he sees
mankind enslaved by religion, the Superman is seduced by nuns and bound
by rosaries. He breaks free and chases after a laughing woman wearing an
Orphan Annie wig. "One cannot be a superman the whole of the time," he
declares. "Sometimes it's a relief to be a mere Hero."

The second "veil," "A Hero's Life," has Strauss disrupting a performance of Richard Wagner's *Tannhäuser* as he ogles the dancers, duels with outraged husbands, and defeats his carping critics. In a series of wicked parodies, Russell lampoons Erich Von Stroheim's *The Merry Widow,* Douglas Fairbanks's swashbucklers, Orson Welles's *Macbeth,* and Cervantes's *Don Quixote.* After charging a religious procession and plunging his lance into an enormous crucifix, he intones, to the music of *Ein Heldenleben:* "The hero's lot is not always a happy one. I was constantly under attack. . . . I am just as important as Alexander the Great or Napoleon; and so, when I composed my *Hero's Life,* I not only paid homage to my own crowning achievement but absolutely demolished the critics as well," whereupon Strauss and an army of women vanquish the critics and lift their trombones over the funereal pyre.

The third veil, "Domestic Symphony," begins with Strauss in bed with his wife. He proclaims his "domestic bliss" as the music from the *Sinfonia Domestica* wells up on the track. The camera pulls back to reveal the bed is surrounded by the players of a symphony orchestra (conducted by Russell himself). As the music and the lovemaking reach a climax, Strauss cries out, "Now!" to the conductor, signaling the consummation of erotic and musical passion.

"I've always had a weakness for women, in my music, that is," says Strauss in the fourth veil, "Heroines." Two female characters from Strauss works, the eponymous Salome from Strauss's opera and Potiphar's Wife from *The Legend of Joseph,* are broadly caricatured. Salome is impersonated by two women seen, alternately, as an enormously fat woman in headdress and as a beautiful young dancer wearing only a body stocking. ("My heroines were too largely conceived for one woman to encompass," Strauss explains.) The women shower gold coins on Joseph. Although this is the most sexually suggestive scene in the film, Russell makes it is clear that Joseph/Strauss is more interested in the gold than in the woman.

In the fifth veil "The Great War," a picnic with Strauss and his wife in the Bavarian Highlands is interrupted by the entrance of wounded soldiers and refugees fleeing the war. As the *Alpine Symphony* is heard on the soundtrack, Strauss has a dream, wherein he is restrained and forced to witness the soldiers's raping of his wife (she seems to enjoy it) and shooting of his child. He wakes up, murmuring: "A life completely away from politics and war — that is what I have always longed for. I saw our beloved Fatherland in need of a leader, the supreme architect who would sweep all the rubble away and redeem our shattered German nation. We needed a Superman."

The sixth veil, "The Nazis," is the longest and most elaborate of the seven veils. It opens to the familiar fanfare of *Also Sprach Zarathustra* as Strauss ascends a podium and begins to conduct the orchestra. Cut to Der Führer and a group of Hitler Youth mocking by the spectacle of a Rabbi and a group of orthodox Jews engaging in the ritual slaughter of a cow. "As I said before and will say again that art and war, like art and politics, should be forever separate," Strauss says, "but there are moments when the base world of politics seems to offer a gleam of hope for the arts. The Nazis offered such a moment. Of course, I never came to terms wit the Nazis. They came to terms with me." Accompanied by the dance music from *Der Rosenkavalier* and *Le bourgeois gentilhomme,* a touring car arrives with Hitler and his retinue. They all drive down the length of a red carpet to Strauss's country estate, where Hitler presents Strauss with an award. "I was the pride of Nazi culture," Strauss continues, "and I conducted everywhere." During a performance of *Der Rosenkavalier,* he is too busy to pay much attention to the two S.S. men in the audience beating up an elderly Jewish couple. "Play louder!" he commands his players in order to drown out the screams. In the next scene he is back in his home, suffering the rebukes of Nazi propagandist Joseph Goebbels for writing to his scenarist, Stefan Zweig, a Jew, a letter critical of the Nazi Party. Strauss is promised that his Jewish daughter-in-law will not be deported if he resigns from the Reichsmusikkammer (RMK), and pens an apology to the Führer. "Mein Führer!," writes Strauss, "My whole life belongs to German music and to an indefatigable effort to elevate German culture. . . . Confident of your high sense of justice, I beg you, my Führer, most humbly to receive me for a personal discussion, to enable me to justify myself in person." As he finishes these lines, his wife appears and slips a mask bearing the features of an old man onto his face. The war over. Strauss, now an old man, walks through the ruins of Munich's once proud opera house, the music of the *Metamorphosen* playing on the soundtrack.

In the concluding veil, "Peace," Strauss sits in the dressing room of London's Albert Hall. He complains to a reporter that he has never received the remuneration owed him from the both world wars: "I was completely exonerated by the de-Nazification court," he says. "But this Jewish stubbornness is enough to — well, it is enough to turn one into an anti-Semite. . . . For me there are only two categories of human beings — those that have talent and those who have not. For me, people exist only when they become an audience." At the sound of a bell, the old man picks up his baton, and ascends the podium once more to the opening fanfare of *Zarathustra* (repeat the scene of the first veil). At the sound of applause, he rips off his face, which is only a mask, to reveal his younger Superman persona. As the end credits roll, we hear Ella Fitzgerald singing George Gershwin's song "By Strauss." (Interestingly, the song was intended to reference Johann Strauss, Jr., not Richard!)

Narcissism, greed, erotic posturing, callousness, anti-Semitism, political opportunism — they are all a part of Russell's searing indictment of the musical and political corruption of Richard Strauss. Seen in hindsight, these broad caricatures and various intertextual references are themselves masks barely concealing an entirely serious intention. *Dance of the Seven Veils,* says biographer Joseph Gomez, is Russell's "most scathing denunciation of the artist as self-server, and it reflects Russell's growing preoccupation with the artist's responsibility to himself and to the world around him."[77] Film historian Robert Kolker calls it "a comic strip which strips the pretensions from a pompous composer and makes him comic."[78] Russell had read George Marek's *Richard Strauss: The Life of a Non-Hero,* the only book up to that time that closely examined Strauss's relationship with the Nazis in a negative light. Marek had refused to accept Strauss's plea of political naïveté. "Marek's book reveals the morally bankrupt response of the composer to the Nazis," writes Gomez, "and presents numerous examples from Strauss' letters which Russell uses in the dialogue of the film."[79] Whereas Marek qualified his attack on Strauss, Russell refuses to soften his portrait. "Everything [Strauss] did, I think, was a glorification of the Master Race," he says. "But no one's ever stood up and said it, or if they have it's been in very half-hearted or pedantic or academic terms."[80] In recent years, Russell has softened his attack: "I didn't dislike Strauss, exactly; he seemed to be an artist in a very difficult situation; and plenty of other people did the same as he did."

The precise nature of Strauss's involvement with the Nazis is too complicated to examine here in detail, save to note that Russell's attacks grow out of a debate that is still unresolved. Indeed, at a recent Bard Music Festival devoted to Strauss, several biographers and commentators convened to sift through the arguments, pro and con. Although Strauss never became officially a Nazi, he occupied under Goebbels the post of director of the Reichsmusikkammer (RMK) from 1933 to 1935. Unlike his colleagues Kurt Weill, Arnold Schoenberg, Ernst Krenek, and Hanns Eisler, he chose to remain in Germany throughout the war. One of Strauss's biographers, Norman Del Mar, rebukes Marek's claims, asserting that Strauss was merely a "useful puppet figurehead" for the Nazis, and that he "was constitutionally unable to grasp" their political manipulations.[81] "However much Strauss' conduct could be ascribed to weakness or self-delusion," concludes Del Mar rather lamely, "it at no time stemmed from malice."[82]

Regardless, points out commentator Michael Tanner, "whatever Strauss' sentiments at the end of the war, there is no clear evidence that he would have minded if the Nazis had won it, having always been fiercely nationalistic."[83] The most considered and balanced assessment can be found in Michael H.

Kater's *Composers of the Nazi Era,* which claims that because Strauss assumed Hitler was interested in the arts—a presumption Strauss described as "the foremost criterion of a German government's worth"—he set out to abolish "un-German aberrations" like operetta, atonality, and serial music and pursue "serious" German art.[84] He also secured copyright reforms for German composers, including Jewish artists. Knowing full well these priorities made Strauss vulnerable, Goebbels promised to support these reforms "in return for the master's clear commitment to serve the wide cultural politics of the new Reich." Far from being an avowed apolitical participant in these affairs, Strauss "was a sincere and dedicated RMK president, and he thought of himself as a consummate politician."[85] However, he was indeed compelled to resign because of his support of Stefan Zweig and his letter criticizing the Nazis. Threats against his daughter-in-law, Alice, compromised any resistance he might offer the party. Kater claims that between 1936 and 1944, "a mutually calculated relationship existed between Strauss and the Third Reich. . . . It required Strauss to show off his regime-marketable qualities and a continuation of the subservient, sometimes groveling, attitude that had first manifested itself in that self-demeaning letter to Hitler in July 1935."[86] By the end of the war he was treated as a "pariah" by the party, and many of his works were banned. Because all his royalties from his works were blocked as long as he remained in Germany, he took refuge in Switzerland with his wife. Ultimately, a de-Nazification board cleared him of "Class-I—Guilty" charges.

The assessment of Leon Botstein at the aforementioned Bard Festival accuses Strauss of personal, rather than political, accommodation. "Here was a man who, on the one hand, was very wise, very profound—a man who could write masterpieces like *Die Frau ohne Schatten* and the *Metamorphosen*—but who chose at this point to put blinders on, not only in his personal life, but in his public life. He really sank to the lowest common denominator of behavior —greed, envy, and political collaboration."[87]

It would be at least two more decades before Russell would make another composer film for British television.

Theatrical Films

The Music Lovers's opening title proclaims it to be "Ken Russell's Film on Tchaikovsky and 'The Music Lovers.'" The first of his composer films to receive theatrical distribution in the United States, it is also now regarded as "the first full-fledged Ken Russell film."[88] What *that* means is worth examining at some length. Certainly it was a particularly personal project, inasmuch as it draws upon Russell's lifelong infatuation (as noted earlier in this chapter) with

the music of Pyotr Tchaikovsky. It also dramatizes with great vitality and complexity the two preoccupations that have already surfaced in his earlier films —
namely, the difficulty artists face in reconciling their genius and their individuality to a world of mediocrity and convention, and how composers exploit the
affective properties of music to express their inner and outer worlds.

Russell is fond of saying that he won over the producers at United Artists
by pitching the film as being "about a homosexual who falls in love with a
nymphomaniac."[89] Indeed, as far as it goes, that is a fair description of the
picture. Initially titled *The Lonely Heart*, later *Opus 74* (the opus number of
his Sixth "Pathetique" Symphony), and finally *The Music Lovers*, it portrays a
homosexual who struggles to contain his sexual nature in order to achieve a
"normal" relationship to a woman who is herself troubled by her own voracious sexual appetites. But, of course, there is so much more than that.
Russell's casual jest conceals far more complex agendas. "To me, Tchaikovsky
personifies nineteenth-century romanticism," he has said, "which is based on a
death wish. People call me self-indulgent, but Tchaikovsky was the most self-
indulgent man who ever lived, insofar as all his problems and hangups are
stated in his music. . . . His music, to me, has more pain in it than any music I
know; self-inflicted pain, despair, suffering, precious little joy and a kind of
hysterical striving for love, a love so intense it could never exist.[90] It is to
Russell's credit that he doesn't try to moderate these musical and temperamental oppositions and extremes; rather, in the grand Romantic tradition, he
allows them full expression. On the surface, the film's flamboyant visual style
bears a superficial resemblance to the madcap antics of *Dance of the Seven
Veils*, but whereas Strauss had been portrayed in that film as a comic-strip
caricature, Tchaikovsky is a complex character embroiled in the contradictions of his personality, sexuality, and art.

When plans fell through to cast Alan Bates as Tchaikovsky, Richard Chamberlain was awarded the part and Glenda Jackson the role of Tchaikovsky's
wife, Nina. Other roles went to Russell standbys Christopher Gable, as Tchaikovsky's lover, Count Anton Chiluvsky; Kenneth Colley as Tchaikovsky's
brother, Modest; Izabella Telezynska as his patron, Nadezhda von Meck; and
Sabine Maydell as his sister, Sasha. These are the "music lovers" of the title;
and each, with the exception of Modest and Chiluvsky (who seem content
with the mediocrity of their shallow lives), are torn apart by the cruel dis-
parities between their private fantasies and worldly realities. In this sense,
Bragg's script departed greatly from its nominal source, Catherine Drinker
Bowen and Barbara von Meck's 1937 biographical study of Tchaikovsky,
"Beloved Friend."[91] Fraught with sentimental effusions and considered spurious by many music historians, this book had carefully skirted the darker

Richard Chamberlain brought Pyotr Tchaikovsky to the screen in Ken Russell's controversial *The Music Lovers* (1970). (Courtesy Photofest/United Artists)

controversies and questions concerning Tchaikovsky's life, notably, the self-destructive nature of his homosexuality; the incestuous implications of his relations with his sister, Sasha; the unsavory character of his wife, Nina; the disastrous consequences of his marriage; the erotic implications behind Madame von Meck's patronage; and the allegation that his sudden, mysterious death was, contrary to received opinion, a suicide.[92]

The Music Lovers begins in 1877 during Tchaikovsky's student days at the Moscow Conservatory as he prepares to premiere his new B-flat Minor Piano Concerto; and it concludes in 1893 with his death from cholera. In between, events include the breakup of a homosexual affair with his lover, Vladimir Chiluvsky; his meeting with and disastrous marriage to Antonina (Nina) Ivanovna Milukove; the association with his patroness, Nadejda von Meck; the composition of many important works (notably, the opera *Eugene Onegin*, the ballet *Swan Lake*, the concert fantasy *Romeo and Juliet*, and the Fourth and Sixth Symphonies); the break with von Meck; the years of public celebrity and touring; and the incarceration of Nina in a madhouse.

The passion, the sweetness, the fantasy, the brutality, and the heartbreak of Tchaikovsky's music ultimately binds together these "music lovers." "There is not one piece of Tchaikovsky's music that is used in the film that is there only for its own sake," Russell has said. "It is all there to reflect some aspect of Tchaikovsky's life and personality."[93] Early in the story, for example, Tchaikovsky's performance of the B-flat Minor Piano Concerto — surely one of the great music sequences in all of Russell's oeuvre — brings everyone together in the concert hall and prefigures the dreams and failures of their subsequent interactions. The music itself is heard both diegetically, as soloist and orchestra perform in concert, and nondiegetically, as it underscores and counterpoints the characters' interior fantasies.

The sequence begins modestly enough: Tchaikovsky enters the hall, bows to the players, seats himself at the keyboard, and launches into the concerto's opening declamatory measures. When the music shifts to the tender lyricism of the slow movement's *andante semplice* (cleverly eliding several minutes by means of a cutaway to von Meck's late arrival to the auditorium), the scene opens up. Tchaikovsky's glance at Sasha triggers a fantasy about frolicking through the sun-drenched woods and meadows with her and her two children. The slow-motion images are sweet almost to the point of saccharinicity ("like the phony dream world of a television shampoo commercial," Russell notes dryly). There is a particularly striking displacement of time and space when the camera tracks the strolling Tchaikovsky to a window where, peering inside, he sees himself and his sister performing the concerto's cello theme. This clever piece of visual sleight-of-hand not only establishes the unusually intimate and artistic union between brother and sister, it seamlessly joins the diegetic performance and extradiegetic background music.

As the gentle music shifts to the skittish prestissimo episode, we return to the concert hall, where Tchaikovsky notices Nina looking on in the audience. It is time for her fantasy: She imagines that she and the soldier seated in front of her are toasting each other with champagne while riding in a briskly moving carriage on their way to marriage ceremony. Then, abruptly, as the music reprises the andante's main theme, we are back in the auditorium, our eyes on Sasha. Her dream seems to pick up the thread of her brother's vision of a woodland idyll — until the intrusive, leering presence of Chiluvsky seduces Tchaikovsky away from her (cut back to the keyboard, as Tchaikovsky catches a suggestive glance from Chiluvsky in the audience). The tension increases now, as the music segues to the cadenza and finale of the last movement. A quick zoom shot isolates the face of von Meck in the balcony. She listens, obviously enraptured, as Tchaikovsky pounds out the double octaves that introduce the orchestra's final peroration. The editing rhythm quickens as the faces of Nina, Sasha, Chiluvsky, and von Meck are reprised in a swift succession of shots. After the thunderous, climactic chords, Tchaikovsky rises from the keyboard to enthusiastic applause. He is dripping with sweat, breathing heavily, and apparently sharing a moment of postcoital exhaustion with all his "music lovers."

Russell has wrought a miracle here. Image and music commingle in an intoxicating whole. In a matter of minutes, sans dialogue, he has sketched the romantic, psychological, and sexual profiles of the principle characters in this music drama, established the foundations of the story line, and musically traversed innocent, lyric sweetness, yearning love, erotic intensity, and triumphant sexual consummation.

This is only the first of several important set pieces that casts music as a "character" in the drama. Consider the famous "Letter Scene" from Act One of Tchaikovsky's opera *Eugene Onegin*. It will be recalled that in this opera, based on a story by Alexander Pushkin, the character of Tatyana pens an impassioned love letter to Onegin. When he rejects her advances, she is devastated. Years later, when the repentant and lovelorn Onegin returns to her, she rebuffs him. It was a story that fascinated Tchaikovsky.[94] Thus, while beginning work on the opera in May 1877, he was astonished to receive a similar avowal of love from Nina, a woman he hardly knew as yet. Intrigued by the parallels this presented to Pushkin's story, and aroused by this romantic effusion, he is also fearful that his refusal of her love might precipitate the sort of crises depicted in his opera. He decides not to follow Onegin's example. He accepts her proposal.

Bragg fleshes out this incident into a complex sequence. "This letter, this declaration, it's right out of the opera," Tchaikovsky tells his brother. "If I don't reply, I know I'll regret it, forever." The pragmatic Modest answers sternly, "Eugene Onegin is a fictitious character, and so is the girl of his dreams. You talk as if they are real." Ignoring him, Tchaikovsky bends to completing the "Letter Scene" music. He rhapsodizes, cryptically, "She's a handsome creature, warm and tender, devoid of all artifice, totally innocent. She sees a man only once, but that once is enough. But when he refuses her offer of love, he is finished." We must ask ourselves at this point to whom Tchaikovsky's words and music refer—Tatyana, the heroine of his opera; the adoring Sasha, his would-be lover, Nina; von Meck, his patroness; or some other creature wholly of his dreams? Russell intentionally leaves us in suspense as he crosscuts back and forth, from Tatyana singing on stage (sung by April Contelo), to Nina furiously penning her love letter, to Sasha embracing him in the parlor, and to von Meck indulging her own erotic fantasies in her lonely mansion. All of them are creatures of their own fantasies, participating in a romantic opera of their own devising.

The *Swan Lake* ballet serves as a useful metaphor for Tchaikovsky's and Nina's ill-starred marriage. As the newlyweds watch an outdoor performance of the ballet, Tchaikovsky is astonished and offended at Nina's ignorance of the story. Turning away from her to attend to the performance, he doesn't notice Chiluvsky's arrival. The wicked Count, stung by his former lover's dismissal, is all too eager to apprise Nina of the opera's tragic plot: "The man is the prince and the woman is called Otile," he says, pointing out the dancers. "He thinks she is the pure, beautiful swan-woman he thinks of marrying." Chiluvsky casts a meaningful glance at Tchaikovsky. "But she'll destroy him." But both Tchaikovsky and Nina are oblivious to the obvious parallels. They blindly pursue the hope that they can find happiness and "normalcy" with each other. "There's so much you don't know about me, Nina," he confesses later; "things in my past you might find difficult to understand. I can change, you'll see. I'll lead a normal life with you. We'll be part of the world."

But of course, that will be denied them both. In the following scene, music again throws into stark relief the futility of their dreams. Tchaikovsky and Nina take the night train on their return to Moscow from their honeymoon. This trip into Hell is one of Russell's cruelest deconstructions of the Romantic dream. As Tchaikovsky get roaring drunk in the cramped confines of the swaying train compartment, the calamitous strains of the *sempre dolente appassionato* of the Sixth Symphony swell on the soundtrack to a noble if overwrought intensity. Sexually aroused, Nina begins to divest herself of her clothes. Startled, the composer shrinks back. Nina falls to the floor and pulls up her skirt and spreads her thighs suggestively. Tchaikovsky can't turn away; there's no escape. He recoils at the gruesome sight of her writhing, stark naked, on the floor. The tilting overhead lamp fitfully illuminates the scene with strobelike stabs of light. Capping the hideous scene are distorted close-ups of his screaming face as the music shifts gear and overwhelms the image with the frenzied convulsions of the main theme of the *Manfred* music. We, too, want to look away, ashamed, embarrassed, and horrified. "The scene is debilitating for its intensity," writes music historian Joseph Horowitz, "and funny for its extravagance. If we enjoy it, we feel guilty; if we don't we are prudes."[95] Although Russell and Bragg have been taken to task for the nightmarish exaggeration of this scene, they received unexpected corroboration years later with the discovery of a letter from Tchaikovsky that acknowledges the anguish and torment he felt during that fateful honeymoon trip.[96]

Perhaps Russell's most extravagant musical fantasy is the *1812 Overture* sequence, which savagely indicts what Russell asserts is Tchaikovsky's sellout to commercialism. "If it's love you want," Modest tells his brother, "an audience will give you that." Music from Tchaikovsky's most popular composition, the *1812 Overture,* a potboiler commemorating Russia's defeat of Napoleon in 1812 (and containing quotations from the Russian national anthem, "God Save the Tsar"), is juxtaposed to scenes of wildly screaming fans who lift him to their shoulders and carry him through clouds of confetti. As Modest capers about, counting stacks of money and firing cannons to decapitate the faithless "music lovers" Chiluvsky, Sasha, and von Meck, Tchaikovsky ascends the podium to conduct his Overture. His gestures, initially spasmodic like a marionette's, gradually acquire enthusiasm as he is caught up in the lust for money and fame.[97] "*The Music Lovers* wasn't so much about a person as an idea," Russell has said, "about the destructive power of fantasy on people's lives." Russell holds Tchaikovsky to blame for much of the anguish suffered by those around him — an opinion echoed years later by biographer Anthony Holden.[98]

Working within the relatively relaxed restrictions of the American Ratings Code, as opposed to the stricter censorial constraints of England, Russell was able to further indulge his penchant for extravagant visual and musical fantasies. Indeed, no biographical portrait had ever looked and sounded like *this* before. In hindsight, *The Music Lovers* seems to be the first "adult" composer biopic to be released in mainstream theaters. General viewers accustomed to the standard, tamer Hollywood composer biopics were understandably astonished, confused, even repelled at the results. The destructive implications of Tchaikovsky's homosexuality — not so much the homosexuality per se but the composer's ill-fated attempts to ignore it in his obsessive drive to achieve a "normal" life ("You wanted a husband," he tells Nina; "I wanted marriage without a wife") — had never been so publicly acknowledged.[99] Likewise outrageous were the film's allegations of Nina's prostitution, von Meck's neurotic obsession with Tchaikovsky ("Tchaikovsky's music alone reminds me that life can be rich and full of meaning"), and the allegation that Tchaikovsky's death was a suicide ("He chose to commit suicide by drinking contaminated water," declares the doctor).[100]

Some viewers were puzzled that the character of Sasha, so crucial to the early scenes, mysteriously disappears in the second half of the film, while, by contrast, Nina seems to dominate much of the second half.[101] And there were complaints that Richard Chamberlain's makeup and hair stylings prettied up the composer too much.[102] Many critics and scholars, meanwhile, went on the attack. Judith Crist, Pauline Kael, and Gary Arnold, for example, branded it, respectively, as "semi-porno," "hyper-Hollywood," and "a monstrosity."[103]

Among the scholars, biographer Poznansky characterized it as a "cinemato-graphic fantasy" that "makes of [Tchaikovsky] a neurotic *bon vivant*, ter-rorized by women, and hideously expiring in the hot bath."[104] And although commentator Gordon Gow praised the "dramatically valid" scenes of gro-tesquerie as "pertinent to the hypersensitive state of mind [Russell] is depict-ing," he complained that such scenes have "a tendency to outweigh the heady splendours of the passages which are superbly aligned with the music it-self."[105] The vitriol and ferocity of some of these attacks prefigured even worse to come.

Melvyn Bragg ruefully acknowledges these criticisms. "Oh, yes, you get the usual feedback for this sort of thing, which is that you are dumped on. But that's what happens to you in this game. The positive side is that you're allowed to do it in the first place. It just about evens out in the end." Bragg defends the flamboyance of the musical fantasies in the Piano Concerto, "Let-ter Song," and the *1812 Overture* sequences. "Ken and I like that sort of story-telling, and I think much of that still looks pretty good. I think the "Let-ter Song," particularly, is still a beautiful eight minutes of film."[106] And while Bragg admits dissatisfaction of his own regarding Chamberlain's perfor-mance, he insists that the inordinate screen time afforded Glenda Jackson was vital to the story.[107] "Richard Chamberlain is obviously a very good actor and in one way was kind of an inspired choice by Ken. But I think in the makeup, the excessive gesturings, the over-pretty makeup, he lost it. He just was not convincing for me as Tchaikovsky. Or maybe my script wasn't good enough. As for my emphasis on Nina, well, she faces the same predicament as Tchai-kovsky, doesn't she? I mean, she can't accept who she is, and her tragedy parallels his."[108]

Ironically, another Tchaikovsky biopic was in production at the time of the release of *The Music Lovers*. Dimitri Tiomkin's *Tchaikovsky* was a Soviet production being shot in Russia. At the time, Tiomkin charged that Russell for his own ends had sensationalized the composer's life and had exploited the advance publicity of the Russian version. Stung by the allegation, Russell shot back: "We did vast research and we screened the truth. The Russians have made a film on the same subject, but because Tchaikovsky is a national hero, they have whitewashed him."[109]

The first few minutes of *Mahler* (1974) proclaim Russell's growing confidence in a more elastic structure and freewheeling style than he had yet allowed himself. Biographer Gomez sees it as "Russell's most experimental work to date," a fragmented film "with brilliant sequences."[110] The opening sequence proves Gomez's point: The first image is of a wooden hut situated near a lake.

Suddenly it bursts into flames. As the strident trumpet blasts from the first movement of the Third Symphony break the silence, a sheathed, white cocoonlike figure lying on the rocky beach wriggles violently. The sheath is burst and, gradually, arms and legs emerge; finally a human form begins to crawl toward a large rock, which resembles Mahler's face, and caresses its stony features. Cut to the figure of Mahler (Robert Powell) in silhouetted profile, sitting silently in a train compartment, the station platform visible through the window behind him. He turns to a lovely blond woman (Georgina Hale as Alma Mahler) next to him and says, "You were a living creature, struggling to be born." She wrinkles her brow and retorts, "At last, you've noticed!" As she quits the compartment, we see through the window a little tableau on the station platform: A young boy dressed in a sailor suit carelessly cavorts about while a middle-aged man dressed in white sits primly on a bench, covertly eyeing him. Music from the "Adagietto" from Mahler's Fifth Symphony tracks the scene. . . .

So much is here, so deftly tossed off in mere minutes — the seaside hut at Steinbach where Mahler spent his summers composing; the white chrysalis as a metaphoric allusion to his wife Alma's struggles to assume an identity on her own as a composer; the rock-image of Mahler's face, suggesting the subtitle of the first movement of Mahler's First Symphony, "What the Rocks Tell Me"; Mahler's last train ride from Paris to Vienna in 1911, having just returned from a sojourn in America; and intertextual references to Luchino Visconti's film, *Death in Venice,* based on the novel by Thomas Mann, which used Mahler's Fifth Symphony "Adagietto" to underpin the story of an older man's blighted hopes for romance with a young boy.

Mahler is not only a fantasy on Mahler's life and work, but it also contains a secondary portrait of Mahler's wife, Alma (who gave Russell permission to make the film). That opening shot of the explosion and conflagration in the seaside hut is like a match touched to the tinder of his subject. Indeed, later in the film, a mysterious character named Nick (Ronald Pickup) talks of this creative blaze when he instructs the child Mahler in the ways of life: "We all have a glimmering of the divine spark, I suppose," he says, "deep down inside us, glowing in the dark. But we all need something, something special to ignite it — to make it burst into flame!"

Mahler's railway journey back to Vienna in 1911, having just concluded his exhausting sojourn in New York City, provides the narrative throughline upon which are hung a series of flashbacks and musical dream fantasies. The flashbacks contain quick, caricatured images of Mahler's childhood, with dear old dad making love to the maid in the hayloft and abusing young Gustav with a stick (in that order), the family swilling soup at the dinner table, and young

Gustav sweating out piano scales; later scenes in his life include the married Gustav playing with his two little girls, his accusations of Alma's infidelities, a visit to the crazed Hugo Wolf in an asylum, his conversion to Catholicism, and the death of his daughter Maria in 1906. By the time the train arrives, a visiting doctor, who has assured the obviously ailing composer that concerns about his health are unnecessary, privately confides that his condition is terminal and that he will not last out the week. Blissful in his ignorance, Mahler and Alma step out onto the platform. "You can go home, doctor," he calls out, "we're going to live forever!" The image freezes. A title informs us he died shortly thereafter, in 1906.

The music fantasies, as usual, constitute the highlights of the film. Two, in particular, stand out. In the first, near the beginning of the film, Mahler is at work in his lakeside hut. He rebukes his wife's remarks about the silence of the area, declaring the "silence" is actually teeming with the sounds of man and nature. His duty as a composer is to create their musical correlatives. "If all the birds and the beasts died tomorrow and the world became a desert," he says, "and people heard my music, they would still know, and feel, what Nature was." In the ensuing montage, nature's sounds blend into — and are replaced by — moments from Mahler's symphonies. The shaking of Alma's baby rattle becomes the opening sleighbell-like notes of the first movement of the Fourth Symphony. The swinging of the church bell is intercut with the ticking of his desk metronome, and in turn blended with an extract from the Third Symphony. Cowbells tinkle and merge with the "Es Sungen Drei Engel" episode, also from the Third Symphony. The shepherd's piping segues into the flute solo from another moment from the Fourth Symphony's first movement. And an oompah band's bleat is transformed into the sturdy melody from the second movement from the First Symphony. Tripping through this interplay of sound and image is the white-clad figure of Alma, anointing, as it were — and silencing — each of these natural sounds as they are replaced by Mahler's musical equivalents. And there's a lovely moment when, accompanied by music from the Third Symphony's first movement, the woodland dissolves into the image of planet Earth, spinning in the spangled cosmos, which in turn dissolves back into the orb of the sun behind Mahler's head. Not since the "Testament of Heiligenstadt" sequence in Abel Gance's *Beethoven* has there been such an adroit and moving visualization of the processes of composing, in which the interior diegesis of musical sounds replicate, transform, and transcend their natural references.[111] Musical creation replaces and, ironically, effectively silences Nature's creations.

The second sequence is much darker in tone and quite affecting in its muted simplicity. The music from two songs from the cycle *Kindertotenlieder* — "In

Ken Russell's *Mahler* (1973) depicted Robert Powell and Georgina Hale as Gustav and Alma Mahler in many imaginative fantasy sequences. (Courtesy Photofest)

diesem Wetter, in diesem Braus" and "Wenn dein Mutterlein tritt zur Tur herein" (sung by Carol Mudie) — accompanies images of the two children scampering about the windy forest, their frilly white jumpers glimmering like fireflies in the darkling wood. Shots of them waving good-bye from atop a balcony and being tucked into bed yield to the image of a small coffin resting atop a piano. Cut to Mahler, in a darkened room, composing. Quietly, he declaims to himself the text of a song as Alma, carrying a candle, silently enters the room: "The mother comes through the door and I turn my head to look at her. Not on her face my first glance falls; but on the place close to her side where your dear face would be, smiling your good night to me as you used to. Little one. When your sweet mother comes through the door and the candles glow, I remember how you always came to me, running before her, to say goodnight." Alma leaves the room and the light fades: "Now in the growing darkness we are left alone. Joy forever gone." This quietly moving scene stands as a rebuke to those who tend to dismiss Russell as a mere showman of bombast and noise.

But speaking of . . . Yes, Mahler the ringmaster is here, too, in two bizarre sequences that recall the comic-strip style of *Dance of the Seven Veils*. The first, a fantasy on Mahler's religious conversion, accompanied by the "Rondo Burlesco" from the Ninth Symphony, is structured and styled in the manner of a silent movie, complete with title cards. In a tacky, pasteboard"Valhalla," Cosima Wagner (Antonia Ellis) is dressed like a storm trooper in drag, complete with helmet and whip. As she struts about, snapping off Nazi salutes, Mahler appears in the costume of a Jewish rabbi and jumps through flaming hoops bearing the emblem of the Christian cross. Like a knife-thrower at a carnival, Alma hurls blades at him. Mahler then transforms into the figure of a Jewish Siegfried who hammers the Star of David into a sword, which he brandishes aloft and turns against a dragon. Emerging victorious from the dragon's cave, he now sports the "Mammy" blackface of Al Jolson. As a reward, Cosima sits him down to a table and brings him a boar's head. "Still kosher?" she asks. Mahler/Siegfried sinks his teeth into the snout. A title card appears: "Along came the Talkies." Cosima now declaims a text to the melody of "The Ride of the Valkyries": "No longer a Jew boy, you're one of us now; now you're a goy!" Mahler and Cosima climb atop a gigantic sword hilt and sit cradled in the crossbars, where they sit and exchange a kiss. In a breathtaking cut, the scene now shifts to Mahler's church conversion ceremony, where the rosary he holds is described as "a passport to heaven, the keys to the kingdom of the Vienna State Opera."

The second example, which symbolizes Mahler's fear of being buried alive, is transpired against excerpts from the "Trauermarsch" of the Fifth Symphony. His body is stacked upright in a coffin, his contorted face visible through a tiny window. Nazi S.S. soldiers march the coffin in goose-step toward a crematorium as Alma dances a high-kicking cancan atop the bier. As the coffin is consigned to the flames, Alma kisses the glass, behind which Mahler's lips move in a silent scream. After the ashes are removed, Alma performs a slinky striptease, cavorting across a series of life-sized, stand-up photographs of the composer. She climbs aboard a gigantic gramophone horn. The camera, positioned directly in front of the horn, now moves toward — and into — its yawning maw.

The references here are obvious enough. Indeed, these and many other musical sequences — including a montage of children's picture books seen against the sounds of the peroration from the last movement of the First Symphony; the boy Mahler's nocturnal stroll through the woodlands, climaxed by his leaping astride a magnificent white stallion to the music of the third movement of the Third Symphony; Mahler's reconciliation with Alma in the film's final scene to the second movement of the Sixth Symphony — all point the viewer/listener toward the strange, sometimes bitter truths surrounding Mahler and his world. Mahler's creative ego superseded phenomenal Nature altogether. He did indeed use the subject of the death of children as a stimulus for composing (although Russell has altered the chronology here). He lived in a viciously anti-Semitic world musically dominated by Cosima Wagner's Aryan Christian agendas. His conversion to Catholicism, while perhaps sincere, did conveniently facilitate his appointment to the Court Theatre in Vienna. His wife, Alma, had indulged in an extramarital affair with the architect Walter Gropius, whom she married in 1915; and it is suggested that after Mahler's death she desecrated his memory by taking on other lovers (even if she did not exactly dance on his grave, as depicted here).[112] The premature burial suggests that in converting to Catholicism, Mahler has become a Jew pretending not to be a Jew—the demise of his faith before that of his flesh. And, as Russell has asserted, his fascist satire of Mahler's harshly militaristic music took its cue from Mahler's "prophetic vision of a nightmarish, jack-booted future."[113]

The film's release in 1973 capitalized on an ongoing resurgence of Mahler's music, led by such stalwarts as Leonard Bernstein and Bernard Haitink (who conducts the music here). Moreover, Russell at long last finally indulged his lifelong fascination with Mahler. "Elgar apart, Mahler is my favourite composer," he wrote in his autobiography, "and I feel we have a lot in common apart from both being Cancerians and living near a lake surrounded by mighty hills."[114] Indeed, both men converted to Catholicism. Both endured hostile attacks on their work. Both believed unabashedly in the programmatic implications of music and that music is inextricably bound up with its creator. Mahler, after all, is a composer who famously said in 1895, "Meine musik ist gelebt" ("My music is lived"). Its wellsprings are at once in himself and in nature. "My music is only 'Naturlaut' [the sound of nature]," he said a year later, "I know of no other program. . . . We probably receive from nature all primeval rhythms and themes."[115] Moreover, Mahler's eclecticism parallels Russell's in its bewildering contrasts and astonishing variety. Russell has noted that Mahler's "bombast" as well as "music that was brutal, vulgar, grotesque, macabre" are the self-same qualities for which he himself is most frequently criticized. Indeed, critic Alex Ross's description of Mahler's music could well stand in for Russell's films: "Everyone knows his swooning intensity of emotion: not only the famous grandeurs and sufferings, but also the intermediate states of waltz-time languor, kitsch-drenched sweetness and sadness, medieval revelation, military rancor, dissonant delirium, adagio lament."[116] Cultural theorist Theodor Adorno's assessment likewise conjures up the films of Russell: "Giant structures are built up, reach to the major-key heavens, then suddenly collapse in downward chromatic swoops and shuddering dissonances."[117]

Lisztomania (1975), along with Charles Vidor's Chopin picture, *A Song to Remember* (1945), may be the best known, if not the most notorious (and condemned) of all composer biopics. Even from a filmmaker who reveled in the excesses of the Romantic sensibility and its many inherent contradictions, *Lisztomania* overreached itself. Russell perhaps pursued too zealously the special empathy he felt with Liszt's assertion "Truly great men are those who combine contrary qualities within themselves." Warner Bros. didn't help things out when it included in the movie's trailer the declaration "You won't understand it, but you'll love every minute of it!" However miscalculated it may have been, one is tempted to agree with biographer Ken Hanke, who wrote, "On the basis of intentions alone, *Lisztomania* is the grandest gesture of Russell's career."[118]

The film is very much a product of the 1970s, owing much to the popularity of the rock opera *Tommy*, which Russell had directed the year before with Roger Daltrey of The Who. The experience with *Tommy* convinced Russell that he should reconsider his audience base and work more specifically to a younger demographic. Despite bringing back Daltrey in the image of nineteenth-century piano virtuoso Franz Liszt—transforming him into a prototype of the rock star of the day (it was Heinrich Heine who coined the term "Lisztomania")—and bringing in rocker Rick Wakeman to give the musical arrangements a contemporary idiom, popular music fans were bewildered by the variety of classical and political references. Classical music aficionados were put off by what seemed to be irresponsibly reckless posturing and distortions of the biographical and musical record. And *everyone*, it seems, balked at what Jack Kroll, writing in *Newsweek*, described as a "mad discord of ideas and images" and a "freaked out charade."[119] Richard Eder in the *New York Times* dismissed it as "a tiny, potentially appealing weed of a picture, absurdly dragged down by a mass of post-Beatles rococo. . . . It is full of flashing lights, satin spacesuits, chrome-lucite furniture and mock agony."[120] On the other hand, there was at least one note of praise. Kevin Thomas in the *Los Angeles Times,* saw it as "an exhilarating and even pleasant wonderment," forsaking reality entirely for fantasy. It is entirely Russell's film, concluded Thomas: "In short, 'Lisztomania' suggests that it [is] far more effective for Russell to present the fantasy inspired by the music of his beloved composers as his rather than theirs."[121]

The film is structured as a succession of satiric allusions to popular culture, including horror movies, glitter rock, comic books, slapstick silent films, television soap operas, and soft-core pornography. Its appropriations of their clichés rip them out of their original contexts and hold them up for fresh, sometimes appalling scrutiny. Certainly it marks Russell's furthest extreme from the more literal and sober-minded *Elgar* of twenty-five years previous. Yet, its guiding agenda is very much in line with his other work, particularly the Strauss and Mahler films—that is, witnessing with a jaundiced eye the failure of artists to cope with the crushing conformity of mass society and popular culture.

The narrative line, such as it is, begins with Liszt's liaison with his mistress, the Countess Marie d'Agoult (Fiona Lewis), and continues with his support of the young Richard Wagner (Paul Nicholas), his popularity as a concert performer, his relationship with the Princess Carolyn von Wittgenstein (Sarah Ketelman), his withdrawal from political revolution during the Dresden riots of 1848, the Princess's failure to get the divorce that would allow her to marry Liszt, Liszt's decision to become an abbé in the church, the symbiotic relationship with Wagner during the years in Munich, Weimar, and Bayreuth, and, finally, an epilogue that depicts Liszt's struggles to overturn the corruptive influences of Wagner on modern music and politics.

The above conveys nothing of the true (non)sense and sensibility of *Lisztomania.* It is in the wildly ranging metaphors, allusions, and absurdist juxtapositions of fact and fantasy, music and image, that we can better divine what Russell is up to. When the outraged husband of d'Agoult discovers his wife and Liszt *in flagrante delicto,* he takes on the composer in a duel choreographed like the swashbuckling antics of Douglas Fairbanks, accompanied by a musical polyglot of funky waltz tunes, blue-grass stylings, and quotations from Liszt's tone poem, *The Battle of the Huns.* Liszt's piano recital is staged in the manner of a seventies rock concert, complete with frenzied groupies, crisscrossing spotlights, and pushy paparazzi. On the platform he alternates his *Rienzi* variations with the banal tune of "Chopsticks" (to the outrage of the young Wagner), who sits seething in the audience.[122] Concert life on the road with d'Agoult is presented as a silent film parody of Charlie Chaplin's *The Gold Rush,* with Liszt and d'Agoult dressed up as Chaplin and his girlfriend singing the sweetly banal lyrics set to Liszt's "Liebestraum" melody.

Liszt's second liaison, with the Princess von Wittgenstein, is conceptualized as a soft-porn exploitation film, accompanied by a Spike Jones–style version of the theme from *Les Preludes* and a quotation from the *Dante Symphony.* In perhaps the most outrageous moment in all of Russell's music fantasies, the Princess, modeled after *Tommy's* Acid Queen, stages a mock castration with a guillotine of Liszt's gargantuan-sized phallus. The subsequent Dresden sequence has the now reclusive, emasculated Liszt living alone in an ivory tower, high above the arena of Wagner's political machinations. But Wagner, desirous of stealing Liszt's creative energies, corners him and sinks his vampire's fangs into his throat, muttering, "I shall write music which will fire the imagination of the German people and bring to life a Man of Iron to forge the shattered fragments of this country into a nation of steel."

Meanwhile, attempts by Liszt and the Princess to secure her divorce from the

Church lead to a meeting with the Pope (Ringo Starr). When his petition is refused, Liszt mutters, "I'll get my revenge on him; I'll get him to support me for the rest of my life. I'll become a priest!" Nonplussed, the Pope mandates Liszt to confront the evil Wagner and "exorcise" his plans for a Master Race. The penultimate sequence, where the priestly Liszt strives to exorcise the villainous Wagner vampire, is staged in the manner of a Universal horror movie — complete with a Gothic castle in which Wagner, personified as Count Dracula, lives with his acolyte, Cosima Liszt (Veronica Quilligan), and his Jonathan Harker–type sycophant, Hans Von Bülow. The music throughout is a crazy blend of themes from the *Totentanz,* the First Piano Concerto, and synthesized-sound versions of the "Magic Fire" and the "Ride of the Valkyries" tunes from Wagner's *Ring.* Although Liszt defeats Wagner with his flame-throwing piano, Wagner's Frankenstein-like monster, a Superman in the guise of Siegfried (with "Siegfried's Funeral Music" on the soundtrack) survives to lay waste to wartorn Europe with his guitar/machine gun.

The epilogue is set in a cotton-candy Heaven, where Liszt and his female acolytes — Marie, Cosima, Carolyn, George Sand, Lola Montes — convene to discuss Wagner's theft of Liszt's music ("I didn't mind him taking it, it was what he did with it that was pretty horrible!"). Declaring that Wagner should be put out of his misery because he's "giving music a bad name," they climb aboard a rocket-shaped pipe organ and, in a sequence presented in the manner of a Flash Gordon serial, dive-bomb the Nazi Wagner–monster, leaving his guitar squashed into the dirt. Thus, pianos, organs, guitars, and machine guns all serve as metaphors for the tools of the artist, by turns "instruments" of creation and destruction. Collectively they constitute a fusion of Orpheus's lyre with engines of destruction. In the end the "Liebestraum" theme is sung one last time by Daltrey, with these sweetly bathetic lines:

> Now Love, sweet Love
> Oh now that Love has won
> Now Love, our Love
> Our Love has ended war
> He'll torture man no more.

Freely interpretive as Russell was with the historical record, he was just as liberal in his treatments of Liszt's and Wagner's music. Save for a few scattered instances in the Strauss and Mahler films, he had never before felt obliged to alter his musical sources, preferring to respect their original orchestrations. Now, with the assistance of Rick Wakeman, he parodied Hollywood's manner of selecting, restructuring, rescoring, and varying a handful of familiar classical tunes — notably, the third "Liebestraum," the theme of the first movement of the First Piano Concerto, a melody from *Les Preludes,* and a tune from the *Hungarian Fantasy* for piano and orchestra — and set them to lyrics by Daltrey and Jonathan Benson. In the manner of techniques employed by a Max Steiner or a Dimitri Tiomkin, Russell deploys a central motto, or thematic motif, that is varied and interwoven throughout the action — a mock "fate" motif derived from the opening seven notes of the Piano Concerto.

In sum, the confused Liszt (torn between his gypsy passions and his religious asceticism), the clinging Marie d'Agoult, the castrating Princess Wittgenstein, and the malevolent despot Wagner and his sycophantic acolytes Hans von Bülow and Cosima Liszt are all pasteboard cutouts moved about by Russell in a reprise of his by now familiar thematic targets — the false excesses of Romanticism and the failure of art and artists to defeat and transcend the seductive corruptions of mass culture and society. As a result, Russell has been accused, with some justification, of simplifying to the point of absurdity these character types and situations.

Yet, although they may seem like crazy burlesques, they are bound up with historical truth. The depiction of Liszt as a rock star, a Chaplinesque tramp, and a priest beautifully sums up Liszt's self-assessment that he was "half Franciscan, half Gypsy" (Russell makes a pun on the name "FRANZ-iscan") and that artists are "useless clowns, ill-fated troubadours." As an artist and performer, Liszt did indeed prefigure the celebrity status of today's popular musicians. He was the first great international superstar and attracted a public already on its way to becoming the mass audience of today's mass culture. Yet in 1847, at the height of his fame, his years of *glanzzeit,* he abjured the concert stage and never again performed publicly for money. Eighteen years later he took Holy Orders (an act that biographer Alan Walker regards as sincere) and was indeed empowered to conduct exorcisms.[123]

Constructing Liszt's relationship with Wagner as a clash between an exorcist and a vampire places Liszt in the appropriate context of a Universal horror film. Russell was surely alluding to Universal's *The Phantom of the Opera* (1943), for example, wherein there is a scene where Liszt (Fritz Leiber) performs a concert on the stage of the Paris Opera while the mad villain, Erik (Claude Rains), thrashes about in his infernal agonies below in the catacombs. Moreover, it was perfectly true that Liszt was exploited by Wagner, who seized some of his musical ideas and opportunistically exploited Liszt's professional contacts and favors (not to mention stealing the daughter away from Liszt's son-in-law, von Bülow).[124] And there is no question that Wagner's anti-Semitism and Aryan posturings were co-opted (with the cooperation of Wagner's descendants) by the Nazis.[125] But even Ken Russell cannot entirely avoid the accusation of carrying things too far. To suggest that Liszt somehow eradicated the

Roger Daltrey's Franz Liszt
suffered vampiric attacks from
Paul Douglas's Richard Wagner
in Ken Russell's erotic fantasy,
Lisztomania (1975). (Courtesy
Photofest/Warner Bros.)

noxious influences of Wagner's life and music influences and that Wagner, in turn, was directly responsible for constructing the musical profile of the Nazi Reich are absurdly simplistic.[126] Yes, it could be argued that Russell mocks these pretensions, but, as critic Richard Eder noted, "Try mocking a quicksand by somersaulting artistically into it."[127] It would be left to another film, Tony Palmer's *Wagner* (1983), to bring the Liszt-Wagner relationship to the screen in a more sober and complex fashion.[128]

Russell himself admits in hindsight to some misgivings about the picture. "Yes, there were all kinds of problems with *Lisztomania*," he said in a recent interview. "I see that now; but even then I think I knew the symbolism and fantasy were pushed too far; and the reality of the characters suffered for that. Maybe I was just tired of making composer biographies. I know I needed to give it a rest for a while."

The South Bank Show

After a hiatus away from television, Russell has returned to the medium in the past two decades with several composer biopics that display a welcome return to the relatively modest dimensions of his first BBC *Monitor* projects. *Portrait of a Composer: Ralph Vaughan Williams* (1984), *The Strange Afflic-tion of Anton Bruckner* (1990), *The Mystery of Dr. Martinu* (1991), *Arnold*

Bax (1992), and *Elgar: Fantasie of a Composer on a Bicycle* (2002) are important, albeit little known biopics. Other musical projects are more difficult to
categorize, such as his *Russell on Russell* and *The ABCs of Music*. Most of
these projects reunited him with Melvyn Bragg, who since *The Debussy Film*
had risen to the ranks of producer of London Weekend Television's *The South
Bank Show*. "Ken is no different from anybody else," says Bragg, "in that
sometimes the quality or direction of work depends to an extent on whom he's
working with. He's a brilliant talent, and I don't buy in to the idea that he has
become some sort of Icarus who, at his height, suddenly plunged back to
earth. When I took over *The South Bank Show*, I welcomed him back. And
he's done some cracking films for me."

Like all of Russell's best work, these late musical portraits are highly personalized tributes to the music and musicians he has loved since his youth. "All of
my recent composer films are like home movies, autobiographical in one way
or another," Russell says. "I guess it's fair to say the obvious, that these portraits of composers are in a way self-portraits. It would be pretty fantastic if I
didn't have something in common with these artists. And didn't Tchaikovsky
and Mahler say that their music is autobiographical, too? When anything
happens to me, I find a way of getting it into my films. For instance, for my
Vaughan Williams movie I took my family along with me, my wife Viv and
daughter Molly. We did a musical tour of the places that inspired his music —
the streets of London, London Bridge, the hills around Lulworth Cove, Stonehenge, the coast of Cornwall."

The telecast of *Portrait of a Composer: Vaughan Williams* was preceded by
a statement from Bragg: "Ken Russell, who made this film especially for the
South Bank Show, has specialized generally in the extraordinary lives of musicians. By his standards, Rafe Vaughan Williams['s] life is uneventful. He was
constrained, for example, for fifty years by his having to nurse his first wife.
Russell has chosen to tell this story in several ways; principally with Ursula
Vaughan Williams, his second wife, who delivers what is in effect a memoir of
her husband. We also look at the music in the nine symphonies, how they
describe the inner life of Vaughan Williams. Russell also tells the story as a tale
for his youngest daughter, Molly."

One gets the impression that Russell had what Vaughan Williams (1872–
1958) might have called "a jolly good time" making this film (more properly, a
film within a film) allowing himself to come out on screen and do what he has
always done behind the scenes — that is, tell stories, conduct viewers on tours
of locations appropriate to music, interpret the meanings of the music at hand,
chat up his film crew, and even venture some opinions as film critic. First, as
storyteller, Russell reads to little Molly from a picture book. As the pages turn,

his narrative, accompanied by shots of photographs, fill in Vaughan Williams's backstory — that he was born on 12 October 1872 in a Gloucester village and as a little boy wrote a piece called "The Robin's Nest" for piano ("He wore a skirt there, you see; boys did; and long hair"); that he later went to Cambridge and married Adeline, a cellist ("Pretty, isn't she?"); that he studied at the Royal College of Music under Hubert Parry and Charles Villiers Stanford; that he went to the Great War as a wagon orderly ("But he finished the war shooting guns"); that he married his second wife-to-be, Ursula, in 1938 ("Their collaboration started then"); and that he subsequently traveled and composed and conducted into his eighties.

Little Molly yawns.

Interspersed throughout these readings are ten musical sequences with Russell as a tour guide of London and environs, accompanied by Molly and the film crew (cinematographer Peter Savage and editor Xavier Russell), and the composer's widow, Ursula. "Getting Ursula Vaughan Williams to accompany him on a tour of the composer's music and places was a charming way to bring off that film," says Bragg. "You must realize that the budgets I gave him were ridiculous. You would have difficulty having a good night in London on those budgets! They're very low for arts programmes. Besides, Ken couldn't afford actors — it was Ursula or nobody."

Each location sequence is keyed either to the composer's nine symphonies or several of his other well-known works. At times, Russell and Ursula playfully discuss and sometimes dispute the meanings inherent in the musical examples; at others, they stroll about with the film crew, partying, exploring, conversing about the various subjects at hand. First, the opening shot discloses a cave opening. Silhouetted against the light of the distant sea, a cloaked figure walks away from the camera. Cut to Ursula, addressing the camera, who relates the composer's use of lines by Walt Whitman in the First Symphony (the so-called "Sea Symphony"). Periodically, she interrupts her monologue to check her lines with an off-camera script consultant ("Did I get it right?"), who reminds her to add lines about the premiere of this work at the Leeds Choral Society on Vaughan Williams's thirty-eighth birthday. Second, as we hear the music from *Fantasia on a Theme of Thomas Tallis,* Ursula strolls about the interior of a church, chatting about her husband's discovery of settings of Tallis's sixteenth-century metrical tunes. Third, music from the Second Symphony ("London") accompanies Russell and Ursula's freewheeling tour of London, by car and on foot. There are shots of the ongoing reconstruction of Big Ben and of Westminster Abbey and the South Bank; scenes of a disco turn with Russell and Ursula (Ursula lovely in the shifting, kaleidoscopic light), a boat ride's view of St. Paul's, and a visit to the Royal Tank Museum (as a tank ominously follows behind Ursula's trek across the grounds). Fourth, music from the Third Symphony accompanies a trip to Gloucester as Ursula talks with violinist Iona Brown about the pastoral affinities the Third Symphony shares with the "Song of the Lark Ascending." Brown performs sections from the "Lark" as she visits a local church and strolls about the surrounding countryside.

Fifth, the Fourth Symphony: During a party scene everyone toasts the music. Russell visits with David Wilcox of the Royal College of Music and the widow Sir John Barbirolli, the conductor and friend of Vaughan Williams. She opines that despite Vaughan Williams's "big human frame," he held within him a "gentleness of spirit and an effervescent humor." Russell interrupts with a blunt "Take Four!" Sixth, the warlike turmoil of the Fifth Symphony: Back inside the Tank Museum we see row upon row of gun barrels. Dummies sit inside the cockpits. Russell and Ursula decide to quit the place, and they walk up the gentle slope of a lovely green meadow. Seventh, the Sixth Symphony is being rehearsed for a studio recording, conducted by Vernon Handley with the London Philharmonic Orchestra. The banks of monitors, seen in split screen, record the progress of the session. Sitting beside the monitor screens, Handley discourses on the music's wide range of expression, of the unusually violent tone ("The more you know of his great range, the more you come to love it"). Eighth, shock cut to ice fields and a platoon of penguins scrambling up a snowy bank. We are temporarily disoriented. "Best acting in the film," says Russell, with a nod toward the penguins. He and Ursula are in a screening room viewing scenes from *Scott of the Antarctic* (1954), whose music score was subsequently converted by Vaughan Williams into his Seventh Symphony ("Symphonia Antarctica"). "I think all these crude sound effects are rather unnecessary against the music," he complains, turning to Ursula. "Your husband was exploring sonorities here." Ursula agrees, "Yes, exploring the sounds of cold and desolation." Ninth, the Eighth Symphony is a clatter of bells, gongs, and cymbals. Russell and Ursula stand on a balcony overlooking the orchestral ensemble. And tenth, "We're approaching the end of the journey, now," says Russell as he and Ursula walk beside the sea. They discuss her collaboration with Vaughan Williams on the masque *Pilgrim's Progress* and its evocations of Salisbury Plain and Stonehenge. The music from the Ninth Symphony wells up on the soundtrack to a visual reprise of the film's key images — the Stonehenge rocks, Big Ben, the sea, the countryside, the performing orchestra, the Antarctic explorers, and finally a dissolve to Ursula, standing alone before Stonehenge. The sequence concludes as a shot of the sea dissolves into a photograph of the aged Vaughan Williams.

In the spirit of collaboration, Russell's visual interpretations of the music are open to dispute. For example, in the first scene Russell confides to the cameraman that he intends to associate music from the First Symphony with the image of a cave mouth opening onto the open sea. "Here, Vaughan Willams is escaping from the ghost of Brahms," he says (at which point we hear the opening, declamatory blast from Brahms's First Symphony). The disrespectful cameraman shrugs off the idea. After declaiming all the musical correlations between the second movement of the "London" Symphony and London's landmarks, Russell is rebuked by Ursula, who denies her husband intended any such thing. Russell replies, undaunted, "But it's got a lot of naturalistic ingredients, like trams and a lavender girl crying her wares, and you can hear the beggars rattling the coins in their hats." Ursula scoffs, "Maybe it's just a horse's harness!" Rather lamely, Russell concludes, "It's a very beautiful sound, anyway." Later, as they listen to the Eighth Symphony, Russell claims to hear "wedding bells" in the music. "I should hardly think so," objects Ursula. "The first performance of that piece was in 1956, and we were married earlier, in 1953." But at least they do agree on the meaning of a folk song heard in the Ninth Symphony, in which Vaughan Williams claimed to hear a death knell for a captured highwayman. Ursula explains that a tolling bell had always represented death to her husband. "It's all there, isn't it?" enthuses Russell. "His love of folk songs, of poets and composers, of history, architecture, the landscape and its people, the sea, and the unknown past, present and future. Incredibly concentrated in this last, great, visionary work." She agrees on this last point: "Yes, it has no finality; it seems more like the beginning of a new exploration. Perhaps that is how all journeys should end."

And that is *almost* where Russell's film ends. But he has one more fanciful moment up his sleeve. As Russell finishes reading the storybook to Molly, he says, "He died in April 1958. That last symphony is his swan song." Asked what a "swan song" is, Russell replies: "Well, a swan song means different things to different people. Just before it dies, a swan begins to sing. Some people hear it as a sad song, because the swan's unhappy at losing its life and friends. But other people think the song is a happy one, because the swan is happy to be meeting God. Now, Rafe didn't know if he believed in God or not; but he knew that no creature in pain ever sings."

The Strange Affliction of Anton Bruckner (1990) is a charming little fable, a gentle forest idyll with an almost transcendental "kick" at the end. When it was first broadcast on London Weekend Television, it was introduced in an on-screen conversation between Russell and Bragg. "I've made films about very complex composers," Russell told him, "like Mahler and Tchaikovsky — very hung up and extraordinary. Well, Bruckner in a sense was too, although he appeared not to be. Until everyone's familiar with him, they won't get the fact that this man was the greatest symphonist since Beethoven. Forget Berlioz, Mendelssohn, Tchaikovsky, Schubert. This man had a vision of the world, the universe, that has never been matched in music."

The film features just three characters, the composer Anton Bruckner (1824–1896, played by Peter MacKriel), a beautiful woman named Gretel (Catherine Nielsen), and her male companion, Hans. It was filmed in Hampshire and Kent. All the musical sequences, except one, are deployed as background accompaniment to the action. We hear excerpts from Bruckner's Fourth, Seventh, Eighth, and Ninth Symphonies (performed by Eugen Jochum and the Berlin Philharmonic Orchestra) and from the F-major String Quintet (played by the Astarte Ensemble). It is a story of cleansing, about an artist healed of a creative block. Despite its rather *Twilight Zone*–like ending, which seems to cast a rather coy wink at what has gone before, Russell has served up a beautifully crafted allegory about an artist's struggles to transcend worldly debilities and limitations. One need not know who Bruckner was, or have heard a note of his music, to share in the curious mixture of fable and transcendence that is this marvelous gem of a film.

Bruckner arrives at a sanitarium situated in the middle of a beautiful greenwood, where he is greeted by two "attendants," a beautiful blond woman and her assistant. He is a quiet little man, neatly dressed in a white suit, with a round face and a quirky smile. Oblivious to his surroundings, he is preoccupied with counting things — the spokes of the carriage wheels, the flowers in the meadow, the rocks on the hillside, the gravestones in the cemetery, even the spoonfuls of food. "I'm only here because of my sister," he protests. "She went and arranged it behind my back with the doctor." Assuring him the doctor will be along soon, Gretel and Hans subject him to several therapies, including immersions in icy baths and a so-called penance of playing Bach at the local church. "That's a nice little organ you have there, Father," he deadpans to the priest. "No fun being a genius," Gretel remarks at one point. "Actually, my music is not like Wagner's, not like Brahms," he protests. "That's my trouble. Brahms' music comes from his brain, Wagner's from his balls, mine comes from God. And He's rather unfashionable these days."

Gradually, the composer calms himself. Gretel tells him the doctor will come soon. In the meantime Bruckner begins to tell her of his life, his schooling in the monastery of St. Florians, his days as a teacher, the death of his mother, the scant time he found to compose, and the many women who rejected his romantic advances. "I fell in love with all my female pupils," he says. "I've lost count of the number of times I've proposed." Gretel inquires if he's ever seen a naked woman. As he considers the unexpected question, she quietly disrobes and climbs into the bed with him. She cradles him in her arms and, in his ensuing monologue, he flashes back to the crisis that triggered his counting mania. He was conductor of the City Guild Chorus of Vienna and teaching at the Vienna Conservatoire when he attended a party at a tavern. His friends pulled a prank on him by blindfolding him and locking him in a room with a woman. "The woman, she was unkind," he says. "And she told them . . . , all my friends. . . . I resigned. I couldn't face them, their sniggers. I stood on the bridge. I wanted to — I wanted to — it would be so easy. Then I saw the boats, and I found myself counting the boats, counting the number of steps I took to get home. The number, the number." He pauses, gazing up through the skylight at the stars overhead. Music from the adagio of the Seventh Symphony wells up on the soundtrack. He stops counting. "Why have you stopped counting?" asks Gretel. "I can't," he replies after a pause, eyes shining. "God alone can count the stars. I cannot. It diminishes glory." The stars glimmer beyond the stained-glass windows. An enormous sun begins to rise above the dark horizon. His hand gently traces the contour of her hip. They lie together, chastely.

Later, alone on his bed, Bruckner hears music coming from another room. He finds a quintet of players performing his F-major String Quintet (the only diegetic use of music in the entire film). The room is empty and bare of furniture, save one chair. He seats himself. "This music has never been played," he says. Gretel explains that these musicians "just wanted you to know you still have friends, friends who love you." Finally, Gretel and Hans escort him out the door to a waiting carriage. He protests he's not seen the doctor yet. "Only people who are ill need to see a doctor, Herr Bruckner," she answers. "And you are not ill. Your sister's looking forward to having you home again." Gretel and Hans wave after the departing carriage. "He's a nice man; I liked him," she tells Hans. Hans asks if she had made love to Bruckner. She silences him: "He might never have written another note of music. Now he will die as he lived, a more or less happy celibate." Clearly, Gretel is the doctor. And now she awaits her next patient. "He's a banker who imagines he's a rooster," she tells Hans. "You'd better find that feather boa of mine!"

"People ask me what I think was really wrong with Bruckner," says Russell, "what the hell was this 'numeromania,' this mania for counting things? I suggest in the film that it was a sexual thing; that he had been 'set up' in some pub with a loose woman and everybody got drunk, and he was ill-prepared to deal with the situation. It was a distasteful encounter for him, and it didn't do him any good. The only way he could connect with reality was to treat it as a mass of data, as something to list and count and itemize." Did any of this really happen? As always, Russell pleads an intuitive process in his storytelling: "I don't stop to analyze myself too much; I just work basically on emotions, not intellect. If an idea comes to me, it comes to me for reasons that I just accept and don't delve into. I can't just depend on historical truth, whatever that is; that and my own feelings about things."

The unprepossessing Bruckner might seem an unlikely choice for the flamboyant Russell — until one remembers that among his finest films are other unlikely portraits — the chilly, ascetic Bártok and the blind and paralyzed Delius. "Bruckner didn't look the way we think a composer should look," Russell says. "I remember people were struck with my *Elgar* because he looked more like a cavalry officer than a poet. Wagner — now Wagner was somebody who really looked the part, with the suave clothes and elegant style. Bruckner wore ill-fitting clothes and looked like a farmer. He was so humble and naïve that after a performance of one of his symphonies, he placed a flower into the conductor's hand and told him to buy himself a drink! Yet this was the guy who Wagner claimed was the greatest symphonist since Beethoven!"

In the character and music of Anton Bruckner, Russell finds the kinds of contradictions he has always been drawn to (and perhaps identifies with) — namely, a life and a body of music that attempts to transcend life's messy contradictions and humiliations and construct an artistic and spiritual self. The essence of Bruckner's struggle, says biographer Derek Watson (and, arguably, of Russell himself) lies in his "reconciliation of opposites, an attempt at finding the harmony and golden measure of the grand design."[129]

Bruckner took little interest in his contemporary surroundings, writes Watson, and his relations with young women were always unsuccessful and unhappy. "His thoughts were in another world, and political events did not touch him in the way they did other composers." As a result of three nervous breakdowns — in 1867, 1887, and 1891 — he side-stepped reality and developed instead an obsession with numbers, both in the meticulous numbering of bars and phrase periods and in what Watson has called "the obsessive and frenzied repetitions of motifs." He kept lists of the numbers of prayers he said each day, the numbers of dances with girls, the number of statues in the park. "He was obsessed with the need to discover the numbers, characteristics, and substance of inanimate objects," continues Watson, "such as the ornamental tops of the municipal towers in Vienna."[130] Yet here, contends another biographer, Robin Holloway, was a man with an unflinching belief in God, who possessed a "colossal drive to create," and within whose textbook psychoses lay "one of the mightiest music-machines ever known."[131]

The Mystery of Dr. Martinu, broadcast by the BBC in 1991, was subtitled *A Revelation by Ken Russell.* Patrick Ryckart portrayed Bohuslav Martinu (1890–1959), with Shauna Baird as his wife, Charlotte, Martin Friend as his psychiatrist, Professor Mirisch, and Hannah King as his mistress, Slava. Written by Russell himself, it is a psychological detective story about a man searching for clues to his lost identity, a breezy blend of the dime-store psychologiz-ings of Alfred Hitchcock's *Spellbound* and the narcissistic musings of Jean Cocteau's *Blood of a Poet* (1930)with a dash of Hitchcock's *Vertigo* thrown in. However, because Martinu and his music are perhaps less well known than most of Russell's other subjects, the film may seem perversely obscure to general audiences. Yet, as is discussed below, it's a story very close to Russell's own tastes and temperament: "My film on Bohuslav Martinu was a challenge because I think in many ways his music is very confrontational. . . . It's amaz-ingly powerful and evocative and full of hidden imagery. I thought to make out of it a visual psychological study."

The first half of the film immediately assaults the unprepared viewer with a barrage of seemingly disconnected images. This lengthy, sustained sequence is limned in sun-drenched, primary colors; and its freely associative editing re-calls the imaginative fantasy sequences of *Mahler, The Music Lovers,* and *Lisztomania.* A brief catalogue of recurring images includes a lighthouse, chil-dren digging in the sand, a hand covered with crawling ants, a model airplane, a miniature Statue of Liberty, a group of Leger–like cardboard cut-out figures, a uniformed man at a ticket booth, the bull-shaped head of a minotaur, and so on. Other characters come and go — a woman named Charlotte sits at a sew-ing machine, a nude woman called Slava races up a spiral stairway. And always, there is the figure of the Dreamer, a male figure, pursuing but never catching Slava — an action repeated, over and over, again and again. Finally, she tumbles over the rail, and the Dreamer follows her. He, too, falls into the abyss . . . Underpinning these images are excerpts from Martinu's Sixth Sym-phony and the cantata *The Opening of the Wells,* the theme from the opera, *Julietta,* and a number of shorter jazz-like pieces.

What can we make of all this? The second half of the film reassembles these images into a psychological profile of Martinu. By contrast to the first half, the narrative is linear, the color palette low-key, and the camera work and editing relatively restrained. The year is 1946. Martinu has fled Europe and is teach-ing in America. As the result of a fall from a second-story balcony (an actual event that occurred in March 1946 while visiting the Berkshire Summer Music School at Tanglewood), he has lost his memory. His only clues to his identity are persistent dreams that assail him with mysterious images of minotaurs, spiral stairs, a tower, the mysterious figure of a woman falling off a balcony. . . .

Martinu relates these dreams to one "Professor Mirisch," a stranger who has accosted him during his walks. Together, the two men begin to make sense of the recurring images: the children playing in the sand represent a Czech folk custom from Martinu's homeland called "The Opening of the Wells"; the lighthouse represents the clock tower of St. Jacob's church in his native Politcka; the woman at the sewing machine is his dressmaker wife, Charlotte;

the pasteboard figures of musicians and the hand crawling with ants signify his devotion to the surrealists Cocteau and Luis Bunuel during his avant-garde years in Paris in the 1920s; the ticket booth and miniature Statue of Liberty reference Martinu's emigration to America; the woman in the tower, called "Slava," is a music student with whom Martinu had an adulterous affair; and the fall from the tower represents the real-life tumble that precipitated Martinu's amnesia and triggered the dreams in the first place.

But what is the "revelation" that Russell hints at in the title of the film? What is the larger truth behind these dreams? Russell turns to the music itself. To begin with, he associates the images of towers and ants with repetitions of the opening measures of the Sixth Symphony. It is no accident that the whirling tangle of notes sounds like the buzzing of insects. "From my room in the tower, the whole of Politcka seemed to be populated with ants," Martinu tells Professor Mirisch, "all scurrying about their business. . . . It was always quite a shock to come down to earth." Russell is convinced such early impressions left a lasting impact on Martinu. "I did go to his home town and went inside the tower," Russell explains, "where as a boy he and his family lived. He spent most of his childhood in that tower, you know, looking down at the world. And if you go to the top of the tower and look down, as he obviously did every day, the people are just tiny dots. And his music sounds like ants busily scurrying around. Obviously, he felt isolated and detached from the world, oblivious to it. Instead, he saw only that horizon that stretched beyond his village." Indeed, Martinu always claimed he would never feel "at home" again, neither in Paris, nor Switzerland, nor later in America. "I am sick for home and yearn for our hills!" Martinu once said. "My work is that of a Czech tied to my homeland by a cord nothing can cut."[132]

As a consequence, Martinu felt isolated and alienated the rest of his life and could never quite settle down to any kind of normalcy, including a conventional marriage to Charlotte — especially when the dream of a woman named Slava was always out there, ever alluring and elusive. Who was Slava? Again, Russell turns to the music and finds the answer in a recurring melody from Martinu's surrealistic opera *Juliette*. This enigmatic and relatively unknown opera, surely one of the seminal products of surrealist music, chronicles the search by Michel, a traveling bookseller, for his former love, Juliette. Tracing her to a village, he hears her haunting melody from every window and in every street. But none of the villagers can help him find her. They seem to have lost their memories. Gradually, Michel realizes that he has entered a world that has neither past nor future, beginning or end, that the mysterious woman he is pursuing is only a dream. Ultimately he, too, finds himself succumbing to that world of dreams.

Russell is convinced that Martinu identified with the character of Michel and that Juliette's melody referred to Martinu's own "dream girl," a childhood friend named Vitezslava Kapralova. As a young woman, she became his pupil and devoted follower. Biographer Brian Large confirms it is likely that Martinu, a married man, was strongly attracted to her, that they might have been lovers, and that she could have been the model for Juliette.[133] Martinu never saw her again after fleeing the Nazis in 1938, and she died two years later. What guilt he may have felt over this adulterous episode (if indeed there was one) we will never know; but Russell constructs a backstory in which the girl and Martinu have a clandestine assignation in the Politcka tower, which is witnessed by his suspicious wife. Angered at the exposure of his infidelity, Martinu momentarily fantasizes that Charlotte falls from the tower to her death.

"Here you are, identifying with the Greek hero Theseus," the professor remarks at this revelation, "wandering through the labyrinth of your mind, disposing of everything that gets between you and your dream girl." The professor explains that Martinu's own lacerating sense of guilt over a real or imagined affair with Slava — as well as the knowledge that he will never find in his marriage the ideal love he so desperately sought with her — conspired to obliterate the terrible event from his mind. Ironically, it is Martinu's accidental fall from the balcony, and his subsequent amnesia, that releases the stream of dream images that, with the help of the professor, eventually brings back the scene on the tower with Slava and Charlotte.

Russell finds clues to this "reawakening" in the music of Martinu's late chamber cantata, *The Opening of the Wells*. "If I can never physically go home again, I can still undertake a spiritual journey to my country," Martinu tells Professor Mirisch. "The music I shall write in celebration will be my homecoming." *The Opening of the Wells* was set to texts by his countryman, Miroslav Bures, and it depicts the Maytime songs and dances of children welcoming the spring season as they clear away the rocks and winter mud from the brooks and streams. According to biographer Large, this music was "a profound affirmation of all that [Martinu] held dear in life."[134] The words of Bures's text are apt:

> With spades and rakes the gay procession goes,
> all laden down with flowers are the lasses. . . .
> They heaved away the stones
> and then the spring like a happy bird awakening began to sing.

By linking this music to Martinu's recurring dream images of children playing in the stream, Russell conveys the composer's moral and spiritual rebirth.

Martinu, like so many artists in Russell's pictures (and perhaps like Russell himself) is an idealist haunted by—and perhaps traumatized by—the splendor of his youth, struggling in middle age to reconcile himself with the tawdry, mundane world and the darker impulses he finds within himself. But when apprised of such interpretations, Russell, ever wary of being pinned down, just shrugs. "People think I was trying to lay Martinu's dreams out on the psychoanalyst's couch and explain them away. Well, I don't presume to solve all of Martinu's problems, just make some suggestions. You can't take it all that seriously, you know."

Arnold Bax was aired on *The South Bank Show* in 1992. For the first time Russell's empathy for a composer reached its logical extreme—he took on the role of Bax himself.[135] "I played him myself because I felt that I *knew* Bax, absolutely," says Russell. "I'm a great fan of his. I financed recordings of his symphonies myself. I also look like him; and I was the same age when I played him. Glenda Jackson got an Emmy for her role as his companion, Harriet Cohen. Before I do any artist, I soak myself for maybe ten years in music and research. So I knew a lot about what was going on in Bax's life when he was writing. I shot some of it at Highcliff, on the beach, and in Hampshire, where I had shot much of the Bruckner film."

There is an elegiac quality to this portrait of an artist facing a midlife crisis. Arnold Bax (1883–1953) had begun his career associated with the fabulously romantic Celtic Revival in Ireland, and his early works *In the Faery Hills* (1909), *The Garden of Fand* (1916), and *Tintagel* (1917) powerfully evoked the mystery, symbolism, myth, and pageantry of Irish folklore. He went on to write seven symphonies of great power, the last of which was dedicated in 1939 to the American people. By the early 1940s his reputation and his prestige—he succeeded Sir Walford Davies as Master of the King's Music—seemed secure. Yet in the next decade he began to feel at odds with the musical establishment and with his audience. Apart from a handful of works, including the score to David Lean's film, *Oliver Twist* (1948), he wrote little. Withdrawing from society, Bax spent more and more time at the White Horse Hotel in the tiny little village of Storrington, Sussex, where he indulged in reading, snooker, and small talk with neighbors and friends. At the end not even the company of pianist Harriet Cohen, his longtime musical champion and sometime lover, could assuage his depression over his sense of lost youth. "When I was young I was thankful for youth," he wrote in his autobiography, *Farewell, My Youth,* "and could have shouted for joy in my consciousness of it—and indeed in my music I frequently did so. I longed to be twenty-two and to remain at that age forever, and I am not sure even now that I was not right."[136] In a letter to Cohen he admitted that nothing but the "Romantic experience," what he described as "untrammeled passion and extasy [*sic*]" could any longer satisfy him. "Within us the desire becomes an agony to live for a single hour with all the might of the imagination, to drown our beings in the proud sunlit tumult of one instant of utter realization, even though it [would] consume us utterly."[137]

In Russell's film Bax seeks to recapture this "proud sunlit tumult" by revisiting — and re-creating — the scene, circumstances, and significance of his composing of *The Garden of Fand*. Written in 1916, Bax had himself assigned it the programmatic connotations of the Celtic saga *The Sick-Bed of Cuchulain*. A tempest casts a group of voyagers onto the shore of a mysterious island. The goddess Fand, Neptune's daughter, appears and her song enchants the men. But then the sea rises up suddenly and engulfs them all. Twilight falls, the sea subsides, and Fand's garden disappears. The music's mixture of impressionism and romanticism, the solo arabesques, muted brass, and winding bass figures all suggest the salt spray, the wheeling sea birds, the enchanted island, and the dance of Fand.

It is likely, suggests Russell, that this music represented for Bax more than just a Celtic dream. It may have memorialized a youthful idyll of love with a woman, probably Harriet. Perhaps Bax, like the other composers in Russell's oeuvre, had been stunned by this single moment, which came to represent an ideal ever seductive, ever elusive, and ultimately impossible to revisit. And now, in his disillusioned middle age, seeking to recapture this romantic ideal, he accosts a lovely young woman, Annie, a feather dancer at a gentlemen's club, and hires her to come to Cornwall and dance for him on the beach. "What kind of dance," she asks teasingly. "Whatever comes to mind," he replies; "your interpretation of 'Greensleeves' was quite moving." She smiles knowingly, "And I bet I know which part was doing the moving." He takes her to a seaside hotel, and the next day on the beach he produces a phonograph and a record. He explains he wants her to dance to the music of his *Garden of Fand* — just at the point "when you come out of the water looking like a sea nymph, diamonds in your hair." Dutifully, she appears before him, clad in a bathing suit adorned with scarlet feathers. For a few moments they dance together, the silver breakers glittering behind them, the music from the phonograph rising to a crescendo. At last he falls back, exhausted, while she continues the dance. Finally, shivering, she stops. "You missed the climax," he shouts. "The story of my life," she retorts.

Back in the hotel room Bax confesses he had been to this beach before, as a youth deeply in love with a woman. Annie bristles. "In your mind she was Fand, just as I'm Fand. Not a woman of flesh and blood. Just some cute pinup girl all dusted up with myths and legends. About time you stopped living in the past." Teasingly, she stands before him, the music of Fand on the phonograph.

Removing her clothes, she dances for a moment before falling into his arms. But their frenzied moment of lovemaking is interrupted by a message that Harriet has suffered a bad fall. Annie angrily breaks the record into pieces and tosses them into the fire. Bax must return to London.

Harriet's accident brings Bax back to reality. They had had several scenes earlier in the film, in which the circumstances of their relationship—particularly her championing of his music and her ongoing frustration at his thirty-year delay in marrying her—were reviewed. "Is there any earthly reason you and I should not get married?" she had accused. "God knows I've waited long enough. Where will it be—Westminster Abbey? Now that you're Master of the King's Music, you've got a right!" Placing a recording of the music *The Garden of Fand* on the phonograph, Harriet remembers a time many years before when things were different, when they had gone to the beach, when she had come up out of the water, "looking like a sea nymph."

Now, reunited in Harriet's flat, Bax tends to her bandaged hand. She fusses that her concert career is over. He reassures her that he'll write for her piano music for the left hand. Unmoved, she instructs him how to change her bandage. "It's easy when you know how," she explains. "The nurse has some time off. I thought it would be nicer, just the two of us, together. Now you start by giving your hands a good scrub." He duly undoes the bandage. "You'll get used to it," she says, as the camera moves in for a close-up of his expression, stoic and inscrutable at the end.

Bax is yet another in a succession of Russell's artist subjects—Martinu was the most recent example—whose clumsy attempts to cling to impossible ideals, to sustain the fantasies of youth and love, are doomed to failure. Having stopped his composing, having lost his public, and now failing to recapture that moment of "sunlit tumult" with the woman on the beach, Bax has no recourse but to return to the grasping, possessive Harriet. It should be remembered that, in a significant irony, the Tchaikovsky of *The Music Lovers* had also found himself trapped by the very "normalcy" he had yearned for. Watching Russell acting out this role cannot help but suggest that Russell is enacting similar struggles in his own life. The difference between him and Bax, of course, is that whereas Bax ceases his search, Russell's will continue. Bax is not "the last great Romantic artist," as Russell described him in the prologue to the film. Rather, Russell may well lay claim to that title.

Return to Elgar

In the summer of 2002, Russell returned to the Malvern Hills and Elgar Country, where he made his first Elgar film forty years before, just as Elgar himself in middle age came back to the countryside of his youth. The identification between filmmaker and composer, begun so long ago in 1962, is now virtually complete. "I have lived with this composer most of my life," Russell says, "and I feel so close to the way his mind works, that I knew there was more I could say, particularly about those so-called 'mysterious women' in his life." Commissioned by Melvyn Bragg on the occasion of the twenty-fifth anniversary of *The South Bank Show, Elgar: Fantasie of a Composer on a Bicycle* was broadcast on 22 September 2002.[138] Narrated by Russell himself and edited by Mike Lane, it is something of a sunny divertissement, dappled with a shadow or two, about the composer and his music. Reminiscent of Russell's first Elgar film are the affectionately gentle tone; recurring images of the composer (James Johnston) bicycling through the Malverns to the music of the *Introduction and Allegro for Strings;* scenes of kite-flying with his daughter, Carice; the ironic juxtaposition of wounded soldiers to the "Pomp and Circumstance" music; and the quotations from *The Dream of Gerontius.*

Other moments bring us some new thoughts about Elgar and his music, rendered in the chamber style of Russell's later composer films. For example, unlike the first film, there are now hints, derived from the musical portraits in the *Enigma Variations* (the most frankly autobiographical of Elgar's symphonic works) that Elgar enjoyed relationships (probably platonic) with other women in his life besides the dutiful and loyal Alice (portrayed here by Russell's wife, Elize; and musically evoked by No. 1, "C.A.E.").[139] Excerpts from the No. 10 ("Dorabella") enhance romantic scenes with Dora Penny, a young student whose stutter is cleverly captured in the tripping patterns of the notes; and the No. 13 ("Romanza") evokes the ill-fated romance with Helen Weaver, Elgar's first love, whose premature death is visualized a la Millais's painting "Ophelia" (itself a reference to Russell's biopic about the Rossetti circle, *Dante's Inferno*). Other source music, excerpts from *Falstaff* and the cadenza of the Violin Concerto, are attached, respectively, to a picnic scene with Rosa Burley, one of Carice's school teachers, and a fantasy image of a gossamer-clad young female dancing along a beach (so reminiscent of the *Garden of Fand* episode from the Bax film). Russell suggests that these women — like the dreamlike figures that haunted Tchaikovsky, Martinu, and Bax — represent the youthful ideals of love that had been thwarted by Elgar's thoroughly respectable, if not entirely romantic marriage.

More musical portraits present themselves, interspersed with shots of the gradually aging Elgar continuing his bicycle ride. For the most part, they are served up with a superb economy that both betrays and transcends Russell's obviously limited budget. It has always been an irony that the seemingly extravagant Russell always rose to the occasion when constrained by budgetary and logistical limitations. What could be more charming than the "Fairies and Giants" episode from the *Wand of Youth* that accompanies a procession of children dressed in toy-soldier costumes as they march around the tiny houses and streets of a miniature town? It is reminiscent of the "Box of Toys" sequence from *The Debussy Film*.[140] What could be more starkly eloquent of the sweetly collaborative nature of his relationship with Alice than hearing the words (by Alice herself) and music of the "In Haven" song from the *Sea Pictures* as Elgar and Alice gaze at us from behind a rain-swept window? And what could be more eerie in its economical way than the so-called "Prophecy" sequence from the Second Symphony, where blurry images of a black-clad Elgar slinking among the gravestones evoke his premonitory visions of the terrors of the oncoming Great War?[141]

The film's epilogue is pure Russell in its highly idiosyncratic commentary about the celebrity status of Elgar the National Monument overtaking the more modest proportions of Elgar the Man. The setting is now the Elgar Birthplace Museum at Broadheath. The shot begins with Russell himself at frame right, silently conversing with a statue of the composer. Panning left, the camera picks up the young, fiercely mustachioed Elgar, in period dress, trundling on his bicycle toward the museum. As the music from the "Nimrod" episode, the No. 9 of the *Enigma Variations* (which Russell here dubs "Elgar's Ghost"), wells up on the soundtrack, Elgar cycles *through* Worcester Cathedral, gliding down the nave, past the pews whipping by in the foreground like so many riffled playing cards.[142] On and on he goes, out the church and back onto the country roads (where, you suspect, he really belongs). "And if you visit Elgar Country today," says Russell's narrative voice, "you'll most certainly make contact with Elgar's ghost—should the mood take you, that is. But don't worry, his spirit is benign; though I can't guarantee that his music won't haunt you for the rest of your life."

Some That Might Have Been

"Looking back I can say that all the film biographies I've done are slightly different, about different people, and about different aspects of their lives." Ken Russell is relaxing over a glass of ale at his favorite pub, Turfcutters, near his home in East Boldre, Brockenhurst, near the New Forest. It is July 2003, and it is time to reflect back on his many films and to toast the memory of some that never made it to the screen. "There's my Percy Grainger project," he sighs wistfully. "I've written a script about Grainger, but it has never been filmed. You remember that Grainger, Delius' good friend, shows up in *Song of Summer*. He literally drops into the frame. What a character! If you ever get to Melbourne, visit the Percy Grainger Museum, where you'll find drawers full of whips and canes! Think about *that* for a moment! Another

Ken Russell (center), Lisi Tribble, and author John C. Tibbetts at Russell's favorite pub, near the New Forest, England. (Courtesy John C. Tibbetts)

project I've been thinking about is Dvořák — the three years he spent in New York in the early 1890s. Imagine him there, near the Bowery, surrounded by black jazz musicians; or at Carnegie Hall; or with Buffalo Bill; or visiting Niagara Falls and Iowa farm country."

Among other as yet unrealized projects are *The Beethoven Secret,* a detective story based on the discovery of Beethoven's "immortal beloved" letter. Russell reports in his autobiography that at one time Anthony Hopkins was cast and costumed as the composer and Jodi Foster and Glenda Jackson as two of the "mystery" women in Beethoven's life before it was shelved.[143] "Film isn't the only medium where I've tried this sort of thing," he continues. "There's radio. I once wrote a script about Alexander Scriabin that started out as a film script. Scriabin always said he was going to write a symphony to end the world, you know. He envisioned thousands of performers and dancers and loving couples and scents and God knows what else. Bells would be suspended from clouds in the Himalayas. The symphony would end with him making love to the most beautiful girl in the world, atop the tallest pile of cushions in the world. And at the very moment he was going to climax with the girl, the orchestra would reach the greatest crescendo any orchestra had ever achieved — and then the world would come to an end! Well. I thought, 'That's pretty good stuff! Big budget.' I was talking to a producer about it, and he suggested I not do it for the movies but for *radio.* 'You can do all that just by suggestion,' he told me. 'If you want a thousand mountain peaks, and thousands of bells, and thousands of

Russian cavalrymen galloping across the steppes — whatever you want — we just get out the old coconuts and it's no problem.' So I changed the Scriabin script into a radio piece." As Russell speaks, the sun is resting on the horizon and a golden light drenches the scene.

"I had a creative moment while planning it," he muses, returning to the subject of his newest Elgar film. "You know, a great challenge in these composer films is visualizing moments of creativity. Inspiration comes only in flashes, I suppose; and I've been trying all my life to get that on film. The location of the Malvern Hills played an important part in Elgar's creative spark. So I knew I had to show these hills in my new film. But what do you do? Just photograph hills? It's so boring! I did manage to come up with one idea: You know, Elgar was a great kite flyer.[144] In my first film I showed him and his daughter flying a kite. Now, after all these years, I knew I wanted to show a similar scene in color; but it would have been even more wonderful to show a kite in the shape of an *ear,* and it would be *Elgar's* ear, 10,000 feet up in the sky, listening to the birds, to the hills, absorbing everything. But it was no go; I was told it was too expensive a prop; and besides, the aerodynamics of an ear are not conducive to flight! Pity."

Indeed, no such scene can be found in the new Elgar film. But it's intriguing to think that somewhere, high above the Malvern Hills there floats an enormous ear, Elgar's ear, tethered by the slimmest thread to the head of the listening Ken Russell.

"A Long, Dark Coda into the Night"
The Composer Films of Tony Palmer

Thus did our life become; it was all a cheat.
Yet filled with hope, men favored deceit.
Trust on, and think tomorrow will repay;
Tomorrow is falser than the former day.
So when at last the dreadful hour
This crumbling pageant shall devour,
Shall trumpet still be heard on high?
No, the dead shall live, the living die,
While music shall untune the sky.
— *John Dryden,* The Song for St. Cecilia's Day, November 22, 1687

"I am fascinated by the relationship between composers and the world they live in," says British filmmaker Tony Palmer. "It doesn't matter what kind of music they write — serious or pop. They are remarkable people who struggle to create something people are interested in."[1] With the exception of his friend and former colleague Ken Russell, no filmmaker on the planet has devoted so much of his or her career to this troublesome genre of biographical film — and aroused more praise and blame in the process. Certainly no filmmaker has been less interested in appeasing a public expecting the standard sophomoric formulas of the Hollywood commercial biopic. "He has

Tony Palmer's many biographical films include portraits of composers, playwrights, jazz artists, and rock stars. (Courtesy John C. Tibbetts)

consistently enraged music, film, and literary critics since the 1960s," wrote a critic in the *Sunday Times* in 1985, "when he appeared as a precociously talented trainee at the BBC."[2] Commentator Elizabeth Dunn noted in 1990, "The fact is that Palmer's films have, over the years, brought him a cultural status to which few remain indifferent. There are those who regard his films as pretentious and far too long, while others cleave to the view that he has single-handedly reformed the nature of the film biography."[3]

Indeed, as Palmer acknowledged in an article he wrote in 1988, making biopics is not a practice for the faint of heart: "Making film profiles of creative artists is a dangerous business. First, you soon realize that more or less everyone knows/knew the subject better than you. . . . Next, you discover that the world is full of 'experts' who are rapidly rewriting history to show themselves in the best possible light. . . . Even more dangerous, assuming, of course, that it's the truth we are seeking, are those participants who seek to 'interpret' the subject's life (and intentions) based on little evidence and less knowledge, except that they happen to be brother/sister/daughter/wife/confidante, etc., and thus (one would assume) possessed of invaluable insight." Most treacherous of all, Palmer continues, is to trust the subject, dead or alive: "He (or she) will twist and turn and cover his tracks and make your search as painful and perverse as he (or she) possibly can."[4]

The same could be said about Palmer himself. As elusive as any of his subjects, he pops up as an author one moment (*Born under a Bad Sign*, 1970), a play director the next (he premiered John Osborne's last play, *Déjà vu,* in May 1992), an opera director (Hector Berlioz's *The Trojans,* Serge Prokofiev's *War and Peace,* Richard Wagner's *Parsifal,* Giacomo Puccini's *Turandot,* and others), a broadcaster for the British Broadcasting Corporation (a founding presenter of BBC Radio 4's *Kaleidoscope*), a music critic (for the *London Observer*), and, of course, the filmmaker of more than ninety documentaries and theatrical films, the latter of which have garnered more than fifty international prizes, including three Italia Prizes, eleven Emmy and BAFTA nominations and awards, and twelve Gold Medals at the New York Film and Television Festival. In 1989 he became the first maker of arts films to be honored with a retrospective of his work at the National Film Theatre in London.

Biography as "Film Essay"

Palmer comes from a generation of post-1960, television-bred historical and political documentarists—notably, Alain Resnais, Chris Marker, Peter Watkins, and others—who might be labeled "postmodernist." Historian Robert Rosenstone, who has written extensively on the subject, contends that postmodernist histories are really a *struggle against history,* that they raise questions about accepted texts and invent micro-narratives as *alternatives* to history. "They speak in a voice that lies somewhere in between the objective voice of scholarship and the subjective voice of fiction and poetry," he explains. "They suspect logic, linearity, progression, and completeness as ways of rendering that past. . . . It is always conscious of itself."[5] Echoing these concepts is commentator Paul Arthur, who adds that these filmmakers work independently, in a highly idiosyncratic and unconventional narrative style. They exploit the television and film medium's multiple discursive levels, the multichannel "stew" of image, speech, shifting time frames, titles, and the diegetic and extradiegetic use of music to make highly personalized essays that take viewers on "a rhetorical journey in which neither an exact route nor final destination are completely spelled out."[6] Dramatic reenactments are juxtaposed with a concoction of found actuality/archival footage, music, on-camera testimonies, and political polemic. Subject matter and point of view are constantly annotated, supported, or undermined by converging angles of inquiry. Moreover, continues Arthur, these "film essays," as he calls them, tend to be oppositional in nature, questioning received wisdom and status quo ideologies. They "gnaw at truth value, cultural contexts, or interpretative possibilities of extant images."[7]

Palmer's films are indeed highly personalized essays that juxtapose fiction and nonfiction, music and image, biographical fact and interpretive fantasy, political invective and poetic lyricism. For all their seemingly freewheeling nature, however, he remains a fierce guardian of historical and poetic truths. The words of George Frideric Handel in Palmer's *God Rot Tunbridge Wells!* (1985) might just as well be his own: "I always drifted to theatricality, but not at the expense of truth." Forswearing facile conclusions, frequently attended by a corrosive, even nihilistic tone, they strike out bravely into what Sergei Rachmaninoff, in Palmer's documentary on the man, *Harvest of Sorrow* (1997), described as the sad ambivalence of life and art, that "long dark coda into the night." Sometimes bewildering in their intertextual complexity and uncompromising in their political and artistic commitments, they make considerable demands on viewers accustomed to the glib formulas of the Hollywood biopics discussed previously in this book. They are visual essays — documents of dreams and dreams of documents — that, in the best sense, take their cue from Samuel Johnson's definition of the written essay, which appeared in his *Dictionary* of 1755: "a loose sally of the mind: an irregular indigested piece; not a regular and orderly composition."

Background and Early Work

Palmer cites Ken Russell, his former mentor at the BBC, for his decision to make a living creating composer documentaries and biopics. After attending Lowestoft Grammar School, the Cambridgeshire High School for Boys, and Cambridge University, his passion for music and theater won him a general traineeship at the BBC. "In the application interviews I rather grandly stated that I wanted to work with Ken Russell," he recalls. "I had seen some of his composer films — the ones on [Edward] Elgar and [Bela] Bartók — and found them completely fascinating."[8]

Before Palmer could realize his dream, however, he was dispatched to Radio Nottingham to gain production experience. "You had to do everything, interviewing people, cutting the tapes, mixing the sound, etc., a real crash course in making programs quickly and inexpensively." This led to a stint as "tea boy" on *The Golden Ring*, a documentary on the production in Vienna of Wagner's *Die Götterdämerung*. "My real education began at that moment, because within two weeks I had met and gotten to know very well Humphrey Burton, the head of Decca Records, John Culshaw, and Georg Solti (Solti would later do the music for my *Wagner*). Suddenly, I felt that this was something that I might be able to do. It was a real 'Road to Damascus' moment in my life."

At last Palmer came to work for Russell as an assistant producer on *Isadora Duncan: The Biggest Dancer in the World* (1966). "I think Tony was influenced by Ken and wanted to compete with him," says Melvyn Bragg, producer of London Weekend Television's *The South Bank Show,* which has presented many films by both Russell and Palmer. "I think almost everybody in this country, all the young people going in to television in the mid-sixties wanted to. Ken was very much the pack leader. Tony had the wit to recognize what was good about Ken, and he wanted to learn from him."[9] Palmer's research chores included scanning contemporary newspapers for reportage on incidents in the life of the legendary dancer. "I learned two absolutely essential things from Ken," says Palmer, "apart from the obvious one that no detail is too small—first, that music is never background, but always foreground. Music has to be a part of the narrative drive of the film. I think too many Hollywood composer films have tended to use music as mere *decoration.* Second, that there are important connections between a composer's life and his or her music. We are both certain that there is not one note—not even a quaver—that is not *meant,* which indicates that he is *trying to tell us something.* The fact that music is open to many interpretations does not disguise the fact that the composer was trying to tell us something, either about the world in which he lived, or about himself—or both. You can't get away from the artist and his times if you want to understand the music."

After making several television documentary series in the late 1960s and early 1970s for London Weekend Television's ITV channel about the history of British and American rock and roll—*All My Loving* and *All You Need Is Love*—Palmer found himself the center of controversy. "What got people going was the message of this music—that it was about full-scale revolution, anti-Vietnam protest, changing the social order. I presented the message to viewers that this was music of the streets, and if you don't listen to what is happening there, you're in deep shit."

Similar energies and social commitments have fed into Palmer's subsequent documentaries about so-called classical composers. Produced throughout his career for the British Broadcasting System and London Weekend Television, they subordinate dramatic reenactments and fictive extrapolations to the factual record of interviews and testimonials, archival photographs, letters and diaries, and actuality film footage. They include, in chronological order, *Benjamin Britten and His Festival* (1967), *A Time There Was . . . A Profile of Benjamin Britten* (1980), *At the Haunted End of the Day* (1981, Sir William Walton), *Once at a Border* (1983, Igor Stravinsky), *Dvořák in Love?* (1988), *Hindemith: A Pilgrim's Progress* (1990), *Gorecki: Symphony of Sorrowful Songs* (1993), *Orff: O Fortuna* (1995), *Parsifal* (1997), *Harvest of Sorrow: Sergei Rachmaninoff* (1997), *Hail Bop!: John Adams* (1997), and *Toward the Unknown Region: Sir Malcolm Arnold* (2004). Compared with the dramatized composer biopics examined elsewhere in this book, they are relatively straightforward documentaries and necessarily lie outside the scope of this book.

The Dramatic Biopics

Palmer's dramatic "theatrical" features have been shown worldwide in theatrical and broadcast venues. They include *Wagner* (1983), *God Rot Tunbridge Wells* (1985), *Puccini* (1985), *Testimony* (1987, Dmitry Shostakovich), *I, Berlioz* (1992), *England, My England* (1995, Henry Purcell), *Brahms and the Little Singing Girls* (1996), and *The Strange Case of Delfina Potocka* (1999, Frédéric Chopin). In each instance, of course, Palmer's trademark fragmented narrative style, political concerns, dramatic reenactments, extensive use of music, and corrosive tone are very much in evidence.

Wagner initiated Palmer's series of theatrical composer films. "I can't go on making documentaries," he had said on several occasions after making the *All You Need Is Love* series, "but I feel if I were to do so — regardless of whether they were good, bad, or indifferent — I'd start repeating myself. My ambitions are slightly different now, and I feel if I am going to make a change I must work with actors." Thus, he considered realizing a long-cherished idea to make a theatrical film about Richard Wagner. He drew upon his experience shooting *The Golden Ring* in Vienna. An associate on that project, critic and record producer John Culshaw, arranged an introduction to fifty-seven-year old Wolfgang Wagner, the grandson of the composer, in Düsseldorf in 1977. At that time Wolfgang was still in control of the family succession at Bayreuth.[10] "We all met and got slightly drunk," declares Palmer. "He told me that if his grandfather were alive today, he would want to work in Hollywood! Wolfgang wished me good luck and offered to help. He gave us the man who was then the dramaturge at Bayreuth, Oswald Bauer, to keep an eye on things. Once the script was finished — that alone took two years — we brought it back to Wolfgang — not so he could veto anything, but so he could just be appraised of the progress. He insisted that my screenwriter, Charles Wood, and I read the whole thing in front of him while his wife, Gudrun, translated it as we went. That script was 480 pages long! Wolfgang didn't react at all, not at first; but when we got to the scene when Ludwig's three ministers were discussing the *Ring* — when John Gielgud's character says, in English, 'And what's more, there's this *Ring* thing' — Gudrun translated it in German as 'Das *Ring* Ding.' Well, Wolfgang thought was the funniest thing he had ever heard. He went on and on, repeating it. Even today, when I see him, he repeats it. At any rate, he approved of the whole project and granted us permission to use anything in Bayreuth we wanted."

The scope was ambitious. Financing came from the London Trust investment corporation and Hungary's Magyar Television, and the budget was ultimately estimated at $11.5 million. The action, researched by Wood from sources that included the newly published massive biography by Martin Gregor-Dellin, ranged across authentic locations and interiors where Wagner lived and worked — Munich, Vienna, Siena, Budapest, Lucerne, Nuremberg, Bayreuth, Wahnfried, and Venice. The star-studded cast included Richard Burton as Wagner, Vanessa Redgrave as Cosima Liszt, Gemma Craven as Minna, Laszlo Galffi as Ludwig II, Ekkehardt Schall as Franz Liszt, Ronald Pickup as Nietzsche, and John Gielgud, Ralph Richardson, and Laurence Olivier as Ludwig II's ministers. The cinematographer was the legendary Vittorio Storaro, and the music was conducted by Georg Solti. The film was released in a seven-hour-and-forty-seven-minute version for the London premiere on 17 April 1983, screened at La Scala on 30 October (the first film ever shown there), cut to three-and-a-half hours for a presentation at the Academy of Motion Picture Arts and Sciences in America, recut to a five-hour version to inaugurate the newly refurbished State Theatre in Sydney, Australia, and shown in January 1984 at the Edinburgh Film Festival. Burton never saw the finished film. His death in 1983 cut short what was predicted to be a resurgence in his failing career.

Typically, Palmer begins the action with a funeral. It is 14 February 1883, and Wagner's funeral boat sails down the Grand Canal. Music from *Siegfried's Tod* underscores the scene. Cosima is draped in black and her young son, Siegfried, is dressed in a sailor's suit. An ironic touch is provided by a montage of shots of the uncrating of memorial busts of Wagner. There they sit, row upon row of identical figurines. The commodification of the composer is already in high gear.

The action then shifts backward to the Dresden uprisings of 1848–49, where the thirty-five-year-old Wagner is serving as Kapellmeister to the doddering king of Saxony (played by Sir William Walton) and inciting artistic and political revolution in the assembly hall. "There are going to be a new theater and a new music," he shouts. "All that comes between the German Volk and their art will be swept away by the coming revolution!" Later, after explaining to his wife, Minna, that he has "arranged" for a doctor to exempt him from service in the Communal Guard, he assesses the current political situation: "In Paris it's about the starving rising up. In Hungary, it's about the oppressed shrugging off Austrian domination, but which in turn will be dominated by the Russian tsar. In Saxony and here in Dresden it's in the form of being given a sop, an assembly in Frankfurt, which purports to be an assembly of all Germany, but isn't. You're still half under Austria and half under Prussia. And it's about the Fatherland, which our King now threatens to dissolve. There isn't a Germany yet. And until there is a Germany, or a German consciousness, I'm not going to have an audience, damn it!" He further describes his vision of a National Theatre and an art form that "embraces everything, music, poetry, drama. . . . Fire, water, destruction, a hero, a German hero." Later, against the flames of his burning State Opera House, Wagner laughs maniacally, shouts, "This is theatre!" and flees the city.

"It was as well that Wagner left Dresden when he did," intones the narrative voice of Minister Pfistermeister (Gielgud), cabinet minister to King Ludwig II of Bavaria, whose voice-over takes up the thread of the story. "Another day, another hour, and he would have been clapped in prison. As it was, a warrant was promptly taken up for his arrest, wherever he might be found." This narrative agency follows subsequent events: Wagner and his wife, Minna, take up temporary residences in Zurich; in Weimar, where Liszt produces *Tannhäuser* and the premiere of *Lohengrin;* and in Bordeaux, where he courts the charms of a patroness, Mrs. Taylor ("Wagner always seemed to find people to support him; it was as if he conjured them up out of his own expectancy"). At a party on Lake Uri in honor of Franz Liszt's birthday, Wagner meets the wealthy silk merchant Otto Wesendonck (Richard Pasco) and his beautiful wife, Mathilde (Marthe Keller). A guest of the Wesendonck's at their estate, he begins his affair with Mathilde, while offering to her husband to depart in exchange for financial support. "Everything is put in the world for him to use," the long-suffering Minna tells the bewildered Mathilde. "He regards the denial of anything he might consider necessary to him—house, money, creature comforts, people, love—he must have love from women."

In Paris during a revised production of *Tannhäuser* (subsidized in part by Wesendonck's money), Wagner endures the hostilities of rival claques of supporters of Giacomo Meyerbeer. He fumes about "the Meyerbeer clique, twittering Nibelungs, maggots deep in the flesh, feeding on the sweet, pretty fleshy confection that is Paris." Meyerbeer angrily denounces his incendiary pamphlet, *Jewishness in Music,* published in 1850. "It was written with you in mind," sniffs Wagner.

Life is harsh back on the road, as Wagner seeks patronage and support, traveling by sledge and wagon to Russia, Hungary, Moldavia, and Vienna. Then, in Stuttgart, despairing and verging on suicide, Wagner is visited by Herr Pfistermeister. He accepts the eighteen-year-old king's invitation to come to Bavaria and arrives in Munich on 4 May 1864. The political situation is tense. War is brewing between Prussia and Austria. "We were eager to be led by our young King," says Pfistermeister, "to be strong enough to stand up to Prussia. We were looking to a new, golden age, though there were some of us (I shall not name names) who sought to gain precedence, the easier to influence the King towards a treaty with Prussia, perhaps toward the surrendering of our sovereignty for the sake of a united Germany at last." Wagner, meanwhile, has gained the adoring support of his "Swan King" ("I shall be true to you to the ends of time," moans the worshipful Ludwig), and he moves into a house in Munich with his young apprentice, Hans von Bülow, and his wife, Cosima (née Liszt). He begins an affair with Cosima right under the nose of von Bülow.

Ludwig sponsors productions of *Lohengrin* and *The Flying Dutchman* while pursuing his plans for building spectacular castles. Soon Wagner is showing Ludwig architectural plans of his own, for what he calls "an amphitheater in the Greek fashion." But rumors of the affair with Cosima reach the court and Pfistermeister warns Wagner of the dangers it could pose to his career. "I am set back on my heels always with scurrility," complains Wagner. Alarmed by Wagner's behavior and favor with the king, Pfistermeister, Baron Ludwig von der Pfordten (Sir Ralph Richardson), and Baron Sigmund von Pfeufer (Sir Laurence Olivier) are aware of the people's resentment of Ludwig's infatuation with Wagner, and they predict disaster if Ludwig continues to finance Wagner's increasingly extravagant ambitions, particularly this *"Ring* Thing" (as the tetralogy is known at this point): "The stage is flooded with water," groans Pfistermeister, "and there is no interval; giants, a dwarf, a rainbow; and nobody is given a chance to sing properly." He continues: "Perhaps art is all right in its way, but to devote oneself to music and castles in the middle of the nineteenth century is perhaps foolish of the King. There is deep resentment among the people of Bavaria because of this King's infatuation with Wagner." But Wagner's relationship with Ludwig deepens, and Wagner advises him to use his power to lead the way toward a united Germany.

After Minna's death Wagner is ensconced with von Bülow and Cosima in his Swiss home at Triebschen on Lake Lucerne, where he begins *Die Meistersinger*. While the outbreak of the brief Austro-Prussian War (the "Seven Weeks War") in which Ludwig's small Bavarian army is defeated, Wagner mounts a campaign of his own, to conceal from the increasingly detached Ludwig his affair with Cosima. "There are those of us artists and strongmen who must be unwaveringly supported," he declares to Cosima, justifying their affair, "so that we may do that which we have to do with conviction and strength. If one understands that, there is nothing dishonest or dishonorable about it." Meanwhile, fissures develop in the relationship with Ludwig. It begins with a dispute over Ludwig's ownership of the *Ring* operas, and it worsens as Wagner asserts his independence by building a Festspielhaus in Bayreuth. Meanwhile,

Wagner himself is the victim of an act of treachery from his new friend, Friedrich Nietzsche (Ronald Pickup), whose book *Human, All Too Human* signals his growing disillusionment with the composer. "All these Germans who flock to Bayreuth," declaims Nietzsche, "all these societies, blowing trumpets, all slashing at each other with sabers, spouting their anti-Semitic rubbish. You're a smalltime theatre manager who through a strange trick of fate has been given the biggest, brightest, most over-decorated barn to call a theatre ever seen. All of Germany must flock to you. In your estimation they have fought their war simply that you may tug down a curtain and shout, 'See the face of art as according to Wagner!' "

The Festspielhaus, strategically located in Bayreuth, midway between Bismarck in Berlin and Ludwig in Munich, is finished in 1876 and Ludwig attends a private performance. "Future generations will envy those of us who have had the incomparable happiness of being with you," Ludwig tells him. "Now, at this moment, long after we have ceased to be, our work will remain." But the performance is a critical and public disaster. "We had to sell everything to pay for it," he tells Liszt, "lighting, machinery, costumes. Then, *Parsifal*. And the money rolled in and I thought, at last, some rest. But no, it always dries up. Concertizing all over Europe just to try to keep a roof on the building. I even thought of going to America."

The years pass. By 1882 Wagner is lamenting the deaths of his friends and celebrating the demise of his foes. He's even repudiating the lifelong loyalty and support of Liszt and mocking Liszt's assumption of Holy Orders. "Now he fancies himself a priest," he grumbles to Cosima. "The old lecher. Get rid of him; I can't stand him anymore." Cosima reminds him, "Wasn't it you who said he inaugurated the New Age?" Wagner retorts, "Yes, in fingering!" A year later Wagner passes his last months in the Palazzo Vendramin, a large house on the Grand Canal in Venice. When Cosima announces a visit by a "Miss Pringle," a singer, there is a terrible row. "That English Flower Maiden, Pringle," shrieks the jealous Cosima. "She says she can't live without you. Hypocrite! Lecher!" Wagner starts up from his desk and then slumps to the floor, dead. This is followed by a shot of Ludwig, alone in Neuschwanstein, when he hears the news. The final image fixes Cosima and Wagner in a beautifully silhouetted tableau as she kneels at her dead husband's feet.

For purposes of clarity, I have given this brief overview in chronological order. It can only fail to do justice to the densely detailed, nonlinear narrative, the wealth of incident and historical allusion, and the superbly appointed and photographed settings. The film's narrative strategy, however, is at times bewilderingly complicated. Two narrative voices, Pfistermeister and Wagner himself, alternate and sometimes collide, both confirming and denying each

other's respective testimonies—a distancing narrative technique Palmer uses
again and again, here and elsewhere in subsequent films. (It should be noted
that as his own spokesperson, Wagner's words can hardly be trusted; ditto for
Pfistermeister, who in reality was bitterly opposed to Wagner's financial excesses and exploitation of the king.) Events flash by in a scrambled sequence.
Frequent flashbacks and flashforwards in time, jump cuts, and abrupt interpolations of images fracture the diegesis. For example, scenes of Wagner's
funeral, Ludwig's death, Cosima's birthing of Siegfried, and dialogues among
Ludwig's ministers appear out of sequence several times. The chronology
of operatic productions is jumbled. Scenes of the Dresden uprising and the
Franco-Prussian War seem interchangeable at times. Assorted images recur
arbitrarily and unexpectedly—a black swan silhouetted against a fiery light,
torch-bearing men running down tunnels, a burning building, a bearded
dwarf hammering on an anvil, Ludwig rushing down labyrinthine corridors,
Wagner's funeral cortege.

Blame for some of the resulting incoherency may be laid at the feet of
circumstantial exigencies over which Palmer had little if any control. As has
been mentioned, the nine-hour picture was too unwieldy for some venues, and
thus it was cut and recut several times, reduced and expanded by turns. It was
serialized in alternate versions for American, British, and German television
presentation; and it was later reformatted on video in an abridged and "complete" version. In sum, it is difficult to know just what constitutes an "original"
version. Complicating matters is Palmer's method of story and musical construction, which, as will be increasingly apparent in the films to come, typically eschews linear diegesis, foregrounds musical performance, and deploys
image systems that constitute a kind of visual equivalent of the Wagnerian
system of "leitmotifs," what commentator Jacques Barzun has described as
"identification tags in sounds."[11] Such a comparison is problematic, to say the
least, but it is evident that Palmer's juxtaposition of recurring images—a network of fundamental shots—against shifting contexts inflects their meanings
(a classic demonstration of the Soviet filmmaker Lev Kuleshov"s "Mozhukin
Experiment"), just as Wagner's repetitions of a simple musical motif to which
he has assigned meanings—Siegfried's sword, the Rhine, and so on—acquire
changing connotations within the varying contexts of operatic scenes and
vocal utterances. Critic Denby Richards has favorably compared the results
with other musical structures: "[Palmer] has produced a film which is formally
based on sonata form; a symphonic poem which is so cast that it develops as it
progresses, and the final section pulls the various threads together in a superb
coda in the Venetian canals."[12]

Palmer's use of music was likewise unsettling in its effect. If Wagner's music *means* something, he insists, it is not necessarily just the surface elements and the emotions of his operas; rather, it's also the interior, frequently contradictory expressions of Wagner's own opportunism, avarice, megalomania, creative throes, and racism. During an orchestra rehearsal at Bayreuth, Wagner peers down through the trap door at conductor Hans Richter and admonishes him to "get off your ass and start playing." At his birthday party Liszt performs his music before a chattering crowd oblivious to his artistry (and he oblivious to their indifference). The music of *Tristan und Isolde* underscores Ludwig's suicide in Lake Starnberg; the terrifying music in the third scene of *Das Rheingold,* the birth of Siegfried; the "Entrance of the Gods into Valhalla," the arriving fat-cat dignitaries at the Bayreuth premiere; and music from *Parsifal,* Wagner's ignominious death scene.

Notwithstanding critical complaints of confusion and historical inaccuracies, there was general applause for the scope of Palmer's achievement.[13] Critic Richard Hornak pronounced it "one of the most beautifully photographed motion pictures in history."[14] Another critic, Barry Millington, called it "a magnificent achievement, a worthy addition to Palmer's series of sensitive composer documentaries and a credit to all concerned in its production." In particular, there was general praise for the musical performances by the London Philharmonic Orchestra and the Vienna Philharmonic Orchestra under Solti; for singers Peter Hofmann, Gwyneth Jones, Jess Thomas, and Yvonne Kenny; and for actors Redgrave as Cosima, Galffi as Ludwig, and Pickup as Nietzsche. Burton's portrayal of Wagner, however, drew a mixed response. "Burton played him with no attempt at winning sympathy," opined critic Richards.[15] And commentator Christopher J. Thomas sniffed that he was "stilted," that "Burton's Wagner never speaks, he declares; he never convinces, he orates. He also manages to mispronounce every German word he uses, whether it be one of his titles or a derogatory description of his opponents."[16] Hornak rightly differentiates between his performance as the young Wagner, when the obvious age discrepancy undermined the conviction of the performance, and his portrayal of the aging composer, when he comes into his own. "He is finally at the age where he can play Wagner with all the appropriate dignity, stature, contradiction and arrogance, Hornak wrote. "The natural physical dissipation that was unsuccessfully concealed through most of the film is now used to advantage, and these are the most moving and memorable moments of Burton's screen career."[17]

Hopes had been high in the year of its release, the centennial of Wagner's death, that Palmer would improve on the rather dismal record of Wagnerian portraits hitherto seen on screen.[18] There had been nothing so far that remotely suggested, in the words of cultural historian Leon Botstein, "Wagner's staggering historical impact, his artistic vision, his musical and dramatic imagination, his sheer persistence, and his perverse but profound belief that in matters of art lie essential aspects of human life." Botstein continues: "As the case of Wagner amply illustrates, art, culture, and the life of the artist cannot be relegated to the periphery of contemporary life."[19] Instead, there had been an aborted project in the 1930s by the visionary Soviet filmmaker Sergei Eisenstein that envisioned a modern *Gesamtkunstwerk* that would bring together theatrical, musical, balletic, and cinematic elements in its depiction of the composer and his world. William Dieterle's *Magic Fire* (1955), despite its location shooting in European theaters, including the Bayreuth Festpielhaus and its musical supervision by the redoubtable Erich Wolfgang Korngold, was a sumptuously upholstered affair, but so drastically cut before its release that it survives today as only a pale shadow of what it might have been (see Chapter One). Luchino Visconti's *Ludwig* (1973), a superbly mounted but chilly and remote portrait of Ludwig II's ill-starred reign, featured Trevor Howard in a secondary role as Wagner, who, by contrast to the idealism of Ludwig (Helmut Berger), is a rampant hedonist and opportunist.[20] Hans Jürgen-Syberberg's perversely obscure polemic, *Ludwig: Requiem for a Virgin King* (1972), contained a wildly eclectic and generally incoherent portrait of Wagner, a conglomeration of photographs, slides, cartoons, agit-prop newsreels in a generally incoherent piece of New German meta-cinema.[21] And Ken Russell's *Lisztomania*, the most notorious of all screen depictions of Wagner (see Chapter Four), portrayed Wagner as a caricature out of *Mad Magazine* — by turns, a musical vampire who sucked the creative juices out of Liszt and a Hollywood "mad doctor" who creates a proto-fascist Hitler monster.

But Palmer had agendas of his own. "It was my first big theatrical film," he remembers. "I've always wondered how a penniless, ruthless, anti-Semitic megalomaniac like Wagner could have 'gotten away' with the things he did. What was there about this man, unpleasant as he must have been, that was so charming? For example, when he first comes to Zurich, absolutely penniless, he finds out who the richest man in Zurich is [Wesendonck], chats him up, has dinner with him, and at the end of the evening not only has his bank account, a cottage at the bottom of the garden, but his wife [Mathilde] as well! We filmmakers could learn a lot from his methods of financing — although we must not run off with anybody's wife! You know, there's an story about Wagner and the first performance of *Parsifal* that tells us what kind of man he was: The first act of *Parsifal* is a quasi-religious ceremony — I think actually a Black Mass to Wagner's own text. At the end, there was silence in the theatre. Absolute silence. Wagner was horrified. And he went running around wondering what had happened. Well, he didn't know that Cosima had already told everybody that this was such a great spiritual moment that it could only be greeted with silence. Applause would be vulgar. Wagner found this out and went about screaming, how dare this horrible woman say that — 'I want applause. I love applause. *Give me applause!* ' "

Indeed, there is no question that the finished film reveals a character who elicits both Palmer's loathing and admiration, just as Thomas Mann had felt the same contradictory fascinations years before, commenting that Wagner was "one of the most splendidly questionable, ambivalent, and fascinating phenomena in all artistic creation."[22] Palmer regards him less as a prophet for "the new music" than as an exemplar of petty bigotry. Indeed, Palmer finds in Wagner the first of what would be many opportunities to come to attack the anti-Semitism that infected not just Wagner and his time but impacted the emergence of Nazism and the Holocaust. As Botstein notes, Wagner viewed Jews "as entirely foreign as a group, incapable of true assimilation even on an individual basis; as the source of cultural and national decline, and as fundamentally diseased and decadent." Moreover, in line with Palmer's conviction that an artist and his work are inseparably linked, Botstein further declares that "the virulent anti-Semitism of the Bayreuth circle around Cosima after 1883 and the appropriation of Wagner by later political anti-Semites, including the Nazis, have deep historical roots in Wagner's work itself."[23]

That Palmer succeeded in venting this acerbic view of Wagner is confirmed by commentator Thomas's review in *Opera Quarterly*. "Indeed, the overwhelming evidence throughout the picture indicates how many of those involved with this project came to detest Wagner the man," Thomas charged, "just as some who knew and loved the historical figure eventually turned against him.[24] There is no doubt that Wagner thought too much about money and women, yet for Palmer this became a fixation."[25]

Puccini, released in 1984 and scripted by Charles Wood, is both a theatricalization of a single episode in Puccini's life — the circumstances behind the suicide in 1909 of a woman presumed to be his mistress — and a documentation of Palmer's own staging of Puccini's opera *Turandot* in 1984 at the Scottish Opera of Glasgow.

A brief recounting of the historical record, whose overheated passions and recriminations resemble nothing so much as a novel by James M. Cain (or an opera by Puccini), is necessary here. In 1880 Puccini began an affair with Elvira Gemignani, the wife of a merchant from Lucca. They married four years later, after her husband's death, and she bore Puccini his only child, Antonio. After the premiere of his opera *Tosca,* they settled near the village of Torre del Lago, ten miles from Pisa, where they engaged the services of a maid, sixteen-year-old Doria Manfredi. By October 1908, Elvira formed suspicions that

Doria had become her husband's mistress, and she spread gossip that Doria was the village whore. She even went to the village priest, Father Michelucci, in an attempt to expel Doria from the village. Puccini, who defended Doria and himself from the accusations, was distraught, and he wrote in a letter to a friend: "It's an appalling torment, and I'm passing through the saddest time of my life! . . . It's enough if I tell you that I don't want to live any longer — certainly not with [Elvira]."[26] Then, on 23 January 1909, Doria swallowed poison in her mother's home, where she died five days later. Her family lodged charges against Puccini. But when it was discovered that she had left behind a note denying the accusations and that she was proven to be a virgin by a subsequent examination by a physician, the charges were withdrawn. Yet the hysterical Elvira remained unconvinced. Biographer Mosco Carner has noted that Elvira, a Catholic, was feeding upon her own past guilt as an adulterer with Puccini. "Admittedly, Puccini's conduct provided abundant justification for her jealousy; everyone in his intimate circle knew of his frequent infidelities, but he was candid enough to confess to them."[27] Eventually, a chastened Elvira returned to Puccini and life at Torre resumed. They relocated to nearby Viareggio in 1921, where they lived for the rest of his life.

Palmer is convinced that the Doria episode, brief as it was, had a profound impact on Puccini's last years, especially in his inability to complete *Turandot*. The composer had himself proposed Carlo Gozzi's *Turandotte* (1762) as the basis for his next project after *Il Trittico*, even though Ferrucio Busoni had already written a two-act opera on the subject in 1917. Beginning in 1920, he labored for four years, ultimately leaving it unfinished. "It is not that Puccini failed to finish *Turandot* because he died of throat cancer," Palmer claims, "there are other reasons." He quotes Puccini's remark that "no one will ever understand this libretto, except me, because no one else will ever know what it is about."[28] Thus, although Palmer is quick to deny too close a parallel between the Doria affair and the *Turandot* story — "I am not suggesting for one moment that the story of *Turandot* is a thinly disguised version of the story of Doria Manfredi" — he does point out that "the character of Liu, the servant girl who dies for love, does not exist in the Gozzi play, nor in the first draft of the libretto."[29] Moreover, Palmer wonders if the relationship between Puccini and Elvira might not have significant parallels in the story of Calaf and the frigid and remote Princess Turandot. If all this be so, there might be an explanation why the opera was never finished: "[The reconciliation between Calaf and Turandot] must have been impossible for [Puccini] to contemplate," says Palmer, "since reconciliation in any heart-warming sense between Puccini and Elvira did not, and could not, take place [and] Puccini simply could not face the emotional and psychological implications of his libretto."[30]

The film's setting is Torre del Lago in 1906.[31] Puccini is laboring to finish

The Girl of the Golden West. Against the lushly photographed idyllic images of the lake, Puccini's voice-over (uttered by actor Robert Stephens in the eponymous role) immediately establishes a melancholy tone: "My life is a sea of sadness in which I am becalmed. Many people say how enviable my life is. I must truly have been born under an unhappy star. I am loved by no one." He feels his creative energies have waned: "The earth slides away from me as I walk. No one to help me write something of *substance*." Moreover, his household, consisting of himself, wife Elvira (Virginia McKenna), son Tonio, and maid Doria (Judith Howarth), is anything but harmonious. When Elvira reproaches him for his casual affairs, he justifies himself: "These affairs of the heart are of no importance to me. Necessary to me only as a fast new car is necessary. Artists need motorcars, speedboats, guns, and women who are not important, who get more out of me than I get out of them. Simple women, women in the fields, ordinary women, shop girls, school teachers. That sort of women. I cultivate them as my 'little gardens,' for my own ends, for my own relief. And that's all." Soon, Elvira shifts her attack to Doria and spreads gossip that she is having an affair with her husband. "We cannot blame the Maestro," the villagers caution the girl. "His wife has told us you are a simple and sensible girl; and that you will confess your behavior and repent fully your sins and wash it away." All poor Doria can do is repeat, over and over, "It isn't true; it isn't true."

As Elvira's recriminations and Puccini's protests grow louder, Doria retreats into a dangerous silence. Finally, desperate, she takes poison. She dies a few days later, screaming in pain, leaving behind a note defending her innocence. Even after a physician's examination proves Doria's virginity, Elvira remains obdurate. In one of the great speeches in the picture, she turns fiercely on Puccini: "You know nothing of love. Love to you is a cushion, soft words, soft flesh, soft, enveloping, fragrant gardens in which you trowel. Just like a little boy who has just discovered this thing, you can put it in wherever you like, whenever you like. Just like a mouse, with sparkling eyes, pomaded hair and elegant whiskers, poking, rutting. You know nothing of hard, cruel love, implacable, relentless, triumphant love."

Later, at Doria's graveside, Puccini stands beside Doria's family. He is utterly disconsolate. The others whisper that he must be going mad. Puccini turns on them and screams, "Leave me alone!" The coffin is lowered into darkness. Hatless in the rain, Puccini stands by, mute and alone.

It is not surprising that Palmer was so attracted to this subject. Despite Puccini's abundance of creative fire and animal sexuality, he was, as Carner writes, in the grip of a perpetual melancholy that was "the ground-bass of Puccini's life and his art"; and the characters in his operas "are troubled, and their world is a harsh one."[32] The music itself, notes actor and commentator

Simon Callow, is full of complexities and perturbation; escape is, in fact, the very last thing it offers."[33] More important, here are themes that have always preoccupied Palmer—namely, the nature of the connections between an artist's life and his creative work. The link in this case resides in the lines from the Vendor's street song in *Tabarro*: "Who lived for love, died for love!" It is an equation of the artist's love (and preoccupation) with death, of his attraction to forces that are both life-enhancing and life-destroying. In the dual role of Elvira/Turandot he sees the source of a female image that reappears in later films—Cosima Liszt in *Wagner,* George Sand in *The Strange Case of Delfina Potocka,* Harriet Smithson in *I, Berlioz,* and Clara Schumann in *Brahms and the Singing Little Girls.*

As was seen in *Wagner,* Palmer breaks up the linear drive of his narrative with frequent flashforwards of Doria's death throes, flashbacks of Puccini's dalliances with young women, interpolations of dream images (Elvira's erotic fantasies of Puccini and Doria in bed), and frequent cutaways to three villagers who comment on ensuing events. It is their conversations that fill us in with the backstory of Puccini, Elvira, and Doria. After Doria's death and exoneration, they discuss the phenomenon of his continued alliance with Elvira: "True love is very rare, very rare indeed," they declaim. Is it a "chemical" thing? A "subtle change in the blood"? The mystery remains.

Also intercut with the dramatic events at Torre del Lago are the rehearsals and premiere of Palmer's Scottish Opera production of *Turandot.* The two narrative lines seem to coexist and intersect in virtual time and space, the characters identical and interchangeable (even down to the fusion of the three Torre del Lago villagers with the ministers Ping, Pang, and Pong). The historical story, shot mostly in close-ups, is presented on two levels. On one hand, there's a prosaic collection of episodes comprised mainly of family disputes, hunting scenes on the lake, Puccini composing at his piano, Doria's funeral. These are intercut, on the other hand, with Puccini and Elvira's subjective world (suggested through overheated histrionics and visual and aural distortions).

The opera production likewise plays out on several levels. First, the rehearsals reveal Palmer wrestling with the details of the production, grappling with the niceties of the staging in much the way (it is suggested) that Puccini bickered and fought with his colleagues and performers. There's humor here, in Palmer's sardonic asides to the players, and there's petty squabbling, particularly between Palmer and the lighting designer.[34] Second, these rehearsal scenes are themselves intercut with moments from the finished stage performance, which Palmer has conceived as a divided platform—the forestage is used for the story in Chinese period scene and dress, while upstage the action transpires in scene and dress appropriate to Puccini's time. In other words, the story is staged simultaneously on both levels, linking the Calaf, Turandot, and

Liu with Puccini, Elvira, and Doria. Third, Palmer's cameras record the opening night of his production. Puccini's granddaughter arrives and talks about Toscanini's premiere of the opera, and how he stopped the performance at the point Puccini had ceased composing.

Emerging from all this, among other considerations, is Palmer's own identification with his work as a filmmaker (and also in this case opera director) and that of Puccini as an opera composer. This is made crystal clear in the penultimate scenes when Palmer reads to the camera the harsh critical notices of his opera production's opening night. "Travesty of the Original" screams one of the headlines. "This production was the most embarrassing experience in the lives of the opera company, and the Scottish Opera doesn't deserve it." Palmer wryly mutters, "I guess they've forgotten that all the nights were sold out." Another notice: "Palmer has simply put on stage his wildly overpraised biographical method of his documentaries. This production will die."

As for the film itself, the critic for *The Listener* charged that Palmer was guilty of stacking his deck: "[It] is not just a story in its own right, but also an attempt to provide the evidence for Palmer's interpretation of *Turandot*. A weakness in this procedure is at once obvious. If Palmer is himself the producer of the biographical part, the evidence it provides is not exactly going to be objective. Palmer knows this, of course. . . . Yet, even on Palmer's evidence, it is hard to believe he is right about *Turandot*. Naturally, Puccini drew on his own emotional experience in some sense in all his music. But the insanely jealous Elvira, apart from her cruelty, seems to have very little in common with Turandot, who guards herself fiercely against the onset of any sexual emotion; while the real and fictional servant-girls are utterly different characters and kill themselves for totally different reasons."[35]

For Palmer, of course, the real "truth" of his conception is that Puccini — and, by extension, Palmer — were living out an opera of their own, on and offstage, both literal and symbolic.

The opening scene of *God Rot Tunbridge Wells* (1985) begins with a modern performance of *Messiah*. There in the audience, sitting amid the twentieth-century suits and ties, is George Frideric Handel himself, attired in his eighteenth-century wig and dressed in ruffles, waistcoat, and breeches. "This night, this very night," he says, addressing the camera, "I was attending a performance of *Messiah* — *my Messiah,* if I may call it so (and I think I may), given by the Amateur Music Club of Tunbridge Wells." The listeners around him lean forward severely to shush him up. "A gathering of such thundering banality," he continues, oblivious to them, "that I would have feigned oncoming deafness, had it not seemed so certain to be at hand, that a deception

Trevor Howard not only portrayed George Frideric Handel in Palmer's *God Rot Tunbridge Wells* (1985) but Richard Wagner in Luchino Visconti's *Ludwig: Mad King of Bavaria* (1972). (Courtesy Isolde Films)

would have been superfluous." He pauses while the music grows louder. "Mediocrity is a great comforter," he concludes, "and why should I take it upon myself to deprive them of their luxury. Nothing will disabuse them, or their kind, of their silly negligence."

Whereupon Handel ceremoniously quits the auditorium and returns home to take to his bed. Feeble and wan, the old man looks about him and addresses camera. He launches into a catalogue of his infirmities: "Shaken with rack of gout, a malady no man dares smirk upon; fevered; paralyzed twice (if only in part), blind these ten years, although I doubt any of it gains more attention than my portliness. . . . Worms destroy this body, impetuous, peremptory. Have I been all that? Yes, yes; even now." Off go his shoes. He loosens his neckpiece. Off goes the shirt. "I am taking to my bed," he confides, his head silhouetted by the strong backlight. "My deserted and no doubt filthy — yes, indeed it is — bed. It is not my intention to slouch off to it in such haste; but events have wrecked my good humor."

In these opening scenes, juxtaposing an exasperated eighteenth-century

Handel with a modern, bombastic concert performance, Palmer has fired a shot across our bow. Here is a Handel, portrayed by Trevor Howard in his last film role, who rails at the fates and the world around him, who catalogues and reproaches his own failings, and who, ultimately, refuses to go gentle into that Good Night. Palmer and his scenarist, John Osborne, have derived their portrait of an irascible, contentious man from an anecdote in Handel's later years. "I had found a letter in which Handel recounted a visit to Tunbridge Wells for a performance of 'our *Messiah,* as they put it,'" says Palmer. "Instead of the twenty-two instruments and choir, that he anticipated, he was subjected to a vast array of musical and vocal forces and a blast of overblown sound. He left after a time and noted in a letter, 'God rot Tunbridge Wells!' I think he knew what posterity was going to make — indeed, already was making — of his music, drowning it with bombast and phony reverence all at the same time."

As the aging composer looks back on his life, occasionally interrupting his narrative to address the camera for periodic salvos against the debilities that assail his body and the mediocrity that debases his world, episodes and fragments of music rapidly come and go in a blur of disjointed continuum of time and space. One moment the young Handel is in his native Halle in the 1690s, performing on the organ for the Duke, the next he is in Lübeck with a prostitute, and still later in Florence, where he is escorted to the bed of an elderly woman. In Rome around 1710 Cardinal Ottoboni arranges a keyboard duel between him and Domenico Scarlatti. In England, "the center and target of everything," he strides down the streets reading *The Spectator*'s attacks on the "pasteboard" exoticisms of Italian opera. He rehearses *Rinaldo* for its premiere at the Haymarket Theatre. He floats down the Thames on a barge in 1717 conducting his *Water Music.* He composes the *Coronation Anthems* in 1727. He rebukes the Archbishop of Canterbury for his attacks on the ceremonial rather than artistic quality of his music — "The ceremony was in the splendor and the art was in both; and he could see neither. It has long seemed to me that clerics and academics hate all art, life, literature, and most surely music." He scorns Bach, who praises God with music that displays "the mechanical repetition of a damned merchant's clock." And he writes, rehearses, and performs more music: scenes from *Acis and Galatea* at the Duke of Chandos's home and from *Messiah* in Dublin in 1742.

"Oratorio and opera, what an absurd war we made of it," he says. "I recall the Pope had banned all opera. In London the opera crowd did not relish my oratorios. It was Dublin that first recognized my seasickness." He becomes a thoroughgoing Londoner — "the premiere Londoner," he says, "the laureate in music of this city." Meanwhile, the political situation keeps changing. Queen Anne, his protector, dies in 1713 and George I of Hanover becomes king, only to be succeeded by Frederick, the Prince of Wales, in 1727. That same year Handel is naturalized as an English subject. Older now, more portly, he wrangles with judges to protect his copyrights and presents damning evidence in court on an anachronistic Edison phonograph. He raises funds for the Foundlings Hospital. Suddenly, he's on a battlefield in the aftermath of the Battle of Culloden. "Was it for this I raised myself, raised myself and all in praise of that great Duke of Cumberland, the Butcher of Cumberland?" He endures a grisly eye operation. Finally, after damning Tunbridge Wells once again and after writing his last oratorio, *Jeptha,* in 1751, he takes to his bed again, complaining of a "paralytic disorder in the head."

He speaks for the last time as we see Andrei Gavrilov in modern dress performing on a modern piano the mighty *Passacaglia:* "I always drifted to theatricality, but not at the expense of truth." A last reprise of scenes and incidents from the film flash before our eyes, culminating with shots of modern-day London, the Royal Academy of Music, the Thomas Coram Foundation (formerly the Foundling Hospital), and Handel's former home, now adorned with a blue plaque duly proclaiming its historical significance.

Needless to say, none of this wealth of incident, anachronistic details, and performance practice is presented in anything resembling chronological order. And the elegiac rant of the composer's "voice" doesn't just belong to Handel; rather, it belongs to actor Trevor Howard (who, like Handel, was facing his own imminent death), to filmmaker Palmer (attendant as always to the gloom and disillusionment of an artist looking back on a wrecked career), and, of course, to playwright John Osborne (himself in the last throes of his creative life). To whom, we ask, do these elegiac words from Handel really belong? "All hid from mortal sight. All our joys to sorrows turning, all our trumpets into mourning, as the night succeeds the day; no certain bliss, no solid peace we mortals know on earth below. Yet, on this maxim we'll obey: Whatever is, is right. Ah, great was the company of preachers."

The critic for the *Sunday Times* had it right when he noted: "It is, as far as I can tell, an extraordinary, rumbustious and funny affair. . . rather more than just a life of Handel or indeed a life of Handel as interpreted by [Tony] Palmer. For [John] Osborne, who wrote the script in just three weeks, has put much of himself into Handel's lines."[36]

"It was one of Osborne's last projects," remembers Palmer.[37] "His last play, *Déjà vu,* which I directed — a sort of sequel to *Look Back in Anger* — had been written before the Handel film. He had wanted to do something like this for a long time. I had known him for many years and knew he was madly passionate about music. In the text of *Déjà vu* there is a reference to Handel's opera *Alcina.* So I rang him up and we talked about the play and the opera reference.

He told me he had listened to Handel all his life — and then he burst out, 'Why don't we make a film about Handel?' And I admitted I had already had a little idea, and that the Tri-Centennial of Handel's birth gave us a great excuse. We had no idea how Handel really felt or what he really said, so what John did was inflect Handel's 'voice' through quotations from the King James Bible and the Book of Common Prayer, which are two of the greatest works of literature in the English language. It's a wonderful device. You end up crafting an invented language for an invented dialogue for invented situations. But I think it gets jolly close to what we know about how Handel really lived and spoke." Osborne may have been speaking of his own script when he has Handel explain his own use of English: "I put my weight into it. Congreve, Dryden, Milton, I served them all, all and more. And most of all, the Bible, Isaiah, Corinthians — what gifts they have been!" At the same time, Palmer claims, "the script may be considered as the third part of John's autobiography, after *Look Back* and *Déjà vu*. He has expressed much about his *own* struggle with the establishment and his own love of the English tradition, which he always felt was being eroded by today's society."

Determining the identity of the 'real' Handel here is an even more complicated affair, considering that five different actors portrayed Handel at various stages in his life. "We made no attempt to make them look physically the same," recalls Palmer. "The next-to-oldest actor was a London taxi driver who looked nothing like Trevor Howard." Thus, if Handel wears many faces and indulges in many moods, musics, and activities, ranging from the carnal to the politically ceremonial to the deeply spiritual, Palmer is everywhere intent on rejecting the standard image of the solemn, heavily jowled, religiously stodgy character that has come down to us over the centuries. Ironically, Handel was the first composer to receive a full biographical treatment, by the Reverend John Mainwaring in 1760. That early attention notwithstanding, however, by the time Newman Flowers wrote his *George Frideric Handel: His Personality and His Times* in 1948, the mythologization was complete.[38] "Of all the great composers," commentator A. Craig Bell has written, "Handel is the most misjudged and misunderstood. By the orgiastic, tasteless Crystal Palace performances of his works Handel was presented as a massively choral and religious composer and nothing else. . . . Thanks to this tradition, the real, vital Handel has been submerged under a wash of religiosity and the whole character of his music misrepresented and misunderstood."[39] It was long presumed, for example, continues Bell, that he preferred serious oratorios to the format of opera; that he wrote nothing of value before 1738 and the "English" oratorios, save the *Water Music* and the "Harmonious Blacksmith"; and that he wrote mostly religious music.[40]

Long before Palmer, the movies had inherited and extended this long tradition. Wilfrid Lawson's 1942 screen portrayal in the Technicolor *The Great Mr. Handel* (discussed in Chapter One), directed by Norman Walker on the occasion of the bicentennial of *Messiah,* was a respectful dramatization that devoted fully one-third of its length to the biblical inspiration behind Handel's writing of *Messiah*. Moreover, shot and released during World War II, it wears its British nationalism on its sleeve and makes of the composer a proper British patriot.[41] Walter Slezak's Hallmark Hall of Fame production *A Cry of Angels,* directed by George Schaefer and written by Sherman Yellen, brought Handel to television in December 1963; it likewise devoted much of its length to the religious inspiration that led to *Messiah*.[42] Simon Callow's film *Honour, Profit, and Pleasure,* directed and written by Anna Ambrose, made two years before Palmer's film, charming as it is, framed Handel's story in a theatrical setting (the Queen's Theatre in London), privileging its generous excerpts from *Rinaldo* and *Acis and Galatea* and pronouncing theatrical stylization over its biographical realism.[43] Only Gérard Corbiau's *Farinelli* (1985), in which Handel (Jeroen Krabbe) is a secondary character, dares to put the composer in a less than favorable light—that is, as a grasping, opportunistic person who stops at nothing to ruin the career of his rival, the castrato Farinelli (Stephano Dionisi).[44]

Palmer tosses all these characteristics into the mixing pot, as it were, subtitling the film, appropriately, as *An Historical, Tragical Comedy; or a Comical, Historical Tragedy; or, What You Will*, and generously spicing the brew with splendid musical performances by the English Chamber Orchestra (conducted by Sir Charles Mackerras), the Academy of Ancient Music (led by Catherine MacIntosh), and solo singers Elizabeth Harwood ("I Know My Redeemer Liveth"), John Shirley-Quirk ("Wake the Ardor of Thy Breast"), and Emma Kirkby ("Who May Abide). Solo instrumentalists include Simon Preston (the Organ Concerto, Opus 7, No. 5) and Andrei Gavrilov (the "Passacaglia"). At times these performers appear as themselves in modern dress and at other times, as period performers in contemporary garb. As usual, Palmer has not hesitated to assign specific meanings and situations to these works. Handel's own words he might have adopted as his own: "All the passions of the heart can be possessed in simple harmony, even without words; yes, its harmony, its unity, its order must prevail."

Palmer looks back with special affection on *God Rot:* "I think it must be about the last performance that Trevor Howard gave. We had to provide him slates for his lines, but he gets things absolutely right. We just wanted to have fun with the character and the period and with the music. Some of the happiest moments in all my career were those times when John Osborne would visit the set and talk with Howard. John admired him so much. Every evening they and their wives would share supper. It was wonderful, comparable to those times when Olivier, Gielgud, and Richardson would get together during the filming of *Wagner*. Sometimes I think that's why I do these films, just to sit at the feet of these great people."

Testimony (1987) is a seminal film in Palmer's career. Rivaling with *Wagner* in ambition, scope, and length, it examines the symbiotic relationship between composer Dmitry Shostakovich and Soviet tsar Joseph Stalin. "It's a work of fiction, of course, *not* a documentary," he insists. But his attention to the myriad details of locations, casting, the historical record, and the extensive use of musical and metaphoric allusion lends a hard-edged, gritty texture to its frightening and, ultimately moving, nightmare. The film is examined in detail in the last chapter of this book.

"I, Louis Hector Berlioz, composer, musician, citizen of France, being now in my sixty-fourth year, tell you in this my last will and testament that my subject has always been . . . WAR." Drum beats and a blast of trombones from *La Symphonie Fantastique* accompany scenes of soldiers on the march. Cut to Berlioz, a man burdened with a world-weary air, sporting a violent shock of reddish hair, sitting at his writing desk, bending over a manuscript. His hair blazes in the light pouring through the window behind him. "At the time of my birth," Berlioz recalls, "year twelve of the Glorious Revolution, war was tearing at the very heart of Europe. By the time I was twelve, my beloved France had been crushed under the boot of Wellington. A military coup against the Emperor Charles when I was not yet thirty. Paris destroyed again in 1848." Music from the "March to the Scaffold" ushers in more scenes of explosions and bloody combat. "For fifty years now revolution, poverty, shame has been my inheritance. And now, as I approach death, Bismarck is at the gates threatening Paris. I feel like I'm an apparition, a ghost."

And so composer Berlioz (Colin Redgrave) and filmmaker Palmer are off and running in *I, Berlioz* (1992), a freewheeling portrait of France's greatest (and most contentious) musical revolutionary, now at the far side of his life, raging at his infirmities and at the reversals of fortune that continue to dog his days. "Of this much I am certain—," Berlioz continues, "the end, when it comes, will be the end of everything."

Another blast of trumpets.

Berlioz was the most incendiary of composers. A contemporary drawing depicts him conducting before the mouth of a cannon, his hair rising like a flame above his brow.[45] He was a volatile character with real and imagined enemies at every hand. He vented with both his pen and in his music a steady stream of hates, protests, and depressions with as much aggressive energy as he proclaimed his loves and his triumphs. All of which makes him an apt subject for Palmer, always attracted to the kind of composer who, as Berlioz biographer Hugh Macdonald writes, "wove his own experience densely into the fabric of his music; neither is intelligible without reference to the other."[46] Palmer thus weaves his narrative out of the multiple strands of the music, Berlioz's *Memoirs* (one of the great autobiographical documents of the nineteenth century), and the thousands of letters he penned to friends and enemies alike.[47] The general tone of these documents is succinctly summed up in a letter to Princess Carolyne Sayn-Wittgenstein, dated 19 October 1864: "I have no faith in the future, but the past tortures me. I suffer, I suffer, I see clearly that I'm absurd, but my lucidity of mind does not relieve my suffering in the slightest."[48] And in the *Memoirs* he writes, "I am in my sixty-first year; past hopes, past illusions, past high thoughts and lofty conceptions. . . . My contempt for the folly and baseness of mankind, my hatred of its atrocious cruelty, have never been so intense. And I say hourly to Death: 'When you will. Why does he delay?' "[49] Macdonald says: "There is no mistaking the sincerity and conviction of these words, . . . [They] annihilate any suspicion that he was a 'poseur,' for falsity and contrivance were remote from the Romantics' world just as the sincerity of belief mattered more than the cause in which one believed. To burn for a cause, even to die for it, was of supreme value, no matter what that cause was."[50]

Palmer rightly nominates Berlioz's opera, *The Trojan's,* as Berlioz's great lost cause. Undoubtedly the greatest and largest of his works, this mighty depiction of the Trojan War and its aftermath was never produced in its entirety in his lifetime.[51] It also provides the organizational model for the film. *The Trojans* uses contrast as its structuring principal: Just as we see the spacious, static layout of Act I followed by the dynamic, compressed action of Act II, and the peaceful portrait of Carthage giving way to the martial intensity of Act III, so too does Palmer organize his film in episodes that contrast the static, framed shots of Berlioz in repose (writing in his study, walking through the forest, lying blissfully atop a high cliff) with abrupt shifts to scenes of war, carnage, and cataclysmic storm.

"Actually, the whole film came out of my minor career as an opera director," recalls Palmer. "I had always wanted to do *The Trojans*, but was told it was impossible. But I did put it on at the Zurich Opera House. It was only the fifth time since Berlioz's lifetime that it was done, complete, in one night. I knew there was a film there. I talked to biographer David Cairns about it. I told Melvyn Bragg we should do it. And so we did. We made what Bragg described as 'a great, thundering film.' The title, *I, Berlioz,* is taken from the first lines of his will, which starts out, 'Je, Berlioz.' "

In the film Berlioz describes *The Trojans:* "Four hours of glorious music which has occupied me most of my life. It is on a grand scale, very grand, describing the fall and destruction of Troy by the Greeks. You will recall the story of the wooden horse? And then the flight of Aeneas and the Trojan heroes to Carthage; his affair with Dido; and finally the founding of Rome and the Roman Empire." As if to atone for the fact that Berlioz never heard much of *The Trojans* in public performance (the first half was never performed in his lifetime), Palmer has taken it upon himself to stage generous portions of it in the film — the "Royal Hunt and Storm" music from Act IV; Cassandra's proph- ecy in Act I, scene 2; the ballet from Act IV, scene 33; Dido and Anna's duet from Act II, scene 24; Dido's farewell from Act V, scene 48; and the Octet and Chorus from Act I, scene 8 ("The horror! The horror! This story will freeze the blood!"). The staging, derived from Palmer's production, is spare yet effective, and the performances by Ludmilla Schmetschuk as Dido, Giorgio Lamberti as Aeneas, Agnes Habereder as Cassandra, Vesselina Karsarova as Anna, and Anne-Sophie von Otter as Ascanius are magnificent. Ralf Weikert conducts the chorus and orchestra of the Zurich Opera House.

"Every time I close my eyes I hear them," writes Berlioz, back in his study, the light behind him limning his fiery hair, "those magnificent trumpets and the steady tap-tap of the drums leading the armies to war." Cut to scenes that alternate between stage action set in fabled Greece and filmed scenes of flame and fire in the Revolution of 1830. "I see it," Berlioz continues, "like some fantastic vision. But you cannot have an entire army marching across the stage, in a theatre, they say. The hell with them. I see it. I shall drive my great Trojan horse across the stage, discharge my armies, and burn their hypocrisies to the ground." Cut to a slow-motion shot of a great stallion, flames surround- ing its flanks, rearing up and galloping away.

Of course, as is his wont, Palmer fractures the chronology of Berlioz's life and works, as if infected by his ferocious drive and impatient distractions. "My head is bursting with ideas [who is saying this, Berlioz or Palmer?] — impossible to write them down quickly enough." The film veers wildly, from war to peace, back and forth. He meets his wife-to-be, actress Harriet Smith- son, and instantly falls in love. "I wrote her letters. She sent them back." He falls in love again, this time with a pianist, Camille Moke. "She also spurned me, so I threatened to kill her and her mother. But then, I met my Harriet again." Cut to the music from *Faust,* "The King of Thule." Tender scenes of the birth of Berlioz's child, Louis, are rudely contrasted with the galloping accents of "The Ride to the Abyss" (with images of plunging horses and an upraised knife). The "Kyrie" from the *Requiem* is counterbalanced by shots of the interior of a gigantic cathedral. Images of trumpets and drums accompany the *Funeral and Triumphal Symphony* ("I shall write a Military Symphony, beginning with a Marche Funebre and demand it be played at my funeral!").

And always we return to *The Trojans*. There is Berlioz himself, frantically rehearsing the performers. Chaos on stage. "How many promises have I been made by the Opera House?" he moans. " 'Eight harps, Mr. Berlioz? Africa? Water on the stage? Rain? A waterfall? Dogs and lightning?' " A claque of horns and jeers interrupts the ballet sequence. "What a surprise that my opera was regarded as absurd and nonsensical," he cries. "Imagine a score lying dismembered in the windows of a music shop, like the carcass of a slaughter-house animal." Cut to a calf, tied and butchered, blood gushing from its throat.[52]

At length, there's a curious little scene of ghoulishly quiet guignol. Berlioz walks through a misty wood to a cemetery. A grave is being opened. The coffin lid is pulled away. The gravedigger lifts out a shapeless black sack of bones. "Then he picked up the hairless head of my poor Harriet, and threw it into my hands," says Berlioz. Preposterous? No. It really happened, as Berlioz recorded in a letter to Wittgenstein, dated 30 August 1864, and related in his *Memoirs:* "The gravedigger bent down and with his two hands picked up the head, already parted from the body—the ungarlanded, withered, hairless head of 'poor Ophelia.' "[53]

The film concludes as it began, with more images of street violence. Bismarck is on the march. "Yet, my *Trojans* shall live," declaims Berlioz. In a quote from John Dryden, he adds: "My trumpets shall 'untune the sky' " (which reappears in Palmer's next film, *England, My England*). An epilogue shows Berlioz at his writing desk, while Palmer's voice provides the valedictory: "Hector Berlioz died in 1869, broken by the failure of his life's work, *The Trojans*. Like his earlier work, *The Damnation of Faust,* it was never performed in his lifetime as he had intended. Indeed, *The Trojans* was not performed complete until twenty-one years after his death. The manuscript was not published complete until one hundred years after his death. And only five complete stage performances have ever been given on one night as Berlioz wanted."

Berlioz has found his match in Palmer (or is it the other way around?). *I, Berlioz* is a welcome corrective to the disappointingly tepid biopic by Christian-Jaque, *La Symphonie Fantastique* (1942), starring Jean-Louis Barrault as the composer. Shot in Paris in 1942 for the German-controlled Continental-Films Studio during the German Occupation (but not released in America until 1947), *La Symphonie Fantastique* presents the life and music of

Berlioz very much in the sentimentalized and reverential formulas of the standard Hollywood-style biopic of the day. Although the film dutifully parades the major events in Berlioz's life — his studies as a medical student, his meeting with Harriet Smithson, the composing of the *Symphonie Fantastique* and *The Damnation of Faust,* his suicidal tendencies, the break with Smithson, his work as a music critic, and the reunion with his estranged son — far too much screen time is devoted to a fictitious and sentimentalized romance with a singer named "Marie" (Renee St. Cyr), who appears to be a combination of two women in Berlioz's life — singer Pauline Viardot, for whom Berlioz had a lasting affection, and Marie Recio, Berlioz's mistress of many years, whom he married in 1854. Of Berlioz's outspoken personal and political agitations, there is little evidence. The film concludes with a spectacularly staged church performance of the "Kyrie" from the *Requiem.* In the gallery sits Victor Hugo, who declaims: "When we were young, we wondered who among us would attain glory. Hector has found it."[54]

I, Berlioz, by contrast, is punctuated with the shot and shell of Berlioz's — and Palmer's — personal and political agitations. I am even tempted to regard the film as a fragment of Palmer's own autobiography. Both director and composer in their respective oeuvres celebrate war and slaughter. Both envision vast artistic projects against impossible odds. Both are habitually assailed by critics. Both have contempt for the "baseless folly of mankind." Both are obsessed with death. And both, above all, believe in the affective properties of music. Biographer Cairns's eulogy for Berlioz fits Palmer just as well: "Sadness, suffering, mark many of his most characteristic utterances . . . the suffering of a nature in love with unattainable beauty, capable of infinite tenderness but estranged from the universe, proud and exalted yet naked to the whips and scorns of time."[55]

England, My England was filmed on the occasion of the tercentenary of the death of Henry Purcell in 1695. It was part of a series of observances that included a series of concerts at London's South Bank Centre and premieres of new works, inspired by Purcell, by composers Gavin Bryars, John Woolrich, Elvis Costello, and Elena Firsova. "Our tercenturians are on the move again —," wrote conductor Andrew Pinnock at the time, "authors, lone and companionable, editors, performers, record companies, television and film producers all heaving for the festival campsite, marching along to the boom-boom of early music drums."[56]

The film begins with a narrative voice (actor Robert Stephens) declaiming: "In Cromwell's time, in and around the year of our Lord, 1660, two things miraculous came about, which, as I shall relate, gave us great hope for the future of this island, this England. The first, the Restoration of Charles Stuart, after many long years in exile in Holland. The second, the birth of Henry Purcell, organist, composer, his father and his uncle both of the Chapel Royal of the Great Abbey of Westminster. From Heaven he came. . . . Their lives were drawn together as if by divine hand. Together, they joined our history forever."

Immediately, we ask, whose voice is that? It can't belong to anyone in our own time, not with that diction and turn of phrase. At other times its timbre and pitch shift to the voice of actor John Shrapnel, who portrays the historical character of diarist and public servant John Pepys. Moreover, this shifting "voice" also exists in a scripted, *theatrical* film, whose dialogue and narrative were written by British playwright John Osborne *in the manner* of the seventeenth century, further inflected by Charles Wood (who came on to the project after Osborne's death) and by Palmer himself. Thus, it is necessary to realize that the proper identity of that "voice" — and that of ensuing narrators and dialogues — is a concatenation of all of them. As the character of the actor-playwright declares at one point, "I'm trying to find a vibrant language to tell the truth, the language of Pepys, of Dryden. That I believe is worthy of our attention."

Thus, this portrait of Restoration England, and its foremost politician and its most celebrated composer, is declaimed by a veritable *chorus* of voices, times past and times present. Palmer's vast canvas of stage plays and players, music and musicians, history and fiction runs for more than two hours, depending upon the version currently available. Viewers come out of the film, exhausted, probably a bit bewildered, and possibly greatly exhilarated. It's been a tussle all around — between a filmmaker and his material, and between the filmic text and its viewers. As the character of Charles II says in the film (in lines that bear some resemblance to Dryden's "Absalom and Achitophel"): "We strain for coherence, for a snatch of harmony. An old trumpet, played upon but not playing. Sounding, but only my head. Alas, coherence conceals as much as it reveals to the lost, like me, who contemplate the wreckage."[57]

G. K. Chesterton says there is something "unreal" about the second half of the seventeenth century: "Almost all the faces in the portraits of that time look, as it were, like masks put on artificially with the perruque [*sic*]. A strange unreality broods over the period."[58] In *England, My England,* Palmer knocks askew some of those masks. Sumptuous, ornate, splendidly costumed the film is, yes; but these are events and people who emerge from the shadow and spit in our face. They sweat, and they bleed. They straddle the seventeenth and eighteenth centuries, partaking of the diction, gestures, and action of both, partaking of them at one and the same time.

Purcell's brief span of thirty-six years encompasses the end of the Commonwealth, the Restoration of the Monarchy (three kings and one queen) and the Anglican church of England, the Great Plague of 1665 (wherein 68,596 people perished), the Fire of London in 1666, the Monmouth Rebellion of 1685, and the Glorious Revolution of 1688, which saw the usurpation of James II by William of Orange. For most of his career, he was closely connected to the court of the Stuart monarchs. He was celebrated in his time. As Pinnock has written, "Purcell had become a public figure, and his death was mourned as a public loss. No one waited for the mysterious 'test of time' to pass judgment: it was clear to his contemporaries that 'a greater musicall [*sic*] genius England never had.' "[59] The seal on his reputation was set as early as Charles Burney's *A General History of Music from the Earliest Ages to the Present Period* in 1789, the standard textbook on English music history until Ernest Walker's *History of Music in England* appeared in 1907.

Yet, Purcell's biographers complain that we know little about him, not even the exact date of his birth, the identity of his parents, and the circumstances of his death (by turns, tuberculosis, influenza, a cold, and so on). Biographer Jonathan Keates has noted, "Hardly any anecdotes exist to fill out the blurred background, made vaguer still by the almost total absence of letters or private papers."[60] And because so much of his music is linked to theatrical contexts (his operas are seldom performed today), it is usually heard out of context. Indeed, until composer Benjamin Britten based his *Young Person's Guide to the Orchestra* on a Purcell tune, his music was scarcely known at all. It is only now, continues Keates, at the end of the twentieth century, "that we have begun to accept the multiplicity of his achievement as something quite astonishing, the reflection of an artistic personality almost supernatural in its gift for being everything at once, abundant and three-dimensional."[61] The best we can do at this point in time, Keates concludes, "is to rely, whatever our Micawberish hope that something more positive will turn up, on those largely chimerical aids to the biographer, ambience, period detail, hypothesis and sheer guesswork."[62]

Enter Tony Palmer. He makes no attempt to conceal the extent of his creative license. As Michael White writes in his liner notes to the compact disc of music released concurrently with the film, "The cinema has, after all, a long track-record for plugging the holes in the lives of long-dead composers with cinematic fantasy, and Osborne has come up with a solution. It wasn't orthodox, but then Palmer's films about composers . . . never are. Essentially there were two possible approaches. One was to fabricate the personal history and show Purcell striding through the fields in search of inspiration, jotting down ideas as he prepared the Sunday lunch, in the time-honored way of film biography. The other way was to take what Palmer calls 'a great leap of imagination' and flesh out the skeleton of known fact with some kind of counter-plot."

In short, Palmer has the audacity to have a character in the play within the film declare that Purcell "is an ideal subject for a play. Nobody knows anything about him. You can make it all up. We can even get an Arts Council grant!"

Characteristically, Palmer has not chosen to arrange events in strict chronology, nor (as has been noted) has he opted to "speak" in just one voice, and he is certainly not content to depict just the time period of the Restoration. Thus, in this, one of his most wildly eclectic intertextual efforts, he fragments the story through the filters of Pepys's *Diary*, Dryden's poetry, the modern-day staging at London's Royal Court Theatre of George Bernard Shaw's *In Good King Charles's Golden Days*,[63] a modern London actor's attempts to write a play about Purcell, and the antiwar and antinuclear protest movements of the 1960s. And, of course, there is the music of the Stuart court, vividly realized in seventeenth-century stage settings and performed (in period costumes) by John Eliot Gardiner's Monteverdi Choir and the English Baroque Soloists.

As if things weren't complicated enough, many of the acting roles are doubled, even tripled. Simon Callow portrays Charles II in the historical story, Charles II in the Shaw play, and an unnamed actor-playwright in the modern day story. Michael Ball portrays Purcell in the historical period, Purcell in the Shaw play, and a stage actor named Harry. Lucy Speed is Nell Gwynn in the historical story, Gwynn in the Shaw play, and the girlfriend of Callow's actor-playwright. And so forth. They step in and out of their roles, costumes, respective time periods, and dramatic contexts as easily as they open a window, pass through a doorway, or walk down a corridor. Call this Palmer's own version of Luigi Pirandello's *Right You Are (If You Think So)*.

Detailed examination of incidents in the film is impossible in this short space. A few highlights must suffice. As a young boy, Purcell is seen scrambling about the choir loft, surreptitiously dropping crumbs of food into the bellows. In the modern setting, the character of the actor-playwright visits the Tower of London and discourses on Restoration history with one of the tour guides, who effortlessly slips into the garb and diction of the king's goldsmith. The music from "Wayward Sisters" (from *Dido and Aeneas*) counterpoints graphically harrowing images of plague-ravaged London in 1665. Back in the modern story, the actor-playwright's girlfriend takes him to an antiwar street riot, and she declares, "I thought you ought to see what the real thing is like." To which he responds, "You're one of those militants that exploits political crises for personal glory; you're both psychopathic and self-righteous." Also in the modern setting, the actor-playwright visits the British Library and marvels at Purcell's hand-written manuscripts: "Written in Purcell's own hand," he muses to himself, "so clear, so beautiful; and with Purcell's own note: 'We play loud or soft, according to our fancy.'" Back in period setting, "Hush, No More" from *The Faerie Queen* is heard as the king in his bedchamber makes gentle love to his mistress. Also in period setting, there is a hilarious moment when Queen Mary (Rebecca Front) entices Purcell into writing martial music. Another moment with the queen, as she enjoys an elaborate stage setting for *King Arthur*, complete with a flying Cupid, while her equally bored and stupefied husband snoozes beside her. Yet another scene with the queen, dying young, her smallpox wracked body oozing from dozens of suppurating wounds. ("The most common disease was rickets," recites the actor-playwright, reading from a statistical survey of the time, "resulting in deformed limbs and scrofula. Above all, smallpox killed two out of every five of the population. . . . Regular bleeding by cutting into the patients' veins is thought to alleviate the suffering, albeit temporarily.") "Queen Mary's Funeral Music" transforms subtly into the Stanley Kubrick–Wendy Carlos version (a delicate homage to Palmer's friend Kubrick). Purcell's dying words, "Remember me"—repeated by the actor-playwright in his dressing room, whereupon he admits to his girlfriend that he's grown weary of portraying Charles II in the Shaw play. "Never mind," she replies, "there's always your play. And there's the telly. They do plays about musicians, don't they?" The actor pauses. "Only from established authors," he says, as he dons his wig peruke and exits.

Best of all is the concluding montage—a kind of visual fugue, if you will—that precedes the final credits. Shots of Britten himself conducting the climactic fugue from the *Young Person's Guide to the Orchestra* are intercut with scenes of modern-day London (street protests, city traffic), brief reprises of scenes with Dryden, Purcell in the tavern, Queen Anne applauding *King Arthur*, the flames of the Great Fire, Charles II's arrival at Torbay, and Purcell as a boy in the Royal Chapel. As the music reaches its magnificent peroration, all the actors in the film/play come to the forestage, hand in hand, and bow toward the camera. It's a magnificent moment and a triumphant affirmation of the theatrical nature of this story.

The film bears the dedication: "In memory of John Osborne, with love from those who made this film." Indeed, as was indicated earlier in this chapter, Osborne's acerbic tone is everywhere in evidence, in the mouths of the historical characters and in the dialogue and monologues of the stage actors in the modern-day story. The message is the same, either way: England's Golden Age has come and gone. Osborne has taken his cue from lines from Dryden's *A Song for St. Cecilia's Day, November 22, 1687*, which are paraphrased in the scene where Purcell visits the afflicted inmates of a lunatic asylum (heard to the music of Purcell's motet, "Thou Knowest Lord, the Secrets of Our Hearts"): "The world was disintegrating. It all was a dream, shadows without substance."[64] It is a voice that surveys modern England with a jaundiced attitude, by turns mournful, satiric, and savage. At one point the actor-playwright declares that Purcell's age was "a country of tolerance, irony, kindliness. Not like today, when the modesty of heroes is dispatched with derision and contempt. God rot the tyranny of equality, streamlining, classlessness! Above all, absurd, irrelevant *correctness!*"

In another scene, he notes, "Charles wanted the crown itself to be extraordinary. Not like today, when the Monarchy is only a tarnished gold filling in a mouthful of decay. The rot set in, of course, with Queen Victoria." Still later, he bemoans the Common Market and the possibility of a united Europe: "England, my England, is shuffling about like an old tramp begging for a pair of boots at the tradesmen's entrance of Europe. The English conscience, for so many years out for hire or rent, is now up for outright purchase. The Common Market — it's about as drab a name for so monumental a swindle since some bright little German adman thought of putting wholesale murder onto the market as National Socialism!"

"John Osborne was writing in his 'Jimmy Porter' vein," recalls Simon Callow. "What he was saying was that modern England is a hell-hole. He has to cling to the ideal of a Golden Age. Any disappointed Romantic has to have a state of grace from which we've fallen. Somebody like Orson Welles and G. K. Chesterton located it in the late Middle Ages. I don't get it, myself, at all. I think Charles II is a most profoundly interesting individual and politician; but to say that he represented everything that is good in England and that has now died is incomprehensible. He ran a very limited court. He was very good at damage control. But a visionary, no. He was a rogue and he intended to keep having his pleasures whatever happened."

Palmer has his own opinions about Osborne's vision: "John was transfixed by the way the 1960s, like the 1660s, were a period of optimism and energy for a better future that did not materialize. Perhaps the parallels here aren't perfect, but for his purposes they were sufficient. They supported a point he wanted to make in the film about the values of 'Englishness' and the way they are under threat in our own times. That's why the film has the title *England, My England* — an expression borrowed from D. H. Lawrence. And in the midst of it all you have this music which, for John Osborne, was the quintessential statement of what was good about being English — nobility of spirit, love of countryside, sense of honour and fairness. All of these sound like terrible clichés, but you *do* find them in Purcell. Just read the text of *King Arthur* — they're values that John saw everywhere under attack in modern Britain. His Jimmy Porter–esque tirades are really laments for the destruction of these values which, as he believed, Purcell enshrined." (At the time of this writing, Palmer had just completed his documentary essay on his late friend, *John Osborne: The Gift of Friendship*, 2004.)

Writing in *The Australian,* critic Philip Adams praised the film and its darkly critical tone "as something that looks and sounds suspiciously like a masterpiece. . . . Osborne was forever shaking his fist at the establishment, academia, the church, the media, women, other writers — just about anything or anyone that presented a target. Beneath the bad temper was a perverse, passionate, disappointed patriotism, and an abhorrence of mediocrity and intellectual fads that made Osborne as interesting as he was infuriating."[65]

Alas, to Palmer's outrage, the film was mutilated when it was shown on American television's Bravo Network. All the modern-day scenes were deleted. Thus, much of the film's complexity, not to mention the original intentions of Palmer and Osborne, was lost. Perhaps the wisest encomium for the film comes from Callow: "I thought Tony's evocation of seventeenth-century England was splendid. And John Eliot Gardiner loved performing in period costume. It is a very odd film. But that's Tony. He just goes for it."

Palmer's *Brahms and the Little Singing Girls* (1996) will come as a shock to those viewers who know their Brahms only from the MGM film *Song of Love* (1947), in which Robert Walker portrayed him as an earnest, clean-shaven young man, devoted to his mentor, Robert Schumann, and Schumann's young wife, Clara (see the discussion in Chapter One). By contrast, Palmer's screen incarnation depicts a portly old man, beard dribbling with food crumbs, cavorting about with his "singing girls" — that is, half-naked prostitutes from the local brothel. Similarly, devotees of the formidable Clara Schumann, portrayed with such noble intensity by Katharine Hepburn in *Song of Love* and with girlish ingenuousness by Nastassja Kinski in *Spring Symphony* (1985) will likewise recoil in stunned amazement at the spectacle of Clara playing piano in a cafe bar, belting out a barrel-house "Hello, My Baby" (the sort of scene one would expect from a Ken Russell film!).[66] And that's not all. There are scenes when the young Brahms plays the piano in the Hamburg brothels and receives the seductive caresses of the female habituées. "To excite the sailors, the little singing girls kissed and caressed me," he recalls, looking back on his youth. "Can you expect me now to honor them? No? Enjoy them, yes!" And we are to believe that Brahms's suit for Clara, newly widowed by the death of her beloved Robert, was dashed when she rejected him. "It is hard," he recalls. "I wrote to her, after years of faithful service, to be nothing more than one more bad experience, as you call it. Well, that must be borne. I am unloved by the one woman who inflamed my heart."

The bare outlines of the story of how young Brahms came into the household of the older Robert Schumann and his pianist wife, Clara, how he was launched into the musical world by his mentor, how he took care of the household while Robert was incarcerated in the mental institution, and how he was thwarted in his hopeless passion for Clara in later years is well known.[67] It is in the details that the biographer quickly runs aground. What exactly was the nature of Brahms's boyhood experiences in the Hamburg night spots? What really happened between him and Clara while her husband was in the asylum? And why did their relationship cool from a mutually felt passion to a slow-burning affection and loyalty that endured for the rest of their lives? We may never know. Too many letters are either lost or burned. (Besides, what kind of trust can we place in letters, anyway?) Both Brahms and Clara were the soul of discretion. Brahms, particularly, guarded his privacy and did his best to foil future biographers.[68] And both took their secrets with them to the grave.

The lacunae in the story is exactly what Palmer seizes upon to flesh out his film. The central conceit in *Brahms and the Singing Girls* is that a cache of newly discovered letters throws new light on the story we thought we knew.[69] Moreover, in the film Brahms (Warren Mitchell) is an old man, looking back on events through the hazy filters of nostalgia, memory, and the bitter realization that death is near. "Now I write only half sentences," he says. "The reader must supply the other half." Palmer is only too happy to oblige.

Despite the sexy hijinks with the "little singing girls," a mood of melancholy, regret, and impending death hangs heavily over the film. Palmer contends that Brahms's emotional life was stunted by a sequence of emotional and sexual traumas — those early years in the brothels, the discovery of his impotence while making love to Agathe von Siebold (a boldly carnal scene), and his rejection by Clara.[70] His sexual activity thereafter was limited to the "singing girls." He says, "my little Singing Girls, when they love they feel no passion; but when they feel passion, they do not love."[71] Against images of fisherman bringing their catch to the Hamburg docks, Brahms muses, "We are like the fish in the sea, born only to die, to feed others by our existence. I remember the great fleets in Hamburg, the smells, the noise. . . . The most you can hope for in life's journey is some knowledge of yourself. But that comes too late and it comes with inextinguishable regrets." Looking back on his lost loves, he glooms, "Who can heal the pain of a man who feels himself poisoned, poisoned by love?" As if to confirm that, we hear lines from one of his songs, "The hoar frost hangs on the linden tree / The light streams forth like silver./ Then I hear your greeting, as cold as the coldest frost." Unable to find spiritual consolation in the great cathedrals, he says, "God is deaf or indifferent. He either hears nothing, or he hears everything and does nothing. Either way, he mocks us. So, will he punish me for my little singing girls?" Late in the film the music from the *German Requiem* wells up on the soundtrack as Brahms arrives late to attend the funeral of Clara Schumann (Lori Piitz). "All flesh is as grass," intone the singers, "and the glory of man is like the flower of grass — it withereth and it falleth away."

The film begins and ends with a lonely figure on a beach, isolated in extreme long shot. "And so, finally, what have I, Hannes Brahms — John Broom to the English — to say for myself?" he asks at last. "That I spent my life pursuing a woman so full of grace of kindness, of all the virtues; but who would not have me? So I was condemned to serenade prostitutes. I loved my little singing girls, and they loved me." His thoughts again turn to Clara, recently dead and gone. "My dearest Clara, soon I no doubt will be joining you and we will be together, side by side for eternity. I have no clear view of the afterlife, nor of immortality; but through my music I do believe I will have achieved a certain emancipation.[72] Indeed, a certain immortality. So, I do believe in immortality . . . that people will keep on for thousands of years talking badly and stupidly about him. . . . but I always was a bit of a fool." The final images reprise the image of a stout old man capering about his room, arms outflung, bearded face flung back.

The nonlinear narrative construction and the juxtapositions of music and image are typically Palmer. Brahms's narrative voice ushers us through a slipstream of images and music, past and present. Brahms is seen, by turns, as an elderly man prowling around his apartment and cavorting with the prostitutes, a handsome young man chasing women (including the reluctant Clara), and a solitary figure on the shore, brooding at the prospect of death. For her part, Clara is seen in a variety of contexts — smiling tenderly upon the newly arrived Brahms, picnicking with him and her children, singing lustily a ragtime song, playing the piano in several extended musical sequences, and staring silently into the face of her own mortality. Graphic images of his youthful erotic encounters contrast with the pathetic musings of the old man shivering beneath his coat while slowly picking his way through the bleak winter landscape. Excerpts from the sprightly *Hungarian Dances* underpin the cafe and brothel scenes; the measured slow movement from the G-Major Sextet, the scenes with Agathe; the stormy First Piano Concerto, his unrequited love for Clara; the Alto Rhapsody, the death of beautiful Julie Schumann; the *German Requiem,* the death of Clara; and the *Vier ernste Gesänge,* Brahms's solitary, melancholy moods. Generous chunks of time are devoted to on-camera performances by musicians Olaf Baer and Susan Chilcott, who sing "The Lullaby," "Es hing der reif," and "Den es gehet." Min Liang sings an excerpt from the *Alto Rhapsody,* and Wilken Rank plays portions of the *Violin Concerto.*

"I think part of my function is to show that these extraordinary people are real human beings," Palmer says. "They do have one thing we lack — their genius. That apart, it's reasonable to assume that everybody has more or less the same feelings — animal feelings, emotional feelings, rows with the bank manager, rows with your wife and your mistress, greed, selfishness, envy, deceit. A whole area of music criticism has come from those familiar photographs of Brahms as an old man with this enormous gray beard and portly girth. And therefore you think the music must be foursquare and rather *lumpen*. But then you look at photos of him as a young man, and my God, he was good looking. He really was a ladies' man. He was sex on legs. And you go back and listen to the music, and you realize that the beginning of the First Symphony, for example, is also sex on legs. That is sex pounding. 'Humping music,' as William Walton always called it. That's a whole new insight into Brahms. And the trouble is that when you begin to show these people as they really were, or at least my interpretation of what they were really like, you do get heavily criticized. I'm always being attacked for that."

The Strange Case of Delfina Potocka (1999) stands with *Testimony* as Tony Palmer's most trenchant statement on the appropriation of art by the authoritarian state for its own ends. Thus, the two films bear several thematic and stylistic similarities. Both base their narratives on historical incidents that occurred in communist countries during the Cold War. Both concern composers, Frédéric Chopin and Dmitry Shostakovich, who have long been assumed to represent the nationalist politics and poetic spirit of their respective countries, Poland and Soviet Russia. Both films are based on texts of disputed authenticity — *Testimony* on the alleged memoirs of Shostakovich, and *Delfina Potocka* on a cache of letters purportedly written by Chopin to his mistress, Potocka.[73] To the horror of the Soviet authorities in Poland and Russia, these documents presented revisionist portraits of their respective subjects — that is, that Shostakovich was a closet dissident who coded his bitterly satiric attacks on the Stalinist regime in his music, and that Chopin was in reality a petty hedonist and anti-Semite who put his patriotism aside when it proved inconvenient for his career ambitions and sensual appetites. In both instances these revelations precipitate an ideological battle over the political control of music. Literally on trial in both films is the question that dominates all of Palmer's work: *What does music mean?* Both films display a nonlinear structure and interpolate black-and-white scenes with fantasy sequences in color. *Delfina Potocka*, however, is not nearly as well known as *Testimony* and does not possess its iconic status as one of the seminal documents in composer biographies. Time will tell. In my opinion it deserves a place alongside it.

The film opens with newsreel footage of the liberation of Poland from Nazi occupation. An officer in the People's Republic of Poland arrives by train in Warsaw with an urn containing Chopin's heart. "This heart, a sacred symbol and a precious relic of our national culture," he declaims in stilted rhetoric to the crowd on the platform, "is returned now, safely, from exile in France. And now, in the renascence of our People's Republic, safely delivered from Nazi domination by our friends and allies of the Union of Soviet Socialist Republics. . . . Chopin's music was and is the purest expression of our Polish national feelings. Let it be for us a stimulus to work and rebuild, together with our allies and friends from the Soviet Union, the greatness of our Fatherland." A blast of steam from the locomotive obliterates his last words. Impatiently, the official waves away the smoke.

In the next scene Paulina Czernicka (Penelope Wilton), a sober, plain-faced woman in her mid-fifties, comes to the office of Professor Iwaszkiewicz (John Shrapnel) with a packet of letters that she claims were written by Chopin to her great-grandmother (on her mother's side), the Countess Delfina Potocka. "A minor love affair," sniffs the professor, with "a loose woman who we know destroyed all her correspondence." However, after reading some extracts from the letters, he is dismayed at lines like these: "The identical energies that are used to fertilize a woman — to create a man — are the identical energies used to create a work of art." As the professor reads on, the black-and-white scene cuts to a scene of blazing color: The young Chopin (Paul Rhys), slim and lithe, strides through a glittering ballroom and seats himself at a piano. As he plays, the professor's recitation from one of the letters continues as a voice-over: "The same life-giving essence that a male squanders for a passing moment of pleasure can also bring moments of joy that can last forever. When a great love overwhelms me and temptations tear me like dogs, I forget about the world and am ready to give everything to a woman."

At the keyboard, meanwhile, Chopin gazes hungrily at the Countess Potocka, standing nearby. "I long to be inside you," continues the "voice" of Chopin's letter, "and kiss your nipples, your legs, taste the sweet smelling entrance to your soul—your 'D-flat,' I shall call it." Cut to Chopin and the Countess in bed, nude, clasped in an erotic embrace. Back and forth, from black-and-white to color, and back again, the sequence continues. The professor, meanwhile, recoils in shock at the erotic nature of the letter.

This and other letters that are quoted in subsequent scenes reveal sexual intimacies that are just short of pornographic. Moreover, the supposedly reticent Chopin who reputedly had always refused to "explain" his music and criticize his contemporaries is here openly discussing his works; making disparaging remarks about cholera-ridden, venereal-diseased Paris; sneering at his mistress, George Sand ("I know we are called Mamselle Chopin and Monsieur George Sand — such an odd couple"); criticizing his contemporaries, such as Franz Liszt ("a rouged Jericho on stilts"); and issuing racist attacks on Jews. This is hardly the image of a "people's composer," a socialist revolutionary hero, that Poland needs right now.

Quickly, officials of the People's Republic of Poland move to discredit the letters and quash their publication. But not before a Warsaw publisher visits Czernicka and urges her to broadcast excerpts of the letters. It is clear that the reputation of Chopin and the interpretation of his music are on trial. Which is to be judged more important — Poland's patriotic ideal of Chopin, the state's fabricated, "official" version of Chopin, or the simple truth of the man himself, whatever that may be?

"Poland needs heroes," says one official. "Now, more than ever. Not charlatans or pornographers."

"Today in Poland we're all charlatans," sniffs another.

"But not pornographers."

"But selling one's heritage to a foreign power for a so-called Union of Europe, is that not pornography?"

"Serving the State, yes; but which state?"

By now Czernicka is alarmed. She hides her letters in the floorboards of her apartment, safely away from the intrusions of the black-clad officials. Finally, she is hauled before a People's Court of the Republic of Poland and ordered to desist broadcast and publication of the letters under threat of imprisonment. The staging of the scene is not unlike that of the denunciation in *Testimony* of Shostakovich by Andrei Zhdanov (again played by John Shrapnel) in the 1948 Conference of Soviet Musicians. The professor denounces the letters as "entirely fraudulent," and that they brand Chopin as "a hypocrite, an anti-Semite, and a vulgar little boy with a pathological obsession with fornication and death." The judge agrees: "That anyone so refined and intelligent as Chopin would have dreamt up such virulent abuse if unthinkable. And your failure to produce the originals is another deciding factor. Consequently, we as representatives of the People's Court of the Republic of Poland, in view of the danger that these forgeries represent to the good name of Chopin, to the Polish people, to the Polish state, hereby confiscate these letters and any other such material as may relate."

Looming over these events is a proposed statue in the town square of Stalin holding a manuscript of Chopin's Preludes.

A subsequent conversation among the officials reveals that Czernicka has fallen to her death from an eight-story window. The ensuing dialogue among the government officials is heavily freighted with irony. It implies that both the suppression of the letters and the circumstances of Czernicka's death were political expediencies:

"It's a pity the original letters were never discovered."

"I thought certain fragments were."

"Ah, yes, but they are safe — now. No one will ever know. The incident will be forgotten."

"What if it were true? His apparent hatred of the Jews?"

"The nineteenth-century was full of anti-Semites. It was even fashionable. Look at Wagner. The Church."

"Yes, but Chopin, whose very name we were forbidden to mention during Nazi times. As if he, too, were one of the oppressed; as if he, too, were a Jew; who was a stain on our conscience."

"Conscience. Are we allowed such luxuries? Would the Comrade General permit such things? [cutaway to a portrait of Stalin on the wall] We always expect our heroes to be perfect—but they never are. Except of course the Comrade General."

"We must never permit ourselves to forget about Chopin. A heart that yearned for freedom and glory. And at what cost."

"Like Madame Czernicka, we all pay a price."

"For our silence."

"For our freedom."

"For our survival."

The film ends with a funeral scene. But there's a mystery here. As we watch, we're not sure if the ceremony is for Chopin, in 1849, or Czernicka in the present day — or both. Palmer has staged and costumed it in such a way that the garb among the mourners appears to be both contemporary and historical. Compounding our confusion is the sight of Czernicka in the crowd. How is it possible that she can be attending her own funeral — or Chopin's, for that matter? Perhaps, as Palmer seems to suggest, this is a burial service that is not consigning the bodies of Chopin or Czernicka to the grave so much as inter-ring the *truth* about them both.

The Strange Case of Delfina Potocka possesses Palmer's typically fractured structure and kaleidoscopic array of images. As Chopin's letters are read — either by Czernicka, the publisher Sydow, the professor, the judges — the black-and-white film slips into color flashbacks and musical fantasy scenes. These include erotic moments with the nude Chopin and Potocka; boyhood Christmas celebrations by Chopin and his sister; Chopin's snooty indignation at the diseased, corpse-strewn Parisian streets; bickerings at Nohant between Chopin and George Sand; rain-sodden treks to the Majorca monastery; Chopin's nightmares of a scythe-wielding figure of death; Chopin's last concert tour through wheezy English and Scottish drawing rooms; and the composer's deathbed scene as he gasps for air, pleading that his corpse be opened up lest he be buried alive.

Palmer clearly enjoys teasing us about the questioned authenticity of the letters. In the best postmodern fashion, he implies they were *both* spurious and authentic. To explain: We see Czernicka at a typewriter in her room, and beside her on the table is a packet of letters. Is she typing fake letters, or is she making copies of the real letters? That she may be the victim of a delusionary obsession about Chopin (thus rendering the letters invalid) is implied by Palmer's casting of actress Penelope Wilton as *both* Czernicka in the black-and-white scenes and Delfina in some of the color sequences. Palmer trumps this ambiguity by placing Paulina, and not Delfina, beside Chopin during his final hours. What are we to make of *that*?

The historical record is not much clearer on these issues. After World War II a woman named Paulina Czernicka, a self-taught musician and admirer of Chopin, did indeed produce packets of letters alleged to have been written by the composer regarding his affair with the Countess Delfina Potocka. Czernicka quoted from several of them in broadcasts on Radio Poznan. When the newly founded Chopin Institute in Warsaw asked her to produce the originals, she claimed she only had photographs of them (the originals having mysteriously disappeared). At various times she offered up different accounts of the photographs' whereabouts—that they were in Australia, in America, in France. Some time later, in 1949, she committed suicide by an overdose of sleeping pills. Many years after, her papers were found and examined, but the photographic originals were never located.

Chopin biographers Adam Zamoyski and the late Chopin authority Arthur Hedley have gone to great lengths to discredit the letters and their claims that Delfina was Chopin's mistress. Writing in 1961, Hedley stated that "the evidence against anything more than a warm friendship is very strong." He added that Chopin was generally averse to sexual relations: "He loved the company of women, but he liked them well bred, well dressed, and unattainable; and the resulting flirtations were little more than an understated game which enlivened his lessons and his social life." Moreover, Hedley scoffs at the notion that Chopin would have invited to his deathbed, in the presence of his confessor and his sister, "a weeping ex-mistress so that her voice might console his last moments with religious melodies."[74] On his part, Zamoyski declares that the authenticity of the letters has never been confirmed, and none of the originals—only some of the copies—were ever produced. "The style of the letters seems Chopinesque enough—too much so, on closer examination—but the texts reveal an entirely new Chopin," writes Zamoyski, "letters full of extraordinarily earthy eroticism, which accords ill with what is known of Chopin's character, style of conduct, and tastes."[75] One of the extant copies, which equates sexual libido with artistic creativity, may have been the model for the quotation in Palmer's film: "Let the creator, whoever he may be, drive women away from him, out of his life, and the strength collecting in his body will not go into his prick and his balls. . . but will return to his brain in the form of inspiration and will perhaps create the most lofty work of art."[76] Zamoyski cites as final damning evidence of their fraudulence the fact that among Czernicka's papers were found books on Chopin with underlined passages that could have been the basis for the fake letters. "There can be no doubt that these texts are in fact forgeries, probably made during the 1930s, and that the forger was almost certainly Paulina Czernicka."[77]

Ultimately, the issue of the authenticity of the letters is of little interest to Tony Palmer. "I don't take sides," he says. "I don't know the truth of the authenticity of those letters. I do know that Paulina Czernicka was hard up; but I also know there was information in the letters she couldn't possibly have known; and that she died mysteriously." More to the point, there is no mistaking the deadly seriousness of Palmer's purpose. What is at stake here are three agendas that drive this — and most of his films. The first is an examination of music's affective properties (in this case, particularly, how Chopin's music influenced the possibly delusional Czernicka). The second is the clash between the public celebrity of an artist and his private life as a man.[78] And the third is the process by which the state seeks to appropriate and distort the artist's life and his works in the service of political agendas. (Ironically, in the instance of both Shostakovich and Chopin there is evidence that neither composer had any overtly activist political sympathies at all!)[79]

Coda: Style and Performance

Tony Palmer's most striking formal and thematic characteristics, his fractured diegesis and imaginative extrapolations of the biographical record, confounds some viewers. "I've never been interested in the standard kind of biographical films," he says. "You know, 'they were born here, and they went there, and then they died' — that sort of thing. You have to include a certain amount of that information, but not necessarily in that order. I read a very funny review of one of my films: 'My God, we had to sit there for two hours before we discovered when this bloke was born!' My films, like Sibelius' symphonies, often go *backwards,* so you get to the theme only when you're quite near the end. But by the time you get there, you understand what has gone in to the making of that theme." Thus the results, which have already been described in general terms as the "documentary essay/theatrical film," are singularly difficult to classify, whether they go backwards or forwards, sideways or up and down.

Moreover, Palmer's most exuberant and freewheeling liberties with the historical record usually turn out to have been calculated on their relative degree of probability. A telling anecdote illustrates how closely the two approaches come together in his work. In the mid-1980s Palmer traveled to the Soviet Union to research what he thought was going to be a documentary on Shostakovich. He needed film footage from the Soviet archives, so he arranged a meeting with Tikon Nikolayevich Khrennikov, the general secretary of the Composer's Union. "Without his say-so, the film wouldn't happen," recalls Palmer. "Khrennikov heard me out and said, 'We're delighted to help. We've got miles of film of Shostakovich, in the bath, on a bicycle, having a picnic, playing the piano, etc.' And indeed they did; they had a huge amount of material, most of which has never been seen in the West. But then, Khrennikov leant over the table and said to me, 'But of course, you will be telling the *true* story of Shostakovich, won't you?' And I knew exactly what he meant — *his* truth, the Party's truth. I glanced at the wall behind him, and there on display were three enormous photographs of Stravinsky, Prokofiev, and Shostakovich. Because of Khrennikov and his like, Stravinsky's music had been banned, Prokofiev's life had been made miserable, and Shostakovich had been denounced. I left. I came away realizing that the only way to get at the truth would be not to make a documentary but instead make a *fictional* film. You see? Fiction can be closer to the truth because at least you *know* this is a fiction. Viewers can accept this is an account of the things *might* have happened had we been there; whereas the mere accumulation of facts can delude us into thinking we know the truth, which we don't, necessarily." Thus, in their most closely observed documentary precision, Palmer's films display dramatic flair; and in the midst of their most theatrically excessive flights of fancy, they contain a documentary core of realism.

Palmer prefers to let the composers tell their stories in their own "voice." But as we have seen, especially in the theatrical films *Wagner, Puccini, Testimony, I, Berlioz, God Rot Tunbridge Wells, England, My England, Singing Girls,* and *Delfina Potocka,* that narrative agency is a collective of many "voices," of letters, diaries, memoirs, and biased accounts that are themselves unstable and untrustworthy. Memory, myth, and autobiography collide and splinter off in all directions. "I have found it useful to have the composers speak to the camera and tell their stories," explains Palmer. "But how are we to trust what they are saying? That allows for the kind of ambiguity between truth and fiction that I need."

The results are served up with a visual panache so distinctive that you can identify any of Palmer's films within a scant few minutes. Some of the techniques stem from his working experiences covering the pop music scene in his early documentaries of the late 1960s and 1970s. For example, there are many distorted, wide-angle steadicam tracking shots that record in real time the characters' flights down endless corridors and winding hallways. These visual metaphors contribute to an overwhelming sense of the artist trapped in the labyrinthine mazes of societal conventions and political bureaucracy. The resulting paranoia is enhanced by a tendency to backlight the characters, throwing them into silhouette, while fog, rain, and smoke envelope the scene, contributing to the carefully modulated chiaroscuro. His years chasing rock performers around the world forced Palmer to shoot "on the wing," as it were. Steadicams proved useful in tracking the unpredictable movements of the performers, on- and offstage. Wide-angle lenses had to be employed to take in the entire stage, to compensate for the close proximity of the cameras to the performers. These devices and techniques tends to produce the kind of image distortion so prevalent in Palmer's work. Moreover, the unusually vivid lighting characteristics of rock concerts, with lots of backlighting and spotlights piercing veils of smoke, likewise lend a dramatic, low-key aspect to the imagery. "Well, we're talking about *theatrical* lighting and dramatic effects in general, aren't we?" asks Palmer. "I love to use smoke pots — sometimes to the point where you can't see the actors!"

By contrast, Palmer's photography of the performance sequences possesses a hallucinatory, hyper-real quality. He employs exceptionally strong side-lighting and carefully modulated fill lights to embrace the players in a kind of sharply edged, golden aura. Ranks of players are viewed in profile and arranged in ranks, shot with narrow-angle lenses that diminish the depth of field. It is only after watching several scenes like this that we begin to realize how strangely stylized and unreal this effect is. These are images that would be impossible to capture in live performance.

"You can't get good pictures of the players while, at the same time, they are doing their best to make a really cracking recording," explains Palmer. "You have to separate the two processes, the playing and the photographing. So very early on, I decided that when we record the music, that's *all* we do. No distracting cameras, except the one on the conductor. Beforehand, I've chosen, from bar to bar, precisely the bits of music I need. So later I line up the ranks of various players for separate filming to a playback. For example, you get the woodwinds lined up with lights, cameras, and playback speakers right in front of them, and hopefully you get perfect pictures to put with the pre-recorded performance. Next come the violins — same chairs, same lights, same camera.

And what you have to remember is, that if the music has a contrapuntal mix of different sections of the orchestra, the violins have to face *this* way, and the cellos have to face *that* way. You need that for effective cutting. More important, a procedure like this allows the musicians to give their best performance without worrying about cameras. All the music heard in *England, My England,* including all the songs, for example, were prerecorded in the studio with John Eliot Gardiner (actually, in George Martin's studio, where the Beatles recorded). So we got absolutely near-perfect takes of every song, including the great "Dido's Lament" at the end. I remember one of the singers was worried about doing it this way. She complained, 'I will never be able to reproduce visually to a playback what I have recorded earlier.' I said, 'I thought you were a singer, and an *actress.* Haven't I seen you on stage somewhere?' By the way, all the musicians thought it was a hoot to appear on camera with their period costumes; and John Eliot Gardiner entirely approved of the way we did it. Everything to a playback."

Which brings us to the *performance* aspects of Palmer's films. Again, perhaps because of his extensive experience in pop music videos, he insists on respecting the music and the integrity of the performance (sometimes, admittedly, at the expense of the narrative drive of the story). He is unique among his peers in this respect. Unlike Ken Russell, who rarely allows music and music performance to be a part of the diegesis—the First Piano Concerto sequence with Tchaikovsky in *The Music Lovers,* the conducting scenes with Richard Strauss in *Dance of the Seven Veils,* and the scenes with Frederick Delius and Eric Fenby composing at the piano in *Song of Summer* are important exceptions—Palmer devotes huge chunks of screen time to source music, rather than background music. Melvyn Bragg sums it up succinctly: "Tony's much more interested in *performance* than in illustration; and Ken is more interested in *illustration* than in performance." Let me be precise here. I do not mean that performers occasionally are seen playing brief and perfunctory snatches of music in the background of the shot; rather, Palmer will either cut away to the musicians and foreground them in uncut performances, or he will *include* the performances as part of the diegesis.

Just a few of many examples have already been cited: pianist Andrei Gavrilov plays the entire Handel "Passacaglia," Emma Kirkby sings "Who May Abide" and Simon Preston plays the Organ Concerto, Opus 7, No. 5 in *God Rot Tunbridge Wells;* Olaf Baer sings several Brahms songs in their entirety in *The Little Singing Girls.* Likewise, there are huge chunks of choral works and operas in abundance, including Berlioz's *The Trojans,* Brahms's *German Requiem,* Wagner's *Parsifal,* Puccini's *Turandot, and* Purcell's *King Arthur.*

Sometimes Palmer will have his little "in" joke with these performance

sequences. Take the marvelous closing visual and musical "fugue" that concludes *England, My England:* "For that scene we used what for me is the
greatest recording ever of the Fugue," recalls Palmer, "which of course was
performed by Britten himself, conducting the English Chamber Orchestra. I
matched that historic audio recording to some film footage I had of Ben conducting. Then I rang up those same musicians — as many as I could find — and
asked them if they could come and be photographed performing to the playback of the record. One of the players was Ossian Ellis, who admitted he had
been amazed at the brisk pace of that recording. He told me that at the time of
the original studio session they had had great difficulty with the Fugue. After a
coffee break, back they came. They began to play at a tremendous pace. By the
time they got past the piccolo and came to the woodwinds, they all thought
they were going too fast. But by now, they were inspired, and they saw it
through to the end. Ben put down the baton and chuckled, and they all applauded. They knew they had done something fantastic. And it's that performance you hear in the film. You will never hear a performance like that again.
The funny thing is, that film I found of Ben conducting — he's conducting
something *else,* not the Fugue!"

Palmer is notoriously difficult to pin down regarding the aesthetic and philo-
sophical aspects of his work. Wisely, he prefers to let the films speak for
themselves. When Palmer does pause long enough to answer my nosy questions, he refuses to pontificate; and above all, he refuses to subject himself to
self-analysis. Better leave that to someone else. "The real purpose of my films,"
says Palmer, with characteristically modest succinctness, "is simply to lay out
the evidence and serve the music, to get it played as well as possible and in a
context that one can understand."

"I love the sense that with Tony all things are possible," comments actor
Simon Callow. " 'We'll just do it,' he will say; 'just do it.' He has a slightly
Orson Wellsian approach that some might describe as quite cavalier. But I like
that. Welles once said that the gap between the impulse to make the film and
the actual execution of the film is so huge that you can lose your sense of why
you're doing it at all. But not with Tony. He gets this huge, reckless excitement
into the making of a film. He has to believe that the composer he's working on
is the greatest composer in history. And by the time he's through, you believe
it, too."

6

Revisionist Portraits

A Medley of Recent Composer Biopics

These are the films that have respected the strangeness of the past, and have accepted that the historical illumination of the human condition is not necessarily going to be an edifying exercise. . . . These are also films that embrace history for its power to complicate, rather than clarify, and warn the time traveler that he is entering a place where he may well lose the thread rather than get the gist.

— *Simon Schama*

In James Lapine's *Impromptu* (1991) a group of artists — including the composers Franz Liszt and Frédéric Chopin, the painter Eugène Delacroix, and the writers George Sand and Alfred de Musset — arrive at the country estate of the Duke and Duchess d'Antan. Disdaining their hosts as coarsegrained nouveaux riches, Liszt haughtily confides to Chopin, "They're probably famished for culture and determined to import it at any cost." Meanwhile, the country squire privately declares to his enraptured wife that their famous guests are nothing but "a gang of parasites" and "perfumed prancers."

Battle lines are drawn. Ensuing events result in a tangle of wounded hearts, outraged temperaments, strategic retreats, willing seductions, and a few incendiary outbursts. Composer biopics have entered a new era. They are assuming a more contentious relationship both with their nominal subjects and with their audiences.

Hugh Grant brought an elegant haughtiness to his Frédéric Chopin in James Lapine's *Impromptu* (1991). (Courtesy Hemdale Pictures)

The breakup of the classical studio oligopoly, post-Vietnam disillusionment and cynicism, collapsing political regimes, reconfigured nation-states, postmodern interrogations of fact and fiction, and global disasters like terrorism and the AIDS epidemic are revising our conventional attitudes toward history and biography. No longer "contained," as outlined in Chapters One, Two, and Three, the composers in Chapters Four and Five have burst their stereotyped frames, climbed off the mountaintop, and, like Frankenstein's monster, run amuck. As we have already seen, Ken Russell and Tony Palmer led the way, replacing the canon of sentimental, love-struck, romantically mad and tragically failed artists with a gallery of fools, cads, opportunists, failed dreamers, and societal victims. The Biedermeier-like worlds of *Blossom Time* and *Swanee River* collapsed, revealing undercurrents of political repression, spiritual corruption, creative failure, and nihilistic despair. Inheriting this legacy are a trilogy of composer portraits outlined in this chapter: *Amadeus* (1984), *Testimony* (1987), and *Mit meinen heissen Tränen* (1987).

Faces and Masks: Amadeus *from Stage to Screen*

Miloš Forman's *Amadeus* opens with a human scream of anguish, accompanied by the two big opening chords from the Overture to Mozart's *Don Giovanni*. "Mozart! Forgive your assassin," screams Antonio Salieri, the esteemed composer to the court of Emperor Joseph II of Austria. "I confess, I killed you!" Friends burst in his door and find him on the floor, blood issuing from his torn throat. There is a sudden blast of music, the stormy opening of Mozart's Symphony No. 25. Later, in an asylum, the aging composer, bandages around his neck, is preternaturally calm as he recounts to a visiting priest his relationship with Mozart. Salieri had known about Mozart since Mozart's celebrity as a child prodigy. Later, as Kapellmeister to the Hapsburg court of Joseph II, he had witnessed the young man's amazing feats of improvisation (at the expense of a little march Salieri had composed). But it is not until Mozart's wife, Constanze, brings Salieri a stack of original manuscripts and pleads for his help that he truly realizes what a gifted rival he has at Joseph's court. "You scorn my attempts at virtue," says Salieri, addressing the God who created this miscreant Mozart, "because You are unjust, unfair, unkind—I will block You! I swear it! I will hinder and harm Your creature on earth as far as I am able! I will ruin Your Incarnation!"

Thereafter, Salieri conspires behind Mozart's back to thwart his efforts to win court favor. He installs a spy, a maid, in Mozart's apartment. He contrives to haunt him with the apparition of a masked, cloaked figure demanding that he write a *Requiem* (which Salieri intends to claim as his own composition). He attempts to thwart a production of *The Marriage of Figaro*. In spite of himself, however, after witnessing a performance of *The Magic Flute* (composed at the behest of the impresario Emanuel Schikaneder), Salieri is forced to acknowledge the man's genius. When Mozart breaks down in the middle of the opera's performance, Salieri takes him to his lodgings. Clearly moved by the agonies of the dying man, Salieri takes Mozart's dictation of the *Requiem*. When Constanze returns to the apartment the next morning, she angrily demands that Salieri leave. At just that moment Mozart breathes his last. In the film's epilogue his body is carted out to a pauper's grave, thrust into the excavation in a sack, and covered with quicklime. Cut back to Salieri, who is concluding his confession. He announces to the startled priest that God has cruelly deprived him of a role in dispatching Mozart. Hereafter, he, Salieri, absolves the world and everyone in it of mediocrities. He wheels his chair through the asylum, past the writhing, anguished, and confused inmates, and dispenses his absolutions. Mozart's cackling laughter is heard as the scene fades to black.

Amadeus began as a play by Peter Shaffer at London's National Theatre in 1979, was transplanted (with revisions) to Broadway a year later, published in book form in 1981, and appeared on the screen (with still more revisions) in a film adapted by Shaffer and produced and directed by the team of Saul Zaentz and Miloš Forman in 1984 (the same team that made *One Flew over the Cuckoo's Nest* in 1975).[1] The film, shot over a six-month period on location in

Miloš Forman's *Amadeus* (1984) cast Tom Hulce as the irrepressible Wolfgang Amadeus Mozart. (Courtesy Photofest/Saul Zaentz)

Prague, budgeted at $18 million, and running almost two-and-a-half hours, subsequently won eight Academy Awards, including Best Picture, Best Director, and Best Actor (F. Murray Abraham's portrayal of Salieri). Despite a firestorm of controversy about the liberties taken with the historical facts by both play and film — including complaints about the exaggerations of Mozart's penury and lack of recognition, the unflattering portrait of the thoroughly respectable and admired Salieri, the implication that Salieri intended to murder Mozart, the suggestion that Salieri himself appeared in disguise to harass Mozart to compose his *Requiem,* the lack of references to Mozart's other children, the portrait of Mozart as a musical rebel, the wholly fabricated deathbed scene, the use of modern musical instruments in the simulation of eighteenth-century orchestral performance, and so on — *Amadeus* stimulated a fresh public and professional interest in the composer.[2] "Almost at once," claims musicologist Robert L. Marshall, "Mozart became the most popular, most well-known, most purchased and, I do believe, the most truly enjoyed of the classical composers, readily displacing Beethoven, Tchaikovsky, and anyone else who, before 1980, might have disputed his claim to that position." Marshall goes so far as to claim that enrollment in college music courses nationwide "saw an unprecedented increase."[3]

The reasons are many. First of all, and perhaps superficially, the film appealed to conspiracy theorists who have continued, since Mozart's death, to speculate about his murder at the hands of a variety of suspects, ranging from Salieri himself to a cabal of Freemasons offended at Mozart's alleged transgressions against their order.[4] More important, Shaffer and Forman had wrought an ingenious fable about the capriciousness of talent to which anyone could relate. Who can fathom how it is that a conscientious, hard-working fellow has to languish in the shadow of the lazy, irresponsible genius at the next desk — who flings his talents about with little reason or discrimination? It is a mystery which appeals to a secular age like ours, not a little dismayed at the toppling of gods and heroes. And embodying this cruel disparity were two superbly and theatrically opposed characters, who just happen to be named Mozart and Salieri.

And there is the music itself. Like so many composer biopics before it, *Amadeus* wears on its sleeve a frank agenda to exploit the "prestige" factor of classical music. Whereas music had been at most a minimal element in the stage version, as is discussed below, on film it leaps to the foreground in all its polished glory, courtesy of Neville Marriner and the Academy of St. Martin-in-the-Fields and vocal and instrumental performers Samuel Ramey, Felicity Lott, June Anderson, Richard Stilwell, Ivan Moravec, and Imogen Cooper. Like the classical Hollywood biopics of yore, it wrenches the music from its original contexts and weaves them into a soundtrack that is a seamless web of themes and textures enhancing and counterpointing the action. At the same, time, however, following a growing trend in biopics since the 1960s, the film also emphasizes *music as performance,* notably, staging excerpts from Schikaneder's riotous satire on Mozartean operas, Mozart's performance of a piano concerto in the open air, and excerpts from *Don Giovanni.*

Three of the film's biggest scenes foreground diegetic and nondiegetic music in ways that throw Salieri and Mozart's complementary characters into sharp relief — Mozart's improvisation on Salieri's "Welcome March," Salieri's wordless encounter with the manuscript sheets Constanze has brought him, and Mozart's deathbed "dictation" to Salieri of the *Requiem*'s Lacrimosa. The first displays an irrepressible Mozart effortlessly tossing off brilliant variations on Salieri's stodgy little tune, to the growing discomfiture of the latter. The second scene has Salieri examining the manuscripts, marveling at first at their immaculate, error-free appearance, then erupting in a vengeful rage that such gifts should have been bestowed upon such a seemingly naughty yet innocent child. The third scene, not present in the original play, may well claim to be the most arresting and vividly remembered moment in the whole picture — as the scribbling Salieri desperately tries to catch up to the dying composer's "dictation" of the "Confutatis Maledictis." All the while, behind Mozart's words, the soundtrack conveys Mozart's internal musical diegesis, which in turn is "heard" by Salieri's own internal diegesis. It is a remarkably astute breakdown of the passage, as Mozart first sets the male chorus's declamation, the trombone instrumentation, the underlying tympani, the female voicings, the agitated ostinato passages in strings, and finally the plangent "Voca Mei" for high voices. The scene ends as Mozart, pale and drawn, falls back on the pillow, exhausted. "Let's stop now," he says, "we'll finished the Lacrimosa later."[5] Not since Frederick Delius's musical dictations to amanuensis Eric Fenby in Ken Russell's *Song of Summer* (see Chapter Four) has such an exciting, almost visceral moment of creation been captured on film. No Hollywood chase scene can rival it.[6] The three scenes bind the film together in a graceful arc — from Salieri's initial amazement, to his growing anger, and, finally, to his recognition of the music's transcendence over petty jealousy and envy (he thrusts a crucifix into a fireplace at the moment of his decision to murder Mozart). At the same time Mozart transforms from a prankster to an unseen musical mystery to a divinely inspired voice of God.

The portrait of Mozart is a compelling blend of the familiar and unfamiliar. On one hand, Shaffer's Mozart bears the likeness of the mythologized Mozart that had persisted since his death at thirty-five in 1791 and had been confirmed as recently as the translation in 1982 of a highly esteemed biography by Wolfgang Hildesheimer. Commentator Nicholas Spice flatly declares that Hildesheimer's portrait of a dysfunctional, childlike Mozart "as a sort of autist, unable to form satisfactory human relationships . . . and incapable of the ordinary range of human feelings" provided a "congenial source for the elaboration of *Amadeus*."[7] This was the myth of Mozart as the "eternal child," the stereotype of the musical genius that is "possessed" by powers beyond his ken and who creates with seemingly no effort at all. Rooted in Plato and later espoused in Schopenhauer, this "possession" theory holds that the muse, or God, speaks through the poet, who is himself naïve and rather childlike but who is gifted with prodigious "natural" talents. It was Mozart's associates and first biographers who first presented him in this light.[8] On the other hand — and what startled the first audiences of the play and film so much — is Shaffer's close-up view of a flawed Mozart, a selfish, self-indulgent character with a high-pitched giggle, a penchant for scatological language, and a style of bohemian behavior quite in keeping with the sensibility of the 1970s. "I am a vulgar man," he says, "but my music is not."

Significantly, neither of these character traits is that far removed from reality. Biographer Maynard Solomon locates the eternal child myth in Mozart's relationship with his father, Leopold, who, for his own ends, determined that his precocious son would never grow up. "In actuality," Solomon writes, "Mozart wanted to leave childhood and its subjections behind, to shatter the frozen perfection of the little porcelain violinist and to put in his place a living man, one with sexual appetites, bodily functions, irreverent thoughts, and selfish impulses, one who needed to live for himself and his loved ones."[9] There is ample evidence that Mozart did indeed write with great speed and facility. "From these and numerous similar stories we can surmise that Mozart must have had a photographic memory and could compose music faster than his pen would write," claims musicologist Erich Hertzman. "He must have worked out many compositions in his head before he sat down to put them on paper."[10] Musicologist Marshall recalls his "amazement bordering on disbelief" of the autograph of the E-flat Piano Concert, K. 482: "With respect to the compositional process, it contained nothing of interest. Indeed, there were almost no corrections of any kind, not even minor ones." As for the giggle and the language, Marshall further confirms that in Mozart's time, particularly in Germany, the use of frank, scatological language was nothing strange or unusual. Moreover, although we know nothing of the sound of Mozart's laughter, it takes only a moment to measure its appropriateness as "the mocking laughter of the gods: laughter directed toward all us common mortals who have been spitefully, maliciously denied the fire of creative genius."[11]

Shaffer and Forman's transformation of *Amadeus* from the stage to the screen offers an object lesson in the adaptive process. "[The cinema's] unverbal essence offers difficulties to anyone living largely by the spoken word," noted Shaffer dryly, and *Amadeus* had to be totally reimagined as a film.[12] The original play, as staged in London and later revised for the American production, is in two acts, divided into twelve and nineteen scenes, respectively. Through subtle lighting techniques and minimal prop changes, his salon serves also as Mozart's last apartment, the Viennese streets, and an opera stage. Salieri is on stage in a wheelchair the whole time, and he entreats the audience members — his "ghosts of the future" — to come to his room in "the smallest hours of dark November, 1823" and hear his tale. The ensuing action is presented in a highly stylized manner with distorting lighting effects, suggestive of the fractured memories of the aging composer. An offstage chorus of whispering voices and two *venticelli*, "purveyors of fact, rumor and gossip," accompany and comment on events. Incidents not retained in the film include scenes with Salieri and his mistress, and suggestions that Mozart betrayed the secret rituals of the Freemasons in *The Magic Flute*. Also not included was Mozart's death scene, in scenes 15 and 16, Act II. It begins with Mozart unmasking Salieri's cloaked figure, whereupon Salieri turns on the dying man. "God does not love you, Amadeus!" he says. "He cares nothing for whom He uses: nothing for whom He denies. . . . You are no use to Him anymore."

Mozart is reduced to infantile behavior. "Behold my vow fulfilled," crows Salieri, "the profoundest voice in the world reduced to a nursery tune." Salieri leaves. Constanze enters and Mozart tells her that Salieri has murdered him. He dies. The scene then shifts back to Salieri in his wheelchair. He tells us that his "confession" of killing Mozart is false, that he only made it to achieve the immortality he craves: "For the rest of the time whenever men say Mozart with love, they will think of Salieri with loathing! . . . *I am going to be immortal after all!* And He is powerless to prevent it." Whereupon he cuts his throat. Dying, he addresses the audience: "Mediocrities everywhere—now and to come—I absolve you all. Amen!"[13]

The characterization of Mozart came as a shock to playgoers. "As an actor on stage I never attempted to give a 'rounded' characterization," says Simon Callow, who originated the part of Mozart opposite Paul Scofield's Salieri in the first London stage production. "I played it as a series of shards, lumps of Mozart, a mind teeming with music, almost giddy with it, like a nuclear explosion going on in front of Mozart's brain. I was the 'vulgar creature,' the strutting punk, the Chanticleer. Here we were in the National Theatre—long before *Jerry Springer* the opera was a glint in Nick Hytner's eye—a grand national institution which had just been taken over by Peter Hall. The memory of Laurence Olivier was still very strong. And here's this Mozart, the most perfect composer, a sublime immortal, who comes on stage about twenty minutes after the action has begun; and when he does, his first utterance is to meow like a pussycat. Then he gets down on his hands and knees and runs around on stage with Felicity Kendall, who was at that time an absolute English rose in everyone's imagination. So I romp after Felicity. I hurl her to the ground, and I say, 'I'd like to shit on your nose!' The audience was horrified. They couldn't believe it. Salieri stands there in a state of rigid shock. Then, a few moments later, he hears the sounds of the slow movement of the Wind Serenade. And it is sublime. The conjunction of those two scenes was a brilliant stroke."[14]

Music, like the action, is mediated through the filters of Salieri's memory. "It's subtle 'treatment,'" says Shaffer, "suggested the sublime work of a genius being experienced by another musician's increasingly agonized mind."[15] Callow explains that Shaffer's first idea was *not* to use music by Mozart. "It should *sound* like Mozart but all be filtered through the faulty memory of Salieri. We started to do that, but Harrison Birtwhistle, the music director, decided instead to do an aural distort on the music. Nothing was played 'straight' at all, and it was used very carefully and sparingly. In that kind of melodramatically distorted atmosphere there was relatively little attempt to simulate keyboard performance. "Paul quite rightly knew that his charisma was such that his audience would believe anything," says Callow. "No matter how carefully I tried to simulate it, Paul rather gave the game away by just flailing away with his arms and hands. He didn't give a damn, and his audience didn't give a damn, either."

How different all this is in the film. "The screenplay was a very different entity from the play," recalls Callow, who was ultimately given the part of Mozart's colorful friend and collaborator, Emanuel Schikaneder,[16] "which was possessed of a wild, distorted energy, an E. T. A. Hoffmann-like exaggeration, lit by candles and filled with monstrous shadows." Salieri's attempted suicide begins, rather than ends, the story. He is in an asylum rather than his apartment. He speaks to a priest, rather than directly to the audience. Because he is not on screen all the time, we tend to accept the flashbacks as real instead of resulting from the distortions of his mind. Events are conveyed in a relatively conventional visual style, instead of the more theatrically stylized sets and lighting. The whispering voices and the *venticelli* are gone. The incidents involving the Masonic rituals are gone. Mozart's role has been greatly expanded from a supporting role to one equal with Salieri. In this more naturalistic environment, he and Salieri are less caricatured as, respectively, the sinister villain and the cruelly infantile Mozart. They emerge more fully fleshed out and more sympathetic characters. "Tom Hulce played the part from a much more psychological point of view," says Callow, "more emotionally retarded, very tender and sweet, very sincere. He brought a natural sweetness of disposition, a tenderness and a delicacy to the role which I could never match. Tom's Wolfie was an over-exuberant child, mine on the stage suffered from Tourette's syndrome."[17]

Similarly, Salieri's character in the film, as played by F. Murray Abraham, was considerably softened. "In the play Salieri was incredibly vain," explains Hulce, "but here in the film he's more sympathetic, very good at his work. He loves Mozart's music but he also hates it because he can't touch it in his own work."[18] (By no means coincidentally, this approach to both characters is reminiscent of Alexander Pushkin's short dramatic dialogue, *Mozart and Salieri*, conceived in 1826, just a year after Salieri's death, wherein Salieri is depicted "as a dedicated musician who was intent on the perfection of his craft" but who is "enraged by Mozart's free, creative spirit and by what he sees as Mozart's light-hearted, almost negligent, relation to the products of his genius.")[19] The death scene was wholly rewritten, a superbly contrived exercise in visual and sound montage. "It is deeply affecting and beautifully observed from a medical point of view," says Callow. "On stage, mine was deliberately grotesque, almost expressionist."[20] And at the end Salieri does not speak directly to us, the audience, to absolve us of our "mediocrities"; rather, he directs his absolutions toward the lunatics in the asylum. And, as has been noted, the musical elements have been greatly amplified (literally), and they saturate the images.

Both Callow and Hulce have left vivid impressions of the transfer from stage to screen. Callow claims that everyone knew that Forman determined to film the play immediately after he saw the London preview in November 1979. "We also knew that for the film he would not want me, or Paul, or Felicity Kendall [Constanze]; he would want huge stars to play these parts. And over the months every major star even faintly eligible came to see the play — Robert Redford, Dustin Hoffman, Robert De Niro. They were all there, every single A-list male star, watching us like hawks, sitting in the third row. It was hilarious. They were like legacy hunters, hovering around the bedside, waiting for us to be gone so they could make the movie. Then, Milos announced suddenly that he wanted 'unknowns.' Before, we hadn't been famous enough; now we were *too* famous!"

Shaffer reports that from the outset there would have to be what he calls a "demolition" of the play's more insistently theatrical elements. "[Forman] pointed out that the film of a play is really a new work," Shaffer explained at the time of the film's release, "another fulfillment of the same impulse which had created the original. The adapter's task was to explore many new paths in order to emerge in the end at the same emotional place. . . . In the case of *Amadeus*, it's operatic stylization would probably have to be made less formal, though not, of course, more juvenile."[21] Forman made it clear that his actors would have to conform to the naturalistic demands of the film medium. "Stage actors are wonderful," he told Callow, "big, generous. But they can't use film, always *acting,* always *doing something.* On film you must BE. And you must *be yourself,* I cast you to be you. Otherwise I cast someone else." Likewise, he told Hulce "that he wanted the approach to be contemporary and bring out as much naturalism and sweat and humor as possible to the characters. Not to put them on pedestals at all, but to make them real and breathing." Callow confirms in his autobiography, *Shooting the Actor,* that for Forman "Mozart was less a creature of Salieri's deceiving imagination, more a real man."[22]

Shooting the film amid so many authentic locations in Prague could only enhance the "realistic" nature of the proceedings. Prague in the early 1980s, recalls Callow, was still "in the Communist decadence of 1982, its hidden city flowing darkly like an underground stream underneath the sometimes glittering, sometimes crumbling metropolis above." At that time Prague offered the most complete baroque and rococo settings in Europe. "It is possible to turn a camera there in a complete circle," says Shaffer, "and see in its frame nothing built after Mozart's death." Even the people of the city were ideally suited to function as period extras. "[They] are not embarrassed by wearing period costume: the smallest bit-player on a day's leave from the factory looks absolutely natural in perruque [*sic*] and pelisse. . . . Contemplating the audiences of extras assembled in the Tyl theatre to watch the Mozart operas being played — the very theatre where *Don Giovanni* was first produced! — one experiences the miraculous feeling of time being reclaimed from oblivion."[23] As Callow and Shaffer walked about the Old Town at night, they realized that this was the selfsame city that Mozart knew well. "You can still see the adjacent hotels where he and his librettist for *Don Giovanni*, Lorenzo da Ponte, stayed. . . . *Giovanni*'s premiere took place in the very theatre where we were filming the opera sequences." At other times, while walking the streets at night, "we would half expect a carriage to draw up and Mozart himself to leap out of it."[24]

And although the details of music performance on stage had been loosely rendered by Callow and Scofield, on film it was a different matter. Hulce, who had had no previous musical training, had to learn to simulate keyboard performance: "It was an act of God and my will power that within a few weeks I could play basically all the pieces you see me play in the film. A real challenge were the brief scenes where you see me writing music with one hand while caroming billiard balls off the cushions of the table with the other. We did endless takes of that scene. I was determined to be accurately writing the music you hear on the track. But in take after take, something would go wrong — the ink would spill, the ball would bounce off the table or scatter the pages. It took hours and hours just to get those few seconds. All of the recording itself was done in a two-week period prior to the start of filming. Neville [Marriner] oversaw all of that. As for conducting, I was just encouraged to 'keep it simple.' Conducting at that time was more a matter of time-keeping than anything else."

Despite its wealth of surface detail and its abundance of music that was transferred to the screen relatively intact, at no time did either Forman or Shaffer claim *Amadeus* to be a history lesson about Mozart. "We were not making an objective Life of Wolfgang Mozart," insisted Shaffer in 1984. "This cannot be stressed too strongly. Obviously *Amadeus* on stage was never intended to be a documentary biography of the composer, and the film is even less of one. . . . We are blatantly claiming the grand license of the storyteller to embellish his tale with fictional ornament and, above all, to supply it with a climax whose sole justification need be that it enthralls his audience and emblazons his theme." At any rate, the famous deathbed scene, the nightlong encounter between the dying Mozart and the "spiritually ravenous" Salieri is

A wholly fabricated moment in *Amadeus* has the dying Mozart dictating his *Requiem* to Antonio Salieri (F. Murray Abraham) (Courtesy Photofest/Saul Zaentz)

justified more for its dramatic plausibility than its historical inaccuracy. "Such a scene never took place in fact," explains Shaffer. "However, our concern at this point was not with facts but with the undeniable laws of drama. It is where — holding fast to the thread of our protagonist's mania — we were finally led."[25]

Perhaps unwittingly, the staging of this deathbed scene confirms the myth that Mozart composed effortlessly, unconsciously, obeying the dictates of a music that already presented itself fully formed in his head. It will be recalled that as Mozart gasps out the notes, key signatures, voices, and instrumentation to Salieri, the appropriate music magically appears, as if on cue, layer by layer, on the soundtrack. Mozart's internal diegesis becomes Salieri's as well, a musical bond between them that had been hitherto denied and which now transforms Mozart from a giggling child to a spiritual presence and Salieri from a vengeful madman into a redeemed soul. "Shaffer was once a music critic," says Hulce, "and for him to write a scene of one composer dictating music to another — and to do it with all the correct technical musicological terminology — was quite a daring thing to do to an audience. I made a bargain with F. Murray Abraham before shooting it that I would know the scene so well that any time he got behind or lost in taking the dictation, he could stop me in character and ask me what to do. Milos set it up to shoot with two cameras at once, so that any accidents that happened could be matched. It was an intensely exciting process. I never knew where 'Salieri' was going to get lost, so there were accidents that happened — it was shot in one continuous take and edited later — that were captured spontaneously on film. At the same time, I had to hum the snatches of music in the same key and in the same tempo as the pre-recorded music. I wore a small transistor speaker in my ear, concealed beneath the hairpiece, which relayed the music to me. It was like I was taking a musical dictation, just like Mozart might have been 'hearing' the music in his head! Three parts of my brain had to be working all at once — speaking my lines, humming and singing the notes, and listening to the music in my earpiece."

If art doesn't exactly imitate life, in this case the movie effectively conveyed and confirmed the myth of Mozart as the passive servant of the Music of the Spheres — or, at least, as the auditor of a performance by Neville Marriner and the Academy of St. Martin-in-the-Fields!

"Noises in the Head": Tony Palmer's Testimony

In the penultimate scene in Tony Palmer's *Testimony,* the dying Dmitry Dmitreyevich Shostakovich — People's Artist of the USSR, three-time recipient of the Order of Lenin, and member of the Communist Party — is visited by Josef Vissarionovich Dzhugashvili (Joseph Stalin), general secretary of the Central Committee and premier of the USSR. Although Stalin has been dead for twenty-two years, his ghost is voluble enough. "I am the enemy you loved, my friend," he says. "I made a great composer of you, while I lived." The ghost pauses. "[We are] together again, I see, the Fool and his Tsar."

Next to his 1982 *Wagner,* Palmer's *Testimony,* an examination of the torturous relationship between Shostakovich and Stalin, is his most ambitious undertaking. "It's a work of fiction, of course, *not* a documentary," he insists.[26] But his attention to the myriad details of locations, casting, the historical record, and musical quotation and allusion lends a hard-edged, gritty texture to its frightening and, ultimately, moving, nightmare. Moreover, it conveys Palmer's conviction that every note in the music of a great composer like Shostakovich *means* something. But what? Indeed, just as historians are applying new findings from recently opened Soviet archives to gaps in extant historiography about Soviet politics and society, so are they learning more about how Soviet artists, like Shostakovich, worked and lived within the Stalinist regime.[27]

Ever watchful of the vicissitudes of party politics, Shostakovich has always seemed the model of the Soviet composer. In his 1959 biography of Shostakovich, D. Rabinovich praised his overcoming the "infantile disorders of modernism" of the West in favor of the "healthy influence" of Soviet social-ist realism.[28] And a recent biography by Laurel Fay seems to confirm this assessment: "He had ceded unconditionally his signature, his voice, his time, and his physical presence to all manner of propaganda legitimizing the Party. Especially since the Tenth Symphony he had even devoted a disproportion-ately large portion of his music to the greater glory of Socialist Realism. He was a role model for the status quo, a malleable symbol of the fusion of civic responsibility with artistic genius, of popularity with professional respect. As an actual member of the Party he could give nothing more."[29]

Shostakovich himself frequently spoke out on behalf of party policies. "I live in the USSR, work actively and count naturally on the worker and peasant spectator," he declared in 1930. "If I am not comprehensible to them I should be deported."[30] In 1948 he appeared before the Central Committee and at-tacked the so-called formalist tendencies in his and others' music, calling upon Soviet musical organizations to accept "criticism and self-criticism."[31] A month later, at the Moscow Congress of Soviet Composers, he reiterated his "con-fession" that the party is right to express "concern for Soviet art and for me, a Soviet composer."[32] At the Waldorf Astoria press conference in 1949 he de-nounced Western "decadent" music and the formalism of Igor Stravinsky and Arnold Schoenberg. "By the late 1950s," writes Fay, "the larger-than-life public image of the most distinguished of Soviet composers—conveyed through the inescapable profusion of speeches, articles, testimonials, photo opportunities, and so forth—was as a sincerely reclaimed loyalist, a cultural pitchman for the causes of the Communist Party and Soviet State."[33]

The call for a "new" Shostakovich gained momentum with the publication in 1979 of *Testimony: The Memoirs of Dmitry Shostakovich*, collected and edited by Solomon Volkov.[34] "I felt it was my duty to tell what I still remembered," says Shostakovich near the end of the volume. Hovering over these recollec-tions, whose authenticity has been in dispute since its publication, is an elegiac, at times bitter, tone: "I have thought that my life was replete with sorrow... and the picture filled me with a horrible depression. I'm sad, I'm grieving all the time.... I have thought that my life was replete with sorrow and that it would be hard to find a more miserable man. But when I started going over the life stories of my friends and acquaintances, I was horrified.... And that made me even sadder. I was remembering my friends and all I saw was corpses, moun-tains of corpses. I'm not exaggerating, I mean mountains."[35]

The alleged authenticity of *Testimony* has become a special issue in Shosta-kovich studies.[36] The book appeared in English in 1979 (there has not been a Russian edition) four years after Shostakovich's death and shortly before the Soviet invasion of Afghanistan in the final days of Cold War tensions. After an initial enthusiastic embrace of the book in the West, doubts crept into the public discussion. In addition to the expected attacks from Moscow branding it as a forgery, the American scholar Laurel Fay noted in *The Russian Review* in 1980 that her requests to view Volkov's manuscript had been refused. She pointed out a number of passages in the book that she contended had been published previously by Soviet sources. "It is clear that the authenticity of *Testimony* is very much in doubt," she wrote. "Volkov's questionable methodology and deficient scholarship do not inspire us to accept his version of the nature and content of the memoirs on faith. . . . Until such tangible proof is offered, we can only speculate about where the boundary lies between Shostakovich's authentic memoirs and Volkov's fertile imagination."[37]

A counterassertion began in 1990 when biographer Ian MacDonald began what has become a decade-long attack on Fay and on all those who dispute *Testimony*'s authenticity. "Leaving aside, for the time being, further evaluation of *Testimony*'s reliability," MacDonald wrote, "it is clear that Volkov's claims are both consistent in themselves and based on firsthand data unavailable to his Western detractors. This makes it vital to consider his outlook thoroughly before moving to a judgement [*sic*] on his methods of purveying it." This reaffirmation of the book's credibility has since been supported by Galina Vishnevskaya, Vladimir Ashkenazy, Russian music historian Daniel Zhitomirsky, and Shostakovich's son, Maxim.[38]

In adapting *Testimony* to film, Palmer immediately sought the cooperation and advice of Shostakovich's son, Maxim. Although Maxim had initially disparaged Volkov's book—Palmer points out that Maxim was still living in Russia at that time, mindful of reprisals against his family—he later endorsed its spirit, if not precisely its letter. Palmer himself went into the film with some questions of his own. "I think in the end the book is what Shostakovich said," he explains, "although I think some of it must have been said when Shostakovich thought he was off the record." Palmer was encouraged when support came from Shostakovich's widow, Irina. "She also had to be careful, because she was then living in Moscow, and she was very nervous. I met with her behind closed doors in a hotel in London with a KGB man standing outside the door. I was so angered by this, I asked him if he would like to come in, but he said no. Irina and I had about a four-hour conversation." After she read David Rudkin's script, she made several corrections, mostly apolitical in nature. "For example, Irina told me that Shostakovich always wrote in ink, because he had things completely finished in his mind before he wrote them down. And she also said that her husband found the whole business of writing music down so boring that he liked to do it on the kitchen table while she was cooking and the children running about."

Eventually Volkov lent his advice to Palmer and co-screenwriter David Rudkin. "Volkov was enormously helpful," notes Palmer, "and subsequently, he came to watch part of the filming (indeed, he is in the film, at the graveside in the opening scenes, just as he was in the real-life event). He had no editorial say, or control, over any of the picture. As far as I know, he approves of it — although he thought he should have been paid more money!"

The filming took five weeks and utilized locations entirely in the United Kingdom, including Wigan, Liverpool, and the Lake District. Cinematographer Nic Knowland, who worked with Vittorio Storaro on Palmer's *Wagner*, lensed the action. In addition to a cast including Ben Kingsley as Shostakovich, Terence Rigby as Stalin, and Ronald Pickup as Marshall Tukhachevsky, an impressive array of musicians is both heard *and* seen, including conductor Rudolf Barshai, whose acquaintance with Shostakovich dated back to the 1940s, singers John Shirley-Quirk and Felicity Palmer, violinist Yuzuko Horigome, and pianist Howard Shelley.

The action encompasses scenes of the composer's boyhood as he watches the brutal repression by tsarist troops of street riots, through his student life at the Petrograd Conservatory with Alexander Glazunov (Peter Woodthorpe), the attacks on his opera, *Lady Macbeth of Mtensk,* his relationships with political ally and personal friend General Tukhachevsky and theater entrepreneur Vsevelod Meyerhold (Robert Stephens) — both of whom would be murdered in the late 1930s at Stalin's directive — his reactions to the siege of Leningrad and the atrocities at Babi Yar, his postwar confrontations with Stalin, his public humiliations of the appearances at the 1948 Conference of Soviet Musicians and the 1949 Peace Congress in New York City, his postwar family life, and his death in 1975.

Such an abbreviated summary gives only a hint of the complexity of Palmer's conception and execution. In the manner of a composer, Palmer introduces his main thematic material at once — the complex relationship between Shostakovich and Stalin — and develops it in a series of variations that move both men freely through a fluid continuum of space and time, reality and fantasy, traversing the varying contexts of life, politics, and art. As noted earlier, its fractured chronology, liberal use of relatively unfamiliar music, throwaway allusions to obscure historical incidents and characters, and juxtaposition of fictive and documentary scenes can leave the unprepared viewer a bit bewildered.[39]

The best approach to understanding the elusive meanings and ambiguities of the man and his music, Palmer decided, was simply not to portray him as solely a patriotic citizen or solely as a secret dissident, but to accept him as both, a divided soul, part responsible Soviet citizen and part dissident artist. In this wise Palmer deploys a central metaphor derived from Volkov's book. This was the *yurodivy,* a hallowed figure in Russian history and folklore dating back to the fifteenth century, a court jester who enjoyed the protection — or at least the tolerance — of the tsar, while critiquing societal ills. "The *yurodivy* has the gift to see and hear what others know nothing about," explains Volkov in *Testimony.* "But he tells the world about his insights in an intentionally paradoxical way, in code. He plays the fool, while actually being a persistent exposer of evil and injustice."[40] The *yurodivy* aren't gone, Volkov quoted Shostakovich, "and tyrants fear them as before. There are examples of it in our day."[41]

Volkov contended that because Shostakovich did not want to enter into open conflict with Stalin over issues of politics and "formalist" music, he sometimes affected "crude and purposely clumsy" words and an eccentric manner to express his antitotalitarian sentiments.[42] As a *yurodivy* composer, he effected in his music an aural correlative to the capering jester in cap and bells — music that was marked, as Esti Scheinberg has examined in his study of ambiguity in Shostakovich's music, by rude dissonances, satiric asides, clownish dances and burlesques, and abrupt shifts in mood that career in seconds from the depths of stark despair to the frenzied jubilation of the circus ring. To a friend, Flora Litvinova, he purportedly once admitted that his music was a kind of disguise. Free of the dictates of the party, he said, "I could have revealed my ideas openly instead of having to resort to camouflage."[43]

Since the attacks on his opera, *Lady Macbeth of Mtensk,* Shostakovich underwent a crash course in becoming a proper socialist realist composer.[44] Palmer resorts to a bit of socialist realist strategy himself in making this subsequent indoctrination painfully clear through the device of an invented dialogue between the composer and his friend and ally, Marshal Tukhachevsky as they discuss Shostakovich's future during a walk down a country road.[45] Tukhachevsky warns him that his creative instincts will get him in trouble. Shostakovich replies, "The Revolution set our creativity free but [Stalin] tells me, step on your own creativity." Tukhachevsky confides that Shostakovich is being "licked into shape" as *the* Soviet composer, but that political patronage exacts a price: "This new sound of yours, violent, black, noises that crush — it's too negative," Tukhachevsky warns. "Such music speaks of conflict; the Revolution resolves all conflict. The symphony must rejoice." Shostakovich defends his music, declaring, "I write what I hear, from within myself. Or else I have no meaning." Tukhachevsky counters with advice: "You are the one true voice by which a truth might still be spoken, and which the people will know for true. You've got to stay alive for that, somehow."

Palmer's portrait of Stalin as the Tsar to Shostakovich's Fool is as bizarre, in its own way, as the image Stalin himself cultivated, or that Hollywood has presented. Essentially a cartoon image, he is a performer in what biographer Jeffrey Brooks has described as "the political theater of high Stalinism."[46] In one scene Shostakovich refers disdainfully to him as a "gardener who dug the Revolution's grave," a "shoeshine boy from the Caucasus, pox pits on his face and neck, little, fat hands, one smaller than the other," who "brooded, and in his brooding our wretched century broke its back." We see his burly, uniformed figure in fragmented glimpses — portrayed by an actor in a film, a figure in a newsreel, and a character from a boys' adventure story ("Koba, Hero of the Caucasus"). Hundreds of masks of his face litter a film studio, his fifteen-foot tall bust bursts into flames, his statue crumbles. The ultimate bureaucrat, he sits alone at his desk in a huge, empty factory, an enormous hammer-and-sickle banner looming above him, stamping execution orders onto a stack of personnel files. The ultimate megalomaniac, he regards himself in the mirror, searching for the greatness he has assumed for himself. And victim of his own mortality, his sick, bloated face balloons out cartoonishly into the wide-angle lens as he gasps his last on his deathbed.

Together, the Fool and his Tsar go through the paces of their own black comedy, like Livia and Emperor Claudius, or like a weirdly distorted version of Laurel and Hardy. Although history tells us the two men met in person only once, Palmer depicts several serio-comic confrontations with diabolical flair. *Testimony* begins with depictions of both their funerals, cross-cutting from Stalin's in 1953 to Shostakovich's in 1975, uniting them in death as they were in life. "Look," intones Shostakovich's narrative voice, "the ravens are here, claiming our corpses." Through flashbacks and a fractured narrative chronology, the two men keep bumping into each other in what might best be described as a series of pratfalls. For example, Stalin directs Shostakovich by telephone to go to America to attend the Congress on World Peace. "You will be the star of the Soviet delegation," he commands. "You are our brightest and most talented." Shostakovich protests that his music has been lately banned. Stalin is unfazed. "In the USSR," he ripostes, with the impeccable timing of a professional straight man, "no work is banned. But there are contexts in which performance is *unwise*." Shostakovich executes a perfect double take. Stalin finishes: "Where that concerns you, we should look into that."

In another example, during a competition held in 1943 for a new national anthem, Stalin embraces Shostakovich and pronounces him the winner. "I like a tune," Stalin tells him in absolute deadpan. After a pause he asks, "Where do they come from, those noises in the head?" Yet again, in a nightmare sequence wherein the dying Stalin gasps his last and falls out of his bed to the floor, Shostakovich mocks, "I'm alive and you're dead," and then falls into a fit of shrieks, sobs, and laughter. Another fantasy scene depicts Stalin's head, inflated to gigantic size, rolling down the street like a bowling ball toward the retreating Shostakovich. Finally, in the aforementioned climactic dream sequence, the ghostly figure of Stalin comes to Shostakovich's own deathbed, and in the ensuing dialogue confirms the symbiotic character of their relationship:

SHOSTAKOVICH: You hijacked my song.

STALIN: Something died from your music when I died. You stopped speaking. I made a great composer of you, while I lived.

SHOSTAKOVICH: You left me a barren tree, to pluck poor fruit.

STALIN: I am the enemy you loved, my friend. Together again, I see, the Fool and his Tsar. I made Russia strong. I found her a medieval pauper. No one tampers with Russia now. What did you do? Squeaks and bangings, thumps, howlings in the head.

SHOSTAKOVICH: My music speaks. It's a warning.

STALIN: I destroyed what you call truthfulness. Yours. You are, my friend, a long bleak coda into the dark. That is your significance.

Palmer creates a rich series of contrapuntal effects, moods, and editorial commentaries in his music-image constructions. The opening measures of the third movement of the Eighth Symphony, pungent and strident, lend the opening credits a premonitory kind of urgency, establishing an uneasy mood that will generally prevail throughout the entire picture. The mocking Polka from the *Age of Gold* ballet deflates the stuffy reception following the premiere of the composer's First Symphony (it is heard again, also in a mocking way, as Shostakovich arrives in America). A jazz band plays his arrangement of "Tea for Two" in a fantasy sequence depicting the arrival of a sinister black train carrying a crowd of partygoers. Measures from the first movement of the Fifth Symphony celebrate — or do they mock? — a montage depicting the frenzied workers' activity during the First Five Year Plan — a wild collection of images of factory workers, smokestacks, wheels, pistons, hammers, molten lead, exercising athletes, and newsreel shots of Stalin reviewing formations of marching athletes. The frenzied, jagged strains of the great *passacaglia* from the First Violin Concerto underpin a lengthy sequence that depicts the low point in Shostakovich's personal and professional life after his humiliation before the Conference of Soviet Musicians — beginning with a montage of his public failure (the tearing down of posters proclaiming his concerts, the replacement by a placard announcing the premiere of the *Tone Poem of the Tractor Workers Cooperative,* by the hated Soviet toady, Khrennikov) — through scenes of a sterile home life and the desertion by his wife. And in one of the most heart-wrenching sequences in the film, music that is disquieting and discordant from the Thirteenth Symphony ("Babi Yar") underlies a lengthy montage of newsreel footage and reenacted scenes depicting Stalin's fall, the assumption of

Khrushchev to power, and Shostakovich's pain and outrage upon visiting the site of the mass extermination of Jews in September 1941 at Babi Yar ("Ravine of Old Women"), a ravine in northwestern Kiev. Intercut with shots of prisoners behind barbed wire and piles of corpses is the image of Shostakovich, striding grimly beneath a leaden sky. In the use of music and arrangement of the mise-en-scène, this scene eloquently evokes memorable lines from Yevgeny Yevtushenko's 1961 poem:

> Wild grasses rustle over Babi Yar,
> The trees look sternly, as if passing judgment.
> Here, silently, all screams, and, hat in hand,
> I feel my hair changing shade to gray.[47]

Three works by Shostakovich appear several times, functioning as veritable leitmotifs throughout the film. The famous March from the first movement of the Seventh Symphony — supposedly, as we have seen, an indictment of the strutting Nazi invasion of Leningrad — appears in several guises in varying contexts. It is first heard as a simple tune Shostakovich whistles to his daughter in an idle moment. "Nobody takes any notice of the tune," he explains to her. He plays it on the keyboard. "We think it's friendly." Again he plays it, louder this time. "Then it gets bigger," he says. "And bigger." Again, still louder. "Before you know it [Stalin] is trampling everybody down. This is the story." By now the childish piping tune has become a relentless hammer blow. After a moment the child asks, "Did somebody kill the giant in the end?" To which Shostakovich quietly mumbles, "Perhaps, perhaps." The next time we hear the motto, the composer is whistling his way into the conservatory full of waiting students. And finally, during the sequence of the siege of Leningrad, the melody is heard in its full symphonic version, this time accompanying images of invading Nazis and the sounds of wartime carnage. At the height of this sequence the music crashes to a halt as Shostakovich ascends to the roof of the conservatory and dons a fireman's helmet for an absurdly posed, propaganda photograph.[48]

The second recurring musical work is the Eleventh Symphony. The relentless rat-a-tat-tat of the second movement underscores scenes of the brutality of the October Revolution — images of gunfire, rampaging mounted horsemen, toppling religious icons, the storming of the Winter Palace (images lifted from Sergei Eisenstein's *October,* 1927, and Vsevelod Pudovkin's *End of St. Petersburg,* 1927). By contrast, the lamenting moan of the opening strains of the first movement lends an ominous tone to the otherwise tender images of the composer at home with his daughter. Not even hearth and home, it seems, can withstand the pervasiveness of the Stalinist Terror. The music appears again in a different context when Shostakovich drunkenly mocks the radio announcement of Stalin's death.

The third recurring work is the second movement from Shostakovich's Piano Concerto.[49] It first is heard while Shostakovich sits at his writing desk with his little son, Maxim. The tender, lyric flow of the music quietly affirms the relationship between a father and the son for whom he wrote this work. The final appearance of this music appears after the nightmare of the Brynkova Ravine, when its gentle melody is heard throughout the extended, imaginary dialogue between Shostakovich and Stalin, continues through the final scenes of the aging Shostakovich walking stiffly through dark streets, and, finally, concludes as a youthful Shostakovich sits at the keyboard. As the music fades, he turns and stares directly into the camera, his face fixing the viewer in a protracted, enigmatic stare. Here, according to the viewer's disposition, the music inflects these final images with either a sense of youthful innocence and sentiment regained, or with a last, ironic reminder of everything that the composer has lost.

Hovering over it all is the huddled figure of Shostakovich, a thin little man with black glasses wearing a black raincoat, clutching at his briefcase, hurrying down an endless, winding corridor. By means of lengthy, uncut tracking shots, Palmer insists that we follow him, even though we never really know where he's been or where he's going. For all we know, he is running yet.

Those who remember life under Stalin, says Palmer, view *Testimony* with a special empathy. He notes with satisfaction that after its premiere in Austria, a long silence ensued, broken finally by a man sitting near the front of the auditorium. "He said, 'I want you all to know this is exactly what life is like in the totalitarian communist regime; I know, I've suffered it.' It was [the celebrated Polish composer] Gyorgy Ligeti." Later, in 1998, Palmer was invited to screen the film in St. Petersburg in the presence of Irina Shostakovich. "I objected, saying that you couldn't expect an Englishman to bring a film about Russia's greatest twentieth century composer to his own home town! Well, we did bring it and it was a terrifying evening. People got very emotional. Mrs. Shostakovich was in tears. I had never understood before why Shostakovich's music was so immensely popular in its own time. But now I know it is because they knew that he was speaking on their behalf, when no one else would."

In the final analysis Palmer resists easy explanations concerning the truth of Shostakovich's politics and musical meanings. Unlike Stalin, Palmer has not tried to pin Shostakovich down and force him to explain himself (where indeed do those "noises in the head" come from?). His Shostakovich is a man who never questions the basic tenets of Communism as a political philosophy, who is constantly striving to fulfill his role as a *Soviet* musician, and who has no desire whatsoever to leave his country. But this is also a Shostakovich who suffers crises of personal integrity and family life, who does what he has to do in order to survive, no matter how appalling the compromises. Having noted all that, we can add that this is the man, who in works like the Fifth Symphony achieved official favor, popular acceptance, *and* deeply felt personal expression. In other words Palmer has wrought a Shostakovich who was not moved so much by a lack of principles as driven by a deep-rooted contradiction of character. "This enabled the composer," writes biographer Richard Taruskin, "to achieve the status of a Soviet 'civic' artist while remaining loyal to his Russian heritage—in effect, to don his Fool's guise to both revile and serve his tsar." Likewise with the music itself, as Taruskin further suggests—and Palmer seems to confirm—its real "meaning" ultimately eludes its specific contexts and arises "out of a process of interaction between subject and object, so that interpretation is never wholly subjective or wholly objective to the exclusion of the other." In short, "we can never merely receive its messages; we are always implicated in their making. . . . It is never just Shostakovich. It is always Shostakovich and us."[50]

Finally, it is worth noting that we feel at times that although Palmer is sympathetic to Shostakovich, he may not *like* him very much—an attitude that some critics have noted in his treatment of other composers, particularly Richard Wagner. In this Palmer proves himself to be a bit of a *yurodivy,* although he denies the suggestion. (In the broader sense his own guise as a kind of jester may convey his self-perception as an independent filmmaker struggling to survive in the sometimes hostile world of mainstream, commercially driven cinema.) Certainly Palmer's strategy in *Testimony* and his other films is to don his own cap and bells and double-tongue his message, revealing his subjects but preserving their—and his own—mystery. To paraphrase G. K. Chesterton, what remains is not the solution by man, only the riddle of God.

"An Unruly Completeness":
 Fritz Lehner's Mit meinen heissen Tränen

"Films about Franz Schubert have presented only a clichéd, unrealistic portrait of the composer," film director Fritz Lehner told this writer in a recent interview. "I grew up with that, and I don't like it. When I made *Mit meinen heissen Tränen* I wanted to show Schubert as a human being, not as some sort of monument, god-like, untouchable. He had been a teacher, and I also had been a teacher; and I was drawn to that."[51]

Lehner's *Mit meinen heissen Tränen* (*With My Hot Tears*) occupies a unique position, not just among the many Schubert biopics, but in the genre at large.

Austrian filmmaker Fritz Lehner's *Mit meinen heissen Tränen (With My Hot Tears)* (1987–1988), took a revisionist look at the life of Franz Schubert. (Courtesy Gabriela Brandenstein)

Shot over a two-year period at an estimated cost of $4 million, it was broadcast on three successive days on Austrian ORF television, from 31 October to 2 November 1986. It was also broadcast and shown theatrically in twenty-six countries, including the United States (where it was presented at Lincoln Center in an abridged version, titled *Notturno (Nocturne)* in 1992 and featured a year later at the 1993 Schubertiad in New York City.[52] Nominated for the Prix Europeen du Cinema in 1988 and winner of a dozen prizes, including the Camera d'Or at the Festival de Cinema de Barcelone, it both amazed and outraged its viewers and critics.[53]

The project had a long gestation. "I began thinking about a Schubert film as early as 1983," Lehner says. "I studied his music, looked at two thousand paintings and researched dozens of books about him and his period, particularly the work of biographer Otto Erich Deutsch. But I didn't want to make a documentary, or an educational film. I wanted to make a dramatic story. You know, Deutsch once said he could account for only *five weeks* out of Schubert's entire life. Everything else is either unknown or open to speculation."

Thus, Lehner's film, like its predecessors, has not stinted on its speculations about incidents in Schubert's life; but unlike them it casts a colder, sharper, more knowing gaze on its subject (see the discussion of *Melody Master* in Chapter One for discussion of the Schubert paradigm on stage and screen). "The great majority of paintings and films of the period portray the Biedermeier ideal of Schubert and his Vienna," he says, "and not the harsh realities, the poverty, the disease, the unsanitary conditions, etc. In that time, the censorship of Metternich refused to acknowledge publicly those conditions. Many of the scenes in the film are my own invention, but they were always based on *what could have happened*. And I don't think anyone can contradict what I have shown, or prove that it could *not* have happened!"

A brief synopsis is in order. *Mit meinen heissen Tränen* consists of three parts — "Der Wanderer" (The Wanderer), "Im Reich des Gartens" (In the Realm of Gardens), and "Winterreise" (Winter Journey). "Der Wanderer" opens in the summer of 1823. A blurred image coalesces into a sharply focused close-up of Schubert's (Udo Samel) disease-ravaged head. The hair is falling out in tufts. He's in a hospital being treated for syphilis. He is rebuked by a visiting monk for the sin of promiscuity. Upon leaving, he dons a wig, which subsequently becomes an object of jest among his friends. At home he speaks with his stepmother, who bestows upon him a prolonged kiss that is decidedly erotic and incestuous in its implication. Outside, the region of the Blutgasse is teaming with carriages, soldiers, citizens, and beggars. Sewage and garbage spill out of the gutters. Schubert sits by the curb a moment, a motionless figure amid the bustle and noise, listening to the bells of St. Stephens. He recognizes a young prostitute and runs to confront her. In a silent rebuke he lifts his wig to reveal the sores on his scalp. "I'm sorry," she says after a moment and walks away. All the while, a legless man dressed in rags and trundling about in a little wheeled cart, is following him. . . .

A few hours later Schubert finds himself with a party of friends traveling by coach to a party at Mauritz von Schwind's country home. Following behind the coach is the legless beggar. Although self-conscious about his new wig, and stinging from an occasional sly insult, Schubert is willing to entertain them by playing some of his German Dances at the piano. At his feet sits the beggar. Schubert is envious of his friend and roommate, Franz von Schober (Daniel Olbrychski), who is flirting with a female companion. When Schober tries to take advantage of the woman, who is obviously drunk, Schubert angrily confronts him. He kicks Schober viciously, and the two grapple on the ground. "Take revenge on your prostitute, not on me," Schober says afterward. "Or are you jealous? Be glad that I took you with me to Spittelberg; otherwise you might still be a virgin. Now, you leave my rooms immediately."

Schubert returns to town, alone, and goes to his father's school. "I need your help," he pleads, ruefully. But Father Schubert only gestures dismissively with his stick and knocks askew his son's wig. The children in the classroom laugh scornfully. "He was once my son and a teacher, like me," his father tells the students, "but now he keeps company with filthy whores." He whacks Schubert with his cane. "Nineteen children have been born to me; ten have been taken away. And you are left alive."

Night grows near. Utterly crestfallen, Schubert crouches at the graveside of his mother. He lifts his face to the twilight sky and removes his wig. "I'm talking to you, mother; do you hear me?" he soliloquizes softly. "You rot in your grave and I am rotting alive. You got uglier with every child, and I inherited the ugliness. Why didn't I die from that? I watch my fingers clumsy on the piano. Young girls close their eyes against me. My beautiful music — it's just markings on paper."

Back at Schober's apartment, Schubert prepares to leave. But as he packs his trunk, a repentant Schober renews his pledge of friendship and invites him to stay. Wordlessly, Schober takes out a small knife, pricks Schubert's finger to draw blood, spills drops of the blood into a wine glass and then, deliberately, meaningfully, drinks it down.

The second part, "Im Reich des Gartens" transpires in one day, autumn 1827. Schubert accompanies his friends Mayrhofer, Schober, von Schwind, Huettenbrenner, and others on an outing in the country. The main action concerns Schubert's brief but intense infatuation with a young woman, Magdalena (Therese Affolter), who he later learns has been hired by his friends to be his companion. Incidents include a wild coach ride through the forest, a fleetingly romantic interlude with Magdalena on a grassy meadow, an excursion to a waterfall, a trip downriver by boat, a visit to an empty church, and a penultimate night scene of a band concert by Johann Strauss, Sr.

Brief but telling vignettes suggest the darker undercurrents beneath the general air of loose hilarity. For example, for the first time there is a hint of homosexual behavior, when Schubert rebuffs overtures by his friend, Huettenbrenner. During the friends' walk through the forest, they watch as a runaway gypsy is hunted down and shot dead by mounted Austrian troops. Meanwhile, a surrealist touch is added when a hot-air balloon, to which is tethered a goat, passes by overhead. The sequence at the waterfall sequence is haunting in its ambiguity. When one of the group breaks a local rule and plunges into the cataract, the waterfall suddenly, mysteriously, ceases its flow. As if in a trance, Schubert ventures into a cleft in the rocky cliff. He stands alone in the dimly lit grotto, surrounded by muffled and indistinct sounds. When he reemerges, the rushing torrent of water resumes.

Most arresting of all is the night scene when, amid the concussions and showers of skyrockets, Schubert clumsily tries to make love to Magdalena. When she shrinks from him, he realizes that Schober has paid her to be his companion that evening. "It's better to let you know," she confesses. "I don't get that much money every day. If you want, I'll lie down with you all night." He staggers back from her. "We all love you," she repeats as he breaks into a run. His retreat blocked by the river. He stands knee-deep in the water, the fitful, intermittent flares of the fireworks limning the abject distress on his face. "I am Franz Schubert," he cries out to the indifferent sky and the curious onlookers jeering at him from the riverbank. "I AM FRANZ SCHUBERT!" he cries again in a mounting frenzy. And then again. . . . In the subsequent epilogue, by contrast, Schubert is alone at break of day. He wanders through the party debris scattered across the grounds. Slowly, deliberately, the camera leaves him and tracks across the meadow, revealing a random assortment of overturned chairs, an abandoned mirror, a tethered goat, a clutch of von Schwind's erotic sketches, a snake trapped inside a bottle, and so on. The party has ended, not on a note of hilarity but with an elegy.

The concluding third of the trilogy, "Winterreise," transpires over a period of a few weeks in November 1828. The action begins as Schubert moves into rooms adjoining the apartment of his brother, Ferdinand (Wolfgang Hübsch). A preternatural quiet envelopes the action like a shroud. Powerful close-ups intensify a sense of mounting claustrophobia. The cramped, boxlike interiors seem to shrink in dimension as the action progresses: the piano room narrows down to the nook that encloses Schubert's tiny writing desk, which is succeeded in turn by the even smaller bedroom, where his fatal convulsions are restrained by attendants and a priest.

The first real intimations of disaster come in a harrowing scene, the more remarkable for its seeming stasis and calm. After picking out the opening measures of the andante of the A Major Piano Sonata (one of last compositions), Schubert leaves the piano and moves to his desk by the window, where in utter and absorbing silence he bends over the manuscript. He rules the staff lines and picks up his quill pen. Slowly, gradually, a montage of extreme close-ups and selective sounds—the rattle of the windowpane, the flutter of a moth at the candle flame, the scratch of the quill, a fly tracking ink across the paper, a shot of another fly trapped in the inkwell—isolate and encapsulate the moment. Then, as we share Schubert's internal diegesis—that is, the sounds of the music itself (the slow buildup to the impassioned outburst midway through the sonata's andante) are heard on the soundtrack. He stops and reaches for another piece of paper. He inscribes the treble clef on the manuscript. But the design is not right. He pauses uncertainly. He tries to draw it again. No. Has he forgotten how to draw it? He's distracted now, puzzled. The ink splatters. He searches frantically through a drawer for another pen. Suddenly, abruptly, he starts back from the desk, overturning the chair. The camera retreats from him, framing his writhing figure in long shot, the lowering, shadow-splashed ceiling dominating the frame and diminishing his figure. The music grows in intensity. He staggers, then collapses to the floor. The sounds of several stark chords hammering away on the soundtrack.

Schubert is in trouble. For now. Later, life goes on, uncaring, indifferent, within and without the tiny apartment. Josepha (Michaela Widhalm), Schubert's fourteen-year-old half sister, is always in the room with him, distracting him as she hums snatches of his melodies and plays with the cat. Through his windows he catches glimpses of the world below and beyond his reach—a clockmaker, a woman tending a flowerpot, birds on a roof, a man and a baby, a little boy getting a haircut, a bird in a cage. Suddenly, he sees a figure standing below his window. The stranger returns Schubert's gaze. The face is Schubert's own—a ghostly *doppelganger*. Later, friends come to visit. One of them stumbles through the B-flat Sonata's first movement. "Don't you have anything easier?" the friend asks. "With music like that you won't be successful. Look at Paganini, Strauss, Rossini; they get more money from one concert than you get in a year." Schubert isn't listening. He sings a verse of a recently composed song, "Die Krähe" ("The Crow"). Ferdinand enters and closes all the windows. "He burns my clothes," observes Schubert; "he's scared that I would infect him and his wife. I'm glad that you came, Spaun—or didn't you know? Best get away from me. It's even worse that you dislike my music."

Brother Ferdinand massages his shoulders. "Watch it, don't get infected," snarls Schubert. He leans down to the keyboard and plays the opening chords to another song, "Der Leiermann" ("The Organ Grinder"). He murmurs to Ferdinand in an aside, "Now go away. You can burn my clothes if you wish. As if dying would be the worst thing. I'm just sad because I don't know what's really wrong with me. Is it my old illness? Nervous fever? That's how my mother died."

Later that night Schubert gazes across the street at a woman framed by her window. He watches, unflinching, as she slowly disrobes, her body outlined behind the transparent nightdress. She returns his gaze. He scribbles drawings onto the pages of a book. The next morning the woman comes to his room. "I was curious what you see when you look my direction," she says, gazing out the window back to her apartment. "I also watch you writing. Are you a poet? Do you write music to dance?" She opens his copy of Heinrich Heine's *Buch der Lieder* and looks dispassionately upon the series of obscene drawings he's scrawled on the page. She pauses, not a flicker of a reaction. "Will you dance with me?" she asks at length. "Come on. I know you want me." They dance, his steps hesitant at first, then more vigorous. They stop, breathing heavily. "We'll dance again soon, I hope," he says. She replies, "Just wave; you watch me all the time anyway."

In bed, Schubert is writing a letter. "Dear Schober," it reads, "I've not eaten in eleven days. Come and help me out with some reading, Cooper's *Last of the Mochicans* and *The Spy*." He looks up. Josepha is hanging up clothes and putting wood onto the fire. He watches her with growing interest. She comes to him and bathes his forehead. He strokes her hair. Then, almost casually, he kisses her forehead, then her lips. She lies down beside him. Music from the second movement of the Ninth Symphony wells up as they embrace in a clumsy, growing frenzy. After a few moments they pause, his face contorted, her breaths coming in gasps. Later, alone, he discovers his brother has locked the door against the other apartment. Schubert is trapped, entombed. He peers out the window and again sees his own figure on the street below. He shrinks back. He takes off his coat and sits down on the bed.

Cut to the doctor, at his bedside measuring out something. "You'll see if the new medicine will help you," explains Ferdinand. Later, a priest arrives. Schubert is singing. Then he murmurs, "Ferdinand, if you're still my brother, send him away. If I never needed him before, I don't need him now." Schubert's face is shining with sweat. He is emaciated. "Ferdinand, I always liked you most, but you have to promise not to prepare me like they did Beethoven, when they cut off his hair; or cut off his head, like Haydn." Ferdinand replies, "Don't worry, the pipe will taste good again. You're getting better every day. You sang so beautifully just now."

Josepha, hearing his delirious voice from the street, quickens her steps, spilling a glass of wine as she runs up the stairs. Inside, she finds him being bathed by an attendant, singing all the while. His mouth is chapped and blistered. Convulsions set in and she retreats to the outer room. Schubert is now completely out of his head. Josepha watches as the priest rushes in to restrain him. The door is closed abruptly in her face.

I have indulged in a certain amount of detail in the foregoing synopsis because, although it hardly scratches the surface of this bleak, densely detailed and dramatically complex portrait of Schubert, it perhaps is enough to convey something of its quiet detachment and its superbly textured aural and visual qualities. Not surprisingly, some viewers were outraged. Biographer Christopher Gibbs observes the film "introduced a darker Schubert — not simply suffering, but alienated, ill, and isolated even among family and friends. It created a considerable stir in Europe."[54] Lehner confirms, "There were many controversies and protests about the film. People were angry that I had ruined the clichés of *Das Dreimäderlhaus* [see the discussion in Chapter One]. People didn't want to admit that Schubert had sexual desires, that he had contracted syphilis, that he had to wear a wig, that he felt alienated from his friends, etc. I even received some death threats!"

Udo Samel's portrayal of Schubert is extraordinary in its nuanced and quiet subtlety. His physical resemblance to extant Schubert portraits is uncanny. "I looked for a year for just the right person to portray Schubert," says Lehner. "Udo was an actor at the Schaubühne Theater in Berlin, working under the directorship of Peter Stein. He had done only one film before coming to my

Fritz Lehner cast stage actor Udo Samel as Franz Schubert in *Mit meinen heissen Tränen* (*With My Hot Tears*). (Courtesy Gabriela Brandenstein)

Schubert project. He had an astonishing resemblance to Schubert and is an excellent actor. He's also a musician who plays the piano and once had ambitions to be a composer. I had to postpone the shooting for a year in order to get him."

Indeed, this is a far cry from the sentimentalized, sweetly suffering Schubert of the *Dreimäderlhaus* paradigm. From the beginning of the first episode, he is depicted as a marginalized figure, diseased, solitary, existing at the fringe of a circle of young people. His ill-fitting wig targets him as a "misfit" everywhere he goes. Music provides him only limited solace. Scenes of him at the piano are few and are either tolerated by his friends as amusing entertainment or are largely ignored altogether. Episodes in the third part clearly demonstrate that his newly composed music finds neither favor nor support among his circle. He is hopelessly estranged from his family. His mother is dead, and his father mocks him. His emotional life is stunted. "Normal" love, as well as the example of the free-and-easy promiscuity of Schober — the only companion whose presence is strongly marked in all three parts and who has obviously drawn him in the past into illicit sexual encounters — is denied him. His only sexual activity here is limited to the wordless encounter with a prostitute in the first part, the aborted romance with Magdalena in the second, and the voyeuristic encounters with the woman in the window in the third. Otherwise, there are only the incestuous implications of the prolonged, intimate kiss exchanged with his stepmother in the first part and the frenzied grapplings with his half sister in the third part. The presence of syphilis, long a controversial topic in Schubert studies, is announced at the beginning and, asserts Lehner, can be inferred as a metaphor for the AIDS epidemic of today. In this light the penultimate scene in the first part, when Schober renews his pledge of friendship with the blood-infected glass of wine, takes on a particularly tragic and horrible significance for both of them. Thus, harbingers of debility and death are omnipresent—from the presence of the legless beggar who follows him throughout the first part to the confrontations with his ghostly self in the doppelganger scenes in the third.

Lehner defends his inclusion of such scenes. "It is true that Schubert's father disliked his friends and was ashamed of Franz's illness," explains Lehner. "Based upon that kind of evidence, I showed Franz' father insulting him and turning his back on him. The character of the beggar was drawn from the many homeless, crippled men who returned from the Napoleonic wars to form little conclaves just outside of Vienna and who came into town to beg. I wanted to show the poverty that people like that endured, and how they had to survive on the trash and food thrown into the streets. I knew little about AIDS at the time I made the film, but I can understand why people might infer that from the scene with Schober and the infected wine glass. I wanted to suggest a homoerotic implication to their relationship—there are hints of that everywhere—but not necessarily that Schubert was actively homosexual. It was just a time when men displayed affection for each other more openly than today. What I really wanted to show was that Schober's gesture with the wine glass demonstrates that he feels responsible for Schubert's illness—it was he who took Schubert to the whore—and that now he shares with him the certainty of death.[55] It's all part of the romantic sensibility of the time: we share life, we share death. You see the same thing in Schober's relationship with the young girl at the outdoor party, who has infected lungs. He kisses her, knowing full well that he might become infected."

The most controversial scene perhaps, the erotic encounter with Josepha, is likewise defended. "Many people have asked me about that scene. It is documented that she really took care of Schubert in a very loving way in the last weeks of his life. I wanted their scene together to suggest innocent love, pure love. But it is a love that will remain unfulfilled. I suggested the same thing in the scene with the woman in the window. When she comes to him, he is unable to dance with her. It has been documented that he *couldn't* dance. All of which is sadly ironic, since he wrote so much music about love and about dance."

Franz Schubert (Udo Samel) plucks the guitar during a country outing in *Mit meinen heissen Tränen* (*With My Hot Tears*). (Courtesy Gabriela Brandenstein)

Other scenes preserve their own mystery, and Lehner is content with that. "The scene at the waterfall is another invented scene. People really believed in miracles at that time. The fact that the waterfall ceased to flow could have a perfectly normal explanation — probably that work of laborers upstream caused it to happen. But Schubert's friends preferred to regard it as a miracle, maybe somehow connected with Schubert's innocence, or with the flow of his creativity. And the strange sounds Schubert heard inside the grotto were probably only the winds acting like a wind harp, although you might want to hear them as musical 'sounds' in his head. All I wanted to do was create a scene open to interpretation."

Meanwhile, we are left with myriads of tiny moments and images that come and go, fleeting, ineffable, inexplicable — the goat tethered to the hot-air balloon, the trapped snake winding its way out the neck of the bottle, the runaway gypsy, Schubert's crudely inscribed obscene drawings, the visit to the empty church, the violent fight with Schober, and so many others too numerous to cite here. Lehner's film belongs to a select company of historical films that reconstructs a vanished world that displays what historian Simon Schama has described as presenting "an unruly completeness." Schama applauds this respect for "the strangeness of the past." These are films, he continues, "that embrace history for its power to complicate, rather than clarify, and warn the time traveler that he is entering a place where he may well lose the thread rather than get the gist."[56]

"The nasty and alluring details of the Vienna of the 1820s can go a long way in illuminating complex and hidden dimensions of Schubert's work," writes cultural historian Leon Botstein.[57] Indeed, it is safe to say that more than any composer biography ever made, *Mit meinen heissen Tränen* closely and tellingly observes the surrounding physical contexts of its subject — the crowded, teeming streets of Vienna in the first part, the forest scenes of part two, and the claustrophobic rooms of Schubert's last apartment. Lehner's unvarnished depiction of Viennese life is grim and graphic. In Schubert's time the city had grown to a population of three hundred thousand, and the density of occupation averaged thirty-eight persons per house. This was an era of declining living standards, deteriorating sanitary conditions, overcrowding, increased poverty, and public begging. Garbage spilled into the streets, sewage flowed freely, refugees and beggars from the late Napoleonic wars crowded the streets, and houses were like honeycombs of narrow, crowded rooms. Cholera was in the air. "Death and its ceremonial rituals — requiems, funeral processions, and burials — were a visible and regular part of daily life," continues Botstein. "Schubert's death at an early age was itself not extraordinary."[58]

"I used many locations in Vienna and in the Vienna Woods and in the Donau Auen meadows next to the Danube, about thirty kilometers outside Vienna," says Lehner. "We do know that Schubert actually went to these locations. Some of the first part I shot in the First District around the Alt Universität, the street called Bäcker Strasse and the Schönlaterngasse. Most of the third part was shot in the studio, except for the street scenes outside. The house opposite Schubert's room was also shot in the studio. I copied it after the room where Schubert died."

What is most astonishing about *Mit meinen heissen Tränen* is, paradoxically enough, its *silence*. It is undoubtedly the quietest movie about a composer ever made. Just as silence can "speak" eloquently in music, so here it commands our attention in the film. Granted, there are many scenes featuring music, most of them nondiegetic, appropriately chosen for the time and context — in particular, excerpts from the slow movement of the C Major Quintet, the A-flat Mass, the Eighth Symphony, the slow movement of the E-flat Piano Trio, the A Major Piano Sonata, and the C Major Fantasie for Violin and Piano, and several songs ("Die Krähe," "Ihr Bild," "Sturmische Morgen," "Der Leiermann," "Die Doppelgänger" — but many protracted sequences transpire in a wordless silence pregnant with the incidental aural textures of

Canadian filmmaker David Devine's series of "Composers' Specials" are targeted to young audiences. *Liszt's Rhapsody* starred
Georgie Johnson and Drew Juracka as Franz Liszt and his young
pupil, Josi Sarai, respectively. (Courtesy Devine Entertainment/
HBO Films)

Schubert's world. "Some people protested that I did not use music all the
time," says Lehner. "So many movies about composers think that music has to
be played *all the time*. But no. You will note I only use it sparingly in the film,
and only then when it is absolutely *meaningful*." The myriad noises of the
Viennese streets, the haunted whispers of the hidden grotto, the scratches of
the quill pen and the buzzings of the flies at Schubert's desk convey meanings
impossible to articulate in words. Indeed, with the exception of a handful of

scenes, the viewer scarcely needs an English translation. At the present time, the film is unavailable in the United States. The interested viewer is advised to contact Austrian Television.

Epilogue: All in the Family

Marking new directions in composer biopics is the series of "Composers Specials," produced and targeted to young viewers, by the Canadian-based Devine Entertainment Corporation. "Young people don't just listen to music," says producer-director David Devine, "they're accustomed to music videos. So we try to accommodate that experience in our own work. Our formula is to introduce children into each story, place them in an adversity situation—loss of a parent, child abuse, racial prejudice, confusion over career goals, etc.— and have a celebrated composer assist them in dealing with it. In the process, the composer achieves solutions to some of his own problems, as well. For both the child and the man, life is dramatized as a series of comebacks."[59]

At this writing, six titles, originally released in 1992 through 1996, have been telecast on HBO and released on videocassette—*Beethoven Lives Upstairs, Bizet's Dream, Bach's Fight for Freedom, Rossini's Ghost, Liszt's Rhapsody,* and *Strauss: The King of ¾ Time.* The best, in my opinion, is *Liszt's Rhapsody.* Directed by Richard Mozer, this charming fable about multiculturalism is based on a true but little-known incident in Liszt's life.[60] Liszt (Georgie Johnson) is impressed when he hears the improvisations of a twelve-year-old gypsy violinist named Josi Sarai (Drew Juracka) and offers to give him lessons. The boy, an untutored and hot-headed rebel, resists at first, but eventually he learns to respect Liszt's musical training. For his part Liszt is inspired by the boy's intuitive handling of gypsy and Hungarian folk tunes. As a result the boy acquires musical and personal discipline, and Liszt strikes out in new creative directions with his *Hungarian Rhapsodies.* "Your music and my music can come together in the world," Liszt tells Josi.

"These excellent videos not only introduce the music in the context of the composers' lives," writes Irene Wood in *Booklist,* "but they also give both meaning and color to the compositions for newcomers to classical music. They are outstanding additions to public libraries and schools."[61] In my opinion filmmakers Devine and Mozer deserve full credit for their commitment to bringing great composers to young people in formats that address their lives and music in ways that are pertinent without being patronizing. They promise new educational and entertainment opportunities for a new generation of viewers.

Notes

Introduction: The Lyre of Light

1. Mark C. Carnes, ed., *Past Imperfect: History According to the Movies* (New York: Henry Holt and Company, 1995), 10.

2. Quoted in Leger Grindon, *Shadows on the Past: Studies in the Historical Fiction Film* (Philadelphia: Temple University Press, 1994), 4.

3. Robert A. Rosenstone, "History in Images/History in Words: Reflections on the Possibility of Really Putting History onto Film," *American Historical Review* 93, no. 5 (December 1988): 1174.

4. Carnes, *Past Imperfect*, 9.

5. Curiously, except for a few passing references, none of the book-length investigations of history and biography on film that have appeared in the past twenty years has devoted any attention to composer biopics.

6. Graham Greene, "Beethoven," *The Spectator,* 23 June 1939; reprinted in David Parkinson, *The Graham Greene Film Reader* (New York: Applause Books, 1995), 306.

7. Quoted in Brian Newbould, *Schubert: The Music and the Man* (Berkeley: University of California Press, 1997), 407.

8. Hector Berlioz, *Evenings with the Orchestra,* ed. and trans. by Jacques Barzun (New York: Alfred A. Knopf, 1956), 298.

9. Quoted in Custen, *Bio/Pic,* 50.

10. James Huneker, *Chopin: The Man and His Music* (London, 1901).

11. Simon Schama, "Clio at the Multiplex," *The New Yorker,* 19 January 1998, 40.

12. Jorge Luis Borges, *Labyrinths: Selected Stories and Other Writings* (New York: New Directions, 1964), 28.

13. Italo Calvino, *Invisible Cities*, trans. by William Weaver (New York: Vintage, 1974), 45–46. This story is also cited as an exemplar of the search for truth and meaning in Teresa de Lauretis, *Alice Doesn't: Feminism, Semiotics, Cinema* (Bloomington: Indiana University Press, 1984), 12.

14. Luigi Pirandello based his 1918 play *Right You Are (If You Think So)* on his 1915 short story "La signora Frola e il signor Ponza suo genero," from which the quote is taken. See Robert S. Dombroski, "Laudisi's Laughter and the Social Dimension of *Right You Are (If You Think So)*," *Modern Drama* 16, nos. 3–4 (December 1973): 337–346.

15. Rosenstone, *Revisioning History*, 7.

16. Hayden White, *Content of the Form: Narrative Discourse and Historical Representation* (Baltimore: John Hopkins University Press, 1990), 4.

17. Hayden White, *Tropics of Discourse: Essays in Cultural Criticism* (Baltimore: Johns Hopkins University Press, 1985), 51.

18. Leo Braudy, *The Frenzy of Renown* (New York: Oxford University Press, 1986), 15.

19. Niall Ferguson, ed., "Introduction" in *Virtual History: Alternatives and Counterfactuals* (London: Papermac, 1997), 83–85.

20. Author's interview with Melvyn Bragg, 21 July 2003, London.

21. Kivy, *Possessor and the Possessed*, 38.

22. Ernst Kris and Otto Kurz, *Legend, Myth, and Magic in the Image of the Artist* (New Haven: Yale University Press, 1979), 11.

23. John Mainwaring's *Memoirs of the Life of the Late George Frideric Handel* (1760) was the first book devoted solely to the life and works of a composer.

24. Kivy, *Possessor and the Possessed*, 27.

25. Kivy, *Possessor and the Possessed*, 34.

26. The mythologizing process was set in motion a full decade before Beethoven's death. For a thorough overview, see Alessandra Comini, *The Changing Image of Beethoven: A Study in Mythmaking* (New York: Rizzoli, 1987), 79.

27. Kivy, *Possessor and the Possessed*, 134.

28. Mozart's first biographical notice was Friedrich Schlichtegroll's *Nekrolog und das Jahr* (1791). In 1798 Franz Niemetschek published the first separate biography of Mozart and only the second biography of a composer (after Mainwaring's *Handel*).

29. Franz Liszt's letter to George Sand, dated 30 April 1837, reprinted in Charles Suttoni, ed., *An Artist's Journey: Lettres d'un bachelier es musique, 1835–1841* (Chicago: University of Chicago Press, 1989), 28.

30. William Weber, "Mass Culture and the Reshaping of European Musical Taste, 1770–1870," *International Review of the Aesthetics and Sociology of Music* 8, no. 1 (June 1977): 15.

31. Quoted in Lawrence W. Levine, *Highbrow Lowbrow: The Emergence of Cultural Hierarchy in America* (Cambridge: Harvard University Press, 1988), 118–121.

32. For information on Anton Seidl's activities, see John Dizikes, *Opera in America: A Cultural History* (New Haven: Yale University Press, 1993), 242–244. For accounts of Jeannette Thurber's National Conservatory of Music of America, see John C. Tibbetts, ed., *Dvořák in America* (Portland, Ore.: Amadeus Press, 1993), 53–81. For an overview

of critic Henry Krehbiel's writings, see Mark N. Grant, *Maestros of the Pen: A History of Classical Music Criticism in America* (Boston: Northeastern University, 1998), 80–86.

33. Charles Hamm, " Dvořák, Stephen Foster, and American National Song," in Tibbetts, ed., *Dvořák in America,* 151.

34. Quoted in Joseph Horowitz, *The Post-Classical Predicament* (Boston: Northeastern University Press, 1995), 147.

35. The David Sarnoff quote and Horowitz's comment are in Horowitz, *Post-Classical Predicament,* 146.

36. Quoted in Gerald Bordman, *American Operetta* (New York: Oxford University Press, 1981), 117.

37. This unidentified author of a music textbook is quoted in Horowitz, *Post-Classical Predicament,* 145.

38. The standard work about this subject is Richard Abel and Rick Altman, *The Sounds of Early Cinema* (Bloomington: Indiana University Press, 2001). A useful, concise discussion is in Kathryn Kalinak, *Settling the Score: Music and the Classical Hollywood Film* (Madison: University of Wisconsin Press, 1992), 40–65.

39. See Philip Kennicott, "What's Opera, Doc?," *Classical,* January 1991, 19–24.

40. For a brief overview, see John C. Tibbetts "The Voice That Fills the House," *Literature/Film Quarterly* 32, no. 1 (2004): 2–11. A more exhaustive examination of opera on film is Ken Wlaschin's invaluable compendium, *Opera on Screen* (Los Angeles: Beachwood, 1997).

41. For full texts of this and other pronouncements by Antonín Dvořák concerning a new American school of music, see Tibbetts, *Dvořák in America,* Appendix A, 355–403.

42. See the discussion of postmodern filmmaking in Robert A. Rosenstone, "Future of the Past," in Vivian Sobchack, ed., *The Persistence of History: Cinema, Television, and the Modern Event* (New York: Routledge, 1996), 201–218.

43. Among the promising signs of new scholarship in these areas is Ewa Mazierska's essay, "Multifunctional Chopin: The Representation of Fryderyk Chopin in Polish Films," *Historical Journal of Film, Radio and Television* 24, no. 2 (2004): 253–268. Two Polish Chopin biopics are examined as representing contrasting constructions of Polish national character. *Mlodosc Chopina (The Youth of Chopin,* 1952), directed by Aleksander Ford, exemplifies the height of socialist realism in the Cold War era and "re-models" the patriotic profile of a man who in real life demonstrated his patriotic sentiments more in his music than in his social and political life. Thus, the film foregrounds Chopin's teenage years, spent mostly in Poland, "when his affinity to Polish culture and people could hardly be questioned" (258). On the other hand, *Chopin—Pragnienie Milosci (Chopin—Desire for Love,* 2002), directed by Jerzy Antczak, reflects the temper of postcommunist Poland. Its portrait of a composer whose love for George Sand tempers and dilutes his patriotic fervor is more in line with a revisionist view of the composer (and, interestingly, with the Hollywood version, *A Song to Remember* [1944], discussed elsewhere in this book).

44. See the chapter "Biopics" in Krin Gabbard, *Jamming at the Margins: Jazz and the American Cinema* (Chicago: University of Chicago Press, 1996), 64–100.

45. Quoted in Gordon S. Wood, "Novel History," *New York Review of Books,* 27 June 1991, 15–16.

Chapter One: The Classical Style

Epigraph: Franz Liszt letter to George Sand, January 1837, in Suttoni, *Artist's Journey,* 14.

1. Thomas Schatz, *The Genius of the System* (New York: Pantheon, 1988), 8–9.

2. For a concise discussion of Balcon's ambitions to promote a national cinema, see Laurence Kardish, "Michael Balcon and the Idea of a National Cinema," in *Michael Balcon: The Pursuit of British Cinema* (New York: Museum of Modern Art, 1984), 34–73.

3. For an overview of the American reception of British cinema during the 1930s and 1940s, see Geoffrey McNabb, *J. Arthur Rank and the British Film Industry* (London: Routledge, 1993), 56–71.

4. Custen, *Bio/Pic,* 26.

5. Cultural historian Jacques Barzun has described the leitmotif system as a strategy devised by Richard Wagner to "tag" a person, idea, or object with a brief musical theme, or motif: See Barzun, *Darwin Marx Wagner,* 16.

6. Theodor Adorno, "On Popular Music," in Richard Leppert, ed., *Essays on Music: Theodor W. Adorno* (Berkeley: University of California Press, 2002), 442.

7. Carol Flinn, "The Most Romantic Art of All: Music in the Classical Hollywood Cinema," *Cinema Journal* 29, no. 4 (Summer 1990): 38.

8. See Tony Thomas, *Music for the Movies* (South Brunswick: A. S. Barnes, 1973), 64–106.

9. For an overview of these composers, see Thomas, *Music for the Movies,* 64–140. See also Kalinak, *Settling the Score,* 66–110; and Alfred W. Cochran, "Cinema Music of Distinction," in Michael Saffle, ed., *Perspectives on American Music, 1900–1950* (New York: Garland, 2000), 323–348.

10. Patrick O'Connor, "Call of the Child," *Times Literary Supplement,* 12 October 2001, 19.

11. Author interview with Simon Callow, 14 July 2003, London.

12. Author interview with Albert Boime, 3 June 1989, Los Angeles.

13. Robert Winter, "Whose Schubert?" *19th-Century Music* 17, no. 1 (Summer 1993): 94–101, 98.

14. Newbould, *Schubert,* 406–407.

15. See Maynard Solomon's "Franz Schubert and the Peacocks of Benvenuto Cellini," *19th-Century Music* 17, no. 1 (Summer 1993): 193–206, in which allegations of Schubert's homosexuality and its possible influence on his music aroused a firestorm of controversy.

16. Elsaesser's discussion concentrates on the biopics of William Dieterle, particularly, *The Story of Louis Pasteur* (1936). See Thomas Elsaesser, "Film History as Social History: The Dieterle/Warner Brothers Bio-Pic," *Wide Angle* 8, no. 2 (1993): 15–31, 26.

17. Braudy, *Frenzy of Renown,* 6. Italics mine.

18. Kivy, *Possessor and the Possessed,* 4–18.

19. The song known as "Ave Maria" was in reality called "Ellen's Gesang" and was composed in 1825 to canto III of Sir Walter Scott's *The Lady of the Lake.* Although it always figures in Schubert films as a church hymn, musicologist John Reed has observed

that its emotion "is secular and aesthetic rather than religious." See Reed, *The Schubert Song Companion* (New York: Universe Books, 1985), 217.

20. Gibbs, "Poor Schubert," 36.

21. Albert Basserman reappears in several composer biopics, including *Rhapsody in Blue* (1946), as George Gershwin's music teacher, and *Night and Day* (1946), as a theater director.

22. Charles Osborne, *Schubert and His Vienna* (New York: Alfred A. Knopf, 1985), 67.

23. Biographer Newbould points out that the work, probably begun in 1822, actually was finished; that the last two movements were sketched out; and that the finale was transplanted to an "Entr'acte" for the overture, *Rosamunde*. See Newbould, *Schubert*, 182.

24. Biographer Osborne, for example, reports that in 1822 Schubert may have attempted to deliver a copy of some variations, but Beethoven was not at home. Early in 1827, friend and amanuensis Anton Schindler brought Beethoven a number of Schubert songs in manuscript. Beethoven purportedly was astonished, proclaiming, "Truly, in Schubert there dwells a divine spark!" and prophesied "that he will still make a great stir in the world!" Osborne also reports that on 19 March 1827 Schubert visited the dying composer, when for the first time they spoke a few words together (*Schubert and His Vienna*, 67). Schubert specialists Christopher H. Gibbs and Maurice Brown, on the other hand, dispute that. For a counterargument, see Gibbs, "Poor Schubert," 39; and Brown, *Schubert: A Critical Biography* (New York: Da Capo Press, 1978), 259.

25. In *Ein Leben in Zwei Setzen* (1953) Schubert is in love with Theresa Grob, a beautiful singer who has expressed an attraction to him since hearing his "Ave Maria" in church. However, prospects of his ability to support her are dim, and she marries instead a baker. Despairing, Schubert realizes he must begin anew his composing. Not long afterward, he dies of a broken heart in his room. His song "Ellen's Gesang" functions as the romantic leitmotif, and it is heard throughout the film many times (despite the fact that in reality its composition in 1825 postdates the romance with Grob).

Das Dreimäderlhaus (1958) directed by Ernst Marischka, stars Karl-Heinz Boehm as Schubert. His love for his music student, Hannerl (Johanna Matz), is thwarted when she gives her heart to his rival, Baron Schober (Rudolf Schock). Hiding his tears, he congratulates her. "You are my best friend's wife," he says. "I wish you the best. Make him very happy. I have my music." After playing the music for her wedding, Schubert slips away and goes alone to his room. He slumps over the piano, while the theme from the first movement of the Eighth Symphony wells up on the soundtrack.

26. Quoted in Newbould, *Schubert*, 407.

27. According to biographer Joseph Wechsberg, "Apart from his music Strauss left few documents and records. . . . Many [of his letters] were lost during the last war when the Nazis requisitioned all material left by Strauss." See Wechsberg, *The Waltz Emperors: The Life and Times and Music of the Strauss Family* (New York: G. P. Putnam's Sons, 1973), 15.

28. Quoted in Wechsberg, *Waltz Emperors*, 12.

29. Donald Spoto, *The Dark Side of Genius: The Life of Alfred Hitchcock* (Boston: Little, Brown and Company, 1983), 134.

30. Jessie Matthews dismisses *Waltzes from Vienna* in just one line: "Alfred Hitchcock directed this one." See Matthews, *Over My Shoulder* (New Rochelle, N.Y.: Arlington House, 1974), 136.

31. For a brief but respectful treatment of the film, see Charles Barr, *English Hitchcock* (Moffat, Scotland: Cameron and Wallis, 1999), 127–130.

32. In his book *Hitchcock's British Films* (Hamden, Conn.: Archon Books, 1977), Maurice Yacowar notes that this scene was not in the original stage production.

33. Barr, *English Hitchcock*, 128–129.

34. "Strauss's Great Waltz," *New York Herald*, 27 April 1935.

35. "Strauss's Great Waltz," *Motion Picture Daily*, 9 April 1935.

36. "The Great Waltz," *Motion Picture Herald*, 5 November 1938.

37. "The Great Waltz," *Film Daily*, 4 November 1938.

38. "The Great Waltz," *Variety*, 2 November 1938.

39. "The Great Waltz," *Motion Picture Herald*, 5 November 1938.

40. Reisch's *Ein Walzer von Strauss* was, he claims, not really about Strauss but about the waltz itself: "The 'Blue Danube' played an integral part in the happenings and continuity of the screenplay: It was about two people in love — I've forgotten the details — who meet during the waltz, dance it together, then are separated. Years later, in totally different circumstances, they are reunited with the waltz. The film was a smashing success." Interview with Walter Reisch by Joel Greenberg, *Song of Scheherazade* folder, Margaret Herrick Library, Academy of Motion Picture Arts and Sciences, Beverly Hills, Calif.

41. Custen, *Bio/Pic*, 50.

42. The Viennese Revolution began on 13 March 1848, when students, burghers, and workers demonstrated at the Ständhaus, demanding freedom of the press, abolition of the monarchy, freedom of science, and the resignation of Prince Metternich. Strauss wrote marches and polkas with revolutionary titles. Somewhat reluctantly, he joined the National Guard; but later, following his political sympathies, he took his band to the barricades, where he played the "Revolution March" and the "Marsaillaise." See Wechsberg, *Waltz Emperors*, 101.

43. In 1938 the Nazis forbade all activities related to Strauss when doubts arose about his Aryan descent (his great-great-grandfather was a Jew). However, later, Joseph Goebbels's *Reichssippenamt*, the government agency entrusted with the investigation of blood lines, confiscated "incriminating" papers and forged papers alleging Strauss's Aryan blood. Now Strauss's music was officially recognized and could be broadcast all over the Third Reich. The Strauss Society was revived in 1945. See Hans Fantel, "Empire of Dreams," *Opera News* 52, no. 8 (January 1988): 12.

44. "The Great Waltz," *Fox West Coast Bulletin*, 5 November 1938.

45. Although Strauss's debut as conductor and composer at Dommayer's Casino on 15 May 1844 was a great success, it was Strauss, Sr., who, until his death in 1849, held the edge as Vienna's most popular waltz composer. During the 1848 insurrection, Strauss the elder composed music for the Loyalist cause and his son composed for the insurgency.

46. *Ewiger Waltz* (1954) was released in America in 1959 under the title *The Eternal Waltz*. It was directed by Paul Verhoeven (no relation to the director of *Total Recall* and *Robocop*). Bernard Wicki portrays Strauss, Jr. The action includes relationships with

Olga Smirnitzki, a Russian woman, and his marriage to three singers, Henriette Treffz, Maria Geistinger, and a woman named Adele. The film is notable for its extravagant sequence depicting a musical "duel" between Strauss and Offenbach (Arnulf Schroeder).

47. Strauss, Jr., made his debut as conductor and composer at Dommayer's Casino on 15 May 1844 to a welcoming crowed.

48. "Blue Danube" was written in 1867 for the Vienna Men's Choral Society, when Vienna was recovering from defeat at the hands of Prussia the year before. In the hope that a new waltz might revive sagging spirits, Strauss seized upon a poem he had once heard that concluded with the lines "An der Donau, an der schönen, blauen Donau" (To the Danube, the beautiful, blue Danube). Although Strauss knew full well that the famous river was greenish-gray and sometimes silvery under the light of the moon, it was never blue. Amazingly, public enthusiasm had to wait for a later performance in Paris. By the time it premiered in London in September 1867, it was an international hit.

49. Franz Hoellering, "The Great Waltz," *The Nation,* 10 December 1938.

50. "The Great Waltz," *Stage,* December 1938.

51. A. Craig Bell, "The Great Mr. Handel," *Music Review* 39, no. 1 (February 1978): 29–30.

52. In *J. Arthur Rank and the British Film Industry,* McNab notes that as early as 1933, Rank "had been inspired by a mission to put religious pictures on the map" (51). To promote that aim, he established the GHW film unit in 1940.

53. Newman Flowers, *George Frideric Handel: His Personality and His Times* (New York: Charles Scribner's Sons, 1948), 270.

54. Bell, "Great Mr. Handel," 27.

55. Quoted in the program notes on the videocassette release of *The Great Mr. Handel* (available from the library of the British Film Institute).

56. " 'The Great Mr. Handel' a Thrill for the Discriminating," *Hollywood Reporter,* 16 June 1944.

57. Braudy, *Frenzy of Renown,* 403.

58. Jeffrey Pulver, *Paganini: The Romantic Virtuoso* (New York: Da Capo Press, 1970), 57.

59. Paganini himself mocked the allegations of demonic associations. In the *Revue Musicale* in 1831 he wrote a letter in which he described the origins of the legend in a concert he played in Vienna: "I played the variations entitled 'Le Streghe,' and they produced some effect. One individual . . . affirmed that he saw . . . while I was playing my variations, the devil at my elbow, directing my arm and guiding my bow. My resemblance to Him was a proof of my origin. He was clothed in red, had horns on his head, and carried his tail between his legs. After so minute a description you will understand . . . they had discovered the secret of what they termed wonderful feats." Quoted in Leslie Sheppard and Herbert R. Axelrod, *Paganini* (Neptune City, N.J.: Paganiniana Publications, 1979), 74.

60. G. I. C. De Courcy, *Paganini: The Genoese,* 2 vols. (Norman: University of Oklahoma Press, 1957), 1:ix.

61. Pressbook for *The Magic Bow,* Margaret Herrick Library, Academy of Motion Picture Arts and Sciences, Beverly Hills, Calif.

62. Jack D. Grant, "The Magic Bow," *Hollywood Reporter,* 13 March 1947.

63. "Cane," "The Magic Bow," *Daily Variety,* 25 September 1946.

64. Pressbook for *Song of Love,* USC Cinema-Television Library, Los Angeles, Calif.

65. Farber and Green, *Hollywood on the Couch,* 56.

66. Quoted in Farber and Green, *Hollywood on the Couch,* 240.

67. Among the many unsolved puzzles of music history, none has been more persistently baffling and hotly debated than the precise nature of the mental and physical illnesses that plagued Schumann and led to his breakdown and incarceration in a mental institution in Bonn-Endenich in 1854. For an overview of these issues, see John C. Tibbetts, "Robert Schumann's Illness," *American Record Guide* (September–October 1994): 41–42.

68. Kivy, *Possessor and the Possessed,* 73–75.

69. For example, Schumann wrote many piano, vocal, choral, and chamber works containing themes and expressions of childhood, ranging from piano pieces (*Album for the Young,* Opus 48) and songs for children (*Song Album for the Young,* Opus 79) to the more psychologically complex *Scenes from Childhood,* Opus 15, several sets of "Fairy Tales" for chamber combinations, and the *Pilgrimage of the Rose* for orchestra and choral ensemble.

70. MGM Production Files, folder no. 1, USC Cinema-Television Library, Los Angeles, Calif.

71. More candid, revisionist appraisals of the Schumann marriage, particularly Robert's opportunistic exploitation of Clara's pianism to promote his career, can be found in Nancy B. Reich's *Clara Schumann: The Artist and the Woman* (Ithaca, N.Y.: Cornell University Press, 1985) and Ostwald, *Schumann.* Among biopics, Peter Schamoni's *Spring Symphony* (1983) and Steve Ruggi's *Schumann's Lost Romance* (1996) speculate, respectively, that Robert's relentless selfish opportunism jeopardized Clara's concert career and that Clara actively endeavored to suppress some of Robert's last compositions.

72. Clara's biographer, Reich, acknowledges the possibility of passionate exchanges between Brahms and Clara during Robert's incarceration but discounts sexual union. See Reich, *Clara Schumann,* 169.

73. Even the suggestion of insanity in Schumann was enough to provoke four of Schumann's grandchildren to sue Loew's Inc. for $9 million on the grounds that the film was "libelous, invaded their right of privacy and misappropriated a property right." The suit was dismissed in 1954. MGM Production Files, folder no. 1, USC Cinema-Television Library, Los Angeles, Calif.

74. Harrowing accounts of Schumann's last days, based on newly discovered medical notes kept by his attending physician, Dr. Richarz, can be found in Judith Chernaik's " 'Guilt Alone Brings Forth Nemesis,' " *Times Literary Supplement,* 31 August 2001, 11–13; and two articles by Eric Frederick Jensen, both entitled "Buried Alive" (*Musical Times* 139, no. 1861 [March 1998]: 10–18; and *Musical Times* 139, no. 1862 [April 1998]: 14–23).

75. The strongest defense of these late works can be found throughout John Daverio's, *Robert Schumann: Herald of a 'New Poetic Age' "* (New York: Oxford University Press, 1997).

76. Quoted in the pressbook for *Song of Love,* USC Cinema-Television Library, Los Angeles, Calif.

77. Bosley Crowther, *New York Times*, clippings file, USC Cinema-Television Library, Los Angeles, *Calif.*

78. "Song to Remember," *Hollywood Reporter*, 21 July 1947.

79. Author interview with William K. Everson, New York City, 12 November 1980.

80. Rimsky-Korsakov, *My Musical Life*, 44–50.

81. The music featured so prominently in the film — *Scheherazade, Capriccio Italien* and the *Russian Easter Festival Overture* — was written much later than the time period of the film, during 1888–1889.

82. It is worth noting that themes from *Capriccio Espagnol* also appear throughout Josef von Sternberg's Marlene Dietrich vehicle, *The Devil Is a Woman*. The musical arranger is uncredited.

83. A concise description of Rimsky-Korsakov's musical and orchestral techniques can be found in Leon Plantinga, *Romantic Music* (New York: W.W. Norton and Company, 1984), 379–380.

84. Jack D. Grant, "Song of Scheherazade," *Hollywood Reporter*, 27 January 1947. Gene Ameels, *Motion Picture Daily*, clippings file, USC Cinema-Television Library, Los Angeles, Calif.

85. Joel Greenberg interview with Walter Reisch, *Song of Scheherazade* folder, Margaret Herrick Library, Academy of Motion Picture Arts and Sciences, Beverly Hills, Calif.

86. The film's chronology of the Gilbert and Sullivan works is accurate, although there are no references to *Patience, Princess Ida, Utopia (Limited)*, and *The Grand Duke*. For the record, it was not until the production of *Pinafore* that the team was known officially as "Gilbert and Sullivan."

87. In his recent *A Most Ingenious Paradox* (New York: Oxford University Press, 2001), Gayden Wren writes that although Gilbert and Sullivan learned to compromise with each other, "neither man was ever forced to yield his artistic intent because of financial considerations, censorship, opinions of the public, the producer or the performers, or any other reason. As a result, their works represent a purer manifestation of artistic purpose than practically any opera or play before or since" (25).

88. The character of Grace is probably modeled after Rachel Scott Russell, the daughter of a distinguished engineer. They became unofficially engaged. As the film suggests, she did indeed urge Sullivan to write "serious" works: "I want you to write an opera — a grand, vigorous great work. . . . I want you to write something for which all the world must acknowledge your talent."

89. Sullivan's desire to be a "serious" composer obsessed him all his life, particularly after he was knighted in 1883. Strongly influenced by the music of Felix Mendelssohn (another favorite of English royalty), Sullivan became the unofficial Composer Laureate and Master of the Queen's Music.

90. It is true that one bone of contention was Sullivan's dislike of Gilbert's melodramatically absurd techniques. "[Sullivan] wanted more serious operas, free of supernatural devices and implausible characters," writes Wren, what Sullivan called "'the elements of topsyturvydom and unreality'" (Wren, *Most Ingenious Paradox*, 163).

91. Geoffrey O'Brien, "Stompin' at the Savoy," *New York Review of Books*, 24 February 2000, 18.

92. See Jonathan Lieberson, "Bombing in Bayreuth," *New York Review of Books,* 10 November 1988, 30.

93. See Barry Millington, ed., *The Wagner Compendium* (London: Thames and Hudson, 1992), 98–99.

94. Quoted in Brendan G. Carroll, *The Last Prodigy: A Biography of Erich Wolfgang Korngold* (Portland, Ore.: Amadeus Press, 1997), 356.

95. In his biography of Liszt, Alan Walker declares that Liszt's objections to the affair between Cosima and Wagner were perhaps more *personal* than official. See Walker, *Franz Liszt: The Final Years, 1861–1886* (New York: Alfred A. Knopf, 1996).

96. For a concise overview of Republic Pictures studio, see Gene Fernett, *Hollywood's Poverty Row* (Satellite Beach, Fla.: Coral Reef Publications, 1973), 75–98.

97. Quoted in Carroll, *Last Prodigy,* 351.

98. Quoted in Carroll, *Last Prodigy,* 351.

99. Carroll, *Last Prodigy,* 354.

100. The most detailed extant treatment of Barton contains no mention of the film, although there is a full account of his career. See Frank T. Thompson, "Charles T. Barton," in Thompson, ed., *Between Action and Cut* (Metuchen, N.J.: Scarecrow Press, 1985), 183–216.

101. In *Song of My Heart,* Tchaikovsky's story is told in flashback by a Soviet official whose father had once been a friend of the composer: Disappointed in his love life with two women — a music student named Sophia Mirova and the Princess Amalya (a stand-in for Nadejda von Meck) — the composer goes to America, where he achieves a great success. He returns and contracts cholera. By the time Princess Amalya arrives at his bedside, he has died. The contemporary framing story contains a scene in which a Russian pianist plays the B-flat Minor Piano Concerto at precisely the moment that the Nazis invade Russia. Music is provided by Albert Coates and the Moscow Conservatory Orchestra.

102. For the record, this is the only Tchaikovsky biopic that alludes to his brief affair with Desiree Artot. In real life, Artot was a Belgian soprano to whom the young Tchaikovsky had considered proposing (he still harbored at this point in his life the conviction that his homosexuality was merely an abnormality that could be averted). The relationship came to nothing, and Artot married a Spanish singer instead. Biographer Anthony Holden insists Tchaikovsky was more interested in her as a musical ideal than as a romantic partner: "It is significant that so much of Tchaikovsky's praise was reserved for the professional rather than the private Artot." See Holden, *Tchaikovsky: A Biography* (New York: Random House, 1997), 66–69.

103. Much ink has been spilled over the identity of the "immortal beloved." Contenders include Giulietta Guicciardi, Dorothea Ertmann, Elise von der Recke, Princess Marie Lichtenstein, and Antonie Brentano. Maynard Solomon's landmark 1977 biography (*Beethoven* [New York: Schirmer Books, 1977], 170–182) asserted convincingly that the woman was Brentano, a married friend of the composer. "The weight of the evidence in her favor is so powerful," writes Solomon, "that it is not presumptuous to assert that the riddle of Beethoven's Immortal Beloved has now been solved." (170). Beethoven did not marry her, concludes Solomon, because of his own "deeply rooted inability to marry" and because he was anguished at betraying his friend Franz Brentano.

However, in a closely argued article, Virginia Oakley Beahrs disputes Solomon's case and claims that Josephine von Deym is the woman. See Beahrs, "Beethoven's *Only* Beloved? New Perspectives on the Love Story of the Great Composer," *Music Review* 54, nos. 3–4 (August–November 1993): 183–197.

104. This transcendence is effectively suggested in the famous "Heiligenstadt mill" sequence, wherein the soundtrack is manipulated to reproduce Beethoven's oncoming deafness. As the outer, natural sounds of the mill, the villagers, and the woodlands cease in his ears, they are replaced by interior, artistic correlatives, the inner, musical tones of the "Pastoral" Symphony. The sequence's sound-image counterpoint was a technical tour de force for its time. Beethoven purists objected that the film was more about filmmaker Gance than composer Beethoven. Gance was as formidable a figure in the cinema as Beethoven had been in music, and he had a comparable ego. He had no compunction about using Beethoven as a vehicle for his own autobiographical psychodrama, a testament to his own sufferings, losses, and triumphs. See James M. Welsh and Steven Kramaer, "Gance's Beethoven," *Sight and Sound* 45, no. 2 (Spring 1976): 109–111.

105. Morrissey's *Beethoven's Nephew* presents a Beethoven for the sexually ambivalent 1980s, an artist (Wolfgang Reichmann) who is an impotent, emotionally spent neurotic who has turned his back entirely on women and art and broods jealously over nephew Karl's love life. "He means more to me than my music," he declares, while lecturing Karl on the horrors of syphilis, spying on him through a telescope, and interfering with his clandestine liaisons with both men and women. Even during the premiere of his Ninth Symphony, Beethoven bolts from the podium in outrage after observing Karl's arrival with a "questionable" female companion. Thus, significantly, it is not his deafness that is identified as Beethoven's primary affliction, but his jealous nature. One character sums up the prevailing tone of the movie quite succinctly: "Nobody loves anybody in just a normal way."

Immortal Beloved brings on all the clichés of bodice-ripping romance novels, positioning the composer "between the passion and the pain, the madness and the music," according to the film's advertisements. Its fractured, flashback-riddled narrative presents everything condoned by the relatively censor-free, tabloid-fraught 1990s — child-custody wrangles, family mysteries, incestuous revelations, and lots of heartbeats on the soundtrack. Bringing his bad boy machismo with him (not to mention a real-life affair with his costar, Isabella Rossellini), actor Gary Oldman lustily wenches and carouses with a succession of beautiful women — Giulietta Guicciardi (Valeria Golino), Countess Anna Maria Erdody (Rossellini), the Brunsvik sisters (Geno Lechner and Claudia Solti), and his sister-in-law, Johanna van Beethoven (Johanna Ter Steege), who is identified as the "immortal beloved." Chameleonlike, this Beethoven is that ideal of the contemporary pop scene, a man for all seasons. At different times, he is alternately a youth fleeing from his abusive father, a drunken wreck lying sprawled in the gutter, and an introspective artist tenderly laying his head on the piano. In a frenzy of carnal lust, Beethoven disrobes a young woman in a country lane, and in an ecstasy of solitary epiphany, he floats supine on the waters of a lake, lost in the starry reflections of the night sky.

For more details on these films, see John C. Tibbetts, "They Oughta Be in Pictures," *American Record Guide* 58, no. 3 (May–June 1995): 6–10.

106. Biographer Leonard Moseley contends that it was Leopold Stokowski who

convinced Disney to make a feature-length animation film, adding music by Bach, Stravinsky, Beethoven, and others to the "Sorcerer's Apprentice" sequence with Mickey Mouse. "Stokowski was in his element," writes Moseley. "He even began to relax about the linking of his name with Mickey Mouse and finally consented to a shot of Mickey shaking his hand at the conclusion of a musical number. But only in silhouette. 'A fabulous little fellow,' he was quoted as saying about Mickey later." See Moseley, *Disney's World* (New York: Stein and Day, 1985), 175.

107. Kansas psychiatrist Karl Menninger has commented on the obsessive urge of Midwesterners like Disney to tidy up their lives. "What is really the nature of the soil? Is it the dirt? Is civilization largely built on overcoming it, or built up on the taboo of dirt, overcoming a natural affection for it?" See Bernard H. Hall, *A Psychiatrist's World: The Selected Letters of Karl Menninger* (New York: Viking Press, 1949), 37.

108. *Fantasia* followed on the heels of other cartoons, notably "The Band Concert," in which Disney attempted to popularize classical music. In that 1935 cartoon Mickey Mouse conducted a program of Rossini to a barnyard audience of animals. *From Mouse to Mermaid: The Politics of Film, Gender, and Culture* (Indianapolis: Indiana University Press, 1995), 8.

109. Walker, *Franz Liszt: The Virtuoso Years*, 3. Walker, who spent almost thirty years researching and writing his three-volume "Life," declared in an interview: "Liszt staged his own life almost as if he were presenting a three-act drama. Reporting the facts of his life is like reading a novel: You have to rub your eyes occasionally and wonder, Did this really happen? Could it have been possible? And usually with Liszt, it was! If anything, you have to suppress interest, lest you be accused of inventing things!" For overviews of my interviews with Walker—in New York City, 2 August 1989, and in Hamilton, Ontario, 25 October 1994—see Tibbetts, "Probing the Liszt Legend," *Christian Science Monitor*, 14 September 1989, 10–11, and Tibbetts, "Mephistopheles as Curate," *The World and I* (September 1996): 285–289.

110. For an overview of these varying portraits, see Tibbetts, "Franz Liszt on Film," 209–222.

111. Karl Storck, trans. and ed., *The Letters of Robert Schumann* (London: John Murray, 1907), 225.

112. Quoted in Suttoni, *Artist's Journey*, 13.

113. Saul Ostrove, "Song without End," *Variety*, 22 June 1960.

114. James Powers, "Song without End," *Hollywood Reporter*, 22 June 1960.

115. For a full account of the artistic aspects of Liszt's relationship with Countess d'Agoult, see Suttoni, *Artist's Journey*.

116. Walker concludes: "The marriage between Liszt and Carolyne did not take place because Carolyne herself lost heart." Arrayed against her were intrigues from members of the church and her own family, which Carolyne feared would hound her into perpetuity. "The burden simply became too much for the Princess to bear. Thereafter she had many opportunities to marry Liszt. . . . [Even after her husband Nicholas died] their marriage plans were never revived. . . . Liszt himself corroborates the idea that it was a mutual decision." See Alan Walker, *Liszt, Carolyne, and the Vatican: The Story of a Thwarted Marriage*, American Liszt Society Studies Series No. 1 (Stuyvesant, N.Y.: Pendragon Press, 1991), 17.

117. For a detailed account of Liszt's taking of the Lower Orders of the priesthood, and his subsequent life divided between churchly and secular matters, see Walker, *Franz Liszt: The Final Years,* 54–94.

118. *Song without End* production file, Special Collections, Margaret Herrick Library, Academy of Motion Picture Arts and Sciences, Beverly Hills, Calif.

119. Author interview with Kevin Brownlow, London, 22 October 2003. See also James Curran and Vincent Porter, eds., *British Cinema History* (Totowa, N.J.: Barnes and Noble Books, 1983), 144–163; and Ernest Betts, *The Film Business: A History of British Cinema, 1896–1972* (London: Allen and Unwin, 1973), 142–153.

120. In particular, see two books by Gregory D. Black, *Hollywood Censored* (New York: Cambridge University Press, 1994) and *The Catholic Crusade against the Movies, 1940–1975* (New York: Cambridge University Press, 1998).

121. Black, *Hollywood Censored,* 1.

122. Richard Maltby, " 'A Brief Romantic Interlude': Dick and Jane Go to 3 ½ Seconds of the Classical Cinema," in David Bordwell and Noel Carroll, eds., *Post-Theory: Reconstructing Film Studies* (Madison: University of Wisconsin Press, 1996), 438–446.

123. *Song of Scheherazade* production file, Special Collections, Margaret Herrick Library, Academy of Motion Picture Arts and Sciences, Beverly Hills, Calif.

124. *The Great Waltz* production file, Special Collections, Margaret Herrick Library, Academy of Motion Picture Arts and Sciences, Beverly Hills, Calif.

125. See *The American Film Institute Catalogue of American Motion Pictures, 1931–1940* (Berkeley: University of California Press, 1993).

126. *Song of Love* production file, Special Collections, Margaret Herrick Library, Academy of Motion Picture Arts and Sciences, Beverly Hills, Calif.

127. *Song of Scheherazade* production file, Special Collections, Margaret Herrick Library, Academy of Motion Picture Arts and Sciences, Beverly Hills, Calif.

Chapter Two: A Song Remembered

1. Unless otherwise noted, all studio publicity citations in this chapter are taken from the *A Song to Remember* pressbook, USC Cinema-Television Library, Los Angeles, Calif.

2. Sherwin Kane, "A Song to Remember," *Motion Picture Daily,* 18 January 1945.

3. Herbert Weinstock, *Chopin: The Man and His Music* (New York: Alfred A. Knopf, 1949), 266.

4. "A Song to Remember," *Hollywood Reporter,* 18 January 1945. The writer was probably referring to the following foreign imports—Abel Gance's *Un grand amour de Beethoven,* which had reached American screens in 1939; a British import about Franz Schubert, *Blossom Time* (1936), starring Richard Tauber; and another British import, *The Great Mr. Handel* (1942), starring Wilfrid Lawson. The critic is incorrect, however, in referring to *A Song to Remember* as "the first venture in this field by American film makers." MGM's big-budget *The Great Waltz,* starring Fernand Gravet as Johann Strauss, Jr., was released in 1938, and several Stephen Foster films had appeared in the 1930s, including *Harmony Lane* (1934) and *Swanee River* (1939), with Douglass Montgomery and Don Ameche, respectively, as Foster.

5. "A Song to Remember," *Variety,* 18 January 1945.

6. "A Song to Remember," *Film Daily,* 18 January 1945.

7. This scene is invariably cited with mingled affection and derision in many of the interviews I undertook for this book with many musicians and film historians.

8. Otis L. Guernsey, Jr., "A Song to Remember," *New York Herald Tribune,* 26 January 1945.

9. T.M.P., "A Song to Remember," *New York Times,* 26 January 1945.

10. Historian Joseph McBride notes the film's rentals through 1985 were $7,430,468 against the original negative cost of $1,607,953. See McBride, *Frank Capra: The Catastrophe of Success* (New York: Simon and Schuster, 1992), 379, fn.

11. See note 5 to the Introduction.

12. In a letter to me, dated 27 February 2004, Columbia Pictures historian Karl Thiede notes: "My Columbia records have a few holes in them and *A Song to Remember* is one of them. Moreover, there is no mention of the film in the *Variety* Anniversary Issue." Archivist Ned Comstock of the USC Cinema-Television Library in Los Angeles confirms that many of Columbia's production records have disappeared.

13. Benita Eisler, *Chopin's Funeral* (New York: Alfred A. Knopf, 2003), 200.

14. Arthur Hedley, "Chopin the Man," in Alan Walker, ed., *Frédéric Chopin: Profiles of the Man and the Musician* (New York: Taplinger Publishing Company, 1967), 2.

15. Jeffrey Kallberg, *Chopin at the Boundaries: Sex, History, and Musical Genre* (Cambridge: Harvard University Press, 1996), iv.

16. In *Lucrezia Floriani,* George Sand depicts "Prince Karol" as something of a monster, an absurdly aloof individual, out of touch with the facts of life, and disdainful, even intolerant, of the imperfections of others. "So accustomed to their own idealistic realm," writes William G. Atwood in his study of the Chopin-Sand relationship—*The Lioness and the Little One* (New York: Columbia University Press, 1980)—"both Karol and Chopin looked down on the less perfect world of everyday life with a certain condescension. To accept or adjust to its imperfections implied a compromise which the two men scorned" (205). Although Sand denied Karol was a disguised—and distorted—portrait of Chopin, no one was fooled. Chopin's friends, the painter Eugene Delacroix and the poet Heinrich Heine, were particularly appalled. "[Sand] has shamefully mistreated my poor friend Chopin in a detestable novel," said Heine. And Franz Liszt dismissed it as a "vulgarity" (209).

17. Pianist Alfred Cortot quoted these passages in his "appreciation" of Chopin, *In Search of Chopin* (New York: Abelard Press, 1952), 8. For a detailed examination of Liszt's book, see Edward N. Waters, "Chopin by Liszt," *Music Quarterly* 47, no. 2 (April 1961): 170–194.

18. Cortot, *In Search of Chopin,* 216–217.

19. Biographer Tad Szulc notes that "Chopin always discouraged relating his musical works to particular events in his life and refused to give actual titles to his compositions (he was furious when his English publisher attempted to do so)." Szulc, *Chopin in Paris,* 43.

20. In *Chopin: The Man and His Music,* biographer Herbert Weinstock claims that the song "Cheek to Cheek" also utilized the polonaise theme. Presumably, he is referring to the song Irving Berlin wrote for the Fred Astaire–Ginger Rogers vehicle *Top Hat* (1935). The similarity is, to the present writer, too tenuous to take seriously (166).

21. "Musical Moments from Chopin" was the first of Walter Lantz's "Musical Minia-

tures" cartoon series. Andy Panda's serious-minded performance of the polonaise is interrupted by the irreverent antics of Woody Woodpecker. See Joe Adamson, *The Walter Lantz Story* (New York: G. P. Putnam's Sons, 1985), 157–158.

22. The morbid and sickly qualities felt to be present in Chopin's music were exploited in MGM's *A Picture of Dorian Gray*. Although this adaptation had nothing to do with Chopin, its music track, adapted by Herbert Stothart, prominently featured Chopin's Twenty-Fourth Prelude (erroneously billed as "Les Preludes") as the musical emblem of Gray's spiritual and physical deterioration. Periodically heard throughout the film, both diegetically in performance and extradiegetically on the soundtrack, its surging minor tonalities consistently connoted Gray's descent into immorality, murder, and self-loathing.

23. In *Frank Capra*, McBride claims that Capra himself worked on the screenplay (360). An entry in the *American Film Institute Catalogue of Feature Films, 1941–1950* (Berkeley: University of California Press, 1999) quotes a letter from the Screen Writers Guild that "the story was derived from a French picture about Frédéric Chopin that was screened years earlier in Europe but never released in the United States" (2274). It is not certain if that film, erroneously cited as *La Valse* (*Valse de l'adieu*), is indeed that source. It is doubtful, however, because a viewing of the picture confirms that the story is more concerned with Chopin's ill-fated romance with Maria Wodzinska than with Sand, who remains a peripheral character.

24. Out of the endless list of such "borrowings" from other composers besides Chopin, a few notable examples from the thirties and forties include Ray Austin's "Tonight We Love," a pop arrangement for bandleader Freddie Martin of the opening theme from Tchaikovsky's First Piano Concerto; Sigmund Romberg's "Song of Love," a transformation of the first theme from Schubert's Eighth Symphony; and Peter DeRose's "The Lamp Is Low," an adaptation of Ravel's *Pavane pour une Infante Defunte*. See Julius Mattfeld, *Variety Music Cavalcade: Musical-Historical Review, 1620–1961* (Englewood Cliffs, N.J.: Prentice-Hall, 1962).

25. Quoted in Atwood, *Lioness and the Little One*, 46.

26. Curtis Cate's *George Sand: A Biography* (Boston: Houghton Mifflin Company, 1975) speculates that a sexual union between Chopin and Sand was probably limited to just one or two years. The quotation is on p. 486.

27. Sand comes off as something of a monster in Benita Eisler's book, *Chopin's Funeral*. Near the end of their relationship Sand was purportedly behaving very badly toward Chopin. Not only did she write a book, *Lucrezia Floriana*, which contained a thinly disguised dissection of her affair with him, but she took on another lover, the sculptor Jean-Baptiste Auguste Clésinger, who soon seduced and married her daughter, Solange. When that misbegotten union went awry, Chopin refused Sand's orders to break off communications with Solange, with whom he had enjoyed a close and sympathetic relationship. Sand countered viciously and implied Chopin was in love with her daughter. Eisler reports that Chopin had proved to be a better parent to Sand's children than Sand herself had been: "He had exposed Sand's image of herself as the perfect mother for a delusion. . . . This was Chopin's unforgivable sin: his knowledge that she had failed her child, a failure from which all of her own miseries flowed" (166–170). In later years Sand described Chopin as a hopeless neurotic with whom she had had only a chaste relationship.

Yet, asserts commentator Angelina Goreau, it was Sand who enabled Chopin to write music for as long as he did. "The attraction that held them together may be explained by the voracious appetite for work they shared. Chopin never wrote so well as when he lived with Sand at Nohant, he worrying the piano all day while she scribbled at night. And in the end, we have the extraordinary body of music, and the novels that tell us what it was like to be a woman in Sand's time. So who is to say it was all a terrible mistake?" See Goreau, "Whatever George Sand Wants . . ." *New York Times Book Review,* 20 April 2003, 29.

28. For a generally more favorable interpretation of Sand's role in the affair with Chopin, see Atwood, *Lioness and the Little One.*

29. Emphasis added in "One must first be a great man and a decent man." As has been indicated, this advice from Breen was not followed. The film's concluding scene has Sand rejecting Elsner's offer to come to the dying composer.

30. A perusal of the production records of *Swanee River,* dating from 31 May to 11 August 1939, reveals the lengths studio chief Darryl F. Zanuck went to rework Stephen Foster's rather colorless personality and uneventful life into a more masculine, activist figure. *Swanee River* file, USC Cinema-Television Library, Los Angeles, Calif.

31. For a concise overview of Sand's political activities, see David Coward, "Liberated Women," *New York Review of Books,* 26 April 2001, 28–31.

32. Mary Ann Doane, *The Desire to Desire: The Woman's Film of the 1940s* (Bloomington: Indiana University Press, 1987), 4.

33. Doane, *Desire to Desire,* 19.

34. Kallberg's *Chopin at the Boundaries* examines the gender implications in Chopin's music, especially the nocturnes. In Chopin's lifetime, and beyond, the nocturnes' filigree detail, sentimental associations, and favor at the hands of female pianists and composers encouraged a presumed "feminine" identity in the music's construction and in its affective properties. "The nocturne was routinely characterized as usually given to a gentle and quiet rapture," explains Kallberg. "Indeed, given the prevailing attitude of the time in which affiliation with women and with effeminacy usually led to a lesser ranking in the aesthetic hierarchy, it would have been odd if the nocturne had escaped unscathed. This grew 'to an almost obsessive preoccupation of writers in the second half of the nineteenth century' who 'obsessively disparaged music that they associated with femininity and effeminacy" (41–42).

35. The films *Humoresque* and *Leave Her to Heaven* present female characters who bear significant resemblances to Sand in *A Song to Remember.* In the first, Joan Crawford is a wealthy patroness of the arts who supports a young musician (John Garfield). Cornel Wilde reappears in *Leave Her to Heaven,* where he comes under the thrall of Gene Tierney, a woman so enamored of him that she finally commits suicide in order to block his love for another woman.

36. Marjorie Rosen, *Popcorn Venus: Women, Movies, and the American Dream* (New York: Coward, McCann and Geoghegan, 1973), 224–225.

37. Konstancia Gladkowska was not a firebrand Polish patriot, as alleged in the film, but a talented singer whom Chopin met in Warsaw in 1829. There is no evidence that they ever enjoyed a romantic relationship.

38. In *Chopin's Funeral,* Eisler claims that Chopin never really wanted to return to

Poland, even after amnesty was granted in 1833 to Polish exiles; that he did not support his family financially during his peak earning years; and that "he was indifferent to politics." Eisler continues: "The conservative loyalties of his family, pious Catholics and servants of the ruling class, and his own rejection of any forms of adolescent rebellion suggest that his apolitical stance was a way of remaining loyal to radical friends while accepting authority whatever its source—his parents, St. Petersburg, Rome, or the local Russian garrison" (31).

39. Szulc, *Chopin in Paris,* 21. The étude was actually completed in Paris late in 1821 or 1832 and published in 1833.

40. The issue is musicologically complicated and technically beyond the scope of this article. In general, according to pianist and Chopin specialist Garrick Ohlsson, "the Polonaises began providing the framework to express depths of personal feeling deeply rooted in his distant, unhappy homeland." See John C. Tibbetts, "Ohlsson Takes on Chopin," *The World and I* 7, no. 12 (December 1992): 162–168.

41. Rozsa and director King Vidor also lavished considerable ingenuity on the film's performance sequences, foregrounding the musical selections in their original piano versions, albeit truncating their length. Chopin's first performance of the *Fantasie Impromptu* at the Wodzinska palace transpires during an elaborately staged dining scene, the shimmering music intercut with shots of a parade of waiters and the annoying chattering of disinterested guests. The meeting with Liszt is staged as a delightful two-piano duet as each plays the polonaise with one hand while shaking hands with the other. Later, at Sand's salon, the lights dim as Liszt seats himself at the keyboard and launches into the dramatic declamations of Chopin's second scherzo. Midway through the piece—Rozsa cleverly abridges the work to half its length—Sand strides through the darkened room, a candelabrum held aloft, and pauses at the piano. The candlelight reveals the performer to be—Chopin himself!

42. Variety; "A Song to Remember," *Film Daily,* 18 January 1945.

43. Custen, *Bio/Pic,* 69.

44. Clayton R. Koppes and Gregory D. Black, "What to Show the World: The Office of War Information and Hollywood, 1942–1945," *Journal of American History* 64, no. 1 (June 1977): 91.

45. Gregory D. Black and Clayton R. Koppes, "OWI Goes to the Movies: The Bureau of Intelligence's Criticism of Hollywood, 1942–43," *Prologue* (Spring 1974): 44–59.

46. Thomas Schatz, *Boom and Bust: Hollywood in the 1940s* (New York: Charles Scribners' Sons, 1997), 204.

47. Useful accounts of the making and reception of *Casablanca* are Howard Koch, *Casablanca: Script and Legend* (Woodstock, N.Y.: Overlook Press, 1992), and Rudy Behlmer, *Behind the Scenes* (Hollywood, Calif.: Samuel French, 1990), 154–176.

48. For an overview of World War II Hollywood films that sympathetically depicted the Soviet struggle, see Robert Fyne, *The Hollywood Propaganda of World War II* (Lanham, Md.: Garland, 1997), 102–113.

49. Rochelle Larkin, *Hail Columbia* (New Rochelle, N.Y.: Arlington House, 1975), 182.

50. McBride, *Frank Capra,* 360–361.

51. Edward Buscombe, "Notes on Columbia Pictures Corporation 1926–41," in Janet

Staiger, ed., *The Studio System* (New Brunswick, N.J.: Rutgets University Press), 30. As an admitted member of the Communist Party from 1938–1945, Buchman refused to name names before HUAC and was subsequently fined and blacklisted. Buscombe points out that half of the Hollywood Ten were employed at Columbia during the 1930s.

52. When Chopin launched his conquest of Paris in the autumn of 1831, he did indeed become involved with the Countess Delfina Potocka, a beautiful and gifted singer and a rather notorious character (she numbered among her lovers the Duke d'Orleans and the Count de Flahault). She and Chopin enjoyed a lifelong relationship, and he dedicated to her his Second Piano Concerto and his D-flat Waltz. See Adam Zamoyski, *Chopin* (Garden City, N.Y.: Doubleday and Company, 1980), 114.

53. In October 1961 a group of linguists and musicologists convened at the Nieborow Conference to examine the letters. The conclusion was that "there was some psychopathic identification of herself with Chopin, which led her to write 'letters' and to put into those letters her own thoughts and imaginings" (quoted in Hedley, "Chopin the Man," 386). In rebuttal, biographer Harasowski published a number of the texts in 1973 in *Music and Musicians* and claimed that 6 of the 118 letters were authentic, while the others — those with the "heavily obscene texts" — were spurious.

54. Kallberg, *Chopin at the Boundaries,* ix–x.

55. Author interview with Ken Russell, 13 June 2003, East Boldre, Brockenhurst, England.

Chapter Three: The New Tin Pan Alley

I would like to thank Frank T. Thompson of Burbank, Calif., for his invaluable assistance in the research and writing of this chapter.

1. Quoted in Fred Andersen, "My God, What an Act to Follow!" *American Heritage* (July–August 1997): 74.

2. See Braudy, *Frenzy of Renown,* 15.

3. Edward Pessen, "The Great Songwriters of Tin Pan Alley's Golden Age: A Social, Occupational, and Aesthetic Inquiry," *American Music* 3, no. 2 (Summer 1985): 193–195.

4. For the record, *Yankee Doodle Dandy:* Despite Cohan's persistent assertions to the contrary, his birth certificate states that he was born on 3 July 1878.

Swanee River: It is doubtful that Foster ever met Christy. Moreover, while actor Ameche might sing beautifully in public, composer Foster's almost terminal shyness prohibited him from such displays. See Ken Emerson, *Doo-Dah! Stephen Foster and the Rise of American Popular Culture* (New York: Simon and Schuster, 1997), 102.

Stars and Stripes Forever: The title song was written in 1896, before the outbreak of the Spanish American War. Sousa himself claimed he wrote it after receiving the news of the death of his manager. See Paul E. Bierley, *The Works of John Philip Sousa* (Columbus, Ohio: Integrity Press, 1984), 85.

Till the Clouds Roll By: Kern's teacher, one "James Hessler," has no basis in fact. *The New Yorker* critic at the time dismissed this fiction sarcastically: "Maybe Guy Bolton, who cooked up the story on which the film is based, confused Hessler with Marie Dressler, for whom Kern was once accompanist, but it doesn't seem likely." "Well, the Songs Are Good," *The New Yorker,* 14 December 1946, 88.

Words and Music: As this chapter later demonstrates, Judy Garland would have been only thirteen at the time of the alleged incident with Hart.

Night and Day: Biographer Charles Schwartz asserts that although little is known about Porter's wartime activities in France, it is probable that he never served in the U.S. Army or the French Foreign Legion, as he alleged, nor did he sustain any war-related injuries. See Schwartz, *Cole Porter,* 45–48.

Three Little Words: The improbable allegations that Kalmar and Ruby preferred careers in magic and baseball to songwriting have at least a basis in fact. Indeed, in 1931 Ruby played an exhibition baseball game with the Washington Senators. In an interview with historian Max Wilk, Ruby recalls: "Of course, everybody knows about us, the two songwriters who always wanted to be something else. When Jack Cummings decided to make our story into a movie, he went into Louis B. Mayer and he said, 'This is gonna be a good musical, because for once we're gonna do a story about songwriters that has a *story!*' And when Mayer asked him what story he had in mind, he said, 'It's a natural — two successful songwriters. One schmuck wants to be a magician and pull rabbits out of a hat; the other one would rather play professional baseball than eat!' " See Wilk, *They're Playing Our Song* (New York: Atheneum, 1973), 31.

Alexander's Ragtime Band: Ragtime had peaked and waned as a national craze long before 1915. As for its introduction to the general public, Edward A. Berlin reports in his biography of Scott Joplin that ragtime "surfaced from its incipient stages in black communities and became known to the wider American public" during the World's Columbian Exposition in Chicago in 1893. See Berlin, *King of Ragtime: Scott Joplin and His Era* (New York: Oxford University Press, 1994), 11–12.

5. Songs attributed to the fictitious "Harrigan and Calhoun" include "K-K-K-Katie," composed by Geoffrey O'Hara in 1918; "America I Love You," by Edgar Leslie and Archie Gottler in 1915; and "Good-Bye Broadway, Hello France!" by Francis Reisner and Billy Baskette in 1917.

6. Jasen, *Tin Pan Alley,* 1–28.

7. Charles Hamm, *Yesterdays: Popular Song in America* (New York: W. W. Norton and Company, 1979), 286.

8. Recent waves of immigration from Eastern Europe had brought a majority of the Jewish emigrants to New York City. It has been estimated that at this time only 36 percent of the city's population was native born, while blacks accounted for sixty thousand and Jews approximately one million. See Hamm, *Music in the New World,* 340–341; and Hamm, *Irving Berlin,* v–x.

9. Neal Gabler, *An Empire of Their Own: How the Jews Invented Hollywood* (New York: Crown Publishers, 1988), 5–6.

10. For a discussion of the influences of European "classical" music and musicians on American musical life, see Alan Howard Levy, "The Search for Identity in American Music, 1890–1920," *American Music* 2, no. 2 (Summer 1984): 70–81.

11. In a remarkably prescient written statement published during his New York sojourn, Dvořák defined what he called "the music of the people" as deriving from "all the

races that are commingled in this great country" — i.e., "the Negro melodies, the songs of the creoles, the red man's chant, the plaintive ditties of the German or Norwegian . . . the melodies of whistling boys, street singers and blind organ grinders." To our modern ears, he seems to have anticipated the rise of the ragtime song and the work of the Tin Pan Alley songwriters. See Antonín Dvořák (assisted by Edwin E. Emerson, Jr.), "Music in America," *Harper's New Monthly Magazine* 90, no. 537 (February 1895): 433. For the full text of this and his other newspaper articles, see Tibbetts, *Dvořák in America* (Portland, Ore.: Amadeus Press, 1993), 355–384. For a discussion of Dvořák's pronouncements, see Tibbetts, "Conference Report: The New Orleans Dvořák Sesquicentennial," *The Sonneck Society Bulletin* 17, no. 3 (Fall 1991): 100–102.

12. The Dvořák "Largo" was transformed into a popular song by William Arms Fisher in 1922 under the title "Goin' Home." Deanna Durbin sang it in *It Started with Eve* (Universal, 1941). The musical "adaptation" of the Dvořák "Largo" in *A Song Is Born* was written by lyricist Don Raye and composer Gene DePaul. The cue sheets from the Goldwyn archives list the entire number as "Long Hair Jam Session Production Routin."

13. Gabbard, *Jammin' at the Margins*, 118–119. Emphasis added.

14. The decade of the 1940s was a period of gloriously bizarre yet clever juxtapositions of pop and classical forms. Even Tex Ritter got into the act: In *Ridin' the Cherokee Trail* (1942), Ritter has a musical "duel" with the villain of the story. When Ritter's adversary, a stuffy fellow who plays the "Moonlight Sonata," scoffs at his western singing, and condemns it as "yodelin' trash," Ritter responds with his own "country-western" versions of "La Donna e mobile" and "March of the Toreadors." To the first, he warbles lyrics about "Old Bandit Pete," and to the second, a variant called "Pete the Bandit." Each rendition is accompanied by appropriate yodels!

15. For a detailed discussion of the influence of *The Jazz Singer* paradigm's influence on popular music films, see Gabbard, *Jammin' at the Margins*, 14–19, 76–100.

16. John Mundy, *Popular Music on Screen: From Hollywood Musical to Music Video* (Manchester: University Press, 1999), 47.

17. George F. Custen, *Twentieth Century's Fox: Darryl F. Zanuck and the Culture of Hollywood* (New York: Basic Books, 1997), 188.

18. Custen, *Bio/Pic*, 78.

19. Custen, *Bio/Pic*, 19.

20. Custen, *Bio/Pic*, 134.

21. Fletcher Hodges, Jr., "Swanee River," *Foster Hall Bulletin*, 4 July 1940, 21.

22. I am grateful to Dr. Deane Root, curator of the Stephen Collins Foster Memorial, for the text of his "Family, Myth, and the Historical Sources: Why We Don't Know the Truth about Stephen Foster," a paper delivered at the American Music at Illinois Conference in Urbana, 29 September 1990. For information about the Stephen Collins Foster Memorial at the University of Pittsburgh, dedicated in June 1937 — the only such memorial to a single American composer — see Tibbetts, "In Search of Stephen Foster," 253–259.

23. Emerson, *Doo Dah!*, 313. See also John Tasker Howard, *Stephen Foster: America's Troubadour* (New York: Thomas Y. Crowell, 1934); and Hamm, *Yesterdays*, 201–227.

24. Herbert J. Yates's Republic Pictures managed to release several "prestige" efforts in between its run of John Wayne and Roy Rogers westerns, including Orson Welles's

Macbeth (1948) and John Ford's *The Quiet Man* (1952). Two more biopics were a Foster remake, *I Dream of Jeanie* (1952), and a Richard Wagner biopic, *Magic Fire* (1954), which is discussed in Chapter Two.

25. *I Dream of Jeanie*, directed by Allan Dwan and starring Bill Shirley as Foster, is a bizarre entry in the series of Foster biopics. It is a more expensively mounted affair than the 1935 version, and it features some elaborately realized blackface minstrel sequences. Foster is still essentially a Schubertian figure, a relatively untutored fellow who possesses musical instincts: "All my life I've heard music in every kind of sound there is," he says, "even in things like squeaky wheels and faucets dripping." Astonishingly, the film ends on a happy note, as Foster reunites with his beloved "Jeanie" and they sail off into the sunset on a steamboat. His later tragic years and demise are entirely omitted. The film's portrait of Foster as an inept, confused, spineless fellow bears out the wisdom of Zanuck's insistence at investing him with "more punch." The critic for the *Hollywood Reporter* agreed in a 5 June 1952 review: "Foster, as portrayed by Bill Shirley, is presented as a befuddled, not very bright young man, with no head for money-making and not much confidence in his music."

26. See Tibbetts, "In Search of Stephen Foster," 253–259.

27. Unless otherwise noted, all quotations from Zanuck in this chapter come from the *Swanee River* file, USC Cinema-Television Library, Los Angeles, Calif.

28. Hodges, "Swanee River," 5.

29. Author interview with Dean Root, Stephen Foster Memorial, University of Pittsburgh, 6 May 1991.

30. Out of loyalty to his family's pro-slavery views, declares Root, "[Foster] never wrote or set lyrics that openly opposed the Democrats' political views. . . . But for the minstrel songs, both comic and tragic, he gradually worked away from the derogatory lyrics so widely associated with the blackface troupes" (Dean Root, "Family, Myth, and the Historical Sources," 11).

31. Root, "Family, Myth, and the Historical Sources," 15.

32. Oddly, although the tune of "Jeanie with the Light Brown Hair" is heard extradiegetically on the soundtrack of *Swanee River,* it is never sung or performed in a full-scale rendition. There has been some dispute as to whether "Jeanie," written in 1854, was a tribute to Foster's wife, Jane Denny McDowell (nicknamed "Jennie"). For a discussion of the issue, see William W. Austin, *Susanna, Jeanie, and the Old Folks at Home: The Songs of Stephen C. Foster from His Time to Ours* (New York: Macmillan Publishing Co., 1975), 89–99.

33. For an overview of definitions and practices, see William A. Everett, "Sigmund Romberg and the American Operetta of the 1920s," *Arti musices* 26, no. 1 (1995): 49–64; and Gerald Bordman, *American Operetta* (New York: Oxford University Press, 1981), 3–15.

34. For a scholarly analysis, see Rick Altman, *The American Film Musical* (Bloomington: Indiana University Press, 1987), 131–199.

35. *The Great Victor Herbert*, a Paramount release produced and directed by Andrew Stone and starring Walter Connolly as Herbert, claims the dubious distinction of having virtually nothing to do with its nominal subject. In a rare moment of candor, the filmmakers provide a title card at the end, which reads: "No attempt has been made in this

picture to depict the actual life of the immortal Victor Herbert. Many of the episodes, incidents, and characters are entirely fictitious. A careful effort has been made, however, to preserve the character and mood of the great composer, whose music serves as the inspiration for this film." Indeed, Herbert is on hand merely to wave a baton at the orchestra and play cupid to the romance between two fictitious singers in his shows, portrayed by Allan Jones and Mary Martin. "If we think of it just as a Paramount musical picture, with an album of twenty-eight Victor Herbert melodies in its score," wrote B.R.C. in the *New York Times,* 7 December 1939, "we shall feel more tolerant toward the distorted portrait it presents of the master." And in *Variety* [n.d.] the critic "Flin." lamented: "Audiences will learn from it very little about Victor Herbert, except that he composed a long list of musical stage hits, and in his spare time concerned himself with the domestic joys and sorrows of actors who played and sang in his shows." "The Great Victor Herbert" file, Paramount Collection, Margaret Herrick Library, Academy of Motion Picture Arts and Sciences, Beverly Hills, Calif.

36. According to biographer William Everett, Romberg's own obfuscations and fabrications about his early years and his musical training create problems for the researcher. At this writing, Everett's book, the first biography to be written about Romberg, is forthcoming from Yale University Press. A title for the work has not yet been determined.

37. Bordman, *American Operetta,* 108–109.

38. Everett, "Sigmund Romberg and the American Operetta," 63.

39. Elliott Arnold, *Deep in My Heart* (New York: Duell, Sloan and Pearce, 1949). Arnold's fictionalized biography shamelessly romanticizes Romberg's life. It depicts a classically trained youth responsive to "the great symphonies, the great operas" of his native Austria, who comes to America determined to blend his Old World training with a New World sensibility: "It was a desire that had been nurtured in new earth and it belonged to where he was now and not to what he left behind" (187).

40. See Emerson's *Doo Dah!* (12–14) for an overview of the influences Foster and his music had on Irving Berlin, George Gershwin, Hoagy Carmichael, Max Steiner, and others.

41. Author interview with Romberg biographer William Everett, 11 December 2003, Kansas City, Mo.

42. Helen Traubel, *Saint Louis Woman* (New York: Duell, Sloan and Pearce, 159), 254.

43. Jack Moffitt, "Deep in My Heart," *Hollywood Reporter,* 1 December 1954.

44. "Deep in My Heart," *Newsweek,* 20 December 1954, 83.

45. There are several versions of this anecdote. The most famous is that Gershwin visited Ravel in Paris in 1928, at which time Ravel declared: "Why should you be a second-rate Ravel when you can be a first-rate Gershwin?" Charles Schwartz concludes that because Gershwin himself spread this and other variants of the story, none of them may be regarded as definitive. See Schwartz, *George Gershwin: His Life and Music* (Indianapolis, Ind.: Bobbs-Merrill, 1973), 125–126. Biographer Joan Peyser notes that it is probable that Gershwin first met Ravel in New York City in 1928 at a party given by Eva Gauthier for the French composer. Gershwin responded by taking Ravel with him for a visit to the Harlem nightclubs. Later that year, while Gershwin was in Paris, Ravel told

an audience in Houston that he hoped the American school of music would "embody a great deal of the rich and diverting rhythm of your jazz and a great deal of sentiment and spirit characteristic of your popular melodies." See Peyser, *The Memory of All That: The Life of George Gershwin* (New York: Simon and Schuster, 1993), 159.

46. *Words and Music* is almost apologetic in its portrayals of Rodgers and Hart as everyday guys. In a prologue actor Tom Drake addresses the camera in the persona of Rodgers: "This is the Metro-Goldwyn-Mayer sound stage No. 1. . . . I'm almost sorry to say there were none of the standard trials and tribulations you would ordinarily expect. In fact, we were just two lucky fellows who had success very young. From the dramatic standpoint, we didn't even have the advantage of being very poor. We weren't very rich, either."

47. It would require a book-length study to detail the number of popular composers, from Sousa to Porter, who harbored "classical" ambitions.

48. There really was a Professor Kleber, a German immigrant who had come to Pittsburgh in 1832. He was a man of many parts in the community—a composer, church organist, teacher, and music store manager. Emerson says Kleber was very eclectic in his musical tastes and "epitomized the genteel tradition and exploited it to the fullest with entrepreneurial energy." See Emerson, *Doo-Dah!* 100–101.

49. "Otto Franck" is probably based on George Gershwin's piano teacher, Charles Hambitzer, who did indeed teach the music of Beethoven, Bach, Chopin, and Ravel. Although he was generally sympathetic to Gershwin's interests in popular music, he insisted on traditional training first. Gershwin concluded his lessons with Hambitzer at age sixteen. Hambitzer died in 1918, bitter over what he regarded as Gershwin's "defection" from the classical world. Gershwin's later teachers included Wallingford Riegger, Henry Cowell, and Rubin Goldmark (a former associate of Antonín Dvořák's at the National Conservatory). By all accounts, Gershwin's evenly divided interests in popular and classical music was genuine. For more information about Hambitzer, see Schwartz, *George Gershwin,* 16–18.

50. Hessler might be modeled after the two music arrangers who played a prominent part in Kern's life: Frank Saddler, who orchestrated the Princess shows, and Robert Russell Bennett, the arranger who worked with him in Hollywood. In either case the professional relationship likely had nothing whatsoever to do with classical music. Indeed, Bennett recalls that Kern once derided the music of Beethoven and Brahms. See Wilk, *They're Playing Our Song,* 20.

51. Laurence Bergreen, *As Thousands Cheer: The Life of Irving Berlin* (New York: Viking, 1990), 359.

52. In his detailed history of the writing and performance of Berlin's "Alexander's Ragtime Band," Charles Hamm contends that, contrary to myth, "it was a hit with audiences from the moment of its first performances" by Emma Carus at the American Music Hall in Chicago, 17 April 1911. However, it was not his first song to attract international attention, nor was it his best-selling song ("White Christmas" enjoys that distinction). (See Hamm, "Alexander and His Band," *American Music* 14, no. 1 (Spring 1996): 65–101. For background on the Fox film, see W. Franklyn Moshier, *The Alice Faye Movie Book* (Harrisburg, Pa.: Stackpole Books, 1974), 101–103.

53. Despite the fact that several later films were virtual cavalcades of Berlin's music—including *You're in the Army Now* (1941) and *There's No Business Like Show Business* (1954)—no "official" biopic on Berlin's life was ever made. Producer Arthur Freed attempted the task in the early 1960s in the never completed *Say It with Music* (the title derived from a song Berlin had written in 1921). The portrait that emerges in *Alexander,* by the way, is now so vaguely conceived that it could also fit several other figures in American music, notably Paul Whiteman (whose career in popularizing ragtime and jazz took him from San Francisco to the concert halls of New York and Europe).

54. *My Gal Sal* file, Seton I. Miller treatment, 13 June 1941, USC Cinema-Television Library, Los Angeles, Calif.

55. *My Gal Sal* file, letter from Darryl F. Zanuck to Robert Bassler, 9 October 1941, USC Cinema-Television Library, Los Angeles, Calif.

56. *My Gal Sal* file, letter to Darryl F. Zanuck from Col. Jason S. Joy, 24 December 1941, Margaret Herrick Library, Academy of Motion Picture Arts and Sciences, Beverly Hills, Calif.

57. "My Gal Sal," *Variety,* 16 April 1942, clippings file, USC Cinema-Television Library, Los Angeles, Calif.

58. "My Gal Sal," *Hollywood Reporter,* 16 April 1942, clippings file, USC Cinema-Television Library, Los Angeles, Calif.

59. "My Gal Sal," *Variety,* 22 April 1942, clippings file, USC Cinema-Television Library, Los Angeles, Calif.

60. Richard Lingeman, *Theodore Dreiser: An American Journey, 1908–1945* (New York: G. P. Putnam's Sons, 1990), 433.

61. Quoted in Wilk, *They're Playing Our Song,* 30.

62. Cohan had attempted a Broadway comeback in 1940 with an original drama, *The Return of the Vagabond,* but the show failed after just seven performances. Cohan's film career is far more extensive than is generally acknowledged. In the assessment of historian Audrey Kupferberg, "*Yankee Doodle Dandy* has done more to keep the memory of George M. Cohan alive than any of his plays or films, any history book or statue." The only detailed information on Cohan's films is Kupferberg, "The Film Career of George M. Cohan," *American Classic Screen* 4, no. 1 (Fall 1979): 43–52. The quotations are from pages 51 and 52.

63. *Yankee Doodle Dandy* file, Hal Wallis letter to Jacob Wilke, 16 January 1941, Warner Bros. Archives, USC Cinema-Television Library, Los Angeles, Calif.

64. Unsigned letter to George M. Cohan, 21 April 1941. Although the copy in the Warner Bros. Museum in Burbank, California, is unsigned, it was probably written by Finlay McDermitt, chief of the Warner Story Department at the time.

65. *Yankee Doodle Dandy* file, George M. Cohan telegram to Robert Buckner, 16 July 1941, Warner Bros. Archives, USC Cinema-Television Library, Los Angeles, Calif.

66. *Yankee Doodle Dandy* file, undated Cohan script treatment, Warner Bros. Archives, USC Cinema-Television Library, Los Angeles, Calif.

67. *Yankee Doodle Dandy* file, Robert Buckner memo to Hal Wallis, 13 August 1941, Warner Bros. Archives, USC Cinema-Television Library, Los Angeles, Calif.

68. The speech written for Cagney/Cohan regarding America's entry into World War I was tailored to refer to the recent Pearl Harbor attack: "Seems it always happens—

whenever we get too high hat and too sophisticated for flag waving, some thug nation decides we're a pushover, all ready to be black-jacked. And it isn't long before we're looking up mighty anxiously to make sure the flag is still waving over us."

69. Kern died of a stroke before the picture was completed. As a result, the original opening, which depicted a birthday party in Kern's Beverly Hills home, was changed, and a new ending was written. Quoted in Hugh Fordin, *The World of Entertainment: Hollywood's Greatest Musicals* (New York: Doubleday and Company, 1975), 181.

70. It is therefore odd that in later years Rodgers would voice his dissatisfaction with the film: "The most terrible lies have been all those Hollywood musicals which purport to be the life story of people like Gershwin, or Porter, or Kern. They give no insight whatsoever into the working patterns of the men they're supposedly about. They did it to Larry and me. The only good thing about that picture was that they had Janet Leigh play my wife. And I found *that* highly acceptable." Interview quoted in Wilk, *They're Playing Our Song,* 66. Rodgers fails to mention the film in his autobiography, *Musical Stages* (New York: Random House, 1975).

71. Quoted in Fordin, *World of Entertainment,* 175.

72. Gerald Bordman, *Jerome Kern: His Life and Music* (New York: Oxford University Press, 1980), 404.

73. *Till the Clouds Roll By* file, Joseph Breen letter to Louis B. Mayer, 9 January 1946, Margaret Herrick Library, Academy of Motion Picture Arts and Sciences, Beverly Hills, Calif.

74. Abel, "Till the Clouds Roll By," *Variety,* 13 November 1946, clippings file, Margaret Herrick Library, Academy of Motion Picture Arts and Sciences, Beverly Hills, Calif.

75. Quoted in Custen, *Bio/Pic,* 119.

76. Schwartz, *Cole Porter,* 223.

77. George Custen, "Night and Day: Cole Porter, Warner Bros., and the Re-Creation of a Life," *Cineaste* 19, nos. 2–3 (1992): 44.

78. *Night and Day* file, letter from Joseph Breen to Jack Warner, 29 December 1944, Margaret Herrick Library, Academy of Motion Picture Arts and Sciences, Beverly Hills, Calif.

79. *Night and Day* file, letter from Joseph Breen to Jack Warner, 16 January 1945, Margaret Herrick Library, Academy of Motion Picture Arts and Sciences, Beverly Hills, Calif.

80. See Schwartz, *Cole Porter,* 102; and Bergreen, *As Thousands Cheer,* 417.

81. Under the heading " 'Particular Applications,' Section II ('Sex'), Subsection 4 of the Motion Picture Production Code, March 1930," appears this prohibition: "Sex perversion or any inference of it is forbidden." (This was amended in 1961 to permit "sex aberration" when treated with "care, discretion, and restraint.") Correspondence from Code executives warned producers to eliminate "pansy action," which was the code word for gay or lesbian behavior (although this did not preclude the ridiculing of same). For a complete text of the 1930 Code, see Jack Vizzard, *See No Evil* (New York: Simon and Schuster, 1970), 366–380.

82. *Night and Day* file, Warner Bros. Archives, USC Cinema-Televison Library, Los Angeles, Calif.

83. *Night and Day* file, Eric Stacey memo, 5 September 1945, Warner Bros. Archives, USC Cinema-Television Library, USC, Los Angeles, Calif.

84. Jack D. Grant, "Night and Day," *Hollywood Reporter,* 9 July 1946.

85. "Night and Day," *Variety,* 9 July 1946.

86. *Words and Music* file, memo 19 January 1946, Warner Bros. Archives, USC Cinema-Television Library, Los Angeles, Calif.

87. *Words and Music* file, contract dated 25 September 1946, Warner Bros. Archives, USC Cinema-Television Library, Los Angeles, Calif.

88. *Words and Music* file, Stephen S. Jackson letter to Louis B. Mayer, 28 April 1948, Warner Bros. Archives, USC Cinema-Television Library, Los Angeles, Calif.

89. *Words and Music* file, Stephen S. Jackson memo (addressee unknown), 7 April 1948, Warner Bros. Archives, USC Cinema-Television Library, Los Angeles, Calif.

90. "Words and Music," *Variety,* 7 December 1948.

91. "Words and Music," *Hollywood Reporter,* 7 December 1948.

92. "Herb," "Words and Music," *Variety,* 8 December 1948.

93. *Rhapsody in Blue* file, Ira Gershwin letter to Elsie Goldberg, 6 October 1942, Warner Bros. Archives, USC Cinema-Television Library, Los Angeles, Calif.

94. *Night and Day* file, Ira Gershwin letter to Elsie Goldberg, 12 July 1943, Warner Bros. Archives, USC Cinema-Television Library, Los Angeles, Calif.

95. *Rhapsody in Blue* pressbook, Warner Bros. Archives, USC Cinema-Television Library, Los Angeles, Calif.

96. *Rhapsody in Blue* pressbook, Warner Bros. Archives, USC Cinema-Television Library, Los Angeles, Calif.

97. *Rhapsody in Blue* file, Ira Gershwin undated letter, Warner Bros. Archives, USC Cinema-Television Library, Los Angeles, Calif.

98. *Rhapsody in Blue* file, Robert Rossen memo, September 1941, Warner Bros. Archives, USC Cinema-Television Library, Los Angeles, Calif.

99. *Rhapsody in Blue* file, Clifford Odets letter to Jack Warner, 13 May 1942, Warner Bros. Archives, USC Cinema-Television Library, Los Angeles, Calif.

100. Sonya Levin scripted *Delicious* for Fox in 1931, which featured many Gershwin tunes. She was also present with Gershwin in the hours before his final collapse.

101. *Rhapsody in Blue* file, R. J. letter to Leo Forbstein, 26 January 1942. Warner Bros. Archives, USC Cinema-Television Library, Los Angeles, Calif.

102. Barry Ulanov, "Rhapsody in Blue," *Morning Telegraph,* 20 August 1945.

103. "Rhapsody in Blue," *Hollywood Reporter,* 27 June 1945.

104. Bosley Crowther, "Rhapsody in Blue," *New York Times,* 28 June 1945.

105. Even in the MGM classical composer biopic about Robert and Clara Schumann, *Song of Love* (1947), the compositions of Clara are neither mentioned nor performed. She is portrayed solely as a *performer,* not as a composer. Acknowledgment of her gifts had to wait for the 1985 biopic *Spring Symphony,* starring Nastassja Kinski as Clara.

106. Gabbard, *Jammin' at the Margins,* 77.

107. The Hall Johnson Choir performs "Old Black Joe" in *Swanee River,* and the Stone Mountain Choir sings "Battle Hymn of the Republic" in *Stars and Stripes Forever.*

108. James Agee, "Till the Clouds Roll By," *Nation* 163 (28 December 1946): 766. George Sidney directed this concluding sequence, which is a veritable movie within a

movie. "All the gaudy and indulgent vulgarity [MGM] had suppressed throughout the picture is slopped all over the screen, as if MGM simply could not hold it in any longer." Moreover, "the spectacle of this scrawny kid [Sinatra] in his bulky white suit singing 'You and me, we sweat and strain' brought audible titters from audiences and a few well-deserved swipes from the press." See Miles Kreuger, *Show Boat: The Story of a Classic American Musical* (New York: Oxford University Press, 1977), 172.

109. When the number first appeared in the *George White Scandals of 1922*, white actors in blackface appeared in the leading roles. Gabbard notes: "The film asks us to side with the daring Gershwin for having the courage to put a sequence on stage in which white actors in blackface perform his short operetta *Blue Monday*." See Gabbard, *Jammin' at the Margins*, 18.

110. Gerald Mast, *Can't Help Singin': The American Musical on Stage and Screen* (New York: Overlook Press, 1987), 231.

111. The celebrated black composer William Grant Still withdrew as the film's music supervisor because the film "degraded colored people." Still is quoted in Daniel J. Leab, *From Sambo to Superspade: The Black Experience in Motion Pictures* (Boston: Houghton Mifflin Company, 1975), 124–130.

112. W. C. Handy, *Father of the Blues* (New York: Macmillan Company, 1955), 12. All subsequent quotations by Handy in this chapter are from his book.

113. Quoted in Steven C. Tracy, *Langston Hughes and the Blues* (Urbana: University of Illinois Press, 2001), 72.

114. Albert Murray, *Stomping the Blues* (New York: McGraw-Hill, 1976), 70.

115. Hugues Panassie, *The Real Jazz* (New York: A. S. Barnes and Company, 1960), 45.

116. Gershwin biographer Schwartz rebuts the contention that the Aeolian Hall concert presented either "experimental" or "jazz" music. It was "essentially a potpourri of popular tunes in a pseudo-jazz style," distinguished primarily for the premiere of the *Rhapsody in Blue*. For a detailed account of this concert, see Schwartz, George *Gershwin*, 83–95.

117. Constantin Bakaleinikoff and his brother, Mischa, both worked in the Hollywood studio system for many years — Mischa for Columbia, Constantin for MGM, RKO, and Paramount. Constantin was born in Moscow in 1896, studied at the Moscow Conservatory, and came to America as a member of the Los Angeles Philharmonic. He became head of RKO's music department in 1941.

118. Gabbard, *Jammin' at the Margins*, 60.

119. In *Father of the Blues*, Handy quotes Deems Taylor's introductory remarks for the concert: "The next number on our program marks an epoch in musical history. There are two schools of thought regarding the invention of the blues. One regards it as an event equal in importance to Edison's invention of the incandescent light" (217–218).

120. In *Father of the Blues*, Handy suggests many times that his music came not from formal training but from an intuitive receptivity to the world around him: "Negroes react rhythmically to everything. That's how the blues came to be. Sometimes I think that rhythm is our middle name. When the sweet good man packs his trunk and goes, that is occasion for some low moaning. When darktown puts on its new shoes and takes off the brakes, jazz steps in. If it's the New Jerusalem and the River Jordan we're studying, we make the spirituals. . . . In every case the songs come from down deep" (82).

121. Gabbard, *Jammin' at the Margins,* 246.

122. Gabbard, *Jammin' at the Margins,* 99.

123. *St. Louis Blues* pressbook, author's collection.

124. William R.Weaver, "St. Louis Blues," *Motion Picture Daily,* 8 April 1958.

125. "Powr." "St. Louis Blues," *Variety,* 8 April 1958.

126. For a more detailed discussion of *Broken Strings,* see Adam Knee, "Class Swings: Music, Race, and Social Mobility in *Broken Strings,*" in Pamela Robertson Wojcik and Arthur Knight, eds., *Soundtrack Available: Essays on Film and Popular Music* (Durham, N.C.: Duke University Press, 2001), 269–294. The quotation is from page 270.

127. "Oh! Susanna" was actually introduced at a gala concert at the Eagle Ice Cream Saloon in Pittsburgh, 11 September 1847. Emerson in *Doo-Dah!* notes its mixture of sources — such as the use of black vernacular in the words and of musical allusions to the European troubadour (the banjo on the singer's knee) and English balladry. The name "Susannah" probably refers to Foster's late sister, Charlotte, whose middle name was Susannah. The song marks "the birth of pop music as we still recognize it today. No popular song is more deeply rooted in American consciousness than 'Oh! Susanna'" (127–130).

128. Contrary to the movie's suggestion, it was Kern, not Hammerstein, who first came up with the idea of writing a musical based on Edna Ferber's novel *Show Boat.* See Kreuger, *Show Boat,* 18.

129. The most notorious example of this sort of lyric-switching is Berlin's "Easter Parade." It began life as an unsuccessful song called "Smile and Show Your Dimple." In 1933 Berlin exhumed the song for a musical, *As Thousands Cheer,* and substituted the lyrics best known today. See Bergreen, *As Thousands Cheer,* 317.

130. Porter's own accounts of the writing of "Night and Day" vary. In one interview he claimed that he had been inspired by hearing the monotonous wail of Moroccan music. But Schwartz contends that it was written for Fred Astaire in 1932 for *The Gay Divorce.* See Schwartz, *George Gershwin,* 142–143.

131. Although Gershwin initially downplayed the programmatic aspects of the work, describing it as "programmatic only in a general impressionistic way," he prepared more detailed program notes with the assistance of Deems Taylor for the work's premiere. The stimulus for *An American in Paris* did indeed derive from two trips to Paris, in April 1923 and March 1928. The taxi-horn inspiration is authentic, and Gershwin brought four French taxi horns back to America with him. Walter Damrosch, who had come to the New York Philharmonic during the 1928–1929 season, premiered the work at Carnegie Hall on 13 December 1928. See Schwartz, *George Gershwin,* 153–170.

132. "Well, the Songs Are Good," *The New Yorker,* 14 December 1946, 88; "Swanee River," *Time,* 15 January 1940, 62; Bosley Crowther, "Rhapsody in Blue," *New York Times,* 28 June 1945, 22.

133. Darryl F. Zanuck allegedly remarked: "No one, in my opinion, will ever pin us down to dates except the later dates in the past two or three years which are clearly remembered." Quoted in Custen, Bio/Pic, 37–38. The remarks concerning *Stars and Stripes Forever* are from a memo addressed to producer William Goetz, dated 12 September 1942. *Stars and Stripes* file, USC Cinema-Television Library/Doheny Library, Los Angeles, Calif.

134. "Yankee Doodle Dandy," *Variety*, 1 June 1942, clippings file, Warner Bros. Archives, USC Cinema-Television Library, Los Angeles, Calif.

135. "Yankee Doodle Dandy," *Hollywood Reporter*, 1 June 1942, clippings file, Warner Bros. Archives, USC Cinema-Television Library, Los Angeles, Calif.

136. Abel, "Yankee Doodle Dandy," *Variety*, 3 June 1942, clippings file, Warner Bros. Archives, USC Cinema-Television Library, Los Angeles, Calif.

137. Philip T. Hartung, "Fascinating Rhythms," *The Commonweal* 42 (6 July 1945): 286.

138. Letter from Harry Ruby to Arthur Freed, 9 July 1946, Warner Bros. Archives, USC Cinema-Television Library Los Angeles, Calif.

Chapter Four: "Just an Innocent Bystander"

Epigraph: G. K. Chesterton, "About Historians," in Chesterton, *As I Was Saying* (London: Methuen, 1936), 152.

1. Ken Russell himself has written about his work in several volumes: *Altered States, The Lion Roars,* and *Directing Film: From Pitch to Premiere* (London: B. T. Batsford, 2000).

2. At this writing, Russell has entered negotiations with Melvyn Bragg concerning a project about Antonín Dvořák.

3. Horowitz, *Post-Classical Predicament*, 23.

4. "I can't read a note," Russell says. "Years ago I tried following miniature scores while playing recordings on a phonograph; but I would get to the end of the last page only to find that the music was still playing on for another five minutes! That's the extent of my musicology! But *as a listener* I know the music I use in my films backwards and forwards."

5. Henry-Louis de la Grange, " 'Meine Musik ist gelebt': Mahler's Biography as a Key to His Works," *Opus* 3, no. 2 (February 1987): 14.

6. Author interviews with Ken Russell, 3 June 2002 and 13 July 2003, Brockenhurst, England. Unless otherwise noted, all Russell quotations in this chapter and these notes are taken from these two interviews.

7. Russell recreates these youthful experiments in amusing fashion in his South Bank film, *Russell on Russell,* broadcast in 1988. The music of Arthur Bliss and Edvard Grieg, respectively, is juxtaposed to scenes from the British futuristic fantasy William Cameron Menzies's *Things to Come* (1936) and Fritz Lang's *Metropolis* (1926).

8. Russell's visual fantasy on Gustav Holst's *The Planets* was made in 1983 and used a wildly varied series of images, including archival footage of space shots, Red Square celebrations, fashion shows, jet planes, movie clips, etc. Absent from Holst's suite is the planet Pluto, which had not been discovered when Holst wrote the piece in 1920.

9. Baxter, *Appalling Talent*, 118.

10. Russell, *Altered States*, 15–16.

11. See the examination of *Song to Remember* in Chapter Two.

12. Russell, *Altered States*, 22.

13. BBC Written Archives, Reading, Norman Swallow memo, 7 April 1959, file T32/1,001/1.

14. BBC Written Archives, Reading, Swallow memo, 1 June 1959, file T32/1033/2 2.

15. The piano playing is provided by Philip Jenkins.

16. Harlow Robinson, *Serge Prokofiev: A Biography* (New York: Viking Press, 1987), 474.

17. Gomez, *Ken Russell,* 185.

18. BBC Written Archives, Reading, file T32/1, 001/1

19. BBC Written Archives, Reading, undated memo, file T32/1033/2.

20. Baxter, *Appalling Talent,* 122.

21. BBC Written Archives, Reading, file T32/1033/2.

22. BBC Written Archives, Reading, file T32/1033/2.

23. BBC Written Archives, Reading, file T32/1033/2.

24. One of the few references to the subject can be found in Michael Kennedy's *Portrait of Elgar* (New York: Oxford University Press, 1987): "The boy's looks belied his physical prowess, for he would ride the Malvern Hills bareback, saving himself from death on one occasion when his horse bolted" (8). Otherwise, there is scant evidence that Elgar ever rode horses. He seems to have always preferred bicycles.

25. BBC Written Archives, Reading, file T32/1033/2.

26. Quoted in Baxter, *Appalling Talent,* 122. Russell later disclosed that Wheldon was also uncomfortable with Russell's inclusion of Catholic iconography in the *Gerontius* sequence. Mimicking Wheldon's stentorian voice, Russell recalls Wheldon's words: "Well, Russell, go and do your Catholic film, but *not too many bloody crucifixes!*" (author interview).

27. The tune appears in the Trio section of the D-major "Pomp and Circumstance March, No. 1," composed in 1901. At King Edward VII's suggestion, patriotic words were written to it, and it was first sung by Clara Butt in London in June 1902. According to commentator John Gardiner, "Elgar never stopped conducting *Land of Hope and Glory,* and his mild irritation at its popularity . . . may simply have been frustration that people did not want to hear his less well-known compositions." See Gardiner, "Variations on a Theme of Elgar: Ken Russell, the Great War, and the Television 'Life' of a Composer," *Historical Journal of Film, Radio, and Television* 23, no. 3 (August 2003): 201.

28. Quoted in Gene Phillips, *Ken Russell* (Boston: Twayne, 1979) 39.

29. Quoted in Phillips, *Ken Russell,* 39.

30. Robert Phillip Kolker further extrapolates this strategy: "It is a conflict in which no one wins: not the subject, not his contemporary world, not the popular myth, and certainly not the audience who come to a biographical film with certain expectations." See Kolker, "Ken Russell's Biopics," 42.

31. Baxter, *Appalling Talent,* 114–115.

32. In a BBC Audience Research Report dated 3 December 1962, the "reaction index" was proclaimed to be an 86, "the highest figure awarded to a *Monitor* programme since the inception of the series at the beginning of 1958." The report went on to cite specific viewer reactions, concluding: "For some viewers, for instance, the manner of presenting this biographical study of a great English composer touched fresh heights in combining imagination with meticulous research ('so that it had appeal both for the music-minded and those people who like facts'). For others, the subject itself was a felicitous choice for *Monitor*'s 'century' edition as a prime example of the series' always stimulating and vivid

approach, it was said, to biographical material." BBC Written Archives, Reading, file T32/1033/2.

33. Subsequent Elgarian scholarship includes Robert Anderson, *Elgar in Manuscript* (Portland, Ore.: Amadeus Press, 1990), Jerrold Northrop Moore's *Edward Elgar: A Creative Life* (New York: Oxford University Press, 1984), and Kennedy's *Portrait of Elgar*.

34. The collapse of the Austro-Hungarian monarchy after 1920 saw a redistribution of its territory, resulting in the loss to Hungary of Transylvania (to Romania), of the "Felvidek" (to Czechoslovakia), and of the Banat (to Yugoslavia). These disruptions — coupled with Bartók's outrage about his native Hungary's accommodation to Hitler's "regime of thieves of murderers" (as he described it), his sorrow at the news of the Anschluss with Austria, and his grief over the death of his mother — caused Bartók to flee to America in the fall of 1940.

35. Agatha Fassett, *The Naked Face of Genius: Béla Bartók's American Years* (Boston: Houghton Mifflin Company, 1958), 3.

36. Gomez, *Ken Russell*, 33.

37. Of these nocturnal investigations, pianist Gyorgy Sandor, also a colleague of Bartók, has noted: "Bartók went back to the earth for his music. He realized that the origins of music lie in the sounds of nature — listen to the fourth movement of the *Out of Doors* suite, to all those little noises of the night, those little stylized twitters and flutings of frogs and insects. He even wrote in his collection, *Mikrokosmos*, a little thing called 'Diary of a Fly.'" Author interview with Gyorgy Sandor, quoted in Tibbetts, "Sandor Recalls Bartók," *The World and I* (September 1995): 98.

38. After his appointment as a professor of piano at the Academy of Music in Budapest, Bartók began his ethnomusicological (the term did not yet exist) researches with his friend and colleague, Zoltan Kodaly. Armed with an Edison phonograph, he spent ten years, from 1904 to 1914, traveling through the peasant villages of Hungary, Slovakia, and Romania in search of "pure" folk songs and dance tunes — musical material vitally close to everyday peasant life and thus quite distinct from the ersatz folk songs and sentimental popular tunes that had been hitherto considered "Hungarian" by Brahms and Liszt. Commentator Malcolm Gillies notes that Bártok, "above all musicians of the century, is credited with bringing the sounds of the swineherd and peasant girl into the concert hall and with putting the urban middle class in touch with a variety of ethnic roots." See Gillies, ed., *The Bartók Companion* (Portland, Ore.: Amadeus Press, 1994), 3.

39. Quoted in John Tibbetts, "Baffling Bartók: Secrets beyond the Seventh Door," *American Record Guide* 58, no. 6 (November–December 1995): 13.

40. BBC Written Archives, Reading, file VR/64/296.

41. *The Miraculous Mandarin* is a wordless, musical pantomime first performed in 1918. It is the story of three thugs who force a beautiful girl to lure men into their attic den so they can rob them. When the eponymous Chinese mandarin enters the room, he is attacked and stabbed. So intense is his erotic frenzy toward the girl, however, that he refuses to die. Not until the girl satisfies his lusts does he expire. See Gyorgy Kroo, "Pantomime: *The Miraculous Mandarin*," in Gillies, *Bartók Companion*, 383–384.

42. Gomez, *Ken Russell*, 35.

43. Another reason for the unavailability of the film was a law suit pressed against the

BBC by Madame de Tinan, a descendant of Debussy, banning exhibition abroad. Brief discussions can be found only in the earliest examinations of Russell's films—Gomez, *Ken Russell,* 33–35; Hanke, *Ken Russell's Films,* 18; Baxter, *Appalling Talent,* 116–117 and 128–129; and Phillips, *Ken Russell,* 46–48.

44. I am grateful to Mr. Russell for the opportunity to view his private print of *The Debussy Film* in his home in East Boldre, Brockenhurst, England.

45. Russell, *Lion Roars,* 100.

46. After *The Debussy Film,* Bragg and Russell cowrote a biopic about Tchaikovsky, *The Music Lovers.* Another project, *Nijinsky,* was begun but never completed. "I still think it was one of the best things I ever wrote," recalls Bragg. "Ken and producer Harry Saltzman both loved it, too. Nijinsky happened to be somebody I knew a lot about. I had read his diaries and all that stuff. Christopher Gable, a wonderful dancer and a fine actor, was going to portray Nijinsky and Oliver Reed was to be Diaghilev. For Oliver to have played a homosexual role in those days would have been a bold stroke. But then Nureyev came on the scene and said he wanted the role. And of course Harry said 'Fine.' Poor Chris Gable. Nureyev even took his place as Principal Dancer at the Royal Ballet. I think I wrote one more draft, but I lost heart. Ken stayed on for awhile, but then he dropped out." Unless otherwise noted, all quotations in this chapter and these chapter notes are from author interviews with Melvyn Bragg conducted at Television Center, London, 17 July 1997 and on 21 July 2003.

47. Russell's own on-set activities paralleled aspects of Debussy's amours. In his autobiography, *Altered States,* Russell reveals that just as Debussy and Gaby were involved in a tumultuous affair, so were Russell and the actress portraying Gaby, Annette Robertson, entering into an ill-fated affair of their own (104–105).

48. Hanke, *Ken Russell's Films,* 35.

49. Russell, *Altered States,* 155. In another volume, *Lion Roars,* he describes his favorite location, the Borrowdale Valley, which "became for me what Monument Valley was for John Ford—a favourite location for every film I made. Though I have to say that the becks, crags, tarns, woods, screes and forces of Borrowdale offer more variety than the sand and stone of Monument Valley" (138).

50. BBC Written Archives, Reading, letter from Estelle Palmley to Kenneth Adam, file T53/118/4.

51. BBC Written Archives, Reading, letter from Ken Russell to Geoffrey Cornell, file T32/1, 095/2.

52. Quoted in Baxter, *Appalling Talent,* 136.

53. BBC Written Archives, Reading, letter from Norman Swallow to Ken Russell, 22 August 1968, file T53/118/2.

54. BBC Written Archives, Reading, letter from Ken Russell to Felix Aylmer, 19 February 1968, file T53/118/4 (A).

55. BBC Written Archives, Reading, treatment by Anthony Wilkinson, dated 27 November 1967, file T53 /118/3.

56. Eric Fenby, *Delius As I Knew Him* (New York: Cambridge University Press, 1981), 8. For additional accounts by Fenby, see his *Delius* (New York: Thomas Y. Crowell Company, 1971) and "Delius," *Music and Musicians* 22, no. 262 (June 1974): 26–28.

57. Fenby, *Delius As I Knew Him,* 125.

58. Quoted in Baxter, *Appalling Talent,* 137.

59. Fenby, "Delius," 26.

60. Fenby, afterword in *Delius As I Knew Him,* 259.

61. Fenby, "Delius," 28.

62. Philip Oyler, "Delius at Grez," *Musical Times* 113, no. 1551 (May 1972): 444–447.

63. Quoted in Baxter, *Appalling Talent,* 136.

64. BBC Written Archives, Reading, clippings file T53/118/4.

65. BBC Written Archives, Reading, John Culshaw letter, 24 July 1968, file T53/118/4.

66. BBC Written Archives, Reading, Estelle Palmley letter, 23 September 1968, file T53/118/4.

67. BBC Written Archives, Reading, Eric Fenby letter to Ken Russell, 16 September 1968, file T53/118/2.

68. BBC Written Archives, Reading, Ken Russell letter to Eric Fenby, 18 September 1968, file T53/118/2. Russell recalls a sad postscript to the association with Fenby: "After the film, Fenby developed a skin complaint of some kind, probably something psychological. His skin was sore to the slightest touch. I think somehow the film brought back all the turmoil of his experience with Delius. He recovered after a year. Then, he came around and asked me for a loan of a hundred pounds. 'I've been asked to come to America to a university close to where I used to work; and I can't afford the fare,' he told me. I never saw him again. But he did write some good music for a Charles Laughton film, *Jamaica Inn.* He felt that he could have been as good as Benjamin Britten." (author's interview, 21 July 2003).

69. BBC Written Archives, Reading, Ken Russell letter to Carlton Hobbs, 20 March 1969, file T53/159/2.

70. BBC Written Archives, Reading, undated treatment, file T53/159/2.

71. BBC Written Archives, Reading, file T53/159/1.

72. BBC Written Archives, Reading, clippings file, T53/159/3.

73. BBC Written Archives, Reading, folder "Dance of the Seven Veils."

74. BBC Written Archives, Reading, file T53/159/4.

75. BBC Written Archives, Reading, file T53/159/4.

76. Quoted in Phillips, *Ken Russell,* 62.

77. Gomez, *Ken Russell,* 69.

78. Kolker, "Ken Russell's Biopics," 43.

79. Gomez, *Ken Russell,* 67.

80. Quoted in Gomez, *Ken Russell,* 69.

81. Norman Del Mar, *Richard Strauss,* vol. 3 (London: Barrie and Jenkins, 1972), 51.

82. Del Mar, *Richard Strauss,* 467.

83. Michael Tanner, "At the Heart of Playfulness," *Times Literary Supplement,* 13 August 1999, 18.

84. Quoted in Michael H. Kater, *Composers of the Nazi Era: Eight Portraits* (New York: Oxford University Press, 2000), 216.

85. Kater, *Composers of the Nazi Era,* 228–229.

86. Kater, *Composers of the Nazi Era,* 249.

87. Quoted in John Tibbetts, "Richard Strauss Re-Examined," *American Record Guide* 55, no. 6 (November–December 1992): 13.

88. Hanke, *Ken Russell's Films,* 75.

89. Russell, *Altered States,* 56.

90. Quoted in Baxter, *Appalling Talent,* 183.

91. Catherine Drinker Bowen and Barbara von Meck, *"Beloved Friend": The Story of Tchaikovsky and Nadejda von Meck* (New York: Random House, 1937).

92. See Anthony Holden, *Tchaikovsky: A Biography* (New York: Random House, 1995); and Alexander Poznansky, *Tchaikovsky's Last Days: A Documentary Study* (Oxford: Clarendon Press, 1996).

93. Quoted in Phillips, *Ken Russell,* 93–94.

94. Tchaikovsky was not *imitating* Pushkin's story so much as attempting to learn from its tragic example. Thus, biographer Holden writes that Tatyana's "Letter Song" may have moved Tchaikovsky not to reject Nina, as Onegin had rejected Tatyana, but to accept her proposal. In any event, continues Holden, "were it not for his confused feelings for Antonina, as she herself poignantly points out, *Eugene Onegin* might not be the affecting imbroglio it is of love lost, promise betrayed" (*Tchaikovsky,* 157).

95. Horowitz, *Post-Classical Predicament,* 28.

96. In an article published in 1982, historian David Brown quotes letters that had been unavailable in the West until 1979. Tchaikovsky described the rail journey in nightmarish terms: "When the carriage started I was ready to cry out with choking sobs. Nevertheless, I still had to occupy my wife with conversation as far as Klin in order that I might earn the right to lie down in my own armchair when it was dark and remain alone by myself. . . . My wife didn't comprehend or even perceive my ill-concealed anguish." Within a few days of the marriage, continues Brown, Tchaikovsky admitted that Nina "has become *totally repugnant* to me" (755). See Brown, "Tchaikovsky's Marriage," *Musical Times* 123, no. 1677 (November 1982): 754–756. In an +interview with the author, Bragg defends his and Russell's intuitive conception of the scene: "The scene of the railway carriage may be regarded as a metaphor for what was going on in this dysfunctional relationship. You could guess that something like that must have happened. Besides, it was very dramatically useful to set such a scene in a railway carriage! But I don't think we outguessed history; I think it was a fluke."

97. The *1812 Overture,* originally entitled *The Year of 1812,* was written in 1882. He purportedly dashed it off at the request of Nikolay Rubinstein to observe the consecration of the Cathedral of Christ the Saviour (which had been built to commemorate the Russian defeat of Napoleon in 1812). In his *Tchaikovsky,* Holden notes it was one of Tchaikovsky's "least favourite compositions" (204).

98. Quoted in Baxter, *Appalling Talent,* 191. In his *Tchaikovsky,* Holden is very critical of Tchaikovsky's self-indulgent and deceitful behavior: "His ambitions to be 'as other men' were doomed, and he was capable of inflicting cruel and unusual treatment on another, quite innocent human being to get his way" (156).

99. Even at the time of Russell's film, details of Tchaikovsky's sexual life had been suppressed. Brother Modest (himself a homosexual) had concealed the truth as much as he could; and later, Soviet censors, for largely political reasons, either withdrew or bowd-

lerized the composer's diaries and letters. According to Holden, in his *Tchaikovsky,* "not merely did he have a dread of scandal; in his heart, as in his letters and diaries, he continued to wish that he were 'as other men.' Although he indulged his predilections on a recklessly promiscuous scale, he ensured that his 'secret vice' was known only to a like-minded sympathetic circle" (199).

100. Published research subsequent to Russell's film largely bears out these claims. Holden, for example, in *Tchaikovsky,* acknowledges that Nina occasionally prostituted herself (125) and bore several illegitimate children after her separation from Tchaikovsky. About von Meck, Holden notes, "Tchaikovsky could not be expected to see it, but Nadezhda von Meck was in love with him—a Platonic love, of course, to be conducted from a safe distance, but a love which wanted him for its own, purchased and paid for in full" (144). As to whether Tchaikovsky's death might have been suicide, that remains one of the most hotly contested issues in music history. The facts are, simply stated, that he died of cholera on 6 November 1993, a few days after drinking a glass of infected water (and just six days after the premiere on 28 October of his Sixth Symphony). Immediately after his death, questions arose disputing the fact that Tchaikovsky died from accidentally imbibing the water; that it may have been suicide, or even murder, as the result of a cabal threatening to disclose his homosexuality. Details of the debate are too complex to detail here. Suffice it to say, after sifting through the literature, biographer David Brown declared in a 1997 article: "There are so many discrepancies and contradictions within the plethora of documents and reports relating to Tchaikovsky's final illness, with individuals sometimes bluntly denying their earlier testimony, that we simply cannot *know* what really happened and whether it was cholera, or indeed, an illness as such—and if it was not, then either he was poisoned by someone, which I find unthinkable, or he took his own life. Let's dig him up, and then perhaps we can all rest in peace." See Brown, "How Did Tchaikovsky Come to Die," 588.

101. Bragg explains that there were unavoidable problems in the casting of Sasha. "Sasha was originally conceived as a central character in the story, placed as she was between Nina and von Meck. You can see that in the early sequences, particularly in the Piano Concerto sequence. But early in the shooting, the actress, Sabine Maydelle, got into a 'state'—I won't say breakdown. We couldn't take her out of the film, because we had already shot three weeks of her key sequences. So we had to do something. As a result, the part had to be reduced and rewritten. We had to shift the dramatic emphasis more toward Glenda. It was bloody hard. The resulting balance was wrong. I hated it. It wasn't what we had set out to do." (Author interview with Bragg, 20 January 1997, London.)

102. "That was another problem," admits Bragg. "The hairdressers and makeup people got to Richard Chamberlain and made him look too pretty. They had too good a time with his hair. 'For God's sake, tone it down,' I said. It was a damned nuisance." (Author interview with Bragg, 20 January 1997, London.)

103. For an overview of critical comments, see Gomez, *Ken Russell,* 97.
104. Poznansky, *Tchaikovsky's Last Days,* 222.
105. Gordon Gow, "The Music Lovers," *Films and Filming* 17, no. 6 (March 1971): 47.
106. Author interview with Bragg, 20 January 1997, London.
107. Gow, "The Music Lovers," 4.

108. Author interview with Bragg, 20 January 1997, London.

109. Quoted in Gomez, *Ken Russell,* 97. For a fuller account of Dimitri Tiomkin's involvement in *Tchaikovsky,* see Christopher Palmer, "St. Petersburg to Hollywood, *Music and Musicians* 21, no. 8 (April 1973): 18–20.

110. Gomez, *Ken Russell,* 183, 188.

111. See James M. Welsh and Steven Kramer, "Gance's Beethoven," *Sight and Sound* 45, no. 2 (Spring 1976): 109–111.

112. Russell, as usual, anchors his fantasies to historical facts. Mahler did indeed request in a letter to Alma that she stop composing: "You have only one profession from now on: to make me happy." See Jonathan Carr, *Mahler: A Biography* (New York: Overlook Press, 1997), 108. Her adulterous affairs and exploitations of the men in her life are documented. In her diary she wrote of herself: "I'm heartless and unloving—things that I only confide, discreetly, to my diary—that I'm incapable of warmth, that everything about me is sheer calculation, cold-blooded calculation." See Antony Beaumont, trans., *Alma Mahler-Werfel: Diaries 1898–1902* (Ithaca, N.Y.: Cornell University Press, 1999), 461.

By contrast to the caricatures of the Russell film, she is more fleshed out in Bruce Beresford's biopic *Bride of the Wind* (2000), starring Sarah Wynter as Alma and Jonathan Pryce as Mahler. See Tibbetts, "Bride of the Wind," *American Historical Review* (April 2002): 673–674; and Max Phillips's novel, *The Artist's Wife* (New York: Henry Holt, 2001).

113. Russell, *Altered States,* 166.

114. Russell, *Altered States,* 165.

115. De la Grange, " 'Meine Musik ist gelebt,' " 15.

116. Alex Ross, "Mahlermania," *The New Yorker,* 4 September 1995, 89–90.

117. Quoted in Ross, "Mahlermania," 92.

118. Hanke, *Ken Russell's Films,* 293.

119. Jack Kroll, "Russellmania," *Newsweek,* 20 October 1975, 99.

120. Richard Eder, "Screen: 'Lisztomania,' " *New York Times,* 11 October 1975.

121. Kevin Thomas, "Lisztomania," *Los Angeles Times,* 17 October 1975.

122. Russell's choice of music from Wagner's *Rienzi* is apt. When Liszt first heard this opera in Dresden in 1844, he was so impressed that he not only composed his variations on *Rienzi's* overture, but he resolved to stage a Wagner opera in Weimar at the first opportunity (which came in 1849).

123. Alan Walker, who spent almost thirty years researching and writing his three-volume series on Liszt known as "Life," declared in my interview with him that "Liszt staged his own life almost as if he were presenting a three-act drama. Reporting the facts of his life is like reading a novel: "You have to rub your eyes occasionally and wonder, Did this really happen? Could it have been possible? And usually with Liszt, it was! If anything, you have to suppress interest, lest you be accused of inventing things!" For accounts of my interviews with Walker—2 August 1989, New York City; and 25 October 1994, Hamilton, Ontario—see Tibbetts, "Probing the Liszt Legend," *Christian Science Monitor,* 14 September 1989, 10–11; and Tibbetts, "Mephistopheles as Curate," *The World and I* 11, no. 9 (September 1996): 285–289.

124. Behind Russell's exaggerations are kernels of truth. Wagner himself confessed his debt to Liszt's innovations in harmony and form. In 1859, after the first performances of

music from *Tristan und Isolde,* Richard Pohl published an article claiming the music had borrowed heavily from Liszt. Wagner's response was enlightening: "There are many matters on which we are quite frank among ourselves—for instance, that since my acquaintance with Liszt's compositions my treatment of harmony has become very different from what it was formerly. But when friend Pohl blurts out this secret before the whole world . . . this is, to say the least, indiscreet" (quoted in Alan Walker, *Franz Liszt: The Weimar Years, 1848–1861* (New York: Alfred A. Knopf), 545.

125. In the wake of the surge of German nationalism in the nineteenth century, and the concomitant anti-Semitic sentiments from both the reactionary fringe and middle-class liberals and progressives, Wagner published his *Das Judentum in der Musik* (*Jewishness in Music,* 1850; republished in 1869). This is his clearest and strongest anti-Semitic polemic. He singled out Felix Mendelssohn for attack as a pernicious influence in German culture. Upon reading the essay, an outraged Liszt demanded an explanation from Wagner. Wagner responded in a letter dated 18 April 1851, in which he redirected his attack against opera composer Giacomo Meyerbeer and poet Heinrich Heine. According to scholar Barry Millington, Wagner inveighed stridently "against Jewish artists who, motivated solely by commercial instincts and lacing a culture of their own, could only imitate the art produced by the host culture." See Millington, ed., *The Wagner Compendium* (London: Midas, 1992), 164.

126. Wagner's place in the ultimate Romantic disaster, Hitler's Third Reich, is a complex subject and exhaustively examined in Burnett James's *Wagner and the Romantic Disaster* (New York: Thames and Hudson, 1983). "Although Richard Wagner was, predictably, Adolf Hitler's favourite composer and the unintending inspirer of many of his most cancerous dreams and asphyxiating visions, it can hardly be laid to Wagner's charge that he was in some malignant way the acting titular head of the Nazi party. Though a passionate German patriot in the larger sense, and a devout celebrant of German nationhood and especially of 'Holy German Art,' Wagner cast suspicious eyes on the muscular pan-Germanism of Bismarck and was not taken in either by the ascendancy of Prussian militarism or the founding of the German Empire. . . . He would surely have spat in the face of the Nazi hierarchy and treated the whole Third Reich with notable contempt" (3–4).

127. Eder, "Screen: Lisztomania," n.p.

128. For overviews of Tony Palmer's *Wagner,* see Richard Hornak, "Epic Project," *Opera News* 49 (November 1984): 10–14; and Christopher J. Thomas, "Richard Burton as Wagner: The Complete Epic," *Opera Quarterly* 15 (Spring 1987): 120–123.

129. Derek Watson, *Bruckner* (New York: Simon and Schuster Macmillan, 1996), x.

130. Watson, *Bruckner,* 45–48.

131. Robin Holloway, "A Colossal Drive to Create," *Times Literary Supplement,* 8 May 1998, 19.

132. Quoted in Brian Large, *Martinu* (London: Gerald Duckworth and Co., 1975), 101.

133. Large, *Martinu,* 72.

134. Large, *Martinu,* 122.

135. Russell's portrayal of Bax is not the first time he has appeared on screen in his films. He played cameo roles as Isadora Duncan's chauffeur in *Isadora* (1966), the film director Rex Ingram in *Valentino* (1977), a village curate in *Song of Summer* (1967), and

a wheelchair-bound invalid in *Tommy* (1975). In *Russell on Russell* and *The ABCs of Music* he appears as a kind of master of ceremonies.

136. Quoted in Colin Scott-Sutherland, *Arnold Bax* (London: J. M. Dent and Sons, 1973), 11.

137. Quoted in Scott-Sutherland, *Arnold Bax,* 192.

138. Bragg first came to Russell in 1999 with the suggestion that he make a new film on Elgar. "But he rejected my first three scripts," recalls Russell. "The first one involved the character of a mysterious woman returning to Malvern on the first anniversary of Elgar's death; and it would later be revealed that she was one of the 'mysterious women' in his life. Then I worked with the playwright, David Pownall, who knew quite a bit about Elgar. But Melvyn didn't like that script, either. My next idea was to be called 'The Elgar Jigsaw,' but we couldn't afford the props. So we finally agreed on a fourth try, the present version." (Author interview, 3 June 2002, East Boldre.)

139. Gardiner, "Variations on a Theme of Elgar," 208, fn 17.

140. *La boite a joujoux* (*The Box of Toys*) was composed originally for piano solo in 1913 after a scenario by Andre Helle, a commercial artist who specialized in figurines and dolls. The subsequent stage production (to an orchestration by Debussy and Andre Caplet) told the story of a toy-box town in which toys live like real people. The temptation to trace similarities between this and Russell's "Wand of Youth" episode is irresistible.

141. There is some controversy as to whether the percussion outburst of the "rondo" section of the Second Symphony could in fact constitute Elgar's direct prophecy of the war, as Russell implies. Gardiner thinks it unlikely that Elgar could have predicted war with Germany in a work begun so many years before the outbreak of hostilities. "Still, the notion that Elgar here was imparting a nightmare vision of the First World War allows Russell's films to reach a compelling climax for those horrified by post-1914 hindsight" See Gardiner, "Variations on a Theme of Elgar," 202.

142. Russell confesses that this particular scene is "a trick." He explains: "We didn't get permission to shoot in Worcester Cathedral. We had to go to Malvern Abbey instead to get that shot." Russell has used actor James Johnston in several of his recent films. "You could project on to him, like he was a blank canvas. And he could play the violin." (Author interview, 3 June 2002, East Boldre.)

143. Russell, *Altered States,* 232.

144. In an article published in 1900, Elgar's friend, F. G. Edwards, described his penchant for kite flying: "His great idea was to invent a kite which would enable him to vary its surface resistance according to the force of the wind that was blowing. . . . He used to have a string of kites, of various shapes and sizes, one under the other. So strong in mid air was their resistance to their captive rope that, on one occasion, he and a friend, pulling with all their might, could not bring the high-flyer down to earth." Reprinted in *Musical Times* 139, no. 1860 (February 1998): 22.

Chapter Five: "A Long, Dark Coda into the Night"

1. Quoted in Stephen Aris, "Tony Palmer's Life of Britten," *Sunday Telegraph,* 30 March 1980.

2. "The Palmer Treatment," *Sunday Times,* 31 March 1985, 11.

3. Elizabeth Dunn, "Palmer's Progress," *Sunday Telegraph,* 15 April 1990, 25.

4. Tony Palmer, "Dogged Days," *The Listener*, 15 September 1988, 4–5.

5. Rosenstone, "Future of the Past," 201.

6. Paul Arthur, "Essay Questions," *Film Comment* 39, no. 1 (January–February 2003): 60.

7. Arthur, "Essay Questions," 59.

8. Unless otherwise indicated, all quotations from Tony Palmer in this chapter and these chapter notes are from author interviews on 26–27 February 2001, Kansas City, Mo.; 12 January 2002, London; 2 June 2002, London; and 24–26 March 2003, Lawrence, Kans.

9. Unless otherwise indicated, all quotations in this chapter and these chapter notes are from author interviews with Melvyn Bragg at Television Centre, London, 20 January 1997 and 21 July 2003.

10. The regime of the aging Wolfgang, in his mid-eighties at the time of this writing, has been under fire since 1984, when his children and his brother Wieland's children requested that he step down. He has rebuffed all such suggestions, however. His son, Gottfried, and his niece, Nike, have published critical accounts of his appropriating artistic control from his brother Wieland. The intrafamily warfare has continued and has gotten extensive coverage in the German press. See Wagner, *Wagners.*

11. This most famous of Wagnerian terms, which may be translated as "leading motif," did not originate with the composer himself, who first referred to the concept as a system of motifs of "anticipation," "recollection," and "reminiscence." Barzun explains that the leifmotif is Wagner's musical designation of a definite person, idea, or object: "This means that when the physical presence of these entities on the stage requires it, the musical development is bound to reintroduce the leitmotif. This not only encourages a mechanical manufacture of the so-called 'unending melody' but it justifies calling Wagner's music 'programmatic' in a stricter sense than usual." See Jacques Barzun, *Darwin Marx Wagner* (Boston: Atlantic Little, Brown, 1947), 16.

12. Denby Richards, "Wagner," *Music and Musicians* (August 1983): 10.

13. For example, the script's historical errors include: Wagner delivering his famous demand that the singers "pay attention to the little notes" during rehearsals of *Tristan* rather than the *Ring;* Ludwig leaving the theater during the premiere of *Tristan* instead of staying for it and for a subsequent performance three days later; adding a reference to Verdi to a quotation from *Mein Leben;* changing the location of Ludwig's tirade about his efforts to reestablish the artistic environment of the medieval Minnesänger from Neuschwanstein to the Hall of Mirrors in Herrenchiemsee; and depicting the waters of Lake Starnberg as icy when Ludwig's suicide occurred in the month of June.

14. Richard Hornak, "Epic Project," *Opera News* 49, no. 5 (November 1984): 62.

15. Barry Millington, "Films," *Musical Times* 124, no. 1685 (July 1983): 445–446; Richards, "Wagner," 11.

16. Christopher J. Thomas, "Videos," *Opera Quarterly* 15, no. 1 (Spring 1987): 122.

17. Hornack, "Epic Project."

18. The centennial year saw *Ring* cycle productions at the English National Opera, the Welsh National Opera, and at Bayreuth under the direction of Sir Peter Hall and Sir Georg Solti.

19. Leon Botstein, "Wagner and Our Century," *19th-Century Music* 11, no. 1 (Summer 1987): 104.

20. In *Ludwig,* Visconti was determined to idealize Ludwig II at the expense of the greedy, power-crazed hedonist Wagner.

21. *Ludwig: Requiem for a Virgin King* is part of a trilogy of Syberberg films dissecting the pernicious influences of four men who influenced modern Germany—Wagner (*The Confessions of Winifred Wagner,* 1975), King Ludwig II, filmmaker Karl May (*Karl May,* 1974), and Adolph Hitler (*Our Hitler: A Film from Germany,* 1977). See John Pym, "Syberberg and the Tempter of Democracy," *Sight and Sound* (Autumn 1977): 227, 230.

22. Quoted in Botstein, "Wagner and Our Century," 93.

23. Botstein, "Wagner and Our Century," 102.

24. It is difficult to find a positive view of Wagner the man. Jonathan Lieberson's general assessment is typical: "He was a consummate borrower, a self-important braggart with an opinion on every subject, something of a crank (though probably not a bore), and treacherous in love. He was not merely a charming rascal, a lesser *Hochstapler,* but unquestionably a genuine swindler, indifferent to the feelings of others, calculating, ruthless, and coarse." See Lieberson, "Bombing in Bayreuth," *New York Review of Books,* 10 November 1988, 30.

25. Thomas, "Videos," 122.

26. Quoted in Mosco Carner, *Puccini: A Critical Biography* (New York: Alfred A. Knopf, 1959), 169.

27. Carner, *Puccini,* 164–165.

28. Biographer Carner has also asserted that Puccini's inability to complete the opera—i.e., the final love duet between Turandot and Calaf—"cannot be ascribed to the onset of his tragic illness; it seems to have sprung from something deep down in himself, from obstacles in his unconscious mind" (*Puccini,* 215). After Puccini's death from throat cancer on 29 November 1924, *Turandot* was completed by Franco Alfano, a friend of Puccini.

29. Did Puccini invent the character of Liu, as Palmer alleges? It is not quite correct that this character does not appear in Gozzi's play. Biographer Carner points out that in Gozzi's play there is a character called Adelma, a rival to Turandot. She is a former Tartar princess and now slave and confidant to Turandot. Because she has fallen in love with Turandot's lover, the Prince, she is sent away from Turandot's court. Carner concludes that she "provided a part-model for Puccini's little slave-girl." The difference is that in Puccini's opera version Liu must die in order for the Prince to win Turandot's heart. "Through it she becomes a tragic figure who, not unlike Butterfly, atones for her 'guilt' of having loved a man entirely out of her own sphere" (*Puccini,* 446).

30. Tony Palmer, "A Vain Quest for Final Reconciliation," *London Times,* 18 April 1984.

31. The locations of Loch Lomond and the village of Luss doubled for Torre del Lago and environs. The real Torre del Lago estate was photographed for the exterior shots.

32. Carner, *Puccini,* 157.

33. Simon Callow, "The Spotlight's on Puccini," *BBC Music Magazine,* September 1995, 27.

34. These scenes reveal Palmer as both director and apologist for his interpretation of the opera. He is seen rehearsing with the chorus and singers, arguing with the set builders, and complaining about the restrictive local fire laws. These scenes seem to prefigure a

later film that also chronicled a behind-the-scenes production of *Turandot,* Allan Miller's *The Turandot Project* (2001), a documentary depicting the staging in 1997 by Zubin Mehta and Zhang Yimou of the opera in Beijing, China.

35. "Score for Scandal," *The Listener,* 29 November 1984.

36. "The Palmer Treatment," *Sunday Times,* 31 March 1985, 11.

37. The influence of John Osborne and his work on Palmer's films can scarcely be overestimated. Palmer has recently paid tribute to Osborne in his 2004 documentary film, *John Osborne: The Gift of Friendship,* produced for London Weekend Television.

38. Flowers described Handel as a man who "dwelt in the pastures of God," who wrote *Messiah* in a state of religious ecstasy: "It was the achievement of a giant inspired — the work of one who, by some extraordinary mental feat, had drawn himself completely out of the world. . . . when he had completed Part II, with the 'Hallelujah Chorus,' his servant found him at the table, tears streaming from his eyes. 'I did think I did see all Heaven before me, and the great God himself!' he exclaimed." See Newman Flowers, *George Frideric Handel: His Personality and His Films* (New York: Charles Scribner's Sons, 1948), 270.

39. Bell, " Great Mr. Handel," 22–24. The tendency to inflate performance practices of *Messiah* typify this tendency over centuries to convert the living Handel into a forbidding monument. Initially, performances of the work, according to conductor Christopher Hogwood, were intimate in scope, deploying no more than forty instrumentalists accompanied by five soloists and nineteen men and boys in the chorus. Beyond that, however, little is known. Beginning around 1784, when the work was performed in Westminster Abbey with 525 singers and instrumentalists, the tradition toward elephantine performances was launched. See Teri Noel Towe, "In Search of the True 'Messiah' with Christopher Hogwood," *Ovation* 5, no. 12 (January 1985): 26–31.

40. In "Great Mr. Handel," Bell laments that even as late as 1958, in an essay appearing in *Men of Music,* Handel's pre-1738 compositions — the operas, the Italian cantatas, the Latin church music, *Acis and Galatea,* the *Coronation* and *Chandos* anthems, the solo and trio sonatas, the *Concerti grossi,* the harpsichord suites — are all "dismissed as 'tragic waste.' "

41. Regarding *The Great Mr. Handel,* Bell observes that even in his adoptive country, England, where his best-known music is set to English texts, Handel's true greatness is realized "in a limited and unsatisfactory way" ("Great Mr. Handel," 27).

42. The Hallmark Hall of Fame production *A Cry of Angels* insists on the essential piety that inspired and underlay the composition of *Messiah.* And, like the earlier film, the creative act is visualized as a series of dream visions suffered by Handel, a wordless series of *tableaux vivant* dissolving in and out of each other, depicting moments from the scriptures and accompanied by pertinent passages from the music.

43. *Honour, Profit, and Pleasure* is unjustly neglected in the canon of composer films. Its exceptionally witty and intelligent script concentrates on Handel's London years and presents cameos of Alexander Pope, Jonathan Swift, and Addison and Steele. Most of Handel's lines were written by Simon Callow himself.

44. In Corbiau's *Farinelli* there are several confrontations with Farinelli in which Handel openly reviles the castrato and his use of exotic costumes, impugning his masculinity and attacking his popularity, which is drawing audiences away from his own produc-

tions. "Because of you, I am forced to exhaust myself composing works unworthy of my talent," Handel rages. "You're causing my music to deviate from its course. I'll never forgive you for that, Farinelli. A castrato's voice is Nature abused, rerouted from its goal in order to deceive. You've subverted your voice to virtuosity without soul, devoted only to artifice. . . . You managed to turn me into what you've always been. You castrated my imagination." The historical record, however, reveals that Handel was enthralled with Farinelli's voice and in the late 1720s sought to employ him in his opera company. For an account of Handel's relationship with Farinelli, see Ellen T. Harris, "Twentieth-Century Farinelli," *Musical Quarterly* 82, no. 2 (Summer 1997): 180–189. It is also worth noting that Corbiau directed another composer film, *Le Roi Danse* (2000), which examined the troubled relationship between two famous artists, composer Jean-Baptiste Lully and playwright Molière during the early reign of Louis XIV. At this writing only a French-language version of that film is available.

45. "Berlioz and His Orchestra" was a famous caricature by Grandville, dated 1846.

46. Macdonald, *Berlioz,* 75. For a concise discussion of the programmatic aspects of Berlioz's music, see Jacques Barzun, "The Meaning of Meaning in Music: Berlioz Once More," *Musical Quarterly* 66, no. 1 (January 1980): 1–20.

47. The *Memoirs* were begun in 1848 and updated in 1854 and 1864. The final pages were completed in 1865 and were published posthumously. See David Cairns's *The Memoirs of Hector Berlioz* (New York: Alfred A. Knopf, 1969).

48. Macdonald, *Selected Letters of Berlioz,* 434.

49. Cairns, *Memoirs of Hector Berlioz,* 497.

50. Macdonald, *Berlioz,* 68.

51. Berlioz began writing *The Trojans* in 1856 at the urging of Princess Carolyne Sayn-Wittgenstein. "So, against his best judgment," writes biographer Macdonald in *Berlioz,* "Berlioz reshaped his life to allow the time and leisure to compose what turned out to be the greatest and largest of his works" (61). For a thorough examination of the opera, see David Cairns, *Berlioz: Servitude and Greatness, 1832–1869* (Berkeley: University of California Press, 1999), 591–627.

52. Palmer has a historical precedent here. In *Berlioz: Servitude and Greatness,* biographer Cairns reports that a contemporary cartoon lambasting *The Trojans* showed an enormous ox being felled by a blast from a tuba. The caption reads: "New method of killing cattle to be introduced at all slaughterhouses" (704).

53. Cairns, *Memoirs of Hector Berlioz,* 497. See also Cairns, *Berlioz: Servitude and Greatness,* 704.

54. Christian-Jaque was the pseudonym of Christian Maudet. With the onset of war, he directed films for Continental-Films, the German-controlled studio in France under the Occupation. His major works of the period include the composer biopic *La Symphonie Fantastique* (1942). In his book *Republic of Images: A History of French Filmmaking* (Cambridge: Harvard University Press, 1992), Alan Williams quotes Goebbels's critique of *La Symphonie Fantastique:* "The film is of excellent quality and amounts to a first-class national fanfare. I shall unfortunately not be able to release it for public showing [in Germany])" (257).

55. Cairns, *Berlioz: Servitude and Greatness,* 779.

56. Andrew Pinnock, "The Purcell Phenomenon," in Michael Burden, ed., *The Purcell Companion* (Portland, Ore.: Amadeus Press, 1994), 14.

57. These lines from Dryden's "Absalom and Achitophel" could stand as an insight into the work of Tony Palmer, as well as constitute an epitaph for the Restoration period: "Some truth there was, but dash'd and brew'd with lies, / To please the fools, and puzzle all the wise. / Succeeding times did equal folly call, / Believing nothing, or believing all" (lines 114–117).

58. G. K. Chesterton, *Five Types* (London, 1911; reprint, New York: Books for Libraries Press, 1969), 69.

59. Pinnock, "Purcell Phenomenon," 5.

60. Jonathan Keates, *Purcell: A Biography* (Boston: Northeastern University Press, 1995), x.

61. Keates, *Purcell*, 277–279.

62. Keates, *Purcell*, x.

63. *Good King Charles' Golden Days* was George Bernard Shaw's fiftieth play. Shaw himself called it a "fancied Page of History" and subtitled it "A True History that Never Happened."

64. Here are Dryden's original lines from *The Song for St. Cecilia's Day, November 22, 1687*: "Thus did our life become; it was all a cheat. / Yet filled with hope, men favored deceit. / Trust on, and think tomorrow will repay; / Tomorrow is falser than the former day. / So when at last the dreadful hour / This crumbling pageant shall devour, / Shall trumpet still be heard on high? / No, the dead shall live, the living die, / While music shall untune the sky."

65. Philip Adams, "Sumptuous with a Capital Sumpt," *The Australian*, 23 November 1995.

66. *Song of Love* was released by MGM in 1947. It was directed by Clarence Brown and starred Katharine Hepburn and Paul Henreid as Clara and Robert Schumann. See Chapter One of this volume for further discussion of the film. *Spring Symphony* was released in 1985. It was directed by Peter Schamoni and starred Nastassja Kinski and Herbert Groenemeyer as the Schumanns. Kinski's performance was described by Michael Wilmington, writing in the *Los Angeles Times*, 26 April 1986, as possessing both "nubility and fire."

67. Of the many biographies of Robert Schumann and Clara Wieck, perhaps the best are John Daverio, *Robert Schumann: Herald of a "New Poetic Age"* (New York: Oxford University Press, 1998), and Nancy B. Reich, *Clara Schumann: The Artist and the Woman* (Ithaca, N.Y.: Cornell University Press, 1985).

68. All of Brahms's biographers attest to his unknowability, a man who, in the words of musicologist Eric Sams, "chose to conceal or dissemble [his] feelings" ("Brahms and His Clara Themes," *Musical Times* 112, no. 1539 [May 1971]: 432–434, 1). Biographer Jan Swafford, in *Johannes Brahms: A Biography* (New York: Alfred A. Knopf, 1997), writes that from the beginning Brahms determined "to live as a revered master with something to hide. In and out of music, he would become adept at masking his feelings, his identity" (30). Moreover, continues Swafford, "Brahms parceled out his life to future generations in all sorts of ways, sometimes by withholding information, sometimes by priming poten-

tial biographers with a few discreet facts and caveats. . . . He was trying to manipulate the future as he manipulated the notes on the page" (394–395).

69. Crucial to Palmer's film are the letters that allegedly piece out the Brahms story. Brahms was notoriously reluctant to allow his letters to be published; indeed, late in life he insisted to his correspondents that they be destroyed. As he admitted to his friend George Henschel, "A person has to be careful about writing letters. One fine day they get printed!" (quoted in Swafford, *Johannes Brahms,* 394). Certainly, he would have been horrified to see them in later years the subject of a film!

70. Although Palmer has some justification in these allegations, some qualifications are necessary. Most problematic are the scenes of the young boy Brahms playing in the brothels of Hamburg, which Palmer hints contributed to his later sexual dysfunction. The brothel story gained currency chiefly from Robert Haven Schauffler's *The Unknown Brahms* (1933) and has been repeated frequently ever since. Denby Richards, writing in 1983, hints that Brahms may have been abused by prostitutes and that he may have been celibate thereafter due to the subsequent trauma (see Richards, "Brahms: The Classic Enigma," *Music and Musicians* [May 1983]: 9). More recently, Swafford flatly states that Brahms played in the brothels, where "between dances the women would sit the pre-pubescent teenager on their laps and pour beer into him, and pull down his pants and hand him around to be played with, to general hilarity. There may have been worse from the sailors — Johannes was as fair and pretty as a girl." As a result, "the Singing Girls marked and molded what he became, and so molded his art" (Swafford, *Johannes Brahms,* 30–32).

Refuting the claim are several scholars: pianist-scholar Charles Rosen writes, "Brahms late in life may have spoken about having played in cafes as a child, but they were certainly respectable cafes" ("Aimez-Vous Brahms?" *New York Review of Books,* 22 October 1998, 64). Commentator Ivan Hewett insists, "Brahms almost certainly never played in a brothel, as entry for anyone under twenty was forbidden under a city statute of 1834, as was any kind of dance music" ("Behind the Beard," *Musical Times* 141, no. 1870 [Spring 2000]: 61). And, most convincingly, in her exhaustive examination of the controversy, Styra Avins declares, "Not only is there no evidence that Brahms played in low-class dives in the sailors' quarter . . . there is also no evidence, only perpetuated rumour, that Brahms played anywhere at all before he was 14 years old." It is a curious set of circumstances, she continues, "that has allowed so much misinformation about Brahms to develop and stay in circulation so long." Rather, when Brahms did begin to work at age fourteen, he played in establishments known as *Schänken,* simple restaurants where food, drink, and entertainment were offered to people of the poorer but respectable classes. See Avins, *Johannes Brahms: Life and Letters* (New York: Oxford University Press, 2001), 3–4.

Palmer is on surer ground regarding Brahms's love for Clara. An indispensable source for this conclusion is Avins's edition of the letters. Writing to a friend, Joseph Joachim, on 19 June 1854, Brahms confessed: "I believe I admire and honour her no more highly than I love and am in love with her. I often have to restrain myself forcibly just from quietly embracing her" (45–46). While Robert Schumann languished in the asylum, Brahms restrained his passion with difficulty. "Why can't I too show you properly how greatly I love and revere you?" he wrote Clara on 30 November 1854 (73). And on 31 May 1856 he gushed, " I constantly want to call you darling and all kinds of other things" (134). However, contrary to Palmer's assertion, it was likely that it was Brahms who ultimately rejected Clara, rather than the other way around. Clara's biographer, Nancy B. Reich, quotes Clara's daughter, Eugenie, to the effect that it was Brahms who "broke away ruthlessly" and who "wounded my mother's feelings at the time" (*Clara Schumann, 206*). Likewise, Rosen cites several reasons for Brahms leaving Clara, none of which imply that it was her fault ("Aimez-Vous Brahms?" 65). And Hewitt declares that Clara was frequently on the receiving end of Brahms's unpredictable, distant moods: "Most long-suffering of all Brahms' victims was, of course, Clara Schumann" ("Behind the Beard," 61). There is general agreement that Brahms and Clara never consummated their relationship. Reich insists that a sexual liaison during Schumann's institutionalization, particularly, would have been entirely out of character for the grieving, practical, and conscientious Clara (*Clara Schumann,* 187).

As far as Agathe von Siebold was concerned, Brahms did indeed spend a golden summer in 1858 of walks and games of hide-and-seek, and they did announce their engagement (eliciting jealousy from Clara). But Brahms got cold feet and broke it off. A sexual liaison with her, declares Swafford, was highly unlikely: "She was too respectable for that, at least in the setting of a small town where everybody knew her proper, prominent Catholic family" (*Johannes Brahms,* 185). Eric Sams concurs with Palmer's suggestion that Brahms coded his love for her in a theme in the first movement of the G-Major Sextet ("Brahms and His Clara Themes," 432–434).

71. Swafford claims that Brahms did indeed in later years frequent brothels and dally occasionally with servant girls. "Probably friends accompanied him to the whorehouses; it was what bachelors and some married men did in Vienna as in many cities. . . . Further, he played the old scamp, the old rogue, flirting with every pretty face and everyone's daughter. But he looked and did not touch beyond a playful squeeze, laughed and held forth and gave lavish gifts but in the end gave nothing of himself beyond his art" (*Johannes Brahms,* 548). Palmer adds, in an interview with this writer: "When he went to Vienna towards the end of his life, the women he really got on with were prostitutes. I would not want to go so far as to say he lived off their earnings — I suspect they lived off *his* earnings (he was quite wealthy). But he clearly enjoyed their company."

72. Brahms was not religious in any traditional sense. Swafford says he was "a humanist and an agnostic" (*Johannes Brahms,* 317).

73. When Chopin launched his conquest of Paris in the autumn of 1831, he became involved with the Countess Delfina Potocka (1807–1877), a beautiful woman, gifted singer, and rather notorious character (she numbered among her lovers the Duke d'Orleans and the Count de Flahault). Rumors of an affair have been generally discounted. Biographer Adam Zamoyski dismisses the gossip: "It is more than likely that Chopin saw her often during his first years in Paris and valued highly both her talent for the piano and her voice." Nothing, of course, is impossible, but evidence, to say the least, is scarce. See Zamoyski, *Chopin* (Garden City, N.Y.: Doubleday and Company, 1980), 114. And biographer Szulc states that their relations "were purely platonic, even though Delfina had an outstanding European reputation in sexual matters." See Szulc, *Chopin in Paris,* 81.

74. Arthur Hedley, ed. and trans., *Selected Correspondence of Fryderyk Chopin* (New York: McGraw-Hill, 1973), 381–382.

75. Zamoyski, *Chopin,* 115.

76. Quoted in Hedley, *Selected Correspondence of Fryderyk Chopin,* 380.

77. Zamoyski, *Chopin,* 338. The debate doesn't end here, however. In October 1961 a group of linguists and musicologists convened at the Nieborow Conference to examine the letters. The conclusion was that "there was some psychopathic identification of herself with Chopin, which led her to write 'letters' and to put into those letters her own thoughts and imaginings" (quoted in Hedley, *Selected Correspondence of Fryderyk Chopin,* 386). In rebuttal, biographer Adam Harasowski published a number of the texts and claimed that 6 of the 118 letters were authentic, while the others—those with the "heavily obscene texts"—were spurious. Harosowski goes on to explain why Czernicka never turned over the letters to the Chopin Institute: "By that time, pressed by financial demands, she started to increase the number of the letters, hoping to make something out of them by paraphrasing and enlarging the existing bits and pieces and inventing new ones, in typewritten copies." See Harosowski, "Fact or Forgery?" *Music and Musicians* 21, no. 247 (March 1973): 33.

78. At the moment of his death, Chopin's body and reputation were already being seized by the public press. See the discussion of the Chopin film *A Song to Remember,* Chapter Two.

79. See the discussion of Chopin's patriotism in Chapter Two.

Chapter Six: Revisionist Portraits

Epigraph: Schama, "Clio at the Multiplex," 41.

1. *Amadeus* was rereleased in 2002 in a "Director's Cut," which extended by twenty minutes the running time to almost three hours.

2. For a litany of historical transgressions, see Walsh, "Mozart: 'Amadeus,' Shameadeus," 51–55. The film and play, accuses Walsh, "continues the honorable tradition of spreading mis- and disinformation about Mozart. For all its protestations of 'authenticity' (within the fundamentally inauthentic context of Shaffer's play), *Amadeus* is surprisingly misleading" (52).

3. Robert L. Marshall, "Film as Musicology: Amadeus," *Music Quarterly* 81, no. 2 (Summer 1997): 177.

4. Within a week of his death, rumors of poisoning were voiced in the newspapers. An early biographer, Franz Xaver Niemetschek, reported that Constanze herself claimed that Mozart in his last days told her he had been poisoned. The Salieri theory refuses to go away, even though reputable biographers like Wheelock Thayer, Maynard Solomon, and Wolfgang Hildesheimer dismiss it out of hand. Beyond the fact that Salieri did indeed use court influence to frustrate his musical competitors (including Mozart), there is no evidence whatsoever of any homicidal inclinations. In his exhaustive examination of the evidence, pro and con, Albert I. Borowitz duly acknowledges that Salieri was reported to have confessed to the murder before he attempted suicide in 1823. But he also speculates that Salieri may at the end of his life thought himself a "murderer" in that his intrigues "poisoned" many an hour of Mozart's existence. See Borowitz, "Salieri and the 'Murder' of Mozart," *Music Quarterly* 59, no. 1 (January 1973): 263–284.

5. Mozart was indeed preoccupied with the *Requiem* during the last months of his

life. It had been commissioned via an anonymous letter in either July or August 1791 — the legend of a "Gray Messenger" has no basis in fact — but it is highly unlikely that he worked on it during his final hours.

6. The factual record of these last days tells a very different story, however: Mozart died attended only by his wife, his sister-in-law, and a medical attendant. The death throes were most unpleasant. Mozart's body by then had become so swollen that he could not move; moreover, the stench from his internal disintegration was unbearable. At the moment of his demise, reported Constanze, he suddenly vomited: "It gushed out of him in an arc — it was brown, and he was dead." See Solomon, *Mozart,* 493.

7. Nicholas Spice, "Music Lessons," *London Review of Books,* 14 December 1995, 3.

8. Biographer Maynard Solomon sums it up: "Mozart's music increasingly came to represent the classical norm against which all other music was measured [and] it became difficult to think of his works as products of subjectivity, for they seemed to have been always in existence, to have issued from an ideal sphere. . . . Mozart's creativity came to be considered as the product of forces external to him; he was regarded as a receptive, neutral instrument or vessel of a vital, perhaps divine force." See Solomon, *Mozart,* 117.

9. Solomon, *Mozart,* 12.

10. Erich Hertzmann, "Mozart's Creative Process," *Music Quarterly* 43, no. 2 (April 1957): 190.

11. Marshall, "Film as Musicology," 176–178.

12. Quoted in Deemer, "Amadeus: Fine-Tuning Villainy," 75.

13. Peter Shaffer, *Amadeus* (New York: Harper and Row, 1981), 88–96.

14. Author interview with Simon Callow, 21 July 2003, London. Unless otherwise indicated, all Callow quotations in this chapter and these notes are taken from this interview.

15. Shaffer, *Amadeus,* xiv.

16. Emanuel Schikaneder was the librettist of *The Magic Flute,* founder of the famous Theater an der Wien, and the most important theater director of his time.

17. Callow, *Shooting the Actor,* 16.

18. Author interview with Tom Hulce, 6 October 1984, Kansas City, Mo. Unless otherwise noted, all Hulce quotations in this chapter and these notes are taken from this interview.

19. Borowitz, "Salieri and the Murder of Mozart," 282–283.

20. Callow notes that director Forman "was absolutely determined that the film had to include this scene. It's lovely, but not true. It did not happen. Of course, it's deeply satisfying for many, many people. But it really disturbed me."

21. Peter Shaffer, "Screen Speak," *Film Comment* 20, no. 5 (October 1984): 56.

22. Callow, *Shooting the Actor,* 16.

23. Shaffer, "Screen Speak," 57.

24. Callow, *Shooting the Actor,* 16.

25. Shaffer, "Screen Speak," 56.

26. Author interviews with Tony Palmer, 26–27 February 2001, Kansas City, Mo.; and 12 January 2002, London. Unless otherwise noted, all quotations from Palmer in this chapter and these notes are taken from these two interviews.

27. For an overview, see Brooks, *Thank You, Comrade Stalin!* 108–125.

28. D. Rabinovich, *Dmitry Shostakovich* (London: Wishart, 1959), 9–10.

29. Laurel Fay, *Shostakovich: A Life* (London: Oxford University Press, 2000), 219.

30. Quoted in Fay, *Shostakovich,* 55.

31. Quoted in Fay, *Shostakovich,* 157

32. Quoted in Fay, *Shostakovich,* 160.

33. Fay, *Shostakovich,* 202.

34. Solomon Volkov, *Testimony: The Memoirs of Dmitri Shostakovich* (New York: Harper and Row, 1979). Volkov was a music reviewer in Leningrad when he first met Shostakovich in 1960. That led, alleges Volkov, to Shostakovich's dictation of a series of memoirs that was published in 1979 as *Testimony* (Volkov had left the Soviet Union in 1976). Volkov claimed that the composer "chose" him to record his memoirs because of his youth — "and it was before youth, more than anyone else, that Shostakovich wanted to justify himself" (xv). Volkov smuggled the manuscript to America, where, as mandated by Shostakovich, it was to be published only after his death.

35. Quoted in Volkov, *Testimony,* 276.

36. At first the West greeted *Testimony* enthusiastically. As Jan Cleave notes: "While observers in the West had long supposed that Shostakovich had put on an iron mask of conformity, they had longed for some statement or other signal allowing them to remove that mask for him. Now they had Shostakovich in the raw, so to speak." See Cleave, "Shostakovich Remembered," *Transition* 3 (10 January 1997): 46–49. To date the book's most fervent advocate is Ian MacDonald; his principal defenses appear in his biography, *The New Shostakovich,* and an article, "Common Sense about Shostakovich." On the other hand, in his recent article "Shostakovich and Us" (in Bartlett, *Shostakovich in Context),* Richard Taruskin flatly declares that *Testimony* is a "shameless book," a "book that falsely purported to be Shostakovich's transcribed oral memoirs." Taruskin goes on to attack MacDonald's book as a "travesty" in which "the author musters all the methods of Soviet music criticism at its most lagging, vulgar, and biased in order to prove that Shostakovich was a 'scornful dissident' and that his creative achievement amounted to nothing less, and nothing more, than an obsessively sustained invective against the Soviet regime and against Stalin personally."

37. Fay, *Shostakovich,* 493.

38. MacDonald writes that Maxim had always admitted that his father had been more of a Russian patriot than a Soviet adherent. In 1986, Maxim came out in support of Volkov's book: "When we take this book in our hands we can imagine what this composer's life was like in this particular situation — how difficult, how awful it was under the Soviet regime." See MacDonald, "Common Sense about Shostakovich," 163.

39. For a variety of critical opinion regarding Palmer's *Testimony,* see Julian Petley, "Testimony," *Monthly Film Bulletin* 55 (January 1988): 81–83; Derek Elley, "Testimony," *Films and Filming* 405 (June 1988): 40; and Anthony Peattie, "Testimony," *BBC Music Magazine,* October 1995, 19.

40. Volkov, *Testimony,* xxv–xxvi, 192. Perhaps this figure could also be compared with Shakespeare's Fools, particularly the one in *King Lear.* Here, explains Northrop Frye, the "fool" is a victim, "the kind of person to whom disasters happen." Indeed, everyone in the play is seen as a Fool: "Everyone on the wrong side of the wheel of fortune is a fool in this sense, and it is in this sense that Lear speaks of himself as 'the natural fool

of fortune.'" See Frye, *Northrop Frye on Shakespeare* (New Haven: Yale University Press, 1986), 111.

41. Quoted in Volkov, *Testimony,* 192.

42. Volkov, *Testimony,* xxvi.

43. Esti Scheinberg's study of ambiguity in Shostakovich's music examines in great detail the "themes of irony, parody, satire and the grotesque [that] are constantly intercalated in Shostakovich's . . . musical works, speeches, and articles." See Scheinberg, *Irony, Satire, Parody and the Grotesque in the Music of Shostakovich* (Burlington, Vt.: Ashgate Publishing Company, 2000), 4. The Shostakovich quotation is taken from Elizabeth Wilson, *Shostakovich: A Life Remembered* (Princeton, N.J.: Princeton University Press, 1994), 425–426.

44. Opera was a likely candidate for the first organized assaults on Soviet music. As Prokofiev's biographer, Harlow Robinson, observes: "Based on literature, opera is more amenable to the doctrine of Socialist Realism, and has always (along with ballet) received more attention from the guardians of Soviet culture than symphonies or concertos or chamber music." Thus, Shostakovich's *Lady Macbeth* was singled out for protest. See Robinson, *Sergei Prokofiev,* 316.

45. Palmer derives this scene from Volkov's *Testimony* in which Shostakovich recalls his relationship with Marshall Tukhachevsky, the "Red Napoleon." They met when the composer was eighteen. An esteemed military hero, Tukhachevsky was passionately fond of music and would become an influential ally. "There was only one single person with supreme power who sincerely liked my music," Shostakovich said, "and that was very important for me" (96). They met often. "He liked driving to the country and he used to take me with him. We would leave the car and go deep into the woods. It was easier to talk freely there" (100).

46. Brooks, *Thank You, Comrade Stalin!* 66. Palmer's imagery is hardly exaggerated. The cult of Stalin pervaded all aspects of Soviet life and culture. A short man with a withered left arm, he nonetheless assumed a public persona of heroic stature and vitality. The press of the late 1930s ritualized him as a sacral figure, a magical persona with power over life itself. Indeed, Brooks asserts "that Stalin filled a void created by the suppression of religion" (66).

47. Shostakovich's Thirteenth Symphony (1962) could almost be regarded as a song cycle, a setting of Yevgeny Yevtushenko's *Babi Yar,* written in 1961. The poem about the Nazi massacre of seventy thousand Jews—the estimates vary in many conflicting accounts—on 28–29 September 1941 in a ravine outside Kiev was a highly controversial indictment of anti-Semitism.

48. This photograph was rendered into a painting for the cover of the 20 July 1942 issue of *Time* magazine.

49. Palmer's quotation of the Second Piano Concerto is ironic in that Shostakovich himself declared, in a letter dated 12 February 1957, that it had "no artistic value." Yet the work, especially noted for its tender and lyric second movement, was so popular that it became a staple on his concert schedule. Quoted in Wilson, *Shostakovich,* 316, fn 49.

50. Taruskin, "Shostakovich and Us," 9.

51. Author interview with Fritz Lehner, 7 January 2003, Vienna. Unless otherwise noted, all Lehner quotations in this chapter and these notes are taken from this interview.

Lehner is a native of Austria and studied filmmaking from 1970 to 1975 at the Film Academy in Vienna. He works for ORF television and freelances as a director.

52. The author wishes to thank Christopher Gibbs, James H. Ottaway Professor of Music at Bard College, one of the organizers of the Schubertiads in New York City, for information about *Mit meinen heissen Tränen*.

53. *Mit meinen heissen Tränen* was a television miniseries consisting of three parts, each of a duration of ninety minutes. It was produced by the Austrian production company TEAM-Film for ORF.

54. Gibbs, " 'Poor Schubert,' " 54.

55. It is true that Schober kept rooms for Schubert when they were needed. Schober wrote texts to several Schubert songs, including "An die Musik," "Todesmusik," and "Am Bach im Frühling," as well as to the opera *Alfonso und Estrella*, on which they collaborated early in 1822. Schober is usually singled out as a regrettable influence on Schubert. As biographer Charles Osborne points out: "Many of the Schubertians were distrustful of Schober's influence over their friend. In particular, they were distressed that Schubert had begun to ape the loose-living ways of Schober, who seemed to delight in initiating others into his own style of life, in which wine and women certainly played as large a part as song." See Charles Osborne, *Schubert and His Vienna* (New York: Alfred A. Knopf, 1985), 90; and Newman Flower, *Franz Schubert: The Man and His Circle* (New York: Frederick A. Stokes Company, 1928), 136–137.

56. Schama, "Clio at the Multiplex," 41.

57. Botstein, "Realism Transformed," 19.

58. Botstein, "Realism Transformed," 29.

59. Author interview with David Devine, 21 October 1997, Toronto. For more information see also Tibbetts, "Composing Lives: New Biopics about Bach, Bizet, Liszt, and Strauss," *Classical Pulse* 17 (August–September 1996): 26; and Mike Boone, "Bizet's Dream," *Montreal Gazette*, 3 December 1994.

60. According to biographer Alan Walker, Liszt later learned the boy had grown up, married, and named his son after him. In a letter to him, Liszt wrote: "I could almost envy you for having escaped from the civilized art of music making, with its limitations and constructions. . . . You have done well, my dear Josi, not to engage in concert-room torture, and to disdain the empty, painful reputation of a *trained* violinist. As a Gypsy, you remain lord of yourself." See Walker, *Franz Liszt: The Virtuoso Years*, 340.

61. Irene Wood, "Making Music," *Booklist* 92, no. 13 (1 March 1996).

Bibliography

Arthur, Paul. "Essay Questions." *Film Comment* 39, no. 1 (January–February 2003): 58–62.

Atwood, William G. *The Lioness and the Little One.* New York: Columbia University Press, 1980.

Austin, William W. *Susanna, Jeanie, and the Old Folks at Home: The Songs of Stephen C. Foster from His Time to Ours.* New York: Macmillan, 1975.

Avins, Styra. *Johannes Brahms: Life and Letters.* New York: Oxford University Press, 2001.

Barr, Charles. *English Hitchcock.* Moffat, Scotland: Cameron and Hollis, 1999.

Bartlett, Rosamund. *Shostakovich in Context.* New York: Oxford University Press, 2000.

Barzun, Jacques. *Darwin Marx Wagner.* Boston: Atlantic Little, Brown, 1947.

———. "The Meaning of Meaning in Music: Berlioz Once More." *Musical Quarterly* 66, no. 1 (January 1980): 1–20.

Baxter, John. *An Appalling Talent: Ken Russell.* London: Michael Joseph, 1973.

Beahrs, Virginia Oakley. "Beethoven's *Only* Beloved? New Perspectives on the Love Story of the Great Composer." *Music Review* 54, nos. 3–4 (August–November 1993): 183–197.

Beaumont, Antony, trans. *Alma Mahler-Werfel: Diaries 1898–1902.* Ithaca, N.Y.: Cornell University Press, 1999.

Bell, A. Craig. "The Great Mr. Handel," *Music Review* 39, no. 1 (February 1978): 22–24.

Berlin, Isaiah. "The Arts in Russia under Stalin." *New York Review of Books.* 19 October 2000. 54–63.

Bordman, Gerald. *Jerome Kern: His Life and Music.* New York: Oxford University Press, 1980.

Bordwell, David, Janet Staiger, and Kristin Thompson. *The Classical Hollywood Cinema.* New York: Columbia University Press, 1985.

Borowitz, Albert. "Salieri and the 'Murder' of Mozart." *Music Quarterly* 59, no. 1 (January 1973): 263–284.

Botstein, Leon. "Realism Transformed: Franz Schubert and Vienna." In *The Cambridge Companion to Schubert,* edited by Christopher H. Gibbs, 15–35. Cambridge: Cambridge University Press, 1997.

———. "Wagner and Our Century." *Nineteenth-Century Music* 11, no. 1 (Summer 1987): 92–104.

Bowen, Catherine Drinker, and Barbara von Meck. *"Beloved Friend": The Story of Tchaikovsky and Nadejda von Meck.* New York: Random House, 1937.

Braudy, Leo. *The Frenzy of Renown.* New York: Oxford University Press, 1986.

Brooks, Jeffrey. *Thank You, Comrade Stalin! Soviet Public Culture from Revolution to Cold War.* Princeton, N.J.: Princeton University Press, 2000.

Brown, David. "How Did Tchaikovsky Come to Die—and Does It Really Matter?" *Music and Letters* 78, no. 4 (November 1997): 581–588.

———. "Tchaikovsky's Marriage." *Musical Times* 123, no. 1677 (November 1982): 754–756.

Buhler, James, Caryl Flinn, and David Neumeyer, eds. *Music and Cinema.* Hanover, N.H.: Wesleyan University Press, 2000.

Burden, Michael, ed. *The Purcell Companion.* Portland, Ore.: Amadeus Press, 1994.

Burke, Richard N. "Film, Narrative, and Shostakovich." *Musical Quarterly* 83, no. 3 (Fall 1999): 413–429.

Cairns, David. *Berlioz: Servitude and Greatness, 1832–1869.* Berkeley: University of California Press, 1999.

———, ed. *The Memoirs of Hector Berlioz.* New York: Norton, 1997.

Callow, Simon. *Shooting the Actor.* New York: Picador, 2003.

Carner, Rosco. *Puccini: A Critical Biography.* New York: Alfred A. Knopf, 1959.

Carr, Jonathan. *Mahler: A Biography.* New York: Overlook Press, 1997.

Carroll, Brendan. *The Last Prodigy: A Biography of Erich Wolfgang Korngold.* Portland, Ore.: Amadeus Press, 1997.

Cates, Curtis. *George Sand: A Biography.* Boston: Houghton Mifflin, 1975.

Custen, George F. *The Bio/Pic: How Hollywood Constructed Public History.* New Brunswick, N.J.: Rutgers University Press, 1992.

———. "Night and Day: Cole Porter, Warner Bros., and the Re-Creation of a Life." *Cineaste* 19, no. 2–3 (1992): 42–44.

———. *Twentieth Century's Fox.* New York: Basic Books, 1997.

de la Grange, Henry-Louis. " 'Meine Musik ist gelebt': Mahler's Biography as a Key to His Works." *Opus* 3, no. 2 (February 1987): 14–18.

Del Mar, Norman. *Richard Strauss.* Vol. 3. London: Barrie and Jenkins, 1972.

Deemer, Chares. "*Amadeus,* Fine-Tuning Villainy: Salieri's Journey." *Creative Screenwriting* 4, no. 4 (Winter 1997): 75–84.

Dunn, Elizabeth. "The Palmer Treatment." *Sunday Times.* 31 March 1985. 11–12.

Dvořák, Antonín. "Music in America." *Harper's New Monthly Magazine* 90, no. 537 (February 1895): 428–434.

Eisler, Benita. *Chopin's Funeral*. New York: Alfred A. Knopf, 2003.

Everett, William A. "Sigmund Romberg and the American Operetta of the 1920s." *Arti Musices* 26, no. 1 (1995): 49–64.

Farber, Stephen. "Russellmania." *Film Comment* 11, no. 6 (November–December 1975): 40–47.

Farber, Stephen, and Mark Green. *Hollywood on the Couch*. New York: William Morrow, 1993.

Fassett, Agatha. *The Naked Face of Genius: Béla Bartók's American Years*. Boston: Houghton Mifflin, 1958.

Fay, Lauren. *Shostakovich: A Life*. London: Oxford University Press, 2000.

———. "Shostakovich versus Volkov: Whose *Testimony?*" *Russian Review* 39, no. 4 (October 1980): 484–493.

Fenby, Eric. *Delius*. New York: Thomas Y. Crowell, 1971.

———. *Delius As I Knew Him*. New York: Cambridge University Press, 1981.

Ferguson, Niall, ed. *Virtual History: Alternatives and Counterfactuals*. London: Macmillan, 1997.

Flinn, Caryl. "The Most Romantic Art of All: Music in the Classical Hollywood Cinema." *Cinema Journal* 29, no. 4 (Summer 1990): 35–50.

Flowers, Newman. *George Frideric Handel: His Personality and His Films*. New York: Charles Scribner's Sons, 1948.

Fulcher, Jane R., ed. *Debussy and His World*. Princeton, N.J.: Princeton University Press, 2001.

Gabbard, Krin. *Jammin' at the Margin: Jazz and the American Cinema*. Chicago: University of Chicago Press, 1996.

Gardiner, John. "Variations on a Theme of Elgar: Ken Russell, the Great War, and the Television 'Life' of a Composer." *Historical Journal of Film, Radio and Television* 23, no. 3 (August 2003): 195–209.

Gibbs, Christopher. "Poor Schubert: Images and Legends of the Composer." In *The Cambridge Companion to Schubert*, edited by Christopher Gibbs, 36–55. Cambridge University Press, 1997.

Gillies, Malcolm, ed. *The Bartók Companion*. Portland, Ore.: Amadeus Press, 1994.

Gomez, Joseph. *Ken Russell*. London: Michael Joseph, 1976.

———. " 'Mahler' and the Methods of Ken Russell's Films on Composers." *Velvet Light Trap* 4 (1975): 45–50.

Gramit, David, "Constructing a Victorian Schubert: Music, Biography, and Cultural Values," *Nineteenth-Century Music* 17, no. 1 (Summer 1993): 65–78.

Greene, Graham. "Beethoven." *The Spectator* (23 June 1939); reprinted in David Parkinson, ed., *The Graham Greene Film Reader*. New York: Applause Books, 1995. 306–307.

Hamm, Charles. *Irving Berlin: Songs from the Melting Pot*. New York: Oxford University Press, 1997.

———. *Music in the New World*. New York: Norton, 1983.

Handy, W. C. *Father of the Blues*. New York: Macmillan, 1955.

Hanke, Ken. *Ken Russell's Films*. Methuen, N.J.: Scarecrow Press, 1984.

Harasowski, Adam. "Fact or Forgery?" *Music and Musicians* 21, no. 247 (March 1973): 33–34.

Hedley, Arthur. "Chopin the Man." In *Frédéric Chopin: Profiles of the Man and the Musician,* edited by Alan Walker, 1–23. New York: Taplinger, 1967.

Holdon, Anthony. *Tchaikovsky: A Biography*. New York: Random House, 1997.

Horowitz, Joseph. *The Post-Classical Predicament*. Boston: Northeastern University Press, 1995.

Howard, John Tasker. *Stephen Foster: America's Troubadour*. New York: Thomas Y. Crowell, 1934.

James, Burnett. *Wagner and the Romantic Disaster*. New York: Thames and Hudson, 1983.

Jasen, David A. *Tin Pan Alley*. New York: Donald I. Fine, 1988.

Kalinak, Kathryn. *Settling the Score: Music and the Classical Hollywood Film*. Madison: University of Wisconsin Press, 1992.

Kallberg, Jeffrey. *Chopin at the Boundaries*. Cambridge: Harvard University Press, 1996.

Kater, Michael. *Composers of the Nazi Era: Eight Portraits*. New York: Oxford University Press, 2000.

Kennedy, Michael. *Portrait of Elgar*. New York: Oxford University Press, 1987.

Kivy, Peter. *The Possessor and the Possessed: Handel, Mozart, Beethoven, and the Idea of Musical Genius*. New Haven: Yale University Press, 2001.

Kolker, Robert Phillip. "Ken Russell's Biopics." *Film Comment* 9, no. 3 (May–June 1973): 42–45.

Kowalke, Kim H. "Burying the Past: Carl Orff and His Brecht Connection." *Musical Quarterly* 84, no. 1 (Spring 2000): 58–83.

Kreuger, Miles. *Show Boat: The Story of a Classic American Musical*. New York: Oxford University Press, 1977.

Kris, Ernst, and Otto Kurz. *Legend, Myth, and Magic in the Image of the Artist*. New Haven: Yale University Press, 1979.

Large, Brian. *Martinu*. London: Duckworth, 1975.

Levine, Lawrence W. *Highbrow/Lowbrow: The Emergence of Cultural Hierarchy in America*. Cambridge: Harvard University Press, 1988.

Levy, Alan Howard. "The Search for Identity in American Music, 1890–1920." *American Music* 2, no. 2 (Summer 1984): 70–81.

Macdonald, Hugh. *Berlioz*. London: J. M. Dent and Sons, 1982.

——, ed. *Selected Letters of Berlioz*. New York: Norton, 1997.

MacDonald, Ian. "Common Sense about Shostakovich: Breaking the 'Hermeneutic Circle.'" *Southern Humanities Review* (1992): 153–167.

——. *The New Shostakovich*. Boston: Northeastern University Press, 1990.

Marshall, Robert L. "Film as Musicology: Amadeus." *Music Quarterly* 81, no. 2 (Summer 1997): 173–178.

Millington, Barry. *The Wagner Compendium*. London: Thames and Hudson, 1992.

Moore, Jerrold Northrop. *Edward Elgar: A Creative Life*. New York: Oxford University Press, 1984.

Murray, Albert. *Stomping the Blues*. New York: McGraw-Hill, 1976.

Newbould, Brian. *Schubert: The Music and the Man*. Berkeley: University of California Press, 1997.

Oestreich, James R. "Schubertizing the Movies." *New York Times*. 30 June 2002, 1, 26–27.

Osborne, Charles. *Schubert and His Vienna*. New York: Alfred A. Knopf, 1985.

Osborne, John. *Almost a Gentleman: An Autobiography, 1955–1966*. London: Faber and Faber, 1991.

Ostwald, Peter. *Schumann: The Inner Voices of a Musical Genius*. Boston: Northeastern University Press, 1985.

———. "Dogged Days." *The Listener*. 15 September 1988. 4–5.

Pearson, Hesketh. *Gilbert: His Life and Strife*. New York: Harper and Brothers, 1957.

Pessen, Edward. "The Great Songwriters of Tin Pan Alleys Golden Age: A Social, Occupational, and Aesthetic Inquiry." *American Music* 3, no. 2 (Summer 1985): 193–195.

Peyser, Joan. *The Memory of All That: The Life of George Gershwin*. New York: Simon and Schuster, 1993.

Poznansky, Alexander. *Tchaikovsky's Last Days: A Documentary Study*. Oxford: Clarendon Press, 1996.

Pulver, Jeffrey. *Paganini: The Romantic Virtuoso*. New York: Da Capo Press, 1970.

Rabinovich, D. *Dmitry Shostakovich*. London: Lawrence and Wishart, 1959.

Reich, Nancy B. *Clara Schumann: The Artist and the Woman*. Ithaca, N.Y.: Cornell University Press, 1985.

Rimsky-Korsakov, Nikolai. *My Musical Life*. New York: Tudor, 1935.

Robinson, Harlow. *Serge Prokofiev: A Biography*. New York: Viking Press, 1987.

Rosenstone, Robert A. "History in Images/History in Words: Reflections on the Possibility of Really Putting History onto Film." *American Historical Review* 93, no. 5 (December 1988): 176–177.

———, ed. *Revisioning History: Film and the Construction of a New Past*. Princeton, N.J.: Princeton University Press, 1995.

Richards, Denby. "Brahms: The Classic Enigma." *Music and Musicians* (May 1983): 9.

Russell, Ken. *Altered States*. New York: Bantam, 1991.

———. *The Lion Roars: Ken Russell on Film*. Boston: Faber and Faber, 1993.

Sams, Eric. "Brahms and His Clara Themes." *Musical Times* 112, no. 1539 (May 1971): 432–434.

———. "Elgar's Enigmas." *Music and Letters* 78, no. 3 (August 1997): 410–415.

Schama, Simon. "Clio at the Multiplex." *The New Yorker* (19 January 1998): 38–43.

Scott-Sutherland, Colin. *Arnold Bax*. London: J. M. Dent and Sons, 1973.

Schwartz, Charles. *Cole Porter*. New York: Da Capo Press, 1979.

Shaffer, Peter. "Mozart Goes to the Movies." *Film Comment* 20, no. 5 (September–October 1984): 56.

———. "Screen Speak." *Film Comment* 20, no. 5 (September–October 1984): 51, 56–57.

Solomon, Maynard. *Beethoven*. New York: Schirmer Books, 1977.

———. "Franz Schubert and the Peacocks of Benvenuto Cellini," *Nineteenth-Century Music* 17, no. 1 (Summer 1993): 202–206.

———. *Mozart*. New York: Farrar, Straus and Giroux, 1995.

Sullivan, Jack. *New World Symphonies*. New Haven: Yale University Press, 1999.

Swafford, Jan. *Johannes Brahms: A Biography*. New York: Alfred A. Knopf, 1997.

Swynnoe, Jan G. *The Best Years of British Film Music, 1936–1958*. London: Boydell Press, 2002.

Szulc, Tad. *Chopin in Paris*. New York: Da Capo Press, 1998.

Thomas, Tony. *Music for the Movies*. South Brunswick: A. S. Barnes, 1973.

Tibbetts, John C. *Dvořák in America*. Portland, Ore.: Amadeus Press, 1993.

——. "Franz Liszt on Film: The Truth in Masquerade." In *Liszt the Progressive*, edited by Hans Kagebeck and Johan Lagerfelt, 209–222. Lewiston, N.Y.: Edwin Mellen, 2001.

——. "In Search of Stephen Foster." *The World and I* 6, no. 7 (July 1991): 525–529.

——. "The Lyre of Light." *Film Comment* 28, no. 1 (January–February 1992): 66–73.

——. "The Missing Title Page: Dvořák and the American National Song." *Music and Culture in America: 1861–1918*, edited by Michael Saffle, 343–365. New York: Garland, 1998.

——. "The New Tin Pan Alley: 1940s Hollywood Looks American Popular Songwriters." In *Music and Culture in America: 1900–1950*, edited by Michael Saffle, 349–384. New York: Garland, 2000.

——. "Probing the Liszt Legend." *Christian Science Monitor*. 14 September 1989. 10–11.

——. "Shostakovich's Fool to Stalin's Czar: Tony Palmer's *Testimony* (1987)." *Historical Journal of Film, Radio and Television* 22, no. 2 (2002): 173–196.

——. "They Oughta Be in Pictures." *American Record Guide* 58, no. 3 (May–June 1995): 6–10.

Towe, Teri Noel. "In Search of the True 'Messiah' with Christopher Hogwood." *Ovation* 5, no. 12 (January 1985): 26–31.

Volkov, Solomon, ed. *Testimony*. New York: Harper and Row, 1979.

——. "Dmitry Shostakovich and 'Tea for Two.'" *Musical Quarterly* 64, no. 2 (April 1978): 223–228.

Wagner, Nike. *The Wagners: The Drama of a Musical Dynasty*. London: Weidenfeld and Nicolson, 2001.

Walker, Alan. *Franz Liszt: The Virtuoso Years, 1811–1847*. New York: Alfred A. Knopf, 1983.

—— —. *Franz Liszt: The Final Years, 1861–1886*. New York: Alfred A. Knopf, 1996.

Walsh, Michael. "Mozart: 'Amadeus,' Shameadeus." *Film Comment* 20, no. 5 (October 1984): 51–55.

Watson, Derek. *Bruckner*. New York: Simon and Schuster, , 1996.

Weber, William. "Mass Culture and the Reshaping of European Musical Taste, 1770–1870." *International Review of the Aesthetics and Sociology of Music* 8, no. 1 (June 1977): 5–21.

Wechsberg, Joseph. *The Waltz Emperors: The Life and Times and Music of the Strauss Family*. New York: G. P. Putnam's Sons, 1973.

Weinstock, Herbert. *Chopin: The Man and His Music*. New York: Alfred A. Knopf, 1949.

Welsh, James M., and Steven Kramer. "Gance's Beethoven." *Sight and Sound* 45, no. 2 (Spring 1976): 109–111.

Wilk, Max. *They're Playing Our Song*. New York: Atheneum, 1973.

Williams, Bernard. "Wagner and Politics." *New York Review of Books* 2 (November 2000): 36–43.

Wilson, Elizabeth. *Shostakovich: A Life Remembered*. Princeton, N.J.: Princeton University Press, 1994.

Winter, Robert. "Whose Schubert?" *Nineteenth-Century Music* 17, no. 1 (Summer 1993): 94–101.

Wlaschin, Ken. *Opera on Screen*. Los Angeles: Beachwood Press, 1997.

Wren, Gayden. *A Most Ingenious Paradox*. New York: Oxford University Press, 2001.

Zamoyski, *Chopin*. Garden City, N.Y.: Doubleday, 1980.

Index

Abraham, F. Murray, xi, 4, 266, 271, 274
Adrian, Max, xii, 170, 172
Aeolian Hall, 140, 141, 147
Alda, Robert, 15
Alexander's Ragtime Band (1939 film), 3,
102, 103, 104, 109, 122, 123; Berlin
biography in, 124–125; production
history of, 125
"Alexander's Ragtime Band" (song), 125,
319n52
*Altered States: The Autobiography of
Ken Russell* (book), 159, 169
Amadeus (1984 film), ix–xii, 1, 4, 22,
264; locations in, 272–273; Mozart
biography in, 266, 267–268; plot of,
264–265; popularity of, 266; Mozart
as "possessed" in, 268; production history of, 264–275; *Requiem* sequence
in, 267–268, 273–275; Tom Hulce on
Mozart role in, 273, 274–275
Amadeus (play), ix, x; death scene in,

269–270; Mozart biography in, 266,
267–268, 269; Mozart as "possessed"
in, 268; production history of, 265,
269–271; Simon Callow on Mozart
role in, ix–x, xi, 270–271; use of music
in, 270–271
Ambrose, Anna, xii, 40
Arnold Bax (1992 film), 169, 200; Bax
biography, 210–211; *Garden of Fand*
sequences in, 211–212; plot of, 211–
212; production history of, 210–212;
as Russell's self-portrait, 210, 212
"Ave Maria" (Schubert), 24, 25–26, 76,
117

"Babi Yar" (Shostakovich's Thirteenth
Symphony), 281–282
Badel, Alan, 64, 66
Bakaleinikoff, Constantin, 21, 145, 146,
148
Barrault, Jean-Louis, xii, 243